Y0-BDZ-084

A TREATISE OF *MUSICK*

Da Capo Press Music Reprint Series

GENERAL EDITOR

FREDERICK FREEDMAN

VASSAR COLLEGE

A TREATISE OF *MUSICK*

SPECULATIVE, PRACTICAL, AND HISTORICAL

BY ALEXANDER MALCOLM

DA CAPO PRESS • NEW YORK • 1970

A Da Capo Press Reprint Edition

This Da Capo Press edition of Alexander Malcolm's *A Treatise of Musick* is an unabridged republication of the first edition published by the author in Edinburgh in 1721.

Library of Congress Catalog Card Number 69-16676

SBN 306-71099-4

Published by Da Capo Press
A Division of Plenum Publishing Corporation
227 West 17th Street, New York, N.Y. 10011

Manufactured in the United States of America

A

TREATISE

OF

MUSICK,

Speculative, Practical, and Historical.

By ALEXANDER MALCOLM.

Hail Sacred Art! *descended from above,*
To crown our mortal Joys: Of thee we learn,
How happy Souls communicate their Raptures;
For thou'rt the Language of the Blest in Heaven.
— Divum hominumq; voluptas.

EDINBURGH,

Printed for the AUTHOR. MDCCXXI.

TO

The moſt Illuſtrious

DIRECTORS

OF THE

Royal Academy of Muſick,

VIZ.

The moſt Noble, *Thomas*, Duke of *Newcaſtle*, Governour,

Lord *Bingley*, Deputy-Governour,

Duke of *Portland*,
Duke of *Queensberry*,
Earl of *Burlington*,
Earl of *Stairs*,
Earl of *Wadeck*,
Lord *Chetwind*,
Lord *Stanhope*,
James Bruce Eſq;
Colonel *Blathwayt*,
Thomas Coke of *Norfolk* Eſq;
Conyers Darcey Eſq;
Brigadier-Gen. *Dormer*,
Bryan Fairfax Eſq;
Colonel *O Hara*,
George Harriſon Eſq;
Brigadier-Gener. *Hunter*,
William Poultney Eſq;
Sir *John Vanbrugh*,
Major-General *Wade*,
Fran. Whitworth Eſq;

My Lords and Gentlemen,

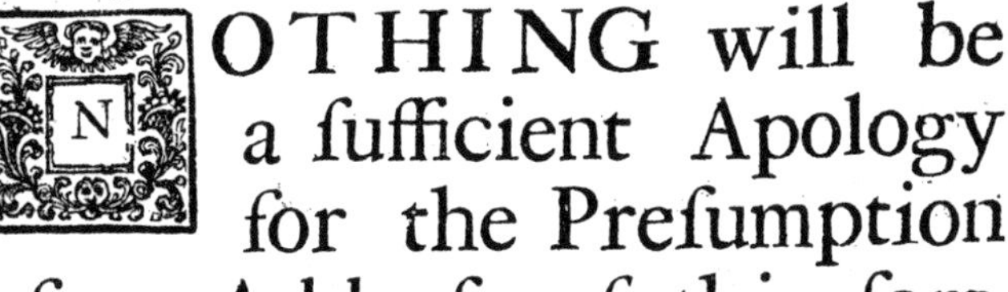

NOTHING will be a ſufficient Apology for the Preſumption of an Addreſs of this ſort, from

from one, ſo much a Stranger as I am, if the Treatiſe, it preſents you, deſerves not a favourable Regard. As you are the beſt Judges of the Work, as well as the greateſt Patrons and Encouragers of the Science, I have taken the liberty to ſend it abroad, under the Sanction of your Names: A Liberty! which I would not have allow'd myſelf to uſe, if I were not conſcious that I have done all I could to deſerve publick Approbation, in explaining the fundamental Grounds and Principles, which are ſo little known or ſtudied, even by ſome celebrated Practiſers of the

Art.

Art. How I have ſucceed-ed, I leave to you to deter-mine. Nor ſhall I be much concern'd at others Cenſure, if you think me not unpro-fitable.

May your Academy long flouriſh, with continual new Improvement, and never want a Body of ſuch gene-rous Patriots to direct and adorn it. Be my Praiſe, at diſtance, to love and admire it. I am,

My Lords and Gentlemen,

Your moſt Obedient,

And moſt Devoted,

Humble Servant,

Alexander Malcolm.

AN

ODE

ON THE

Power of MUSICK,

Inſcrib'd to

Mr. MALCOLM,

AS A

Monument of Friendſhip,

By Mr. MITCHELL.

I.

WHEN *Nature* yet in *Embrio* lay,
Ere Things began to be,
The ALMIGHTY from eternal Day
Spoke loud his deep Decree:
The Voice was tuneful as his Love,
At which Creation ſprung,
And all th' *Angelick* Hoſts above
The Morning Anthem ſung.

II. At

II.

At *Musick*'s sweet prevailing Call,
Thro' boundless Realms of Space,
The Atoms danc'd, obsequious all,
And, to compose this wondrous Ball,
In Order took their Place.
How did the Piles of Matter part,
And huddled Nature from her Slumber start?
When, from the Mass immensely steep,
The Voice bid Order sudden leap,
To usher in a World.
What heavenly Melody and Love
Began in ev'ry Sphere to move?
When Elements, that jarr'd before,
Were all aside distinctly hurl'd,
And *Chaos* reign'd no more.

III.

Musick the mighty Parent was,
Empower'd by GOD, the sovereign Cause.
Musick first spirited the lifeless Waste,
Sever'd the sullen, bulky Mass,
And active Motion call'd from lazy Rest.
Summon'd by *Musick*, *Form* uprear'd her Head,
From Depths, where Life it self lay dead,
While sudden Rays of everliving Light
Broke from the Abyss of ancient Night,
Reveal'd the new-born Earth around and its fair Influence spread.
GOD saw that all the Work was good;
The Work, the Effect of Harmony, its wondrous Offsprings stood.

IV. *Musick*

IV.

Musick, the beſt of Arts divine,
Maintains the Tune it firſt began,
And makes ev'n Oppoſites combine
To be of Uſe to Man.
Diſcords with tuneful Concords move
Thro' all the ſpacious Frame;
Below is breath'd the Sound of Love,
While myſtick Dances ſhine *Above*,
And *Musick*'s Power to nether Worlds proclaim.
What various Globes in proper Spheres,
Perform their great Creator's Will?
While never ſilent never ſtill,
Melodiouſly they run,
Unhurt by Chance, or Length of Years,
Around the central Sun.

V.

The little perfect World, call'd Man,
In whom the *Diapaſon* ends,
In his Contexture, ſhews a Plan
Of Harmony, that makes Amends,
By God-like Beauty that adorns his Race,
For all the Spots on Nature's Face.
He boaſts a pure, a tuneful Soul,
That rivals the celeſtial Throng,
And can ev'n ſavage Beaſts controul
With his inchanting Song.
Tho' diff'rent Paſſions ſtruggle in his Mind,
Where Love and Hatred, Hope and Fear are joyn'd.
All, by a ſacred Guidance, tend
To one harmonious End.

VI. Its

VI.

Its great Original to prove,
And ſhew it bleſs'd us from above,
In creeping Winds, thro' Air it ſweetly flotes,
And works ſtrange Miracles by Notes.
Our beating Pulſes bear each bidden Part,
And ev'ry Paſſion of the maſter'd Heart
Is touch'd with Sympathy, and ſpeaks the Wonders of the Art.
Now Love, in ſoft and whiſpering Strains,
Thrills gently thro' the Veins,
And binds the Soul in ſilken Chains.
Then Rage and Fury fire the Blood,
And hurried Spirits, riſing high, ferment the boiling Flood;
Silent, anon, we ſink, reſign'd in Grief:
But ere our yielding Paſſions quite ſubſide,
Some ſwelling Note calls back the ebbing Tide,
And lifts us to Relief.
With Sounds we love, we joy, and we deſpair,
The ſolid Subſtance hug, or graſp deluſive Air.

VII.

In various Ways the Heart-ſtrings ſhake,
And different Things they ſpeak.
For, when the meaning Maſters ſtrike the *Lyre*,
Or *Hautboys* briskly move,
Our Souls, like Lightning, blaze with quick Deſire,
Or melt away in Love.
But when the martial *Trumpet*, ſwelling high,

Rolls

Rolls its ſhrill Clangor thro' the ecchoing
Sky;
If, anſwering hoarſe, the ſullen *Drum's* big
Beat
Does, in dead Notes, the lively Call repeat;
Bravely at once we break o'er Nature's Bounds;
Snatch at grim Death, and look, unmov'd,
on Wounds.
Slumb'ring, our Souls lean o'er the trembling
Lute;
Softly we mourn with the complaining *Flute*;
With the *Violin* laugh at our Foes,
By Turns with the *Organ* we bear on the Sky,
Whilſt, exulting in Triumph on *Æther* we
fly,
Or, falling, grone upon the *Harp*, beneath a
Load of Woes.
Each Inſtrument has magick Power
To enliven or deſtroy,
To ſink the Heart, and, in one Hour,
Entrance our Souls with Joy.
At ev'ry Touch, we loſe our raviſh'd Thoughts,
And Life, it ſelf, in quivering clings, hangs o'er
the varied Notes.

VIII.

How does the ſtarting *Treble* raiſe
The Mind to rapt'rous Heights;
It leaves all Nature in Amaze,
And drowns us with Delights.
But, when the manly, the majeſtick, *Baſs*
Appears with awful Grace,

What

What ſolemn Thoughts are in the Mind infus'd?
And how the Spirit's rous'd?
In ſlow-plac'd Triumph, we are led around,
And all the Scene with haughty Pomp is crown'd;
Till friendly *Tenor* gently flows,
Like ſweet, meandring Streams,
And makes an Union, as it goes,
Betwixt the Two Extremes.
The blended Parts in *That* agree,
As Waters mingle in the Sea,
And yield a Compound of delightful Melody.

IX.

Strange is the Force of modulated Sound
That, like a Torrent, ſweeps o'er ev'ry Mound!
It tunes the Heart at ev'ry Turn;
With ev'ry Moment gives new Paſſions Birth;
Sometimes we take Delight to mourn;
Sometimes enhance our Mirth.
It ſooths deep Sorrow in the Breaſt;
It lul's our waking Cares to Reſt,
Fate's clouded Brow ſerenes with Eaſe,
And makes ev'n Madneſs pleaſe.
As much as Man can meaner Arts controul,
It manages his maſter'd Soul,
The moſt invet'rate Spleen diſarms,
And, like *Aurelia*, charms:
Aurelia! dear diſtinguiſh'd Fair!
In whom the Graces center'd are!
Whoſe Notes engage the Ear and Mind,

As

As Violets breath'd on by the gentle Wind;
Whose Beauty, *Musick* in Disguise!
Attracts the gazing Eyes,
Thrills thro' the Soul, like *Haywood's* melting Lines,
And, as it certain Conquest makes, the savage Soul refines.

X.

Musick religious Thoughts inspires,
And kindles bright poetick Fires;
Fires! such as great *Hillarius* raise
Triumphant in their Blaze!
Amidst the *vulgar versifying* Throng,
His Genius, with Distinction, show,
And o'er our *popular Metre* lift his Song
High, as the Heav'ns are arch'd o'er Orbs below.
As if the Man was pure Intelligence,
Musick transports him o'er the Heights of Sense,
Thro' Chinks of Clay the Rays above lets in,
And makes Mortality divine.
Tho' Reason's Bounds it ne'er defies,
Its Charms elude the Ken
Of heavy, gross-ear'd Men,
Like Mysteries conceal'd from vulgar Eyes.
Others may *that* Distraction call,
Which *Musick* raises in the Breast,
To *me* 'tis Extasy and Triumph all,
The Foretastes of the Raptures of the Blest.
Who knows not this, when *Handel* plays,
And *Senesino* sings?

Our

Our Souls learn Rapture from their Lays,
While rival'd Angels ſhow Amaze,
And drop their golden Wings.

XI.

Still, God of Life, entrance my Soul
With ſuch Enthuſiaſtick Joys;
And, when grim Death, with dire Controul,
My Pleaſures in this lower Orb deſtroys,
Grant this Requeſt whatever you deny,
For Love I bear to Melody,
That, round my Bed, a ſacred Choir
Of skilful Maſters tune their Voice,
And, without Pain of agonizing Strife,
In Conſort with the *Lute* conſpire,
To untie the Bands of Life;
That, dying with the dying Sounds
My Soul, well tun'd, may raiſe
And break o'er all the common Bounds
Of Minds, that grovel here below the Skies.

XII.

When Living die, and dead Men live,
And Order is again to *Chaos* hurl'd,
Thou, *Melody*, ſhalt ſtill ſurvive,
And triumph o'er the Ruins of the World.
A dreadful Trumpet never heard before,
By Angels never blown, till then,
Thro' all the Regions of the Air ſhall rore
That Time is now no more:
But lo! a different Scene!
Eternity appears.

Like

Like Space unbounded and untold by Years.
High in the Seat of Happineſs divine
Shall Saints and Angels in full *Chorus* joyn.
In various Ways,
Seraphick Lays
The unceaſing Jubile ſhall crown,
And, whilſt Heav'n ecchoes with his Praiſe,
The ALMIGHTY's ſelf ſhall hear, and look, delighted, down.

XIII.

Who would not wiſh to have the Skill
Of tuning Inſtruments at Will?
Ye Pow'rs, who guide my Actions, tell!
Why I, in whom the Seeds of *Muſick* dwell,
Who moſt its Pow'r and Excellence admire
Whoſe very Breaſt, it ſelf's, a *Lyre*,
Was never taught the heav'nly Art
Of modulating Sounds,
And can no more, in Conſort, bear a Part
Than the wild *Roe*, that o'er the Mountains bounds?
Could I live o'er my Youth again,
(But ah! the Wiſh how idly vain!)
Inſtead of poor deluding Rhime,
Which like a *Syren* murders Time,
Inſtead of dull, ſcholaſtick Terms,
Which made me ſtare and fancy Charms;
With *Gordon*'s brave Ambition fir'd,
Beyond the tow'ring *Alps*, untir'd,

To

To tune my Voice to his ſweet Notes, I'd
roam ;
Or ſearch the Magazines of Sound,
Where *Muſick*'s Treaſures ly profound,
With *M*---- here at Home.
M----, the dear, deſerving Man,
Who taught in Nature's Laws,
To ſpread his Country's Glory can
Practiſe the Beauties of the Art, and ſhew its
Grounds and Cauſe.

* * *

TABLE OF CONTENTS.

§ 2. *Of*

CHAP.

§ 4. *Of*

§ 1. *Of*

INTRODUCTION.

I Have no ſecret Hiſtory to entertain my *Reader* with, or rather to be impertinent with, concerning the Occaſion of my ſtudying, writing, or publiſhing any Thing upon this Subject: If the Thing is well done, no matter how it came to paſs. And tho' it be ſomewhat unfaſhionable, I muſt own it, I have no Apology to make: My Lord *Shaftsbury*, indeed, aſſures me, that the Generality of Readers are not a little raiſed by the Submiſſion of a confeſſing Author, and very ready on theſe Terms to give him Abſolution, and receive him into their good Grace and Favour; whatever may be in it, I have Nothing of this Kind wherewith to bribe their Friendſhip; being neither conſcious of *Lazineſs*, *Precipitancy*, or any other *wilful Vice*, in the Management of this Work, that ſhould give me great Uneaſineſs about it; if there be a Fault, it lies ſomewhere elſe; for, to be plain, I have taken all the Pains I could.

I

I have always thought it as impertinent for an Author to offer any Performance to the World, with a flat Pretence of ſuſpecting it, as it is ridiculous to commend himſelf in a conceited and ſaucy Manner; there is certainly ſomething juſt and reaſonable, that lies betwixt theſe Extremes; perhaps the beſt Medium is to ſay Nothing at all; but if one may ſpeak, I think he may with a very good Grace ſay, he has deſigned well and done his beſt; the Reſpect due to Mankind requires it, and as I can ſincerely profeſs this, I ſhall have no Anxiety about the Treatment my Book may meet with. The *Criticks* therefore may take their full Liberty: I can loſe Nothing at their Hands, who examine Things with a true Reſpect to the real Service of Mankind; if they approve, I ſhall rejoyce, if not, I ſhall be the better for their judicious Correction: And for thoſe who may judge raſhly thro' Pride or Ignorance, I ſhall only pity them.

BUT there is one common Place of Criticiſm I would beg Leave to conſider a little. Some People, as ſoon as they hear of a new Book upon a known Subject, ask what Diſcovery the Author has made, or what he can ſay, which they don't know or cannot find elſewhere? I might deſire theſe curious Gentlemen to read and ſee; but that they may better underſtand my Pretences, and where to lay their Cenſures, let them conſider, there are Two Kinds of Diſcoveries in Sciences; one is that of new *Theorems* and *Propoſitions*, the other is of the proper

Re-

Relation aad *Connection* of the Things already found, and the eafy Way of reprefenting them to the Underftanding of others; the firft affords the Materials, and the other the Form of thefe intellectual Structures which we call Sciences: How ufelefs the firft is without the other, needs no Proof; and what an Odds there may be in the Way of explaining and difpofing the Parts of any Subject, we have a Thoufand Demonftrations in the numerous Writings upon every Subject. An Author, who has made a Science more intelligible, by a proper and diftinct Explication of every fingle Part, and a juft and natural Method in the Connection of the Whole; tho' he has faid Nothing, as to the Matter, which was not before difcovered, is a real Benefactor to Mankind: And if he has gathered together in one *Syftem*, what, for want of knowing or not attending to their true Order and Dependence, or whatever other Reafon, lay fcattered in feveral Treatifes, and perhaps added many ufeful Reflections and Obfervations; will not this Author, do ye think, be acquitted of the Charge of *Plagiarifm*, before every reafonable Judge; and be reckoned juftly more than a mere Collector, and to have done fomething new and ufeful? If you appeal to a very wife and learned ANCIENT, the Queftion is clearly determined. — *Etiamfi omnia a veteribus inventa funt, tamen erit hoc femper novum, ufus & difpofitio inventorum ab aliis.* SENECA *Ep.* 64. How far this Character of a new Author will be found in the following TREATISE, depends

pends upon the Ability and Equity of my Judges, and I leave it upon their Honour.

BUT you muſt have Patience to hear another Thing, which Juſtice demands of me in this Place. It is, to inform you, that the 13 *Ch.* of the following Book was communicated to me by a Friend, whoſe Modeſty forbids me to name. The ſpeculative Part, and what elſe there is, beſides the Subject of that *Chapter*, were more particularly my Study: But I found, there would certainly be a Blank in the Work, if at leaſt the more general Principles of Compoſition were not explained; and whatever Pains I had taken to underſtand the Writers on this Branch, yet for want of ſufficient Practice in it, I durſt not truſt my own Judgment to extract out of them ſuch a Compend as would anſwer my Deſign; which I hope you will find very happily ſupplied, in what my Friend's Genius and Generoſity has afforded: And if I can judge any Thing about it, you have here not a mere Compend of what any Body elſe has done, but the firſt Principles of *harmonick Compoſition* explained in a Manner peculiarly his own.

AFTER ſo long a perſonal Conference, you'll perhaps expect I ſhould ſay ſomething, in this *Introduction*, to my Subject; but this, I believe, will be univerſally agreeable, the Experience of ſome Thouſand Years giving it ſufficient Recommendation; and for any Thing elſe I have little to ſay in this Place: The Contents you have in the preceeding Table, and I ſhall only make this ſhort Tranſition to the Book it ſelf.

THE

Of the *original* and various *Significations* of the Word *Musick*, you'll have an Account in the Beginning of *Chap.* 14. For, an historical Account of the *ancient Musick* being one Part of my Design, I could not begin it better, than with the various Use of the Name among the *Ancients*. It shall be enough therefore to tell you here, that I take it in the common Sense, for that Science which considers and explains those Properties and Relations of Sounds, that make them capable of exciting the agreeable Sensations, which the Experience of all Mankind assures us to be a natural Effect of certain Applications of them to the Ear. And for the same Reason I forbear to speak, in this Place, any Thing particularly of the *Antiquity*, *Excellency*, and various *Uses* and *Ends* of *Musick*, which I shall at large consider in the forementioned *Chapter*, according to the Sentiments and Experience of the *Ancients*, and how far the Experience of our Times agrees with that.

Corrigenda.

PAge 52. l. 16. *read* 3 : 2. p. 55. l. 3. *D.* *r.* *C.* p. 76. l. 32. two. *r.* one. l. 33. fundamental *r.* acute Term. p. 77. l. 2. 2. *r.* 1. acute Term *r.* fundamental. p. 125. l. 24. *r.* $\frac{3}{5}$ by $\frac{2}{3}$. p. 146. l. 11. *r.* 2 : 3. p. 158. l. 5. 3. *r.* 2. p. 227. l. 18. *r.* in harmonical (as one Word) p. 256. l. 1. *r.* *C*--*c.* l. 5. D. *r.* d. p. 295. l. 14. ♭ *r.* b. p. 301. l. 11. *r.* Plate 2 Fig. 2. p. 319.

p. 319. l. 26. Tune or *r.* human. l. 30 *dele* in. p. 341. l. 11. a *r.* or. p. 356. l. 27. g✱, e♭. *r.* a♭, d✱. p. 435. l. 7. the *r.* in the. p. 452. l. 29. *dele* other. p. 458. l. 22. are *r.* is. l. 23. least *r.* best. p. 550. l. 10. Objects *r.* Subjects.

Pray excuse a few smaller Escapes which the Sense will easily correct.

Addenda.

PAge 408. l. 8. after Bar, *add*, or of any particular Note. p. 411. l. 1. after Crotchets, *add*, in the Triples $\frac{6}{4}$ $\frac{12}{4}$ $\frac{9}{4}$. p. 413. *add at the End*; and if ♭ or ✱ is annexed to these Figures, it signifies *lesser* or *greater*, so 3✱ is *3d g*, and 6♭ is *6th l.* p. 415. l. 21. *after* Example, *add* Plate 4. *and* mind, *that all the Examples of Plates* 4, 5, 6. *belong to the* 13 Chap. p. 485. l. 11. *after* Memory, *add*, we have a very old and remarkable Proof of this Virtue of Musick.

N. B. In the Table of Examples *Page* 258. the different Characters of Letters are neglected; but the Numbers of each Example will discover what they ought to be, in Conformity to *Fig.* 5. *Plate* 1. from whence they are taken.

N. B. See *Page* 50. at *Line* 7. and consequently, *&c.* A wrong Conclusion has here escaped me, *viz.* that since the Chord passes the Point O, therefore it is accelerated. I own the only Thing that follows from its passing that Point is, that the Chord in every Point *d.* (of a single Vibration) has more Force than would retain it there: And the true Reason of Acceleration, is this, *viz.* in the outmost Point *D.* it has just as much Force as is equal to what would keep it there: This Force is supposed not to be destroyed, but at the next Point *d.* to receive an Addition of as much as would keep it in that Point, and so on through every Point till it pass the straight Line, and that it loses its Force by the same Degrees; from whence follows the Law of Acceleration mentioned.

N. B. See *Plate* 6. *Example* 35. the 2d, 3d, 4th, 5th, and 6th Notes of the Bass ought to be each a Degree lower.

A TREATISE OF *MUSICK*.

CHAP. I.

Containing an Account of the *Object* and *End* of MUSICK, and the Nature of the Science, in the *Definition* and *Division* of it.

§ 1. *Of* SOUND: *The Cause of it; and the various Affections of it concerned in Musick.*

MUSICK is a Science of *Sounds*; whose *End* is *Pleasure*. *Sound* is the *Object* in general; or, to speak with the *Philosophers*, it is the *material Object*. But it is not the Business of *Musick*, taken in a strict and proper Sense, to consider every Phenomenon and Property of Sound; that belongs to a more universal Philosophy: Yet, that we may understand what it is in Sounds upon

upon which the *Formality of Musick* depends, *i. e.* whereby it is distinguished from other Sciences, of which *Sound* may also be the Object: *Or*, What it is in Sounds that makes the particular and proper Object of *Musick*, whereby it obtains its End; we must a little consider the Nature of Sound.

SOUND is a Word that stands for every Perception that comes by the *Ear* immediately. And for the Nature of the Thing, it is now generally agreed upon among Philosophers, and also confirmed by Experience, to be the Effect of the mutual Collision, and consequent tremulous Motion in Bodies communicated to the circumambient Fluid of *Air*, and propagated thro' it to the Organs of Hearing.

A Treatise that were designed for explaining the Nature of *Sound* universally, in all its known and remarkable *Phænomena*, should, no doubt, examine very particularly every Thing that belongs to the Cause of it; *First*, The Nature of that Kind of Motion in Bodies (excited by their mutual Percussion) which is communicated to the Air; *then*, how the Air receives and propagates that Motion to certain Distances: And, *lastly*, How that Motion is received by the Ear, explaining the several Parts of that Organ, and their Offices, that are employed in *Hearing*. But as the Nature and Design of what I propose and have *essayed* in this Treatise, does not require so large an Account of Sounds, I must be content only to consider such *Phænomena* as belong properly to *Musick*,

Musick, or serve for the better Understanding of it. In order to which I shall a little further enlarge the preceding general Account of the Cause of *Sound*. And,

First, That *Motion* is necessary in the Production of *Sound*, is a Conclusion drawn from all our Experience. *Again, that Motion* exists, first among the small and insensible Parts of such Bodies as are *Sonorous*, or capable of *Sound*; excited in them by mutual Collision and Percussion one against another, which produces that tremulous Motion so observable in Bodies, especially that have a free and clear Sound, as Bells, and the Strings of musical Instruments; *then*, this Motion is communicated to, or produces a like Motion in the Air, or such Parts of it as are apt to receive and propagate it: For no Motion of Bodies at Distance can affect our Senses, (or move the Parts of our Bodies) without the Mediation of other Bodies, which receive these Motions from the Sonorous Body, and communicate them immediately to the Organs of Sense; and no other than a Fluid can reasonably be supposed. But we know this also by Experience; for a Bell in the exhausted Receiver of an Air-pump can scarcely be heard, which was loud enough before the Air was drawn out. In the *last Place*, This Motion must be communicated to those Parts of the Ear that are the proper and immediate Instruments of Hearing. The Mechanism of this noble Organ has still great Difficulties, which all the Industry of the most capable and curious Enquirers has not surmounted: There

There are Queſtions ſtill unſolved about the Uſe of ſome Parts, and perhaps other neceſſary Parts never yet diſcovered: But the moſt important Queſtion among the Learned is about the laſt and immediate Inſtrument of Hearing, or that Part which laſt receives the ſonorous Motion, and finiſhes what is neceſſary on the Part of the Organ. Conſult theſe with the Philoſophers and Anatomiſts; I ſhall only tell you the common Opinion, in ſuch general Terms as my Deſign permits, *thus:* Next to the external viſible Cavity or Paſſage into the Ear, there is a Cavity, of another Form, ſeparate from the former by a thin Membrane, or Skin, which is called the Tympan or Drum of the Ear, from the Reſemblance it has to that Inſtrument: Within the Cavity of this Drum there is always Air, like that external Air which is the Medium of Sound. Now, the external Air makes its Impreſſion firſt on the Membrane of the Drum, and this communicates the Motion to the internal Air, by which it is again communicated to other Parts, till it reaches at laſt to the auditory Nerve, and there the Senſation is finiſhed, as far as Matter and Motion are concerned; and then the *Mind*, by the Laws of its Union with the Body, has that Idea we call *Sound*. It is a curious Remark, that there are certain Parts fitted for the bending and unbending of the Drum of the Ear, in order, very probably, to the perceiving Sounds that are raiſed at greater or leſſer Diſtances, or whoſe Motions have different Degrees of Force, like what we are more ſenſible

ſenſible of in the Eye, which by proper Muſcles (which are Inſtruments of Motion) we can move outwards or inwards, and change the very Figure of, that we may better perceive very diſtant or near Objects. But I have gone far enough in this.

LEST what I have ſaid of the Cauſe of Sound be too general, particularly with reſpect to the Motion of the ſonorous Body, which I call the original Cauſe, let us go a little farther with it. That Motion in any Body, which is the immediate Cauſe of its ſounding, may be owing to two different Cauſes; one is, the mutual Percuſſion betwixt it and another Body, which is the Caſe of Drums, Bells, and the Strings of muſical Inſtruments, *&c.* Another Cauſe is, the beating or daſhing of the ſonorous Body and the Air immediately againſt one another, as in all Kind of Wind-inſtruments, Flutes, Trumpets, Hautboys, *&c.* Now in all theſe Caſes, the Motion which is the Conſequence of the mutual Percuſſion betwixt the whole Bodies, and is the immediate Cauſe of the ſonorous Motion which the Air conveys to our Ears, is an inviſible tremulous or undulating Motion in the ſmall and inſenſible Parts of the Body. To explain this;

ALL viſible Bodies are ſuppoſed to be compoſed of a Number of ſmall and inſenſible Parts, which are of the ſame Nature in every Body, being perfectly hard and incompreſſible: Of theſe infinitely little Bodies are compoſed others that are ſomething greater, but ſtill inſenſible, and theſe are different, according to the different Figures and

and Union of their component Parts: These are again supposed to constitute other Bodies greater, (which have greater Differences than the last) whose different Combinations do, in the last Place, constitute those gross Bodies that are visible and touchable. The first and smallest Parts are absolutely hard; the others are compressible, and are united in such a Manner, that being, by a sufficient external Impulse, compressed, they restore themselves to their natural, or ordinary, State: This Compression therefore happening upon the Shock or Impulse made by one Body upon another, these small Parts or Particles, by their restitutive Power (which we also call elastick Faculty) move to and again with a very great Velocity or Swiftness, in a tremulous and undulating Manner, something like the visible Motions of grosser Springs, as the Chord of a musical Instrument; and this is what we may call the *Sonorous Motion* which is propagated to the Ear. But observe that it is the insensible Motion of these Particles next to the smallest, which is supposed to be the immediate Cause of Sound; and of these, only those next the Surface can communicate with the Air; their Motion is performed in very small Spaces, and with extreme Velocity; the Motion of the Whole, or of the greater Parts being no further concerned than as they contribute to the other.

And this is the Hypothesis upon which Monsieur *Perrault* of the Royal Society in *France*, explains the Nature and *Phænomena* of Sound, in his curious Treatise upon that Subject, *Essais de Physique*; *Tom.*

Tom. II. *Du Bruit.* How this Theory is ſupported I ſhall briefly ſhew, while I conſider a few Applications of it.

Of thoſe hard Bodies that ſound by Percuſſion of others, let us conſider a Bell: Strike it with any other hard body, and while it ſounds we can diſcern a ſenſible Tremor in the Surface, which ſpreads more ſenſibly over the Whole, as the Shock is greater. This Motion is not only in the Parts next the Surface, but in all the Parts thro' the whole Solidity, becauſe we can perceive it alſo in the inner Surface of the Bell, which muſt be by Communication with thoſe Parts that are immediately touched by the ſtriking Body. And this is proven by the ceaſing of the Sound when the Bell is touched in any other Part; for this ſhews the eaſy and actual Communication of the Motion. Now this is plainly a Motion of the ſeveral ſmall and inſenſible Parts changing their Situations with reſpect to one another, which being ſo many, and ſo cloſely united, we cannot perceive their Motions ſeparately and diſtinctly, but only that Trembling which we reckon to be the Effect of the Confuſion of an infinite Number of little Particles ſo cloſely joyned and moving in infinitely ſmall Spaces. Thus far any Body will eaſily go with the Hypotheſis: But Monſieur *Perrault* carries it farther, and affirms, That that viſible Motion of the Parts is no otherwiſe the Cauſe of the Sound, than as it cauſes the inviſible Motion of the yet ſmaller Parts, (which he calls *Particles*, to diſtinguiſh them from the other which he calls

calls *Parts*, the leaſt of all being with him *Corpuſcles*.) And this he endeavours to prove by other Examples, as of Chords and Wind-inſtruments. Let us conſider them.

TAKE a Chord or String of a Muſical Inſtrument, ſtretched to a ſufficient Degree for Sounding; when it is fixt at both Ends, we make it ſound by drawing the Chord from its ſtraight Poſition, and then letting it go; (which has the ſame Effect as what we properly call Percuſſion) the Parts by this drawing, whereby the Whole is lengthned, being put out of their natural State, or that which they had in the ſtraight Line, do by their Elaſticity reſtore themſelves, which cauſes that vibratory Motion of the Whole, whereby it moves to and again beyond the ſtraight Line, in Vibrations gradually ſmaller, till the Motion ceaſe, and the Chord recover its former Poſition. Now the ſhorter the Chord is, and the more it is ſtretched in the ſtraight Line, the quicker theſe Vibrations are: But however quick they are, Monſieur *Perrault* denies them to be the immediate Cauſe of the Sound; becauſe, ſays he, in a very long Chord, and not very ſmall, ſtretched only ſo far as that it may give a diſtinct Sound, we can perceive with our Eye, beſides the Vibrations of the whole Chord, a more confuſed Tremor of the Parts, which is more diſcernible towards the Middle of the Chord, where the Parts vibrate in greater Spaces in the Motion of the Whole; this laſt Motition of the *Parts* which is cauſed by the firſt Vibrations of the Whole, does again occaſion a Motion

Motion in the leſſer Parts or *Partitles*, which is the immediate Cauſe of the Sound. And this he endeavours to confirm by this Experiment, *viz.* Take a long Chord (he ſays he made it with one of 30 Foot) and make it ſound; then wait till the Sound quite ceaſe, and then alſo the viſible Undulations of the whole Chord will ceaſe: If immediately upon this ceaſing of the Sound, you approach the Chord very ſoftly with the Nail of your Finger, you'll perceive a tremulous Motion in it, which is the remaining ſmall Vibrations of the whole Chord, and of the *Parts* cauſed by the Vibrations of the Whole. Now theſe Vibrations of the *Parts* are not the immediate Cauſe of Sound; elſe how comes it that while they are yet in Motion they raiſe no Sound? The Anſwer perhaps is this, That the Motion is become too weak to make the Sound to be heard at any great Diſtance, which might be heard were the Tympan of the Ear as near as the Nail of the Finger, by which we perceive the Motion. But to carry off this, Mr. *Perrault* ſays, That as ſoon as this ſmall Motion is perceived, we ſhall hear it ſound; which is not occaſioned by renewing or augmenting the greater Vibrations, becauſe the Finger is not ſuppoſed to ſtrike againſt the Chord, but this againſt the Finger, which ought rather to ſtop that Motion; the Cauſe of this renewed Sound therefore is propably, That this weak Motion of the *Parts*, which is not ſufficient to move the *Particles* (whoſe Motion is the Firſt that ceaſes) receives ſome Aſſiſtance from the daſhing

dashing against the Nail, whereby they are enabled to give the *Particles* that Motion which is necessary for producing the Sound. But lest it should still be thought, that this Encounter with the Nail may as well be supposed to increase the Motion of the Parts to a Degree fit for sounding, as to make them capable of moving the *Particles*; we may consider, That the Particles being at Rest in the *Parts*, and having each a common Motion with the whole *Part*, may very easily be supposed to receive a proper and particular Motion by that Shock; in the same Manner that Bodies which are relatively at Rest in a Ship, will be shaked and moved by the Shock of the Ship against any Body that can any thing considerably oppose its Motion. Now for as simple as this Experiment appears to be, I am afraid it cannot be so easily made as to give perfect Satisfaction, because we can hardly touch a String with our Nail but it will sound.

But Mr. *Perrault* finishes the Proof of his Hypothesis by the Phenomena of Wind-instruments. Take, for example, a *Flute*; we make it sound by blowing into a long, broad, and thin Canal, which conveys the Air thrown out of the Lungs, till 'tis dashed against that thin solid Part which we call the Tongue, or Wind-cutter, that is opposite to the lower Orifice of the foresaid Canal; by which Means the *Particles* of that Tongue are compressed, and by their restitutive Motion they communicate to the Air a Sonorous Motion, which being immediately thrown against the inner concave Surface of the Flute, and

and moving its *Particles*, the Motion communicated to the Air, by all these *Particles* both of the Tongue and inner Surface, makes up the whole Sound of the Flute.

Now to prove that only the very small *Particles* of the inner Surface and Edge of the Tongue are concerned in the Sound of the Flute, we must consider, That Flutes of different Matter, as Metal, Wood, or Bone, being of the same Length and Bore, have none, or very little sensible Difference in their Sound; nor is this sensibly altered by the different Thickness of the Flute betwixt the outer and inner Surface; nor in the last place, is the Sound any way changed by touching the Flute, even tho' it be hard pressed, as it always happens in Bells and other hard Bodies that sound by mutual Percussion. All this Mr. *Perrault* accounts for by his Hypothesis, thus: He tells us, That as the *Corpuscles* are the same in all Bodies, the *Particles* which they immediately constitute, have very small Differences in their Nature and Form; and that the specifick Differences of visible Bodies, depend on the Differences of the *Parts* made up of these *Particles*, and the various Connections of these Parts, which make them capable of different Modifications of Motion. Now, hard Bodies that sound by mutual Percussion one against another, owe their sounding to the Vibrations of all their *Parts*, and by these to the insensible Motions of their *Particles*; but according to the Differences of the Parts and their Connections, which make

make them, either Silver, or Braſs, or Wood, *&c.* ſo are the Differences of their Sounds. But in Wind-inſtruments (for example, Flutes) as there are no ſuch remarkable Differences anſwering to their Matter, their Sound can only be owing to the inſenſible Motion of the Particles of the Surface; for theſe being very little different in all Bodies, if we ſuppoſe the Sound is owing to their Motions only, it can have none, or very ſmall Differences: And becauſe we find this true in Fact, it makes the Hypotheſis extremely probable. I have never indeed ſeen Flutes of any Matter but Wood, except of the ſmall Kind we call Flageolets, of which I have ſeen Ivoryo nes, whoſe Sound has no remarkable Difference from a wooden one; and therefore I muſt leave ſo much of this Proof upon Monſieur *Perrault*'s Credit. As to the other Part, which is no leſs conſiderable, That no Compreſſion of the Flute can ſenſibly change its Sound, 'tis certain, and every Body can eaſily try it. To which we may add, That Flutes of different Matter are ſounded with equal Eaſe, which could not well be if their *Parts* were to be moved; for in different Bodies theſe are differently moveable. But I muſt make an End of this Part, in which I think it is made plain enough, That the Motion of a Body which cauſes a ſounding Motion in the Air, is not any Motion which we can poſſibly give to the whole Body, wherein all the Parts are moved in one common Direction and Velocity; but it is the Motion of the ſeveral ſmall and undiſtinguiſhable Parts,

Parts, which being compressed by an external Force, do, by their elastick Power, restore themselves, each by a Motion particular and proper to it self. But whether you'll distinguish *Parts* and *Particles* as Mr. *Perrault* does, I leave to your selves, my Design not requiring any accurate Determination of this Matter. And now to come nearer to our Subject, I shall next consider the Differences and Affections of Sounds that are any way concern'd in *Musick*.

SOUNDS are as various, or have as many Differences, as the infinite Variety of Things that concur in their Production; which may be reduced to these general Heads: 1*st*, The Quantity, Constitution, and Figure of the sonorous Body; with the Manner of Percussion, and the consequent Velocity of the Vibrations of the Parts of the Body and the Air; also their Equality and Uniformity, or Inequality and Irregularness. 2*dly*, The Constitution and State of the fluid Medium through which the Motion is propagated. 3*dly*, The Disposition of the Ear that receives that Motion. And, 4*thly*, The Distance of the Ear from the sonorous Body. To which we may add, *lastly*, the Consideration of the Obstacles that interpose betwixt the sonorous Body and the Ear; with other adjacent Bodies that, receiving an Impression from the Fluid so moved, react upon it, and give new Modification to the Motion, and consequently to the Sound. Upon all these do our different Perceptions of Sound depend.

THE

The Variety and Differences of Sounds, owing to the various Degrees and Combinations of the Conditions mentioned, are innumerable; but to our preſent Deſign we are to conſider the following Diſtinctions.

I. *SOUNDS*, come under a ſpecifick Diſtinction, according to the Kinds of Bodies from which they proceed: Thus, Metal is eaſily diſtinguiſhed from other Bodies by the Sound; and among Metals there is great difference of Sounds, as is diſcernible, for Example, Betwixt Gold, Silver, and Braſs. And for the Purpoſe in hand, a moſt notable Difference is that of ſtringed and Wind-inſtruments of Muſick, of which there are alſo Subdiviſions: Theſe Differences depend, as has been ſaid, upon the different Conſtitutions of theſe Bodies; but they are not ſtrictly within the Conſideration of *Muſick*, not the *Mathematical* Part of it at leaſt, tho' they may be brought into the *Practical*; of which afterwards.

II. Experience teaches us, That ſome Sounds can be heard, by the ſame Ear, at greater Diſtances than others; and when we are at the ſame Diſtance from two Sounds, I mean from the ſonorous Body or the Place where the Sound firſt riſes, we can determine (for we learn it by Experience and Obſervation) which of the Two will be heard fartheſt: By this Compariſon we have the Idea of a Difference whoſe oppoſite Terms are called *LOUD* and *LOW*, (or *ſtrong* and *weak*.) This Difference depends both upon the Nature of different Bodies, and upon

upon other accidental Circumſtances, ſuch as their *Figure*; or the different Force in the Percuſſion; and frequently upon the Nature of the circumjacent Bodies, that contribute to the ſtrengthning of the Sound, that is a Conjunction of ſeveral Sounds ſo united as to appear only as one Sound: But as the Union of ſeveral Sounds gives Occaſion to another Diſtinction, it ſhall be conſidered again, and we have only to obſerve here that it is always the Cauſe of *Loudneſs*; yet this Difference belongs not ſtrictly to the Theory of Muſick, tho' it is brought into the Practice, as that in the Firſt Article.

III. THERE is an Affection or Property of Sound, whereby it is diſtinguiſhed into ACUTE, *ſharp* or *high*; and GRAVE, *flat* or *low*. The Idea of this Difference you'll get by comparing ſeveral Sounds or Notes of a muſical Inſtrument, or of a human Voice ſinging. *Obſerve* the Term, *Low*, is ſometimes oppoſed to *Loud*, and ſometimes to *acute*, which yet are very different Things: *Loudneſs* is very well meaſured by the Diſtance or Sphere of Audibility, which makes the Notion of it very clear. *Acuteneſs* is ſo far different, that a Voice or Sound may aſcend or riſe in Degree of *Acuteneſs*, and yet loſe nothing of its *Loudneſs*, which can eaſily be demonſtrated upon any Inſtrument, or even in the Voice; and particularly if we compare the Voice of a Boy and a Man.

THIS Relation of *Acuteneſs* and *Gravity* is one of the principal Things concerned in Muſick, the Nature of which ſhall be particularly con-

considered afterwards; and I shall here observe that it depends altogether upon the Nature of the sonorous Body it self, and the particular Figure and Quantity of it; and in some Cases upon the Part of the Body where it is struck. So that, for Example, the Sounds of two Bells of different Metals, and the same Shape and Dimensions, being struck in the same Place, will differ as to *Acuteness* and *Gravity*; and two Bells of the same Metal will differ in *Acuteness*, if they differ in Shape or in Magnitude, or be struck in different Parts: So in Chords, all other Things being equal, if they differ either in Matter, or Dimensions, or the Degree of Tension, as being stretched by different Weights, they will also differ in *Acuteness*.

BUT we must carefully *remark*, That *Acuteness* and *Gravity*, also *Loudness* and *Lowness* are but relative Things; so that we cannot call any Sound *acute* or *loud*, but with respect to another which is *grave* or *low* in reference to the former; and therefore the same Sound may be *acute* or *grave*, also *loud* or *low* in different Respects. *Again*, These Relations are to be found not only between the Sounds of different Bodies, but also between different Sounds of the same Body; for different Force in the Percussion will cause a *louder* or *lower* Sound, and striking the Body in different Parts will make an *acuter* or *graver* Sound, as we have remarkably demonstrated in a Bell, which as the Stroke is greater gives a greater or *louder* Sound, and being struck nearer the open End,

gives

gives the *graver* Sound. How theſe Degrees are meaſured, we ſhall learn again, only *mind* that theſe Degrees of *Acuteneſs* and *Gravity* are alſo called different and diſtinguiſhable *Tones* or *Tunes* of a Voice or Sound; ſo we ſay one Sound is in *Tune* with another when they are in the ſame Degree: *Acute* and *Grave* being but Relations, we apply the Name of *Tune* to them both, to expreſs ſomething that's conſtant and abſolute which is the Ground of the Relation; in like manner as we apply the Name *Magnitude* both to the Things we call *Great* and *Little*, which are but relative Idea's: Each of them have a certain Magnitude, but only one of them is great and the other little when they are compared; ſo of Two Sounds each has a certain *Tune*, but only one is *acute* and the other *grave* in Compariſon.

IV. THERE is a Diſtinction of *Sounds*, whereby they are denominated *long* or *ſhort*; which relates to the *Duration*, or continued, and ſenſibly uninterrupted Exiſtence of the *Sound*. This is a Thing of very great Importance in *Muſick*; but to know how far, and in what reſpect it belongs to it, we muſt diſtinguiſh betwixt the *natural* and *artificial Duration* of Sound. I call that the *natural Duration* or *Continuity* of *Sound*, which is leſs or more in different Bodies, owing to their different Conſtitutions, whereby one retains the Motion once received longer than another does; and conſequently the Sound continues longer (tho' gradually weaker) after the external Impulſe ceaſes; ſo Bells of different Metals, all other Things being equal and alike

alike, have different Continuity of Sound after the Stroke: And the ſame is very remarkable in Strings of different Matter: There is too a Difference in the ſame Bell or String, according to the Force of the Percuſſion. This Continuity is ſometimes owing to the ſudden Reflection of the Sound from the Surface of neighbouring Bodies; which is not ſo properly the ſame Sound continued, as a new Sound ſucceeding the Firſt ſo quickly as to appear to be only its Continuation: But this Duration of Sound does not properly belong to Muſick, wherefore let us conſider the other. The *artificial* Continuity of Sound is, that which depends upon the continued Impulſe of the efficient Cauſe upon the ſonorous Body for a longer or ſhorter Time. Such are the Notes of a Voice, or any Wind-inſtrument, which are longer or ſhorter as we continue to blow into them; or, the Notes of a Violin and all ſtring'd Inſtruments that are ſtruck with a Bow, whoſe Notes are made longer or ſhorter by Strokes of different lengths or Quickneſs of Motion; for a long Stroke, if it is quickly drawn, may make a ſhorter Note than a ſhort Stroke drawn ſlowly. Now this kind of Continuity is properly the Succeſſion of ſeveral Sounds, or the Effect of ſeveral diſtinct Strokes, or repeated Impulſes, upon the ſonorous Body, ſo quick that we judge it to be one continued Sound, eſpecially if it is continued in one Degree of Strength and Loudneſs; but it muſt alſo be continued in one Degree of *Tune*, elſe it cannot be called one Note in Muſick. And this leads me naturally ly to consider the very old and notable Distinction of a twofold Motion of Sound, thus.

SOUND may move thro' various Degrees of *Acuteness* in a continual Flux, so as not to rest on any Degree for any assignable, or at least sensible Time; which the Ancients called the *continuous Motion* of Sound, proper only to Speaking and Conversation. Or, 2*do.* it may pass from Degree to Degree, and make a sensible Stand at every Pitch, so as every Degree shall be distinct; this they called the *discrete* or *discontinued Motion* of Sound, proper only to Musick or Singing. But that there may be no Obscurity here, *consider*, That as the Idea's of *Motion* and *Distance* are inseparably connected, so they belong in a proper Sense to *Bodies* and *Space*; and whatever other Thing they are applied to, it is in a figurative and metaphorical Sense, as here to Sounds; yet the Application is very intelligible, as I shall explain it. *Voice* or *Sound* is considered as one individual Being, all other Differences being neglected except that of *Acuteness* and *Gravity*, which is not considered as constituting different Sounds, but different States of the same Sound; which is easy to conceive: And so the several *Degrees* or Pitches of *Tune*, are considered as several Places in which a Voice may exist. And when we hear a Sound successively existing in different Degrees of *Tune*, we conceive the Voice to have moved from the one Place to the other; and then 'tis easy to conceive a Kind of Distance between the

two

two Degrees or Places; for as Bodies are ſaid to be diſtant, between which other Bodies may be placed, ſo two Sounds are ſaid to be at Diſtance, with reſpect to *Tune*, between which other Degrees may be conceived, that ſhall be *acute* with reſpect to the one, and *grave* with reſpect to the other. But when the Voice continues in one Pitch, tho' there may be many Interruptions and ſenſible Reſts whereby the Sound doth end and begin again, yet there is no Motion in that Caſe, the Voice being all the Time in one Place. Now this Motion, in a ſimple and proper Senſe, is nothing elſe but the ſucceſſive Exiſtence of ſeveral Sounds differing in *Tune*. When the ſucceſſive Degrees are ſo near, that like the Colours of a Rainbow, they are as it were loſt in one another, ſo that in any ſenſible Diſtance there is an indefinite Number of Degrees, ſuch kind of Succeſſion is of no uſe in *Muſick*; but when it is ſuch that the Ear is Judge of every ſingle Difference, and can compare ſeveral Differences, and apply ſome known Meaſure to them, there the Object of Muſick does exiſt; or when there is a Succeſſion of ſeveral Sounds diſtinct by ſenſible Reſts, tho' all in the ſame Tune, ſuch a Succeſſion belongs alſo to Muſick.

FROM this twofold Motion explain'd, we ſee a twofold *Continuity* of Sound, both ſubject to certain and determinate Meaſures of *Duration*; the one is that ariſing from the continuous Motion mentioned, which has nothing to do in *Muſick*; the other is the Continuity or uninterrupted Exiſtence of Sound in one

one Degree of *Tune*. The Differences of Sounds in this reſpect, or the various Meaſures of *long* and *ſhort*, or, (which is the ſame, at leaſt a Conſequence) *ſwift* and *ſlow*, in the ſucceſſive Degrees of Sound, while it moves in the ſecond Manner, make a principal and neceſſary Ingredient in *Muſick*; whoſe Effect is not inferior to any other Thing concerned in the Practice; and is what deſerves to be very particularly conſidered, tho' indeed it is not brought under ſo regular and determinate Rules as the Differences of *Tune*.

V. SOUNDS are either *ſimple* or *compound*; but there is a twofold Simplicity and Compoſition to be conſidered here; the Firſt is the ſame with what we explain'd in the laſt Article, and relates to the Number of ſucceſſive Vibrations of the Parts of the ſonorous Body, and of the Air, which come ſo faſt upon the Ear that we judge them all to be one continued Sound, tho' it is really a Compoſition of ſeveral Sounds of ſhorter Duration. And our judging it to be *one*, is very well compared to the Judgment we make of that apparent Circle of Fire, cauſed by putting the fired End of a Stick into a very quick circular Motion; for ſuppoſe the End of the Stick in any Point of that Circle which it actually deſcribes, the Idea we receive of it there continues till the Impreſſion is renewed by the ſudden Return; and this being true of every Point, we muſt have the Idea of a Circle of Fire; the only Difference is, that the End of the Stick has actually exiſted in every Point of the Circle, whereas

whereas the Sound has had Interruptions, tho' insensible to us because of their quick Succession; but the Things we compare are, the Succession of the Sounds making a sensible Continuity with respect to Time, and the Succession of the End of the Stick in every Point of the Circle after a whole Revolution; for 'tis by this we judge it to be a Circle, making a Continuity with respect to Space. The Author of the *Elucidationes Physicæ* upon *D' Cartes* Musick, illustrates it in this Manner, says he, As standing Corns are bended by one Blast of Wind, and before they can recover themselves the Wind has repeated the Blast, so that the Corn's standing in the same inclined Position for a certain Time, seems to be the Effect of one single Action of the Wind, which is truly owing to several distinct Operations; in like Manner the small Branches (*capillamenta*) of the auditory Nerve, resembling so many Stalks of Corn, being moved by one Vibration of the Air, and this repeated before the Nerve can recover its Situation, gives Occasion to the Mind to judge the whole Effect to be one Sound. The Nature of this kind of *Composition* being so far explain'd, we are next to consider what *Simplicity* in this Sense is; and I think it must be the Effect of one single Vibration, or as many Vibrations as are necessary to raise in us the Idea of Sound; but perhaps it may be a Question, Whether we ever have, or if we can raise such an Idea of Sound: There may be also another Question, Whether any Idea of Sound can exist in the Mind for an indivisible Space of of Time; the Reaſon of this Queſtion is, That if every Sound exiſts for a finite Time, it can be divided into Parts of a ſhorter Duration, and then there is no ſuch Thing as an abſolute Simplicity of this Kind, unleſs we take the Notion of it from the Action of the external Cauſe of Sound, *viz.* the Number of Vibrations neceſſary to make Sound actually exiſt, without conſidering how long it exiſts; but as it is not probable that we can ever actually produce this, *i. e.* put a Body in a ſounding Motion, and ſtop it preciſely when there are as many Vibrations finiſhed as are abſolutely neceſſary to make Sound, we muſt reckon the Simplicity of Sound, conſidered in this Manner, and with reſpect to Practice, a relative Thing; that being only ſimple to us which is the moſt ſimple, either with reſpect to the Duration or the Cauſe, that we ever hear: But whether we conſider it in the repeated Action of the Cauſe or the conſequent Duration, which is the Subject of the laſt Article, there is ſtill another Simplicity and Compoſition of Sounds very different from that, and of great Importance in Muſick, which I ſhall next explain.

A *ſimple Sound* is the Product of one Voice or individual Body, as the Sound of one Flute or one Man's Voice. A *compound Sound* conſiſts of the Sounds of ſeveral diſtinct Voices or Bodies all united in the ſame individual Time and Meaſure of Duration, *i. e.* all ſtriking the Ear together, whatever their other Differences may be. But we muſt here diſtinguiſh a *natural*
and

and *artificial Compoſition*; to underſtand this, remember, That the Air being put into Motion by any Body, communicates that Motion to other Bodies; the *naturalCompoſition* of Sounds is therefore, that which proceeds from the manifold Reflexions of the Firſt Sound, or that of the Body which firſt communicates ſounding Motion to the Air, as the Flute or Violin in one's Hand; theſe Reflexions, being many, according to the Circumſtances of the Place, or the Number, Nature, and Situations of the circumjacent Bodies, make Sounds more or leſs *compound.* This is a Thing we know by common Experience; we can have a hundred Proofs of it every Day by ſinging, or ſounding any muſical Inſtrument in different Places, either in the Fields or within Doors; but theſe Reflexions muſt be ſuch as returning very ſuddenly don't produce what we call an *Eccho*, and have only this Effect, to increaſe the Sound, and make an agreeable Reſonance; but ſtill in the ſame Tune with the original Note; or, if it be a Compoſition of different Degrees of Tune, they are ſuch as mix and unite, ſo that the Whole agrees with that Note. But this Compoſition is not under Rules of Art; for tho' we learn by Experience how to diſpoſe theſe Circumſtances that they may produce the deſired Effect, yet we neither know the Number or different Tunes of the Sounds that enter into this Compoſition; and therefore they come not under the Muſician's Direction in what is hereafter called the *Compoſition of Muſick*; his Care being only about

bout the *artificial Composition*, or that Mixture of several Sounds, which being made by Art, are separable and distinguishable one from another. So the distinct Sounds of several Voices or Instruments, or several Notes of the same Instrument, are called *simple Sounds*, in Distinction from the artificial *Composition*, in which to answer the End of Musick, the *Simples* must have such an Agreement in all Relations, but principally and above all in *Acuteness* and *Gravity*, that the Ear may receive the Mixture with Pleasure.

VI. THERE remains another Distinction of Sounds necessary to be considered, whereby they are said to be *smooth* and *evenly*, or *rough* and *harsh*; also *clear* or *blunt*, *hoarse* and *obtuse*, the Idea's of these Differences must be sought from Observations; as to the Cause of them, they depend upon the Disposition and State of the sonorous Body, or the Circumstances of the Place. *Smooth* and *rough* Sounds depend upon the Body principally; We have a notable Example of a *rough* and *harsh* Sound in Strings that are unevenly and not of the same Constitution and Dimension throughout; and for this Reason that their Sounds are very grating, they are called false Strings. I will let you in few Words hear how Monsieur *Perrault* accounts for this. He affirms that there is no such Thing as a simple Sound, and that the Sound of the same Bell or Chord is a Compound of the Sounds of the several Parts of it; so that where the Parts are homogeneous, and the Dimensions or Figure uniform, there is always such a perfect Union and

and Mixture of all these Sounds that makes one uniform, smooth and evenly Sound; and the contrary produces Harshness; for the Likeness of Parts and Figure makes an Uniformity of Vibrations, whereby a great Number of similar and coincident Motions conspire to fortify and improve each other mutually, and unite for the more effectual Production of the same Effect. He proves his Hypothesis by the Phenomena of a Bell, which differs in *Tone* according to the Part you strike, and yet strike it any where there is a Motion over all the Parts; he considers therefore the Bell as composed of an infinite Number of Rings, which according to their different Dimensions have different *Tones*; as Chords of different Lengths have (*cæteris paribus*) and when it is struck, the Vibrations of the Parts immediately struck specify the *Tone*, being supported by a sufficient Number of consonant Tones in other Parts: And to confirm this, he relates a very remarkable Thing; He says, He happen'd in a Place where a Bell sounded a *Fifth* acuter than the Tone it used to give in other Places; which in all Probability, says he, was owing to the accidental Disposition of the Place, that was furnished with such an Adjustment for reflecting that particular Tone with Force, and so unfit for reflecting others, that it absolutely prevailed and determined the Concord and total Sound to the *Tone* of that *Fifth*. If we consider the Sound of a Violin, and all string'd Instruments, we have a plain Demonstration that every Note is the Effect of seve-

ſeveral more ſimple Sounds; for there is not only the Sound reſulting from the Motion of the String, but alſo that of the Motion of the Parts of the Inſtrument; that this has a very conſiderable Effect in the total Sound is certain, becauſe we are very ſenſible of the tremulous Motion of the Parts of the Violin, and eſpecially becauſe the ſame String upon different Violins ſounds very differently, which can be for no other Reaſon but the different Conſtitution of the Parts of theſe Inſtruments, which being moved by Communication with the String increaſe the Sound, and make it more or leſs agreeable, according to their different Natures: But *Perrault* affirms the ſame of every String in it ſelf without conſidering the Inſtrument; he ſays, Every Part of the String has its particular Vibrations different from the groſs and ſenſible Vibrations of the Whole, and theſe are the Cauſes of different Motions (and Sounds) in the *Particles*; which being mix'd and unite, as was ſaid of the Sounds that compoſe the total Sound of a Bell, make an uniform and evenly Compoſition, wherein not only one Tone prevails, but the Mixture is ſmooth and agreeable; but when the Parts are unevenly and irregularly conſtitute, the Sound is harſh and the String from that called falſe. And therefore ſuch a String, or other Body having the like Fault, has no certain and diſtinct *Tone*, being a Compoſition of ſeveral *Tones* that don't unite and mix ſo as to have one Predominant that ſpecifies the *total Tone*.

AGAIN

Again for *clear* or *hoarſe* Sounds, they depend upon Circumſtances that are accidental to the ſonorous Body; ſo a Man's Voice, or the Sound of an Inſtrument will be hollow and hoarſe, if it is raiſed within an empty Hogſhead, which is clear and bright out of it; the Reaſon is very plainly the Mixture of other and different Sounds raiſed by Reflexion, that corrupt and change the Species of the primitive and direct Sound.

Now that Sounds may be fit for obtaining the End of *Muſick* they ought to be *ſmooth* and *clear*; eſpecially the Firſt, becauſe if they have not one certain and diſcernible *Tone*, capable of being compared to others, and ſtanding to them in a certain Relation of *Acuteneſs*, whoſe Differences the Ear may be able to judge of and meaſure, they cannot poſſibly anſwer the End of *Muſick*, and therefore, are no Part of the Object of it.

But there are alſo Sounds which have a certain *Tone*, yet being exceſſive either in Acuteneſs or Gravity, bear not that juſt Proportion to the Capacity of the Organs of Hearing, as to afford agreeable Senſations. Upon the Whole then we ſhall call that *harmonick* or *muſical Sound*, which being *clear* and *evenly* is agreeable to the *Ear*, and gives a certain and diſcernible *Tune* (hence alſo called *tunable Sound*) which is the Subject of the whole Theory of Harmony.

Thus we have conſidered the Properties and Affections of Sound that are any way neceſſary

cessary to the Subject in hand; and of all the Things mentioned, the Relation of *Acuteness* and *Gravity*, or the *Tune* of Sounds, is the principal Ingredient in *Musick*; the Distinctness and Determinateness of which Relation gives sound the Denomination of *harmonical* or *musical*: Next to which are the various Measures of *Duration*. There is nothing in Sounds without these that can make *Musick*; a just *Theory* whereof abstracts from all other Things, to consider the Relations of Sounds in the Measures of *Tune* and *Duration*; tho' indeed in the *Practice* other Differences are considered (of which something more may be said afterwards) but they are so little, compared to the other Two, and under so very general and uncertain *Theory*, that I don't find they have ever been brought into the Definition of *Musick*.

---

§ 2. *Containing the* Definition *and* Division *of* Musick.

WE may from what is already said affirm, That *Musick* has for its Object, in general, *Sound*; and particularly, *Sounds* considered in their Relations of *Tune* and *Duration*, as under that *Formality* they are capable of affording agreeable Sensations. I shall therefore define MUSICK, *A* SCIENCE *that teaches how* SOUNDS, *under certain Measures of* TUNE *and*

and TIME, *may be produced; and ſo ordered or diſpoſed, as in* CONSONANCE (i. e. *joynt ſounding*) *or* SUCCESSION, *or both, they may raiſe agreeable Senſations.*

PLEASURE, I have ſaid, is the immediate End of *Muſick*; I ſuppoſe it therefore as a *Principle*, That the Objects propoſed are capable, being duly applied, to affect the Mind agreeably; nor is it a precarious Principle; Experience proves, and we know by the infallible Teſtimony of our Senſes, that ſome *ſimple* Sounds ſucceed others upon the Ear with a poſitive Pleaſure, others diſagreeably; according to certain Relations of Tune and Time; and ſome *compound* Sounds are agreeable, others offenſive to the Ear; and that there are Degrees and Variety in this Pleaſure, according to the various Meaſures of theſe Relations. For what Pretences are made of the Application of *Muſick* to ſome other Purpoſes than mere Pleaſure or Recreation, as theſe are obtain'd chiefly by Means of that Pleaſure, they cannot be called the immediate End of it.

FROM the *Definition* given, we have the Science divided into theſe two general Parts. *Firſt*, The *Knowledge* of the MATERIA MUSICA, or, how to produce Sounds, in ſuch relations of *Tune* and *Time* as ſhall be agreeable in *Conſonance* or *Succeſſion*, or both. I don't mean the actual producing of theſe Sounds by an Inſtrument or Voice, which is merely the *mechanical* or *effective* Part; But the Knowledge of the various Relations of *Tune* and *Time*, which

which are the essential Principles out of which the Pleasure sought arises,and upon which it depends. This is the pure *speculative* Part of *Musick*. *Second*, How these Principles are to be applied; or, how Sounds, in the Relations that belong to *Musick* (as these are determined in the First Part) may be ordered, and variously put together in *Succession* and *Consonance* so as to answer the End; which Part we rightly call THE ART of COMPOSITION; and it is properly the *practical* Part of *Musick*.

SOME have added a Third Part, *viz*. The *Knowledge* of INSTRUMENTS; but as this depends altogether upon the First, and is only an Application or Expression of it, it could never be brought regularly into the Definition; and so can be no Part of the Division of the Science; yet may it deserve to be treated of, as a Consequent or Dependent of it, and necessary to be understood for the *effective* Part. As this has no Share in my Design, I shall detain you but while I say, in a few Words, what I think such a Treatise should contain. And 1*mo*, There should be a *Theory* of *Instruments*, giving an Account of their Frame and Construction, particularly, how, supposing them completely provided of all their *Apparatus*, each contains in it the *Principles* of *Musick* *i. e.* how the several Degrees of *Tune* pertaining to *Musick* are to be found upon the *Instruments*. The *Second Part* should contain the Practice of Instruments, in such Directions as might be helpful for the dextrous and nice handling of them, or the elegant Performance

of

of *Musick*: And here might be annex'd Rules for the right Use of the *Voice*. But after all, I believe these Things will be more successfully done by a living Instructor, I mean a skilful and experienced Master, with the Use of his Voice or Instrument; tho' I doubt not such might help us too by Rules; but I have done with this.

YOU must next *observe* with me, That as the *Art* of common *Writing* is altogether distinct from the Sciences to which it is subservient by preserving what would otherwise be lost, and communicating Thoughts at Distance; so there is an *Art* of *Writing* proper to *Musick*, which teaches how, by a fit and convenient Way of representing all the Degrees and Measures of Sound, sufficient for directing in the *executive Part* one who understands how to use his Voice or Instrument: The *Artist* when he has invented a Composition answering the Principles and End of Musick, may preserve it for his own Use, or communicate it to another present or absent. To this I have very justly given a Place in the following Work, as it is a Thing of a general Concern to *Musick*, tho' no Part of the Science, and merely a Handmaid to the Practice; and particularly as the Knowledge of it is necessary for carrying on my Design. I now return to the Division above made, which I shall follow in explaining this Science.

THE First general Branch of this Subject, which is the *contemplative* Part, divides naturally into these. *First*, the Knowledge of the Relations and Measures of *Tune*. And *Secondly*, of *Time*.

Time. The First is properly what the Ancients called HARMONICA, or the Doctrine of *Harmony* in Sounds; because it contains an Explication of the Grounds, with the various Measures and Degrees of the Agreement (*Harmony*) of Sounds in respect of their *Tune.* The other they called *Rythmica*, because it treats of the Numbers of Sounds or Notes with respect to *Time*, containing an Explication of the Measures of *long* and *short*, or *swift* and *slow* in the Succession of Sounds.

The Second general Branch, which is the PRACTICAL Part, as naturally divides into Two Parts answering to the Parts of the First: That which answers to the *Harmonica*, the Ancients called *Melopœia*; because it contains the Rules of making Songs with respect to *Tune* and *Harmony* of Sounds; tho' indeed we have no Ground to believe that the Ancients had any Thing like Composition in Parts. That which answers to the *Rythmica*, they called *Rythmopœia*, containing the Rules concerning the Application of the *Numbers* and *Time.* I shall proceed according to this natural Division, and so the *Theory* is to be first handled.

CHAP.

CHAP. II.

Of Tune, *or the Relation of* Acuteneſs *and* Gravity *in Sounds*; particularly, *of the* Cauſe *and* Meaſure *of the Differences of* Tune.

§ 1. *Containing ſome neceſſary* Definitions *and* Explications, *and the particular* Method *of treating this Branch of the Science concerning* Tune *or* Harmony.

FIRST, The Subject to be here explained is, That Property of Sounds which I have called their *Tune*; whereby they come under the Relation of *acute* and *grave* to one another: For as I have already obſerved, there is no ſuch Thing as *Acuteneſs* and *Gravity* in an abſolute Senſe, theſe being only the Names given to the Terms of the Relation; but when we conſider the Ground of the Relation which is the *Tune* of the Sound, we may juſtly affirm this to be ſome thing abſolute; every Sound having its own proper and peculiar *Tune*, which muſt be under ſome determinate Meaſure in the Nature of the Thing, (but the Denominations of *acute* and *grave* reſpect always another Sound.) Therefore as to *Tune*, we muſt remark that the only Difference can poſſibly be betwixt one *Tune* and another, is is in their Degrees, which are naturally infinite; *that is*, we conceive there is ſomething poſitive in the Cauſe of Sound which is capable of leſs and more, and contains in it the Meaſure of the Degrees of *Tune*; and becauſe we don't ſuppoſe a leaſt or greateſt Quantity of this, therefore we ſay the Degrees depending on theſe Meaſures are infinite: But commonly when we ſpeak of theſe Degrees, we call them ſeveral Degrees of *Acuteneſs* and *Gravity*, without ſuppoſing theſe Terms to expreſs any fixt and determinate Thing; but it implies ſome ſuppoſed Degree of *Tune*, as a Term to which we tacitely compare ſeveral otherDegrees; thus we ſuppoſe any one given or determinate Meaſure of *Tune*, then we ſuppoſe a Sound to move on either Side, and acquire on the one greater Meaſures of *Tune*, and on the other leſſer, *i. e.* on the one Side to become gradually more *acute*, and on the other more *grave* than the given *Tune*, and this *in infinitum*: Why I aſcribe the greater Meaſure to *Acuteneſs* will appear, when we ſee upon what that Meaſure depends. Now tho' theſe Degrees are infinite, yet with reſpect to us they are limited, and we take ſome middle Degree, within the ordinary Compaſs of the human Voice, which we make the Term of Compariſon when we ſay of a Sound that it is very *acute* or very *grave*, or, as we commonly ſpeak, very *high* or very *low*.

II. If Two or more Sounds are compared in the Relation we now treat of, they are either

ther *equal* or *unequal* in the Degree of *Tune*: Such as are *equal* are called *Unisons* with regard to each other, as having one *Tune*; the *unequal*, being at Distance one from another (as I have already explain'd that Word) constitute what we call an *Interval* in *Musick*, which is properly the Difference of *Tune* betwixt Two Sounds. Upon this Equality or Difference does the whole Effect depend; and in respect of this we have these Relations again divided into,

III. *Concord* and *Discord*. *Concord* is the Denomination of all these Relations that are always and of themselves agreeable, whether applied in *Succession* or *Consonance* (by which Word I always mean a mere sounding together;) *that is*, If two simple Sounds are in such a Relation, or have such a Difference of *Tune*, that being sounded together they make a Mixture or *compound* Sound which the Ear receives with Pleasure, that is called *Concord*; and whatever Two Sounds make an agreeable Compound; they will always follow other agreeably. *Discord* is the Denomination of all the Relations or Differences of *Tune* that have a contrary Effect.

IV. *Concords* are the essential Principles of Musick; but their particular Distinctions, Degrees and Names, we must expect in another Place. *Discords* have a more general and very remarkable Distinction, which is proper to be explained here; they are either *concinnous* or *inconcinnous Intervals*; the *concinnous* are such as are apt or fit for *Musick*, next to and

in

in Combination with *Concords*; and are neither very agreeable nor very disagreeable in themselves; they are such Relations as have a good Effect in *Musick* only as, by their Opposition, they heighten and illustrate the more essential Principles of the Pleasure we seek for ; or by their Mixture and Combination with them, they produce a Variety necessary to our being better pleased; and therefore are still called *Discord*, as the Bitterness of some Things may help to set off the Sweetness of others, and yet still be bitter: And therefore in the Definition of *Concord* I have said *always and of themselves agreeable*, because the *concinnous* could have no good Effect without these, which might subsist without the other, tho' less perfectly. The other Degrees of *Discord* that are never chosen in *Musick* come under the Name of *inconcinnous* and have a greater Harshness in them, tho' even the greatest Discord is not without its Use. Again the *concinnous* come under a Distinction with respect to their Use, some of them being admitted only in *Succession*, and others only in *Consonance*; but enough of this here.

V. Now to apply the Second and Third Article observe, *Unisons* cannot possibly have any Variety, for there must be Difference where there is Variety, therefore *Unisonance* flowing from a Relation of Equality which is invariable, there can be no Species or Distinction in it; all *Unisons* are *Concord*, and in the First and most perfect Degree; but an *Interval* depending upon a Difference of *Tune* or a Relation

lation of Inequality; admits of Variety, and ſo the Terms of every *Interval*, according to the particular Relation or Difference, make either *Concord* or *Diſcord.* Some indeed have reſtrained the Word *Concord* to *Intervals*, making it include a Difference of *Tune*; but it is precarious; for as the Word *Concord* ſignifies an Agreement of Sounds, 'tis certainly applicable to *Uniſons* in the Firſt Degree.

OBSERVE, the Words *Concord* ard *Harmony* are of the ſame Senſe; yet they are arbitrarily made different Terms of Art; *Concord* ſignifies the agreeable Effect of two Sounds in *Conſonance*; *Harmony* is applied to the Agreement of any greater Number of Sounds in *Conſonance*. Again *Harmony* always ſignifies *Conſonance*, but *Concord* is applied ſometimes alſo to *Succeſſion*, yet never but when the Terms can ſtand agreeably in *Conſonance*: The Effect of an agreeable *Succeſſion* of ſeveral Sounds being particularly called *Melody*.

VI. INTERVALS differ in *Magnitude*; and in this there is an infinite Variety, according to the poſſible Degrees of *Tune*; for there is no Difference ſo great or little but a greater or leſs is further imaginable: But if we conſider it with regard to what's practicable, there are Limits, which are the leaſt and greateſt *Intervals* our Ears are Judges of, and can be actually produced by Voice or Inſtruments; beſides which there is yet a further Limitation from what's uſeful for attaining the Ends of *Muſick.*

VII.

VII. INTERVALS are diſtinguiſhed into *ſimple* and *compound*; a *ſimple Interval* is without Parts or Diviſion; a *compound* conſiſts of ſeveral leſſer *Intervals*. Now 'tis plain this Diſtinction has a Regard to Practice only, becauſe there is no ſuch Thing as a leaſt *Interval*: Beſides, by a *ſimple Interval* is not meant here the leaſt practiſed, but ſuch as, tho' it were equal to Two or more leſſer which are in Uſe, yet, when we would make a Sound move ſo far up or down, we always paſs immediately from its one Term to the other; what is meant then by a *compound Interval* will be very plain, it is ſuch whoſe Terms are, in Practice, taken either in immediate Succeſſion, or we make the Sound to riſe and fall from the one to the other by touching ſome intermediate Degrees, ſo that the Whole is a Compoſition of all the *Intervals* from one Extreme to the other. What I call a *ſimple Interval* the Ancients called a *Diaſtem*; and they called the *compound* a *Syſtem*: Each of theſe has Differences; even of the *ſimple* there are ſome greater and leſſer, and they are always *Diſcord*; but of the *compound* or *Syſtem*, ſome are *Concord*, ſome *Diſcord*. But again,

VIII. SYSTEMS of the ſame Magnitude (and conſequently of the ſame Degree of *Concord* and *Diſcord*) may differ in reſpect of their Compoſition, as containing and being actually divided into more or fewer *Intervals*. And when that Number is equal, yet the Parts may differ in Magnitude. *Laſtly*, when they conſiſt of the very

ſame

ſame Parts or leſſer Intervals, there may be a Difference of the Order and Poſition of them betwixt the Extremes.

IX. A moſt remarkable Diſtinction of *Syſtems* is into *concinnous* and *inconcinnous*. How theſe Words are applied to ſimple Intervals we have already ſeen; but to *Syſtems* they are applied in a twofold Manner, thus, In every *Syſtem* that is concinnouſly divided, the Parts conſidered as ſimple Intervals muſt be *concinnous* in the Senſe of Article *Third*; but not only ſo, they muſt be placed in a certain Order betwixt the Extremes, that the Succeſſion of Sounds from one Extreme to the other, may be agreeable, and have a good Effect in Practice. An *inconcinnous Syſtem* therefore is that where the ſimple Intervals are *inconcinnous*, or ill diſpoſed betwixt the Extremes.

X. A *Syſtem* is either *particular*, or *univerſal*, containing within it every particular Syſtem that belongs to *Muſick*, and is called, The Scale of Musick, which may be defined, *A Series of Sounds riſing or falling towards* Acuteness or Gravity *from any given Sound, to the greateſt Diſtance that is fit and practicable, thro' ſuch intermediate Degrees, as make the Succeſſion moſt agreeable and perfect, and in which we have all the concording Intervals moſt concinnouſly divided.*

The right Compoſition of ſuch a *Syſtem* is of the greateſt Importance in *Muſick*, becauſe it will contain the whole Principles; and ſo the Task

Task of this Part may be concluded in this, *viz.* To explain the Nature, Conſtitution and Office of the *Scale of Muſick*; for in doing this, the whole fundamental Grounds and Principles of *Muſick* will be explain'd; which I ſhall go through in this Order. 1*mo.* I ſhall explain upon what the *Tune* of a Sound depends, or at leaſt ſomething which is inſeparably connected with it; and how from this the *relative Degrees of Tune*, or the *Intervals* and *Differences* are determined and meaſured. 2*do.* I ſhall conſider the Nature of *Concord* and *Diſcord*, to explain, or at leaſt ſhow you what has been or may be ſaid to explain the Grounds of their different Effects. 3*tio* and 4*to.* I ſhall more particularly conſider the Variety of *Concords*, with all their mutual Relations: In order to which I ſhall deliver as ſuccinctly as I can the *harmonical Arithmetick.* teaching how muſical Intervals are compounded and reſolved, in order particularly to find their Differences and mutual Relations, Connections with, and Dependencies one on another. 5*to.* I ſhall explain what may be called *The geometrical* Part of the Theory, or, how to expreſs the *Degrees* and *Intervals* of *harmonick Sound* by the Sections and Diviſions of right Lines. 6*to.* I ſhall explain the *Compoſition* and *Degrees* of *Harmony* as that Term is already diſtinguiſhed from *Concord.* 7*mo.* I ſhall conſider the *concinnous Diſcords* that belong to *Muſick*; and explain their Number and Uſe; how with the *Concords* they make up the *univerſal Syſtem*, or conſtitute what we call *The Scale*

Scale of Musick, whose Nature and Office I shall very particularly explain ; wherein there will be several Things handled that are fundamental to the right understanding of the *practical Part*; particularly, 8*vo.* The Nature of *Modes* and *Keys in Musick* (see the Words explain'd in their proper Place:) And 9*no.* The Consequences with respect to Practice, that follow from having a Scale of fix'd and determinate Sounds upon Instruments; and how the Defects arising from this are corrected.

---

§ 2. *Of the* Cause *and* Measure *of* Tune ; *or upon what the Tune of a Sound depends ; and how the relative Degrees or Differences of Tune are determined and measured.*

IT was first found by Experience, That many Sounds differing in *Tune*, tho' the Measures of the Differences were not yet known, raised agreeable Sensations, when applied either in *Consonance* or *Succession* ; and that there were Degrees in this Pleasure. But while the Measures of these Differences were not known, the Ear must have been the only Director; which tho' the infallible Judge of what's agreeable to its self; yet perhaps not the best Provisor: *Reason* is a superior Faculty, and can make use of former Experiences of Pleasure to contrive and invent new ones ; for, by examining the Grounds and Causes of Pleasure in one Instance,

ſtance, we may conclude with great Probability, what Pleaſure will ariſe from other Cauſes that have a Relation and Likeneſs to the former; and tho' we may be miſtaken, yet it is plain, that *Reaſon*, by making all the probable Concluſions it can, to be again examined by the Judgment of Senſe, will more readily diſcover the agreeable and diſagreeable, than if we were left to make Experiments at Random, without obſerving any Order or Connection, *i. e.* to find Things by Chance. And particularly in the preſent Caſe, by diſcovering the Cauſe of the Difference of *Tune*, or ſomething at leaſt that is inſeparably connected with it, we have found a certain Way of meaſuring all their relative Degrees; of making diſtinct Compariſons of the Intervals of Sound; and in a Word, we have by this Means found a perfect Art of raiſing the Pleaſure, of which this Relation of Sounds is capable, founded on a rational and well ordered *Theory*, which Senſe and Experience confirms. For unleſs we could fix theſe Degrees of *Tune*, *i. e.* meaſure them, or rather their Relations, by certain and determinate Quantities, they could never be expreſt upon Inſtruments: If the Ear were ſufficient for this as to *Concords*, I may ſay, at leaſt, that we ſhould never otherwiſe have had ſo perfect an Art as we now have; becauſe, as I hope to make it appear, the Improvement is owing to the Knowledge of the Numbers that expreſs theſe Relations: Without which, again, how could we know what

Pro-

Progreſs were made in diſcovering the Relations of *Tune* capable to pleaſe; for in all Probability it was with this, as much more of our Knowledge, the firſt Diſcovery was by Accident, without any deliberate Enquiry, which Men could never think of till ſomething accidental as to them made a Firſt Diſcovery; nor could we at this Day be reaſonably ſure that ſome ſuch Accident ſhall not diſcover to us a new *Concord*, unleſs we ſatisfied our ſelves by what we know of the Cauſe of *Acuteneſs* and *Gravity*, and the mutual Relations of *concording Intervals*, which I am now to explain.

ACCORDING to the Method I have propoſed in this *Eſſay*, you muſt expect in another Place, an Account of the Firſt Enquirers into the Meaſures of *Acuteneſs* and *Gravity*; and here I go on to explain it as our own Experience and Reaſon confirms to us.

THIS Affection of Sounds depends, as I have already ſaid, altogether upon the ſonorous Body; which differs in *Tune*, 1*mo*. According to the ſpecifick Differences of the Matter; thus the Sound of a Piece of Gold is much *graver* than that of a Piece of Silver of the ſame Shape and Dimenſions; and in this Caſe the *Tones* are proportional to the ſpecifick Gravities, (*cæteris paribus*) *i. e.* the Weights of Two Pieces of the ſame Shape and Dimenſion. Or, 2*do*. According to the different Quantities of the ſame ſpecifick Matter in Bodies of the ſame Figure; thus a ſolid Sphere of Braſs one Foot Daimeter will ſound *acuter* than one of the ſame Braſs Two Foot

Foot Diameter; and here the *Tones* are proportional to the Quantities of Matter, or the abſolute Weights.

But neither of theſe Experiments can reaſonably ſatisfy the preſent Enquiry. There appears indeed no Reaſon to doubt that the ſame *Ratio*'s of Weights (*cæteris paribus*) will always produce Sounds with the ſame Difference of *Tone*, *i. e.* conſtitute the ſame *Interval*; yet we don't ſee in theſe Experiments, the immediate Ground or Cauſe of the Differences of *Tone*; for tho' we find them connected with the Weights, yet it is far from being obvious how theſe influence the other; ſo that we cannot refer the Degrees of *Tone* to theſe Quantities as the immediate Cauſe; for which Reaſon we ſhould never find, in this Method of determining theſe Degrees, any Explication of the Grounds of *Concord* and *Harmony*; which can only be found in the Relations of the Motions that are the Cauſe of Sound; in theſe Motions therefore muſt we ſeek the true Meaſures of *Tune*; and this we ſhall find in the Vibrations of Chords: For tho' we know that the Sound is owing to the vibratory Motion of the Parts of any Body, yet the Meaſures of theſe Motions are tolerably plain, only in the Caſe of Chords.

It has been already explained; that Sounds are produced in Chords by their vibratory Motions; and tho' according to what has been explained in the preceeding *Chapter*, theſe ſenſible Vibrations of the whole Chord are not the immediate

ate Caufe of the Sound, yet they influence thefe infenfible Motions that immediately produce it; and, for any Reafon we have to doubt of it, are always proportional to them; and *therefore* we may meafure Sounds as juftly in thefe, as we could do in the other if they fell under our Meafures. But even thefe fenfible Vibrations of the whole Chord cannot be immediately meafured, they are too fmall and quick for that; and therefore we muft feek another Way of meafuring them, by finding what Proportion they have with fome other Thing: And this can be done by the different *Tenfions*, or *Groffnefs*, or *Lengths* of *Chords* that are in all other refpects, except any one of thefe mentioned, equal and alike; the Chords in all Cafes being fuppofed evenly and of equal Dimenfions throughout: And of all Kind of Chords Metal or Wire-ftrings are beft to make the following Experiments with.

Now, in *general*, we know by Experience that in two Chords, all Things being equal and alike except the *Tenfion* or the *Thicknefs* or the *Length*, the *Tones* are different; there muft therefore be a Difference in the Vibrations, owing to thefe different Tenfions, *&c.* which Difference can only be in the Velocity of the Courfes and Recourfes of the Chords, thro' the Spaces in which they move to and again beyond the ftraight Line: We are therefore to examine the Proportion between that Velocity and the Things mentioned on which it depends. And *mind* that to prevent faying fo oft *cæteris paribus*,

bus, you are always to suppose it when I speak of Two Chords of different *Tensions*, *Lengths*, or *Grossness*.

PROPOSITION I. *If the elastick Chord* AB. (*Plate* 1. *Fig*. 1.) *be drawn by any Point* o, *in the Direction of the Line* o D, *every Vibration it makes will be in a lesser Space as* o d, *till it be at perfect Rest in its natural Position* A o B; *and the elastick or restituent Force at each Point* d *of the Line* o D (i. e. *at the Beginning of each Vibration*) *will be in a simple direct Proportion of the Lines* o D, o d, o d.

DEMONSTRATION. That the Vibrations become gradually less till the Chord be at Rest, is plain; and that this must proceed from the Decrease of the elastick Force is as plain; *lastly* that this Force decreases in the Proportion mentioned, is proven by this Experiment made upon a Wire-string, *viz.* that being stretched lengthwise by any Weight, if several Weights are applied successively to the Point o, drawing the Chord in the same Direction as o D, they bend it so that the Distances o D, o d, to which the several Weights draw it, are in simple direct Proportion of these Weights: But Action and Reaction are equal and contrary, *therefore* the Resistance which the Chord by its Elasticity makes to the Weight, is equal to the Gravity or drawing Force of that Weight, *i. e.* the restituent Forces in the Points D, d, are as the Lines o D, o d; now it is the same Case whether the Chord be stretcht by Weight or any other Force; for when we suppose it stretcht

ſtretcht to D, or d, the elaſtick Force is the ſame Thing, and in the ſame Proportion at theſe Points, whatever the bending Force is; therefore the Propoſition is true.

COROLLARY. The Vibrations of the ſame Chord are all performed in equal Time; *becauſe* in the Beginning of each Vibration, the reſtituent or moving Force, is as the Space to be gone thro'; for it is as the half Space o D, but Halfs are as the Wholes.

SCHOLIUM. In the preceeding Experiment (which is Dr. *Graveſande*'s) the Vibrations are taken very ſmall, *that is*, at the greateſt bending the Line o D is not above a Quarter of an Inch, the Chord being Two Foot and a Half long. And if the Propoſition be but phyſically true with reſpect to the very ſmall Vibrations, it will ſufficiently anſwer our Purpoſe; for indeed Chords while they ſound vibrate in very ſmall Spaces.

BUT *again*, as to the *Corollary*, which is the principal Thing we have uſe for, it will perhaps be objected, that I have only conſidered the Motion of the Point o or D, without proving that the elaſtick Force in the reſt of the Points are alſo proportional to the Diſtances; but as the whole bending Force is immediately applied to one Point, (tho' thereby it acts upon them all) the reſtitutive Force may be referred all to the ſame Point; *or*, we may conſider the whole *Area* A B D, which is the Effect of the bending, as the Space to be run thro' by the whole Body or Chord A B D, and theſe *Areas* are as the Lines

Lines o D, o d, *viz.* The Altitudes of different Figures having the ſame common Baſe A B, and a ſimilar Curve A D B, and A d B; for ſtrictly ſpeaking the Chord is a Curve in its Vibrations; and if we take A D, and D B for ſtraight Lines, as they are very nearly, and without any ſenſible Variation in ſuch ſmall Vibrations as we now ſuppoſe, then it will be more plain that theſe *Areas* are as the Lines o D, o d; and becauſe in this Way we conſider the Action upon, and Reaction of all the Points of the Chord, *therefore* the Objection is removed.

But there remains one Thing more, *viz.* That the Concluſion is drawn from the Forces or Velocities in the ſeveral Points D, d, as if they were uniform thro' all the Space; whereas in the Nature of the Thing they are accelerated from D to o, and in the ſame Proportion retarded on the other Side of o: The *Anſwer* to this is plainly, that ſince the Acceleration is of the ſame Nature in all the Vibrations, it muſt be the ſame Caſe with reſpect to the Time as if the Motion were uniform.

Now from the Conſideration of this Acceleration, there is another *Demonſtration* drawn of the preceeding *Corollary*; and that I may ſhow it, let me *firſt* prove that there muſt be an Acceleration, and *then* explain the Nature of it. *Firſt.* Suppoſe any one Vibration from D to o, in that the Point D muſt move into d, d, ſucceſſively, before it come to O; and if there were no Acceleration, but that the Point D, in every

every Poſition of the Chord, as A d B, had no more elaſtick Force than is equal to a Force that could keep it in that Poſition; 'tis plain it could never paſs the Point o; *becauſe* theſe Forces are as the Diſtances, and therefore it is nothing in the Point o; but it actually paſſes that Point, and *conſequently* the Motion is accelerated; and the Law of the Acceleration is this, In every Point of the ſame Vibration, the Point D is accelerated by a Force equal to what would be ſufficient to retain it in that Poſition; but theſe Points being as the Diſtances o d, o d, the Motion of the Point D agrees with that of a Body moving in a *Cycloid*, whoſe Vibrations the Mathematicians demonſtrate to be of equal Duration (*vid.* KEIL's *Introductio ad veram phyſicam*) and therefore the Times of the Vibrations of the Chord are alſo equal (*vid.* GRAVESANDE's *mathematical Elements of Phyſicks.* Book I. Chap. 26.)

BEFORE we proceed farther, I ſhall apply this Propoſition to a very remarkable *Phænomenon*; that Experience and our Reaſonings may mutually ſupport one another. It is a very obvious Remark, That the Sound of any Body ariſing from one individual Stroke, tho' it grows gradually weaker, yet continues in the ſame *Tone*: We ſhall be more ſenſible of this by making the Experiment on Bodies that have a great Reſonance, as the larger Kind of Bells and long Wire-ſtrings.

NOW ſince the *Tone* of a Sound depends upon the Nature of theſe Vibrations, whoſe Dif-

Differences we can conceive no otherwise than as having different Velocities; and since we have proven that the small Vibrations of the same Chord are all performed in equal Time; and *lastly*, since it is true in Fact that the *Tone* of a Sound which continues for some Time after the Stroke, is from first to last the same; it follows, I think, that the *Tone* is necessarily connected with a certain Quantity of Time in making every single Vibration; *or*, that a certain Number of Vibrations, accomplished in a given Time, constitutes a certain and determinate *Tone*; for this being supposed we have a good Reason of that *Phænomenon* of the Unity of *Tone* mentioned: And this mutually confirms the Truth of the *Proposition*, that the Vibrations are all made in equal Time; for this Unity of *Tone* supposes an Unity in that on which the *Tone* depends, or with which our Perception of it is connected; and this cannot be supposed any other Thing than the Equality of the Vibrations, in the Time of their Courses and Recourses: For the absolute Velocity, or elastick Force, in the Beginning of each Vibration is unequal, being proportional to the Power that could retain it in that Position.

Again, if we could absolutely determine how many Vibrations any Chord, of a given *Length*, *Thickness* and *Tension*, makes in a given Time, this we might call a *fix'd Sound* or rather a *fix'd Tone*, to which all others might be compared, and their Numbers be also deter-

mined

mined; but this is a mere Curiosity, which neither promotes the Knowledge or Practice of *Musick*; it being enough to determine and measure the *Intervals* in the Proportions and relative Degrees of *Tone*, as in the following *Propositions*.

PROPOSITION II. *Let there be Two elastick Chords* A *and* C (*Plate* 1. *Fig.* 2.) *differing only in* Tension, i. e. *Let them be stretcht Length-wise by different Weights which are the Measures of the* Tension; *the Time of a Vibration in the one is to that of the other inversely as the square Root of the* Tensions *or Weights that stretch them. For Example, if the Weights are as* 4 : 9. *the Times are as* 3 : ~~4~~.2.

DEMONSTRATION. If Two Chords C and A (*Plate* 1. *Fig.* 2.) differ only in *Tension*, they will be bended to the same Distance O D by Weights (similarly applied to the Points o) which are directly proportional to their *Tensions*; this is found by Experiment (*vid.* Gravesande's *Elements.*) *Again*, these Two Chords bended equally, may be compared to Two Pendulums vibrating in the same or like *Cycloid* with different accelerating Forces; in which Case, the Mathematicians know, it is demonstrated, that the Times are inversely as the square Roots of the *Tensions*, which are as the accelerating, *i. e.* the bending Forces, when they are drawn to equal Distances; but the Proposition is true whether the Distances O D be equal or not;

be-

becauſe all the Vibrations of the ſame Chord are of equal Duration by *Prop.* 1.

COROLLARY. *The Numbers of the Vibrations accompliſhed in the ſame Time are directly as the ſquare Roots of their Tenſions. For Example, If the Tenſions are as 9 to 4. the Numbers of Vibrations in the ſame Time will be as* 3 *to* 2.

PROPOSITION III. *The Numbers of Vibrations made in the ſame Time by Two Chords,* A *and* B (*Plate* 1. *Fig.* 3.) *that differ only in* Thickneſs, *are inverſely as the ſquare Roots of the Weights of the Chords,* i. e. *as the Diameters of their Baſes inverſely.*

DEMONSTRATION. We know by common Experience that the *thicker* and *groſſer* any Chord is, being bended by the ſame Weight, it gives the more *grave* Sound; ſo that the *Tone* is as the *Thickneſs* in general: But for the particular Proportion, we have this *Experiment*, *viz.* Take Two Chords B and C (*Plate* 1. *Fig.* 3.) differing only in *Thickneſs*; let the Weights they are ſtretched with be as the Weights of the Chords themſelves, *i. e.* as the Squares of their Diameters; their Sounds are *uniſon*, therefore the Number of Vibrations in each will be equal in the ſame Time: And conſequently if the thick *Chord* B be compared to another of equal Length A (in the ſame *Figure*) ſtretched with the ſame Weight, but whoſe *Thickneſs* is only equal to that of the ſmaller Chord C laſt compared to it; the Numbers of Vibrations of B and A will be

as

as the ſquare Roots of the Weights of the Chords inverſely: That is, inverſely as the Diameters of their Baſes, or the Bores thro' which the Wire is drawn.

PROPOSITION IV. *If Two Chords* A *and* B, *in Plate* 1. *Fig.* 2. *differ only in their* Lengths, *the Time of a Vibration of the one is to that of the other as the* Lengths *directly; and conſequently as the Number of Vibrations in the ſame Time inverſely. For Example, Let the one be Three Foot and the other Two, the Firſt will make Two Vibrations and the other Three in the ſame Time.*

DEMON. 'Tis Matter of common Obſervation, that if you take any Number of Chords differing only in *Length*, their Sounds will be gradually *acuter* as the Chords are *ſhorter*; and for the Proportion of the *Lengths* and Vibrations, it will be plain from what has been already ſaid; for the ſame *Tone* is conſtitute by the ſame Number of Vibrations in a given Time; and we know by *Experience* that if Two Chords C and B (*Plate* 1. *Fig.* 2.) differing only in *Length*, are tended by Weights which are as the Squares of their *Lengths*, their Sounds are *uniſon*; therefore they make an equal Number of Vibrations in the ſame Time. But *again*, by *Propoſition* 2. the Number of Vibrations of the longeſt of theſe Two Chords C, is to the Number in the ſame Time, of an equal and like Chord A (in the ſame *Figure*) leſs tended, as the ſquare Roots of the Tenſions directly; therefore if A is

A is tended equally with the ſhorter Chord B (whoſe Vibrations are equal to thoſe of the longer Chord D that's moſt tended)'tis plain the Number of Vibrations of theſe two muſt be as their Lengths, becauſe theſe Lengths are directly as the ſquare Roots of the unequal Tenſions.

OBSERVE, that if we ſuppoſe this Proportion of the Time and Lengths to be otherwiſe demonſtrated, then what is here advanced as an Experiment will follow as a Conſequence from this *Propoſition* and the Second. But I think this Way of demonſtrating the *Propoſition* very plain and ſatisfying. You may alſo ſee from what Conſiderations Dr. *Graveſande* concludes it. Or we may prove it independently of the Second *Propoſition*, after the Manner of the Firſt by the following

EXPERIMENT. *Viz.* If the ſame or equal Weight is ſimilarly applied to ſimilar Points O o, of Two elaſtick Chords A and B (*Plate* 1. *Fig.* 2.) that differ only in Lengths; the Points O, o will be drawn to the Diſtances O D, o d, that ſhall be as the Lengths of the Chords A, B; ſo that the Figures ſhall be ſimilar, and the whole Areas proportional to the Lengths of the Chords.

NOW the bending Forces in D and d are equal and equally applied, therefore the reſtituent Forces are equal; the Times conſequently are as the Spaces, *i. e.* as the Areas or the Chords A, B, and this holds whatever the Difference of o d and O D is, ſince all the Vibrations

rations of the ſame Chord are made in equal Time; and therefore, *laſtly*, the Numbers of Vibrations in a given Time are as theſe Lengths inverſely.

OBSERVE. From this Demonſtration and the Experiment uſed in the former Demonſtration, we ſee the Truth of *Propoſition* 2. in anoher View.

GENERAL *Corollary* to the preceeding *Propoſitions*. *The Numbers of Vibrations made in the ſame Time by any Two Chords of the ſame Matter, differing in Length, Thickneſs and Tenſion, are in the compound* Ratio *of the Diameters and Lengths inverſely, and the ſquare Roots of the Tenſions directly.*

NOW let us ſum up and apply what has been explained, and, *firſt*, We have concluded that the Differences of *Tone* or the *Intervals* of *harmonick Sound* are neceſſarily connected with the Velocity of the Vibrations in their Courſes and Recourſes, *i. e.* the Number of Vibrations made in equal Time by the Parts of the ſonorous Body: And becauſe theſe Numbers cannot be meaſured in themſelves immediately, we have found how to do it in Chords, by the Proportions betwixt them and the different *Tenſions* or *Thickneſs* or *Lengths*; we have not ſought any abſolute and determinate Number of Vibrations in any Chord, but only the *Ratio* or Proportion betwixt the Numbers accompliſhed in the ſame Time, by ſeveral Chords differing in *Tenſion* or *Thickneſs* or *Length*, or in all theſe; *therefore* we have diſcovered the

true

true and just Measures of the relative Degrees of *Tone*, not only in *Chords*, but in all other Bodies; for if it is reasonable to conclude, from the Likeness of Causes and Effects, that the same *Tone* is constitute in every Body, by the same Number of Vibrations in the same Time, it follows, that whatever Numbers express the *Ratio* of any Two Degrees in one kind of Body, they express the *Ratio* of these Two Degrees universally: But this would hold without that Supposition, because we can find Two Chords, whose *Tones* shall be *unison* respectively to any other Two Sounds; and therefore all the Conclusions we can make from the various Compositions and Divisions of these *Ratio*'s will be true of all Sounds, whatever Differences there be in the Cause.

It follows *again*, that in the Application of Numbers to the different *Tones* of Sound, whereby we express the Relations of one Degree to another, the *grave* is to the *acute* as the lesser Number to the greater, because the *graver* depends upon the least Number of Vibrations: But if we apply these Numbers to the Times of the Vibrations, then, the *grave* is represented by the greater Number, and the *acute* by the lesser.

If we express the same *Tones* by the Quantity of the different *Tensions* of Chords that are otherwise equal and like, then the *Ratio* will be different, because the *Tensions* are as the Squares of the Vibrations, and the *grave* will be to the *acute* as the lesser to the greater: But the Reason why we ought not to use these Num-

Numbers is, that tho' different *Tensions* make different *Tones*, yet we can only examine the Grounds of *Concord* and *Discord*, in the *Ratio*'s of the Vibrations, which are immediately the Cause of Sound ; and this is a more accurate Way, because these represent something that's common in all Sounds; and besides, being always lesser Numbers (*viz.* the square Roots of the other) are more convenient for the easy Comparison of *Intervals*. As to the *Diameters* or *Lengths* of different Chords, because they are in a simple Proportion of the Numbers of Vibrations, therefore the same Numbers represent either them or the Vibrations, but inversely ; so that the *graver* Tone is represented by the *longer* or *grosser* Chord : And because *Experiments* are more easily made with Chords differing only in Lengths; and also because these Proportions are more easily conceived, and more sensibly represented by right Lines; *therefore* we also represent the Degrees of *Tone* by these Lengths, tho' in examining the Grounds of *Concord* we must consider the Vibrations, which are exprest by the same Numbers.

THIS brings to Mind a Question which *Vincenzo Galilei* makes in his Dialogues upon *Musick*; he asks, Whether the expressing of the Interval which we call an *Octave* by the *Ratio* of 1:2. be reasonably grounded upon this, That if a Chord is divided into Two equal Parts, the *Tone* of the Half is an *Octave* to that of the Whole? The Reasons of his Doubt he proposes thus,

thus, says he, There are Three Ways we can make the Sound of a Chord *acuter*, *viz.* by *shortning* it, by a *greater Tension*, and by making it *smaller*, *cæteris paribus*. By *shortning* it the *Ratio* of an *Octave* is 1 : 2. By *Tension* it is 1 : 4. and by lessening the *Thickness* it is also 1 : 4. He means in the last Case, when the Tones are measured by the Weights of the Chord. Now he would know why it is not as well 1 : 4. as 1 : 2. which is the ordinary Expression : I think this Difficulty we have sufficiently answered above ; for these Weights are not the immediate Cause of the Sound; it is true we may say that the *acute* Term of the *Octave* is to the *grave* as 4. to 1. meaning only that the *acute* is produced by Four Times the Weight which determines the other ; and if *Intervals* are compared together by *Ratio*'s taken this Way, we can compound and resolve them, and find their mutual Connections and Relations of Quantity, as truly as by the other Expressions ; but the Operations are not so easy, because they are greater Numbers : *And* then, if the Sounds are produced any other Way than by Chords of different *Tensions* or *Thickness*, the *Tones* are to one another as these Numbers in a very remote Sense ; for they express nothing in the Cause of these Sounds themselves, but only tell us, that Two Chords being made *unisons* to these Sounds, their *Tensions* or *Thickness* are as these Numbers: But, all Sounds being produced by Motion, when we express the *Tones* by the Numbers of Vibrations in the same Time, we represent something that's that's proper to every Sound; this therefore is the only Thing that can be considered in examining the Grounds of *Concord* and *Discord*: And because the same Numbers express the Vibrations and Lengths of Chords, we apply them sometimes also to these Lengths, for Reasons already said.

WE have also gained this further Definition of *Acuteness* and *Gravity*, *viz.* That *Acuteness* is a relative Property of Sound, which with respect to some other is the Effect of a greater Number of Vibrations accomplished in the same Time, or of Vibrations of a shorter Duration; and *Gravity* is the Effect of a lesser Number of Vibrations, or of Vibrations of a shorter Duration. And by considering that the Vibrations proceeding from one individual Stroke are gradually in lesser Spaces till the Motion cease, and that the Sound is always louder in the Beginning, and gradually weaker, therefore we may define *Loudness* the Effect of a greater absolute Velocity of Motion or a greater Vibration made in the same Time; and *Lowness* is the Effect of a lesser.

BEFORE I end this *Chapter*, let us consider a Conclusion which *Kircher* makes, in his *Musurgia universalis*. Having proven in his own Way, the Equidiurnity of the Vibrations of the same Chord, he draws this Conclusion, That the Sound of a Chord grows gradually more *grave* as it ceases (tho' he owns the Difference is not sensible) because the absolute Velocity of Motion becomes less, *i. e.* That Velocity whereby by the Chord makes a Vibration of a certain Space in a certain Time. By this Argument he makes the Degrees and Differences of *Tune* proportional to the abſolute Velocity: But if this is a good Hypotheſis, I think it will follow, contrary to Experience, that two Chords of unequal Length (*cæteris paribus*) muſt give an equal *Tune*; for to demonſtrate the reciprocal Proportion of the Lengths and the Number of Vibrations, he ſuppoſes the *Tenſion* or elaſtick Force, which is the immediate Cauſe of the abſolute Velocity, to be equal when the Chords are drawn out to proportional Diſtance; for by this Equality the ſhorter Chord finiſhes its Vibrations in ſhorter Time, in Proportion as the Spaces are leſſer, which are as the Lengths. *Again*, the Elaſticity of the Chord diminiſhes gradually, ſo that in any aſſignable Time there is at leaſt an indefinite Number of Degrees; and ſince the Elaſticity has ſuch a gradual Decreaſe, it ſeems odd that the Differences of *Tune*, if they have a Dependence on the abſolute Velocity, ſhould not be ſenſible. But in the other Hypotheſis, where I ſuppoſe the Degrees of *Tune* are connected with and proportional to the Duration of a ſingle Vibration, and conſequently to the Number of Vibrations in a given Time, there can no abſurd Conſequence follow. I am indeed aware of a Difficulty that may be ſtarted, which is this, That the Duration of a ſingle Vibration is a Thing the Mind has nothing whereby to judge of, of, whereas it can eafily judge of the Difference of abfolute Velocity by the different Percuffions upon the Ear; and the Defenders of this Hypothefis may further alledge, that the Vibrations that produce Sound are the fmall and almoft infenfible Vibrations of the Body; fo far infenfible at leaft that we can only difcern a Tremor, but no diftinct Vibrations; and we cannot, fay they, be furprized if the Differences of *Tune* are infenfible. But I fuppofe the Degrees of *Tune* of the firft Vibrations are predominant, and determine the particular *Tune* of the Sound; and then it is no lefs unaccountable how Two Chords drawn out to fimilar Figures, as in *Prop.* 4. fhould not give the fame *Tune*, and indeed it feems impoffible to be otherwife in this Hypothefis, which yet is contrary to Experience; and for the Difficulty propofed in the other Hypothefis it is at leaft but a Difficulty and no Contradiction, efpecially if we fuppofe it depends immediately on a certain Number of Vibrations in a given Time, which is the Confequence of a fhorter Duration of every fingle Vibration; and this again, I own, fuppofes there can be no Sound heard till a certain Number of Vibrations are accomplifhed, the contrary whereof I believe will be difficult to prove. I fhall therefore leave it to the *Philofophers*, becaufe I think the chief Demand of this particular Part is fufficiently anfwered, which was to know how to take the juft Meafures of the relative Degrees of Tune, and their Intervals or Differences. You'll remember too, what Reafon I have already

already alledged for expreſſing the Degrees of *Tune* by the Numbers of Vibrations accompliſhed in the ſame Time; for whether the Cauſe of our perceiving a different *Tone* lies here or not, the only Way we have of accounting for the *Concord* and *Diſcord* of different *Tones*, is the Conſideration of theſe Proportions, and whatever may be required in a more univerſal Enquiry into the Nature and *Phænomena* of Sound, this will be ſufficient to ſuch a Theory, as by the Help of Experience and Obſervation, may guide us to the true Knowledge of the Science of Muſick.

BESIDES, in this Account of the Cauſe of the Differences of *Tune*, I follow the Opinion not only of the Ancients but of our more modern Philoſophers; Dr. *Holder*'s whole Theory of the natural Grounds and Principles of *Harmony*, is founded on this Suppoſition; take his own Words, *Chap.* 2. " The Firſt and great " Principle upon which the Nature of *harmonical* Sounds is to be found out and diſcovered is this: That the *Tune* of a Note (to ſpeak " in our vulgar Phraſe) is conſtituted by the " Meaſure and Proportion of Vibrations of the " ſonorous Body; I mean, of the Velocity of " theſe Vibrations in their Recourſes, for the " frequenter theſe Vibrations are, the more *acute* is the Tune; the ſlower and fewer they " are in the ſame Space of Time, by ſo much " the more *grave* is the Tune. So that any " given Note of a Tune is made by one certain Meaſure of Velocity of Vibrations, *viz.*

" ſuch

" ſuch a certain Number of Courſes and Re-
" courſes, *e. g.* of a Chord or String in ſuch a
" certain Space of Time, doth conſtitute ſuch
" a determinate Tune.

DOCTOR *Wallis* in the *Appendix* to his Edition of *Ptolomey*'s Books of *Harmony*, owns this to be a very reaſonable Suppoſition; yet he ſays he would not poſitively affirm, that the Degrees of *Acuteneſs* anſwer the Number of Vibrations as their only true Cauſe, becauſe he doubted whether it had been ſufficiently confirm'd by Experience. Now that Sound depends upon the Vibrations of Bodies, I think, needs no further Proof than what we have; but whether the different Numbers of Vibrations in a given Time, is the true Cauſe, on the Part of the Object, of our perceiving a Difference of Tune, is a Thing I don't conceive how we can prove by Experiments; and to the preſent Purpoſe 'tis enough that it is a reaſonable Hypotheſis; and let this be the only true Cauſe or not, we find by Experience and Reaſon both, that the Differences of *Tune* are inſeparably connected with the Number of Vibrations; and therefore theſe, or the Lengths of Chords to which they are proportional, may be taken for the true Meaſure of different *Tunes*. The Doctor owns that the Degrees of *Acuteneſs* are reciprocally as the Lengths of Chords, and thinks it ſufficiently plain from Experience; ſince we find that the ſhorter Chord (*cæteris paribus*) gives the more *acute* Sound, *i. e.* that the *Acuteneſs* increaſeth

as

as the Length diminisheth; and therefore the *Ratios* of these Lengths are just Measures of the Intervals of *Tune*, whatever be the immediate Cause of the Differences, or whatever Proportion be betwixt the Lengths of the Chords and their Vibrations. So far he owns we are upon a good Foundation as to the arithmetical Part of this Science; but then in *Philosophy* we ought to come as near the immediate Cause of Things as possibly we can; and where we cannot have a positive Certainty, we must take the most reasonable Supposition; and of that we judge by its containing no obvious Contradiction; and then by its Use in explaining the Phenomena of nature; how well the present Hypothesis has explained the sensible Unity of *Tune* in a given Sound we have already heard, and the Success of it in the Things that follow will further confirm it.

I shall end this Part with observing, that as the Lengths of Chords determine the Measure of the Velocity of their Vibrations, and this determines the Measure of their *Gravity* and *Acuteness*, so 'tis thus that *Harmony* is brought under Mathematical Calculation; the True object of the Mathematical Part of *Musick* being the Quantity of the Intervals of Sounds; which are capable of various Additions, Substractions, &c. as other Quantities are; tho' performed in a Manner suitable to the Nature of the Thing.

CHAP.

CHAP. III.

Of the Nature of CONCORD *and* DISCORD *as contained in the Causes thereof.*

§ 1. *Wherein the* Reasons *and* Characteristicks *of the several Differences of* Concords *and* Discords *are enquired into.*

WE have already considered the Reason of the Differences of *Tune*, and the Measures of these Differences, or of the *Intervals* of Sound arising from them: We now enquire into the Grounds and Reasons of their different Effects. When Two Sounds are heard in immediate Succession, the Mind not only perceives Two simple Ideas, but by a proper Activity of its own, comparing these Ideas, forms another of their Difference of *Tune*, from which arise to us various Degrees of Pleasure or Offence; these are the Effects we are now to consider the Reasons of.

BUT it will be fit in the First Place to know what is mean'd by the Question, or what we propose and expect to find; in order to this *observe*, That there is a great Difference betwixt knowing what it is that pleases us, and why we are pleased with such a Thing: Plea-

sure

ſure and Pain are ſimple Ideas we can never make plainer than Experience makes them, for they are to be got no other Way; and for that Queſtion, Why certain Things pleaſe and others not, as I take it, it ſignifies this, *viz.* How do theſe Things raiſe in us agreeable or diſagreeable Ideas? Or, What Connection is there betwixt theſe Ideas and Things? When we conſider the World as the Product of infinite Wiſdom, we can ſay, that nothing happens without a ſufficient Reaſon, I mean, that whatever is, its being rather than not being is more agreeable to the infinite Perfection of GOD, who knew from Eternity the whole Extent of Poſſibility, and in his *perfect Wiſdom* choſe to call to a real Exiſtence ſuch Beings, and make ſuch a World, as ſhould anſwer the beſt and wiſeſt End. The Actions of the SUPREME BEING flow from *eternal Reaſons* known and comprehenſible only to his *infinite Wiſdom*; and here lies the ultimate Reaſon and Cauſe of every Thing. To know how *perfect Wiſdom* and *Omnipotence* exerted it ſelf in the Production of the World; to find the *original Reaſon* and Grounds of the Relations and Connection which we ſee among Things, is altogether out of the Power of any created Intelligence; but not to carry our Contemplation beyond what the preſent Subject requires, I think the Reaſon of that Connection which we find by Experience betwixt our agreeable and diſagreeable Ideas, and what we call the Objects of Senſe, our *Philoſophy* will never reach; and for any Thing

Thing we ſhall ever find (at leaſt in our mortal State) I believe it will remain a Queſtion whether that Connection flows from any Neceſſity in the Nature of Things, or be altogether an arbitrary Diſpoſition; for to ſolve this, would require to know Things perfectly, and underſtand their whole Nature; which belongs only to that GLORIOUS BEING on whom all others depend. We ſhall therefore, as to this Queſtion, be content to ſay, in the *general*, that 'tis the Rule of our Conſtitution, whereby upon the Application of certain Objects to the Organ of Senſe, conſidered in their preſent Circumſtances, an agreeable or diſagreeable Idea ſhall be raiſed in the Mind. We have a conſcious Perception of the Exiſtence of other Things beſides our ſelves, by the irreſiſtible Impreſſions they make upon us; if the Effect is Pleaſure we purſue it farther; if it is Pain we far leſs doubt of the Reality: And ſo in our Enquiries into Nature, we muſt be ſatisfied to examine Obſervations already made, or make new ones, that from Nature's conſtant and uniform Operations we may learn her Laws. Things are connected in a regular Order; and when we can diſcover the *Law* or *Rule* of that Order, then we may be ſaid to have diſcovered the *ſecondary Reaſon* of Things; for Example, tho' we are forced to reſolve the Cauſe of *Gravitation* into the arbitrary Will of GOD; yet having once diſcovered this Rule in Nature, that all the Bodies within the Atmoſphere of the Earth have a Tendency downward

ward perpendicularly as to a common Centre within the Earth, and will move towards it in a Right Line, if no other Body interposes; upon this Principle we can give a good Reason why Timber floats in Water, and why Smoke ascends. I call it a *secondary Reason*, because is is founded on a Principle of which we can give no other Reason but that we find it constantly so. Accordingly in Matters of Sense we have found all we can expect, when we know with what Conditions of the Object and Organs of Sense our Pleasure is connected; so in the *Harmony* of Sounds we know by Experience what Proportions and Relations of *Tune* afford Pleasure, what not; and we have also found how to express the Differences of *Tune* by the Proportion of Numbers; and if we could find any Thing in the Relation of these Numbers, or the Things they immediately represent, with which *Concord* and its various Degrees are connected; by this Means we should know where Nature has set the Limits of *Concord* and *Discord*; we should with Certainty determine what Proportions constitute *Concord*, and the Order of Perfection in the various Degrees of it; and all other Relations would be left to the Class of *Discords*. And this I think is all we can propose in this Matter; so that we don't enquire why we are pleased, but what it is that pleases us; we don't enquire why, for Example, the *Ratio* of 1 : 2 constitutes *Concord*, and 6 : 7 *Discord*, *i. e.* upon what *original Grounds* agreeable or disagreeable Idea's are connected with these Relations; and the pro-

proper Influence of the one upon the other; but what common Property they agree in that make *Concord*; and what Variation of it makes the Differences of *Concord*; by which we may alſo know the Marks of *Diſcord*: *In ſhort*, I would find, if poſſible, the diſtinguiſhing Character of *Concord* and *Diſcord*; or, to what Condition of the Object theſe different Effects are annexed, that we may have all the Certainty we can, that there are no other *Concords* than what we know already; or if there are we may know how to find them; and have all poſſible Aſſiſtance, both from Experience and Reaſon, for improving the moſt innocent and raviſhing of all our ſenſual Entertainments; and as far as we are baffled in this Search, we muſt ſit down content with our bare experimental Knowledge, and make the beſt Uſe of it we can. Now to the Queſtion.

BY EXPERIENCE we know, that theſe *Ratios* of the Lengths of Chords, are all *Concord*, tho' in various Degrees, *viz.* 2 : 1, 3 : 2, 4 : 3, 5 : 4, 6 : 5, 5 : 3, 8 : 5, *that is*, Take any Chord for a Fundamental, which ſhall be repreſented by 1. and theſe Sections of it are *Concord* with the Whole, *viz.* $\frac{1}{2}$, $\frac{2}{3}$, $\frac{3}{4}$, $\frac{4}{5}$, $\frac{5}{6}$, $\frac{3}{5}$, $\frac{5}{8}$, for, as 2 to 1, ſo is 1 to $\frac{1}{2}$, and ſo of the reſt. The firſt Five you ſee, are found in the natural Order of Numbers 1, 2, 3, 4, 5, 6; but if you go on with the ſame Series, thus, 7 : 6, 8 : 7, we find no more Agreement; and for theſe Two 3 : 5, and 5 : 8, they depend upon the others, as we ſhall ſee. There are alſo other *Intervals* that are

Con-

Concord besides these, yet none less than 2 : 1, (the *Octave*) or whose *acute* Term is greater than $\frac{1}{2}$; nor any greater than *Octave*, or whose *acute* Term is less than $\frac{1}{2}$, but what are composed of the *Octave* and some lesser *Concord*, which is all the Judgment of Experience.

I suppose it agreed to that the vibratory Motion of a Chord is the Cause, or at least proportional to the Motion which is the immediate Cause of its Sound; we have heard already that the Vibrations are quicker, *i. e.* the Courses and Recourses are more frequent, in a given Time, as the Chord is shorter; I have observed also that *acute* and *grave* are but Relations, tho' there must be something absolute in the Cause of Sound, capable of less and more, to be the Ground of this Relation which flows only from the comparing of that less and more; and whether this be the absolute Velocity of Motion, or the Frequency of Vibrations, I have also considered, and do here assume the last as more probable. We have also proven that the Lengths of Chords are reciprocally as the Numbers of Vibrations in the same Time; and therefore their *Ratios* are the true Measures of the *Intervals* of Sound. But I shall apply the *Ratios* immediately to the Numbers of Vibrations, and examine the Marks of *Concord* and *Discord* upon this Hypothesis.

Now then, the universal Character whereby *Concord* and *Discord* are distinguished, is to be sought in the Numbers which contain and express the *Intervals* of Sound: But not in these Numbers abſtractly; we muſt conſider them as expreſſing the very Cauſe and Difference of Sound with reſpect to *Tune*, *viz.* the Number of Vibrations in the ſame Time: I ſhall therefore paſs all theſe Conſiderations of Numbers in which nothing has been found to the preſent Purpoſe.

UNISONS are in the Firſt Degree of *Concord*, or have the moſt perfect Likeneſs and Agreement in *Tune*; for having the ſame Meaſure of *Tune* they affect the Ear as one ſimple Sound; yet I don't ſay they produce always the beſt Effect in *Muſick*; for the Mind is delighted with Variety; and here I conſider ſimply the Agreement of Sounds and the Effect of this in each *Concord* ſingly by it ſelf. *Uniſonance* therefore being the moſt perfect Agreement of Sounds, there muſt be ſomething in this, neceſſary to that Agreement, which is to be found leſs or more in every *Concord*. The Equality of *Tune* (expreſt by a *Ratio* of Equality in Numbers) makes certainly the moſt perfect Agreement of Sound; but yet 'tis not true that the nearer any Two Sounds come to an Equality of *Tune* they have the more Agreement, therefore 'tis not in the Equality or Inequality of the Numbers ſimply that we are to ſeek this ſecondary Reaſon of the Agreement or Diſagreement of Sounds, but in ſome other Relation of them, or rather of the Things they expreſs.

IF we conſider the Numbers of Vibrations made in any given Time, by Two Chords of equal *Tune*, they are equal upon the Hypotheſis laid down; and ſo the

Vi-

Vibrations of the Two Chords coincide or begin together as frequently as possible with respect to both Chords, *viz.* at the least Number possible of the Vibrations of each; for they coincide at every Vibration: And in this Frequency of Coincidence or united Mixture of the Motions of the Two Chords, and of the Undulations of the Air caused thereby, not in the Equality or Inequality of the Number of Vibrations, must we seek the Difference of *Concord* and *Discord*; and therefore the nearer the Vibrations of Two Strings accomplished in the same Time, come to the least Number possible, they seem to approach the nearer to the Condition, and consequently to the Agreement of *Unisons*. Thus far we reason with Probability, but let us see how Experience approves of this Rule.

If we take the natural Series 1, 2, 3, 4, 5, 6, and compare every Number to the next, as expressing the Vibrations (in the same Time) of Two Chords, whose Lengths are reciprocally as these Numbers; we find the Rule holds exactly; for 1 : 2. is best than 2 : 3, *&c.* and the Agreement diminishes gradually; so that after 6 the *Consonance* is unsufferable, because the Coincidences are too rare; but there are other *Ratio*'s that are agreeable besides what are found in that continued Order, whereof I have already mentioned these Two, *viz.* 3 : 5, and 5 : 8 which with the preceeding Five are all the *concording* Intervals within, or less than *Octave* 1 : 2. *i. e.* whose acute Term is greater than

than $\frac{1}{2}$, the Fundamental being 1. Now to judge of these by the Rule laid down, 3 : 5 will be preferr'd to 4 : 5, because being equal in the Number of Vibrations of the *acuter* Term, there is an Advantage on the Side of the Fundamental in the *Ratio* 3 : 5, where the Coincidence is made at every Third Vibration of the Fundamental, and 5*th* of the *acute* Term: Again as to the *Ratio* 5 : 8 'tis less perfect than 5 : 6, because tho' the Vibrations of the fundamental Term of each that go to one Coincidence are equal, yet in the *Ratio* 5 : 6 the Coincidence is at every 6 of the *acute* Term, and only at every 8 in the other Case. Thus does our Rule determine the Preference of the *Concords* already mentioned; nor doth the Ear contradict it; so that these *Concords* stand in the Order of the following Table, where I annex the Names that these Intervals have in Practice, and which I shall hereafter assume till we come to the proper Place for explaining the Original and Reason of them.

	Vibrations.		
	acute,		*grave*,
Unison.	1	:	1
Octave.	2	:	1
Fifth.	3	:	2
Fourth.	4	:	3
Sixth greater.	5	:	3
Third greater.	5	:	4
Third lesser.	6	:	5
Sixth lesser.	8	:	5
	grave,		*acute.*
	Lengths.		

Now

Now you muſt *obſerve* that this Frequency of Coincidence does not reſpect any abſolute Space of Time; for 'tis ſtill an *Octave*, for Example, whatever the Lengths of the Chords are, if they be to one another as 1 : 2; and yet 'tis certain that a longer Chord, *cæteris paribus*, takes longer Time to every Vibration: It has a Reſpect to the Number of Vibrations of both Chords accompliſhed in the ſame Time: It does not reſpect the Vibrations of the *Fundamental* only, for then 1 : 2 and 1 : 3 would be equal in *Concord*, and ſo would theſe 4 : 7 and 4 : 5 which they are not nor can be; for where the *Ratios* differ there muſt the Agreement differ from the very Nature of the Thing, becauſe it depends altogether on theſe *Ratios*; ſo that equal Agreement muſt proceed from an equal (*i. e.* from the ſame) *Ratio*; nor can it reſpect the *acuter* Term only, elſe 3 : 5 and 4 : 5 would be equal; therefore neceſſarily a Conſideration muſt be made of the Number of Vibrations of both Chords accompliſhed in equal Time. And if from the known *Concords* within an *Octave*, we would make a *general Rule*, it is this, *viz.* that when the Coincidences are moſt frequent with reſpect to both Chords (*i. e.* with reſpect to the Numbers of Vibrations of each that go to every Coincidence) there is the neareſt Approach to the Condition of *Uniſons*: So that when in Two Caſes we compare the ſimilar Terms (*i. e.* the Number of Vibrations of the *Fundamental* of the one to that of the other,

and

and the *acute* Term of the one to the *acute* Term of the other) if both ſimilar Terms of the one are leſs than theſe of the other, that one is preferable; and any one of the ſimilar Terms equal and the other unequal, that which has the leaſt is the preferable *Interval*, as we find by the Judgment of the Ear in all the *Concords* of the preceeding Table.

Now if this be the true Rule of Nature, and an univerſal Character for judging of the comparative Perfection of Intervals, with reſpect to the Agreement of their Extremes in *Tune*; then it will be approven by Experience, and anſwer every Caſe: But it is not ſo, for by this Rule 4:7 or 5:7, both *Diſcords*, are preferable to 5:8 a *Concord*, tho' indeed in a low Degree; and 1:3, an *Octave* and *Fifth* compounded, will be preferable to 1:4 a double *Octave*, contrary to Experience. But ſuppoſe the Rule were good as to ſuch Caſes where both ſimilar Terms of the one Caſe compared are leſs than theſe of the other, or the one ſimilar Term equal and the other not; yet there are other Caſes to which this Character will not extend, *viz.* when there is an Advantage (as to the Smalneſs of the Number of Vibrations to one Coincidence) on the Part of the *Fundamental* in one Caſe, and on the Part of the *acute* Term in the other; which Advantage may be either equal or unequal, as here 5:6 and 4:7; the Advantages are equal, the Coincidence in the Firſt being made ſooner, by Two Vibrations of the *Fundamental*, than in the Second

Second, which again makes its Coincidences ſooner by ½ Vibrations of the *acute* Term. If we were to draw a Rule from this Compariſon, where the Ear prefers 5 : 6 a 3d leſſer, to 4 : 7 a *Diſcord*, then we ſhould always prefer that one, of Two Caſes whoſe mutual Advantages are equal, which coincides at the leaſt Number of *Vibrations* of the *acute* Term. But Experience contradicts this Rule, for 3 : 8, an *Octave* and 4th compounded, is better than 4 : 7; ſo that we have nothing to judge by here but the Ear. If, *laſtly*, the mutual Advantages are unequal, we find generally that which has the greateſt Advantage in whatever Term is preferable, tho' 'tis uncertain in many Caſes. Upon the Whole I conclude that there is ſomething beſides the Frequency of Coincidence to be conſidered in judging of the comparative Perfection of *Intervals*; which lies probably in the Relation of the Two Terms of the Interval, *i. e.* of their Vibrations to every Coincidence; ſo that it is not altogether leſſer Numbers, but this joined with ſomething elſe in the Form of the *Ratio*, which how to expreſs ſo as to make a complete Rule, no Body, that I know, has yet found.

As to the *Concords* of the preceeding *Table* ſome have taken this Method of comparing them: They find the relative Number of Coincidences that each of them makes in a given Time, thus, Find the leaſt common Dividend to all the Numbers that expreſs the Vibrations of the Fundamental to one Coincidence; take this for a Number of Vibrations made in any Time by a common *fundamental* Chord; if it it is divided ſeverally by the Numbers whoſe common Dividend it is, *viz.* the Terms of the ſeveral *Ratios* that expreſs the Vibrations of the Fundamental to one Coincidence; the Quotes are the relative Numbers of Coincidences made in the ſame Time by the ſeveral Concords; thus, the common Dividend mentioned is 60, and it is plain while the common Fundamental makes 60 Vibrations, there are 60 Coincidences of it with the *acute Octave*, and 30 Coincidences with the *5th*, and ſo on as in the *Table* annexed.

THE Preference in this Method is according to greater Number of Coincidences, and where that is equal the Preference is to that *Interval* whoſe *acuteſt* Term has fewer Vibrations to one Coincidence. And ſo the Order here is the ſame as formerly determined; but we are left to the ſame Difficulties and Uncertainty as before; for this Rule refers all to the Conſideration of the Vibrations of the Fundamental to one Coincidence; and therefore of Two Caſes that whoſe leſſer Term is leaſt will be preferable, whatever Difference there be of the other Term, which is contrary to Experience.

	Ratios	*Coin.*
8ve,	2 : 1	60
5th,	3 : 2	30
4th,	4 : 3	20
6th gr.	5 : 3	20
3d gr.	5 : 4	15
3d leſſ.	6 : 5	12
6th leſſ.	8 : 5	12

Merſennus, in his *Book* I. of *Harmony*, *Art.* 1. of *Harmonick* Numbers, has a Propoſition which promiſes an univerſal Character, for diſtinguiſhing the Perfection of Intervals as to the

the Agreement of their Extremes in *Tune*: The Subſtance of the whole *Art*. I ſhall give you briefly in the ſeveral *Propoſitions* of it, becauſe it may help to explain or confirm what I have delivered; and then I ſhall examine that particular Propoſition which reſpects the Thing directly before us; he tells us, That, 1*mo*. Every Sound has as many Degrees of *Acuteneſs* as it conſiſts of Motions of the Air, *i.e.* as oft as the Tympan of the Ear is ſtruck by the Air in Motion. 'Tis plain he means that the Degree of Acuteneſs depends on the Number of Vibrations of the Air, and conſequently of the ſonorous Body, accompliſhed in a given Time, agreeable to what I have ſaid of it above, elſe I do not underſtand the Senſe of the Propoſition. 2*do*. The Perception of *Concord* is nothing but the comparing of Two or more different Motions, which in the ſame Time affect the auditory Nerve. 3*tio*. We cannot make a certain Judgment of any *Conſonance* until the Air be as oft ſtruck in the ſame Time, by Two Chords, or other Inſtruments, as there are Unites in each Number, expreſſing the *Ratio* of that *Concord*: For Example, We cannot perceive a 5*th*, till 2 Vibrations of the one Chord, and 3 of the other are accompliſhed together, which Chords are in Length as 3 to 2. 4*to*. The greater Agreement and Pleaſure of *Conſonance* ariſes from the more frequent Union (or Coincidence) of Vibrations. But, *obſerve*, this is ſaid without determining what this Frequency has reſpect to; and how incomplete a Rule it is, I think we have already

already ſeen. *5to.* That Number of Motions (or Vibrations) is the Cauſe that the *arithmetical* Diviſion of *Conſonancies* (or Intervals) has more agreeable Effects than the *harmonical*; but this cannot be undreſtood till afterwards. Now follows the *Propoſition* which is the *4th* in *Merſennus*, but placed laſt here, becauſe 'tis what I am particularly to examine. *6to.* The more ſimple and *agreeable Conſonancies* are generated before the more *compound* and *harſh*. Example. Let 1, 2, 3, be the Lengths of Three Chords, 1 : 2. is an *Octave*, 2 : 3 a *5th*; and it is plain 1 : 3 is an *Octave* and *5th compounded*, or a *Twelfth*. But the Vibrations of Chords are reciprocally as their Lengths, therefore the Chord 2 vibrates once while the Chord 1 vibrates twice, and then exiſts an *Octave*; but the 12*th* does not yet exiſt, becauſe the Chord 3 has not vibrated once, nor the Chord 1 vibrated thrice (which is neceſſary to a 12*th*;) again for generating a *5th*, the Chord 2 muſt vibrate thrice, and the Chord 3 twice, which cannot be unleſs the Chord 1 in the ſame Time vibrate 6 Times, and then the 12*th* will be twice produced, and the *Octave* thrice, as is manifeſt; for the Chord 2 unites its Vibrations ſooner with the Chord 1 than with the Chord 3, and they are ſooner conſonant than the Chord 1 or 2 with 3. Whence many of the Myſteries of Harmony, *viz.* concerning the Preference of Concords and their Succeſſion may be deduced, by the ſagacious Practiſer. Thus far *Merſennus*; and *Kircher* repeats his very Words.

But

BUT when we examine this Propoſition by other Examples, it will not anſwer; and we are. as far as ever from the univerſal Character ſought. Take this Example, 2 : 3 : 6, the very ſame Intervals with *Merſennus*'s Example, only here the *Octave* is betwixt the Two greateſt Numbers, which was formerly betwixt the Two leſſer; now here the Chord 2 unites every Third Vibration with every Second Vibration of the Chord 3, and then the 5*th* exiſts; but alſo at every Third Vibration of the ſame Chord 2 there is a Coincidence of every ſingle Vibration of the Chord 6 (becauſe as 2 to 6 ſo 1 to 3) and then doth the 12*th* exiſt, and alſo the *Octave*, becauſe at every ſecond Vibration of the Chord 3, and every ſingle Vibration of the Chord 6, there is an *Octave*; ſo that in 3 Chords whoſe Lengths are as 2 : 3 : 6, containing the *Octave* : 5*th* : 12*th*, all the Three are generated in the ſame Time, *viz.* while the Chord 2 makes Three Vibrations; for when the Chord 3 has made Two, preciſely then the 5*th* exiſts; at the ſame Time alſo the Chord 6 has made 1 Vibration, and then doth the 12*th* firſt exiſt: But while the Chord 3 vibrates twice (*i. e.* while the Chord 2 vibrates thrice) the Chord 6 vibrates once, and not till then doth the *Octave* exiſt. From this Example 'tis plain the *Propoſition* is not true in the Senſe in which *Merſennus* explains it, or at leaſt, that I can underſtand it in: It is true that taking the Series 1, 2, 3, 4, 5, 6, 8, and comparing every Three of them immediately next other in the Manner

of

of the preceeding Example, the Preference will be determined the ſame way as has been already done, *viz.* *Octave* : *5th* : *4th* : *6th*, greater; *3d* greater, *3d* leſſer, *6th* leſſer: But yet it will not hold of the very ſame Concords taken another way, as is made ſufficiently plain in the laſt Example. Take this other, 6 : 4 : 3, containing a *5th*, *4th*, and *Octave*; while the Chord 4 makes 3 Vibrations, the Chord 3 makes 4 Vibrations; and then there is a *4th*: Alſo while the Chord 4 makes 3 Vibrations, the Chord 6 makes 2 Vibrations, and then there is a *5th*: So that we have here a *5th* and *4th* generated in the ſame Time; tho' if you take the ſame *Concords* in another Order, thus, 2 : 3 : 4; then the Rule will hold. Take laſtly this Example: Suppoſe Three Chords *a* : *b* : *c*, where *a* : *b*, is as 4 : 7, and *b* : *c* as 5 : 6, while *b* vibrates 4 Times, *a* vibrates 7 *Times*, and then that *Diſcord* 4 : 7 exiſts; but the *3d* leſſer, 5 : 6, is not generated till *b* has vibrated 6 Times, ſo that the *Diſcord* 4 : 7 is generated before the *Concord* 5 : 6. It will be ſo alſo if you take them thus; ſuppoſe *a* : *b* as 8 : 5, and *a* : *c* as 7 : 4, here the *Diſcord* exiſts whenever *a* has made 4 Vibrations, and the *Concord* not till *a* has made 5 Vibrations. Now if this were a juſt Rule, it would certainly anſwer in all Poſitions of the Intervals with reſpect to one another, which it does not; or there muſt be a certain Order wherein we ought to take them; but no one Rule with reſpect to the Order will make this Character anſwer to Experience in every Caſe.

Now

Now after all our Enquiry for an universal Character, whereby the Degrees of *Concord* may be determined, we are left to our Experience, and the Judgment of the Ear. We find indeed that where the radical Numbers which express any Interval are great, it is always gross *Discord*; and that all the *Concords* we know are exprest by small Numbers: And of all the *Concords* within an *Octave*, these are best which are contained in smallest Numbers; so that we may easily conclude that the frequent Coincidences of Vibrations is a necessary Condition in the Production of *Harmony*; but still we have no certain general Rules that afford an universal Character for judging of the Agreement of any Two Sounds, and of the Degree of their Approach to the Perfection of *Unisons*; which was the Thing we wanted in all this Enquiry: However, as to the Use of what we have already done, I think I may say, that in a Philosophical Enquiry, all our Pains is not lost, if we can secure our selves from false and incomplete Notions, and taking such for just and true; not that I say 'tis a wrong Notion of the Degrees of *Concord*, to think they depend upon the more and less frequent uniting the Vibrations, and the Ear's being consequently more or less uniformly moved; for that this Mixture and Union of Motions is the true Principle, or at least a chief Ingredient of *Concord*, is sufficiently plain from Experience; but I speak thus, because there seems to be something in the Proportion of the Two Motions that we have not yet

yet found, which ought to be known, in order to our having an univerſal Rule, that will infallibly determine the Degrees of *Concord*, agreeable to Senſe and Experience. And if any Body can be ſatisfied with the general Reaſon and Principle of *Concord* and *Diſcord* already found, they may take this *Definition, viz. That* Concord *is the Reſult of a frequent Union and Coincidence of the Vibrations of Two ſonorous Bodies, and conſequently of the undulating Motions of the Air, which being cauſed by theſe Vibrations, are like and proportional to them; which Coincidence the more frequent it is with reſpect to the Number of Vibrations of both Bodies performed in the ſame Time,* cæteris paribus, *the more perfect is that* Concord, *till the Rarity of the Coincidence in reſpect of one or both the Motions become* Diſcord.

I can find no better or more particular Account of this Matter among our modern Enquirers; you have already heard *Merſennus*, and I ſhall give you Dr. *Holder*'s Definition in his own Words, who has written chiefly on this One Point, as the Title of his Book bears: Says he, "*Conſonancy* (the ſame I call *Concord*) is the "Paſſage of ſeveral tunable Sounds through the "Medium, frequently mixing and uniting in "their undulated Motions cauſed by the well "proportioned commenſurate Vibrations of the "ſonorous Bodies, and conſequently arriving "ſmooth and ſweet and pleaſant to the Ear. "On the contrary, *Diſſonancy* is from diſpropor-"tionate Motions of Sounds, not mixing, but "jarring

" jarring and clashing as they pass, and arriving " to the Ear harsh and grating and offen- " sive.' If the Dr. means by our Pleasure's being a Consequence of the frequent Mixture of Motions, any other Thing than that we find these Things so connected, I do not conceive it; but however he understood this, he has applied his *Definition* to the Preference of *Concord* no further than these Five, 1 : 2, 2 : 3, 3 : 4, 5 : 4, 5 : 6. Yet after all I hope we shall, in what follows, find other Considerations to satisfie us, that we have discovered all the true natural Principles of musical Pleasure, with respect to the *Harmony* of the different Tunes of Sound; and I should have done with this Part, but that there are some remarkable Phenomena, depending on the Things already explained, which are worth our Observation.

---

§ 2. *Explaining some remarkable Appearances relating to this Subject, upon the preceeding Grounds of* Concord.

I. IF a Sound is raised with any considerable *Intenseness*, either by the human Voice, or from any sonorous Body; and if there is another sonorous Body near, whose *Tune* is *unison* or *octave* above that Sound, this Body will also sound its proper Note *unison* or *octave* to the given Note, tho' nothing visibly has touched it. The Experiment can be made most sensibly with the Strings of a musical In-stru-

ſtrument; for if a Sound is raiſed *uniſon* or *octave* below the Tune of any open String of the Inſtrument, it will give its Sound diſtinctly. And we might make a pleaſant Experiment with a ſtrong Voice ſinging near a well tuned Harpſichord. We find the ſame *Phænomenon* by raiſing Sound near a Bell, or any large Plate of ſuch Metal as has a clear and free Sound, or a large chryſtal drinking Glaſs. Now our *Philoſophers* make Uſe of the Hypotheſis already laid down to explain this ſurprizing Appearance; they tell us, That, for Example, when one String is ſtruck, and the Air put in Motion, every other String within the Reach of that Motion receives ſome Impreſſion from it; but each String can move only with a certain determinate Velocity of Recourſes in vibrating, becauſe all the Vibrations from the greateſt to the leaſt are equidiurnal ; again, all *Uniſons* proceed from equal or equidiurnal Vibrations, and other *Concords* from other Proportions, which as they are the Cauſe of a more perfect Mixture and Agreement of Motion, *that is*, of the undulated Air, ſo much better is that *Concord* and nearer to *Uniſon* : Now the *uniſon* String keeping an exact equal Courſe with the ſounded String, becauſe it has the ſame Meaſure of Vibrations, has its Motion continued and improven till it become ſenſible and give a diſtinct Sound; and other concording Strings have their Motions propagated in different Degrees, according to the Commenſurateneſs of their Vibrations with theſe of the ſounded String ; the

Octave

Octave moſt ſenſibly, then the 5th; but after this the croſſing of the Motions hinders any ſuch Effect: And they illuſtrate it to us in this Manner; ſuppoſe a Pendulum ſet a moving, the Motion may be continued and augmented, by making frequent light Impulſes, as by blowing upon it, when the Vibration is juſt finiſhed and the Pendulum ready to return; but if it is touched before that, or by any croſs Motion, and this done frequently, the Motion will be ſo interrupted as to ceaſe altogether; ſo of Two *uniſon* Strings, if the one is forcibly ſtruck it communicates Motion by the Air, to the other; and being equidiurnal in their Vibrations, they finiſh them preciſely together; and the Motion of that other is improven by the frequent Impulſes received from the Vibrations of the Firſt, becauſe they are given preciſely when that other Chord has finiſhed its Vibrations, and is ready to *return*; but if the Two Chords are unequal in Duration, there will be a croſſing of Motions leſs or more, according to the Proportion of that Inequality; and in ſome Caſes the Motion of the untouched String is ſo checked as never to be ſenſible, or at leaſt to give any Sound; and in Fact we know, that in no Caſe is this *Phænomenon* to be found but the *Uniſon*, *Octave* and *Fifth*; moſt ſenſibly in the Firſt, and gradually leſs in the other Two, which are alſo limited to this Condition, that the *graver* will make the *acuter* Sound, but not contrarily. And as this is a tolerable Explication of the Matter, it confirms in a great Degree the Truth

Truth of the Equidiurnity of the Vibrations of the ſame Chord, and the Proportion of the Lengths and Duration of the Vibrations; for we know that the Sound of the untouched Chord is weaker than that of the other, and its Vibrations conſequently leſs; now if they were not equidiurnal, and if the Proportion mentioned were not alſo true, we ſhould not have ſo good a Reaſon of the *Phænomenon*, which joyned with the ſenſible Identity of the *Tune*, is ſufficient without other Demonſtrations to make it highly probable that the Vibrations are all performed in equal Time, and that the Duration of a ſingle Vibration of the one is to that of the other directly, or the Number of Vibrations in a given Time reciprocally as the Lengths of the Chords (*cæteris paribus.*)

II. I cannot omit to mention in this Place, how the Gentlemen of the Academy of Sciences in *France* apply this Hypotheſis of *harmonick Motion*, for explaining the ſtrange Recovery of one who has been bitten by the *Tarantula*, the Effect of which is a Lethargy and Stupifying of the Senſes; I ſhall not here repeat the whole Story, but in ſhort, the Recovery is by Means of *Muſick*; 'tis not every Kind that will recover the ſame Perſon, nor the ſame Kind every Perſon; but having tried a great many various Meaſures and Combinations of *Tune* and *Time*, they hit at random on the Cure, which excites Motion in the Patient by Degrees, till he is recovered. To account for this, theſe *Philoſophers* tell us, that there is a certain Aptneſs in in theſe particular Motions, to give Motion to the Nerves of that Perſon (for they ſuppoſe the Diſeaſe lies all there) in their preſent Circumſtances, as one String communicates Motion to another, which neither a greater nor leſſer, nor any other Combination can do; being excited to Motion the Senſes return gradually.

III. THERE are other Inſtances of this wonderful Power, and, if I may call it ſo, ſympathetick Virtue in ſonorous Motions; I have felt a very ſenſible tremulous Motion in ſome Parts of my Body when near a baſs Violin, upon the ſounding of certain Notes ſtrongly ſtruck, tho' the Sound of a Cannon would not produce ſuch an Effect. And from all our Obſervations we are aſſured that it is not a great or ſtrong Motion in the Parts of one Body that is capable to produce Motion by this Kind of Communication in the Parts of another, but it depends on a certain inexpreſſible Likeneſs and Congruity of Motions; whereof take this one Example more, which is not leſs ſurpriſing than the reſt: If a Man raiſes his Voice *uniſon* to the Tune of a drinking Glaſs, and continue to blow for ſome time in it with a very intenſe or ſtrong Voice, he ſhall not only make the Glaſs ſound, but at laſt break it; whereas a Motion much ſtronger, if it is out of Tune to the Glaſs, will never make it ſound and far leſs break it (I have known perſons to whom this Experiment ſucceeded.) The Reaſon of this ſeems very probably to be, that when the Glaſs ſounds, its Parts are put into a vibratory or tremulous Motion, which being continued long by by a ſtrong Voice, their Coheſion is quite broken; but ſuppoſe another Voice much ſtronger, yet if 'tis out of Tune, there will be ſuch a croſſing of Motions that prevents both the Sound of the Glaſs and the breaking of it. It is a noted Experiment, that by preſſing one's Finger upon the Brim of a Glaſs, and ſo moving it quickly round, it will ſound; and to demonſtrate that this is not effected without a very ſwift Motion of the inſenſible Parts of the Glaſs, we need but fill ſome Liquor into it, and then repeating the Experiment, we ſhall have the Liquor put gradually into a greater Motion, till the Glaſs ſound very diſtinctly, and continuing it with a brisk Motion, the Liquor will be put into a very Ferment. The Conſideration of this may perhaps make the Explication of the laſt Caſe more reaſonable.

IV. DOCTOR *Holder*, to confirm his general Reaſon of *Conſonancy* alledges ſome Experiments that happened to himſelf, particularly, " ſays he, " Being in an arched ſounding Room
" near a ſhrill Bell of a Houſe-clock, when the A-
" larm ſtruck I whiſtled to it, which I did with
" Eaſe in the ſame Tune with the Bell ; but
" endeavouring to whiſtle a Note higher or lower,
" the Sound of the Bell and its croſs Motions
" were ſo predominant, that my Breath and
" Lips were checked, ſo that I could not
" whiſtle at all, nor make any Sound of it in
" that diſcording Tune. After I ſounded a
" ſhrill whiſtling Pipe, which was out of Tune
" to the Bell, and their Motions ſo claſhed
that

" that they ſeemed to ſound like ſwitching one " another in the Air." To confirm this of the Doctor's, there is a common Experiment, that if Two Sounds, ſuppoſe the Notes of a muſical Inſtrument, are brought to uniſon *Octave* or *5th*, and then one of them raiſed or depreſſed a very little, there will be a Claſhing of the Two Sounds, like a Beating, as if they ſtrove together; and this will continue till they are reſtored to exact *Concord*, or carried a little further from it, for then alſo this Beating will ceaſe, tho' the *Diſcord* will perhaps increaſe. Now if we conſider that *Concords* are ſuch a Mixture and Agreement of Sounds that the compound ſeems not to partake more of the one Simple than of the other, but they are ſo evenly united that the one does not prevail over the other ſo as to be more obſervable; We ſee that this ſtriving, in which we find an alternate prevailing of either Sound, ought naturally to happen when they are neareſt to their moſt perfect Agreement, but when they are farther removed, the one has gained too much upon the other not to make that one moſt obſervable. All theſe Things ſerve to ſhow us how neceſſary an Ingredient in the Cauſe of *Concord* the Union and Conicidence of the Motions is, and I ſhall beg a little more of your Patience to conſider the following Illuſtration.

IT is not an unpleaſant Entertainment to contemplate the beautiful Uniformity of Nature in her ſeveral Productions; the Reſemblance diſcovered among Things, if it don't let us farther into

into the Knowledge of the Eſſence and original Reaſon of them, it does at leaſt increaſe our Knowledge of the common Laws of Nature; and we are helped to explain and illuſtrate one Thing by another. To the Matter in Hand, we may compare *Sight* and *Hearing*, and to manage the Compariſon to greateſt Advantage, let us conſider, *Senſation* is the ſame Thing with reſpect to the Mind that perceives, whatever be the Inſtrument of Senſe, *i. e.* without diſtinguiſhing the external Senſe (as *Philoſophers* ſpeak) the internal is the ſame, which is properly *Senſation*, as this implies a certain Mode of the Mind cauſed by the Admittance (or, with Mr. *Lock*, the actual Entrance) of an Idea into the Underſtanding by the Senſes; which is a Definition plainly unconfin'd to one or other of the Five Ways whereby Ideas enter, when the Mind is ſaid to perceive by the Senſes; hence we have good Reaſon to think, that it is not improper to compare one Senſe with another, as Seeing and Hearing; for tho' their Objects are different, and the Means whereby they make their Impreſſion on the Mind be ſuited to them, by which Senſations very diſtinct are produced; yet they may be equally agreeable in their Kind, and have ſome common Principle in both Caſes neceſſary to that Agreeableneſs. We believe that Nature works by the moſt ſimple and uniform Ways; accordingly we find by Experience that ſimple Ideas have a much eaſier Acceſs than compound; and the more Difficulty the leſs Pleaſure; yet the more eaſy

are

are not always the moſt agreeable; for as we have no Pleaſure in what falls confuſedly on the Senſes, and wearies the Mind with the manifold and perplex'd Relations of its Parts; neither does that afford much Pleaſure that is too eaſily perceived, at leaſt we are ſoon cloyed with it; but a middle betwixt theſe Extremes is beſt. *Again*, we know that Variety entertains, both of ſimple Ideas and theſe variouſly connected and joyned together. And becauſe the Mind is beſt pleaſed with Order, Uniformity, and the diſtinct Relation of its Ideas, the compound Idea ought to have its Parts uniform and regularly connected, and their Relations ſo diſtinct that the Mind may perceive them without Perplexity: In ſhort, when the Cauſe is moſt uniform, and involves not too great Multiplicity in the Senſation, the Idea will be entertained with the more Pleaſure; hence it is that a very intricate Figure, perplex'd with many Lines, and theſe not very regular, nor their *Ratios* diſtinct, does not pleaſe the Eye ſo well as a Figure of fewer Lines and in a more diſtinct Relation.

But the Compariſon muſt run between the Eye and Ear in Perceptions that have ſomething common: *Motion* is the Object of Sight very properly; and tho' it be not ſo of Hearing immediately; yet Sound being the immediate Product of Motion, we may conclude that if the Eye is gratify'd with the Uniformity of Motion, for the ſame Reaſon (whatever it be in its ſelf) will the Ear be with Uniformity in Sounds,

Sounds, which ow themſelves to Motion, and are in a Manner nothing elſe but Motion forcing on us a Perception of its Exiſtence by other Organs than the Eye, and therefore makes that different Idea we call *Sound.* In *Seeing* the Thing is plain; for if Two Motions are at once in our View, where the Senſe attends to nothing but the Motion, then, as the Relation of the Velocities is more diſtinct, we compare the Motions, and view them with the greater Pleaſure; but were the Relation leſs ſenſible, there could but little Pleaſure ariſe from theſe Ideas: Thus, were it obvious that the one Motion were to the other as 2 : 1 or 3 : 2 uniformly and conſtantly, we could look on them with Delight; but were the *Ratio* leſs perceiveable as 13 : 7; or the one being uniform Motion, and the other irregularly accelerate; the Mind would weary in the Compariſon, and perhaps never reach it, therefore find no Pleaſure: I do not ſay that in many Caſes, which might be viewed with Satisfaction, we could be determinately ſure what were the *Ratio* of Velocity; but from Experience we know, that the more commenſurable the Extremes are to one another, it is the more agreeable, becauſe diſtinct; therefore it is certain we perceive the one more than the other: And in many Caſes there would be a Pain in viewing ſuch Objects, the Irregularity of the Motion creating a Giddineſs in the Brain, while we endeavour to entertain both the Motions; and by Experience we know

know, that to follow very quick Motions with the Eye, especially if circular, this is constantly the Effect. It is the same Way in Hearing, some simple Sounds are painful and harsh, because the Quickness of the Vibrations bears no Proportion to the Organs of Sense, which is necessary to all agreeable Sensation. But we have a particular Example that comes nearer the Purpose.

LET us view the Motion of Two Pendulums; if they are of equal Length, and let fall from equal Height they describe equal Arches; their Motions continue equal Time, and their Vibrations begin always together: The Motions of these Two Pendulums are like and equal, so that if we suppose the Eye to follow the one, and describe an equal Arch with it (which would be if the visual Ray in every Point of the Arch were perpendicular to the pendulum Chord) then that one would always eclipse the other, and the Eye perceive but one Motion; and suppose the Eye at a considerable Distance, it would not perceive Two different Motions, tho' it self moved not; consequently there could be no jarring of these Ideas: This is exactly the Case of Two Chords every way the same, and equally impelled to Motion; for their Vibrations give the Parts of the Air alike and equal Motion, so that the Ear is always struck equally and at the same Time, hence we perceive but one simple Sound; and with respect to the Effect it is no more a compound Idea than Two Bottles of Water from the same Fountain make

a

a compound Liquor, which only increaſe the Quantity; as the foreſaid Uniſons only fill the Ear with a greater Sound increaſing the Intenſeneſs.

IF in the ſame Caſe we ſuppoſe the Eye ſo ſituated as to ſee diſtinctly the Motion of both Pendulums; or ſuppoſe the Pendulums fall from different Heights, then this Variety would afford a greater Pleaſure; for the Mind perceives a Difference, but a very diſtinct Relation; becauſe we ſee the Vibrations begin always at the ſame Time; and this explains the greater Pleaſure we have in *Uniſons* which proceed from Chords differing in ſome Circumſtances, as if the one were more intenſe or of a different Species; in which we perceive the Unity of Acuteneſs, but theſe other different Circumſtances make them perceiveably diſtinct ſimple Sounds, which heightens the Pleaſure. If we carry this Compariſon further, we'll find, that if Two Pendulums of unequal Length be let fall together from ſimilar Points of their Arch, they begin not every Vibration together, but they will coincide more or leſs frequently, according to a certain Proportion of their Lengths, which is always reciprocally ſubduplicate; and tho' this is quite another Proportion than that of ſimple Chords which are in reciprocal ſimple Proportion of their Number of Vibrations to every Coincidence, yet the Illuſtration drawn from this Compariſon ſtands good, becauſe we conſider only the *Ratios* of the Number of Vibrations to each Coincidence in both Caſes; and in this we find it true in general, that the more

more frequently the Vibrations coincide, the Prospect is the more agreeable; but it is alſo according to the Number of Vibrations of both Pendulums in the ſame Time, in ſo much that the ſame Numbers which make leſs or more Concord in Sound, will alſo give a greater or leſs pleaſant Proſpect, if the Pendulums are ſo proportioned, according to the known Laws of their Motion; and if the Pendulums ſeldom or never coincide, or begin their Vibrations together, there will be ſuch a thwarting of the Images as cannot miſs to offend the Sight.

CHAP. IV.

Containing the Harmonical Arithmetick.

HERE I propoſe to explain as much of the *Theory* of Numbers as is neceſſary to be known, for making and underſtanding the Compariſons of *muſical Intervals*, which are expreſt by Numbers; in order to our finding their mutual Relations, Compoſitions and Reſolutions But I muſt premiſe Two Things. *Firſt*: That I ſuppoſe the Reader acquainted with the more general and common Properties and Operations of Numbers; ſo that I ſhall but barely propoſe what of theſe I have Uſe for, without any Demonſtration, and demonſtrate Things that are leſs

leſs common. *Second.* That I confine my ſelf to the principal and more neceſſary Things; leaving a Thouſand Speculations that may be made, as leſs uſeful to my Deſign, and alſo becauſe theſe will be eaſily underſtood when you meet with them, if the fundamental Things here explained be well underſtood.

---

§ 1. *Definitions.*

I. THERE is a twofold *Compariſon* of Numbers, in both of which we diſtinguiſh an *Antecedent* or Number compared, and *Conſequent* or Number to which the other is compared. By the *Firſt* we find how much they differ, or by how many Units the *Antecedent* exceeds or comes ſhort of the *Conſequent*; which Difference is called the *arithmetical Ratio* (or *Exponent* of the *arithmetical Relation* or *Habitude*) of theſe Two Numbers: So if 5 and 7 are compared, their *arithmetical Ratio* is 2; and all Numbers that have the ſame Difference, whatever they are themſelves, are in the ſame *arithmetical Habitude* to one another. By the *Second* Compariſon we find how oft or how many Times the *Antecedent* contains (if greateſt) or is contained (if leaſt) in the other; and this Number is called the *geometrical Ratio* (or *Exponent* of the *geometrical Relation*) of the Numbers compared;

red; so compare 12 to 4, the *Ratio* is 3, signifying that 12 contains 4, or that 4 is contained in 12, thrice.

THE *geometrical Ratio* thus conceived is always the *Quote* of the greater divided by the lesser: But *observe* when the lesser is *antecedent* to the greater, the Sense of the Comparison is also this, *viz.* To find what Part or Parts of the greater that lesser is equal to; and according to this Sense the *geometrical Ratio* of Two Numbers is made universally the *Quote* of the *Antecedent* divided by the *Consequent*, and is exprest by setting the *Antecedent* over the *Consequent* Fraction-wise; so that if the *Antecedent* is greatest, the *Ratio* is an improper Fraction, equal to some whole or mix'd Number, and signifies that the *Antecedent* contains the *Consequent* as many Times, and Parts of a Time, as that *Quote* contains Units and Parts of an Unit. *Example.* The *Ratio* of 12 to 4 is $\frac{12}{4}$ equal to 3 (for 12 contains 4 thrice.) The *Ratio* of 18 to 7 is $\frac{18}{7}$ equal to $2\frac{4}{7}$, signifying that 18 contains 7 Two Times and $\frac{4}{7}$ Parts of a Time, *i. e.* $\frac{4}{7}$ Parts of 7; which is plainly this, that 18 contains 2 Times 7, and 4 over. But if the *Antecedent* is least, the *Ratio* is a proper Fraction, signifying that the *Antecedent* is such a Part of the *Consequent*; so the *Ratio* of 7 to 9 is $\frac{7}{9}$, *i. e.* that 7 is $\frac{7}{9}$ Parts of 9.

IN what follows I shall take the *geometrical Ratio* of Numbers both ways, as it happens to be most convenient.

II.

II. An Equality of *Ratios* conſtitutes *Proportion*, which is *arithmetical* or *geometrical* as the *Ratio* is. A *Ratio* exiſts betwixt Two Terms, but *Proportion* requires at leaſt Three; ſo theſe 1, 2, 3, are in *arithmetical Proportion*, or theſe, 2, 5, 8, becauſe there is the ſame Difference betwixt the Numbers compared, which are 1 to 2, and 2 to 3, or 2 to 5, and 5 to 8. *Again* theſe are in *geometrical Proportion*, 2, 4, 8, or 9, 3, 1, becauſe as 2 is a Half of 4, ſo is 4 of 8, alſo as 9 is triple of 3 ſo is 3 of 1.

Observe, 1*mo*. In all *Proportion*, as there are at leaſt Two Couple of Terms, ſo the Compariſon muſt run alike in both, *i. e.* if it is from the leſſer to the greater, or contrary, in the one Couple, it muſt be ſo in the other alſo; *thus* in 2, 6, 9 the Proportion runs, as 2 to 6 ſo is 6 to 9, or as 9 to 6 ſo 6 to 2.

2*do*. If three proportional Numbers are right diſpoſed, it will always be, as the 1*ſt* to the 2*d*, ſo the 2*d* to 3*d*, as above; but 4 Numbers are in Proportion when the 1*ſt* is to the 2*d* as the 3*d* to the 4*th*, without conſidering the *Ratio* of the 2*d* and 3*d*; as here 2 : 4 : 3 : 6; for in a proper Senſe *Proportion* is the Equality of the *Ratios* of Two or more Couples of Numbers, whether they have any common Term or not; and ſo, ſtrictly, there muſt be Four Terms to make *Proportion*, tho' there need be but Three different Numbers.

III. From the laſt Thing explained we have a Diſtinction of *continued* and *interrupted Proportion*

portion Continued Proportion is when in a Series of Numbers there is the same *Ratio* of every Term to the next, as of the 1*st* to the 2*d*; as here 1 : 2 : 3 : 4 : 5, which is *arithmetical* and 1, 2, 4, 8, 16, which is *geometrical*. *Interrupted* is when betwixt any Two Terms of the Series there is a different *Ratio* from that of the rest; as 2 : 5 : 6 : 9, *arithmetical*, where 2 is to 5 as 6 : 9 (*i. e.* differing by 3,) but not so 5 and 6, or 2, 4, 3, 6; *geometrical*, where 2 is to 4 as 3 to 6 (*i. e.* a *Half*,) but not so 4 to 3; and *observe* that of 4 Terms, if there is any Interruption of the *Ratio* it must be betwixt the 2*d* and 3*d*, else these 4 are not *proportional*.

IV. Out of these Two *Proportions* arises a Third Kind, which we call *harmonical Proportion*, thus constituted; of Three Numbers, if the 1*st* be to the 3*d* in *geometrical Proportion*, as the Difference of the 1*st* and 2*d* to the Difference of the 2*d* and 3*d*, these Three Numbers are in *harmonical Proportion*. *Example*. 2 : 3 : 6 are *harmonical*, because 2 : 6 :: 1 : 3 are *geometrical*. And Four Numbers are *harmonical*, when the 1*st* is to the 4*th*, as the Difference of the 1*st* and 2*d* to the Difference of the 3*d* and 4*th*, as here 24 : 16 : 12 : 9 are *harmonical*, because 24 : 9 :: 8 : 3 are *geometrical*.

AGAIN, of 4 or more Numbers, if every Three immediate Terms are *harmonical*, the Whole is a Series of *continual harmonical Proportionals* as 30 : 20 : 15 : 12 : 10. or if every 4 immediately next are *harmonical*, 'tis also a *continued* Series,

Series, but of another Species, as 3, 4, 6, 9 18, 36.

How this came by the Name of *harmonical Proportion* ſhall be ſhewn afterwards; and here I ſhall explain the fundamental Properties of this Kind, having firſt propoſed as much of the Doctrine of *arithmetical* and *geometrical Proportion* as is neceſſary for the Explanation of the other.

---

§ 2. *Of* Arithmetical *and* Geometrical Proportion.

THEOREM I. If any Number is given as the Firſt of a Series of Proportionals, and alſo the common *Ratio*, the Series may be continued thus: 1*mo*. In *arithmetical Proportion* by adding the *Ratio* (or common Difference) to the 1*ſt* Term given, and then to the Sum; and ſo on to every ſucceeding Sum; theſe ſeveral Sums are the Terms ſought in an *increaſing Series*, which may be continued *in infinitum*. But to make a *decreaſing Series*, ſubſtract the *Ratio* from the Firſt Term, and from every ſucceeding Remainder; the ſeveral Remainders are the Terms ſought. But 'tis plain this Series has Limits, and cannot deſcend *in infinitum*. *Example*. Given 3 for the 1*ſt* Term of an increaſing Series, and 2 the *arithmetical Ratio*, or common Difference; the Series is 3, 5, 7, 9, *&c.* Or, given 8 the 1*ſt* Term, and

and 3 the common Difference in a decreasing Series, it is 8, 5, 2, and can go no further in positive Numbers. 2*do.* In *geometrical Proportion*, by multiplying the given Term into the *Ratio* (which I take here for the Quote of the greater Term divided by the lesser) and that Product again by the *Ratio*, and so on every succeeding Product by the *Ratio*; the several Products make the Series sought increasing, but for a decreasing Series divide. *Example.* Given 2 the 1*st* Term, and 3 the *Ratio* for an increasing Series it is 2 : 6 : 18, 54, 162 *&c.* Or, given 24 the 1*st* Term and the *Ratio* 2, the decreasing Series is 24 : 12 : 6 : 3. 1½, *&c.* It is plain a *geometrical Series* may increase or decrease *in infinitum* in positive Numbers.

THEOREM II. If Three Numbers are in *arithmetical* or *geometrical Proportion*, the *Sum* of the Extremes in the first, and the *Product* in the second Case, is equal to double the middle Term in the 1*st*, and to the Square of the middle Term in the second Case. *Example.* 3 : 7 : 11 *arithmetical*, the Sum of the Extremes 3 and 11 is equal to twice 7, *viz.* 14. And in these, 4 : 6 : 9 *geometrical*, the *Product* of 4 and 9, *viz.* 36, is equal to the Square of 6, or 6 Times 6.

COROLLARY. Hence the Rule for finding a Mean proportional, either *arithmetical* or *geometrical*, betwixt Two given Numbers is very obvious, *viz.* Half the Sum of the Two given Numbers is an *arithmetical* Mean, and the Square Root of their Product is a *geomtrical* Mean.

THEOR.

THEOREM III. If Four Numbers are in *Proportion arithmetical* or *geometrical*, whether *continued* or *interrupted*, the Sum of the Extremes in the first Case, and *Product* in the 2*d*, is equal to the Sum of the middle Terms in the 1*st* and the Product in the 2*d* Case. *Example*. In these, 2 : 3 : 4 : 5 *arithmetical*, the Sum of 2 and 5 is equal to the Sum of 3 and 4; and these *geometrical* 2 : 5 : 4 : 10. the *Product* of 2 and 10 is equal to that of 5 and 4, *viz*. 20.

COROLLARY. If Four Numbers represented thus, $a : b :: c : d$, are *proportional* either *arithmetically* or *geometrically*, comparing a to b and c to d; they will also be *proportional* taken *inversely*, thus, $d : c :: b : a$, or *alternately* thus, $a : c :: b : d$, or *inversely* and *alternately* thus, $d : b :: c : a$. The *reason* is obvious, because in all these Forms the Extremes and the middle Terms are the same, whose Sums, if they are *arithmetical*, or *Products* if *geometrical*, being equal, is a Sign of their Proportionality by this *Theorem*.

THEOREM IV. In a Series of *continued Proportionals*, *arithmetical* or *geometrical*, the Two Extremes with the middle Term, or the Extremes with any Two middle Terms at equal Distance from them, are also *proportional*. *Example*. 2, 3, 4, 5, 6, 7, 8 *arithmetical*, here 2, 5, 8, are *arithmetically proportional*, also 2, 4, 6, 8, or 2 : 3 : 7 : 8. *Again* in this *geometrical* Series, 2 : 4 : 8 : 16 : 32 :

64 : 128, these are *geometrically proportional* 2 : 16, 128, or 2 : 8, 32 : 128.

THEOREM V. If Two Numbers in any *geometrical Ratio* are added to, or substracted from other Two in the same *Ratio* (the less with the less and greater with the greater) the *Sums* or *Differences* are in the same *Ratio*. *Example.* 6 : 3 :: 10 : 5 are *proportional*, the common *Ratio* being 2, and 6 added to 10 makes 16, as 3 to 5 makes 8, and 16 to 8 are in the same *Ratio* as 6 to 3 or 10 to 5; and again 16 being to 8 as 6 to 3, their Differences 10 and 5 are in the same *Ratio*.

THE Reverse of this *Proposition* is true, *viz.* That if to or from any Two Numbers be added or substracted other Two, then, if the Sums or Differences are in the same *geometrical Ratio* of the First Two, the Numbers added or substracted are in the same *Ratio*.

COROLLARY. If any Two given Numbers are equally multiplied or divided, *i. e.* multiplied or divided by the same Number, the Two *Products* or *Quotes* are in the same *Ratio* with the given Numbers, *i. e.* are proportional with them. *Example.* 3 and 5 multiplied each by 7 produce 21 and 35, and these are proportional 3 : 5, 21 : 35. *Again* 24 and 16, divided each by 8 *quote* 3 and 2 and these are proportional 24 : 16, 3 : 2.

IT follows also that if every Term of any continued Series is equally multiplied or divided it is still a *continued* Series in the same *Ratio*.

THEOREM.

THEOREM VI. If Two Numbers in any *arithmetical Ratio* be added to other Two in the ſame *Ratio* (the leſs to the leſs and greater to the greater) the *Sums* are in a doub e *Ratio*, *i. e.* their *Difference* is double that of the reſpective Parts added; ſo, if to theſe 3 : 5, you add theſe 7 : 9 the Sums are 10, 14 whoſe Difference 4 is double the Difference of 3 : 5 or 7 : 9. And if to this Sum you add other Two in the ſame *Ratio*, the Difference of the laſt Sum will be triple the Difference of the Firſt Two, and ſo on.

OBSERVE. If Two Numbers in any *arithmetical Ratio* are ſubſtracted from other Two in the ſame *Ratio* (the leſs from the leſs, *&c.*) the *arithmetical Ratio* of the Remainders is 0, ſo from 7 : 9 take 3 : 5 the Remainders are 4, 4.

COROLLARY. If Two Numbers in any *arithmetical Ratio* be both multiplied by the ſame Number, the *Difference* of the *Products* ſhall contain the Firſt *Difference*, as oft as the Multiplier contains Unity; ſo 3, 5 multiplied by 4 produce 12, 20, whoſe Difference 8 is equal to 4 Times 2 (the Difference of 3 and 5) and ſo if any *continued arithmetical* Series has each Term multiplied by the ſame Number, the Products will make a *continued* Series with a Difference containing the former Difference as oft as the Multiplier contains Unity. But if divided, the Difference of the Quotes will be ſuch a Part of the Firſt Difference as the Diviſor denominates.

THEOREM.

THEOREM VII. If Two Numbers in any *Ratio arithmetical* or *geometrical*, be added to, or multiplied by other Two in any other *Ratio* of the ſame Kind (the leſſer by the leſſer, and the greater by the greater) the *Sums* in the one Caſe and *Products* in the other are in a *Ratio* which is the Sum or Product of the *Ratios* of the Numbers added, or multiplied: An *Example* will explain it, Let 2 : 4 and 3 : 9 be added in the Manner mentioned, the Sums are 5, 13, whoſe *arithmetical Ratio* or Difference is 8 the Sum of 2 and 6 the Differences of the Numbers given; or if they are multiplied, *viz.* 2 by 3, and 4 by 9, the Products 6 and 36 are in the *geometrical Ratio* of 6, equal to the Product of 2 and 3 the *Ratios* of the given Numbers.

THEOREM VIII. If any Two Numbers are multiplied by ſame Number, and the Products taken for the Extremes of a Series, they will admit of as many middle Terms as the Multiplier contains Units leſs one; and the whole Series will be in the *arithmetical Ratio* of the Firſt Numbers; ſo let 3 and 7 be multiplied by 4 the Prodncts are 12 and 28 (in the ſame *geometrical Ratio* as 3 and 7 by *Corollary* to *Theorem 5th*) and their *arithmetical Ratio* or Difference 16, is 4 Times as great as that of 3 and 7, which is 4 (by *Corol.* to *Theor.* 6.) and therefore they are capable of 3 ſuch middle Terms as that the common Difference of the whole Series ſhall be 4; the Series is 12 : 16,

20 : 24 : 28. *Corollary.* Hence we have a Solution to this *Problem.*

PROBLEM I. To find an *arithmetical Series*, of a given Number of Terms, whose Extremes shall be in the *geometrical Ratio*, and the intermediate Terms in the *arithmetical Ratio* of Two given Numbers; the *Rule* is, Multiply the given Numbers by the Number of Terms less 1, and then fill up the middle Terms by the given *Ratio. Example.* Let 3 to 5 be given for the *Ratio* of the Extremes, and 10 for the Number of Terms; I multiply 3 and 5 by 9, which produces 27 and 45, and the Series is 27, 29, 31, 33, 35, 37, 39, 41, 43, 45.

LET us now compare the *arithmetical* and *geometrical* Proportions together.

THEOREM IX. If there is a Series of Numbers in continued *arithmetical Proportion*, then the *geometrical Ratios* of each Term to the next must necessarily differ; and from the least Extreme to the greatest, these *Ratios* still increase; but from the greatest they decrease, comparing always the lesser to the greater; but contrarily if we compare the greater to the lesser. *Example.* In this *arithmetical Series* 1, 2, 3, 4, 5, 6. the *geometrical Ratios* are $\frac{1}{2}$, $\frac{2}{3}$, $\frac{3}{4}$, $\frac{4}{5}$, $\frac{5}{6}$, increasing from $\frac{1}{2}$, and consequently decreasing from $\frac{5}{6}$. *Again*, if we take a *continued geometrical Series*, the *arithmetical Ratios* or Differencesincre ase from the least Extreme to the greatest, and contrarily from the greatest to the least. *Example.* 1, 2, 4, 8, 16, the *arithmetical Ratios* are 1, 2, 4 8.

COROL-

COROLLARY. It is plain, that if an *arithmetical Mean* is put betwixt Two Numbers, the *geometrical Ratios* betwixt that middle Term and the Extremes are unequal; and that of the leſſer Extreme to the middle Term is leſs than that of the ſame middle Term to the other Extreme. *Example.* 2, 4, 6 the two *geometrical Ratios* are $\frac{1}{2}$ and $\frac{2}{3}$ comparing the leſſer Number to the greater; but it is contrary if we compare the greater to the leſſer.

---

§ 3. *Of* Harmonical Proportion.

THEOREM X. If Three or Four Numbers in *harmonical Proportion* are multiplied or divided by any the ſame Number, the *Products* or *Quotes* will alſo be in *harmonical Proportion*; becauſe as the Products or Quotes made of the Extremes are in the ſame *Ratio* of the Extremes, ſo the Differences of the Products of the intermediate Terms, tho' they are greater or leſſer than the Differences of theſe Terms, yet they are proportionally ſo, being equally multiplied or divided. *Example.* If 6, 8, 12, which are *harmonical*, be divided by 2, the Quotes are 3, 4, 6, which are alſo *harmonical*; and reciprocally, ſince 3, 4, 6, are *harmonical*, their Products by 2, *viz.* 6, 8, 12 are *harmonical*.

THEOREM.

THEOREM XI. If double the *Product* of any Two Numbers be divided by their *Sum*, the *Quote* is an *harmonical Mean* betwixt them. *Example.* Let 3 and 6 be given for the Extremes to find an *harmonical Mean*, their Product is 18, which doubled is 36; this divided by 9 (the *Sum* of 3 and 6) quotes 4, and these Three are in *harmonical Proportion*, *viz.* 3 : 4 : 6.

To them that have the least Knowledge of *Algebra*, the following *Demonstration* will be plain; suppose any Two Numbers *a* and *b*, and *a* the greater, let the *harmonical Mean* sought be *x*; from the Definition of *harmonical* Proportion, we have this true in *geometrical* Proportion, *viz.* $a : b :: a-x : x-b$. And by *Theorem 3d*, $ax-ab=ab-xb$: Then, $ax+bx=2ab$; and lastly, $x=\frac{2ab}{a+b}$ *W. W. D.*

THEOREM XII. Take any Two Numbers in Order, and call the one the First Term, and the other the Second; if you multiply them together, and divide the Product by the Number that remains, after the Second is substracted from double the First, the Quote is a Third in *harmonical* Proportion, to be taken in the same Order. *Example*, Take 3 : 4 their Product is 12, which being divided by 2 (the Remainder after 4 is taken from 6 the double of the First) the Quote is 6, the Third *harmonical* Term sought: Or reversely, take 6, 4, their Product is 24, which divided by 8 (the Difference of 4 and 12) quotes 3, the Third Term sought.

DE-

DEMONSTRATION. Take a and b known Numbers, and a the greateſt; let x be the Third Term ſought, leſs than b; then, ſince theſe are *harmonical*, *viz.* a, b, x, theſe are *geometrical*, *viz.* $a : x :: a-b : b-x$ (by *Definition* 4. § 1. of this *Chapter*) then, taking the Products of the Extremes and Means, we have $ab-ax=ax-xb$; and $ab=2ax-xb$. And laſtly $x=\frac{ab}{2a-b}$ *W. W. D.* The *Demonſtration* proceeds the ſame way when a is ſuppoſed leſs than b, and x greater.

OBSERVE. When a is greater than b, then x can always be found becauſe in the Diviſor $(2a-b)$ $2a$ is neceſſarily greater than b. But if a is leſs than b, it may happen that $2a$ ſhall be equal to or leſs than b, and in that Caſe x is impoſſible. *Example.* Take 3 and 6, if a 3*d* greater than 6 be required it cannot be found; for $2a$, *viz.* twice 3, or 6, is equal to b or 6; and ſo the Diviſor is 0; or if $2a$ be greater than b, as here 3, 5, where twice 3 or 6 is greater than 5, then it is more impoſſible.

HENCE again *obſerve*, that from any given Number a Series of *continued harmonical Proportionals* (of the 1*ſt* Species, *i. e.* where every 3 immediate Terms are *harmonical*) may be found decreaſing *in infinitum* but not increaſing.

LASTLY, *obſerve* this remarkable Difference of the Three Kinds of Proportionals, *viz.* That from any given Number we can raiſe by *Theorem* 1. a *continued arithmetical Series* increaſing *in infinitum*; but not decreaſing. The *harmonical* is decreaſable but not increaſable *in infinitum* by by the present *Observe*; the *geometrical* is both (by *Theorem* 1.)

THEOREM XIII. Take any Three Numbers in Order, multiply the 1*st* into the 3*d*, and divide the Product by the Number that remains after the middle or 2*d* is substracted from double the 1*st*; and that Quote shall be a 4*th* Term in *harmonical Proportion* to the Three given. *Example*. Take these Three, 9, 12, 16, a 4*th* will be found by the Rule to be 24.

DEMONSTRATION. Let any Three given Numbers be a, b, c, and a less than b, let the Number sought be x greater than c, then by *Definition* 4*th*, it is $a : x :: b-a : x-c$, and $ax-ac=bx-ax$, lastly $x=\frac{ac}{2a-b}$. The Demonstration is the same when a is greater than b, and x less then c. *Observe* here also that if b is equal to or greater than $2a$, then there can be no 4*th* found, so that x is impossible. But this can only happen when the Terms increase, *i. e.* when a is less than b, and c less than x. See this *Example*, 1, 2, 3, to which a 4*th* harmonical is impossible.

THEOREM XIV. Take any Series of *continued arithmetical Proportionals*, and out of these may be made a Series of *continued harmonical Proportionals* of the first Species, where every Two Terms shall be in a reciprocal *geometrical* Proportion of the correspondent Terms of the *arithmetical* Series. The *Rule* is, Take the Two first Couplets of the arithmetick Series, set them down in a reverse Order, (as in the Operation below) multiply each of the 1*st* Couple by the greater of the 2*d*, and the lesser of the one by the lesser

leſſer of the other; and ſet down the Products; then, take the next Couplet, and multiply each of the laſt Products by the greater of this Couplet, and alſo the leaſt of theſe Products by the leaſt of this Couplet, and ſet down theſe new Products: Repeat this Operation with every Couplet, and the laſt Line of Products is the Series ſought. The following *Example* and Operation will make it plain.

Arithmetical Series.

2 : 3 : 4 : 5 : 6, *&c.*

---

3 : 2
4 : 3

---

12 : 8 : 6
5 : 4

---

60 : 40 : 0 : 24
6 : 5

---

360 : 240 : 180 : 144 : 120, *&c.*

Harmonical Series.

NOTE, After this Operation is finiſhed, the Series found may be reduced by equal Diviſion, if poſſible; ſo the Series found in this *Example*, is reduced to this, 30, 20, 15, 12, 10.

THE *Demonſtration* of this Rule is eaſily made, 1*mo.* If we take any Three Numbers in *arithmetical Proportion*, and multiply them according to the Rule, 'tis manifeſt the Products will be *harmonical*; for the Two Extremes of the Three *arithmetical* being multiplied by the ſame middle Term, their Products (which are the Extremes of the Three *harmonical*) are in the ſame *geometrical Ratio*; and then the Two Extremes being multiplied together, and the Product made the middle Term, it muſt be an *harmonical Mean*,

Mean, becaüse the *arithmetical Ratio* of the Two Couplets being equal, and the 1*st* Couplet being multiplied by the greater Extreme, and the other by the lesser Extreme, the Differences of the Products are increased in Proportion of these Multipliers (*viz.* the Extremes) *consequently* the Three Products are in *harmonical Proportion*, according to the *Theorem*. But the same being true of every Three Terms immediately next in the *arithmetical* Series thus multiplied; and it being also true by *Theorem* 10. that the Terms of any *harmonical* Series being equally multiplied the Products are also *harmonical*, and in the same *geometrical Ratio*, it will be evident that working according to the Rule we must have an *harmonical Series*.

THE *Reverse* of this *Theorem* is also true, *viz.* that if you take a Series of continued *Harmonicals* of the 1*st* Species, and multiply them in the Manner prescribed in the Rule, there will come out a Series of *Arithmeticals*, whose every Two Terms shall be reciprocally in the *geometrical Ratio* of their correspondent *Harmonicals*. *Example.* Take 3, 4, 6, the Products according to the Rule are 24 : 18 : 12; or by Reduction 4 : 3 : 2, which are *arithmetical*; see the Operation. The *Reason* is plain, for the Difference of the Two Couplets 4 : 3 and 6 : 4 being *geometrically* as the Extremes 3 : 6, when the 1*st* Couplet is multiplied by the greater Extreme, and the other by the least, the

3 : 4 : 6
4 : 3
6 : 4
24 : 18 : 12

Dif-

Differences of the Products must be equal; every Thing else is plain.

COROLLARY. From the *Demonstration* of this *Theorem* it follows, that taking any Series of whatever Nature, another may be made out of it, whose every Two Terms shall be respectively in a reciprocal *geometrical Proportion* of their Correspondents in the given Series.

THEOREM XV. In a Series of *continued Harmonicals* of the 1*st* Species, any Term with any Two at equal Distance from it are in *harmonical Proportion*. *Example*. 10, 12, 15, 20, 30, 60; because every Three immediate Terms are *harmonical*, therefore these are so, 10, 15, 30; and these, 12, 20, 60. The Reason is easily deduced from the last. But of *Harmonicals* of the 2*d* Species, (See *Definition* 4.) it will not always hold that any Two with any other Two at equal Distance are also *harmonical*; an *Example* will demonstrate this: See here 3, 4, 6, 9, 18, 36, tho' every Four next other are *harmonical*, yet these are not so, 3 : 6 : 9 : 36.

THEOREM XVI. If there are Four Numbers disposed in Order, whereof one Extreme and the Two middle Terms are in *arithmetical Proportion*, and the same middle Terms with the other Extreme are in *harmonical Proportion*, the Four are in *geometrical Proportion*, as here, 2 : 3 : 4 : 6, which are *geometrical*, and whereof 2 : 3 : 4 are *arithmetical*, and 3, 4, 6 *harmonical*.

DEM-

DEMONSTRATION. This *Theorem* contains 4 Cases. 1*mo.* If the First Three Terms are *arithmetical* increasing, and the last Three *harmonical*, the Four together are *geometrical*. *Demonstration.* Let $a : b : c : d$ be Three Numbers, whereof a, b, c are *arithmetical* increasing from a, and b, c, d *harmonical*; then are a, b, c, d, *geometrical*; for since out of the *Harmonicals* we have this *geometrical Proportion*, viz. $b : d :: c\text{-}b : d\text{-}c$ and also $b\text{-}a = c\text{-}b$ (since a, b, c are *arithmetical*) therefore $b : d : b\text{-}a : d\text{-}c$; and consequently (by *Theor.* 5.) $b : d :: a : c$, or $a : b :: c : d$. *W. W. D. Example.* 2, 3, 4, 6. 2*do.* If the First Three are *harmonical* decreasing, and the last Three *arithmetical*, the Four are *geometrical*; this is but the Reverse of the last Case, and needs no other Proof. 3*tio.* If the First Three are *arithmetical* decreasing, and the other Three *harmonical*, the Four are *geometrical*, suppose a, b, c are *arithmetical* decreasing, and b, c, d, *harmonical*, then a, b, c, d, are *geometrical*, for out of the *Harmonicals* we have this *geometrical Proportion*, viz. $b : d :: b\text{-}c\ (=a\text{-}b) : c\text{-}d$, therefore $b : d :: a : c$, and $a : b :: c : d$. *Example.* 8 : 6 :: 4 : 3. 4*to.* If the first Three are *harmonical* increasing, and the other Three *arithmetical*, the Four are *geometrical*; this is the Reverse of the last.

OBSERVE. It must hold reciprocally that if Four Numbers are *geometrical*, and the first Three *arithmetical* or *harmonical*, the other Three must be contrarily *harmonical* or *arithmetical*; for to the same Three Numbers there can be but

one

one individual Fourth *geometrical*, and to the Two laſt of them but one individual Third *arithmetical* or *harmonical*, therefore the *Obſerve* is true.

THEOREM XVII. If betwixt any Two Numbers you put an *arithmetical* Mean, and alſo an *harmonical* one, the Four will be in *geometrical Proportion*. *Example*. Betwixt 2 and 6 an *arithmetical Mean* is 4, and an *harmonical* one is 3, and the Four are 2 : 3 : : 4 : 6 *geometrical*; the *Demonſtration* you'll find here : Let a and b be Two given Numbers, an *arithmetical Mean* by *Theor*. 2. is $\frac{a+b}{2}$ and an *harmonical Mean* by *Theor*. 11. $\frac{2ab}{a+b}$, and theſe Four are *geometrical* $a : \frac{a+b}{2} : : \frac{2ab}{a+b} : b$, which is proven by the equal Products of the Extremes and Means.

---

§ 4. *The* Arithmetick *of* Ratios geometrical, *or of the Compoſition and Reſolution of* Ratios.

BY the preceeding *Definitions*, the Exponent of the *geometrical Relation* of Two Numbers is a proper Fraction, when we compare the leſſer to the greater, ſignifying that the leſſer is ſuch a Part or Parts of the greater ; ſo the *Ratio* of 2 to 3 is $\frac{2}{3}$, ſignifying that 2 is Two thirds of 3. Or, if we compare the greater to the leſſer, it is an improper Fraction, which being reduced to its equivalent Whole

or

or mix'd Number, expresses how many Times and Parts of a Time the greater contains the lesser; so the *Ratio* of 13 to 5 is $\frac{13}{5}$ or $2\frac{3}{5}$, for 13 is equal to 2 Times 5, and 3 over: Or being kept in the fractional Form signifies that the greater is equal to so many Times such a Part of the lesser as that lesser denominates; and this Difference of comparing the greater as *Antecedent* to the lesser, or the lesser to the greater, constitutes Two different Species of *Ratios*.

ONE Number is said to be composed of others, when it is equal to the Sum of these others; the *Compound* therefore must be greater than any of these of which it is composed; and this is the proper Sense of Composition of Numbers, so 9 is composed of 4 and 5, or 6 and 3, &c. also $\frac{2}{3}$ is composed of, or equal to the Sum of $\frac{3}{7}$ and $\frac{5}{21}$. But tho' *Ratios* are Fractions proper or improper, as they express what Part or Parts, or how many Times such a Part of one Number another Number is equal to; yet in the *Arithmetick* proposed they are taken in a Notion very different from that of mere Numbers; for if we take the *Exponents* of Two Relations as Numbers, and add them together, the Sum is a Number compounded of the Numbers added, but it is not a *Ratio* or the Exponent of a Relation compounded of the other Two *Ratios*; so that *Composition* and *Resolution* of *Ratios* is not adding and substracting them as Numbers. What it is see in the following *Definition*, wherein I take the *Ratio* or *Exponent* of the *Relation* of Two

Num-

Numbers to be the Quote of the *Antecedent* divided by the *Consequent.*

DEFINITION. One *Ratio* is said to be compounded of others, when it is equal to the *Ratio* betwixt the continual Product of the *Antecedents* of these others, and the continual Product of their *Consequents* multiplied as Numbers (*i. e.* by the Rules of common *Arithmetick*) *or thus*, one *Ratio* is compounded of others, when, as a Number, it is equal to the continual Product of these others considered also as Numbers. *Example.* The *Ratio* of 1 to 2 is compounded of the *Ratios* of 2 to 3, and 3 to 4, because $\frac{1}{2}$ is equal to $\frac{2}{3}$ multiplied by $\frac{3}{4}$, also 40 to 147 is in the compound *Ratio* of these, *viz.* 2 : 3, 5 : 7 and 4 : 7.

THEOREM XVIII. Take any Series whatever, the *Ratio* of the First Term to the last considered as a Number, is equal to the continual Product of all the intermediate *Ratios* multiplied as Numbers, taking every Term in Order from the First as an *Antecedent* to the next. For *Example.* In this Series 3, 4, 5, 6, the *Ratio* of 3 and 6 is $\frac{1}{2}$, equal to the continual Product of these $\frac{3}{4}$, $\frac{4}{5}$, $\frac{5}{6}$, for when all the *Numerators* are multiplied together, and all the *Denominators*, it is plain the Products are as 3 to 6, because all the other Multipliers are common to both Products; and it must be true in every Series for the same Reason.

COROLLARY. If the Series is in *continued geometrical Proportion*, the *Ratio* of the Extremes is equal to the common *Ratio* taken and

mul-

multiplied into it ſelf, as a Number, as oft as there are Terms in the Series leſs one.

PROBLEM II. To find a Series of Numbers which ſhall be to one another (comparing them in Order each to the next) in any given *Ratios*, taken in any Order aſſigned. RULE. Multiply both Terms of the 1*ſt Ratio* by the *Antecedent* of the 2*d*, and the *Conſequent* of this by the *Conſequent* of the 1*ſt*; and thus you have the 1*ſt* Two *Ratios* reduced to Three Terms, which multiply by the *Antecedent* of the 3*d Ratio*, and the *Conſequent* of this by the laſt of theſe Three, and you have the 1*ſt* Three *Ratios* reduced to 4 Terms: Go on thus, multiplying the laſt Series by the *Antecedent* of the next *Ratio*, and the *Conſequent* of this by the laſt Term of that laſt Series. The Juſtneſs of the Rule appears from this, That the Terms of each *Ratio* are equally multiplied. *Example*. The *Ratios* of 2 : 3, of 4 : 5 and 6 : 7 are reduced to this Series 48 : 72 : 90 : 105. See the Operation.

2 : 3
    4 : 5
8, 12, 15
        6 : 7
48 : 72 : 90 : 105

OBSERVE. From the Operation of this Rule it is plain, that the Extremes of the Series found are, *the One* equal to the continual Product of all the *Antecedents*, and *the other* to the continual Product of all the *Conſequents* of the given *Ratios*; ſo that theſe Extremes are in the *compound Ratio* of the given Ones; which is otherwiſe

wiſe plain from the laſt *Propoſition*, ſince all the intermediate Terms of this Series are in the *Ratios* given reſpectively. And it follows alſo, that where any Number of *Ratios* are reduced to a Series, tho' the Number of the Series will differ according to the different Orders, yet becauſe the intermediate *Ratios* are the ſame in every Order, the Extremes muſt ſtill be in the ſame *Ratio*.

THEOREM XIX. Every *Ratio* is compoſed of an indefinite Number of other *Ratios*; for, by *Corol.* to *Theor.* 5. if any Two Numbers are equally multiplied, the Products are in the ſame *geometrical Ratio*, and by *Corol.* to *Theor.* 6. their Difference contains the Firſt Difference, as oft as the Multiplier contains Unity; therefore it is plain that theſe Products are the Extremes of a Series, which can have as many middle Terms as their Difference has Units leſs one; and conſequently by taking the Multiplier greater you make the Difference of the Products greater, which admitting ſtill a greater Number of middle Terms, reduces the *Ratio* given into more intermediate Ones: So take the *Ratio* of 2 : 3, multiply both Terms by 4, the Products are 8 : 12, and the Series is 8 : 9 : 10 : 11 : 12, but multiply by 7, the Series is 14 : 15 : 16 : 17 : 18 : 19 : 20 : 21.

OBSERVE. We may fill up the middle Terms very differently, ſo as to make many different Series betwixt the ſame Extremes: And hereby we learn how to take a View of all the

mean

mean *Ratios*, of which any other is compofed.

THEOREM XX. The *geometrical Ratio* of any Two Numbers taken as a proper Fraction, (*i. e.* making the leffer Number the *Antecedent*) is lefs than that of any other Two Numbers which are themfelves refpectively greater, and yet have the fame *arithmetical Ratio* or Difference. *Example.* The *Ratio* 2 : 3 taken as a Fraction is $\frac{2}{3}$ lefs than that of 3 : 4, *viz.* $\frac{3}{4}$, or than 5 : 6, *viz.* $\frac{5}{6}$.

DEMONSTRATION. Let a and $a+b$ reprefent any Two Numbers, let $a+c$ and $a+c+b$ reprefent other Two which are refpectively greater than the firft Two, but have the fame Difference b; take them Fraction-wife thus, $\frac{a}{a+b}$ and $\frac{a+c}{a+c+b}$, if we reduce them to one common Denominator, the new Numerators will be found $aa+ac+ab$, and $aa+ac+ab+bc$, which is greater than the other by bc; therefore the Firft Fraction, to which the Numerator $aa+ac+ab$ correfponds, is leaft.

PROBLEM III. To reduce any Number of *Ratios* to one common *Antecedent* or *Confequent*. RULE. Multiply all their *Antecedents* continually into one another, that Product is the common *Antecedent* fought: Then multiply each *Confequent* into all the *Antecedents* (except its own) continually, and the laft Product is the *Confequent* correfpondent to the *Confequent* that was now multiplied. Or, multiply all the *Confequents* for a common *Confequent*, and each *Antecedent* into all the *Confequents* (except its own) for a new *Antecedent*. So thefe these *Ratios*, 2 : 3, 3 : 4, 4 : 5 reduced to one *Antecedent*, are 24 : 36, 24 : 32, 24 : 30, which in one Series are 24 : 36 : 32 : 30.

THE *Reason* of the Rule is plain from this, that the Terms of each *Ratio* are equally multiplied.

ADDITION of *RATIOS*.

PROBLEM IV. To add one or more *Ratios* together, or to find the Compound of these *Ratios*. RULE. Multiply all the *Antecedents* continually into one another, and all the *Consequents*; the Two Products contain the *Ratio* sought; which is plainly this; Take the *Ratios* Fraction-wise, (the *Antecedent* of each, whether 'tis greater or lesser than the *Consequent*, being the Numerator, and the *Consequent* the Denominator) and as fractional Numbers multiply them continually into another, the last Product is the *Exponent* of the *Relation* sought. *Example:* Add the *Ratios* of 2 : 3, 5 : 7 and 8 : 9, the *Sum* or *compound Ratio* sought is 80 : 189. The *Reason* of the *Rule* is plain from the *Definition* of a compound *Ratio* in § 4. of this *Chapter*.

OBSERVE 1*mo*. To understand in what Sense this Operation is called *Addition* of *Ratios*, we must consider that to compound Two or more *Ratios* is in effect this, *viz.* to find the Extremes of a Series whose intermediate Terms are respectively in the *Ratios* given; so to compound, or add the *Ratios*, 2 : 3 and 4 : 5, is to find the Extremes of Three Numbers, whereof the 1*ſt* ſhall be to the 2*d* as 2 to 3, and the 2*d* to the 3*d* as 4 to 5. Such a Series may in any Caſe be found by *Probl.* 2. and in this *Example* it is 8 : 12 : 15, for 8 is to 12 as 2 to 3, and 12 : 15 as 4 : 5, and 8 : 15 is the *compound Ratio* ſought, which is called the *Sum* of the given *Ratios*, becauſe it is the Effect of taking to the *Conſequent* of the 1*ſt Ratio*, conſidered now as an *Antecedent*, a new *Conſequent* in the 2*d Ratio*; and ſo of more *Ratios* added.

2*do*. There is no Difference, as to this *Rule*, whether all the *Ratios* to be added are of one Species or not, *i. e.* whether all the *Antecedents* are greater than their *Conſequents*, or all leſs, or ſome greater ſome leſs. For in this Rank 3 : 4 : 5 : 2 the *Ratio* of 3 to 2 is compounded of the intermediate *Ratios* 3 : 4, 4 : 5, and 5 : 2: tho' the laſt is of a different Species from the other Two; what Difference there is in the Application to *muſical Intervals* ſhall be explained in its Place.

SUBSTRACTION of *RATIOS*.

PROBLEM V. To ſubſtract one *Ratio* from another. RULE. Multiply the *Antecedent* of the Subſtrahend into the *Conſequent* of the Subſtractor, that Product is *Antecedent* of the Remainder ſought; then multiply the *Antecedent* of the Subſtractor into the *Conſequent* of the Subſtrahend, and that Product is the *Conſequent* of of the Remainder ſought; which is plainly this; Take the Two *Ratios* Fraction-wiſe, and divide the one by the other according to the Rules of Fractions. *Example.* To ſubſtract the *Ratio* of 2 : 3 from that of 3 : 5; the Remainder is 9 : 10, for $\frac{3}{5}$ divided by $\frac{2}{3}$ quotes $\frac{9}{10}$.

THE *Reaſon* of this Rule is plain; for, as the Senſe of Subſtraction is oppoſite to Addition, ſo muſt the Operation be; and to ſubſtract one *Ratio* from another ſignifies the finding a *Ratio*, which being added (in the ſenſe of *Probl.* 4.) to the Subſtracter, or *Ratio* to be ſubſtracted, the Compound or Sum ſhall be equal to the Subſtrahend; and therefore, as Addition is done by multiplying the *Ratios* as Fractions, ſo muſt Subſtraction be done by dividing them as Fractions; and ſo in this Series 6 : 9 : 10, the *Ratio* 6 : 10 (or 3 : 5) is compoſed of 6 : 9 (or 2 : 3) and 9 : 10; which Compoſition is done by multiplying $\frac{9}{10}$ into $\frac{2}{3}$ whoſe Product is $\frac{18}{30}$ or $\frac{3}{5}$: So to ſubſtract 6 : 9 or 2 : 3 from 6 : 10 or 3 : 5, it muſt be done by a reverſe Operation dividing $\frac{3}{5}$ by $\frac{2}{3}$ whoſe Quotient is $\frac{9}{10}$.

OBSERVE. As in Addition, the *Ratios* added may be of the ſame or different Species, ſo it may be in Subſtraction; but it is to be obſerved here that the Two given *Ratios* to be ſubſtracted, being conſidered as Fractions, and both proper Fractions, then, the leaſt being ſubſtracted from the greater, the Remainder is a *Ratio* of a different Species, as in this Series, 5 : 2 : 7, for take $\frac{2}{7}$ from $\frac{5}{7}$ the Remainder is $\frac{5}{2}$: But take the

the greater from the leſſer, and the Remainder is of the ſame Species; ſo $\frac{2}{7}$ from $\frac{2}{7}$ there remains $\frac{5}{7}$, as in this Series 2 : 5 : 7. *Again* ſuppoſe both the given *Ratios* are improper Fractions (*i. e.* the *Antecedents* greater than the *Conſequents*) if the leaſt is ſubſtracted from the greater, the Remainder is of the ſame Species; but the greater from the leſſer and the Remainder is of a different Species. *Example.* $\frac{7}{5}$ from $\frac{7}{2}$ remains $\frac{5}{2}$, as in this Series 7 : 5 : 2. But $\frac{7}{2}$ from $\frac{7}{5}$ remains $\frac{2}{5}$, as here 7 : 2 : 5; theſe Obſervations are all plain from the *Rule*.

MULTIPLICATION of *RATIOS*.

PROBLEM VI. To multiply any *Ratio* by a Number. This Problem has Two *Caſes*.

CASE I. To multiply any *Ratio* by a whole Number. RULE. Take the given *Ratio* as oft as the Multiplier contains Unity, and add them all by *Probl.* 4*th*. *Example.* 2 : 3 multiplied by 4, produces 16 : 81; or thus, Take the *Ratio* as a Fraction, and raiſe it to ſuch a Power as the Multiplier expones, that is, to the Square if 'tis 2, to the *Cube* if 3, and ſo on.

FOR the Reaſon of the *Rule* conſider, That as the multiplying any Number ſignifies the adding it to it ſelf, or taking it ſo many Times as the Multiplier contains Unity, ſo to multiply any *Ratio* ſignifies the adding or compounding it with it ſelf, ſo many Times as the Multiplier contains Unity, *i. e.* to find a new *Ratio* that ſhall be equal to the given one ſo oft compounded ed, thus, to multiply the *Ratio* of 2 : 3 by the Number 4 signifies the finding a *Ratio* equal to the *compound Ratio* of 2 : 3 taken 4 Times, which is 16 : 81; for 2 : 3, 2 : 3, 2 : 3, 2 : 3, being added by *Probl.* 4. amount to 16 : 81, and to fill up the Series apply *Probl.* 2.

OBSERVE. The Product is always a *Ratio* of the same Species with the given *Ratio*; as is plain from the *Rule*. And if you'll complete the Series by *Probl.* 2. *i. e.* turn the given *Ratio* so oft taken as the Multiplier expresses into a Series, it will be a *continued geometrical* one. Thus, 2, 3 multiplied by 4, produces 16, 81, and the Series is 16 : 24 : 36 : 54 : 81; and this Series shows clearly the Import of this Multiplication, that it is the finding the Extremes of a Series, whose intermediate Terms have a common *Ratio* equal to the given *Ratio*, and which contains that *Ratio* as oft repeated as the Multiplier contains 1.

CASE II. To multiply any *Ratio* by a Fraction, *that is*, to take any Part of a given *Ratio*. RULE. Multiply it by the Numerator of the Fraction, according to the last *Case*, and divide that Product which is also a *Ratio* by the Denominator, after the Method of *Case* 1. of the following *Probl.* the Quote is the *Ratio* sought. *Example.* To multiply the *Ratio* 8 : 27, by $\frac{2}{3}$. *First*, I multiply 8 : 27 by 2, the Product is 64 : 729, and this divided by 3, according to the next *Probl.* quotes the *Ratio* 4 : 9, so that the *Ratio* 4 : 9 is $\frac{2}{3}$ Parts of the *Ratio* 8 : 27.

THE

THE *Reason* of the Operation is this, since $\frac{2}{3}$ Parts of 1 (*i. e.* of once the *Ratio* to be multiplied) is equal to $\frac{1}{3}$ Part of 2 (or of twice the R*atio* to be multiplied) therefore having taken that *Ratio* twice, I must take a Third of that Product, to have the true Product sought: And so of other *Cases*. The Sense of this *Case* will appear plain in this Series 8:12:18:27 which is in *continued geometrical Proportion*, the common *Ratio* being that of 2:3; consequently 8:27: contains 2:3 Three Times; or 2:3 multiplied by 3 produces 8:27: Also 8:18 (equal to 4:9) contains 2:3 twice, and consequently is equal to $\frac{2}{3}$ Parts of 8:27.

OBSERVE. It produces the same Thing to divide the given *Ratio* by the Denominator of the given Fraction, and multiply the Quote (which is a *Ratio*) by the Numerator; because, for Example, 2 Times $\frac{1}{3}$ of a Thing is equal to $\frac{1}{3}$ of twice that Thing.

COROLLARY. To multiply a *Ratio* by a mix'd Number, we must multiply it separately, *First*, By the integral Part (by *Case* 1.) and then by the fractional Part (by *Case* 2.) and sum these Products (by *Probl.* 4.) or reduce the mix'd Number to an improper Fraction, and apply the *Rule* of the last *Case*. *Example*. To multiply 4:9 by $1\frac{1}{2}$ or $\frac{3}{2}$, the Product is 8:27, for in this Series 8:12:18:27, it is plain 8:27 is 3 Times 2:3. And this is $\frac{1}{2}$ of 4:9 (equal to 8:18) consequently 8:27 is equal to 3 Halfs or 1 and $\frac{1}{2}$ of 4:9.

DI-

DIVISION of *RATIOS.*

PROBLEM VII. To divide any *Ratio* by a Number. This *Probl.* has Three *Cases.*

CASE I. To divide any *Ratio* by a whole Number, *that is,* to find ſuch a *Ratio* as being multiplied (or compounded into it ſelf) as oft as the Diviſor contains Unity, ſhall produce the given *Ratio,* RULE. Out of the *Ratio,* taken as a Fraction, extract ſuch a Root as the Diviſor is the Index of, *i. e.* the ſquare Root if the Diviſor is 2, the cube Root if the Diviſor is 3, *&c.* and that Root is the *Exponent* of the *Relation* ſought. *Example.* To divide the *Ratio* of 9 : 16 by 2, the ſquare Root of $\frac{9}{16}$ is $\frac{3}{4}$ which is the *Ratio* ſought.

THE *Reaſon* of this *Rule* is obvious, from its being oppoſite to the like Caſe in Multiplication; and is plain in this Series, 9 : 12 : 16, which is in the *continued Ratio* of 3 : 4. and ſince the multiplying 3 : 4 by 2, to produce 9 : 16, is performed by multiplying $\frac{3}{4}$ by $\frac{3}{4}$, or ſquaring $\frac{3}{4}$, the Diviſion of 9 : 16 by 2 to find 3 : 4, can be done no other ways than by extracting the ſquare Root of $\frac{9}{16}$, which is $\frac{3}{4}$; and ſo of other Caſes; which will be all very plain to them who underſtand any Thing of the Nature of Powers and Roots. Or ſolve the *Probl.* thus; Find the firſt of as many *geometrical Means* betwixt the Terms of the given *Ratio* as the Diviſor contains of Units leſs one, that compared with the leſſer Term of the given *Ratio* contains

tains the *Ratio* ſought; thus 9 : 12 is the Anſwer of the preceeding *Example.*

CASE II. To divide a *Ratio* by a Fraction, *that is*, to find a *Ratio* of which ſuch a Part or Parts as the given Fraction expreſſes ſhall be equal to the given *Ratio*. RULE. Multiply it by the Denominator (by *Probl.* 6. 1 *Caſe*) and divide the Product by the Numerator (by *Caſe* 1 of this *Probl.*) the Quote is the *Ratio* ſought. Or divide the *Ratio* by the Numerator, and multiply the Quote by the Denominator. *Example.* To divide 4 : 9 by $\frac{2}{3}$ or to find $\frac{2}{3}$ Parts of 4 : 9, I take the *Cube* of $\frac{4}{9}$, it is $\frac{64}{729}$, whoſe ſquare Root is $\frac{8}{27}$ the *Ratio* ſought. The *Reaſon* of the Operation is contained in this, that it is oppoſite to *Caſe* 2. of Multiplication. And becauſe 8 : 27 multiplied by $\frac{2}{3}$, produces 4 : 9, ſo 4 : 9 divided by $\frac{2}{3}$ ought to quote 8 : 27.

COROLLARY. To divide a *Ratio* by a mix'd Number; reduce the mix'd Number to an improper Fraction, and divide as in the laſt *Caſe.*

CASE III. To divide one *Ratio* by another, both being of one Species; *that is*, to find how oft the one is contained in the other; or how oft the one ought to be added to it ſelf to make a *Ratio* equal to the other. RULE. Subſtract the Diviſor from the Dividend (by *Probl.* 5.) and the ſame Diviſor again from the laſt Remainder; and ſo on continually, till the Remainder be a *Ratio* of Equality; and then the Number of Subſtractions is the Number

Number ſought; or, till the Species of the *Ratio* change, and then the Number of Subſtractions leſs one is the Number of Times the whole Diviſor is found in the Dividend, and the laſt Remainder except one is what the Dividend contains over ſo many Times the Diviſor. *Example.* To divide the Ratio 16 : 81 by 2 : 3, I ſubſtract 2 : 3 from 16 : 81, the Remainder is 48 : 162 equal to 8 : 27; from this I ſubſtract 2 : 3, the 2*d* Remainder is 24 : 54, equal to 4 : 9; from this I ſubſtract 2 : 3, the 3*d* Remainder is 12 : 18 or 2 : 3; from this I ſubſtract 2 : 3, the 4*th* Remainder is 6 : 6 or 1 : 1, a *Ratio* of Equality; therefore the Quote ſought is the Number 4, ſignifying that the *Ratio* 2 : 3 taken 4 Times, is equal to 16 : 54; as you ſee it all in this Series 16 : 24 : 36 : 54 : 81. *Example* 2. To divide 12 : 81 by 2 : 3, proceed in the ſame Manner as before, and you'll find the Remainders to be 2 : 9, 1 : 3, 1 : 2, 3 : 4, 9 : 8, and becauſe the laſt changes the Species, I juſtly conclude that the *Ratio* 12 : 81 does not contain 2 : 3 five Times, but it contains it 4 Times and 3 : 4 over; for 2 : 3 multiplied by 4 produces 16 : 81, which added to 3 : 4 makes exactly 12 : 81, as in this Series 16 : 24 : 36 : 54 : 81 : 108 whoſe Extremes 16 : 108, (equal to 12 : 81) is in a *Ratio* compounded of 16 : 81 and 81 : 108 (equal to 3. 4.)

OBSERVE. The Two *Ratios* given muſt be of one Species; becauſe the Senſe of it is, to find how oft the Diviſor muſt be added to it ſelf to make a *Ratio* equal to the Dividend; and

and in multiplying, any *Ratio* by a whole Number, that *Ratio* and the Product are always of one Species, as was obſerved in *Probl.* 6. therefore 'tis plain that the *Ratio* of the Dividend, taken as a Fraction, muſt be leſſer than the Diviſor ſo taken, the *Antecedent* being leaſt, *i. e.* theſe Fractions being proper, and contrarily if they are improper; the *Reaſon* is plain, becauſe in an increaſing Series, *i. e.* where all the *Antecedents* are leſſer than their *Conſequents*, the *Ratio* of the Firſt to the leaſt Extreme is leſs than the *Ratio* of any Two of the intermediate Terms, and yet, according to the Nature of *Ratios*, contains them all in it; but in a decreaſing Series, *i. e.* where all the *Antecedents* are greater than the *Conſequents*, the 1*ſt* to the leaſt, or the greateſt *Antecedent* to the leaſt *Conſequent*, is in a greater *Ratio* than any of the intermediate, and alſo contains them all : So in this Series 2 : 3 : 4 : 5, the *Ratio* 2 : 5 contains all the intermediate *Ratios*, and yet $\frac{2}{5}$ is leſs than $\frac{2}{3}$ or $\frac{3}{4}$ or $\frac{4}{5}$; but take the Series reverſely, then $\frac{5}{2}$ is greater than $\frac{5}{4}$ or $\frac{4}{3}$ or $\frac{3}{2}$.

§ 5

---

§ 5. *Containing an Application of the preceeding Theory of Proportion to the* INTERVALS *of Sound.*

IT has been already ſhewn that the Degrees of *Tune* are proportional to the Numbers of Vibrations of the ſonorous Body in a given Time, or their Velocity of Courſes and Recourſes; which being proportional, in Chords, to their Lengths (*cæteris paribus*) we have the juſt Meaſures of the relative Degrees of *Tune* in the *Ratios* of theſe Lengths; the *grave* Sound being to the *acute* as the greater Length to the leſſer.

THE Differences of *Tune* make *Diſtance* or *Intervals* in *Muſick*, which are greater and leſſer as theſe Differences are, whoſe Quantity is the true Object of the mathematical Part of *Muſick*. Now theſe *Intervals* are meaſured, not in the ſimple Differences, or *arithmetick Ratios* of the Numbers expreſſing the Lengths or Vibrations of Chords, but in their *geometrical Ratios*; ſo that the ſame Difference of *Tune*, *i. e.* the ſame *Interval* depends upon the ſame *geometrical Ratio*; and different Quantities or *Intervals* ariſe from a Difference of the *geometrical Ratios* of the Numbers expreſſing the Extremes, as has been already ſhewn; *that is*, equal

equal *geometrical Ratios* betwixt whatever Numbers, conſtitute equal *Intervals*, but unequal *Ratios* make unequal *Intervals*.

But now *obſerve*, that in comparing the Quantity of *Intervals*, the *Ratios* expreſſing them muſt be all of one Species; otherwiſe this Abſurdity will follow, that the ſame Two Sounds will make different *Intervals*; for *Example*, Suppoſe Two Chords in Length, as 4 and 5, 'tis certainly the ſame *Interval* of Sound, whether you compare 4 to 5, or 5 to 4, yet the *Ratios* of 4 : 5 and 5 : 4 taken as Numbers, and expreſt Fraction-wiſe would differ in Quantity, and therefore different *Ratios* cannot without this Qualification make in every Caſe different *Intervals*.

In what Manner the Inequality of *Intervals* are meaſured, ſhall be explained immediately and here take this general Character from the Things explained, to know which of Two or more *Intervals* propoſed are greateſt. *If all the* Ratios *are taken as proper Fractions, the leaſt Fraction is the greateſt Interval.* But to ſee the Reaſon of this, take it thus; The *Ratios* that expreſs ſeveral *Intervals* being all of one Species, reduce them (by *Probl.* 3. of this *Chap.*) to one common *Antecedent*, which being leſſer than the *Conſequents*, that *Ratio* which has the greateſt Conſequent is the greateſt *Interval*. The Reaſon is obvious, for the longeſt Chord gives the *graveſt* Sound, and therefore muſt be at greateſt Diſtance from the common *acute* Sound. Or contrarily, reduce them to one common Conſequent greater than the Antecedents,

dents, and the leſſer Antecedent expreſſes the *acuter* Sound, and conſequently makes with that common fundamental or *graveſt* Sound, the greater *Interval*.

It follows that if any Series of Numbers are in *continual arithmetical Proportion*, comparing each Term to the next, they expreſs a Series of *Intervals* differing in Quantity from firſt to laſt; the greateſt *Interval* being betwixt the Two leaſt Numbers, and ſo gradually to the greateſt, as here 1 : 2 : 3 : 4. 1 : 2 is a greater *Interval* than 2 : 3, as this is greater than 3 : 4. The Reaſon why it muſt hold ſo in every Caſe is contained in *Theor.* 20. where it was demonſtrated that the *geometrical Ratio* of any Two Numbers taken as a proper Fraction (*i. e.* making the leſſer the Antecedent) is leſs than that of any other Two Numbers, which are themſelves reſpectively greater, and yet have the ſame *arithmetical Ratio* or Difference: And by what has been explained we ſee that the leſſer proper Fraction makes the greater *Interval*.

Thus we can judge which of any *Intervals* propoſed is greateſt, and which leaſt, in general; but how to meaſure their ſeveral Differences or Inequalities is another Queſtion; that whoſe Extremes make the leaſt Fraction is the greateſt *Interval*, and ſo, in general, the Quantities of ſeveral *Intervals* are reciprocally as theſe Fractions; but this is not always in a ſimple Proportion. For *Example*, The Interval 1 : 2, is to the Interval 1 : 4 exactly as $\frac{1}{4}$ to $\frac{1}{2}$ (or as 1 to 2) the Quantity of the laſt being double the other.

But

But 2 : 3 to 4 : 9 is not as $\frac{4}{9}$ to $\frac{2}{3}$, but as 1 to 2, as ſhall be explained. Sounds themſelves are expreſſed by Numbers, and their Intervals are repreſented by the *Ratios* of theſe Numbers, ſo theſe *Intervals* are compared together by comparing theſe *Ratios*, not as Numbers, but as *Ratios*; and I ſuppoſe every given *Interval* is expreſſed by expreſſing diſtinctly the Two Extremes, *i. e.* their relative Numbers.

I ſhall now explain the *Compoſition* and *Reſolution* of *Intervals*, which is the Application of the preceeding *Arithmetick* of *Ratios*; and this I ſhall do, *Firſt* in general, without Regard to the Difference of *Concord* and *Diſcord*, which ſhall imploy the reſt of this *Chapter*; and in the next make Application to the various *Relations* and *Compoſitions* of *Concords*; and after that of *Diſcords* in their Place.

IN what Senſe *Ratios* are ſaid to be added and ſubſtracted, *&c.* has been explained, but in the *Compoſition* of *Intervals* we have a more proper Application of the true Senſe of adding and ſubſtracting, *&c.* The Notions of Addition and Subſtraction, *&c.* belong to Quantity; concerning which it is an *Axiom*, that the Sum or what is the Reſult of Addition, muſt be a Quantity greater than any of the Quantities added, becauſe it is equal to them all: And in ſubſtracting we take a leſſer Quantity from a greater, and the Remainder is leſs than that greater, which is equal to the Sum of the Thing taken away and the Remainder. A mere Relation cannot properly be called

Quan-

Quantity, and therefore the *geometrical Ratio* of Numbers can be no otherwise called Quantity than as by taking the *Antecedent* and *Consequent* Fraction-wise, they express what Part or how many Times such a Part of the *Consequent* the *Antecedent* is equal to; and then the greater Fraction is always the greater *Ratio*. But the *Composition* of *Ratios* is a Thing of a quite different Sense from the *Composition* of mere Numbers or Quantity; for in Quantities, Two or more added make a Total greater than any of them that are added; but in the *Composition* of *Ratios*, the *Compound* consider-ed as a Number in the Sense abovementioned, may be less than any of the component Parts. Now we apply the Idea of Distance to the Difference of Sound in *Acuteness* and *Gravity* in a very plain and intelligible Manner, so that we have one universal Character to determine the greater or lesser of any Intervals proposed; according to which Notion of Greatness and Littleness all Intervals are added and substracted, *&c.* and the Sum is the true and proper Compound of several lesser Quantities; and in Substraction we actually take a lesser Quantity from a greater; but the Intervals themselves being expressed by the *geometrical Ratio* of Numbers applied to the Lengths of Chords (or their proportional Vibrations) the Addition and Substraction, *&c.* of the Quantities of *Intervals* is performed by Application of the preceeding *Arithmetick* of *Ratios*.

NOTE.

NOTE. In the following *Problems* I conſtantly apply the Numbers to the Lengths of Chords, and ſo the leſſer of Two Numbers that expreſs any *Interval* I call the *acute* Term and the other the *grave*.

ADDITION of *INTERVALS*.

PROBLEM VIII. To add Two or more *Intervals* together. RULE. Mutiply all the *acute* Terms continually, the Product is the *acute* Term ſought; and the Product of the *grave* Terms continually multiplied, is the *grave* Term ſought; *that is*, Take the *Ratios* as proper Fractions; and add them by *Probl.* 4. *Example.* Add a *5th* 2 : 3 and, a *4th* 3 : 4, and a 3*d g.* 4 : 5, the Sum is 24 : 60 equal to 2 : 5. a 3*d g.* above an *Octave*.

OBSERVE. This is a plain Application of the RULE for adding of *Ratios*, and to make it better underſtood, ſuppoſe any given Sound repreſented by *a*, and another Sound, *acuter* or *graver* in any *Ratio*, repreſented by *b*; if again we take a Third Sound ſtill *acuter* or *graver* than *b*, and call it *c*, then the Sound of *c* being at greater Diſtance from *a*, towards *Acuteneſs* or *Gravity*, than *b* is, the *Interval* betwixt *a* and *c* is equal to the other Two betwixt *a b* and *b c*. And ſo let any Number of *Intervals* be propoſed to be added, we are to conceive ſome Sound *a* as one Extreme of the *Interval* ſought; to this we take another Sound *b acuter* or *graver* in any given *Ratio*; then a Third Sound *c acuter* or *graver* than *b* in

an-

another given *Ratio*, and a 4*th* Sound *d acuter* or *graver* than *c*, and so on; every Sound always exceeding another in *Acuteness* or *Gravity*, and all of them taken the same way, *i. e.* all *acuter*, or all *graver* than the preceeding, and consequently than the first Sound *a*; and then the first and last are at a Distance equal to the Sum of the intermediate Distances. For *Example*, If 5 Sounds are represented by *a*, *b*, *c*, *d*, *e* exceeding each other by certain *Ratios* of *Acuteness* or *Gravity* from *a* to *e*, the *Interval* *a* : *e* is equal to the Sum of the *Intervals* *a* : *b*, *b* : *c*, *c* : *d*, *d* : *e*.

Now that the Rule for finding the true Distance of *a* : *e* is just, you'll easily perceive by considering that Intervals are represented by *Ratios*; therefore several *Intervals* are added by compounding the *Ratios* that express them; for if the given *Intervals* or *Ratios* are reduced, by *Probl.* 2. to a Series continually increasing or decreasing, wherein every Number being *antecedent* to the next, they shall contain in Order the *Ratios* given, *i. e.* express the given *Intervals*, 'tis plain the *Ratio* of the Extremes of this Series shall be composed of all the intermediate (which are the given) *Ratios*, and therefore be the Sum of them according to the true Sense in which *Intervals* are added, as it has been explained; so in the preceeding *Example*, in which we have added a 5*th* 2 : 3, a 4*th* 3 : 4 and a 3*d g.* 4 : 5, the Compound of these *Ratios* is 24 : 60 or 2 : 5; for take them in the Order proposed they

are

are contained in this simple Series, 2 : 3 : 4 : 5, which represents a Series of Sounds gradually exceeding each other in *Gravity* from 2 to 5 by the intermediate Degrees or *Ratios* proposed; so that 2 : 5 being the true Sum of these *Intervals*, and the true *Compound* of the given *Ratios*, shews the *Rule* to be just.

AGAIN take Notice, that tho' in the *Composition* of *Ratios* it is the same Thing whether they are all of one Species or not, yet in their Application to *Intervals* they must be of one Kind. I have already shewn what Absurdity would follow if it were otherwise, but you may see more of it here; suppose Three Sounds represented by 4 : 5 : 3, tho' 4 : 3 is the true *Compound* of these *Ratios* 4 : 5 and 5 : 3, yet it cannot express the Sum of the *Intervals* represented by these; for if 4 represent one Extreme and 5 the middle Sound (*graver* than the former) 3 cannot possibly represent another Sound at a greater Distance towards Gravity, because 'tis *acuter* than 5, and therefore instead of adding to the Distance from 4, it diminishes it; but it is the same *Interval* (tho' in some Sense not the same *Ratio*) whether the lesser or greater is *antecedent*; and the Sum of these Two *Intervals* cannot be represented but by the Extremes of a Series continually increasing or decreasing from the least or greatest of the Numbers proposed, because they cannot otherwise represent a Series of Sounds continually rising or falling, the *Ratio* of the Extremes of which Kind of Series can only be

cal-

called the Sum of the intermediate Diſtances or nterval of Sound; and ſo the preceeding Example muſt be taken thus, 3 : 4 : 5, where 3 : 5 is not only the *compound Ratio* of 3 : 4 and 4 : 5, but expreſſes the true Sum of the *Intervals* repreſented by theſe *Ratios*.

It is plain then from this Explication, that in Addition of *Intervals* the Sum is a greater Quantity than any of the Parts added, as it ought to be, according to the juſt Notion of the Quantity of *Intervals*; but it would be otherwiſe and abſurd if the *Ratios* expreſſing *Intervals* were not taken all one way; ſo in the preceeding Example tho' 4 : 3 is the Compound of 4 : 5 and 5 : 3, yet conſidered as a Fraction $\frac{3}{4}$ it is greater than $\frac{3}{5}$, and conſequently a leſſer *Interval*, by the Character already eſtabliſhed.

PROBLEM IX. To add Two or more *Intervals*, and find all the intermediate Terms; a certain Order of their Succeſſion being aſſigned, from the *graveſt* or the *acuteſt* Extreme.

RULE. If the given *Intervals* are to proceed in Order from the *acuteſt* Term, make the leſſer Numbers *Antecedents*; if from the *graveſt*, make the greater *Antecedents*, and then apply the Rule of *Probl.* 2.

EXAMPLE. To find a Series of Sounds, that from the *acuteſt* to the *graveſt* ſhall be in Order (comparing the 1*ſt* to the 2*d*, and the 2*d* to the 3*d*, and ſo on) a 3*d g* : 4*th* : 3*d l* : 5*th*. Working by the *Rule* I find this Series 120 : 150 :

200

200 . 240 : 360, or reduced to lower Terms by Division they are 12 : 15 : 20 : 24 : 36. See the Operation here. But if the same *Intervals* are to proceed in that Order from the *gravest* Extremes, the Series is 90 : 72 : 54 : 45 : 30.

4 : 5 - - - - - - 3*d* gr.
3 : 4 - - - - - 4*th*.
12 : 15 : 20
5 : 6 - - 3*d* less.
60 : 75 : 100 : 120
2 : 3 - 5*th*.
120 : 150 : 200 : 240 : 360

OBSERVE. In adding several *Intervals* in a continued Series, the Sum or *Ratio* of the Extremes must always be the same, whatever Order they are taken in; because in any Order the *Ratio* of the Extremes is the true Compound of all the intermediate *Ratios*, or the *Ratios* added, which being individually the same, only in a different Order, the Sum must be the same; but then according to the different Orders the Series of Numbers will be different, so if we add a 4*th* 3 : 4, 3*d gr*. 4 : 5 and a 3*d less*. 5 : 6, they can be taken in Six different Orders, which are contained in these Six different Series, which contain all the different Orders both from *Gravity* and *Acuteness*.

3	:	4	:	5	:	6
4	:	5	:	6	:	8
5	:	6	:	8	:	10
16	:	8	:	10	:	20
12	:	15	:	20	:	24
15	:	20	:	24	:	30

SUB-

SUBSTRACTION of *INTERVALS.*

PROBLEM X. To ſubſtract a leſſer *Interval* from a greater. RULE. Multiply the *acute* Terms of each of the given Intervals by the *grave* Term of the other, and the Two Products are in the *Ratio* of the Difference ſought, *that is*, take the *Ratios* given as proper Fractions, and ſubſtract them by *Probl* 5.

EXAMPLE. Subſtract a 5*th* 2 : 3 from an *Octave* 1 : 2, the Remainder or Difference is a 4*th* 3 : 4. See the *Intervals* in this Series (made by reducing both the *Intervals* given to a common Fundamental by *Probl.* 3) 6 : 4 : 3 the Extremes 6 : 3 are *Octave*, the intermediate *Ratios* are 6 : 4 a 5*th*, and 4 : 3 a 4*th*, therefore any one of them taken from *Octave* leaves the other.

THE *Reaſon* and Senſe of the Rule is obvious; for as Subſtraction is oppoſite to Addition, ſo muſt the Operation be; and this is a plain Application of the Subſtraction of *Ratios*, with the ſame Limitation as in Addition, *viz.* that the *Ratios* muſt be taken both one way, ſo that we take always a leſſer Quantity from a greater, and the Remainder is leſs than that greater, according to the true Character whereby the greater and leſs *Intervals* are diſtinguiſhed.

OBSERVE. The Difference of any Two *Intervals* expreſſes the mutual Relation betwixt any Two of their ſimilar Terms, *i. e.* Suppoſe any Two *Intervals* reduced to a common *acute* or *grave* Term, their Difference is the *Interval* contained betwixt the other Two Terms; and the *Ratio* expressing it is called the mutual Relation of the Two given *Intervals*; so the Difference or mutual Relation of an *Octave* and *5th* is a *4th*

MULTIPLICATION of *INTERVALS*.

BECAUSE it is the same *Interval* whether the greater or lesser Number be *Antecedent* of the *Ratio*, and in all Multiplication the Multiplier must be an absolute Number, therefore Multiplication of *Intervals* is an Application of *Probl.* 6. without any Variation or Limitation. I need therefore only make Examples, and refer to that *Problem* for the *Rule*.

PROBLEM XI. *Case* 1. To multiply an *Interval* by a whole Number. *Example.* To multiply a *5th* 2 : 3 by 4. the Product is 16 : 81 the *4th* Power of 2 and 3; and the Series of intermediate Terms being filled up is 16 : 24 : 36 : 54 : 81, expressing 4 *Intervals* in the continued *Ratio* of 2 : 3.

CASE II. To multiply an *Interval* by a Fraction. *Example.* Multiply the *Interval* 8 : 27 by $\frac{2}{3}$, the Product, *i. e.* $\frac{2}{3}$ Parts of the given *Interval* is 4 : 9, for $\frac{4}{9}$ is the Square of the cube Root of $\frac{8}{27}$. See this Series, 8 : 12 : 18 : 27, in the *continued Ratio* of 2 : 3, where 8 : 18 (or 4 : 9) is plainly 2 Thirds of 8 : 27.

NOTE. If these Two Cases are joyned we can multiply any *Interval* by any mixt Number: Or we may turn the mixt Number to an improper Fraction, and apply the 2d *Case*. Co-

Corollary. From the Nature of Multiplication it is plain, that we have in these Cases a *Rule* for finding an *Interval*, which shall be to any given one, as any given Number to any other; for 'tis plain if we take these given Numbers in form of a Fraction, and by that Fraction multiply the given *Interval*, we shall have the *Interval* sought, which is to that given as the Numerator to the Denominator; so in the preceeding *Example*, the *Interval* 4 : 9 is to 8 : 27 as 2 to 3. But *observe*, if the Root to be extracted cannot be found, then the *Problem*, strictly speaking, is impossible, and we can express the *Interval* sought only by irrational Numbers. *Example*. To multiply a 4th 3 : 4 by $\frac{2}{3}$, *i.e.* to take $\frac{2}{3}$ Parts of it, it can only be expressed by the *Ratio* of the Cube Root of 9 to the Cube Root of 16, or the Square of the Cube Root of 3, to the Square of the Cube Root of 4. And the best we can do with such Cases, if they are to be reduced to Practice, is to bring the Extraction of the Root as near the Truth as may serve our Purpose without a very gross Error.

But if 'tis proposed to find Two *Intervals* that are as Two given Numbers, this can easily be done by multiplying any *Interval*, taken at Pleasure, by the Two given Numbers severally; 'tis plain the Products are in the *Ratio* of these Numbers.

DIVISION of *INTERVALS.*

HERE alſo there is nothing but the Application of *Probl.* 7. to which I refer for the *Rules*, and only make *Examples*.

PROBLEM XII. *Caſe* 1. To divide an *Interval* by a whole Number, *i. e.* to find ſuch an *aliquot* Part of that *Interval* as the give nNumber denominates.

Example. Divide the *Interval* 4 : 9 by 2, *that is*, find the Half of it; the Anſwer is a 5*th* 2 : 5, for Two 5*hts* make 4 : 9, as in this *Series*, 4 : 6 : 9.

CASE II. To divide an *Interval* by a Fraction, *that is*, to find an *Interval* that ſhall be to the given one, as the Denominator of the Fraction to the Numerator.

Example. Divide the *Interval* 1 : 4 by $\frac{2}{3}$, the Quote is 1 : 8, which is to 1 : 4, as 3 to 2. See this Series, 1, 2, 4, 8.

NOTE. To divide by a mixt Number, we can turn it to an improper Fraction, and do as in *Caſe* 3.

OBSERVE. As Multiplication and Diviſion are directly oppoſite, ſo we have by Diviſion as well as by Multiplication, a *Rule* to find an *Interval*, which ſhall be to a given one, as any given Number to another: Thus, if the *Interval* ſought muſt be greater than the given one, make the leaſt of the given Numbers the Numerator, and the other the Denominator of a Fraction, by which divide the given *Interval*; but

but if the fought *Interval* muft be leffer than the given, make the greater Number the Numerator; which is all directly oppofite to the Rule of Multiplication: And, as I have already obferved in Multiplication, if the Roots to be extracted by the Rule cannot be found, then there is no *Interval* that is accurately to the given one as the Two given Numbers.

CASE III. To divide one *Interval* by another, *that is*, to find how oft the leffer is contain'd in the greater. *Rule.* Subftract (by *Probl.* 10.) the leffer from the greater, and the fame Divifor from the laft Remainder continually till the Remainder be a *Ratio* of Equality, or change the Species; the Number of Subftractions, if you come to a *Ratio* of Equality, is the Number of Times the whole Divifor is to be found in the Dividend: But if the Species change, the Number of Subftractions preceeding that in which the Remainder changed, is the Number fought: But then, there is a Remainder which belongs alfo to the Quote, and it is the Remainder of the Operation preceeding that which changed; fo that the Dividend contains the Divifor fo oft as that Number of Subftractions denotes and contains that Remainder over, which is properly the Remainder of the Divifion.

EXAMPLE I. To find how oft the *Interval* 64 : 125 contains 4 : 5. By the *Rule* I find Three Times.

EXAMPLE II. To find how oft an 8*ve* 1 : 2 contains a 3d *g.* 4 : 5. you'll find Three Times, and

and this *Interval* over, *viz.* 125 : 128. For, *First*, I ſubſtract 4 : 5 from 1 : 2, the firſt Remainder is 5 : 8 ; from this I ſubſtract 4 : 5, the 2*d* Remainder is 25 : 32 ; from this I ſubſtract 4 : 5, the 3*d* Remainder is 125 : 128 ; from this I ſubſtract 4 : 5, the 4*th* Remainder is 625 : 512, which is of a different Species, the Antecedent being here greateſt, which in the other *Ratio* is leaſt ; therefore the Quote is 3, and the *Ratio* or *Interval* 125 : 128 over. See the Proof in this Series, 64 : 80 : 100 : 125 : 128. which is in the continued *Ratio* of 4 : 5. 64 : 125 is equal to Three times 4 : 5, and 64 : 128 is equal to 1 : 2.

THUS far only I proceeded with the Anſwer in *Caſe* 3. of *Probl.* 7. for dividing of one *Ratio* by another. Now I add, that if we would make the Quote complete and perfect, ſo that it may accurately ſhew how many Times and Parts of a Time the Dividend contains the Diviſor, (if 'tis poſſible) then proceed thus, *viz.* Take the Remainder preceeding that which changed, by it divide the given Diviſor, until you come to a *Ratio* of Equality, or till the Species change, and then take the Remainder (preceeding that which changed of this Diviſion) and by it divide the laſt Diviſor ; and ſo on continually till you find a Diviſion that ends in a *Ratio* of Equality ; then take the given Dividend and Diviſor, and the Remainders of each Diviſion, and place them all in order from Left to Right, as in the following Example. Now, each of theſe *Ratios* having been divided by the next

next towards the right Hand, they have all been Dividends except the least (or that next the right) therefore over each I write the Quote or whole Number of Times the next lesser was found in it; then numbring these Dividends and Quotes from the Right, I set the first Quote under the first Dividend, and multiplying the first Quote by the second, and to that Product adding 1, I set the Sum under the 2*d* Dividend: Again, I multiply that last Sum by the 3*d* Quote, and to the Product add the Quote set under the first Dividend; and this Sum I set under the 3*d* Dividend; again, I multiply the last Sum by the 4*th* Quote, and to the Product add the Number set under the 2*d* Dividend, and I set this Sum under the 4*th* Dividend; and so on continually, multiplying the Number set under every Dividend by the Quote set over the next Dividend (on the Left), to the Product I add the Number set under the last Dividend (on the Right): When all this is done, the Numbers that stand under each Dividend, express how oft the last Divisor (which is the first Number on the Right of the Series of Dividends) is contained in each of these Dividends; and consequently these Dividends are to one another as the Number set under them: Therefore, in the *last* Place, if the Numbers under the given Dividend and Divisor are divided, the greater of them by the lesser, the Quote signifies how oft the *Interval* given to be divided contains the other given one.

EXAMPLE.

EXAMPLE. Divide the *Interval* 1 : 2048 by 1 : 16. According to the *Rule* I ſubſtract 1 : 16 from 1 : 2048, and have two Subſtractions, with a Remainder 1 : 8 (for the 4*th* Subſtraction changes the Species) then I ſubſtract 1 : 8 from 1 : 16, and after one Subſtraction there remains 1 : 2 (the 2*d* Subſtraction changing.) Again I ſubſtract 1 : 2 from 1 : 8, and after Three Subſtractions there remains a *Ratio* of Equality. Now place theſe according to the Rule, as in the following Scheme, and divide 11 by 4, the Quote ſhews, that the given Dividend 1 : 2048, contains the Diviſor 1 : 16, 2 and $\frac{3}{4}$ Parts of a Time, *i. e.* that it contains 1 : 16 twice; and moreover. 3 4*th* Parts of 1 : 16, which you may view all in this *Series* 1 : 2 : 4 : 8 : 16 : 32 : 64 : 128 : 256 : 512 : 1024 : 2048, in the *continual Ratio* of 1 : 2; in which we ſee 1 : 16 contained two Times, as in theſe three Terms 1 : 16 : 256, then remains 256 : 2048, equal to 1 : 8. which you ſee is equal to 3 4*th* Parts of 1 : 16, *viz.* three Times 1 : 2, which is a 4*th* of 1 : 16, as you ſee in the *Series*.

	2	1	3	
1 : 2048,	1 : 16,	1 : 8,	1 : 2	
	11	4	3	

FOR a more general *Demonſtration*, ſuppoſe any *Quantity*, *Number* or *Interval*, repreſented by *a* and a leſſer by *b*; let a contain *b* Two Times (which Two is ſet over *a*) and *c* the Remainder. Again let *b* contain *c* Three times (which Three is ſet over *b*) and *d* the Re-

Remainder. Then let *c* contain *d* Five times (which Five is ſet over *c*) and *e* the Remainder. *Laſtly*, Let *d* contain *e* Four times (ſet over *d*) and no Remainder (*i. e.* a *Ratio* of Equality.) Now becauſe *d* contains *e* Four times, I ſet 4 under *d*, then *c* containing *d* Five times, and *d* containing *e* Four times, therefore *c* muſt contain *e* as many times as the Product of Five into Four, *viz.* Twenty times; but becauſe *c* is equal to Five times *d* and to *e* over, and *e* is contained in the Remainder, *viz.* it ſelf once, therefore *e* is contained in *c* Twenty one times. Again *b* contains *c* Three times and *d* over, and *c* contains *e* Twenty one times preciſely, therefore *b* muſt contain *e* as oft as the Sum of Three times 21, *viz.* 63 and 4 which is 67; then *a* contains *b* Two times and *c* over, alſo *b* contains *e* Sixty ſeven times, therefore *a* contains *e* as oft as the Sum of Two times Sixty ſeven, *viz.* 134 and 21, which is 155. The other Inferences are plain, *viz.* 1*mo.* That each of thoſe Intervals *a*: *b*: *c*, &c. are to one another, as the Numbers ſet under them; for theſe are the Numbers of Times they contain a common Meaſure *e*. And conſequently, 2*do.* If any of theſe Numbers be divided by another, the Quote will ſhew how oft the *Interval* under which the Dividend ſtands, contains the other.

2	3	5	4	
a:	*b*:	*c*:	*d*:	*e*
155 :	67 :	21 :	4	

COROLLARY. Thus we have found a Way to diſcover the *Ratio* betwixt any Two *Intervals*,

vals, if they are commensurable; so in the preceeding *Example*, the *Interval* 1 : 2048 is to 1 : 16, as the Number 11 to 4. But *observe*, if the *Divisions* never came to a *Ratio* of Equality, the given *Intervals* are not commensurable, or as Number to Number; yet we may come near the Truth in Numbers, by carrying on the Division a considerable Length.

CHAP. V.

Containing a more particular Considera-tion of the Nature, Variety *and* Composition *of* Concords, *in Application of the preceeding* Theory.

WE have already distinguished and defined *simple* and *compound Intervals*, which we shall now particularly apply to that Species of *Intervals* which is called Concord.

Definition. A *simple* Concord is such, whose Extremes are at a Distance less than the Sum of any Two other *Concords*. A *compound* Concord is equal to Two or more *Concords*. This in general is agreeable to the common Notion of *simple* and *compound*; but the *Definition* is also taken another Way among the Writers on *Musick*; thus an *Octave*

1 :

1 : 2, and all the leſſer *Concords* (which have been already mentioned) are called *ſimple* and *original* CONCORDS; and all greater than an *Octave* are called *compound* CONCORDS, becauſe all *Concords* above an *Octave* are compoſed of, or equal to the Sum of one or more *Octaves*, and ſome ſingle *Concord* leſs than an *Octave*; and are ordinarily in Practice called by the Name of that *ſimple Concord*; of which afterwards.

---

§ 1. *Of the* original CONCORDS, *their Riſe and Dependence on each other*, &c.

SEe theſe *original Concords* again in the following *Table*, where I have placed them in Order, according to their Quantity.

Table of ſimple CONCORDS.

5 : 6	a 3d *l.*
4 : 5	a 3d *g.*
3 : 4	a 4th.
2 : 3	a 5th.
5 : 8	a 6th *l.*
3 : 5	a 6th *g*
1 : 2	a 8ve.

LET us now firſt examine the *Compoſition* and *Relations* of theſe *original Concords* among themſelves.

IF we apply the preceeding Rules of the Addition and Subſtraction of *Intervals* to theſe *Concords*, we ſhall find them divided into *ſimple* and *compound*, according to the

the firſt and more general Notion, in the Manner expreſſed in the following *Table*.

Simple.	*Compound.*				*Proof in Numb.*
5 : 6. a 3d *l.*	5th.	composed of	3d *g.* &	3d *l.*	4. 5. 6.
	6th *l.*		4th,	3d *l.*	5. 6. 8.
4 : 5. a 3d *g*	6th *g.*		4th,	3d *g.*	3. 4. 5.
			5th,	4th. *or*	2. 3. 4.
3 : 4. a 4th.			6th *g.*	3d *l.* *or*	3. 5. 6.
	8*ve.*		6th *l.*	3d *g.* *or*	4. 5. 8.
			3d *g.*	3d *l.* 4th.	4. 5. 6. 8.

The 3*d l.* 3*d g.* and 4*th*, are equal to the Sum of no other *Concords*; for the 3d *l.* is it ſelf the leaſt *Interval* of all *Concords*. The 3d *g.* is the next, which is equal to the 3d *l.* and a Remainder which is *Diſcord*. The 4*th* is equal to either of the 3*ds* and a *Diſcord* Remainder; and theſe Three are therefore the leaſt Principles of *Concord*, into which all other *Intervals* are diviſible: For the Compoſition of the 5*th*, 6*th* and 8*ve*, you ſee it proven in the Numbers annexed; and that they can be compounded of no other *Concords*, you'll prove by applying the Rules of Addition and Subſtraction.

As to the Proofs in Numbers which are annex'd, they demonſtrate the Thing, taking the component Parts in one particular Order; but it is alſo true in whatever Order they are taken, as is proven in *Probl.* 2. *Chap.* 4. Or ſee all the Variety in this Table; in the laſt Column of which you ſee the Names of all the component Parts ſet down in the ſeveral Orders of which

which they are capable, either from the *acutest* Term or the *gravest*.

TABLE of the various Orders of the harmonical Parts of the greater Concords.

Concord	Orders	Composition
5th, 2 : 3	4 . 5 . 6	*3d g. 3d l.*
	10 . 12 . 15	*3d l. 3d g.*
6th, l. 5 : 8	5 . 6 . 8	*3d l. 4th.*
	15 . 20 . 24	*4th. 3d l.*
6th, g. 3 : 5	3 . 4 . 5	*4th, 3d g.*
	12 . 15 . 20	*3d g. 4th.*
8ve 1 : 2	2 . 3 . 4	*5th, 4th.*
	3 . 4 . 6	*4th, 5th.*
	3 . 5 . 6	*6th g. 3d l.*
	5 . 6 . 10	*3d l. 6th g.*
	4 . 5 . 8	*3d g. 6th l.*
	5 . 8 . 10	*6th l. 3d g.*
	3 . 4 . 5 . 6	*4th, 3d g. 3d l.*
	4 . 5 . 6 . 8	*3d g. 3d l. 4th.*
	5 . 6 . 8 . 10	*3d l. 4th. 3d g.*
	10 . 12 . 15 . 20	*3d l. 3d g. 4th.*
	12 . 15 . 20 . 24	*3d g. 4th. 3d l.*
	15 . 20 . 24 . 30	*4th, 3d l. 3d g.*

Here you may observe, that the Varieties of the Composition of Octave *by Three Parts*, viz. 3d g. 3d *l.* 4th, *include the other Three Ways by Two Parts*; *and also all the Varieties of the Composition of the* 5th *and* 6th.

WE

WE have already, by Addition of the various *Concords* within an *Octave*, found and proven that the *5th*, *6ths* and *8ve*, are equal to the Sum of lesser *Concords*, as in the preceeding *Table*: Now we shall consider, by what Laws of Proportion these *Intervals* are resolvable back into their component Parts; or, how to put such middle Numbers betwixt the Extremes of these *Intervals*, that the intermediate *Ratios* shall make *harmonical Intervals*; by which we shall have a nearer View of the Dependence of these *original Concords* upon one another.

OF the Seven *original Concords* we examine their *Composition* among themselves, *i. e.* what lesser ones the greater are equal to; therefore the *Octave* being the greatest, its *Resolutions* must include the *Resolutions* of all the rest.

PROPOSITION I. If betwixt the Extremes of an *Octave* we place an *arithmetical Mean* (by *Corol.* to *Theor.* 2. *Chap.* 4.) it shall resolve it into Two *Ratios*, which are the *Concords* of *5th* and *4th*; and the *5th* shall be next the lesser Extreme: So betwixt 1 and 2 an *arithmetical Mean* is $1\frac{1}{2}$; or because 1 and 2 can have no middle Term in whole Numbers; therefore if we multiply them by 2, the Products 2 and 4 being in the same *Ratio*, can receive one *arithmetical Mean* (by *Theor.* *8th*) which Mean is 3, and the Series 2 : 3 : 4, *viz.* a *5th* and a *4th*.

PROPOSITION II. If betwixt the Extremes of an *Octave* we take an *harmonical Mean*, by *Theor.* *11th*, the intermediate *Ratios* shall be a a *4th* and a *5th*, and the *4th* next the leſſer Extreme; ſo betwixt 1 : 2 an *harmonical Mean* is $1\frac{1}{3}$; or multiplying all by 3, to bring them to whole Numbers, the Series is 3, 4, 6, which is *harmonical.*

COROLLARY. 'Tis plain, that if betwixt the Extremes of the *Octave* we put Two *Means*, one *arithmetical* and one *harmonical*, the Four Numbers ſhall be in *geometrical Proportion*, as here, 6, 8, 9, 12. The *Reaſon* is, that the *4th* and *5th* are the Complements of each other to an *Octave*; and therefore a *4th* to the lower Extreme leaves a *5th* to the upper, and contrarily: And in this Diviſion of the *Octave*, we have the Three Kinds of *Proportion*, ARITHMETICAL, HARMONICAL *and* GEOMETRICAL, mixt, for 6 : 9 : 12. *viz.* the *5th*, *4th*, and *8ve*, are *arithmetical*; 6 : 8 : 12, the *4th*, *5th*, and *8ve*, are *harmonical*; and 6 : 8 : 9 : 12, *geometrical.*

OBSERVE. The *5th* and *4th* are the Reſult of the immediate and moſt ſimple Diviſion of the *Octave* into Two Parts: The *4th* is not reſolvable into other *Concords*, ſince the only leſſer *Concords* are the *3d g.* and *3d l.* and either of theſe taken from a *4th*, leaves a *Diſcord*; and therefore 'tis in vain to ſeek any *mean* Terms that will reſolve it into *Concords*. 'Tis natural therefore next to enquire into the *Reſolutions* of the *5th*, which by a remarkable Uniformity, we find reducible into its conſtituent leſſer *Concords* by the ſame Laws of Proportion.

PRO-

PROPOSITION III. An *arithmetical Mean* put betwixt the Extremes of a *5th*, reſolves it it into a *3d g.* and a *3d l.* with the *3d g.* next the leſſer Extreme, as here, 2 : 2 $\frac{1}{2}$: 3. which multiplied by 3 are reduced to theſe whole Numbers 4 : 5 : 6.

PROPOSITION IV. An *harmonical Mean* put betwixt the Extremes of a *5th*, reſolves it into a *3d g.* and *3d l.* with the *3d l.* next the leſſer Extreme; as 2 : $2\frac{2}{5}$: 3, which multiplied by 5 are reduced to theſe, 10 : 12 : 15.

COROLLARY. The ſame Thing follows here as from the two firſt Propoſitions, *viz.* That taking both an *arithmetical* and *harmonical Mean* betwixt the Extremes of a *5th*, the Four Numbers are in *geometrical Proportion*, as in theſe, 20, 24, 25, 30.

NOW out of the various Mixtures of theſe ſimple Diviſions of the *8ve* and *5th*, we can bring not only all the *Reſolutions* of the *6th*, and the other *Reſolutions* of the *8ve*, but all the Varieties with reſpect to the Order in which the Parts can be taken, as follows, *viz.*

1*mo.* IF with the *arithmetical* Diviſion of the *Octave*, we mix the *arithmetical* Diviſion of the *5th*, *i. e.* if we put an *arithmetical Mean* betwixt the Extremes of the *Octave*, and then another *arithmetical Mean* betwixt the leſſer Extreme and the laſt *mean* Term found, and reduce all the 4 to whole Numbers, then we have this Series 4, 5, 6, 8, in which we have the *Octave* reſolved into its three conſtituent *Concords*, *3d* greater, *3d* leſſer, and *4th*; and within

within that Series the *5th* resolved into its two constituent *Concords*, 3*d* greater, and 3*d* lesser: And if we consider the Extremes of the *Octave* with the least of the two middle Terms 5, then these 4, 5, 8 shew us the *Octave* resolved into a 3*d g.* and a *6th l.* *Lastly.* It shews us the *6th l.* resolved into a 3*d l.* and a *4th*, *viz.* 5, 6, 8.

2*do.* IF we mix the *harmonical* Division of *Octave*, with the *arithmetical* Division of the *5th*, *i. e.* if we put an *harmonical Mean* betwixt the Extremes of *Octave*, and then an *arithmetical Mean* betwixt the greatest Extreme and middle Term last found, as in this Series, 3, 4, 5, 6, then we have the *Resolution* of the *Octave* into a *6th g.* and 3*d l.* as in these 3, 5, 6; also the *6th g.* *resolved* into a *4th* and 3*d g.* in these, 3, 4, 5; and taking the whole Series, we have a 2*d* Order of the Three Parts of the *Octave.*

WE have seen all the *harmonical* Parts of the *Octave* and *5th*, and both the *6ths*; and as to the Variety of Order in which these may be placed betwixt the Extremes, it may all be found by other Mixtures of the Parts of the *Octave*, and *5th* or *6th*; as you'll easily find by comparing the 6 Orders of the *Composition* of *Octave* by 3 *Concords*, in the preceeding *Table.*

OR, you may find them all in one Series, if you'll divide the *Octave* thus, *viz.* Put both an *arithmetical* and *harmonical Mean* betwixt its Extremes, and you'll have a *4th* and *5th* to each of the Extremes; both of which *5ths* divide

arith-

arithmetically and alſo *harmonically*, and at every Diviſion reduce all to a Series of whole Numbers; and 'tis plain you'll have a Series of 8 Terms, among which you'll have Examples of the 7 *original Concords* with their *Compoſitions*, and all the different Orders in which their Parts can be taken. Or, you may make the Series by taking the 7 *Concords*, and reducing them to a common *Fundamental*, by *Problem* 3. the Series is 360 : 300 : 288 : 270 : 240 : 225 : 216 : 180. See *Plate* 1. *Fig*. 4. wherein I have connected the Numbers ſo as all the *Compoſition* may be eaſily traced.

THERE is this remarkable in that Series, that you have all the *Concords* in a Series, both aſcending toward *Acuteneſs* from a common *Fundamental*, or greateſt Number 360, and deſcending towards *Gravity*, from a common *acute* Term 180. and for that Reaſon the Series has this Property, that taking the Two Extremes, and any other Two at equal Diſtance, theſe 4 are in *geometrical Proportion*.

Nota. IF betwixt the Extremes of any *Interval* you take Two middle Terms, which ſhall be to the Extremes in the *Ratios* of any Two component Parts of that *Interval*, *i. e.* if the two middle Terms divide the *Interval* into the ſame Parts only in a different Order, the Four Numbers are always *geometrical*.

NOW, from the Things laſt explained, we ſhall make ſome more *particular Obſervations* concerning

concerning the *Dependence* of the *original Concords* one upon another.

THE *Octave* is not only the greatest Interval of the Seven *original Concords*, but the first in Degree of Perfection; the Agreement of whose Extremes is greatest, and in that respect most like to *Unisons*: As it is the greatest *Interval*, so all the lesser are contained in it; but the Thing most remarkable is, the Manner how these lesser *Concords* are found in the *Octave*, which shews their mutual Dependences; by taking both an *harmonical* and *arithmetical Mean* betwixt the Extremes of the *Octave*, and then both an *arithmetical* and *harmonical Mean* betwixt each Extreme, and the most distant of the Two Means last found, *viz.* betwixt the lesser Extreme, and the first *arithmetical Mean*, also betwixt the greater Extreme and the first *harmonical Mean* we have all the lesser *Concords*: Thus if betwixt 360 and 180 the Extremes of *Octave*, we take an *arithmetical Mean*, it is 270, and an *harmonical Mean* is 240; then betwixt 360, the greatest Extreme, and 240, the *harmonical Mean*, take an *arithmetical Mean*, it is 300, and an *harmonical Mean* is 288; again, betwixt 188 the lesser Extreme of the *Octave*, and 270 the first *arithmetical Mean*, take an *arithmetical Mean*, it is 225, and an *harmonical* it is 216, and the whole Numbers make this Series, 360 : 300 : 288 : 270 : 240 : 216 : 180.

OBSERVE. The immediate Division of the *Octave* resolves it into a *4th* and *5th*; the *arithmetical*

rithmetical Diviſion puts the *5th* next the leſſer Extreme, as here 2, 3, 4, and the *harmonical* puts it next the greater Extreme, as here 3 : 4 : 6 ; and you may ſee both in theſe four Numbers 6, 8, 9, 12. *Again* the immediate Diviſion of the *5th* produces the Two *3ds* ; the *arithmetical* Diviſion puts the leſſer *3d*, and the *harmonical* the greater *3d* next the leſſer Extreme ; as in theſe 4, 5, 6, and 10, 12, 15 ; or ſee both in one Series, 20, 24, 25, 30. The two *6ths* are therefore found by Diviſion of the *Octave*, tho' not by any immediate Diviſion. The ſame is true alſo of the two *3ds*; ſo that all the other *ſimple Concords* are found by Diviſion of the *Octave*. The *5th* and *4th* ariſe immediately and directly out of it, and the *3ds* and *6ths* proceed from an accidental Diviſion of the *Octave* ; for the *3ds* ariſe immediately out of the *5th*, which having one Extreme common with the *Octave*, the mean Term which divides it directly, divides the *Octave* in a Manner accidentally.

NOW, if we conſider how perfectly the Extremes of an *Octave* agree, that when they are ſounded together, 'tis impoſſible to perceive two different Sounds ; ſo great is their Likeneſs, and the Mixture ſo evenly, that it is impoſſible to conceive a greater Agreement ; we ſee plainly there is no Reaſon to expect that there ſhould be any other *Concord* within the Order of Nature that comes nearer, or ſo near to the Perfection of *Uniſons* : And if we conſider again, how theſe Seven *original Concords* gradually
decreaſe

decreaſe from the *Octave* to the leſſer *6th*, which has but a ſmall Degree of *Concord*; and with that Conſideration joyn this of the mutual Dependence of theſe Seven *Concords* upon one another, and eſpecially how they all riſe out of the Diviſion of the *Octave*, according to a moſt ſimple Law, *viz.* The taking an *arithmetical* and *harmonical Mean* betwixt its Extremes which gives the Two *Concords* next in Perfection to the *Octave*, whereof the *5th* is beſt; and the ſame Law being applied to this, diſcovers all the reſt of the *Concords*; for out of the *5th* ariſe immediately the two *3ds*, whoſe Complements to *Octave* are the two *6ths*; and for that Reaſon theſe *6ths* and *3ds* are ſaid to riſe accidentally out of the *Octave*; (and afterwards we ſhall ſee how by the ſame Law, ſome other principal *Intervals* belonging to the Syſtem of *Muſick* are found.) Upon all theſe Conſiderations we may be ſatisfied, that we have diſcovered the true natural Syſtem of *Concords* within the *Octave*; and that we have no reaſonable Ground to believe there are any more, nor even a Poſſibility of it, according to the preſent State and Order of Things.

Now as to the Order of their Perfection, we have already ſtated them according to the Ear thus, *Octave*, *5th*, *4th*, *6th gr.* *3d gr.* *3d leſſ.* *6th leſſ.* In which Order we find this Law, That the beſt *Concords* are expreſt by leaſt Numbers. Yet, as I obſerved, this is not an univerſal Character; and we are only certain of this from Experience, that the frequent Coincidence of Vibrations,

brations, is a neceſſary Part of the Cauſe of *Harmony*; Senſe and Obſervation muſt ſupply the reſt, in determining the Preference of *Concords*; and ſo we take theſe 7 *original Concords* in the Order mentioned; and upon what Conſiderations they are otherways ranked by practical *Muſicians*, ſhall be explain'd in its proper Place.

YET before I go further, let us notice this one Thing concerning the Difference of the *arithmetical* and *harmonical* Diviſion. An *arithmetical* or *harmonical Mean* put betwixt the Extremes of any *Interval*, divides it into two unequal Parts; the *arithmetical* puts the greateſt *Interval* next the leſſer Extreme, the *harmonical* contrarily, as in theſe, 2 : 3 : 4, and 3 : 4 : 6, where the *Octave* is divided into its conſtituent *5th* and *4th*; or the Reſolutions of the *5th*, as here 4 : 5 : 6, and 10 : 12 : 15. Now let us apply theſe Numbers either to the Lengths of Chords or their Vibrations, and we find this Difference, that applied to the Vibrations, the *arithmetical* Diviſion puts the beſt *Concord* next the *fundamental*, or *grave Extreme*, and the *harmonical* puts it next the *acute* Extreme; but contrarily in both when applied to the Lengths of Chords. As theſe two Diviſions reſolve the *Octave* or *5th* into the ſame Parts, they are in that reſpect equal; but if we ſuppoſe the Extremes of the *Octave* or *5th*, with their *arithmetical* or *harmonical Means*, to be ſounded all together, there will be a conſiderable Difference; and that Diviſion which

which puts the beſt *Concord* loweſt is beſt, which is the *arithmetical* if the Numbers are applied to the Vibrations, but the *harmonical* if applied to the Lengths of Chords. The obſerving this ſhall be enough here; I ſhall more fully explain it when I treat of *compound Sounds*, under the Name of *Harmony*. This however we find true, That *geometrical Proportion* affords no *ſimple Concords* (how it comes among the *compound* ſhall be ſeen preſently) and it has no Place in the Relation and Dependence of the *original Concords*, but ſo far as a Mixture of the *arithmetical* and *harmonical* produces it, as in theſe, 6, 8, 9, 12. And here I ſhall obſerve, That the *harmonical* Proportion received that Denomination from its being found among the Numbers, applied to the Length of Chords, that expreſs the chief *Concords* in *Muſick*, *viz.* the *Octave*, *5th*, and *4th*, as here, 3, 4, 6. But this Proportion does not always conſtitute *Concords*, nor can poſſibly do, becauſe betwixt the Extremes of any *Interval* we can put an *harmonical Mean*, yet every *Interval* is not reſolvable into Parts that are *Concords*; therefore this Definition has been rejected, particularly by *Kepler*; and for this he inſtitutes another Definition of *harmonical Proportion*, *viz.* When betwixt the Extremes of any *Ratio* or *Interval*, one or more middle Terms are taken, which are all *Concord* among themſelves, and each with the Extremes, then that is an *harmonical* Diviſion of ſuch an *Interval*; ſo that *Octave*, *6th* and *5th* are capable of of being *harmonically* divided in this Senſe; all the Variety whereof you ſee in a Table at the Beginning of this Chapter: And theſe middle Terms will be in ſome Caſes *arithmetical* Means, as 1 : 2 : 3; in ſome *geometrical*, as 1, 2, 4; in ſome *harmonical* (in the firſt Senſe) as 3 : 4 : 6; and in others they will depend on no certain *Proportion*, as 5, 6, 8.

HITHERTO we have conſidered the *Reſolution* and *Compoſition* of *Intervals*, as they are expreſt by *Ratios* of Numbers; but there are other Ways of deducing the Relation and Dependence of the *Concords*, not from the Diviſion or Reſolution of a *Ratio*, but the Diviſion of a ſimple Number, or rather of a Line expreſt by that Number, which may be call'd the *geometrical* Part of this *Theory*. But it will be better if I firſt conſider and explain the remaining *Concords* belonging to the *Syſtem* of *Muſick*, which are particularly called *compound Concords*.

---

§ 2. *Of*

§ 2. *Of* COMPOUND CONCORDS; *and of the* Harmonick Series; *with ſeveral Obſervations relating to both ſimple and compound Concords.*

HITHERTO we have taken it upon Experience, That there are no *concording Intervals* greater than *Octave*, but what are compoſed of the 7 *original Concords* within an *Octave*; the *Reaſon* of which is deduced from the Perfection of the *Octave*. We have ſeen already how all the other *ſimple* and *original Concords* are contained in, and depend upon the *Octave*, and derive their Sweetneſs from it, as they ariſe more or leſs directly out of it: We have obſerved, that it has in all Reſpects the greateſt Perfection of any *Interval*, and comes neareſt to *Uniſons*; and tho' there ſeems to be ſomething ſtill wanting, to make a general Character, by which we may judge of the Approach of any *Interval* to the perfect Agreement of *Uniſons*, yet 'tis plain the *Octave* 1 : 2 comes neareſt to it; for 'tis contained not only in the leaſt of all Numbers, but that Proportion is of the moſt perfect Kind, *viz. Multiple*; and of all ſuch it is the moſt ſimple, which makes the greateſt Degree of Commenſurateneſs or Agreement in the Motions of the Air that produce theſe Sounds. Let me add this other

other Remark, That if Wind-inſtruments are overblown, the Sound will riſe firſt to an *Octave*, and to no other *Concord*; why it ſhould not as well riſe to a *4th*, *&c.* is owing probably to the Perfection of *Octave*, and its being next to *Uniſon*. Again, take into the Conſideration that ſurpriſing *Phænomenon* of Sound being raiſed from a Body which is touched by nothing but the Air, moved by the ſonorous Motion of another Body; particularly that if the Tune of the untouched Body be *Octave* above the given Sound, it will be moſt diſtinctly heard; and ſcarcely will any other but the *Octave* be heard.

FROM this ſimple and perfect Form of the *Octave*, ariſes this remarkable Property of it, that it may be doubled, tripled, *&c.* and ſtill be *Concord*, *i. e.* the Sum of Two or more *Octaves* are *Concord*, tho' the more *compound* will be gradually leſs agreeable; but it is not ſo with any other *Concord* leſs than *Octave*, the Double, *&c.* of theſe being all *Diſcords*; and as continued *geometrical Proportion* conſtitutes a Series of equal *Intervals*, ſo we ſee that ſuch a Series has no Place in *Muſick* but among *Octaves*, the Continuation of other *Concords* producing *Diſcord*. Theſe Things remarkably confirm to us the Perfection of the *Octave*: There is ſuch a Likeneſs and Agreement betwixt its Extremes, that it ſeems to make a Demonſtration *a priori*, that whatever Sound is *Concord* to one Extreme of the *Octave*, will be ſo to the other alſo; and in Experience it is ſo.

We

We have ſeen already, that whatever Sound betwixt the Extremes of an *Octave*, is *Concord* to the one, is in another Degree *Concord* to the other alſo; for we found that the *Octave* is reſolvable into *Concords*. *Again*, if we add any other *ſimple Concord* to an *Octave*, we find by Experience that it agrees to both its Extremes; to the neareſt Extreme it is a *ſimple Concord*, and to the fartheſt it is a *compound Concord*: Now, take this for a Principle, That whatever agrees to one Extreme of *Octave*, agrees alſo to the other, and we eaſily conclude, That there cannot be any *concording Interval* greater than an *Octave*, but the *Compounds* of an *Octave* and ſome leſſer *Concord*: For if we ſuppoſe the Extremes of any *Interval* greater than an *Octave* to be *Concord*, 'tis plain we can put in a middle Term, which ſhall be *Octave* to one Extreme of that *Interval*, conſequently the other Extreme ſhall be alſo *Concord* with this middle Term, and be diſtant from it by an *Interval* leſs than an *Octave*; and therefore if we add a *Diſcord* to one Extreme of an *Octave*, it will be alſo *Diſcord* to the other; the ſame will apply alſo to the *Compounds* of Two or more *Octaves*; but the Agreement will ſtill be leſs as the Compoſition is greater.

I cannot but mention here how *D' Cartes* concludes this Principle to be true; he obſerves, what I have done, *That the Sound of a Whiſtle or Organ-pipe will riſe to an* Octave, *if 'tis forcibly blown; which proceeds,* ſays

ſays he, *from this, That it differs leaſt from* Uniſon. *Hence again*, ſays he, *I judge that no Sound is heard, but its acute* Octave *ſeems ſome way to eccho or reſound in the Ear; for which Reaſon it is that with the groſſer Chords* (*or thoſe which give the graver Sound*) *of ſome ſtringed Inſtruments* (he mentions the *Teſtudo*) *others are joyned an* Octave acuter, *which are always touched together, whereby the* graver *Sound is improven, ſo as to be more diſtinctly heard.* From this he concludes it plain, *That no Sound which is* Concord *to one Extreme of an* Octave, *can be* Diſcord *to the other.* From all this we ſee how the *Octave* comprehends the whole *Syſtem* of *Concords*, (excepting the *Uniſon*) becauſe they are all contained in it, or compoſed of it and theſe that are cotained in it.

THE Author already mentioned of the *Elucidationes Phyſicæ* upon *D' Cartes's Compend of Muſick*, advances an *Hypotheſis* to explain how this happens, which *D' Cartes* affirms, *viz.* That the *Fundamental* never ſounds but the *acute Octave* ſeems to do ſo too. He ſuppoſes that the Air contains in it ſeveral Parts of different Conſtitution, capable, like different Chords, of different Meaſures of Vibrations, which may be the Reaſon, ſays he, that the human Voice or Inſtruments, and chiefly theſe of Metal never ſound, but ſome other *acuter* Sounds are heard to reſound in the Air.

IN the Beginning of this *Chapter* I obſerved two different Senſes in which *Concords* were called *ſimple* and *compound*: The *Octave* and all

all within it are called *simple* and *original Concords*; and all greater than an *Octave*, are *compound*, because all such are composed of an *Octave*, and some lesser *Concord*. Now, the 5*th*, 6*ths* and *Octave* are also composed of the 3*ds* and 4*ths* which are the most *simple Concords*; but then all the 7 *Concords* within an *Octave* have different Effects in *Musick*, whereas the *compound Concords* above an *Octave* have all in Practice the same Name and Effect with these simple ones, less than an *Octave*, of which with the *Octave* they are composed; so a 5*th* and an *Octave* added make 1 : 3, and is called a *compound* 5*th*. Now as there are 7 *original Concords*, so these 7 added to *Octave*, make 7 *compound Concords*; and added to two *Octaves*, make other 7 more compound, and so on. We have seen already, in *Prob.* 8. how to add *Intervals*, and according to that *Rule* I have made the following *Table* of *Concords*, which I place in Order, according to the Quantity of the *Interval*, beginning with the least. I suppose 1 to be a common *fundamental* Chord, and express the *acute* Term of each *Concord* by that Fraction or Part of the *Fundamental* that makes such *Concord* with it, and have reduced each to its radical Form, *i. e.* to the lowest Number; so an *Octave* and 5*th* added, is in the *Ratio* 2 : 6, equal by Reduction to 1 : 3; and others.

Follows the general Table of CONCORDS,

Octaves

	Simple Concords	Compounds above one *Octave*	Compounds above two *Octaves.*	
Octaves	1/2	1/4	1/8	1/16 &c.
6th g.	3/5	3/10	3/20	&c.
6th l.	5/8	5/16	5/32	
5th	2/3	1/3	1/6	
4th	3/4	3/8	3/16	
3d g.	4/5	2/5	1/5	
3d l.	5/6	5/12	5/24	

THESE *Compounds* are ordinarly called by the Name of the *simple Concord* of which they are composed, tho' they have also other Names, of which in another Place.

IF this Table were continued infinitely, 'tis plain we should have all the possible *harmonical Ratios*, and in their radical Forms; 'tis also certain, that there should be no other Numbers found in it than these, 1, 3, 5, and their Multiples by 2, *i. e.* their Products by 2, which are 2, 6, 10, and the Products of these by 2, *viz.* 4,12,20,and so on *in infinitum*,multiplying the last Three Products by 2. The *Reason* of which is,that in this Series 1, 2, 3, 4, 5, 6, 8, we have no other Numbers but 1, 3, 5, and their Products by 2; and we have here also all the Numbers that belong to the *simple original Concords*; and if we consider how the *Compounds* are raised by adding an *Octave* continually, we see plainly that no no new Number can be produced, but the Product of these that belong to the *simple Concords* multiplied by 2 continually. All which Numbers make up this Series, *viz.* 1, 2, 3, 4, 5, 6, 8, 10, 12, 16, 20, 24, 32, 40, 48, 64, 80, *&c.* which is continued after the Number 5, by multiplying the last Three by 2, and their Products *in infinitum* by 2; whereby 'tis plain, we shall have all the Multiples of these original Numbers 1, 3, 5, arising from the continual Multiplication of them by 2. And this I call the HARMONICAL SERIES, because it contains all the possible *Ratios* that make *Concord*, either *simple* or *compound*: And not only so, but every Number of it is *Concord* with every other, which I shall easily prove: That it contains all possible *Concords* is plain from the Way of raising it, since it has no other Numbers than what belong to the preceeding general *Table* of *Concords*; and that every Number is *Concord* with every other is thus proven: After the Number 5 every Three Terms of the Series are the Doubles of the last Three; but the Numbers 1, 2, 3, 4, 5, are *Concord* each with another, and consequently each of these must be *Concord* with every other Number in the Series, since all the rest are but Multiples of these; for whatever *Concord* any lesser Number of these 5 makes with another of them that is greater, it will with the Double of that greater make an *Octave* more, and with the Double of the last another *Octave* more, and so on: Thus, 2 to 3, is a *5th*, and 2 to 6 is a *5th* and *8ve*; but, comparing any greater

greater Number of these Five with a lesser, whatever *Concord* that is, it will with the Double of that lesser be an *8ve* less, providing that Double be still less than the Number compared to it, (so 5 to 2 is a *3d g.* and *8ve*, and 5 to 4 is only a *3d g.*) But if 'tis greater, then it will be the Complement of the first *Concord* to *8ve*, *i.e.* the Difference of it and *8ve*, (so 5 to 6 is a *3d l.* the Complement of a *6th g.* 5 : 3 to an *8ve*) and taking another Double it will be an *8ve* more than the last, and so on. Now the Thing being true of these Five Numbers compared together, and with all the other Numbers in the Series, it must hold true of all these others compared together, because they are only Multiples of the first. The Use of this *harmonick Series* you'll find in the next *Chapter*. I shall end this with some further Observations relating to the *harmonical Numbers*, and the whole *System* of *Concords* both *simple* and *compound*.

IN the preceeding *Chapter* I have endeavoured to discover some Character, in the Proportion of *musical Intervals*, whereby their various Perfections may be stated, tho' not with all the Success to be wished; so that we are in a great Measure left to Sense and Experience. We have seen that the principal and chief *Concords*, are contain'd within the first and least of the natural Series of Numbers; the *Octave*, *5th*, *4th*, and *3ds*, in the natural Progression 1, 2, 3, 4, 5, 6; and the Two *6ths* arise out of the Division of the *Octave*, and are contain'd in these Numbers 3, 5, 8. Considering what a necessary Condition

dition of *Concord*, frequent Union and Coincidence of Motion is, we have concluded, that the ſmaller Numbers any Proportion conſiſts of, *cæteris paribus*, the more perfect is the *Interval* expreſſed by ſuch a Proportion of Numbers. But then I obſerved, that beſides this Smalneſs of the Numbers on which the Coincidence depends, there is ſomething ſtill a Secret in the Proportion or Relation of the Numbers that repreſent the Extremes of an *Interval*, that we ought to know for making a general Character, whereby the Degrees of *Concord* may be determined; ſo 4 : 7 is *Diſcord*, and yet 5 : 6 is *Concord*, and 5 : 8. Now again we ſee in this *Table* of *Concords*, that the Smalneſs of the Numbers does not abſolutely determine the Preference, elſe 1 : 3 an *Octave* and *5th*, would be better than 1 : 4 a double *Octave*, which it is not, and ſo would all the other *compound 5ths in infinitum*. Again, the *compound 3d* 1 : 5 would be better than either the *compound Octave* 1 : 8, or the *compound 5th* 1 : 6, which is all contrary to Experience; and this demonſtrates, that there muſt be ſomething elſe in it than barely the Smalneſs of the Numbers. *D' Cartes* obſerves here, that the 3*d* 1 : 6, compos'd of Two *Octaves*, is better than either the *ſimple 3d*, 4 : 5, or the firſt *Compound* 2 : 5; and gives this Reaſon, *viz*. that 1 : 5 is a multiple Proportion, which the others are not; and out of multiple Proportion, he ſays, the beſt *Concords* proceed, becauſe it is the moſt ſimple Form, and eaſily perceived: By the ſame Reaſon all the

the *compound* *5ths* are better than the *ſimple* *5th*; and *D' Cartes* himſelf makes the firſt *compound* *5th* 1 : 3 the moſt perfect, becauſe it is Multiple, and in ſmaller Numbers than the *ſimple* *5th*. But we muſt obſerve, that every multiple Proportion will not conſtitute *Concord*, ſo 1 : 9 is groſs *Diſcord*, being equal to Three *Octaves*, and this *Diſcord* 8 : 9. Now conſider either the Numbers or their multiple Proportion, and this of 1 : 9 ſhould be better than 3 : 8, or than 3 : 16; yet it is otherwiſe, for theſe are *compound* *4ths*, which are *Concord*; we muſt therefore refer this to ſome other thing, in the Relation of the Numbers, that we cannot expreſs.

Observe next how *D' Cartes* ſtates theſe *Concords*; he puts them in this Order, *Octave*, *5th*, *3d* g. *4th*, *6th* g. *3d* l. *6th* l. and gives this Reaſon, *viz.* That the Perfectiou of any *Concord* is not to be taken from its *ſimple* Form only, but from a joynt Conſideration of all its *Compounds*; becauſe, ſays he, it can never be heard alone ſo ſimply, but there will be heard the Reſonance of its *Compound*; as in the *Uniſon*, or a ſingle given Sound, the Reſonance of the *acute* *Octave* is contained; and therefore he places the *3d* g. before the *4th*, becauſe being contain'd in leſſer Numbers, it is more perfect. But we muſt obſerve again, that as *Concord* does not depend altogether upon multiple Proportion, neither does it upon the Smalneſs of the Numbers; for then *D' Cartes* ſhould have put the *5th* before the *Octaves*, becauſe all its

Com-

Componuds are contained in leſſer Numbers than the *Octaves*. We ſee then how difficult it is to deduce the Perfection of the *Concords* from the Numbers that expreſs them.

LET us conſider this other Remark of *D' Cartes*, he obſerves that only the Numbers 2, 3, 5, are ſtrictly *muſical* Numbers, all the other Numbers of the Table being only *Compounds* or Multiples of theſe Three, which belong in the firſt Place to the *Octave*, 5*th*, and 3*d g.* which he calls *Concords* properly, and *per ſe*, as he calls all others *accidental*, for Reaſons I ſhall ſhow you immediately.

NOW, tho' the *compound* 5*ths* are contain'd in leſſer Numbers than the *Octaves*, perhaps the Preference of the *Octaves* is due to the radical Number 2, which belongs originally and in the firſt Place to that *Concord*; whereas the *compound* 5*ths* depend on the Number 3 which is more complex: But we ſhall leave this Way of Reaſoning as uncertain and chimerical; yet this we have very remarkable, that the firſt ſix of the natural Series of Numbers, *viz.* 1, 2, 3, 4, 5, 6, are *Concords* comparing every one with every other, which is true of no other Series of Numbers, except the Equimultiples of theſe 6, which, in reſpect of *Concord*, are the ſame with theſe. Again, if each of theſe Numbers be multiplied by it ſelf, and by each of the reſt, and theſe Products be diſpoſed in a Series, each Number of that Series with the next conſtitutes ſome *Interval* that belongs to the Syſtem of *Muſick*, tho' they are not at all *Concord*, as will

will appear afterwards: That Series is 1. 2. 3. 4. 5. 6. 8. 9. 10. 12. 15. 16. 18. 20. 24. 25. 30. 36. It would be of no great Uſe to repete what wonderful Properties ſome Authors have found in the Number 6, particularly *Kircher*, who tells us, that it is the only Number that is abſolutely *harmonical*, and clearly repreſents the *divine Idea* in the Creation, about which he imploys a great deal of Writing. But theſe are fine imaginary Diſcoveries, that I ſhall leave every one to ſatisfy himſelf about, by conſulting their Authors or Propagators.

ANOTHER Thing remarkable in this *Syſtem* of *Concords* is, that the greateſt Number of Vibrations of the *Fundamental* cannot be above 5, or, there is no *Concord* where the *Fundamental* makes more than 5 Vibrations to one Coincidence with the *acute* Term: For ſince it is ſo in the *ſimple Concords*, it cannot be otherwiſe in the *Compounds*, the *Octave* being $\frac{1}{2}$, which by the *Rule* of Addition can never alter the leſſer Number of any *ſimple Concord* to which it is added. It is *again* to be *remarked*, that this Progreſs of the *Concords* may be carried on to greater Degrees of Compoſition *in infinitum*; but the more *compound* ſtill the leſs agreeable, if you'll except the Two Caſes abovementioned of the 5*th* 1 : 3, and 3*d* 1 : 5; ſo a ſingle *Octave* is better than a double *Octave*, and this better than the Sum of 3 *Octaves*, &c. and ſo of 5*ths* and other *Concords*. And *mind*, tho' a *compound Octave* is the Sum of 2 or more *Octaves*, yet by a *compound* 5*th* or other *Concord*,

cord, is not meant the Sum of Two or more *5ths*, but the Sum of an *Octave* and *5th*, or of Two *Octaves* and a *5th*, &c. Now, tho' this Composition of *Concords* may be carried on infinitely, yet 3 or 4 *Octaves* is the greatest Length we go in ordinary Practice; the old Scales of *Musick* were carried no further than 2, or at most 3 *Octaves*, which is fully the Compass of any ordinary Voice: And tho' the *Octave* is the most perfect *Concord*, yet after the Third *Octave* the Agreement diminishes very fast; nor do we go even so far at one Movement, as from the one Extreme to the other of a triple or double *Octave*, and seldom beyond a single *Octave*; yet a Piece of Musick may be carried agreeably thro' all the intermediate Sounds, within the Extremes of 3 or 4 *Octaves*; which will afford all the Variety of Pleasure the *Harmony* of Sounds is capable to afford, or at least we to receive: For we can hardly raise Sounds beyond that Compass, either by Voice or Instruments, that shall not offend the *Ear*. *Chords* are fittest for raising a great Variety of Degrees of Sound; and if we suppose any *Chord* ½ Foot long, which is but a small Length to give a good Sound, the Fourth *Octave* below must be Eight Foot, which is so long, that to give a clear Sound, it must have a good Degree of Tension; and this will require a very great Tension in the ½ Foot *Chord:* Now if we go beyond the Fourth *Octave*, either the *acute* Term will be too short, or the *grave* Term too long; and if in this the Length be supplied by the Greatness

neſs of the *Chord*, or in the other the Shortneſs be exchanged with the Smalneſs, yet the Sound will by that means become ſo blunt in the one, or ſo ſlender in the other, as to be uſeleſs.

D' Cartes ſuppoſes we can go no further than Three *Octaves*, but he muſt mean only, that the Extremes of any greater *Interval* heard without any of the intermediate Terms, have little *Concord* to our Ears; but it will not follow, that a Piece of *Muſick* may not go thro' a greater Compaſs, eſpecially with many Parts.

CHAP. VI.

Of the Geometrical *Part of* Muſick; *or, how to divide right Lines, ſo as their Sections or Parts one with another, or with the Whole, ſhall contain any given* Interval *of* Sound.

THE *Degrees* of Sound with reſpect to *Tune*, are juſtly expreſt by the Lengths of Chords or right Lines; and the Proportions which we have hitherto explained being found, firſt by Experiments upon Chords, and

and again confirmed by Reaſoning; the Diviſion of a right Line into ſuch Parts as ſhall conſtitute one with another, or with the Whole, any *Interval* of Sound is a very eaſy Matter: For in the preceeding Parts we have all along ſuppoſed the Numbers to repreſent the Lengths of *Chords*; and therefore they may again be eaſily applied to them, which I ſhall explain in a few *Problems*.

---

§ 1. *Of the more general Diviſion of* Chords.

PROBLEM I. TO aſſign ſuch a Part of any right Line, as ſhall conſtitute any *Concord* (or other *Interval*) with the Whole.

Rule. Divide the given Line into as many Parts, as the greateſt Number of the *Interval* has *Units*; and of theſe take as many as the leſſer Number; this with the Whole contains the *Interval* ſought. *Example.* To find ſuch a Part of the Line *A B*, as ſhall be a 5*th* to the Whole. The 5*th* is 2 : 3, therefore I divide the Line into Three Parts, whereof 2, *viz.* *A C*, is the Part ſought; that is, Two Lines, whoſe Lengths are as *A B* to *A C*, *cæteris paribus*, make a 5*th*.

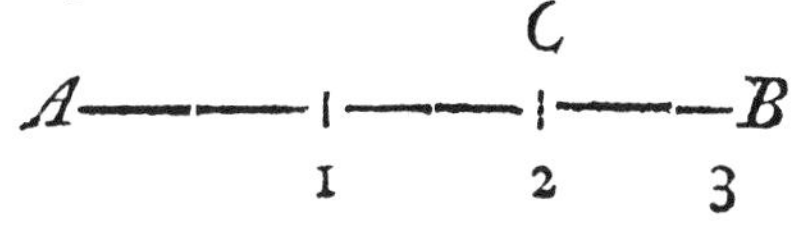

COROL-

COROLLARY. Let it be propofed to find Two or more different Sections of the Line *A B.* that fhall be to the Whole in any given Proportion. 'Tis plain, we muft take the given *Ratios*, and reduce them to one *Fundamental* (if they are not fo) by *Probl.* 3. *Chap.* 4. and then divide the Line into as may Parts as that *Fundamental* has *Units* ; fo, to find the Sections of the Line *A. B.* that fhall be *Octave*, 5*th* and 3*d g*, I take the *Ratios* 1 : 2, 2 : 3, and 4 : 5, and reduce them to One *Fundamental*, the Series is 30 : 24, 20 : 15. the *Fundamental* is 30, and the Sections fought are 24 the 3*d g.* 20 the 5*th*, and 15 the *Octave*.

PROBLEM II. To find feveral Sections of a Line, that from the leaft gradually to the Whole, fhall contain a given Series of *Intervals*, in a given Order, *i. e.* fo as the leaft Section to the next greater fhall contain a certain *Interval*, from that to the next fhall be another; and fo on. *Rule*. Reduce all the *Ratios* to a continued Series, by *Probl.* 2. *Chap.* 4. Then divide the Line into as many Parts as the greateft Extreme of that Series ; and number the Parts from the one End to the other, and you have the Sections fought, at the Points of Divifion anfwering the feveral Numbers of the Series. *Example*. To find feveral Sections of the Line *A B*, fo that the leaft to the next greater fhall contain a 3*d g.* that to the next greater a 5*th*, and that to the Whole an *Octave*. The Three *Ratios* 4 : 5, 2 : 3, 1 : 2, reduced to One Series, make 8 : 10 : 15 : 30. So the Line

A

A B being divided into Thirty equal Parts, we have the Sections sought at the Points *C D* and *E*, so as *A C* to *A D* is a 3*d g*. *A D* to *A E* a 5*th*, and *A E* to *A B* *Octave*.

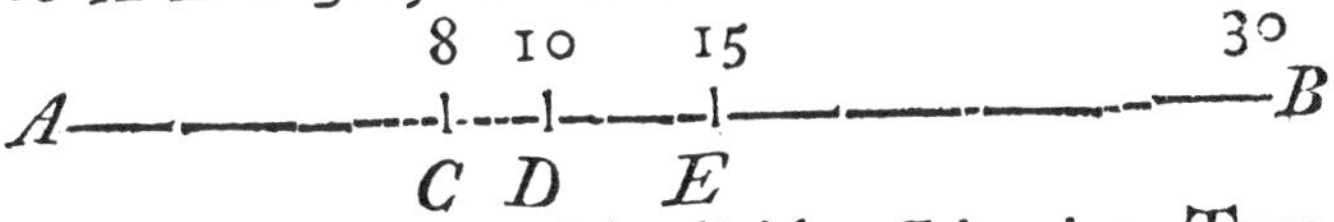

8 10 15 30
A————————\|——\|————\|——————————————*B*
C D E

PROBLEM III. To divide a Line into Two Parts, which shall be any given *Interval*. *Rule*. Add together the Numbers that contain the *Ratio* of that *Interval*, and divide the Line into as many Parts as that Sum; the Point of Division answering to any of the given Numbers is the Point which separates on either Hand the Parts sought. *Example*. To divide the Line *A B* into Two Parts which shall contain betwixt them a 4*th*, I add 3 and 4, and divide the Line into 7 Parts, and the Point 4 or *C* gives the Thing sought, for *A C* is 4, and *C B* is 3. *A*——\|——\|——\|——\|(4, *C*)——\|——\|——(7)*B*.

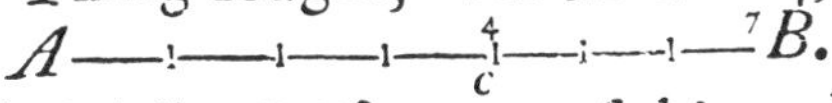

NOTA. The Difference of this and the last *Problem* is, that there we found several Sections of the Line which were not considered as altogether precisely equal to the Whole; but here the Point sought must be such as their Sum shall be exactly equal to the Whole.

COROLLARY. If it is proposed to divide a Line into more than Two Parts, which shall be to one another as any given *Intervals* from the least to the greatest; we must take the given *Ratios*, and reduce them to one continued Series, as in the last *Probl.* and add them all together; then divide the Line into as many Parts as that Sum. *Ex-*

Example. To divide the Line *AB* into 4 Parts, which ſhall contain among them, from the leaſt to the greateſt, a 3*d g.* 4*th* and 5*th*, I take the *Ratios* 4 : 5, 3 : 4 and 2 : 3, which reduced to one Series, it is 12 : 15 : 20 : 30, whoſe Sum is 77; let the Line be divided into 77 Parts; and if you firſt take off 12, then 15, then 20, and laſtly 30 Parts, you have the Parts ſought equal to the Whole.

THE preceeding *Problems* are of a more general Nature, I ſhall now particularly treat of the *harmonical* Diviſion of Chords.

§ 2. *Of the* harmonical *Diviſion of* Chords.

I Explained already Two different Senſes in which any *Interval* is ſaid to be *harmonically* divided; the *Firſt*, When the Two Extremes with their Differences from the middle Term are in *geometrical Proportion*; the 2*d*, when an *Interval* is ſo divided, as the Extremes and all the middle Terms are *Concord* each with another. *Now*, we are to conſider, not the *harmonical* Diviſion of an *Interval* or *Ratio*, but the Diviſion of a ſingle Number or Line, into ſuch Sections or Parts as, compared together and with the Whole, ſhall be *harmonical* in either of the Two Senſes mentioned, *i.e.* either with reſpect to the Proportion of their Quantity, which is the firſt Senſe, or of their Qua-

Quality or *Tune*, which is the ſecond Senſe of *harmonical* Diviſion.

PROBLEM IV. To find Two Sections of a Line which with the whole ſhall be in *harmonical* Proportion of their Quantity. To anſwer this Demand, we may take any Three Numbers in *harmonical* Proportion, as 3, 4, 6, and divide the whole Line into as many Parts as the greateſt of theſe Three Numbers (as here into 6), and at the Points of Diviſion anſwering the other two Numbers (as at 3 and 4) you have the Sections ſought. And an infinite Number of *Examples* of this Kind may be found, becauſe betwixt any Two Numbers given, we can put an *harmonical Mean*, by *Theor.* 11. *Chap.* 4.

NOTE. The *harmonical* Sections of this *Problem* added together, will ever be greater than the Whole, as is plain from the Nature of that Kind; and this is therefore not ſo properly a Diviſion of the Line as finding ſeveral Sections, or the Quotes of ſeveral diſtinct Diviſions.

Theſe Sections with the Whole, will alſo conſtitute an *harmonical* Series of the 2*d* Kind, but not in every Caſe; for *Example*, 2, 4, 6, is *harmonical* in both Senſes; alſo 2 : 3 : 6; but 21, 24, 28 is *harmonical* only in the Firſt Senſe becauſe there is no *Concord* amongſt them but betwixt 21, 28, (equal to 3 : 4.)

To know how many Ways a Line may be divided *harmonically* in both Senſes, ſhall be preſently explained.

PROBLEM V. To find Two Sections of a Line, that together and with the Whole ſhall be *har-*

harmonical in the Second Senſe ; *that is*, in reſpect of Quality or *Tune*. *Rule*. Take any Three Numbers that are *Concord* each with another, and divide the Line by the greateſt, the Points of Diviſion anſwering the other Two give the Sections ſought : Take, for Example, the Numbers 2, 3, 8, or 2, 5, 8, and apply them according to the *Rule*.

I obſerved in the former *Problem*, That the Two Sections together are always greater than the whole Line ; but here they may be either greater, as in this *Example*, 2, 3, 4, or leſs, as in this *Example*, 1, 2, 5, or equal, as here, 2, 3, 5, which laſt is moſt properly Diviſion of the Line, for here we find the true conſtituent Parts of the Line : They may alſo be *harmonical* in the firſt Senſe, as 2 : 3 : 6, or otherwiſe as 2 : 3 : 4.

Now, to know all the Variety of Combinations of Three Numbers that will ſolve this *Problem*, we muſt conſider the preceeding *general Table* of *Concords*, *Pag*. 172. and the *harmonical Series* made out of it, which contains the Numbers of the *Table* and no other. I have ſhewn that all the Numbers of the *Table* of *Concords*, are *Concords* one with another, as well as theſe that are particularly connected : We have alſo ſeen that, tho' the *Table* were carried on *in infinitum*, the leſſer Number of every *Ratio* is one of theſe, 1. 2. 3. 4. 5; and the greater Number of each *Ratio* one of theſe, 2. 3. 5. or their Products by 2. *in infinitum*. 'Tis plain therefore, that if we ſuppoſe this *Table* of *Con-*

cords

cords carried on *in infinitum*, we can find in it infinite Combinations of Three Numbers that ſhall be all *Concord*. For *Example*, Take any Two that have no common Diviſor, as 2 : 3, you'll find an Infinity of other Numbers greater to joyn with theſe; for we may take any of the Multiples *in infinitum* of either of theſe Two Numbers themſelves, or the Number 5, or its Multiples: But if we ſuppoſe the Table of *Concords* limited(as with reſpect to Practice it is) ſo will the Variety of Numbers ſought be: Suppoſe it limited to Three *Octaves*, then the *harmonical Series* goes no farther than the Number 64, as here, 1. 2. 3. 4. 5. 6. 8. 10. 12. 16. 20. 24. 32. 40. 48. 64, *&c.* and as many Combinations of Three Numbers as we can find in that Series, which have not a common Diviſor, ſo many Ways may the *Problem* be ſolved. But beſides theſe we muſt conſider again, that as many of the preceeding Combinations as are *arithmetically* proportional (ſuch as 2. 3. 4, and 2. 5. 8) there are ſo many Combinations of correſpondent *Harmonicals* (in the firſt Senſe) which will ſolve this *Problem*. Theſe joyned to the preceeding, will exhauſt all the Variety with which this *Problem* can be ſolved, ſuppoſing 3 *Octaves* to be the greateſt *Concord*. *Again*, we are to take Notice, that of that Variety there are ſome, of which the Two leſſer Numbers will be exactly equal to the greateſt, as 1. 2. 3. tho' the greater Numbers are otherwiſe.

I ſhall

I ſhall now in Two diſtinct *Problems* ſhow you, *Firſt*, The Variety of Ways that a Line may be cut, ſo as the *Sections* compared together and with the Whole ſhall be *harmonical* in both the Senſes explained ; and 2*do*. How many Ways it may be divided into Two Parts equal to the Whole, and be *harmonical* in the Second Senſe; for theſe can never be *harmonical* in the Firſt Senſe, as ſhall be alſo ſhewn.

Problem VI. To find how many Ways 'tis poſſible to take Two Sections of a Line, that with the Whole ſhall conſtitute Three Terms *harmonical* both in Quantity and Quality.

From the *harmonical Series* we can eaſily find an Anſwer to this Demand : In order to which conſider, *Firſt*, That every Three Numbers in *harmonical Proportion* (of Quantity) have other Three in *arithmetical Proportion* correſponding to them, which contain the ſame *Intervals* or *geometrical Ratios*, tho' in a different Order ; and reciprocally every *arithmetical Series* has a correſpondent *Harmonical*, as has been explained in *Theor*. 14. *Chap*. 4. Let us *next* conſider, That there can no Three Numbers in *arithmetical Proportion* be taken, which ſhall be all *Concord* one with another, unleſs they be found in the *harmonical Series* : Therefore it is impoſſible that any Three Numbers which are in *harmonical Proportion* (of Quantity) can be all *Concord* unleſs their correſpondent *Arithmeticals* be contain'd in the *harmonical* Series. Hence 'tis plain, that as many Combinations of Three Numbers in *arithmetical Proportion* as can

can be found in that Series, so many Combinations of Three Numbers in *harmonical Proportion* are to be found, which shall be *Concord* each with another; and so many Ways only can a Line be divided *harmonically* in both Senses.

And in all that Series 'tis impossible to find any other Combination of Numbers in *arithmetical Proportion*, than those in the following *Table*; with which I have joyned their *correspondent Harmonicals*.

Arithmet.	*Harmon.*
1 . 2 . 3	2 . 3 . 6
2 . 3 . 4	3 . 4 . 6
3 . 4 . 5	12 . 15 . 20
4 . 5 . 6	10 . 12 . 15
1 . 3 . 5	3 . 5 . 15
2 . 5 . 8	5 . 8 . 20

Now, to show that there are no other Combinations to be found in the Series to answer the present Purpose, *observe*, the Three *arithmetical* Terms must be in radical Numbers, else tho' it may be a different *arithmetical Series*, yet it cannot contain different *Concords*, so 4 : 6 : 8 is a different Series from 2 : 3 : 4, yet the *geometrical Ratios*, or the *Concords* that the Numbers of the one Series contain, being the same with these in the other, the correspondent *harmonical* Series gives the same Division of the Line. Now by a short and easy Induction, I shall show the Truth of what's advanced: Look on the *harmonical Series*, and you see, 1*mo*. That if we take the Number 1, to make an *arithmetical Series* of Three

Three Terms, it can only be join'd with 2 : 3. or 3 : 5, for if you make 4 the middle Term, the other Extreme muſt be 7, which is not in the Series; or if you make 5 the Middle, the other Extreme is 9, which is not in the Series: Now all after 5 are even Numbers, ſo that if you take any of theſe for the middle Term, the other Extreme in *arithmetical Proportion* with them, muſt be an odd Number greater than 5, and no ſuch is to be found in the Series: Therefore there can be no other Combination in which 1 is the leſſer Extreme, but theſe in the *Table*.

2*do*. Take Two for the leaſt Extreme, and the other Two Terms can only be 3 : 4, or 5 : 8; for there is no other odd Number to take as a middle Term, but 3 or 5; and if we take 4 or any even Number, the other Extreme muſt be an even Number, and theſe Three will neceſſarily reduce to ſome of the Forms wherein 1 is concerned, becauſe every even Number is diviſible by 2, and 2 divided by 2 quotes 1. 3*tio*. Take 3 for the leſſer Extreme, the other Two Terms can only be 4, 5; for if 5 is the middle Term, the other Extreme muſt be 7, which is not in the Series: But there are no other Numbers in the Series to be made middle Terms, 3 being the leſſer Extreme, except even Numbers; and 3 being an odd Number, the other Extreme muſt be an odd Number too, but no ſuch is to be found in the *Series* greater than 5. 4*to*. The Number 4 can only joyn with 5, 6, for all the reſt are even Numbers, and where the

the Three Terms are all even Numbers, they are reducible. *5to.* There can be no Combination where 5 is the leaſt Extreme, becauſe all greater Numbers in the *Series* are even; for where one Extreme is odd, the other muſt be odd too, the middle Term being even. *Laſtly.* All the Numbers above 5 being even, are reducible to ſome of the former Caſes: *Therefore* we have found all the poſſible Ways any Line can be divided, that the Sections compared together and with the Whole, may be *harmonical* both in Quantity and Quality, as theſe are explain'd.

PROBLEM VII. To divide a Line into Two Parts, equal to the Whole, ſo as the Parts among themſelves, and each with the Whole ſhall be *Concord*; and to diſcover all the poſſible Ways that this can be done. For the firſt Part of the *Problem*, 'tis plain, that if we take Three Numbers which are all *Concord* among themſelves, and whereof the Two leaſt are equal to the greateſt, then divide the given Line into as many Parts as that greateſt Number contains *Units*, the Point of Diviſion anſwering any of the leſſer Numbers ſolves the *Problem*: So if we divide a Line *A B* into Three Parts, one Third *A C*, and Two Thirds *C B*, or *A D* and *D B* are the Parts ſought, for all theſe are *Concord* 1 : 2, 2 : 3, 1 : 3. *A*—$^{1}_{C}$—$^{2}_{D}$—^{3}*B*

I ſhall next ſhew how many different Ways this *Problem* can be ſolved; and I affirm, that there can be but Seven Solutions contained in the

the following *Table*, in which I have diſtingui-ſhed the Parts and the Whole.

THAT theſe are *harmonical Sections* is plain, becauſe there are no other Numbers here but what belong to the *harmonical Series*; and 'tis remarkable too, that there are no other here but what belong to the *ſimple Concords*. But then to prove, that there can be no other *harmonical Sections*, conſider that no other Number can poſſibly be any radical Term of a *Concord*, beſides theſe of the preceeding *harmonical Series*. Indeed we may take any *Ratio* in many different Numbers, but every *Ratio* can have but one radical Form, and only theſe Numbers are *harmonical*; ſo 5 : 15 is a *compound 5th*, yet 15 is no *harmonical* Number, becauſe 5 : 15 is reducible to 1 : 3; alſo 7 : 14 is an *Octave*, yet neither 7 nor 14 are *harmonical*, ſince they are reducible to 1 : 2. Now ſince all the poſſible *harmonical Ratios*, in their radical Forms, are contained in the *Series*, 'tis plain, that all the poſſible *harmonical Sections* of any Line or Number are to be found, by adding every Number of the *Series* to it ſelf, or every Two together, and taking theſe Numbers for the Two Parts, and their Sum for the whole Line. Now let us conſider how many of ſuch Additions will produce *harmonical Sections*,

Parts.				*Whole.*
1	+	1	=	2
1	+	2	=	3
1	+	3	=	4
1	+	4	=	5
1	+	5	=	6
2	+	3	=	5
3	+	5	=	8

ctions, and what will not: It is certain, that if the Sum of any Two Numbers of the Series be a Number which is not contain'd in it, then the Division of a Line in Two Parts, which are in Proportion as these Two Numbers, can never be *harmonical*; for *Example* the Sum of 3 and 4 is 7, which is not an *harmonical Section*, because 7 is no *harmonical* Number, or is not the radical Number of any *harmonical Ratio*. Again 'tis certain, That if any Two Numbers, with their Sum, are to be found all in the Series, these Numbers constitute an *harmonical Section*. But observe, if the Numbers taken for the Parts are reducible, they must be brought to their radical Form; for the *Concords* made of such Parts as are reducible, must necessarily be the same with these made of their radical Numbers; so if we take 4 and 6 their Sum is 10, and 4 : 6 are harmonical Parts of 10; but then the Case is not different from 2. 3. 5. *Next*, We see that all the Numbers in that Series after the Number 5, are Compounds of the preceeding Numbers, by the continual multiplying of them by 2; therefore we can take no Two Numbers in that Series greater than 5, (for Parts) but what are reducible to 5, and some Number less, or both less; and if we take 5 or any odd Number less, and a Number greater than 5, they can never be harmonical Parts, because their Sum will be an odd Number, and all the Numbers in the Series greater than 5, are even Numbers; therefore that Sum is not in the Series; and if we take

an

an even Number leſs than 5, and a Number greater, the Sum is even and reducible; therefore all the Numbers that can poſſibly make the Two Parts of different *harmonical* Sections, are theſe, 1. 2. 3. 4. 5; and if we add every Two of theſe together, we find no other different *harmonical* Sections but theſe of the preceeding Table, becauſe their Sum is either odd or reducible; and when the Parts are equal, 'tis plain there can be but one ſuch Section, which is 1 : 1 : 2, becauſe all other equal Sections are reducible to this.

---

§ 3. *Containing further Reflections upon the Diviſion of* CHORDS.

WE have ſeen, in the laſt *Table*, that the *harmonical* Diviſions of a Line depend upon the Numbers 2. 3. 4. 5. 6. 7. 8; and if we reflect upon what has been already obſerved of theſe 1. 2. 3. 4. 5. 6. *viz.* That they are *Concord*, comparing every one with every other, we draw this Concluſion, That if a Line is divided into 2 or 3, 4, 5 or 6 Parts, every Section or Number of ſuch Parts with the Whole, or one with another, is *Concord*; becauſe they are all to one another as theſe Numbers 1. 2. 3. 4. 5. 6. I ſhall add now, that, taking in the Number 8, it will ſtill be true of the Series, 1. 2. 3. 4,

4. 5. 6. 8. that every Number with every other is *Concord* ; and here we have the whole *original Concords*. And as to the Conclusion last drawn, it will hold of the Parts of a Line divided into 8 Parts, except the Number 7, which is *Concord* with none of the rest. So that we have here a Method of exhibiting in one Line all the *simple* and *original Concords*, *viz.* by dividing it into 8 equal Parts, and of these, taking , 1. 2. 3. 4. 5. 6. and comparing them together, and with the whole 8.

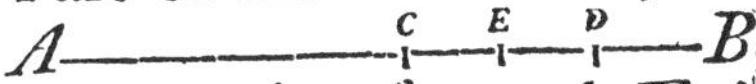

But if it be required to show how a Line may be divided in the most simple Manner to exhibite all these *Concords*; here it is : Divide the Line *A B* into Two equal Parts at *C*; then divide the Part *C B* into Two equal Parts at *D*; and again the Part *C D* into Two equal Parts at *E*. 'Tis plain that *A C* or *C B*, are each a Half of *A B*; and *C D* or *B D* are each equal to a 4*th* Part of the Line *A B*; and *C E* or *E D* are *A*————C—E—D——*B*, each an 8*th* Part of *A B* ; therefore *A E* is equal to Five 8*th* Parts of *A B* ; and *A D* is Six 8*th* Parts, or Three 4*th* Parts of it ; and *A E* is therefore Five 6*th* Parts of *A D*. Again, since *A D* is Three 4*th* Parts of *A B*, and *A C* is a Half, or Two 4*ths* of *A B*, therefore *A C* is Two 3*d* Parts of *A D* ; *then*, because *A E* is Five 8*th* Parts of *A B*, and *A C* Four 8*ths* (or a Half) therefore *A C* is Four 5*ths* of *A E*. *Lastly*, *E B* is Three 8*ths* of *A B*. *Consequently A C* to *A B* is an *Octave*; *A C* to *A D* a 5*th* ; *A D* to *A B*, a 4*th*; *A C* to to *A E* a 3*d g*. *A E* to *A D* a 3*d l*. *A E* to *E B* a 6*th g*. *A E* to *A B* a 6*th l*. which is all agreeable to what has been already explained; for *A C* and *A B* containing the *Octave*, we have *A D* an *arithmetical Mean*, which therefore gives us the 5*th*, with the *acute* Term *A C*, and a 4*th* with the lower Term *A B* of the *Octave*. Again, *A E* is an *arithmetical Mean* betwixt the Extremes of the 5*th* *A C* and *A D*, and gives us all the rest of the *Concords*.

IT will be worth our Pains to consider what *D' Cartes* observes upon this Division of a Line: But in order to the understanding what he says here, I must give you a short Account of some general Premisses he lays down in the Beginning of his Work. Says he, 'Every Sense is capable 'of some Pleasure, to which is required a certain Proportion of the Object to the Organ: 'Which Object must fall regularly, and not very 'difficultly on the Senses, that we may be able 'to perceive every Part distinctly: Hence, 'these Objects are most easily perceived, whose 'Difference of Parts is least, *i. e.* in which there 'is least Difference to be observed; and there-'fore the Proportion of the Parts ought to be '*arithmetical* not *geometrical*; because there 'are fewer Things to be noticed in the *arith-metical Proportion*, since the Differences are 'every where equal, and so does not weary the 'Mind so much in apprehending distinctly e-'very Thing that is in it. He gives us this 'Example: Says he, 'The Proportion of these

'Lines

' Lines $\begin{smallmatrix}2 \\ 3 \\ 4\end{smallmatrix}$ is easier distinguished by the ' Eye, than the Proportion of these $\begin{smallmatrix}2 \\ \sqrt{8} \\ 4\end{smallmatrix}$ ' because in the first we have nothing to notice ' but that the common Difference of the Lines ' is 1.' He makes not the Application of this expresly to the Ear, by considering the Number of Strokes or Impulses made upon it at the same Time, by Motions of various Velocities; and what Similitude that has to perceiving the Difference of Parts by the Eye: He certainly thought the Application plain; and takes it also for granted, That one Sound is to another in *Tune*, as the Lengths of Two Chords, *cæteris paribus*. From these Premisses he proceeds to find the *Concords* in the Division of a Line, and observes, That if it be divided into 2, 3, 4, 5, or 6 equal Parts, all the Sections are *Concord*; the first and best *Concord Octave* proceeds from dividing the Line by the first of all Numbers 2, and the next best by the next Number 3, and so on to the Number 6. But then, says he, we can proceed no further, because the Weakness of our Senses cannot easily distinguish greater Differences of Sounds: But he forgot the *6th* lesser, which requires a Division by 8, tho' he elsewhere owns it as *Concord*. We shall next consider what he says upon the preceeding Division of the Line *A B*, from which he proposes to show how all the other *Concords* are contained in the *Octave*, and proceed from the Division of it, that their Nature may be more distinctly known. Take it in his own

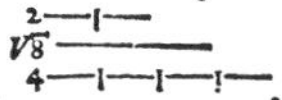

own Words, as near as I can tranſlate them.
" *Firſt* then, from the Thing premiſed it is
" certain,this Diviſion ought to be *arithmetical*,
" or into equal Parts, and what that is which
" ought to be divided is plain in the Chord *A B*,
" which is diſtant from *A C* by the Part *C B*;
" but the Sound of *A B*, is diſtant from the
" Sound of *A C* by an *Octave*; therefore the
" Part *C B* ſhall be the Space or *Interval* of an
" *Octave*: This is it therefore which ought to
" be divided into Two equal Parts to have the
" whole *Octave* divided, which is done in the
" Point *D*; and that we may know what *Con-*
" *cord* is generated properly and by it ſelf (*pro-*
" *prie & per ſe*, as he calls it) by this Diviſion,
" we muſt conſider, that the Line *A B*, which
" is the *lower* or *graver* Term of the *Octave*,
" is divided in *D*, not in order to it ſelf (*non*
" *in ordine ad ſeipſum*, I ſuppoſe he means not
" in order to a Compariſon of *A D* with *A B*)
" for then it would be divided in *C*, as is al-
" ready done (for *A C* compared to *A B* makes
" the *Octave*) neither do we now divide the
" *Uniſon* (*viz.* *A B*) but the *Octave*, (*viz.* the
" *Interval* of 8*ve*,which is *C B*,as he ſaid alrea-
" dy) which conſiſts of Two Terms; therefore
" while the *graver* Term is divided,that's done
" in order to the *acuter* Term, not in order to
" it ſelf. Hence the *Concord* which is properly
" generated by that Diviſion, is betwixt
" the Terms *A C* and *A D*, which is a 5*th*,
" not betwixt *A D*, *A B*, which is a 4*th*; for
" the Part *D B* is only a Remainder, and
" generates

" generates a *Concord* by Accident, becauſe
" that whatever Sound is *Concord* with one
" Term of *Octave*, ought alſo to be *Concord*
" with the other." In the ſame Manner he argues, that the *3d g.* proceeds *properly*, *& per ſe* out of the Diviſion of the *5th*, at the Point *E*, whereby we have *A E* a *3d g.* to the *acute* Term of the *5th*, *viz.* to *A C* (for *A C* to *A D* is *5th*) and all the reſt of the *Concords* are accidental; and thus alſo he makes the *tonus major* (of which afterwards) to proceed directly from the *3d g.* and the *tonus minor* and *Semitones* to be all accidental: And to ſhow that this is not an imaginary Thing, when he ſays, the *5th* and *3d g.* proceed *properly* from the Diviſion of *Octave*, and the reſt by Accident, he ſays, He found it by Experience in ſtringed Inſtruments, that if one String is ſtruck, the Motion of it ſhakes all the Strings that are *acuter* by any Species of *5th* or *3d g.* but not theſe that are *4th* or other *Concord*; which can only proceed, ſays he, from the Perfection of theſe *Concords*, or the Imperfection of the other, *viz.* that the firſt are *Concords per ſe*, and the others *per accidens*, becauſe they flow neceſſarily from them. *D' Cartes* ſeems to think it a Demonſtration *a priori* from his Premiſſes, that if there is ſuch a Thing as *Concord* among Sounds, it muſt proceed from the *arithmetical* Diviſion of a Line into 2. 3, *&c.* Parts, and that the more ſimple produce the better *Concords*. 'Tis true, that Men muſt have known by Experience, that there was ſuch a Thing as *Concord* before they

they reaſoned about it; but whether the general Reflection which he makes upon Nature, be ſufficient to conclude that ſuch Diviſion muſt infallibly produce ſuch *Concords*, I don't ſo clearly ſee; yet I muſt own his Reaſoning is very ingenious, excepting the ſubtil Diſtinction of *Concords per ſe & per accidens*, which I don't very well underſtand; but let every one take them as they can.

CHAP. VII.

Of HARMONY, *explaining the Nature and Variety of it, as it depends upon the various Combinations of* concording *Sounds.*

IN *Chap.* II. § 1. I ſhewed you the Diſtinction that is made betwixt the Word *Concord*, which is the Agreement of Two Sounds conſidered either in *Conſonance* or *Succeſſion*, and *Harmony*, which is the Agreement of more, conſidered always in *Conſonance*, and requires at leaſt Three Sounds. In order to produce a perfect *Harmony*, there muſt be no *Diſcord*

cord found between any Two of the simple Sounds; but each must be in some Degree of *Concord* to all the rest. Hence *Harmony* is very well defined, *The Sum of* CONCORDS arising from the Combination of Two or more *Concords*, *i. e.* of Three or more simple Sounds striking the Ear all together; and different Compositions of *Concords* make different *Harmony*.

To understand the Nature, and determine the Number and Preference of *Harmonies*, we must consider, that in every *compound* Sound, where there are more than Two *Simples*, we have Three Things observable, 1*st*. The *primary Relation* of every *simple* Sound to the *Fundamental* (or *gravest*) whereby they make different Degrees of *Concord* with it. 2*dly*. The *mutual Relations* of the *acuter* Sounds each with another, whereby they mix either *Concord* or *Discord* into the *Compound*. 3*dly*. The *secondary Relation* of the Whole, whereby all the Terms unite their Vibrations, or coincide more or less frequently.

THE Two first of these depend upon one another, and upon them depends the last. Let us suppose Four Sounds *A. B. C. D.* whereof *A* is the *gravest*, *B* next *acuter*, then *C*, and *D* the *acutest*; *A* is called the *Fundamental*, and the Relations of *B*, *C*, and *D*, to *A*, are *primary Relations*: So if *B* is a 3*d g.* above *A*, that *primary Relation* is 4 to 5; and if *C* is 5*th* to *A*, that *primary Relation* is 2 to 3; and if *D* is 8*ve* to *A*, that is 1 to 2. *Again*, to find the *mutual Relations* of all the *acute* Terms

B C,

B, *C*, *D*, we muſt take their *primary Relations* to the *Fundamental*, and ſubſtract each leſſer from each greater, by the Rule of *Subſtraction* of *Intervals*; ſo in the preceeding *Example*, *B* to *C* is 5 to 6, a 3*d l*. *B* to *D* is 5 to 8, a 6*th l*. and *C* to *D* 3 to 4, a 4*th*. Or, if we take all the *primary Relations*, and reduce them to one common *Fundamental*, by *Probl*. 3. *Chap*. 4. we ſhall ſee all the *mutual Relations* in one Series; ſo the preceeding *Example* is 30. 24. 20. 15.

AGAIN, having the *mutual Relations* of each Sound to the next in any Series, we may find the *primary Relations*, by *Addition* of *Intervals*; and then by theſe all the reſt of the *mutual Relations*; or reduce the given Relations to a continued Series by *Probl*. 2. *Chap*. 4. and then all will appear at once. *Laſtly*, to find the *ſecondary Relation* of the Whole, find the leaſt common Dividend to all the leſſer Terms or Numbers of the *primary Relations*, *i. e.* the leaſt Number that will be divided by each of them exactly without a Remainder; that is the Thing ſought, and ſhows that all the ſimple Sounds coincide after every ſo many Vibrations of the *Fundamental* as that Number found expreſſes: So in the preceeding *Example*, the leſſer Terms of the Three *primary Relations* are 4. 2. 1. whoſe leaſt common Dividend is 4, therefore at every Fourth Vibration of the *Fundamental* the Whole will coincide; and this is what I call the *ſecondary Relation* of the Whole. I ſhall firſt ſhow how in every Caſe you may find

find this leaſt Dividend, and then explain how it expreſſes the Coincidence of the Whole.

PROBLEM. To find the leaſt common Dividend to any given Numbers. *Rule.* 1*mo.* If each greater of the given Numbers is a Multiple of each leſſer, then the greateſt of them is the Thing ſought; as in the preceeding *Example.* 2*do.* If 'tis not ſo, but ſome of them are commenſurable together, others not; take the greateſt of all that are commenſurable, and, paſſing their *aliquot* Parts, multiply them together, and with the reſt of the Numbers continually, the laſt Product is the Number ſought. *Example.* 2. 3. 4. 6. 8. Here 2. 4. 8, are commenſurable, and 8 their leaſt Dividend; alſo 3. 6 commenſurable and 6 their leaſt Dividend: Then 8. 6. multiplied together produce 48, the Number ſought. Take another *Example.* 2. 3. 5. 4. Here 2 . 4 are commenſurable and all the reſt incommenſurable, therefore I multiply 3. 4. 5. continually, the Product is 60 the Number ſought. 3*tio.* If all the Numbers are incommenſurable, multiply them all continually, and the laſt Product is the Anſwer. *Example.* 2. 3. 5. 7. the Product is 210. The Reaſon of this *Rule* is obvious from the Nature of *Multiplication* and *Diviſion.*

NOW I ſhall ſhow that the leaſt common Dividend to the leſſer Terms of any Number of *primary Relations*, expreſſes the Vibrations of the *Fundamental* to every Coincidence. Thus, of the Numbers that expreſs the *Ratio* of any *Interval*, the leſſer is the Length of the *acuter* Chord,

Chord, and the greater the Length of the *graver*: Or reciprocally, the leſſer is the Number of Vibrations of the longer, and the greater the Vibrations of the ſhorter Chord, that are performed in the ſame Time; *conſequently* the leſſer Numbers of all the *primary Relations* of any *compound* Sound, are the Numbers of the Vibrations of the common *Fundamental* which go to each Coincidence thereof with the ſeveral *acute* Terms; but 'tis plain if the *Fundamental* coincide with any *acute* Term after every 3 (for *Example*) of its own Vibrations, it will alſo coincide with it after every 6 or 9, or other Multiple, or Number of Vibrations which is diviſible by 3, and ſo of any other Number; conſequently the leaſt Number which can be exactly divided by every one of the Numbers of Vibrations of the *Fundamental*, which go to a Coincidence with the ſeveral *acute* Terms, muſt be the Vibrations of that *Fundamental* at which every total Coincidence is performed. For *Example*, ſuppoſe a common *Fundamental* coincide with any *acute* Term after 2 of its own Vibrations, and with another at 3; then whatever the *mutual Relation* of theſe Two *acute* Terms is, it is plain they cannot both together coincide with that *Fundamental*, till Six Vibrations of it be finiſhed; and at that Number preciſely they muſt; for the *Fundamental* coinciding with the one at 2, and with the other at 3, muſt coincide with each of them at Six; and no ſooner can they all coincide, becauſe 6 is the leaſt Multiple to both 2 and 3: Or thus,
the

the *Fundamental* coinciding with the one after 2, muſt coincide with that one alſo after 4. 6. 8. *&c.* ſtill adding 2 more; and coinciding with the other after 3. muſt coincide with it alſo after 6. 9. 12. *&c.* ſtill adding 3 more; ſo that they cannot all coincide till after 6. becauſe that is the leaſt Number which is common to both the preceeding Series of Coincidences. Next for the Application of this to *Harmony.*

HARMONY is a *compound* Sound conſiſting (as we take it here) of Three or more *ſimple* Sounds; the proper Ingredients of it are *Concords*; and therefore all *Diſcords* in the *primary Relations* eſpecially, and alſo in the *mutual Relations* of the ſeveral *acute* Terms are abſolutely forbidden.

'TIS true that *Diſcords* are uſed in *Muſick*, but not for themſelves ſimply; they are uſed as Means to make the *Concords* appear more agreeable by the Oppoſition; but more of this in another Place.

NOW any Number of *Concords* being propoſed to ſtand in *primary Relation* with a common *Fundamental*; we diſcover whether or no they conſtitute a perfect *Harmony*, by finding their *mutual Relations*. *Example.* Suppoſe theſe *primary Intervals*, which are *Concords*, *viz.* 3*d g.* 5*th*, 8*ve*, their *mutual Relations* are all *Concord*, and therefore can ſtand in *Harmony*; for the 3*d g.* and 5*th*, are to one another as 5 : 6 a 3*d. l.* The 3*d g.* and *Octave* as 5 : 8, a 6*th l.* the 5*th* and *Octave* are as 3 : 4, a

4*th*

4th; as appears in this Series to which the given Relations are reduced, *viz.* 30 : 24 : 20 : 15. *Again*, take *4th*, *5th*, and *Octave*, they cannot ſtand together, becauſe betwixt the *4th* and *5th* is a *Diſcord*, the *Ratio* being 8 : 9. Or ſuppoſing any Number of Sounds, which are *Concord* each to the next, from the loweſt to the higheſt; to know if they can ſtand in *Harmony* we muſt find their *primary Relations*, and all the other *mutual Relations*, which muſt be all *Concord*; ſo let any Number of Sounds be as 4 : 5 : 6 : 8 they can ſtand in *Harmony*, becauſe each to each is *Concord*; but theſe cannot 4. 6. 9, becauſe 4 : 9 is *Diſcord*.

WE have conſidered the neceſſary Conditions for making *Harmony*, from which it will be eaſy to enumerate or give a general Table of all the poſſible Variety; but let us firſt examine how the Preference of *Harmonies* is to be determined; and here comes in the Conſideration of the *ſecondary Relations*. Now upon all the Three Things mentioned, *viz.* the *primary*, *ſecondary*, and *mutual Relations*, does the Perfection of *Harmonies* depend; ſo that Regard muſt be had to them all in making a right Judgment: It is not the beſt *primary Relation* that makes beſt *Harmony*; for then a *4th* and *5th* muſt be better than a *4th* and *6th*; yet the firſt Two cannot ſtand together, becauſe of the *Diſcord* in their *mutual Relation*: Nor does the beſt *ſecondary Relation* carry it; for then alſo would a *4th* and *5th*, whoſe *ſecondary Relation* with a common *Fundamental*

damental is 6, be better than 3*d l.* and 5*th*, whose *secondary Relation* is 10; but here also the Preference is due to the better *mutual Relation* of the 3*d l.* and 5*th*, which is a 3*d g.* and a 4*th* and *Octave* would be equal to a 6*th g.* and *Octave*, the *secondary Relation* of both being 3, which cannot possibly be, the Ingredients being different. As to the *mutual Relations*, they depend altogether upon the *primary*, yet not so as that the best *primary Relation* shall always produce the best *mutual Relation*; for 'tis contrary when two Terms are joyned to a *Fundamental*; so a 5*th* and *Octave* contain betwixt them a 4*th*; and a 4*th* and *Octave* contain a 5*th*. But the *primary Relations* are by far more considerable, and, with the *secondary*, afford us the following Rule for determining the Preference of *Harmony*, in which that must always be taken for a necessary Condition, that there be no *Discord* among any of the Terms; therefore this is the Rule, that comparing Two *Harmonies* (which have an equal Number of Terms) that which has both the best *primary* and *secondary Relation*, is most perfect; but in Two Cases, where the Advantage is in the *primary Relations* of the one, and in the *secondary* of the other, we have no certain Rule; the *primary Relations* are the principal and most considerable Things; but how the Advantage here ought to be proportioned to the Disadvantage in the *secondary*, or contrarily, in order to judge of the comparative Perfection, is a Thing we know not how to determine;

and

and therefore a well tuned Ear muſt be the laſt Reſort in theſe Caſes.

LET us next take a View of the poſſible Combinations of *Concords* that conſtitute *Harmony*; in order to which conſider, That as we diſtinguiſhed *Concords* into *ſimple* and *compound*, ſo is *Harmony* diſtinguiſhable: That is *ſimple Harmony*, where there is no *Concord* to the *Fundamental* above an *Octave*, and it is *compound*, which to the *ſimple Harmony* of one *Octave*, adds that of another *Octave*. The Ingredients of *ſimple Harmony* are the 7 *ſimple original Concords*, of which there can be but 18 different Combinations that are *Harmony*, which I have placed in the following *Table*.

TABLE of HARMONIES.

	2*dry* *Rel.*		2*dry* *Rel.*	
5th *8ve*	2	*3d g. 5th*	4	*3d g. 5th, 8ve*
4th *8ve*	3	*3d l. 5th*	10	*3d l. 5th, 8ve*
6th g. 8ve	3	*4th, 6th g.*	3	*4th, 6th g. 8ve*
3d g. 8ve	4	*3d g. 6th g.*	12	*3d g. 6th g. 8ve*
3d l. 8ve	5	*3d l. 6th l.*	5	*3d l. 6th l. 8ve*
6th l. 8ve	5	*4th, 6th l.*	15	*4th, 6th l. 8ve.*

IF we reflect on what has been explained of theſe *original Concords*, we ſee plainly that here are all the poſſible Combinations that make *Harmony*; for the *Octave* is compoſed of a *5th* and *4th*, or a *6th* and *3d*, which have a Variety of greater and leſſer: Out of theſe are the

the firſt Six Harmonies compoſed ; then the *5th* being compoſed of *3d g.* and *3d. l.* and the *6th* of *4th* and *3d*, from theſe proceed the next Six of the Table ; then an *Octave* joyned to each of theſe Six, make the laſt Six.

Now the firſt 12 Combinations have each 2 Terms added to the *Fundamental*, and their Perfection is according to the Order of the Table : Of the firſt 6 each has an *Octave* ; and their Preference is according to the Perfection of the other leſſer *Concord* joyned to that *Octave*, as that has been already determined ; and with this alſo agrees the Perfection of their *ſecondary Relations.* For the next 6, the Preference is given to the Two Combinations with the *5th*, whereof that which hath the *3d g.* is beſt ; then to the Two Combinations with the *6th g.* of which that which has the *4th* is beſt : Then follows the Combinations with the *6th l.* where the *3d l.* is preferred to the *4th*, for the great Advantage of the *ſecondary Relation*, which does more than balance the Advantage of the *4th* above the *3d l.* So that in theſe Six we have not followed the Order of the *ſecondary Relations*, nor altogether the Order of the *primary*, as in the laſt Caſe. Then come in the laſt Place the Six Combinations ariſing from the Diviſion of the *Octave*, into 3 *Concords*, which I have placed laſt, not becauſe they are leaſt perfect, but becauſe they are moſt *complex*, and are the Mixtures of the other 12 one with another ; and for their Perfection, they are plainly preferable to the immediately pre-

preceeding Six, because they have the very same Ingredients, and an *Octave* more, which does not alter the *secondary Relation*, and so are equal to them in that Respect; but as they have an *Octave*, they are much preferable; and being compared with the first Six, they have the same Ingredients, with the Addition of one *Concord* more, which does indeed alter the *secondary Relations*, and make the Composition more sensible, but ye adds an agreeable Sweetness, for which in some Respect they are preferable.

FOR *compound Harmony*, I shall leave you to find the Variety for your selves out of the Combinations of the *simple Harmonies* of several *Octaves*. And *observe*, That we may have *Harmony* when none of the *primary Intervals* are within an *Octave*, as if to a *Fundamental* be joyned a *5th* above *Octave*, and a double *Octave*. Of such *Harmonies* the *secondary Relations* are ever equal to those of the *simple Harmonies*, whose *primary Intervals* have the same Denomination; and in Practice they are reckoned the same, tho' seldom are any such used.

I have brought all the Combinations of *Concords* into the Table of *Harmony* which answer to that general Character, *viz.* That there must be no Discord among any of the Terms; yet these few Things must be observed. 1*mo*. That in Practice *Discords* are in some Circumstances admitted, not for themselves, simply considered, but to prepare the Mind for a greater Relish of the succeeding more perfect *Harmony*. 2*do*. That tho' the *4th*, taken by it self, is *Concord*, and

and in the next Degree to the *5th*; yet in Practice 'tis reckoned a *Discord* when it ſtands next to the *Fundamental*; and therefore theſe Combinations of the preceeding Table, where it poſſeſſes that Place, are not to be admitted as *Harmonics*; but 'tis admitted in every other Part of the *Harmony*, ſo that the *4th* is *Concord* or *Discord*, according to the Situation; for Example, if betwixt the Extremes of an *Octave* is placed an *arithmetical Mean*, we have it divided into a *4th* and a *5th* 2. 3. 4. which Numbers, if we apply to the Vibrations of Chords, then the *5th* is next the *Fundamental*, and the *ſecondary Relation* is in this Caſe, 2. But take an *harmonical* Mean, as here 3. 4. 6. and the *4th* is next the *Fundamental*, and the *ſecondary Relation* is 3. Now in theſe Two Caſes, the component Parts being the ſame, *viz.* a *4th*, *5th*, *8ve*, differing only in the Poſition of the *4th* and *5th*, which occaſions the Difference of the *ſecondary Relation*, the different Effects can only be laid on the different Poſitions of the *4th* and *5th*; which Effect can only be meaſured by the *ſecondary Relation*; and by Experience we find that the beſt *ſecondary Relation* makes the beſt Compoſition, ſo 2. 3. 4. is better than 3 : 4 : 6 : And thus in all Caſes, where the ſame *Interval* is divided into the ſame Parts differently ſituated, the Preference will anſwer to the *ſecondary Relation*, the leſſer making the beſt Compoſition, which plainly depends upon the primary Relation; but the *4th* next the *Fundamental* is not only worſe than the

5th

5*th*, but is reckoned *Discord* in that Position; and therefore all the other Combinations of the Table are preferr'd to it, or rather it is quite rejected; the Reason assigned for this is, that the *graver* Sounds are the most powerful, and raise our Attention most; so that the 4*th* being next the *Fundamental*, its Imperfection compared with the *Octave* and 5*th* is made more remarkable, and consequently it must be less agreeable than when it is heard alone; whereas when it stands next the *acute* Term of the *Octave*, that Imperfection is drowned by its being between the 5*th* and *Octave*, both in *primary* Relation to the *Fundamental*. But this does not hold in the 6*th* and 3*d*, because they differ not in their Perfection so much as the 5*th* and 4*th*. But we shall hear *D' Cartes* reasoning upon this. Says he, *Hæc infælicissima*,&c. *The* 4th *is the most unhappy of all the* Concords, *and never admitted in Songs, but by Accident* (he means not next the *Fundamental*, but as it falls accidentally among the mutual Relations) *not that it is more imperfect than the* 3d *or* 6th, *but because it is too near the* 5th, *and loses its Sweetness by this Neighbourhood; for understanding which we must notice, That a* 5th *is never heard, but the acuter* 4th *seems some way to resound, which is a Consequent of what was said before, that the* Fundamental *never sounds but the* acuter Octave *seems to do so too.*

LET the Lines A C *and* D B *be a* 5th, *and the Line* E F, *an* acuter Octave *to* A C, *it will be a* 4th *to* D B; *and if it resound to the* Fundamental

damental, *then, when the* 5th *is sounded with the* Fundamental, *this Resonance is a* 4th *above the* 5th *that always follows it, which is the Reason it is not admitted next the* Bass; *for since all the rest of the* Concords *in* Musick *are only useful for varying of the* 5th, *certainly the* 4th *which does not so is useless, which is plain from this, That if we put it next the* Bass, *the* acuter 5th *will resound, and there the Ear will observe it out of its Place, therefore the* 4th *would be very displeasing, as if we had the Shadow for the Substance, an Image for the real Thing.* Elsewhere he says it serves in Composition where the same Reason occurs not, which hinders its standing next the Bass. It is well observed, that the rest of the *simple Concords* serve only for varying the *5th*; Variety is certainly the Life of all sensual Pleasure, without which the more exquisite but cloy the sooner; and in *Musick*, were there no more *Concords* but *Octave* and *5th*, it would prove a very poor Fund of Pleasure; but we have more, and agreeable to *D' Cartes*'s Notion, we may say, They are all designed to vary the *5th*, for they all proceed from it, as we saw in the Divisions of the upper and lower *5th* of the *Octave* in *Chap.* 5. and that all the Variety in *Musick* proceeds from these *3ds* and *6ths* arising from the Division of the *5th* directly or accidentally, as we shall see more particularly afterwards: Mean time observe, that as the *4th* rises naturally from the Division of the *Octave*, so it serves

ſerves to vary it, and accordingly is admitted in Compoſition in every Part but next the *Fundamental* or *Baſs*; for the 5*th* being more perfect and capable of Variety (which the 4*th* is not, ſince no leſſer *Concord* agrees to both its Extremes) by Means of the 3*ds*, ought to ſtand next the *Fundamental*. Now if the 4*th* muſt not ſtand with the *Fundamental*, then this 4*th*, with the *Octave*, muſt not be reckoned among *ſimple Harmonies*. To prove that the 4*th* conſidered by it ſelf is a *Concord*, *Kircher* makes a very odd Argument. Says he, A 4*th* added to a 5*th* makes an *Octave*, which is Concord; but *nothing gives what it has not*, therefore the 4*th* is a Concord: But by the ſame Argument you may prove that any *Interval* leſs than *Octave* is a *Concord*.

I have obſerved of the Series 1. 2. 3. 4. 5. 6. 8. that they are *Concords* each with other. They contain all the *original Concords*, and the chief of the *compound*; and they ſtand in ſuch Order that Seven Sounds in the Proportions and Order of this Series joyned in one *Harmony* is the moſt complete and perfect that can be heard: For here we have the chief and principal of all the *Harmonies* of the preceeding Table, as you'll ſee by comparing theſe Numbers with that *Table*; ſo that in this ſhort and ſimple Series we have the whole eſſential Principles and Ingredients of *Muſick*; and all at once the moſt agreeable Effect that Sounds in *Conſonance* can have.

LET-

LET us now consider how these Sounds may be raised; this will be easily found from the Things already explained; but we must first observe, that there will be a great Difference betwixt applying these Numbers to the Lengths of Chords, and to their Vibrations: If they are applied to the *Chords*, then 'tis easy to find Seven Chords which shall be as these Seven Numbers; but 8 being the longest Chord, the less perfect *Concords* stand in *primary Relation* to the *Fundamental*; and the secondary Relation is 15: But if we have Seven Sounds whose Vibrations are as these Numbers, then 1 is the Vibration of the *Fundamental*, and so on in Order to 8 the Vibration of the *acutest* performed in the same Time: And thus the best *Concords* stand in *primary* Relation to the *Fundamental*, and 1 is the *secondary* Relation: . Therefore to afford this most perfect *Harmony*, we must find Seven Sounds which from the lowest to the highest shall be as 1 : 2 : 3 : 4 : 5 : 6 : 8, the least Number representing the *gravest* Sound. Now, to do this, let us mind that the Lengths of Chords are in simple reciprocal Proportion of their Vibrations accomplished in the same Time, out of which I shall draw the Two following *Problems*, whereof the first shall solve the Question in hand.

PROBLEM I. To find the Lengths of several Chords, whose Vibrations performed in the same Time, shall be as a given Rank of Numbers. *Rule*. Take the given Series, and out of it find another reciprocal to it, by *Theor*. 14.

Chap.

Chap. 4. which, according to the Demonſtration there given, and what I have premiſed here, is the Series of Lengths ſought, ſo the preceeding Series 1. 2. 3. 4. 5. 6. 8. being given as a Series of Vibrations performed in the ſame Time, the Lengths of Seven Chords, to which that Series of Vibrations agrees, are 120. 60. 40. 30. 24. 20. 15. And theſe Seven Chords being in every other Reſpect equal and alike, and all ſounded together, ſhall produce the *Harmony* required.

PROBLEM II. The Lengths of ſeveral Chords being given, to find the Number of Vibrations of each performed in the ſame Time. This is done the ſame Way as the former: And ſo if the Series 1. 2. 3. 4. 5. 6. 8. *&c.* be the Length of Seven Chords, their Vibrations ſought are 120. 60. 40. 30. 24. 20. 15.

NOTE, From what has been explained in *Theor.* 14. *Chap.* 4. we ſee that if one of theſe, *viz.* the Lengths of ſeveral Chords, or their Vibrations accompliſhed in the ſame Time, make a *continued arithmetical* or *harmonical* Series, the other will be reciprocally an *harmonical* or *arithmetical* Series, ſo the preceeding Series 1. 2. 3. 4. 5. 6. being *continuedly arithmetical*, its correſpondent Series 120. 60. 40. 30. 24. 20. is *continuedly harmonical*; but the Number 8 in the firſt Series interrupts the *arithmetical Proportion*, and ſo is the *harmonical Proportion* interrupted by its Correſpondent 15. But as in the firſt, 2. 4. 6. 8. are *continuedly arithmetical*, ſo are theſe correſpondent to them in the other

harmo-

harmonical, *viz.* 60 : 30 : 20 : 15. Alſo it will hold univerſally, that taking any Numbers out of the one Series in *continued arithmetical* or *harmonical Proportion*, their Correſpondents in the other will be reciprocally *harmonical* or *arithmetical.*

CHAP. VIII.

Of concinnous Intervals, *and the* Scale of Muſick.

§ 1. *Of the Neceſſity and Uſe of* concinnous Diſcords, *and of their Original and Dependence on the* Concords.

WE have, in the preceeding *Chapters*, conſidered the firſt and moſt eſſential Principles [as far as concerns the firſt Part of the Definition] of *Muſick*, *viz.* theſe Relations of Sound in *Acuteneſs* and *Gravity* whoſe Extremes are *Concord*; for without theſe there can be no *Muſick*: The indefinite Number of other *Ratios* being all *Diſcord*, belong not eſſentially to *Muſick*, becauſe of themſelves felves they produce no Pleafure; yet fome of them are admitted into the *Syftem* as neceffary to the better being of it, both with refpect to *Confonance* and *Succeffion*, but moft remarkably in this; and fuch are called *concinnous Intervals*, as being apt or fit for the Improvement of *Mufick*: All other *Difcords* are called *inconcinnous*. To explain what thefe *concinnous Intervals* are, their Number, Nature and Office, fhall employ this *Chapter*.

IN order to which, I fhall firft offer the following Confiderations, to prove that fome other than the *harmonical Intervals* of Sound (*i. e.* fuch whofe Extremes are *Concord*) are neceffary for the Improvement or better Being of *Mufick*.

WE know by Experience how much the Mind of Man is delighted with Variety: It can ftand no Difpute, whether we confider intellectual or fenfible Pleafures; every one will be confcious of it to himfelf: If you ask the Reafon, I can only anfwer, That we are made fo: And if we apply this Rule to *Mufick*, then it is plain the more Variety there is in it, it will be the more entertaining, unlefs it proceed to an Excefs; for fo limited are our Capacities, that too much or too little are equally fatal to our Pleafures. Let us then confider what muft be the Effect of having no other but *harmonical Intervals* in the *Syftem* of *Mufick*, and,

Firft, With refpect to a fingle Voice, if that fhould move always from one Degree of *Tune* to another, fo as every Note or Sound to the next

next were in the *Ratio* of ſome *Concord*, the Variety which we happily know to be the Life of *Muſick* would ſoon be exhauſted. For to move by no other than *harmonical Intervals*, would not only want Variety, and ſo weary us with a tedious Repetition of the ſame Things; but the very Perfection of ſuch Relations of Sounds would cloy the Ear, in the ſame Manner as ſweet and luſcious Things do the Taſte, which are therefore artfully ſeaſoned with the Mixture of ſowr and bitter: And ſo in *Muſick* the Perfection of the *harmonical Intervals* are ſet off, and as 'twere ſeaſoned with other Kinds of *Intervals* that are never agreeable by themſelves, but only in order to make the Agreement of the other more various and remarkable. *D' Cartes* has a Notion here that's worth our conſidering. He obſerves, that an *acute* Sound requires a greater Force to produce it either in the Motion of the vocal Organs of an Animal, or in ſtriking a String; which we know by Experience, ſays he, in Strings, for the more they are ſtretched they become the *acuter*, and require the greater Force to move them: And hence he concludes, that *acute* Sounds, or the Motion of the Air that produce them immediately, ſtrike the Ear with more Force: From which Obſervations he thinks may be drawn the true and primary Reaſon why *Degrees* (which are *Intervals* leſs than any *Concord*) were invented; which Reaſon he judges to be this, Leſt if the Voice did always proceed by *harmonical* Diſtances, there ſhould be too great Diſproportion

tion or Inequality in the *Intenseness* of it (by which *Intenseness* he plainly means that Force with which it is produced, and with which also it strikes the Ear) which would weary both Singer and Hearer. For *Example.* Let *A* and *B* be at the Distance of a greater 3*d*, if one would ascend from *A* to *B*, then because *B* being acuter strikes the Ear with more Force than *A*; lest that Disproportion should prove uneasy, another Sound *C* is put between them, by which as by a Step we may ascend more easily, and with less unequal Force in raising the Voice. Hence it appears, says he, that the *Degrees* are nothing but a certain *Medium* contrived to be put betwixt the Extremes of the *Concords*, for moderating their Inequality, but of themselves they have not Sweetness enough to satisfy the Ear, and are of Use only with regard to the *Concords*; so that when the Voice has moved one Degree, the Ear is not yet satisfied till we come to another, which therefore must be *Concord* with the first Sound. Thus far *D' Cartes* reasons on this Matter; the Substance of what he says being plainly this, *viz.* That by a fit Division of the *concording Intervals* into lesser Ones, the Voice will pass smoothly from one Note to another, and the Hearer be prepared for a more exquisite Relish of the perfecter *Intervals*, whose Extremes are the proper Points in which the Ear finds the expected Rest and Pleasure. Yet moving by *harmonical* Distances is also necessary, but not so frequently: The Thing therefore required as

to

to this Part is, ſuch *Intervals* leſs than any *harmonical* one, which ſhall divide theſe, in order that the Movement of a Sound from their one Extreme to another, by theſe *Degrees*, may be ſmooth and agreeable; and by the Variety improve the more eſſential Principles of *Muſick* to a Capacity of affording greater Pleaſure, and all together make a more perfect *Syſtem*.

2*dly*. LET us conſider *Muſick* in *Parts*, *i. e.* when Two or more Voices joyn in *Conſonance*; the *general Rule* is, That the ſucceſſive Sounds of each be ſo ordered, that the ſeveral Voices ſhall always be *Concord*. Now there ought to be a Variety in the Choice of theſe *ſucceſſive Concords*, and alſo in the Method of their Succeſſions; but all this depends upon the Movements of the ſingle *Parts*. And if theſe could move in an agreeable Manner only by *harmonical* Diſtances, there are but a few different Ways in which they could remove from *Concord* to *Concord*; and hereby we ſhould loſe very much of the Raviſhment of Sounds in *Conſonance*. As to this Part then, the Thing demanded is, a Variety of Ways, whereby each ſingle Voice of more in *Conſonance* may move agreeably in their *ſucceſſive* Sounds, ſo as to paſs from *Concord* to *Concord*, and meet at every Note in the ſame or a different *Concord* from what they ſtood at in the laſt Note. In what Caſes and for what Reaſons *Diſcords* are allowed, the *Rules* of *Compoſition* muſt teach: But joyn theſe Two Conſiderations, and you ſee manifeſtly how imperfect *Muſick* would be without

out any other *Intervals* than *Concords*; tho' these are the principal and most essential, and the others we now enquire into but subservient to them, for varying and illustrating the Pleasure that arises immediately out of the *harmonical Kind*.

But, *lastly*, consider, that tho' the *Melody* of a single Voice is very agreeable, yet no *Consonance* of *Parts* can have a good Effect separately from the other; therefore the Degrees which answer the first Demand, must serve the other too, else, however perfect the *System* be as to the first Case, it will be still imperfect as to the last.

When a *Question* is about the Agreeableness of any Thing to the Senses, the last Appeal must be to Experience, the only infallible Judge in these Cases; and so in *Musick* the Ear must inform us of what is good and bad; and nothing ought to be received without its Approbation. We have seen to what Purposes other *Intervals* than the *harmonical* are necessary; now we shall see what they are; and agreeable to what has been said, we shall make *Experience* the Judge, which approves of those, and those only, with their *Dependents* (besides the *harmonical Intervals*) as Parts of the true *natural System* of *Musick*, *viz.* whose *Ratios* are 8 : 9. called a *greater Tone*, 9 : 10 called a *lesser Tone*, and 15 : 16 called a *Semitone*: And these are the lesser *Intervals*, particularly called *Degrees*, by which a Sound can move upwards or downwards successively, from one Extreme

treme of any *harmonical Interval* to another, and produce true *Melody*; and by Means whereof alſo ſeveral Voices are capable of the neceſſary Variety in paſſing from *Concord* to *Concord.* By the *Dependents* of theſe Degrees, I mean their Compounds with *Octave*, (which are underſtood to be the ſame Thing in Practice, as we obſerved in another Place of *compound Concords*) and their *Complements* to an *Octave* (or Differences from it) *viz.* 9 : 16, 5 : 9, 8 : 15, which are alſo a Part of the *Syſtem*, tho' more imperfect, but of theſe afterwards: As to the *Semitone*, 'tis ſo called, not that it is geometrically the Half of either of theſe which we call *Tones* (for 'tis greater) but becauſe it comes near to it; and 'tis called the *greater Semitone*, being greater than what it wants of a *Tone*.

NOTE, Hitherto we have uſed the Words, *Tone* and *Tune* indifferently, to ſignify a certain Quality of a ſingle Sound; but here *Tone* is a certain *Interval*, and ſhall hereafter be conſtantly ſo uſed, and the Word *Tune* always applied to the other.

OUR next Work ſhall be to explain the *Original* of theſe *Degrees*, and their different Perfections; and then ſhew how they anſwer the Purpoſes for which they were required; and, in doing this, I ſhall make ſuch Reflections upon the Connection and Dependence of the ſeveral Parts of the *Syſtem*, that we may be confirmed both by Senſe and Reaſon in the true *Principles* of *Muſick.*

As to the *Original* of theſe *Degrees*, they ariſe out of the *ſimple Concords*, and are equal to their Differences, which we take by *Probl.* 10. *Chap.* 4. Thus 8 : 9 is the Difference of a 5*th* and 4*th*. 9 : 10 is the *Difference* of a 3*d l.* and 4*th*, or of 5*th* and 6*th g.* 15 : 16, the *Difference* of 3*d g.* and 4*th*, or of 5*th* and 6*th l.*

We ſhall preſently ſee the Reaſon why no other *Degrees* than ſuch as are the Differences of *Concords* could be admitted; but there are other Differences among the *ſimple Concords*, beſides theſe (which you may obſerve do all ariſe from a Compariſon of the 5*th* with the other *Concords*) yet none elſe could anſwer the Deſign, which I ſhall ſhew immediately, and give you in the mean Time a *Table* of all theſe Differences of *ſimple Concords*, which are not *Concords* themſelves.

Differences of			*Ratios.*
3*d l.* and	3*d g.*	=	24 : 25
	4*th*	=	9 : 10
	6*th g.*	=	18 : 25
3*d g.* and	4*th*	=	15 : 16
	6*th l.*	=	25 : 32
4*th* and 5*th*		=	8 : 9
5*th* and	6*th l.*	=	15 : 16
	6*th g.*	=	9 : 10
6*th l.* and	6*th g.*	=	24 : 25

I ſhall now explain how theſe *Degrees* contribute to the Improvement of the *Syſtem* of *Muſick*: In doing which I ſhall

ſhall endeavour to give the Reaſon why theſe only are proper and natural to that End.

Degrees were required both for improving the *Melody* of a ſingle Voice conſidered by it ſelf; and that ſeveral Voices, while they move melodiouſly each by it ſelf, might alſo joyn together in an agreeable Variety of *Harmony*; and therefore I obſerved, that the *Degrees* required muſt anſwer both theſe Ends, if poſſible; accordingly, Nature has bounteouſly afforded us theſe neceſſary Materials of our Pleaſure, and made the preceeding *Degrees* anſwer all our Wiſh, as I ſhall now explain.

I ſhall firſt conſider it with reſpect to the *Conſonance* of Two or more Voices. *Suppoſe* Two Voices *A* and *B*, containing between them any *Concord*; they can change into another *Concord* only Two Ways. 1*mo*. If the one Voice as *A* keeps its Place, and the other *B* moves upward or downward (*i. e.* becomes either *acuter* or *graver* than it was before.) Now if the Movement of *B* can only be agreeable by *harmonical Intervals*, they can change only in theſe Caſes, *viz.* if the firſt *Concord* be *Octave*, then by *B*'s moving nearer the Pitch of *A*, either by the Diſtance of a *6th*, *5th*, *4th* or 3*d*, the Two Voices will *concord* in a 3*d*, *4th*, *5th* or *6th*, which is plain from the Compoſition of an *Octave*: And conſequently by *B*'s moving farther from *A*, the Voices can again change from any of theſe leſſer *Concords* to an *Octave*. Or ſuppoſe them at firſt at a *6th*, by *B*'s moving either a *4th* or 3*d*, they will meet in a 3*d* or

4*th*,

4th, or being at a *4th* or *3d*, they may meet in a *6th*, because a *6th* is composed of *4th* and *3d*. And *lastly*, being at a *5th*, they may meet in a *3d*, and contrarily. But by the Use of these *Degrees* the Variety is increased; for now suppose *A* and *B* distant by any *simple Concord*, if *B* moves up or down one of these *Degrees* 8 : 9, or 9 : 10, or 15 : 16, there shall always be a Change into some other *Concord*, because these *Degrees* are the very Differences of *Concords*. Then, 2*do*. If we suppose both the Voices to move, they may move either the same Way (*i. e.* both become *acuter* or *graver* than they were) or move contrary to one another; and in both Cases they may increase their first Distance, or contract it, so as to meet in a different *Concord*; but then if the Movements be by *harmonical Intervals*, the Variety will be far less here than in the first Supposition; but this is abundantly supplied by the Use of the *Degrees*. You must *observe* again, that besides the Want of Variety in most of the Changes that can be made, from *Concord* to *Concord*, by the single Voices moving in *harmonical Distances*, there will be too great a Disproportion or Inequality of the *Concord* you pass from, and that you meet in, which must have an ill Effect: For by Experience we are taught, that *Nature* is best pleased, where the Variety and Changes of our Pleasure (arising from the same *Objects*) are gradual and by smooth Steps; and therefore moving from one Extreme to another is to be seldom practis'd; for this Reason also the

the *Degrees* are of neceſſary Uſe for making the Paſſage of the *Concords* eaſy and ſmooth, which generally ought to be from one *Concord* into the next, which is conſiſtent with the Motion of one or both Voices. But let me make this laſt Remark, which we have alſo confirmed from Experience, *viz.* That of Two Sounds in *Conſonance*, 'tis required not only that every Note they make together be *Concord* (I have ſaid already that there are ſome Exceptions to this Rule) but that, as much as poſſible, the preſent Note of the one Voice be *Concord* to the immediately preceeding Note of the other; which can be done by no Means ſo well as by ſuch *Degrees* as are the Differences of *Concords* (where theſe happen to be *Diſcord*, *Muſicians* call it particularly *Relation inharmonical.*) And indeed upon this Principle it can eaſily be ſhewn, that 'tis impoſſible there can be any other *Degrees* admitted, than what are equal to the Differences of *ſimple Concords*: If only one Voice move, the Thing is plain; if both move, let us ſuppoſe *A B* at any *Concord*, and to move into another, and there let the Two new Notes be expreſſed by *a b*. Then ſince *a B* muſt be *Concord*, it follows, that the Diſtance of *a* and *A* is equal to the Difference of the Two *Concords A B*, and *a B*; the ſame Way 'tis proven that *b B* is the Difference of the *Concords A B*, and *b A*.

'T IS a very obvious Queſtion here, why the ſucceſſive Notes of Two different Voices may not as well admit of *Diſcords*, as theſe of the ſame

ſame Voice; to which the Anſwer ſeems plainly to be this, that in the ſame Voice, the *Degrees*, which are the only *Diſcords* admitted, are regulated by the *harmonical Intervals* to which they are but ſubſervient; and the *Melody* is conducted altogether with reſpect to theſe; for the *Degrees* of themſelves without their Subſerviency to the *Concords* could make no *Muſick*, as ſhall be further explained afterwards: But in the other Caſe, the ſucceſſive Motions can be brought under no ſuch Regulation, and therefore muſt be *harmonical* as much as poſſible, leſt it diminiſh the Pleaſure of the ſucceeding *Concord*; beſides, conſider the *Diſcords* that are moſt ready to occur here, are greater than the *Degrees*, and would be intolerable in any Caſe.

But now, ſuppoſing that only theſe *Diſcords* belong to the *Syſtem* of *Muſick*, which are the Differences of *Concords*, you'll ask why the other Differences marked in the preceeding *Table* are excluded, *viz.* 24 : 25 the Difference of the Two 3*ds*, or the Two 6*ths*; 18 : 25 the Difference of the 3*d l.* and 6*th g.* 25 : 32 the Difference of 3*d g.* and 6*th l.* To ſatisfie this, we are to conſider, *Firſt*, that the Paſſage of ſeveral Voices from *Concord* to *Concord* does not need them, there being a ſufficient Variety from the other Differences; but chiefly the Reaſon ſeems to be, that they don't anſwer the Demands of a ſingle Voice, which I ſhall explain in the next §, and deſire you here only to obſerve

ſerve that they ariſe out of the *imperfect Concords*, *viz.* *3ds* and *6ths*.

---

§ 2. *Of the Uſe of* Degrees *in the Conſtruction of the* Scale of Muſick.

WE have already obſerved, that the *Concords* are the eſſential Principles of *Muſick* as they afford Pleaſure immediately and of themſelves: Other Relations belong to *Muſick* only as they are ſubſervient to theſe. We have alſo explained what that Subſerviency required is, *viz.* That by a fit Diviſion of the *harmonical Intervals* a ſingle Voice may paſs ſmoothly from one Extreme to another, whereby the Pleaſure of theſe perfect Relations may be heightned, and we may have a Variety neceſſary to our more agreeable Entertainment: It follows, that to anſwer this End, the *Intervals* ſought, or ſome of them at leaſt, muſt be leſs than any *harmonical* one, *i. e.* leſs than a 3*d l.* 5 : 6 ; and that they ought all to be leſs, will preſently appear from the Nature of the Thing. For the *Degrees* ſought we have already aſſigned theſe, *viz.* 8 : 9 called a *greater Tone*, 9 : 10 called a *leſſer Tone*, and 15 : 16 called a *greater Semitone* : Now that every *harmonical Interval* is compoſed of, and conſequently reſolvable into a certain Number of theſe *Degrees*, will appear from the following *Table*,

Table, wherein I give you the Number and Kinds of theſe *Degrees* that each *Concord* is e-qual to, which you can prove by the *Addition* of *Intervals*, *Chap*. 4. Or you'll find it more ea-ſily afterwards, when you ſee them all ſtand in order in the *Scale*; we ſhall afterwards conſider in what Order theſe *Degrees* ought to be taken in the Diviſion of any *Interval*.

TABLE of the component Parts of Concords.

3*d l.*	contains	1 *tg*,	& 1 *ſ*	
3*d g.*		1 *tg*,	1 *tl*,	
4*th*		1 *tg*,	1 *tl*,	1 *ſ*
5*th*		2 *tg*,	1 *tl*,	1 *ſ*
6*th l.*		2 *tg*,	1 *tl*,	2 *ſ*
6*th g.*		2 *tg*,	2 *tl*,	1 *ſ*
8*ve*		3 *tg*,	2 *tl*,	2 *ſ*

NOTE, That as in this *Table*, ſo afterwards I ſhall for Brevity mark a *greater Tone* thus *t g*, a *leſſer* thus *t l*, a *Semitone* thus *ſ*.

BUT now, *obſerve*, that ſince we can conceive a Variety of other *Intervals* that will divide the *Concords* beſides theſe, we are therefore to conſider for what Reaſon they are preferable to any other: To do this, I ſhall firſt ſhew you, that no other but ſuch as are equal to the Differences of *Concords* are fit for the Purpoſe, and then for what Reaſon only theſe Three are choſen.

FOR the *Firſt*, conſider, that every greater *Concord* contains all the leſſer within it, in ſuch a Manner, that betwixt the Extremes of any greater *Concord*, as many middle Terms may be be placed as there are leſſer *Concords*; which middle Terms ſhall be to any one Extreme of that greater *Concord* in the *Ratio* of theſe leſſer *Concords*; ſo betwixt the Extremes of the 8*ve* may be placed 6 Terms, which ſhall make all the leſſer *Concords* with any one of the Extremes, as in this Series,

$$1 : \frac{5}{6} : \frac{4}{5} : \frac{3}{4} : \frac{2}{3} : \frac{5}{8} : \frac{3}{5} : \frac{1}{2}$$

where comparing each Term with 1, you have all the *ſimple Concords* in their gradual Order, 3*d l.* 3*d g.* 4*th*, 5*th*, 6*th l.* 6*th g.* 8*ve*; and the mutual Relations of the Terms immediately next other in the Series are plainly the Differences of the *Concords* which theſe Terms make with the Extreme. Now it is natural and reaſonable that if we would paſs by *Degrees* from one Extreme to another of any greater *harmonical Interval*, in the moſt agreeable Manner, we ought to chooſe ſuch middle Terms as have an *harmonical Relation* to the Extremes of that greater, rather than ſuch as are *Diſcord*; for the *ſimple Concords* being different in Perfection, vary the Pleaſure in this Progreſſion very agreeably; but we could not bear to hear a great many Sounds ſucceeding one another, among which there were no *Concord*, or where only the laſt is *concord* to the Firſt: And therefore it is plain that the *Degrees* required ought to be equal to the Differences of *Concords*, as you ſee evidently they muſt be where the middle Terms are *Concord* with

with one or both the Extremes. But of all the *discord Differences* of *Concords*, only these are agreeable, *viz.* 8 : 9, 9 : 10, 15 : 16; the other Three are rejected, *viz.* 24 : 25, 18 : 25, 25 : 32; the Reason of which seems to be, that the Two last are too great, and the first too small; but particularly 25 : 32 is an *Interval* greater than a *4th*, as 18 : 25 is greater than a *3d g.* and therefore would make such a disproportioned and unequal Mixture with the other *Degrees*, that would be insufferable. Then for 24 : 25 it is too small, and would also make too much Inequality among the *Degrees*. But at last we shall take Experience for the infallible Proof that we have chosen the only proper *Degrees*: Our Reason in Cases like this can go no further than the making such Observations upon the Dependence and Connection of Things, that from the Order and Analogy of *Nature* we may draw a probable Conclusion that we have discovered the true natural Rule. And of this Kind we shall immediately have further Demonstrations that the only true *natural Degrees* are these already assign'd.

WE come now to consider the Order in which the *Degrees* ought to be taken, in this Division of the *harmonical Intervals*, for constituting the *Scale* of *Musick*; for tho' we have the true *Degrees*, yet it is not every Order and Progression of them that will produce true *Melody*. For *Example*, Tho' the greater *Tone* 8 : 9 be a true *Degree*, yet there could be no *Musick* made of any Number of such *Degrees*, because no Number

ber of them is equal to any *Concord*; the ſame is true of the other Two *Degrees*; which you may prove by adding Two or Three, *&c.* of any one Kind of them together, till you find the Sum exceed an *Octave*, which it will do in 6 *greater Tones*, or 7 *leſſer Tones*, or 11 *Semitones*; and compare the Sum of 2, 3, 4, *&c.* of them, till you come to that Number, you'll find them equal to no *Concord.* Therefore there is a Neceſſity that theſe *Degrees* be mixt together to make right *Muſick*; and 'tis plain they muſt be ſo mixt, that there ought never to be Two of one Kind next other. But this we ſhall have alſo confirmed in examining the Order they ought to be taken in.

THE *Octave* containing in it all the other *ſimple Concords*, and the *Degrees* being the Differences of theſe *Concords*, 'tis plain that the Diviſion of the *Octave* will comprehend the Diviſions of all the reſt: Let us therefore joyn all the *ſimple Concords* to a common *Fundamental*, and we have this Series.

I :	$\frac{5}{6}$:	$\frac{4}{5}$:	$\frac{3}{4}$:	$\frac{2}{3}$:	$\frac{5}{8}$:	$\frac{3}{5}$:	$\frac{1}{2}$
Fund.	*3d l.*	*3d g.*	*4th,*	*5th*	*6th l.*	*6th g.*	*8ve.*

NOW if we ſhould aſcend to an *Octave* by theſe Steps, 'tis evident we have all the poſſible *harmonical Relations* to the *Fundamental*; and if we examine what *Degrees* are in this Aſcent

ſcent, or the mutual Relations of each Term to the next, they are theſe.

$$\frac{5}{6} \cdot \frac{24}{25} \cdot \frac{15}{16} \cdot \frac{8}{9} \cdot \frac{15}{16} \cdot \frac{24}{25} \cdot \frac{5}{6}$$

But this we know is far from being a *melodious* Aſcent; there is too great Inequality among theſe *Degrees*; the firſt and laſt are each a 3*d l.* which ought alſo to be divided; it is equal to a *tg.* and *ſ.* and ſo inſtead of $\frac{5}{6}$ we ſhall have theſe Two Degrees 8 : 9 and 15 : 16. But when this is done, yet the Diviſion of the *Octave* will not be perfect; for we have too many *Degrees*, and an Exceſs is as much a Fault as a Defect: So many ſmall *Degrees* would neither be eaſily raiſed, nor heard with Pleaſure: The Two 3*ds* and Two 6*ths* have ſo ſmall a Difference, 24 : 25, that the Diviſion of the *Octave* does not require nor admit them both together, the Progreſs being ſmoother where we have but one of the 3*ds* and one of the 6*ths*: If this Degree 24 : 25 be expelled, then will 9 : 10 have Place in the Series, which is not only a better Relation of it ſelf, as it conſiſts of leſſer Numbers, but it has a nearer Affinity with the other Two 8 : 9 and 15 : 16, all theſe Three proceeding from the 5*th*, as I have already noted.

Now then if we take only one of the 3*ds* and one 6*th* in the Diviſion of the 8*ve* we have theſe Two different Series,

THE

Fund.	*3d l.*	*4th,*	*5th,*	*6th l.*	*8ve*
1 .	$\frac{5}{6}$.	$\frac{3}{4}$.	$\frac{2}{3}$.	$\frac{5}{8}$.	$\frac{1}{2}$.
1 .	$\frac{4}{5}$.	$\frac{3}{4}$.	$\frac{2}{3}$.	$\frac{3}{5}$.	$\frac{1}{2}$
Fund.	*3d g.*	*4th,*	*5th,*	*6th g.*	*8ve*

THE 3*d l.* and 6*th l.* are taken together, as the 3*d g.* and 6*th g.* because their Relation is the *Concord* of a 4*th*; whereas the 3*d l.* and 6*th g.* also the 3*d g.* and 6*th l.* are one to the other a gross *Discord*; and 'tis better how many *Concords* are among the middle Terms; but if in some particular Cases of Practice this Order is changed, 'tis done for the sake of some other Advantage to the *Melody*, of which I have an Occasion to speak afterwards. But the 3*ds* next each Extreme are yet undivided, which ought to be done to complete the Division of the *Octave*.

IN the first of the preceeding Series we have the 3*d l.* next the *Fundamental*, and the 3*d g.* next the other Extreme: In the Second we have the 3*d g.* next the *Fundamental*, and the 3*d l.* next the *acute* Extreme. Now it is plain what *Degrees* will divide these 3*ds*, because we see them divided in the Divisions already made; for in the first Series, betwixt the 3*d l.* and the 5*th* we have a 3*d g.* (which is their Difference) divided into these *Degrees*, and in this Order ascending, *viz. t l.* and *t g.* and betwixt the 4*th* and 6*th l.* we have a 3*d l.* (which is their Dif-

Difference) divided into *t g.* and *ſ.* We have the ſame *Intervals* divided in the other Series betwixt the *3d g.* and *5th*, and betwixt the *4th* and *6th g.* but the Order of the *Degrees* here is reverſe of what it is in the other Series: And the Queſtion now is, what is the moſt natural Order for the Diviſion of theſe *3ds* that ly next the Extremes in the *Octaves*? It may at firſt ſeem that we have got a fair and natural Hint from theſe Places mentioned, and that the *3ds* ought to be ordered the ſame Way towards the Extremes of each Series, as they are in theſe Places of it. In the *3ds* next the *Fundamental* I have followed that Order, but not for that Reaſon; and in the upper *3ds* I have taken the contrary Order, which ſee in the Two following Series, where I have marked the *Degrees* from every Term to the next; and you ſee I have divided

with a *3d l.* - $1 : \frac{8}{9} : \frac{5}{6} : \frac{3}{4} : \frac{2}{3} : \frac{5}{8} : \frac{5}{9} : \frac{1}{2}$

tg. ſ. tl. tg. ſ. tg. tl.

with a *3d g.* - $1 : \frac{8}{9} : \frac{4}{5} : \frac{3}{4} : \frac{2}{3} : \frac{3}{5} : \frac{8}{15} : \frac{1}{2}$

tg. tl. ſ. tg. tl. tg. ſ.

the *3d g.* (which is in the upper Place of the one and lower of the other Series) in this Order aſcending, *viz. t g.* and *t l.* And the *3d l.* (which is alſo in the upper Place of the one

and

and lower of the other) in this Order afcen-ding, *viz.* *t g.* and *f.* The Reafon of this Choice I fhall thus account for. *Firft*, As to the 3*d* next the *Fundamental*, I place the *t g.* loweft, becaufe it is the *Degree* which a natural Voice can moft eafily raife, being the moft perfect of the Three, and we find it fo by Experience; and if you confider, that it is the Difference of a 4*th* and 5*th*, which two *Concords* the Ear is perfectly Judge of, by practifing thefe one learns very eafily how to raife a *t g.* with Exactnefs: But for the *t l.* (the other Part of the 3*d g.*) it is not fo eafily learned, for the Difference betwixt the Two Tones being but fmall, one cannot be fure of it, but will readily fall into the more perfect. It is true, that in rifing from any *Fundamental* to a 3*d g.* we take a *t l.* at the fecond Step; but then I believe, our taking it exactly here, is owing to the Idea of the *Fundamental*, to which the Ear feeks the *harmonical* Relation of 3*d g.* where it refts with Pleafure; and whenever a Reafon like this occurs, the Voice will eafily take a *t l.* even at the firft Step; for *Example*, Suppofe Two Voices concording in a 6*th g.* if one of them keeps its *Tune*, and the other moves to meet it in a 5*th*, then muft that Movement be a *t l.* which is the Difference of 6*th g.* and 5*th*: As to the Parts of the 3*d l.* *obferve*, that the *t g.* and *f.* being remarkably different, there would be no Hazard of taking the one for the other; therefore as to that, any of them might ftand next the *Fundamental*, yet the *t g.* being a more

more perfect Relation, it is easier taken, and makes a more agreeable Ascent, tho' I know that in some Circumstances the *f.* is placed next the *Fundamental* (as I shall mark in its proper Place.) *Now* for the *Degrees* of the upper Third, the *t g.* is set in the lowest Place in both the Series; the Effect of which is, that the middle Term proceeding from that Order, is in an *harmonical* Relation to more, and the more principal of the other Terms in the Series. *Kepler* upon *harmonical Proportions* places the *t g.* next both the Extremes in the *Octave*, and gives this Reason for it, lest the second and seventh Term of the one Series differ from these in the other (for it seems he would have them differ as little as possible, *viz.* only in the 3*ds* and 6*ths*) and this he concludes with a Kind of Triumph against the Authorities of *Ptolomy*, *Galileus* and *Zarline*, whom he mentions as contrary to him in this Point. But indeed I cannot see the Sufficiency of this Reason, there is nothing in it drawn from the Nature of the Thing: And as to 3*d* in the upper Place, the Order in which I've placed its *Degrees*, is approven by Experience, and is I think the constant Practice.

THUS we have the *Octave* completely divided into all its *concinnous Degrees*, and in it the Division of all the lesser *Concords*, with the most natural and agreeable Order in which these *Degrees* can follow, in moving from any given Sound through any *harmonical Interval*. There are only these Three different

De-

Degrees, viz. *t g.* 8 . 9, *t l.* 5 : 6, and *ſ.* 15 : 16. And how many of each Kind every *harmonical Interval* contains, is to be ſeen in the preceeding Series, which eaſily confirms and proves the *Table* of *Degrees* given a little above, where you ſee alſo the natural Order, *viz.* in aſcending, it is *t g. t l. ſ. t g. t l. t g. ſ.* —— Or this, *t g. ſ. t l. t g. ſ. t g. t l.* according as you choſe the 3*d l.* or 3*d g.* to aſcend by; and in deſcending we take that Order juſt reverſe, by taking the ſame individual middle Terms.

Now the Syſtem of *Octave* containing all the *original Concords*, and the *compound Concords* being the Sum of *Octave* and ſome leſſer *Concord*, therefore 'tis plain, that if we would have a Series of *Degrees* to reach beyond an *Octave*, we ought to continue them in the ſame Order thro' a ſecond *Octave* as in the firſt, and ſo on thro a third and fourth *Octave*, &c. and ſuch a Series is called *The Scale of Muſick*, which as I have already defin'd, expreſſes a Series of Sounds, riſing or falling towards *Acuteneſs* or *Gravity*, from any given Pitch of *Tune*, to the greateſt Diſtance that is fit or practicable, thro' ſuch intermediate *Degrees* as makes the Succeſſion moſt agreeable and perfect; and in which we have all the *harmonical Intervals* moſt *concinnouſly* divided. And of this we have Two different Species according as the 3*d l.* or 3*d g.* and *6th l.* or *6th g.* are taken in, which cannot both ſtand together in relation to one *Fundamental*, and make an *harmonical*

monical Scale. But if either of theſe Ways we aſcend from a *Fundamental* or given Sound to an *Octave*, the Succeſſion is very *melodious*, tho' they make different Species of *Melody*. It is true, that every Note to the next is *Diſcord*, but each of them is *Concord* with the *Fundamental*, except the 2*d* and 7*th*, and many of them among themſelves, which is the Ground of that Agreeableneſs in the Succeſſion; for we muſt reflect upon what I have elſewhere obſerved, that the *graver* Sounds are the more powerful, and are capable of exciting Motion and Sound in Bodies whoſe *Tune* is *acuter* in a Relation of *Concord*, particularly 8*ve* and 5*th*, which an *acute* Sound will not effect with reſpect to a *grave*. And this accounts for that *Maxim* in Practice, That all *Muſick* is counted *upwards*; the Meaning is, that in the Conduct of a ſucceſſive Series of Sounds, the lower or *graver* Notes influence and regulate the *acuter*, in ſuch a Manner that all theſe are choſen with reſpect to ſome *fundamental* Note which is called the *Key*; but of this only in general here, in another Place it ſhall be more particularly conſidered.

WE have expreſt the ſeveral Terms of the *Scale* by the proportional *Sections* of a Line repreſented by 1, which is the *Fundamental* of the Series; but if we would expreſs it in whole Numbers, it is to be done by the Rules of *Ch.* 4. by which we have the Two following Series, in each of which the greateſt Number expreſſes

expresses the longest *Chord*, and the other Numbers the rest in Order.

540 : 480 : 432 : 405 : 360 : 324 : 288 : 270
tg. tl. s. tg. tl. tg. s.

216 : 192 : 180 : 162 : 144 : 135 : 120 : 108
tg. s. tl. tg. s. tg. tl.

THE first Series proceeds by a *3d g.* and the other by a *3d l.* and if any Number of Chords are in these Proportions of Length, *cæteris paribus*, they will express the true *Degrees* and *Intervals* of the *System* of *Musick*, as 'tis contain'd in an *8ve concinnously* divided in the Two different Species mentioned.

§ 3. *Containing further Reflections upon the Constitution of the* Scale *of* Musick; *and explaining the Names of* 8ve, 5th, &c. *which have been hitherto used without knowing all their Meaning; shewing also the proper Office of the* Scale.

WE considered in *Chapter* 5. the Division of the *Concords*, in order only to find what *Intervals* they were immmediately divisible into: We find that either an *harmonical* or *arithmetical Mean* divides the *8ve* into a *5th* and

and *4th*, with this Difference, that the *harmonical* puts the *5th*, and the *arithmetical* the *4th* next the *Fundamental*: And from this the Invention of the *tg* (which is the Difference of *4th* and *5th*) was very obvious. These Divisions of the *8ve* we suppose indeed made only for discovering the immediate *harmonical* Parts of it; but taking in both these middle Terms, then we see the *8ve* resolved into these Three Parts, and in this Order, *viz.* a *4th*, a *tg* and a *4th*, as in these Numbers 6 : 8 : 9 : 12. where 6 and 12 are *8ve*; 8 is an *harmonical* Mean, and 9 an *arithmetical* Mean; 6 : 8 is a *4th*; 8 : 9 a *tg.* and 9 : 12 a *4th*; that these Two middle Terms are at a Distance proper for making *Melody*, and consequently that their Relation 8 : 9 is a *concinnous Interval*, we have infallible Assurance of from Experience.

BUT I proposed to make some Observations on the Connection and Dependence of the several Parts of the *System* of *Musick*; and *First*, we are to remark, that this *Degree* 8 : 9 proceeds from the Two *Concords* that are of the next perfect Form to *8ve*, *viz.* *4th* and *5th*, which are the *harmonical* Parts of it; and stands so in the middle betwixt the upper and lower *4th*, that added to either of them it makes up the *5th*, and so joyns the *harmonical* and *arithmetical* Division of *8ve* in one Series: and this *tg* being the Difference of Two *Concords* of which the Ear is perfectly Judge, we very easily learn to raise it; and in Fact we know it is the *Degree* which a natural Voice can with most Ease

and

and Certainty raiſe from a *Fundamental* or given Sound. *Again*, we found that the ſame Law of an *harmonical* and *arithmetical Mean* reſolved the *5th* into *3d l.* and *3d g.* By the *harmonical* the *3d g.* being next the greater Number, as here 10 : 12 : 15, and by the *arithmetical* the *3d l.* loweſt, as here 4 : 5 : 6; and applying this to the upper and lower *5th* proceeding from the immediate Diviſion of the *8ve*, we have 4 more middle Terms within the *8ve*, whereof the lower Two are *3ds* to the *Fundamental* and *6ths* to the other Extreme, and the upper Two are *6ths* to the *Fundamental*, and *3ds* to the other Extreme, as you ſee in the preceeding Series : And this produces Two new *Degrees*, *viz.* 24 : 25. the Difference of *3d l.* and *3d g.* or of *6th l.* and *6th g.* and 15 : 16, the Difference of *3d g.* and *4th*, or of *5th* and *6th l.* but this *Degree* 24 : 25 is too ſmall, and upon that Account rejected, as I have already ſaid. Now we are to find why this *Degree* 24 : 25 is *inconcinnous*, and 15 : 16 *concinnous*, from ſome ſettled Conſtitution and Rule in Nature, which we ſhall have from this Obſervation, *viz.* That if we apply the ſame Law which reſolved the *8ve* and *5th* into their *harmonical* Parts, to the *3d g.* we have it divided into a *t g.* and a *t l.* as in this *arithmetical* Series 8 : 9 : 10; or this *harmonical*, 36 : 40 : 45; and if we conſider this *Analogy*, it ſeems to determine theſe Two Degrees of *t g.* 8 : 9 and *t l.* 9 : 10, to be the true *concinnous* Parts of *3d g.* and thereby excludes 24 : 25, and conſequently the Two *3ds* and

Two

two *6ths* from ſtanding both together in one *Scale*. And *now*, ſince the *5th* does not admit of both theſe middle Terms together which proceed from its *harmonical* and *arithmetical* Diviſion, it ſeems to be but the following of Nature, if we apply the ſame Kind of Diviſion to the upper and lower *5th* of the *8ve*; the Effect of which is, that as by the *harmonical* Diviſion of the lower *5th* we have a *3d g.* next the *Fundamental*; ſo by the *harmonical* Diviſion of the upper *5th* we have a *6th g.* to the *Fundamental*; and by the *arithmetical* Diviſions we have contrarily the *3d l.* and *6th l.* next the *Fundamental*, as you ſee in the preceeding Series: And this is a Kind of natural Proof that the *3d l.* and *6th l.* alſo the *3d g.* and *6th g.* belong to one Series; and here we have the Diſcovery of the *t l.* which lies narally betwixt the *3d l.* and *4th*, or betwixt the *5th* and *6th g.* But tho' the Two *3ds* and Two *6ths* cannot ſtand together, yet there muſt none of them be loſt, and therefore they conſtitute Two different *Scales*. But the Diviſion of the *8ve* is not finiſhed, for the *3ds* that ly next the Extremes are undivided; as to the *3d g.* we ſee how naturally 'tis reſolved into a *t g.* and *t l.* which is another Way of diſcovering theſe *Degrees*; and 'tis worth remarking, that the ſame general *Rule* which by a gradual Application reſolved the *8ve* immediately into a *5th* and *4th.* and then the *5th* immediately into *3d g.* and *3d l.* (by which Diviſions the Two *6ths* were alſo found indirectly) being applied to the *3d g.* produces immediately the Two principal

cipal *concinnous Intervals* ; and for the Original of the *ſ.* 15 : 16. we ſee 'tis the Difference of 3*d g.* and 4*th*, and riſes not from the immediate Diviſion of any other *Interval*, but falls here by Accident, upon the Application of the preceeding general *Rule* to the 8*ve* and 5*th*. But we have yet the 3*d l.* which is next the Extremes to conſider ; of what *concinnous* Parts it conſiſts was eaſy to ſee betwixt the 3*d g.* and 5*th*. *viz.* a *ſ.* and *t g* ; but next the Extremes of the 8*ve* they muſt be in this Order aſcending, *viz. t g.* and *ſ.* Of the Reaſon of this I have ſaid enough already: And now the Diviſion of the *Octave* being completed, we have the whole *original Concords* concinnouſly divided, and theſe *Intervals* added to the *Syſtem*, *viz.* 8 : 9, 9 : 10, and 15 : 16. which have all this in common, that they are the Differences of the 5*th* and ſome other *Concords*.

Of the particular Names of Intervals, *as* 8ve, 5th, &c.

WE have conſidered the *concinnous* Diviſion of every *harmonical Interval*, and we find the 8*ve* contains 7 *Degrees* ; the 6*th*, whether leſſer or greater, has 5 ; the 5*th* has 4 ; the 4*th* has 3 ; the 3*d*, leſſer or greater, has 2 : And if we number the Terms or Sounds contained within the Extremes (including both) of each *harmonical Interval*, there will be one more than there are of *Degrees*, *viz.* in the 8*ve* there are 8. in

8. in the *6th* 6. in the *5th* 5. in the *4th* 4. and in the *3d* 3. And now at laſt we underſtand from whence the Names of *8ve*, *6th*, *5th*, &c. come; the Relations to which theſe Names are annexed are ſo called, becauſe in the *natural Scale* of *Muſick* the Terms that are in theſe Relations to the *Fundamental* are the *Third*, *Fourth*, *&c.* in order from that *Fundamental* incluſively. Or thus, becauſe theſe *harmonical Intervals* being *concinnouſly* divided, contain betwixt their Extremes (including both) ſo many Terms or Notes as the Names *8ve*, *6th*, *&c.* bear. For the ſame Reaſon alſo, the *Tone* or *ſ.* (whichever of them ſtands next the *Fundamental*) is called a *2d*, particularly the *Tone* (whoſe Difference of greater and leſſer is not ſtrictly regarded in common Practice) is called the *2d g.* and *ſ.* the *2d l.* Alſo that Term which is betwixt the *6th* and *8ve*, is called the *7th*, which is alſo the greater 8 : 15, or the leſſer 5 : 9. Concerning this *Interval* we muſt here remark, that as it ſtands in *primary Relation* to the *Fundamental* in the Diviſion of the *8ve*, it does in this reſpect belong to the *Syſtem* of *Muſick*: But it is alſo uſed as a *Degree* without Diviſion, *that is*, in Practice we move ſometimes the Diſtance of a *7th* at once; but it is in ſuch Circumſtances as removes the Offence that ſo great a *Diſcord* would of it ſelf create; of which we ſhall hear more in the next *Chapter*; and here *obſerve*, that it is the Difference of *8ve* and the *Degrees* of *Tone* and *Semitone*.

As to the Order in which the *Degrees* of this *Scale* follow, we have this to remark, that if either Series, (*viz.* that with the 3*d l.* or with the 3*d g.*) be continued *in infinitum*, the Two *Semitones* that fall naturally in the Division of the 8*ve*, are always asunder 2 *Tones* and 3 *Tones* alternately, *i. e.* after a *Semitone* come 2 *Tones*, then a *Semitone*, and then 3 *Tones*; and of the Two *Tones* one is a greater and the other a lesser; of the Three, one is lesser in the middle betwixt Two greater. If you continue either Series to a double *Octave*, and mark the *Degrees*, all this will be evident. *Observe* also, that this is the *Scale* which the *Ancients* called the DIATONICK *Scale*, because it proceeds by these *Degrees* called *Tones* (whereof there are Five in an 8*ve*) and *Semitones* (whereof there are Two in an *Octave*) But we call it also the NATURAL *Scale*, because its *Degrees* and their Order are the most agreeable and *concinnous*, and preferable, by the Approbation both of Sense and Reason, to all other Divisions that have ever been instituted. What these other are, you shall know when I explain the *ancient Theory* of *Musick*; but I shall always call this, *The Scale of Musick*, without Distinction, as 'tis the only true *natural System*.

WE have already observed, that if the *Scale* of *Musick* is to be carried beyond an *Octave*, it must be by the same *Degrees*, and in the same Order thro' every successive *Octave* as thro' the first. How to continue the Series of Numbers by a continual Addition, is sufficiently explain'd al-

already; and for the Names there are Two Ways, either to compound the Names of the *simple Interval* with the *Octave* thus, *viz. tg.* or *f.* or 3*d*, &c. above an *Octave*, or above Two *Octaves*, &c. or name them by the Number of *Degrees* from the *Fundamental*, as 9*th*, 10*th*, &c. but the first Way is more intelligible, as it gives a more distinct and simple Idea of the Distance, just as we conceive a certain Quantity of Time more easily, by calling it, for *Example*, 9 Weeks, than 63 Days. But that you may readily know how far any Note is removed from the *Fundamental*, if you know how far it is above any Number of *Octaves*. See the following *Table*, wherein the first Line contains the Names of the Notes within one *Octave*; the second Line the Names (with respect to the first *Fundamental*) of these Terms that are as far above one *Octave*, as these standing over them in the first are above the *Fundamental*; and the Third Line the Names of these above Two *Octaves*.

Fund. 1	2*d*	3*d*	4*th*	5*th*	6*th*	7*th*	8*th*
	9*th*	10*th*	11*th*	12*th*	13*th*	14*th*	15*th*
	16*th*	17*th*	18*th*	19*th*	20*th*	21*st*	22*d*

And this *Table* may be continued as far as you please; or if you take the Columns of Figures downward, then each Column gives the Names of the Notes or Terms that are equally removed from the *Fundamental*, from the first *Octave*,

ctave, the ſecond *Octave*, &c. Thus the firſt Column on the left ſhews the Names of ſuch as are a 2*d* above the *Fundamental*, above the firſt *Octave*, &c. if we conſider what is practical then the *Scale* is limited to Three or Four *Octaves*, otherwiſe 'tis infinite. Again *obſerve*, that let the *Scale* be continued to any Extent, every *Octave* is but a Repetition of the firſt; and therefore an *Octave* is ſaid to be a perfect *Scale* or *Syſtem*, which comprehends Eight Notes with the Extremes; but the Eighth being ſo like the firſt, that in Practice it has the ſame Name, and is the ſame Way *fundamental* to the *Degrees* of a ſecond *Octave*, and ſo on from one *Octave* to another, gave Occaſion to ſay there are but ſeven different Notes in the *Scale* of *Muſick*; or that all *Muſick* is comprehended in ſeven Notes; becauſe if we take other ſeven Notes higher, they are but Repetitions of the firſt ſeven in *Octave*, and have the ſame Names.

Of the Office of the SCALE.

The *Conſtitution* of the *Scale* being already explained, the Office and Uſe of it ſhall be next treated of, which you have expreſt in general in the preceeding Definition of it; but that you may have a diſtinct and clear Notion, I ſhall be a little more particular. The Deſign then of the *Scale* of *Muſick* is to ſhow how a Voice may riſe or fall, leſs than any *harmonical Interval*, and thereby move from the one Ex-

treme

treme of any of these to the other, in the most agreeable Succession of Sounds: It is a *System* which ought to exhibite tousthe whole *Principles* of *Musick*, which are either *Concords* or *concinnous Intervals*: The *Concords* or *harmonical Intervals* are the *essential Principles*, the other are subservient to them, for making their Application more various. Accordingly we have in this *Scale* the whole *Concords*, with all their *concinnous Degrees*, placed in such Order as makes the most perfect Succession of Sounds from any given *Fundamental*, which I suppose represented in the preceeding Series by 1; so that the true Order of *Degrees* thro' any *harmonical Interval* is, that in which they ly from 1 upwards, to the *acute* Term of the given *Concord*, as to $\frac{1}{2}$ for the *Octave*, $\frac{2}{3}$ for the *5th*, &c. or downwards from these Terms to the *Fundamental* 1. The Divisions of the *Octave*, *5th* and *4th* are different, according to the Difference of the *3ds*, and these *Intervals* are to be found in *primary Relation* to the *Fundamental*, in both the preceeding *Scales*; but the *3d l.* and *6th l.* belong to the one, and *3d g.* and *9th g.* to the other *Scale*.

THIS *Scale* not only shews us, by what *Degrees* a Voice can move agreeably, but gives us also this *general Rule*, that Two *Degrees* of one Kind ought never to follow other immediately in a progressive Motion upwards or downwards; and that no more than Three *Tones* (whereof the middle is a lesser *Tone*, and the other Two greater *Tones*) can follow other, but

but a *ſ.* or ſome *harmonical Interval* muſt come next; and every *Song* or *Compoſition* within this *Rule* is particularly called *diatonick Muſick*, from the *Scale* whence this *Rule* ariſes; and from the Effect we may alſo call it the only *natural Muſick*: If in ſome Inſtances there are Exceptions from this *Rule*, as I ſhall hereafter have more particular Occaſion to obſerve, 'tis but for Variety, and very ſeldom practis'd: But this *general Rule* may be obſerved, and yet no good *Melody* follow; and therefore ſome more particular *Rules* muſt be ſought from the *Art* of *Compoſition*. While we are only upon the *Theory*, you can expect but *Theory* and *general Notions*, yet I ſhall have Occaſion afterwards to be more particular on the Limitations, which are neceſſary for the Conduct of the true *muſical Intervals* in making good *Melody*, as theſe Limitations are contained in the Nature of the *Scale* of *Muſick*. But don't miſtake the Deſign of this *Scale* of *Degrees*, as if a Voice ought never to move up or down by any other immediate Diſtances, but by *Degrees*; for tho' that is the moſt frequent Movement, yet to move by *harmonical Diſtances* at once is not excluded, and 'tis abſolutely neceſſary: For the Agreeableneſs of it, you may conſider the *Degrees* were invented only for Variety, that we might not always move up and down by *harmonical Intervals*, which of themſelves are the moſt perfect, the others deriving their Agreeableneſs from their Subſerviency to them. *Obſerve*, theſe *Tones* and *Semitones* are the *Diaſtems* or or *ſimple Intervals* of the *natural* or *diatonick Scale.* In *Ch.* 2. § 1. I have defined a *Diaſtem*, ſuch an Interval as in Practice is never divided, tho' there may be of theſe ſome greater ſome leſſer. To underſtand the Definition perfectly, take now an *Example* in the *diatonick Scale:* A *Semitone* is leſs than a *Tone*, and both are *Diaſtems*; we may raiſe a *Tone* by *Degrees*, firſt raiſing a *Semitone*, and then ſuch a Diſtance as a *Tone* exceeds a *Semitone*, which we may call another *Semitone*, *i. e.* from *a* to *b* a *Semitone*, and then from *b* to *c* the Remainder of a *Tone* which is ſuppoſed betwixt *a c.* But this is never done if we would preſerve the Character of *diatonick Muſick*, becauſe in that *Scale* Two *Semitones* are not to be found together; and if we riſe to the Diſtance of a *Tone*, it muſt be done at once; all greater *Intervals* are diviſible in Practice of this Kind of *Melody*; but in other Kinds practis'd by the *Ancients*, we find that the *Tone* was a *Syſtem*, and ſome greater *Intervals* were practis'd as *Diaſtems*, which ſhall be explain'd in another Place.

WE ſhall ſtill want ſomething toward a complete and finiſhed Notion of the Uſe and Office of the *Scale* of *Muſick*, till we underſtand diſtinctly what a *Song* truly and naturally *concinnous* is, and particularly what that is which we call the *Key* of a *Song*; and the true Notion of theſe we ſhall eaſily deduce from the Things already explain'd concerning the Principles of *Muſick*; but I find it convenient firſt to diſpatch ſome remaining Conſiderations of the *Intervals*

of

of *Musick*, particularly as they regard the *Scale*.

---

§ 4. *Of the accidental* Discords *in the* System *of* Musick.

WE have considered these *Intervals* and Relations of *Tune* that are the immediate Principles of *Musick*, and which are directly applied in the Practice; I mean these *Intervals* or Relations of *Tune*, which, to make true *Melody*, ought to be betwixt every Note or Sound and the immediately next; these we have considered under the Distinction of *Concords* and *concinnous Intervals*. But there are other *discord* Relations that happen unavoidably in *Musick*, in a kind of accidental and indirect Manner; thus, in the Succession of several *Notes* there are to be considered not only the Relations of these that succeed other immediately, but also of these betwixt which other *Notes* intervene. *Now* the immediate Succession may be conducted so as to produce good *Melody*, yet among the distant Notes there may be very gross *Discords*, that would not be tolerated in immediate *Succession*, and far less in *Consonance*. But particularly let us consider how such *Discords* are actually contained in the *Scale* of *Musick*: Let us take any one Species, suppose

ſuppoſe that with the 3*d g*. as here, in which I mark the Degrees betwixt each Term, and the next.

Names	*Fund.*	2*dg*.	3*dg*.	4*th*,	5*th*,	6*thg*.	7*thg*.	8*ve*
Ratios.	1	$\frac{8}{9}$	$\frac{4}{5}$	$\frac{3}{4}$	$\frac{2}{3}$	$\frac{3}{5}$	$\frac{8}{15}$	$\frac{1}{2}$
Degr.		*tg*	*tl*	*ſ*	*tg*	*tl*	*tg*	*ſ*.

NOW tho' the Progreſſion is *melodious*, as the Terms refer to one common *Fundamental*, yet there are ſeveral *Diſcords* among the *mutual Relations* of the Terms, for *Example*, from 4*th* to 7*th g*. is 32 : 45, alſo from 2*d g*. to 6*th g*. is 27 : 40, and from 2*d g*. to 4*th* is 27 : 32, all *Diſcords*. And if we continue the Series to another *Octave*, then 'tis plain we ſhall find all the *Diſcords*, leſs than *Octave*, that can poſſibly be in ſuch a *Scale*, by comparing every Term, from 1 in order upwards, to every other, that's diſtant from it within an *Octave*; and tho' there be Difference of the Two *Scales* of Aſcent, the one uſing the 3*d l*. and 6*th l*. and the other the 3*d g*. and 6*th g*. yet all the Relations that can poſſibly happen in the one, will alſo happen in the other, as I ſhall immediately ſhow you.

LET us therefore take any one of theſe Series, as that with the 3*d g*. and 6*th g*. and continue it to a double *Octave*, and then examine the Relations of each Term to each. In order to this, I ſhall anticipate a little upon that Part

Part where I am to explain the *Art* of *writing Musick*; and here suppose several Sounds in the Order of the preceeding *Scale* to be represented by so many Letters; and because every *Octave* is but the Repetition of the 1*st*, so that from every Term to the 8*th inclusive*, is always a just *Octave* in the Relation of 1 : 2; therefore to represent such a Scale by Letters, we need but 7 different ones, A, B, C, D, E, F, G, which will answer the first 7 Terms of the *Octave*, and the 8*th* will be represented by the first Letter; and so in order again to another *Octave*. And that all Things may be as distinct as possible, we shall make every 7 Letters in order from the Beginning of a different Character; but for a Reason that will appear afterwards, instead of beginning with *A*, I shall begin with *C*, and proceed in this Order,

C : D : E : F : G : A : B : *c* : *d* : *e* : *f* : *g* : *a* : *b* :: *cc*.

where C represents the *Fundamental* and lowest Note of the *Scale*; and the rest are in order *acuter*. And now when any *Interval* is expressed by Two Letters, it will be easy to know in which *Octave* (*i. e.* whether in the first or second in order from the *Fundamental*) each Extreme is; for if they be both one Kind of Character, then they are both in one *Octave*, as *C*-*F*; otherwise they are in different *Octaves*, as *A* - *f*. And it will be easily known whether the *Interval* be equal to, or greater or less than an *Octave*; for from any Letter to the like Letter is is an *Octave*, or Two *Octaves*, as *c-c* is an *Octave*, or *C-cc* Two *Octaves*, consequently *A-b* is known at Sight to be greater than an *Octave*, even as far as *b* is above *a*; and *B-D* to be less. *Again*, by this Means we easily know whether the Example is taken ascending or descending, so 'tis plain, that from *D* to *a* is ascending, or from *d* to *g*; but from *f* to *d* is descending, or from *d* to *E*: The Order of the several Letters, and their different Characters determine all these Things with great Ease.

ACCORDING to this Supposition, then, I have express'd the *Scale* by these Letters, in a Table calculated for the Purpose of this *Section*, (See *Plate* 1. *Fig.* 5.) In the first Column on the left you have the Names of the *Intervals*, as they proceed in Order from a common *Fundamental*; in the 2*d* you have the Progression of *Degrees* from every Term to the next; in the 3*d* you have the several Terms expressed by Letters; in the 4*th* Column you have the Numbers that express the Relations of every Term to the *Fundamental C* (which is 1) as far as Two *Octaves*, taken in the natural Order of the *concinnous* Parts of the *Octave*, as above divided and explained, these being supposed to be fixed Relations; then in the other Columns you have expressed the Relations of every Term, in order upwards from *C*, to all these above them, as far as an *Octave*; reduced to a common *Fundamental* 1, which is the first Number in every Column, and signifies that the Letter

or

or Note againſt which it ſtands, is ſuppoſed to be a common *Relative* to the 7 Terms that ſtand next above it, *i. e.* That the other Numbers of that Column compared to 1, expreſs the Relations which the Notes, or Letters againſt which they ſtand, bear to that againſt which the 1 of that Column ſtands, according to the fixt Relations ſuppoſed in the Fourth Column of Numbers. The 11th Column is the ſame with the 1*ſt*; and if we would carry on that Table *in infinitum*, it would be but a Repetition of the preceeding 7 Columns of Numbers; which ſhews us that Two *Octaves* was ſufficient to diſcover all the ſimple *Diſcords* that could poſſibly be in the *Scale*. I have carried theſe Columns no further than one *Octave*, except the firſt, becauſe all above are but an 8*ve*, and ſome leſſer compounded; and therefore we needed only to find all the ſimple *Diſcords* leſs than an 8*ve*: But the 1*ſt* Column is carried to Two 8*ves*, becauſe the reſt are made out of it; for theſe other expreſs the mutual Relations of each Term of the 1*ſt* Column to all above it within an *Octave*, reduced to a common *Fundamental* 1.

I'll next ſhow you that there are no other Relations in the other Series, which aſcends by a 3*d l.* and 6*th l.* than what are here. The two Species differ only in the 7*ths*, 6*ths* and 3*ds*, and if you'll look but a little back, you'll ſee the true Relation of the Terms of that other Series to the *Fundamental*, which if you compare with that Column in this Table, which begins againſt *E*, you'll find them the ſame in every Term

Term but one; for here the 2*d* Term is 15 : 16 which there is 8 : 9; but if you compare the Column which begins against *A*, you'll find that agree with the *Scale* we are speaking of in every Term but the 4*th*, which is here 20 : 27, and there 3 : 4, the one wants the true 2*d*, and the other the true 4*th*; but both these are in the first Column which begins at *C*; therefore 'tis plain that if these Columns are continued, we must find in them all the Relations that can possibly be in that Scale; which a little Examination will soon discover.

Now besides the *harmonical Intervals* and *Degrees* already explained, we have in this Table the following *discord* Relations, which proceed from the Differences of the *Degrees*, and the particular Order in which they follow other in the Scale; for we may conceive a great Variety of other *Discords* from different Combinations of these *Degrees*, but the Speculation would be of no Use; 'tis enough to consider what are inavoidable in the Order of the *Scale* of *Musick*, which are these mentioned.

Exa. From	To		*Ratios*
D	*F*	=	27 : 32
F	*B*	=	32 : 45
A	*D*	=	20 : 27
D	*A*	=	27 : 40
B	*F*	=	45 : 64
F	*D*	=	16 : 27
D	*C*	=	9 : 16

Again, from the Table we find plainly that from any Note or Letter of the *Scale*, to the 2*d*, 3*d*, 4*th*, 5*th*, &c. *inclusive*, either above or below, is not always the same *Interval*; because tho' there is an an equal Number of *Degrees* in every ſuch Caſe, yet there is not always an equal Number of the ſame *Degrees* ; ſo, from *C* to *F*, there are three Degrees, whereof 1 is a *t g.* 1 is *t l.* and 1 a *ſ.* but from *F* to *B* there are Three *Degrees*, whereof 2 are *t g.* and 1 is a *t l.*

WE have already ſettled the Definitions of a 3*d*, 4*th*, &c. as they are *harmonical Intervals*, they are either to be taken from the true *Ratios* of their Extremes ; or, reſpecting the *Scale* of *Muſick*, from the Number and particular Kinds of *Degrees* ; yet we may make a general Definition that will ſerve any Part of the *Scale*, and call that *Interval*, which is from any Letter of the *Scale* to the 2*d*, 3*d*, 4*th*, &c. *incluſive*, a 2*d*, a 3*d*, a 4*th*, &c. But then we muſt make a Diſtinction, according as they are *harmonical* or not ; under which Diſtinction the *Octaves* will not come, because every Eight Letter *incluſive* is not only the ſame, but is a true *Octave* in the *Ratio* of 1 : 2 ; which is plain from this, That every *Octave* in order from the *Fundamental* or loweſt Note of the *Scale*, is divided the ſame Way, into the ſame Number of the ſame Kind of *Degrees*, and in the ſame Order : And for other *Intervals* leſs than an *Octave*, we have Three of each Kind, differing in Quantity ; which Differences ariſe from the Three different *Degrees*, as I have expreſſed them in the following *Table*, wherein the greateſt ſtands uppermoſt, and ſo in Order.

2ds.	3ds.	4ths.	5ths.	6ths.	7ths.
8 : 9	4 : 5	32 : 45	2 : 3	16 : 27	8 : 15
9 : 10	5 : 6	20 : 27	27 : 40	3 : 5	5 : 9
15 : 16	27 : 32	3 : 4	45 : 64	5 : 8	9 : 16

THE Three 2*ds* or *Degrees* are all *concinnous Intervals*; of the 3*ds* one is *Discord*, viz. 27 : 32, and therefore called a *false* 3*d*; the other Two are particularly known by the Names of 3*dg.* and 3*d l.* of the 4*ths* and 5*ths* Two are *Discords*, and called *false* 4*ths* and 5*ths*; and therefore when we speak of a 4*th* or 5*th*, without calling it *false*, 'tis understood to be of the true *harmonical* Kind; of the 6*ths* one is *false*, and the other Two which are *harmonical*, are called 6*th g.* and 6*th l.* the 7*ths* are neither *harmonical* nor *concinnous Intervals*, yet of Use in *Musick*, as I have already mentioned; the Two greater are particularly known by the Name of greater or lesser 7*th*, tho' some I know make the least 9 : 16 the 7*th* lesser; I mean they make that *Ratio* a Term in the Division of the *Octave* by 3*d l.* and 6*th l.* but I shall have Occasion to consider this more particularly in another Place. *Now*, as to the Composition of the *Octave* out of the *Intervals* of this last *Table*, we have this to remark, that if we compare the 2*ds* with the 7*ths*, or the 3*ds* with the 6*ths*, or 4*ths* with 5*ths*, the greater of the one added to the lesser of the other, or the Middle of the one added to the Middle of the

the other, is exactly equal to *Octave*; and generally add the greatest of any Species of *Intervals* (for *Example 5ths*) to the lesser of any other (as 3*ds*) and the least of that to the greater of this; also the Middle of the one to the Middle of the other, the Three *Sums* or *Intervals* proceeding from that Addition are equal.

WE shall next consider what the Errors of these *false Intervals* are. The Variety, as to the Quantity, of *Intervals* that have the same Number of *Degrees* in the *Scale*, arises, as I have already said, from the Differences of the Three *Degrees*; and therefore the Differences among *Intervals* of the same Species and Denomination, *i. e.* the Excesses or Defects of the *false* fromthe *true*, are no other than the Differences of these *Degrees*, viz. 80 : 81, the Difference of a *tg.* and *tl.* which is particularly called a *Comma* among *Musicians*; 24 : 25, the Difference of a *tl.* and *f.* which is sometimes called a lesser *Semitone*, because it is less than 15 : 16; then 128 : 135, the Difference of a *tg.* and *f.* which is a greater Difference than the last, and is also called a lesser *Semitone*, and is a Middle betwixt 15 : 16, and 24 : 25. Betwixt which of the greater *Intervals* these Differences do particularly exist, will be easily found, by looking into the former *Table*, and applying *Problem* 10. of *Chap.* 4. that is, multiplying the Two *Ratios* compared cross-ways, the greater Number of the one by the lesser of the other, the Products contain the *Ratio* or Dif-

Difference ſought. *Obſerve* alſo, that the greateſt of the *4ths*, viz. 32 : 45 is particularly called a *Tritone*, for 'tis equal to 2 *t g.* and 1 *t l.* and its Complement to an *Octave*, viz. 45 : 64, which is the leaſt of the *5ths*, is particularly called a leſſer *5th* or *Semidiapente* (the Original of the laſt Name you'll hear afterwards.) Theſe Two are the *falſe 4th* and *5th*, which are uſed as *Diſcords* in the Buſineſs of *Harmony*, and they are the Two *Intervals* which divide the *Octave* into Two Parts neareſt to Equality, for their Difference is only this very ſmall *Interval* 2025 : 2048. And becauſe in common Practice the Difference of *t g.* and *t l.* is neglected, tho' it has its Influence, as we ſhall hear of, therefore theſe *Intervals* are only called *falſe*, which exceed or come ſhort by a *Semitone* ; and upon this Suppoſition therefore there is no *falſe 3d* or *6th*, nor any *falſe 4th* or *5th*, except the *Tritone* and *Semidiapente* mentioned, which with the *7ths* and *2ds* are all the *Diſcords* reckoned in the *Syſtem*; however when we would know the Nature of Things accurately, we muſt neglect no Differences.

THE Diſtinctions already made of the *Intervals* of the *Scale* of *Muſick*, regard their Contents as to the Number and Kind of *Degrees* ; but in the *Scale* we find *Intervals* of the ſame Extent, differing in the Order of their *Degrees*. We ſhall eaſily find the whole Variety, by examining the *Scales* of *Muſick* ; for the Variety is increaſed by the Two different *Series* or *Scales* above explained, there being ſome in the one that

that are not to be found in the other. I ſhall leave it to your ſelves to examine and find out the Examples, and only mention here the *Octaves*, whereof there are in this reſpect ſeven different Species in each *Scale*, proceeding from the ſeven different Letters; for it is plain at ſight, that the Order of *Degrees* from each of theſe Letters upward to an *Octave* is different; and that there can be no more Variety if the *Scale* were continued *in infinitum*, becauſe from the ſame Letter taken in any Part of the *Scale*, there is always the ſame Order. What Uſe has been made of this Diſtinction of *Intervals*, and particularly *Octaves*, falls to be conſidered in another Place; I ſhall only obſerve here, that tho' all this Variety happens actually within the Compaſs of Two *Octaves*, yet if you ask, what is the moſt natural and agreeable Order in the Diviſion of the *Octave*, it is that which belongs to the *Octave* from *C* in the preceeding *Scale*; or change the 3*d*, 6*th* and 7*th* from greater to leſſer, and that makes another *concinnous* Order; the *Degrees* of each as they follow other, you have already ſet down. Now if you begin and carry on the *Series* in any of theſe Two Orders to a double *Octave*, none of the accidental *Diſcords* will give any Offence to the Ear, becauſe their Extremes are not heard in immediate Succeſſion; and the *Diſcord* is rendred altogether inſenſible by the immediate Notes; eſpecially by the *harmonious* Relation of each Term to the common *Fundamental*, and the manifold *Concords* that are to be found among

among the ſeveral middle Terms. For the Poſitions of the *Degrees*, which occaſion theſe *Diſcords*, if we conſider them with reſpect to the *Fundamental C*, they are truly *concinnous*, but with reſpect to the loweſt of Two Notes, betwixt which they make the *Diſcord*, they follow *inconcinnouſly* from it, becauſe they were not deſigned to follow it as a *Fundamental*; and ſo are not to be referred to it: Therefore in all the *Scale*, only *C* can be made *fundamental*, becauſe from none of the other Six Letters do the *Degrees* follow in a right *concinnous* Order, unleſs, as I ſaid before, we neglect the Difference of *t g.* and *t l.* and then the *Octave* from *A* will be a right *concinnous* Series, proceeding by a 3*d l.* when it proceeds by a 3*d g.* from *C*, and contrarily; and hereby we ſhall have both the Species in one Series; otherwiſe there are Three Terms that are variable, which are the 3*d*, 6*th* and 7*th* from the *Fundamental*, i. e. *E*, *A*, *B*, when the *Fundamental* is called *C*; and this muſt be carefully minded when we ſpeak of the *Scale* of *Muſick*. How unavoidable theſe Kinds of *Diſcords* are among the Notes of the *Scale*, we have ſeen; but, as I have already obſerved, there are other Succeſſions that are *melodious*, beſides a conſtant Succeſſion of *Degrees*; for theſe are mixt in Practice with *harmonical Intervals*: And here alſo the immediate Succeſſion many be *melodious*, tho' there be many *Diſcords* among the diſtant Notes, whoſe Harſhneſs is rendred altogether inſenſible from their Situation, eſpecially becauſe of the *harmonical*

Relation

Relation of the ſeveral Notes to ſome *fundamental* or principal Note, which is called the *Key*, with a particular Reſpect to which the reſt of the Notes are choſen.

CHAP. IX.

Of the Mode *or* Key *in* Muſick; *and a further Account of the true End and Office of the* Scale *of* Muſick.

§ 1. *Of the* Mode *or* Key.

WE have already divided the Application of the *Tune* of *Sounds* into theſe Two, *Melody* and *Harmony*. When ſeveral ſimple Sounds ſucceed other agreeably in the Ear, that Effect is called *Melody*; the proper Materials of which are the *Degrees* and *harmonious Intervals* above explained. But 'tis not every Succeſſion of theſe that can produce this Pleaſure; Nature has marked out certain Limits for a general Rule, and left the Application to the Fancy and Imagination; but always under the Direction of the Ear. The other chief Ingredient in *Muſick* is the *Duration*, or Difference of Notes with reſpect to their uninterrupterrupted Continuance in one *Tune*, and the Quickneſs or Slowneſs of their Succeſſion; taking in both theſe, a *melodious Song* may be brought under this general Definition, *viz. A Collection of Sounds or Notes (however produced) differing in* Tune *by the* Degrees *or* harmonious Intervals *of the* Scale *of* Muſick, *which ſucceeding other in the Ear, after equal or unequal* Duration *in their reſpective* Tunes, *affect the Mind with Pleaſure.* But the Deſign of this *Chapter* is only to conſider the Nature and general Limits of a Song, with reſpect to *Tune*, which is properly the *Melody* of it; and obſerve, That by a Song I mean every ſingle Piece of *Muſick*, whether contrived for a Voice or Inſtrument.

A *Song* may be compared not abſurdly to an Oration; for as in this there is a *Subject*, *viz.* ſome *Perſon* or *Thing* the Diſcourſe is referred to, that ought always to be kept in View, thro' the Whole, ſo that nothing unnatural or foreign to the *Subject* may be brought in; in like Manner, in every regular and truly *melodious Song*, there is one Note which regulates all the reſt; the Song begins, and at leaſt ends in this, which is as it were the principal Matter, or *muſical Subject* that demands a ſpecial Regard to it in all the other Notes of the Song. And as in an Oration, there may be ſeveral diſtinct Parts, which refer to different Subjects, yet ſo as they muſt all have an evident Connection with the principal Subject which regulates and influences the Whole; ſo in *Melody*, there may be be ſeveral ſubprincipal Subjects, to which the different Parts of that Song may belong, but theſe are themſelves under the Influence of the principal Subject, and muſt have a ſenſible Connection with it. This principal Note is called the *Key* of the Song, or the *principal Key* with reſpect to theſe others which are the *ſubprincipal Keys.* But a Song may be ſo ſhort, and ſimply contrived, that all its Notes refer only to one *Key.*

THAT we may underſtand this Matter diſtinctly, let us reflect on ſome Things already explained: We have ſeen how the *Octave* contains in it the whole Principles of *Muſick*, both with reſpect to *Conſonance* (or *Harmony*) as it contains all the original *Concords*, and the *harmonical* Diviſion of ſuch greater, as are equal to the Sum of leſſer *Concords* ; and with reſpect to *Succeſſion* (or *Melody*) as in the *concinnous* Diviſion of the *Octave*, we have all the *Degrees* ſubſervient to the *harmonical Intervals*, and the Order in which they ought to be taken to make the moſt agreeable Succeſſion of Sounds, riſing or falling gradually from any given Sound, *i. e.* any Note of a given and determined Pitch of *Tune*; for the *Scale* ſuppoſes no Pitch, and only aſſigns the juſt Relations of Sound which make true *muſical Intervals* : But as the 3*ds* and 6*ths* are each diſtinguiſhed into greater and leſſer, from this ariſe Two different Species in the Diviſion of the *Octave*. We have alſo obſerved, That if either *Scale* (*viz.* That which proceeds by the 3*d l.* or by the 3*d g.*) is is continued to a double *Octave*, there ſhall be in that Caſe 7 different Orders of the *Degrees* of an 8*ve*, proceeding from the 7 different Letters with which the Terms of the *Scale* are marked; none of which Orders but the firſt, *viz.* from *C* is the natural Order; and tho' in raiſing the Series from *C* to the double *Octave*, we actually go through the Degrees in each of theſe Orders, yet *C* only being the *Fundamental*, to which all the Notes of the Series are referred, there is nothing offenſive in theſe different Orders, which are but accidental; ſo that in every *Octave* concinnouſly divided, there are 7 different *Intervals* relative to the *Fundamental*, whoſe acute Terms are the eſſential Notes of the *Octave*, and they are theſe, *viz.* the 2*d g.* 3*d g.* 4*th*, 5*th*, 6*th g.* 7*th g.* 8*ve*, or 2*d g.* 3*d l.* 4*th*, 5*th*, 6*th l.* 7*th l.* 8*ve*.

NOW, let us ſuppoſe any given Sound, *i. e.* a Sound of any determinate Pitch of *Tune*, it may be made the *Key* of a *Song*, by applying to it the Seven eſſential or natural Notes that ariſe from the *concinnous* Diviſion of the 8*ve*, as I have juſt now ſet them down, and repeating the 8*ve* above or below as oft as you pleaſe. The given Sound is applied as the principal Note or *Key* of the *Song*, by making frequent *Cloſes* or *Cadences* upon it; and in the Courſe or Progreſs of the *Melody*, none other than theſe Seven natural Notes can be brought in, while the *Song* continues in that *Key*, becauſe every other Note is foreign to that *Fundamental* or *Key*.

To

To understand all this more distinctly, let us consider, That by a *Close* or *Cadence* is meant a terminating or bringing the *Melody* to a Period or Rest, after which it begins and sets out anew, which is like the finishing of some distinct Purpose in an Oration; but you must get a perfect Notion of this from Experience. Let us suppose a Song begun in any Note, and carried on upwards or downwards by *Degrees* and *harmonical Distances*, so as never to touch any Notes but what are referable to that first Note as a *Fundamental*, *i. e.* are the true Notes of the *natural Scale* proceeding from that *Fundamental*; and let the *Melody* be conducted so through these natural Notes, as to close and terminate in that *Fundamental*, or any of its 8*ves* above or below; that Note is called the *Key* of the *Melody*, because it governs and regulates all the rest, putting this general Limitation upon them, that they must be to it in the Relation of the Seven essential and natural Notes of an 8*ve*, as abovementioned; and when any other Note is brought in, then 'tis said to go out of that *Key*: And by this Way of speaking of a Song's continuing in or going out of a *Key*, we may observe, that the whole 8*ve*, with all its natural and *concinnous* Notes, belong to the *Idea* of a *Key*, tho' the *Fundamental*, being the principal Note which regulates the rest, is in a peculiar Sense called the *Key*, and gives Denomination to it in a System of fixt Sounds, and in the Method of marking Sounds by Letters, as we shall hear of more particularly afterwards.

And

And in this Application of the Word *Key* to one *fundamental* Note, another Note is ſaid to be out of the *Key*, when it has not the Relation to that Fundamental of any of the natural Notes that belong to the *concinnous* Diviſion of the 8*ve*. And here too we muſt add a neceſſary Caution with reſpect to the Two different Diviſions of the 8*ve*, *viz.* That a Note may belong to the ſame *Key*, *i. e.* have a juſt muſical Relation to the ſame *Fundamental* in one Kind of Diviſion, and be out of the *Key* with reſpect to the other: For *Example*, If the Melody has uſed the 3*d g.* to any *Fundamental*, it requires alſo the 6*th g.* and therefore if the 6*th l.* is brought in, the *Melody* is out of the firſt *Key*.

NOW a Song may be carried thro' ſeveral *Keys*, *i e.* it may begin in one *Key*, and be led out of that to another, by introducing ſome Note that is foreign to the firſt, and ſo on to another: But a regular Piece muſt not only return to the firſt *Key*, theſe other Keys muſt alſo have a particular Connection and Relation with the firſt, which is the principal Key. The Rule which determines the Connection of *Keys*, you'll find diſtinctly explained in *Chap.* 13. for we may not change at random from one *Key* to another; I ſhall only obſerve here, that theſe other *Keys* muſt be ſome of the Seven natural Notes of the *principal Key*, yet not any of them; for which ſee the *Chapter* referred to.

BUT that you may conceive all this yet more clearly, we ſhall make *Examples*. Suppoſe the following *Scale* of Notes expreſt by Letters, where-

wherein I mark the Degrees thus, *viz.* a *t g.* with a *Colon* (:) a *t l.* with a *Semicolon* (;) *Semitone* with a Point (.) And here I mark the Series that proceeds with the 3*d g*, &c.

C : D ; E . F : G ; A : B . c : d ; e . f : g ; a : b . c

The first Note represents any given Sound, and the rest are fixt according to their Relations to it, exprest by the Degrees: Let the first Note of the Song, which is also the designed *Key*, be taken *Unison* to *C.* (which represents any given Sound) all the rest of the Notes, while it keeps within one *Key*, must be in such Relation to the first, as if placed according to their Distances from it in a direct Series, they shall be *unison* each with some Note of the preceeding *Scale*: The *Example* is of a *Key* with the 3*d g*, &c. which is easily applied to the other Species. Let us now suppose the Conduct of the *Melody* such, that after a Cadence in *C* the Song shall make the next Cadence in a 3*d g.* above, *viz.* in *E*, and this is a new *Key* into which the *Melody* goes.

WE have observed in the preceeding *Chap.* that the Order of Degrees from each of the Letters of the *diatonick Scale*, is different; and therefore while the Relation of these Notes are supposed fixt, 'tis plain none of the Notes of that *Scale* except *C* can be made a *Key*, because the Seven Notes within the 8*ve* are not in the true Relation of the essential and natural Notes of an 8*ve* concinnously divided; and

and therefore the *natural Scale* (*i.e.* the Order from *C*) muſt be applied anew from every new *Key*; as in the preceeding *Example*, the 2*d Key* is *E*, which in that *Scale* has a 3*d l.* at *G*, but it has not all its Seven Notes in juſt Relation to the *Fundamental*, the firſt Degree being a *ſ.* which ought to be *t g*; and therefore if the *Melody* in that *Key* be ſo managed as to have Uſe for all the Seven natural Notes, they cannot be all found in the Series that proceeds *concinnouſly* from *C*, but requires the Application of the *natural Scale* to that new Pitch, *i. e.* requires that we make a Series of *concinnous* Degrees from that new *Fundamental*; which we may expreſs either by calling it *C*, and applying the ſame Names to the whole 8*ve*, above or below it, as to the former *Key*, or retaining ſtill the Names *E F*, &c. to an 8*ve*, but ſuppoſing their Relations changed.

A Song may be ſo ordered, that it ſhall not require all the Seven natural Notes of the *Key*; and if the *Melody* be ſo contrived in the *ſub-principal Keys* of the *Song*, that it ſhall uſe none of the eſſential Notes of theſe *Keys*, but ſuch as coincide with theſe of the *principal Key*, then is the whole of that *Song* more ſtrictly limited to the *principal Key*: So that in a good Senſe it may be said never to go out of it; but then there will be leſs Variety under ſuch Limitations: And if a Song may be ſuppoſed to go through ſeveral *Keys*, the principal being always perfect as from *C*, and the Subprincipals taken with ſuch Imperfections as they unavoidably have, when

we

we are confined to one individual Series of determinate Sounds, the *Musick* may be said also in this Case never to depart from the *principal Key*; but 'tis plain, that the using such *Intervals* with respect to the *subprincipal Keys*, will make the *Melody* imperfect, and also occasion Errors of worse Consequence in the *Harmony* of Parts so conducted.

'Tis Time now to consider the *Distinctions* of *Keys*. We have seen that to constitute any Note or given Sound a *Key* or *fundamental* Note, it must have these Seven essential or natural Notes added to it, *viz.* 2*d g.* 3*d g.* or 3*d l.* 4*th*, 5*th*, 6*th g.* or 6*th l.* 7*th g.* or 7*th l.*. 8*ve* out of which, or their 8*ves*, all the Notes of the *Song* must be taken while it keeps within that *Key*, *i. e.* within the Property of that *Fundamental*; 'tis plain therefore, that there are but Two different Species of *Keys*, according as we joyn the greater or lesser 3*d*, which are always accompanied with the 6*th* and 7*th* of the same Species, *viz.* the 3*d g.* with the 6*th g.* and 7*th g*; and the 3*d l.* with the 6*th l.* and 7*th l*; and this Distinction is marked with the Names of A Sharp Key, which is that with the 3*d g*, &c. and A Flat Key with the 3*d l*, &c. Now from this it is plain, that however many different Closes may be in any Song, there can be but Two *Keys*, if we consider the essential Difference of *Keys*; for every *Key* is either *sharp* or *flat*, and all *sharp Keys* are of the same Nature, as to the *Melody*, and so are all *fla[t] Keys* for *Example*, Let the *principal Key* o[f]

a

a Song be *C* (with a 3*d g.*) in which the final Cofe is made, let other Clofes be made in *E* (the 3*d* of the *principal Key*) with a 3*d g.* and in *A* (the 6*th* of the *principal Key*) with a 3*d l.* yet in all this there are but Two different *Keys*, *ſharp* and *flat*: But *obſerve*, in ommon Practice the *Keys* are ſaid to be different when nothing is conſidered, but the different *Tune* or Pitch of the Note in which the different Cloſes are made; and in this Senſe the ſame Song is ſaid to be in different Keys, according as it is begun in different Notes or Degrees of *Tune*. But that we may ſpeak accurately, and have Names anſwering to the real Differences of Things, which I think neceſſary to prevent Confuſion, I would propoſe the Word *Mode*, to expreſs the *melodious Conſtitution* of the *Octave*, as it conſiſts of Seven eſſential or natural Notes, beſides the *Fundamental*; and becauſe there are Two Species, let us call that with a 3*dg.* the *greater Mode*, and that with a 3*d l.* the *leſſer Mode*: And the Word *Key* may be applied to every Note of a Song, in which a *Cadence* is made; ſo that all theſe (comprehending the whole *Octave* from each) may be called different *Keys*, in reſpect of their different *Degrees* of *Tunes*, but with reſpect to the eſſential Difference in the Conſtitution of the *Octaves*, on which the *Melody* depends, there are only Two different *Modes*, the greater and the leſſer. Thus the Latin Writers uſe the Word *Modus*, to ſignify the particular *Mode* or Way of conſtituting the *Octave*;

and

and hence they also called it *Constitutio*; but of this in its own Place.

'TIS plain then, that a *Mode* (or *Key* in this Sense) is not any single Note or Sound, and cannot be denominated by it, for it signifies the particular Order or Manner of the *concinnous Degrees* of an 8*ve*, the *fundamental* Note of which may in another Sense be called the *Key*, as it signifies that principal Note which regulates the rest, and to which they refer: And even when the Word *Key*, applied to different Notes, signifies no more than their different Degrees of *Tune*, these Notes are always considered as *Fundamentals* of an 8*ve concinnously* divided, tho' the Mode of the Division is not considered when we call them different *Keys*; so that the whole 8*ve* comes within the *Idea* of a Key in this Sense also: Therefore to distinguish properly betwixt *Mode* and *Key*, and to know the real Difference, take this Definition, *viz.* an 8*ve* with all its natural and *concinnous* Degrees is called a *Mode*, with respect to the Constitution or the Manner and Way of dividing it; and with respect to the Place of it in the *Scale* of *Musick*, *i. e.* the *Degree* or Pitch of *Tune*, it is called a *Key*, tho' this Name is peculiarly applied to the *Fundamental*. Hence it is plain, that the same *Mode* may be with different *Keys*, that's to say, an *Octave* of Sounds may be raised in the same Order and Kind of *Degrees*, which makes the same *Mode*, and yet be begun higher or lower, *i. e.* taken at different *Degrees* of *Tune*, with respect to the Whole, which makes different

Keys.

Keys. It follows alſo from theſe Definitions, that the ſame *Key* may be with different *Modes*, that is, the Extremes of Two *Octaves* may be in the ſame *Degree* of *Tune*, and the Diviſion of them different. The Manner of dividing the *Octave*, and the *Degree* of *Tune* at which it is begun, are ſo diſtinct, that I think there is Reaſon to give them different Names; yet I know, that common Practice applies the Word *Key* to both; ſo the ſame *Fundamental* conſtitutes Two different *Keys*, according to the Diviſion of the *Octave*; and therefore a Note is ſaid to be out of the *Key*, with reſpect to the ſame *Fundamental* in one Diviſion, which is not ſo in another, as I have explained more particularly a little above; and the ſame Song is ſaid to be in different *Keys*, when there is no other Difference, but that of being begun at different Notes. Now, if the Word *Key* muſt be uſed both Ways, to keep up a common Practice, we ought at leaſt to prevent the Ambiguity, which may be done by applying the Words *ſharp* and *flat*. For *Example*. Let the ſame *Song* be taken up at different Notes, which we call *C* and *A*, it may in that reſpect be ſaid to be in different *Keys*, but the Denomination of the *Key* is from the Cloſe; and Two Songs cloſing in the ſame Note, as *C*, may be ſaid to be in different *Keys*, according as they have a greater or leſſer 3*d*; and to diſtinguiſh them, we ſay the one is in the *ſharp Key C*, and the other in the *flat Key C*; and therefore, when *ſharp* or *flat* is added to the Letter or Name by which any

funda-

fundamental Note is marked, it expreſſes both the *Mode* and *Key*, as I have diſtinguiſhed them above; but without theſe Words it expreſſes nothing but what I have called the *Key* in Diſtinction from *Mode*. But of the Denominations of *Keys* in the *Scale* of *Muſick*, we ſhall hear particularly in *Chap.* 11.

Obſerve next, that of the natural Notes of every *Mode* or *Octave*, Three go under the Name of the *eſſential Notes*, in a peculiar Manner, *viz.* the *Fundamental*, the 3*d*, and 5*th*, their *Octaves* being reckoned the ſame, and marked with the ſame Letters in the *Scale*; the reſt are particularly called *Dependents*. But again, the *Fundamental* is alſo called the *final*, becauſe the Song commonly begins and always ends there: The 5*th* is called the *Dominante*, becauſe it is the next principal Note to the *final*, and moſt frequently repeted in the Song; and if 'tis brought in as a new *Key*, it has the moſt perfect Connection with the *principal Key*: The 3*d* is called the *Mediante*, becauſe it ſtands betwixt the *Final* and *Dominante* as to its Uſe. But the 3*d* and 5*th* of any *Mode* or *Key* deſerve the Name of *eſſential Notes*, more peculiarly with reſpect to their Uſe in *Harmony*, becauſe the *Harmony* of a 3*d*, 5*th* and 8*ve*, is the moſt perfect of all others; ſo that a 3*d* and a 5*th*, applied in *Conſonance* to any *Fundamental*, gives it the Denomination of the *Key*; for chiefly by Means of theſe the Cadence in the *Key* is performed. The *Baſs* being the governing Part with reſpect to the *Harmony*, ought finally to

cloſe

close in the *Key*; and the Relation or *Harmony* of the Parts at the final Close, ought to be so perfect, that the Mind may find entire Satisfaction in it, and have nothing further to expect. Let us suppose Four Voices, making together the *Harmony* of these Four Notes *G* -- *c* -- *e* -- *g*, where *G* is the *Fundamental*, *c* a 4*th*, *e* a 6*th g*. and *g* an 8*ve*; so that *c* - *e* is a 3*d g*. and *e* -- *g* a 3*d l*. and *c* -- *g* a 5*th*. The Ear would not rest in this Close, because there is a Tendency in it to something more perfect; for the true *Key* in these Four is *c*, to which the 3*d* and 5th is applied; the *Bass* closing in *G* puts the 5*th* out of its proper Place, for it ought to stand next the *Fundamental*; nor can the 3*d* be separate from the 5*th*, which can stand with no other. Now the Thing required is, to restore the 5*th* to its due Place, and this is done, by removing the 4*th* to the upper Place of the *Harmony*; so in the preceeding *Example*, suppose the *Bass* moves from *G* to *c*, and the rest move accordingly till the Four make these *c* -- *e* -- *g* -- *cc*, in which *c* -- *e* is 3*d g*. *c* -- *g* a 5*th*; then we have a perfect Close, and the *Musick* is got into the true and principal *Key*, which is *c*.

WE have one Thing more to observe as to the 7*th*, which is natural to every *Mode*; in the *greater Modes* or *sharp Keys* 'tis always the 7*th g*. but *flat Keys* use both the 7*th g*. and 7*th l*. in different Circumstances: The 7*th l*. most naturally accompanies the 3*d l*. and 6*th l*. which constitute a *flat Key*, and belongs to it necefneceſſarily, when we conſider the *concinnous* Diviſion of the *Octave*, and the moſt agreeable Succeſſion of *Degrees*; and it is uſed in every Place, except it is ſometimes toward a Cloſe, eſpecially when we aſcend to the *Key*, for then the *7th g.* being within a *ſ.* of the *Key*, makes a ſmooth and eaſy Paſſage into it, and will ſometimes alſo occaſion the *6th g.* to be brought in. Again, 'tis by Means of this *7th g.* that the Tranſition from one *Key* to another is chiefly performed; for when the *Melody* is to be tranſferred to a new *Key*, the *7th g.* of it (whether 'tis a *ſharp* or *flat Key*) is commonly introduced: But you ſhall have more of this in *Chap.* 13.

I have ſaid, that the *7th* is uſed in *Melody* as a ſingle *Degree*, but in ſuch Circumſtances as removes the Harſhneſs of ſo great a *Diſcord*, as particularly in quick Movements; and we may here conſider, that a *7th* being the Complement of a true *Degree* to *Octave*, partakes of the Nature of a *Degree* ſo far, that to move upward by a *Degree*, or downwards by its Correſpondent *7th*, and contrarily downwards by a *Degree*, or upwards by a *7th*, brings us into the ſame Note; and from this Connection of it with the true *Degrees*, 'tis frequently uſeful.

---

§ 2. *Of the Office of the* Scale *of* Muſick.

NOw from what has been explained, we very eaſily ſee the true and proper *Office* of the *Scale of Muſick*, which, ſtrictly ſpeaking, is all comprehended in an *Octave*, what is above or below

below being but a Repetition. The *Scale* ſuppoſes no determinate Pitch of *Tune*, but that being aſſigned to the *Fundamental*, it marks out the *Tune* of the Reſt with relation to it. We learn here how to paſs by *Degrees* moſt *melodiouſly*, from any given Note to any *harmonical* Diſtance. The *Scale* ſhews us, what Notes can be naturally joyned to any *Fundamental*, and thereby teaches us the juſt and natural Limitations of *Melody*. It exhibites to us all the *Intervals* and Relations that are eſſential and neceſſary in *Muſick*, and contains virtually all the. Variety of Orders, in which theſe Relations can be taken ſucceſſively; if a Song is confined to one *Key*, the Thing is plain, if 'tis carried thro' ſeveral *Keys*, it may ſeem to require ſeveral diſtinct Series; yet the *Muſick* in every Part being truly *diatonick*, 'tis but the ſame natural *Scale* (with its Two different Species) applied to different *fundamental* Notes. And this brings us to conſider the Effect of having a Series of Sounds fixt to the Relations of the *Scale*: If we ſuppoſe this, it will eaſily appear how inſufficient ſuch a *Scale* is for all the agreeable Variety of *Melody*: But then, this Imperfection is not any Defect in the natural *Syſtem*, but follows accidentally, upon its being confined to this Condition: For this is not the *Nature* and *Office* of the *Scale of Muſick*, that ſuppoſing its Relations all expreſſed in a Series of determinate Sounds, that individual Series ſhould contain all the Variety of Notes, that can *melodiouſly* ſucceed other; unleſs

leſs you'll ſuppoſe every Song ought to be limited to one *Key*; but otherwiſe one individual *diatonick* Series of fixt Sounds is not ſufficient. Let us ſuppoſe the *Scale* of *Muſick* thus defin'd, *viz.* a Series of Sounds, whoſe Relations to one another are ſuch, that in one individual Series, determined in theſe Relations, all the Notes may be found that can be taken ſucceſſively to make true *Melody*; ſuch a *Syſtem* would indeed be of great Uſe, and be juſtly reckoned a *perfect Syſtem*; but if the Nature of Things will not admit of ſuch a Series, then 'tis but a *Chimera*; and yet it is true, that the natural *Scale* is a *juſt* and *perfect Syſtem*, when we conſider its proper Office as I have expreſt it above, and as we ſhall underſtand further from the next *Chapter*, in which I ſhall conſider more particularly the *Defect* of *Inſtruments* having fixt and determinate Sounds, and the Remedy applied to it; and comparing this with the Capacity of the *human Voice*, we ſhall plainly underſtand, in what different Senſes the *Scale* of *Muſick* explained, ought to be called a *perfect* or *imperfect Syſtem*.

CHAP.

CHAP. X.

Concerning the Scale *of* Musick *limited to fixed Sounds, explaining the* Defects *of* Instruments, *and the Remedies thereof; wherein is taught the true* Use *and* Original *of the Notes we commonly call* sharp *and* flat.

§ 1. *Of the* Defects *of* Instruments, *and of the Remedy thereof in general, by the Means of what we call* Sharps *and* Flats.

THE Use of the *Scale* of *Musick* has been largely explain'd, and the general Limitations of *Melody* contained in it. Why the *Scale* exhibited in the preceeding *Chapters* is called the *natural*, and the *diatonick Scale*, has been also said, and how *Musick* composed under the Limitations of that *Scale* is called *diatonick Musick*.

LET us now conceive a Series of Sounds determined and fixt in the Order and Proportions of that *Scale*, and named by the same Letters. Suppose, for *Example*, an *Organ* or *Harpsichord*, the lowest or gravest Note being taken at any Pitch of *Tune*; it is plain, 1*mo*. That we can proceed from any Note only by one particular Order of of *Degrees*; for we have ſhewn before, that from every Letter of the *Scale* to its *Octave*, is contain'd a different Order of the *Tones* and *Semitones*. 2*do*. We cannot for that Reaſon find any *Interval* required from any Note or Letter upward or downward; for the *Intervals* from every Letter to all the reſt are alſo limited; and therefore, 3*tio*. A *Song* (which is truly *diatonick*) may be ſo contrived, that beginning at a particular Letter or Note of the Inſtrument, all the *Intervals* of the *Song*, that is, all the other Notes, according to the juſt Diſtances and Relations deſigned by the Compoſer, ſhall be found exactly upon that Inſtrument, or in that fixt Series; yet ſhould we begin the Song at any other Note, we could not proceed. This will be plain from *Examples*, in order to which, view the *Scale* expreſſed by Letters, in which I make a *Colon* (:) betwixt Two Letters, the Sign of a greater *Tone* 8 : 9, a *Semicolon* (;) the Sign of a leſſer *Tone* 9 : 10, and a *Point* (.) the Sign of a *Semitone* 15 : 16. And theſe Letters I ſuppoſe repreſent the ſeveral Notes of an Inſtrument, tuned according to the Relations marked by theſe *Tones* and *Semitones*——

C : D ; E . F : G ; A : B . *c* : *d* ; *e* . *f* : *g* ; *a* : *b* . *cc*

Here we have the *diatonick* Series with the 3*d* and 6*th* greater, proceeding from C; and therefore, if only this Series is expreſſed, ſome Songs compoſed with a *flat Melody*, i. e. whoſe *Key* has a leſſer 3*d*, &c. could not be performed on on this Inſtrument, becauſe none of the *Octaves* of this Series has all the natural *Intervals* of the *diatonick* Series, with a 3*d* leſſer, as they have been ſhewn in *Chap.* 8. For *Example*, the *Octave* proceeding from *E* has a 3*d l.* but inſtead of a *t g.* next the *Fundamental*, it has a *Semitone*. *Again*, the *Octave A* has a 3*d l.* but it has a *falſe* 4*th* from *A* to *d*, being Two greater *Tones* and a *Semitone* in the *Ratio* of 20 : 27. Let us then ſuppoſe, that a Note is put betwixt *c* and *d*, making a true 4*th* with *A*, to make the *Octave A* a true *diatonick* Series. By this Means we can perform upon this Inſtrument moſt Songs, that are ſo ſimple as to be limited within one *Key*, I mean that make *Cloſes* or *Cadences* only in one Note; for every Piece of *diatonick Melody* being regulated by the *Intervals* of that *Scale*, and every *Key* or *Mode* being either the *greater* or *leſſer* (i. e. having either a 3*d* greater or leſſer, with the other *Intervals* that properly accompany them, which have been already ſhewn) 'tis plain, that beginning at *A* or *E* on this Inſtrument, we can find the true Notes of any ſuch ſimple Song, as was ſuppoſed; unleſs the *Melody* in the *flat Key* is ſo contrived, as to uſe the 6*th* and 7*th* greater, as I have ſaid it may do in ſome Circumſtances, for then there will be ſtill a Defect, even as to ſuch ſimple Songs.

BUT there are many other conſiderable Reaſons why this Inſtrument is yet very imperfect. And 1*mo*. Conſider what has been already ſaid concerning the Variety of *Keys* or *Cloſes*, which may

may be in *one Piece of Melody*; and then we ſhall find that this fixt Series will be very inſufficient for a Song contrived with ſuch Variety; for *Example*, a Song whoſe principal *Key* is *C* with its 3*d g*. may modulate or change into *F*; but on this Inſtrument *F* has a falſe 4*th* at *B*, and if a true 4*th* is required in the Song, 'tis not here; or if it modulate into *D*, then we have a falſe 3*d* at *F*, and a falſe 5*th* at *A*, which are altogether inconſiſtent with right *Melody*; 'tis true that the Errors in this laſt Caſe are only the Difference of a greater and leſſer *Tone*, as you'll find by conſidering how many, and what Kind of *Degrees* the true 3*d* and 5*th* contains; or by conſidering their Proportions in Numbers, in the Tables of *Chap.* 8. And this Difference is in the common Account neglected, tho' it has an Influence, of which I ſhall ſpeak afterwards; but where the Error is the Difference of a *Tone* and *Semitone*, it is ſo groſs, that it can in no Caſe be neglected; as the falſe 4*th* betwixt *F* and *B*; or when a *Semitone* occurs where the *Melody* requires a *Tone*; for *Example*, if from the *Key C* there is a Change into *E*, to which a *tg*. is required, we have in the Inſtrument only a *Semitone*. And, to ſay it all in few Words, 1*mo*. The *harmonical* and *concinnous Intervals* of which all true *Melody* conſiſts, may be ſo contrived, or taken in *Succeſſion*, that there is no Letter or Note of this Inſtrument at which we can begin, and find all the reſt of the Notes in true Proportion, which yet is not the Fault of the *Scale*, that not

being

being the Office of it. 2*do*. When the ſame Song is to be performed by an Inſtrument and a Voice, or by Two Inſtruments in *Uniſon*, it may be required, for accommodating the one to the other, either to alter the Pitch of the Tuning, ſo as the whole Notes may be equally *lower* or *higher*; or, becauſe this is in ſome Caſes inconvenient, and in others impoſſible, as when any Wind-inſtrument, as *Organ* or *Flute*, is to accompany a Voice, and the Note at which the Song is begun on the Inſtrument is too high or low for the Voice to carry it thro' in; in ſuch Caſes the only Remedy is to begin at another Note, from which, perhaps, you cannot proceed and find all the true Notes of the Song, for the Reaſons ſet forth above; or let it be yet further illuſtrated by this *Example*. A Song is contrived to proceed thus, *Firſt*, upward a *tg*. then a *tl*. then a *Sem*. &c. ſuch a Progreſs is *melodious*, but is not to be found from any Note of the preceeding *Scale*, except *c*; and therefore we can begin only there, unleſs the Inſtrument has other Notes than in the Order of the *diatonick Scale*.

WE ſee then plainly the Defect of *Inſtruments*, whoſe Notes are fixt; and if this is curable, 'tis as plain that it can only be effected by inſerting other Notes and Degrees betwixt theſe of the *diatonick Series*: How far this is, or may be obtained, ſhall be our next Enquiry; and the firſt Thing I ſhall do, is, to demonſtrate that there cannot poſſibly be a perfect *Scale* fixed upon Inſtruments, *i. e.* ſuch as from any Note

Note upward or downward, ſhall contain any *harmonical* or *concinnous Interval* required in their exact Proportions.

SINCE the Inequality of the *Degrees* into which the *natural Scale* is divided, is the Reaſon that Inſtruments having fixt Sounds are imperfect; for hence it is that all *Intervals* of an equal Number of Degrees, or whoſe Extremes comprehend an equal Number of Letters, are not equal; ſo from *C* to *E* has Two Degrees, and *E* to *G* has as many; but the Degrees, which are the component Parts of theſe *Intervals*, differ, and ſo muſt the whole *Intervals*: Therefore it is manifeſt, that if there can be a *perfect Scale* (as above defined) fixt upon Inſtruments, it muſt be ſuch as ſhall proceed from a given Sound by equal Degrees falling in with all the Diviſions or Terms of the *natural Scale*, in order to preſerve all its *harmonious Intervals*, which would otherwiſe be loſt, and then it could be no *muſical Scale*.

IF ſuch a Series can be found, it will be abſolutely perfect, becauſe its Diviſions falling in with theſe of the *natural Scale*, each *Degree* and *Interval* of this will contain a certain Number of that new *Degree*; and therefore we ſhould have, from any given Note of this *Scale*, any other Note upward or downward, which ſhall be to the given Note in any *Ratio* of the *diatonick Scale*; and conſequently any Piece of *Melody* might begin and proceed from any Note of this Scale indifferently: But ſuch a Diviſion is impoſſible, which I ſhall demonſtrate thus.

thus. 1*mo.* If any Series of Sounds is expreſſed by a Series of Numbers, which contain betwixt them the true *Ratios* or *Intervals* of theſe Sounds, then if the Sounds exceed each other by equal Degrees or Differences of *Tune*, that Series of Numbers is in *continued geometrical Proportion*, which is clear from what has been explained concerning the Expreſſion of the *Intervals* of Sound by Numbers. 2*do.* Since it is required that the new Degree ſought, fall in with the Diviſions of the *natural Scale*, 'tis evident that this new Degree muſt be an exact Meaſure to every *Interval* of that *Scale*; *that is*, This Degree muſt be ſuch, that each of theſe *Intervals* may be exactly divided by it, or contain a certain preciſe Number of it without a Remainder; and if no ſuch Degree or common Meaſure to the *Intervals* of the *natural Scale* can be found, then we can have no ſuch *perfect Scale* as is propoſed. But that ſuch a Degree is impoſſible is eaſily proven; *conſider* it muſt meaſure or divide every *diatonick Interval*, and therefore to prove the Impoſſibility of it for any one *Interval* is ſufficient; take for Example the *Tone* 8 : 9, it is required to divide this *Interval* by putting in ſo many *geometrical* Means betwixt 8 and 9 as ſhall make the Whole a continued Series,with theſe Qualifications, *viz.* That the common *Ratio*, (which is to be the firſt and common Degree of the new *Scale*) may be a Meaſure to all the other *diatonick Intervals*: But chiefly, 2*do.* 'Tis required that it be a rational Quantity, expreſſible in rational or known

known Numbers. Now ſuppoſe one *Mean*, it is the ſquare Root of 72 (*viz.* of 8 multiplied by 9) which, not being a ſquare Number, has no ſquare Root in rational Numbers; and *univerſally*, let n repreſent any Number of *Means*, the firſt and leaſt of them, is by an *univerſal Theorem* (as the *Mathematicians* know) thus expreſt $\overline{8^n \times 9|}^{\frac{1}{n+1}}$, equal to this $\overline{8^n|}^{\frac{1}{n+1}} \times 9^{\frac{1}{n+1}}$: But ſuppoſe n to be any Number you pleaſe, ſince 9 is a figurate Number of no Kind but a Square, therefore this *Mean* will in every Caſe be *ſurd* or irrational, and conſequently the *Tone* 8 : 9 cannot be divided in the Manner propoſed; and ſo neither can the *diatonick Scale.*

AGAIN, if the Diviſion cannot be made in rational Numbers, we can never have a *muſical Scale*; for ſuppoſe that by ſome *geometrical* Method we put in a certain Number of Lines, *mean Proportionals* betwixt 8 and 9, yet none of theſe could be Concord with any Term or Note of the *diatonick Scale*; becauſe the Coincidence of Vibrations makes *Concord*, but Chords that are not as Number to Number, can never coincide in their Vibrations, ſince the Number of Vibrations to every Coincidence are reciprocally as the Lengths, which not being as Number to Number, they could not make a *muſical Scale.* In the laſt Place, Let us ſuppoſe the *Interval* 8 : 9 divided by any Number of ſuch *geometrical Means*, and ſuppoſe (tho' abſurd) that they make *Concord* with the rational Terms of the *Scale*, yet it is certain we could never find a common Meaſure to the whole *Scale*; for

for every Term of a *geometrical* Series multiplied by the common *Ratio*, produces the next Term; but the *Ratio* here is a ſurd Quantity, *viz.* $\overline{8^n \times 9}|^{\frac{1}{n+1}} : 8$, and therefore, tho' it were multiplied *in infinitum* with any rational Number, could never produce any Thing but a Surd; and conſequently never fall in with the Terms of the *natural Scale*: Therefore, ſuch a perfect Series or *Scale* of fixt Sounds is impoſſible.

THO' the Defects of Inſtruments cannot be perfectly removed, yet they are in a good Meaſure cured, as we ſhall preſently ſee; in order to which let me premiſe, that the nearer the *Scale* in fixt Sounds, comes to an Equality of the Degrees or Differences of every Note to the next, providing always that the natural *Intervals* be preſerved, the nearer it is to abſolute Perfection; and the Defects that ſtill remain after any Diviſion, are leſs ſenſible as that Diviſion is greater, and the Degrees thereby made ſmaller and more in Number; but by making too many we render the Inſtrument impracticable; the Art is to make no more than that the Defects may be inſenſible, or very nearly ſo, and the Inſtrument at the ſame Time fit for Service.

I know that ſome Writers ſpeak of the Diviſion of the *Octave* into 16, 18, 20, 24, 26, 31, and other Numbers of Degrees, which, with the Extremes, make 17, 19, 21, 25, 27, and 32 Notes within the Compaſs of an *Octave*; but 'tis eaſily imagined how hard and difficult a Thing it muſt be to perform upon ſuch an Inſtrument; ſuppoſe a *Spinet*, with 21 or 32 Keys

Keys within the Compaſs of an *Octave*; what an Embaraſſment and Confuſion muſt this occaſion eſpecially to a Learner. Indeed if the Matter could not be tolerably rectified another Way, we ſhould be obliged patiently to wreſtle with ſo hard an Exerciſe: But 'tis well that we are not put to ſuch a difficult Choice, either to give up our Hopes of ſo agreeable Entertainment as *muſical Inſtruments* afford, or reſolve to acquire it at a very painful Rate; no, we have it eaſier, and a *Scale* proceeding by 12 Degrees, *that is*, 13 Notes including the Extremes, to an *Octave*, makes our Inſtruments ſo perfect that we have no great Reaſon to complain. This therefore is the preſent *Syſtem* for Inſtruments, *viz.* betwixt the Extremes of every *Tone* of the *natural Scale* is put a Note, which divides it into Two unequal Parts called *Semitones*; and the whole may be called the *ſemitonick Scale*, containing 12 *Semitones* betwixt 13 Notes within the Compaſs of an *Octave*: And to preſerve the *diatonick* Series diſtinct, theſe inſerted Notes take the Name of the *natural* Note next below, with this Mark ✱ called a *Sharp*, as *C*✱ or *C ſharp*, to ſignify that it is a *Semitone* above *C* (*natural*;) or they take the Name of the *natural* Note next above, with this Mark ♭, called a *Flat*, as *D*♭ or *D flat*, to ſignifie a *Semitone* below *D* (*natural*;) and tho' it be indifferent upon the main which Name is uſed in any Caſe, yet, for good Reaſons, ſometimes the one Way is uſed, and ſometimes the other, as I ſhall have Occaſion to explain: But that I may

may proceed here upon a fixt Rule, I denominate them from the Note below, excepting that betwixt *A* and *B*, which I always mark ♭ simply without any other Letter; underſtand the ſame of any other Character of theſe Letters; as always when I name any Letters for Examples, I ſay the ſame of all the other Characters of theſe Letters, *i. e.* of all the Notes through the whole *Scale* that bear theſe Names; and thus the whole *Octave* is to be expreſſed, *viz.* *C. C*✻. *D. D*✻ *E. F. F*✻ *G. G*✻ *A.* ♭. *B. C*—

The *Keys* of a Spinet repreſent this very diſtinctly to us; the foremoſt Range of continued *Keys* is in the Order of the *diatonick Scale*, and the other *Keys* ſet backward are the *artificial* Notes.

Why we don't rather uſe 12 different Letters; will appear afterwards. The Two *natural Semitones* of the *diatonick Scale* being betwixt *E F* and *A B* ſhew that the new Notes fall betwixt the other natural ones as they are ſet down. Theſe new Notes are called *accidental* or *fictitious*, becauſe they retain the Name of their *Principals* in the *natural Syſtem*: And this Name does alſo very well expreſs their Deſign and Uſe; which is not to introduce or ſerve any new Species of *Melody* diſtinct from the *diatonick* Kind; but, as I have ſaid in the Beginning of this Chapter, to ſerve the Modulation from one *Key* to another in the Courſe of any Piece, or the Tranſpoſition of the Whole to a different Pitch, for accommodating Inſtruments to a Voice, that beginning at a convenient Note, the Inſtrument may accompany the Voice

Voice in *Unison*. How far the Luxury, if I may so call it, of the present *Musick* is carried, so as to change the Species of *Melody*, and bring in something of a different Character from the true *Diatonick*, and for that Purpose have Use for a *Scale* of *Semitones*, I shall have Occasion to speak of afterwards: But let us now proceed to shew how these Notes are proportioned to the *natural* ones, *i. e.* to shew the Quantity of the *Semitones* occasioned by these *accidental* Notes, and then see how far the *System* is perfected by them.

---

§ 2. *Of the true Proportions of the* Semitonick Scale, *and how far the System is perfected by it.*

THERE is great Variety, or I may rather call it Confusion, in the Accounts that Writers upon *Musick* give of this Matter; they make different Divisions without explaining the Reasons of them. But since I have so clearly explained the Nature and Design of this Improvement, it will be easy to examine any Division, and prove its Fitness, by comparing it with the End: And from the Things above said, we have this *general Rule* for judging of them, *viz.* That, the Division which makes a Series, from whose every Note we can find any *diatonick Interval*, upward or downward, with least and fewest Errors, is most perfect.

THERE are Two Divisions that I propose to explain here; and after these I shall explain the ordi-

ordinary and most approven Way of bringing Spinets and such kind of Instruments to Tune; and shew the true Proportion that such Tuning makes among the several Notes.

THE *first Division* is this: Every *Tone* of the *diatonick* Series is divided into Two Parts or *Semitones*, whereof the one is the *natural Semitone* 15 : 16, and the other is the Remainder of that from the *Tone*, *viz*. 128 : 135 in the *tg*. and 24 : 25 in the *tl*. and the *Semitone* 15 : 16 is put in the lowest Place in each, except the *tg*. betwixt *f* and *g*, where 'tis put in the upper Place; and the whole *Octave* stands as in the following Scheme, where I have written the *Ratios* of each Term to the next in a Fraction set betwixt them below.

SCALE of *SEMITONES*.

c . *c*✱ . *d* . *d*✱. *e* . *f* . *f*✱. *g* . *g*✱ . *a* . ♭ . *b* . *cc*.

$\frac{15}{16}$ $\frac{128}{135}$ $\frac{15}{16}$ $\frac{24}{25}$ $\frac{15}{16}$ $\frac{128}{135}$ $\frac{15}{16}$ $\frac{15}{16}$ $\frac{24}{25}$ $\frac{15}{16}$ $\frac{128}{135}$ $\frac{15}{16}$

IT was very natural to think of dividing each *Tone* of the *diatonick Scale*, so as the *Semitone* 15 : 16 should be one Part of each Division; because this being an unavoidable and necessary Part of the *natural Scale*, would most readily occur as a fit Degree in the Division of the *Tones* thereof; especially after considering that this Degree 15 : 16 is not very far from the exact Half of a *Tone*. *Again* there must be some Reason for placing these *Semitones* in one Order rather than another, *i. e.* placing 15 : 16 uppermost in the *Tone f : g*, and undermost in all

all the reſt; which Reaſon is this, that hereby there are fewer Errors or Defects in the *Scale*; particularly, the 15 : 16 is ſet in the upper Place of the *Tone f : g*, becauſe by this the greateſt Error in the *diatonick Scale* is perfectly corrected, *viz.* the falſe *4th* betwixt *f* and *b* upward, which exceeds the true *harmonical 4th* by the *Semitone* 128 : 135, and this *Semitone* being placed betwixt *f* and *f*※, makes from *f*※ to *b* a true *4th*; and corrects alſo an equal Defect in the *Interval b-f* taken upward, which inſtead of a true *5th* wants 128 : 135, and is now juſt, by taking *f*※ for *f*, *that is*, from ♭ up to *f*※ is a juſt *5th*. There were the ſame groſs Errors in the *natural 8ve* proceeding from *f*, which are now corrected by the altered *b viz.* ♭, which is a true *4th* above *f*, whereas *b* (natural) is to the *f* below as 32 : 45 exceeding a true *4th* by 128 : 135; alſo from *b* (natural) up to *f* is a falſe *5th*, as 45 : 64, but from ♭ to *f* is a juſt *5th* 2 : 3; and therefore reſpecting theſe Corrections of ſo very groſs Errors, we ſee a plain Reaſon why the greater *Semitone* 15 : 16 is placed betwixt *f*※ and *g*, and betwixt *a* and ♭: For the Place of it in the other *Tones*, I ſhall only ſay, in general, that there are fewer Errors as I have placed them than if placed otherwiſe; and I ſhall add this Particular, that we have now from the Key *c* both the *diatonick Series* with the *3d l.* and *3d g.* and their Accompanyments all in their juſt Proportions, only we have 9 : 16, *viz.* from *c* to ♭ for the leſſer *7th*, which tho' it make not ſo ſo many *harmonious* Relations to the other *diatonick* Notes as 5 : 9 would do, yet conſidering a *7th* is ſtill but a *Diſcord*, and for what Reaſon *b*. was made a greater *Semitone* 15 : 16 above *a*. This *7th* ought to be accounted the beſt here ; yet the other 5 : 9 has Place in other Parts of the *Scale* ; I ſhall preſently ſhew you other Reaſons why 9 : 16 is the beſt in the Place where I have put it, *viz.* betwixt *c* and *b*.

CONCERNING this *Scale* of *Semitones*, *Obſerve* 1*mo*, From any Letter to the ſame again comprehending Thirteen Notes is always a true 8*ve*, as from *c* to *c*, or from *c*✱ to *c*✱. 2*do*. We have Three different *Semitones* 15 : 16 the *greateſt*, 128 : 135 the *middle*, and 24 : 25 the *leaſt*, which, when I have Occaſion to ſpeak of, I ſhall mark thus, *ſg*. *ſm*. *ſl*. The firſt is the Difference of a 3*d g*. and 4*th*; the ſecond the Difference of *t g*. and *ſ g*. and the Third the Difference of *t l*. and *ſ g*. (or of 3*d g*. and 3*d l*. or 6*th g*. and 6*th l*.) 3*tio*. We have by this Diviſion alſo Three different *Tones*, *viz*. 8 : 9 compoſed of *ſ g*. and *ſ m*. as *c* : *d* ; then 9 : 10 compoſed of *ſ g*. and *ſ l*. as *d* ; *e* ; and 225 : 256 compoſed of Two *ſ g*. as *f*✱ : *g*✱, which occurs alſo betwixt *b* and *c*✱, and no where elſe, all the reſt being of the other Two Kinds which are the true *Tones* of the *natural Scale*. And tho' we might ſuppoſe other Combinations of theſe *Semitones* to make new *Tones*, yet their Order in this *Scale* affording no other, we are concerned no further with them. Now *obſerve*, this laſt *Tone* 225 : 256 being equal to 2 *ſ g*. muſt

must be also the greatest of these Three *Tones*; so that what is the greatest of the Two *natural Tones*, is now the Middle of these Three, and therefore when you meet with *t g.* understand always the *natural Tone* 8 : 9, unless it be otherwise said.

4*to*. LET us now consider how the *Intervals* of this *Scale* shall be denominated; we have already heard the Reason of these Names 3*d*, 4*th*, 5*th*, &c. given to the *Intervals* of the *Scale* of *Musick*; they are taken from the Number of Notes comprehended betwixt the Extremes (*inclusive*) of any *Interval*, and express in their principal Design, the Number of Notes from the *Fundamental* of an 8*ve concinnously* divided to any *acute* Term of the Series, tho' to make them of more universal Use they are also applied to the *accidental Intervals*. See *Chap.* 8. So that whatever *Interval* contains the same Number of Degrees is called by the same Name; and hence we have some *Concords* some *Discords* of the same Name; so in the *diatonick Scale*, from *c* to *e* is a 3*d g*. *Concord*, and from *e* to *g* a 3*d l*. and from *d* to *f* is also called a 3*d*, because *f* is the 3*d* Note *inclusive* from *d*, yet it is *Discord*. See *Chap*. 8. If we consider next, that the Notes added to the *Scale* are not designed to alter the Species of *Melody*, but leave it still *diatonick*, only they correct the Defects arising from something foreign to the Nature and Use of the *Scale* of *Musick*, *viz.* the limiting and fixing of the Sounds; then we see the Reason why the same Names are still

con-

continued : And tho' there are now more Notes in an *Octave*, and ſo a greater Number of different *Intervals*, yet the *diatonick* Names comprehend the whole, by giving to every *Interval* of an equal Number of Degrees the ſame Name, and making a Diſtinction of each into greater and leſſer. Thus an *Interval* of 1 *Semitone* is called a leſſer Second or *2d l.* of 2 *Semitones* is a *2d g.* of 3 *Semitones* a *3d l.* of 4, a *3d g.* and ſo on as in this *Table*.

Denominations.	*2d l.*	*2d g.*	*3d l.*	*3d g.*	*4th l.*	*4th g.*	*5th.*	*6th l.*	*6th g.*	*7th l.*	*7th g.*	*8ve.*
Num. of *Sem.*	1	2	3	4	5	6	7	8	9	10	11	12.

In which we have no other Names, than theſe already known in the *diatonick Scale*, except the *4th* greater, which for equal Reaſon might be called a *5th* leſſer, becauſe 'tis a Middle betwixt *4th* and *5th*, i.e. betwixt 5 and 7 *Semitones*; and therefore we may call all *Intervals* of 6 *Semitones Tritones* (for 6 *Semitones* make 3 *Tones*) and theſe of 5 *Semitones* call them ſimply *4ths*; and ſo all the Names of the *diatonick Scale* remain unaltered, and we have only the Name of *Tritone* added, which yet is not new, for I have before obſerved, that it is uſed in the *diatonick Scale*, and thus all is kept very diſtinct; and if we proceed above an *Octave*, we compound the Names with an *Octave* and theſe below. Again take Notice, that as in the pure *diatonick Scale*, the Names of *3d*, *4th*, &c. anſwer to the Number of Letters which are betwixt the Extremes (incluſive) of any *Interval*, whereby the Denomination of the *Interval* is known, by knowing the Letters by which the

the Extremes of it are expreſt, ſo in this new *Scale* the ſame will hold, by taking any Letter with or without the *Sharp* or *Flat* for the ſame Letter, and applying to the *accidental* Notes, in ſome Caſes the Letter of the Note below with a *Sharp*, and in others that of the Note above with a *Flat*: For *Example.* *d*※--*g* is a 3*d*, and includes 4 Letters; but if for *d*※ we take *e*♭, then *e*♭--*g*, which is the ſame individual *Interval*, contains but 3 Letters; alſo if for ♭ we take *a*※, then *a*※--*c*※, which is a true 3*d l.* includes 3 Letters, whereas ♭--*c*※ has but Two. There is only one Exception, for the *Interval* *b*-*f*, which is a 4*th g.* contains 5 Letters, and cannot be otherwiſe expreſt, unleſs you take *e*※ which is equal to *f natural*; or take *c*♭, which is equal to *b natural*; but this is not ſo regular, and indeed makes too great a Confuſion; tho' I have ſeen it ſo done in the Compoſitions of the beſt Maſters, which yet will not make it reaſonable, unleſs in the particular Caſe where 'tis uſed, it could not have been ſo conveniently ordered otherwiſe: But if we call the ſame *Interval* a 5*th* leſſer, then the *Rule* is good; yet if we call every *Tritone* a 5*th*, we ſhall ſtill have an Exception, for then *f*--*b* contains only 4 Letters; and therefore 'tis beſt to call all *Intervals* of 6 *Semitones*, *Tritones*, and then they are not ſubject to this *Rule.* In this therefore we ſee a Reaſon, why 'tis better that the *accidental* Note ſhould be named by the Letter of the *natural Note*, than to make Twelve Letters in an *Octave*; beſides, the *Melody* being ſtill *diatonick*,

theſe

these *accidental* Notes are only in place of the others; and by keeping the same Names, we preserve the Simplicity of the *System* better.

5*to.* Having thus settled the Denominations of the *Intervals* of this *semitonick Scale*, we must next *observe*, that of each Denomination there are Differences in the Quantity, arising from the Differences of the *Semitones* of which they are composed, as is very obvious in the *Scale* : And these again may be distinguished into *true* and *false*, i. e. such as are either *harmonical* or *concinnous Intervals* of the *natural Scale*, and such as are not; and in each Denomination we find there is one that is *true*, and all the rest are *false*, except the *Tritones* which are all *false*, tho' they are used in some very particular Cases.

6*to.* Let us next enquire into all the Variety and the precise Quantity of every *Interval* within this new *Scale*, that we may thereby know what Defects still remain. We have already observed, that there are Three different *Semitones* and as many *Tones*; hence it is plain, there are neither more nor less than Three different 7*ths* of each Species, *i. e.* lesser and greater, which are the Complements of these *Semitones* and *Tones* to *Octave*, as here.

Semit. *7th g.*	*7th l.* *Tone.*
15 - 16 - 30	128 - 225 - 256
128 - 135 - 256	9 - 16 - 18
24 - 25 - 48	5 - 9 - 10

And

And to know where each of theſe *7ths* lies, and all the *Examples* of each in the *Scale*, 'tis but taking all the *Examples* of theſe *Semitones* and *Tones*, which are to be found at Sight in the *Scale* marked with the *Semitones*, as you ſee in Page 294. and you have the correſpondent *7ths* betwixt the one Extreme of that *Semitone* or *Tone*, and the *Octave* to the other Extreme. Then for the other *Intervals*, viz. *3ds*, *6ths*, *4ths*, *5ths*, which are *harmonical*, I have in the *Table-plate*, *Fig.* ſet all the *Examples* of ſuch of them as are *falſe*, with their reſpective *Ratios*; and with the *Ratios* of the *6th* and *5th* I have ſet an *e* or *d*, to ſignify an exceſſive, or a deficient *Interval* from the true *Concord*; and conſequently their correſpondent *3ds* and *4ths* will be as much on the contrary deficient or exceſſive. All the reſt of the *Intervals* of theſe ſeveral Denominations, containing 3, 4, 5, 7, 8 or 9 *Semitones*, are true of their ſeveral Kinds, whoſe *Ratios* we have frequently ſeen, and ſo they needed not be placed here. Then for the *Tritones*, you have in the laſt Part of the *Table* all their Variety and *Examples*; by the Nature of this *Interval* it exceeds a *true 4th*, and wants of a *true 5th*; you'll eaſily find the Difference by the *Ratio*.

Now we have ſeen all the Variety of *Intervals* in this new *Scale*; and by what's explain'd we know where all the Extremes of each ly: and it will be eaſy to find the true *Ratio* of any *Interval*, the Letters or Names of whoſe Extremes in the *Scale* are given, *viz.* by finding in the

the *Scale* how many *Semitones* it contains, and thereby the Denomination of it, by which you'll find its *Ratio* in the preceeding *Table*, unless it be a true *Concord*, and then it is not in the *Table*, which is a Sign of its being *true*. And as to this *Table*, observe, that I have no Respect to the different Characters of Letters, and you must suppose every *Example* to be taken upward in the *Scale*, from the first Letter of the *Example* to the second, counting in the natural Order of the Letters.

7mo. WE are now come to consider how far the *Scale* is perfected; and first *observe*, that there are no greater or lesser, and precisely no other Errors in it, than the Differences of the Three *Semitones*, which are these following; of which the uppermost is the least, and the lower the greatest Error.

Diff. of			
	sg. and *sm.*	=	2025 : 2048
	sm. and *sl.*	=	80 : 81
	sg. and *sl.*	=	125 : 128

In the *diatonick Scale* some *Intervals* erred a whole *Semitone*, and all the rest only by a *Comma* 80 : 81; here we have one Error a very little greater, and another lesser: All the *5ths* and *4ths* except Three, are *just* and *true*; of the *3d l.* and *6th g.* there are as many *true* as *false*; and of the *3d g.* and *6th l.* we have Five *false* and Seven *true*. These Errors are so small, that in a single Case the Ear will bear it, especially in the *imperfect Concords* of *3d* and *6th*; but when many of these Errors happen in a Song, and especially in the prin-

principal *Intervals* that belong to the *Key*, it will interrupt the *Melody*, and the Inſtrument will appear out of Tune (as it really is with reſpect to that Song :) But then we muſt *obſerve*, that as the Order of theſe *Semitones* is different in every *Octave*, proceeding from each of the Twelve different *Keys* or Letters of the *Scale* ; ſo we find that ſome Songs will proceed better, if begun at ſome Notes, than at others. If we compare one *Key* with another, then we muſt prefer them according to the Perfection of their principal *Intervals*, viz. the 3*d*, 5*th* and 6*th*, which are Eſſentials in the *Harmony* of every *Key* : And let any Two Notes be propoſed to be made *Keys* of the ſame *Species*, viz. both with the 3*d l*, &c. or 3*d g*, &c. We can eaſily find in the preceeding *Table* what *Intervals* in the *Scale* are *true* or *falſe* to each of them; and accordingly prefer the one or the other: But I ſhall proceed to

THE *ſecond Diviſion* of the 8*ve* into *Semitones* which I promiſed to explain, and it is this: Betwixt the Extremes of the *t g.* and *t l.* of the *natural Scale* is taken an *harmonical Mean* which divides it into Two *Semitones* nearly equal, thus, the *t g.* 8 : 9 is divided into Two *Semitones* which are 16 : 17 and 17 : 18, as here 16 : 17 : 18, which is an *arithmetical* Diviſion, the Numbers repreſenting the Lengths of Chords; but if they repreſent the Vibrations, the Lengths of the Chords are reciprocal, *viz.* as $1 : {}^{16} : \frac{8}{9}$ which puts the greater *Semitone* $\frac{16}{17}$ next the lower Part of the *Tone*, and the leſſer $\frac{17}{18}$ next the

the upper, which is the Property of the *harmonical* Diviſion : The ſame Way the *t l*, 9 : 10 is divided into theſe Two Semit. 18 : 19, and 19 : 20, and the whole 8*ve* ſtands thus.

c .	*c*✱ .	*d* .	*d*✱ .	*e* .	*f* .	*f*✱ .	*g* .	*g*✱ .	*a* .	♭ .	*b* .	*c*
$\frac{16}{17}$	$\frac{17}{18}$	$\frac{18}{19}$	$\frac{19}{20}$	$\frac{15}{16}$	$\frac{16}{17}$	$\frac{17}{18}$	$\frac{18}{19}$	$\frac{19}{20}$	$\frac{16}{17}$	$\frac{17}{18}$	$\frac{15}{16}$	

IN this Scale we have theſe Things to obſerve, 1*mo*. That every *Tone* is divided into Two, *Semit*. whereof I have ſet the greater in the loweſt Place. 2*do*. We have hereby Five different *Semitones* ; out of which as they ſtand in the Scale we have Seven different *Tones*, as here.

Sem.				*Tones.*
$\frac{16}{17}$	✠	$\frac{17}{18}$	=	$\frac{8}{9}$
$\frac{17}{18}$	✠	$\frac{18}{19}$	=	$\frac{17}{19}$
$\frac{18}{19}$	✠	$\frac{19}{20}$	=	$\frac{9}{10}$
$\frac{19}{20}$	✠	$\frac{15}{16}$	=	$\frac{57}{64}$
$\frac{15}{16}$	✠	$\frac{16}{17}$	=	$\frac{15}{17}$
$\frac{19}{20}$	✠	$\frac{16}{17}$	=	$\frac{76}{85}$
$\frac{17}{18}$	✠	$\frac{15}{16}$	=	$\frac{85}{96}$

CONSIDERING how, by a *harmonical Mean*, the 8*th*, 5*th*, and 3*d g*. were divided into their *harmonical* or *concinnons* Parts, it could not but readily occur to divide the *Tones* the ſame Way, when a Diviſion was found neceſſary ; but we are to conſider what Effect this Diviſion has for perfecting of Inſtruments. It would be more troubleſom than difficult to calculate a *Table* of all the Variety of *Ratios* contain'd in this *Scale*; I ſhall leave you to this Exercise for your Diverſion, and only tell you here, that having

ving calculate all the *5ths* and *4ths*, I find there are only Seven true *5ths*, and as many *4ths*, whereas in the former *Scale* there were Nine; and then for the Errors, there are none of them above a *Comma* 80 : 81; in short, there is one false *5th* and *4th* whose Error is a *Comma*, and the rest are all very much less; and, tho' there are fewer true *5ths* and *4ths* here, yet the Errors being far less and more various, compensate the other Loss: As to the *3ds* and *6ths*, there are also here more of them false than in the preceeding *Scale*, for of each there are but Four true *Intervals*, but the Errors are generally much less, the greatest being far less than the greatest in the other *Scale*.

I shall say no more upon this, only let you know, That Mr. *Salmon* in the *Philosophical Transactions* tells us, That he made an Experiment of this *Scale* upon Chords exactly in these Proportions, which yielded a perfect Consort with other Instruments touched by the best Hands: But observe, that he places the lesser *Semit.* lowest, which I place uppermost; and when I had examined what Difference this would produce, I found the Advantage would rather be in the Way I have chosen. And this brings to mind a Question which Mr. *Simpson* makes in his *Compend* of *Musick*, *viz.* Whether the greater or lesser *Semitone* lies from *a* to ♭; he says 'tis more rational to his Understanding, that the lesser *Semitone* ly next *a*; but he does not explain his Reason; he speaks only of the *arithmetical* Division of a Chord into equal Parts,

Parts, but has not minded the *harmonical* Division of an *Interval*, by which we have seen the *diatonick Scale* so naturally constituted, whereby the greater Part is always laid next the gravest Extreme: But in short, when we speak of the Reason of this, we must consider the Design of these *Semitones*, and which one in such a Place answers the End best, and then I believe there will be no Reason found why it should be as Mr. *Simpson* says, rather than the other Way.

---

§ 3. *Of the common Method of Tuning* Spinets, *demonstrating the Proportions that occur in it; and of the Pretence of a nicer Method considered.*

THE last Thing I proposed to do upon this Subject, was to explain the ordinary Way of tuning Spinets and that Kind of Instruments; for whether it be, that the tuning them in accurate Proportions in the Manner mentioned is not easily done, or that these Proportions do not sufficiently correct the Defects of the Instrument, there is another Way which is generally followed by *practical Musicians*; and that is Tuning by the Ear, which is founded upon this Supposition, that the Ear is perfectly Judge of an 8*ve* and 5*th*. The *general Rule* is, to begin at a certain Note as *c*, taken toward the Middle of the

the Inſtrument, and tuning all the 8*ves* up and down, and alſo the 5*ths*, reckoning Seven *Semitones* to every 5*th*, whereby the whole will be tuned; but there are Differences even in the Way of doing this, which I ſhall explain.

SOME and even the Generality who deal with this Kind of Inſtrument, tune not only their *Octaves*, but alſo their 5*ths* as perfectly *Concord* as their Ear can judge, and conſequently make the 4*ths* perfect, which indeed makes a great many Errors in the other *Intervals* of 3*d* and 6*th* (for the *diſcord Intervals*, they are not ſo conſiderable;) others that affect a greater Nicety pretend to diminiſh all the 5*ths*, and make them deficient about a Quarter of a *Comma*, in order to make the Errors in the reſt ſmaller and leſs ſenſible: But to be a little more particular, I ſhall ſhew you the Progreſs that's made from Note to Note; and then conſider the Effect of both theſe Methods. In order to this, let us view again the *Scale* with its 12 *Semitones* in an *Octave*; but we have Uſe for Two *Octaves* to this Purpoſe. Then 1*mo*. Beginning at *c* take it at a certain Pitch, and tune all its *Octaves* above and below; then 2*do*. Tune *g* a 5*th* above *c*, and next tune all the *Octaves* of *g*; 3*tio*. Take *d* a 5*th* above *g*, and then tune all the *Octaves* of *d*. 4*to*. Take *a* a 5*th* above *d*, then tune all the *Octaves* of *a*. 5*to*. Take *e* a 5*th* above *a*, and tune all the *Octaves* of *e*: Then, 6*to*. Take *b* (natural) a 5*th* above *e*, and tune all the *Octaves* of *b*. 7*mo*. Take *f*✻ a 5*th* above *b*, then

then tune all the *Octaves* of *f*♯. 8*vo*. *c*♯ a 5*th* above *f*♯, and then all the *Octaves* of *c*♯. 9*no*. Take *g*♯ a 5*th* above *c*♯, then all its *Octaves*; and having proceeded so far, we have all the *Keys* tuned except *f*, *d*♯, and ♭; for which, 10*mo*. Begin again at *c*, and take *f* a 5*th* downward, then tune all the *f*s. 11*mo*. Take ♭ a 5*th* downward to *f*, and tune all the ♭s. *Lastly*. Take *d* ♯a 5*th* below ♭, and then tune all the *Octaves* of *d*♯; and so the whole Instrument is in Tune. And *observe*, That having tuned all the *Octaves* of any *Key*, the next Step being to take a 5*th* to it, you may take that from any of the Keys of that Name.

Now supposing all these *Octaves* and 5*ths* to be in perfect Tune, we shall examine the Effects it will have upon the rest of the *Intervals*; and in order to it, I have exprest this Tuning in *Plate* 1. *Fig*. 6. by drawing Lines betwixt every Note, and another, according to the Method of Procedure; but I have only marked the 5*ths*, supposing the *Octaves* to be tuned all along as you proceed; then I have marked the Progress from 5*th* to 5*th* by Numbers set upon them to signify the 1*st*, 2*d*, &c. Step; and in the Method there taken you see all the Notes tuned from *c* to *f*♯ above its *Octave*: We suppose all the other Notes above and below in the Instrument to have been tuned by *Octaves* to these, but for the Thing in Hand we have Use for no more of the *Scale*. *Observe* next, That I have marked the *Semitones* betwixt every Note by the Letters *g*, *l*. *viz*.

viz. greater and leſſer; for there are only Two Kinds in this *Scale*, as we ſhall preſently ſee, and alſo what they are, for the natural *Sem.* 15 : 16 is not to be found here; and while I ſpeak of this *Scale* and of *Semitones* greater and leſſer, I mean always theſe Two, unleſs it be ſaid otherwiſe.

If we find the Degrees of this *Scale* in the *Tones* or *Semitones*, we ſhall by theſe eaſily find the Quantity of every other *Interval*; and in the following Calculations I take all the *Examples* upward from the firſt Letter named, and therefore I have made no Diſtinction in the Character of the Letters: To begin, from *c* to *g* is a *5th* 2 : 3, and from *g* to *d* a *5th*, therefore from *c* to *d* is Two *5ths* 4 : 9; out of this take an *Octave*, the Remainder is 8 : 9 a *tg.* and conſequently *c-d* is a *tg.* 8 : 9; by this Method you'll prove that each of theſe *Intervals* marked in the following *Table* is a *tg.* 8 : 9. In the next Place, conſider, from *a* to *e* is a *5th*, therefore from *e* to *a* is a *4th*: But from *f* to *a* there are Two *tg.* as in the preceeding *Table*, whoſe Sum is 64 : 81, which taken from a *4th* 3 : 4, leaves this *Semitone* 243 : 256 for *e* : *f* (which is leſs than 15 : 16 by a *Comma*) then if we ſubſtract this from a *Tone* 8 : 9, it leaves 2048 : 2187, a greater *Semitone* than the former, and if we mark the one *l.* and the other *g.* all the *Semi-*

All greater Tones 8:9			
	c	-	*d*
	d	-	*e*
	d※	-	*f*
	e	-	*f*※
	f	-	*g*
	f※	-	*g*※
	g	-	*a*
	a	-	*b*
	♭	-	*c*

Semitones from *d* to *a*, will be as I have marked them in the *Fig.* referred to; for since *e* : *f*※ is a *t g.* and *e* . *f* is a *s l.* therefore *f* . *f*※ is a *s g.* and so of the rest, every Two Semitones from *d* to *a* being a *t g.* Again since *f* - *c* is a 5*th*, and also *e* - *b*, taking away what's common to both, *viz.* *f* - *b*, there remains on each Hand these equal Parts *e* . *f* and *b* . *c*, so that *b* . *c* is also a *s l.* and since ♭ : *c* is a *t g.* and *b* . *c* a *s l.* ♭ . *b* must be a *s g.* and also *a* . ♭ a *s l.* because *a* : *b* is a *t g.* *Next*, from *c*※ to *g*※ is a 5*th*, also from *d*※ to ♭, and taking away *d*※-*g*※ out of both, there remains *c*※ : *d*※ equal to *g*※-♭, which contains Two *s l.* but *d* . *d*※ is already found to be a *s l.* therefore *c*※ . *d* is *s l.* and *c* : *d* being a *t g.* *c* . *c*※ must be a *s g.*

Thus we have discovered all the *Semitones* within the *Octave*; of which as they stand in the Scale, we have only Two different *Tones*, *viz.* the *t g.* 8 : 9 and another which is lesser 59049 : 65536 composed of Two of the lesser *Semitones*, as you see betwixt *c*※ : *d*※, and also betwixt *g*※ : ♭ ; in every other Place of the Scale it is a *t g.*

Let us next consider the other *Intervals*, and *first*, We have all the *Octaves* and 5*ths* perfect except the 5*th* *g*※ - *d*※ which is 531441 : 786432, wanting of a true 5*th* more than a *Comma*, *viz.* the Difference of the *s g.* and *s l.* as is evident in the Scheme, for *g* - *d* is a true 5*th* but the *Interval* *g*※ - *d* is common to *g* - *d*, and *g*※ - *d*※, and being taken from both,

leaves

leaves in the firſt the *ſg. g . g*※, and in laſt the *ſl. d . d*※; then all the 4*ths* are of conſequence perfect, except *d*※ - *g*※, which exceeds as much as its correſpondent 5*th* is deficient. But *Laſtly*, For the 3*ds* and 6*ths* they are all falſe, plainly for this Reaſon, that in the whole Series there is no leſſer *Tone* 9 : 10, which with the *tg*. 8 : 9 makes a true 3*d g*. nor any of the greater *Semitone* 15 : 16, which with *tg* makes a 3*d l*. And for the Errors they are eaſily diſcovered, in the 3*d g*. (and the Correſpondent 6 *l*.) the Error is either an Exceſs of a Comma 80 : 81 the Difference of *tg*. and *tl*. of the *natural Scale*; which happens in theſe Places where Two *tg*. ſtand together, as in the 3*d g*. from *c* to *e*; or it is a Deficiency equal to the Difference of the leſſer *Tone* 9 : 10, and the *Tone* above mentioned 59049 : 65536, which *Tone* is leſs than 9 : 10 by this Difference 32768, 32805 (as in the 3*d g*. *c*※ : *f*) which is greater than a Comma; and for the 3*d l*. (and its 6*th g*.) it has the ſame Errors, and is either deficient a Comma, *viz*. the Difference of the *ſg*. 15 : 16 and the *ſl*. 243 : 256, as in the 3*d l*. *c* : *d*※, or exceeds by the Difference of the new *ſg*. 2048 : 2187 and the *ſg*. 15 : 16 which is leſs than the other by this Difference 32768 : 32805 which is greater than a Comma.

Now the 5*ths* and 4*ths* are all perfect but one, yet the 3*ds* and 6*ths* being all falſe, there is no Note in all the *Scale* from which we have a true *diatonick* Series; and the Errors

rors being equal to a Comma in ſome and greater in others, makes this *Scale* leſs perfect than any yet deſcribed; at leaſt than the firſt Diviſion explained, in which there were only 3 falſe *5ths*, whereof Two err by a Comma, and the other by a leſſer Difference; and having many true *3ds* and *6ths*, ſeems plainly a more perfect Scale. Theſe Errors may ſtill be made leſs by multiplying the *artificial Keys*, and placing them betwixt ſuch Notes of the preceeding *Scale* as may correct the greateſt Errors of the moſt uſual *Keys* of the *diatonick* Series, aud of ſuch Diviſions you have Accounts in *Merſennus* and *Kircher*; but a greater Number than 13 Keys in an *Octave* is ſo great a Difficulty for Practice, that they are very rare, and our beſt Compoſitions are performed on Inſtruments with 13 Notes in the *Octave*, and as to the tuning of theſe,

LET us now conſider the Pretences of the nicer Kind of *Muſicians*; they tell us, That in tuning by *Octaves* and *5ths*, they diminiſh all the *5ths* by a Quarter of a *Comma*, or near it (for the *Ratio* 80 : 81 cannot be divided into 4 equal Parts, and expreſt in rational Numbers) in order to make the Errors through the whole Inſtrument very ſmall and inſenſible: I ſhall not here trouble you with Calculations made upon this Suppoſition, becauſe they can be eaſily done by thoſe who underſtand what has been hitherto explained upon this Subject; therefore I ſay no more but this, That it muſt be an extraordinary Ear that can judge exactly of a Quarter *Comma*, and I

ſhall

ſhall add, That ſome Practiſers upon *Harpſi-chords* have told me they always tune their *5ths* perfect, and find their Inſtrument anſwer very well. 'Tis true they cannot deny that the ſame Song will not go equally well from every *Key*, which argues ſtill the Imperfection of the Inſtrument; but there is no Song but they can find ſome *Key* that will anſwer. If a very juſt and accurate Ear can diminiſh the Errors, ſo as to make them yet ſmaller and more equal thro' the whole Inſtrument, I will not ſay but they may make more of the *Octaves* like other, and conſequently make it an indifferent Thing which of theſe *Keys*, that are brought to ſuch a Likeneſs, you begin your Song at; but even theſe cannot deny that a Song will do better from one *Key* than another; ſo that the Defects are not quite removed even as to Senſe.

DR. *Wallis* has a Diſcourſe in the *Philoſophical Tranſactions* concerning the Imperfection of Organs, and the Remedy applied to it; the Imperfection he obſerves is the ſame I have already ſpoken of, *viz.* That from every Note you cannot find any *Interval* in its juſt Proportion. 'Tis true indeed the Doctor only conſiders the Imperfection of a *Scale* of *Semitones*, and particularly one conſtituted in the *Ratio* of the 2*d* Kind of Diviſion abovementioned; he does not ſay directly for what Reaſons a *Scale* of *Semitones* was neceſſary; but, as if he ſuppoſed that plain enough, he ſays there are ſtill ſome Defects; and therefore, ſays he, *Inſtead of theſe Proportions* (*of the* Semitones) *it is ſo ordered, if I miſtake*

miſtake not the Practice, that the 13 *Pipes within an* Octave, *as to their Sounds, with reſpect to* acute *and* grave, *ſhall be in continual Proportion, whereby it comes to paſs that each Pipe doth not expreſs its proper Sound, but ſomething varying from it, which is called* Bearing ; *and this,* ſays he, *is an Imperfection in this noble Inſtrument.* Again, he ſays, That the *Semitones* being all made equal, they do indifferently anſwer all Poſitions of *mi* (*i.e.* of the Two *natural Semitones* in an *Octave* ; of the Uſe of this Word *mi*, we ſhall hear again) and tho' not exactly to any, yet nearer to ſome than to others ; whence it is that the ſame Song ſtands better in one Key than another. I have ſhewn above, that a *Scale* of *Degrees* accurately equal, which will coincide with the Terms of the *natural Scale* is not poſſible ; and now let me ſay, That tho' the *Octave* may be divided into 12 equal *Semitones* by *geometrical* Methods, *that is,* 13 Lines may be conſtructed, which ſhall be in continued *geometrical Proportion,* and the greateſt to the leaſt be as 2 to 1, yet none of theſe Terms can be expreſt by rational Numbers, and ſo 'tis impoſſible that ſuch a *Scale* could expreſs any true *Muſick,* and hence I conclude, that this *Bearing* does not make the *Semitones* exactly equal, tho' they may be ſenſiby ſo in a ſingle Compariſon of one with another ; and ſuppoſing them equal, the Doctor ſays the ſame Song will ſtand better at one *Key* than another ; which may be very true, becauſe none of the Terms of ſuch a *Scale* can poſſibly

possibly fall in with these of the *natural Scale*, which are all exprest by rational Numbers, and the other are all Surds; whereas had we a Scale of equal Degrees, coinciding with the *natural Scale*, every *Key* would necessarily be alike for] every Song. These Imperfections, says the Doctor, might be further remedied by multiplying the Notes within an *Octave*, yet not without something of bearing, unless to every *Key* (he means of the Seven *natural* ones) be fitted a distinct Scale or Set of Pipes rising in the true Proportions, which would render the Instrument impracticable: But even this I think would not do; for let us suppose that from any one *Key* as *c*, we have a Series of true *diatonick* Notes, in both the Species of *sharp* and *flat Key*, let a Song be begun there as the *principal Key*, and suppose it to change into any or all of the *consonant Keys* within that *Octave*, then 'tis plain that if a Series is fitted to all these *natural* Notes of the *Key c*, the Instrument is so perfected for *c*, that any Piece of true *diatonick Musick* may begin there; but suppose, for the Accommodation of one Instrument to another, we would begin the Piece in *g*, 'tis plain this cannot be done with the same Accuracy as from *c* perfected as we have supposed, unless to these Notes that proceed *concinnously* from *g*, and are now considered as the *natural* Notes of that Key, be also fitted other Scales for answering the Modulations of the Song from the *principal Key* (which is now *g*) to the other *consonant Keys*. And if we should but perfect Two Keys of of the whole Inſtrument in this Manner, what a Multitude of Notes muſt there be? But I have done with this.

---

§ 4. *A brief Recapitulation of the preceeding Sections.*

THE *Amount* of all that has been ſaid upon this Subject of the *Syſtem* of *Muſick*, with reſpect to Inſtruments having fixt Sounds, is in ſhort this. 1*mo*. Becauſe the Degrees of the true *natural diatonick Scale* are unequal; ſo that from every Note to its *Octave* contains a different Order of *Degrees*; therefore from any Note we cannot find any *Interval*, in a Series of fixt Sounds conſtituted in theſe *Ratios*; which yet is neceſſary, that all the Notes of a Piece of *Muſick* which is carried thro' ſeveral Keys, may be found in their juſt Tune; or that the ſame Song may be begun indifferently at any Note, as will be neceſſary or at leaſt very convenient for accommodating ſome Inſtruments to others, or theſe to the human Voice, when it is required that they accompany each other in *Uniſon*. 2*do*. 'Tis impoſſible that ſuch a *Scale* can be found; yet Inſtruments are brought to a tolerable Perfection, by dividing every *Tone* into Two *Semitones*, making of the whole *Octave* 12 *Semitones*, which in a ſingle Caſe are ſenſibly equal

qual. 3*tio.* These *Semitones* may be made in exact Proportions, according to the Methods above explained; or the Instrument tun'd by the Ear, as is also explained, which reduces all to the particular Kinds of Degrees and Order also shown above. 4*to.* The *diatonick* Series, beginning at the lowest Note, being first settled upon any Instrument, and distinguished by their Names *a . b . c . d . e . f . g.* the other Notes are called *fictitious* Notes, taking the Name or Letter of the Note below with a ※ as *c*※, signifying that 'tis a *Semitone* higher than the Sound of *c* in the *natural* Series, or this Mark ♭ with the Name of the Note above signifying a *Semitone* lower, as *d* ♭; which are necessary Notes in a *Scale* of fixt Sounds, for the Purposes mentioned in the last Article; what Reasons make them to be named sometimes the one, sometimes the other Way shall be shewn afterwards; and *observe*, that since there is no Note betwixt *e* and *f*, which is the *natural Semitone*, therefore *f* cannot be marked ♭, for with that Mark it would be *e*; nor can *e* be marked ※, which would raise it to *f*; but *e* is capable of a ♭, as *f* is of a ※. So *b . c* being the other *natural Semitone*, *b* is incapable of a ※, which would make it coincide with *c*, but it properly takes a ♭, and when this Mark is set alone it expresses *flat b*; again *c* receives not a ♭, for *c* ♭ is equal to *b natural*, but it takes a ※. All the rest of the Notes *d . g . a* are made either ♭ or ※ because they have a *Tone* on either Hand above and below. Hence it is, that *b* and *e* are said to be *naturally* *naturaly ſharp*, as *c* and *f* naturally *flat*; and yet in ſome Caſes I have ſeen *c* and *f* marked ♭, and *b* and *e* marked ✳, which makes theſe Letters ſo marked coincide with the natural Notes next below and above. 3*tio*. Becauſe the *Semitones* are very near equal, therefore in *Practice* (upon ſuch Inſtruments at leaſt) they are all accounted equal, ſo that no Diſtinction is made of *Tones* into greater and leſſer; and for the other *Intervals* they are alſo conſidered here without any Differences, every Number of *Semitones* having a diſtinct Name, according to the Rule already laid down; and therefore when a true 3*d* or 4*th*, &c. is required from any Note, we muſt take ſo many *Semitones* as make an *Interval* of that Denomination in general, which will in ſome Caſes be true, and in others a falſe *Interval*, and cannot be otherwiſe in ſuch Inſtruments. 4*to*. The Differences among the *Semitones*, in the beſt tuned Inſtruments, is the Reaſon that a Song will go better from one Note or *Key* of the Inſtrument than another; becauſe the Errors occur more frequently in ſome Combinations and Succeſſions of Notes than in others; and happen alſo in the more principal Parts of one *Key* than another.

AND becauſe the Deſign of theſe new Notes is not to alter the Species of the true *diatonick* Melody, but to correct the Defects ariſing not from the Nature of the Syſtem of *Muſick* it ſelf, but the Accident of limiting it to fixt Sounds; therefore beginning at any Note, if we take an 8*ve concinnouſly* divided by *Tones* and *Semi-*

tones

tones in the *diatonick* Order (which will be ſound more exact from ſome Notes than others becauſe of the ſmall Errors that ſtill remain) that may be juſtly called a *natural Series*, and all theſe Notes *natural Notes* with reſpect to the Firſt or *Fundamental* from which they proceed; and yet in the common Way of ſpeaking about theſe Things, no 8*ve* is called a *natural Key* that takes in any of theſe Notes marked ※ or ♭, in order to make it a concinnous Series. And, as I have obſerved in another Place, there is no *Key* called *natural* in the whole Scale but *C* and *A*. I have alſo explained that there are properly but Two Kinds of *Keys* or *Modes*, the *greater* with the 3*d g*, &c. as in the 8*ve C*, and the *leſſer* with the 3*d l*, &c. as in *A*; but whenever in any Syſtem of fixt Sounds we can find a Series that is a true Key (or ſo near that we take it for one) there is no other Reaſon of calling that an *artificial Key*, than the arbitrary Will of thoſe who explain theſe Things to us, unleſs they make the Word *artificial* include the Imperfections of theſe *Keys*, which I believe they don't mean, becauſe they ſuppoſe the Errors are inconſiderable; for with reſpect to the Tune or Voice, 'tis equally a natural Key, begin at what Pitch you will; and we can ſuppoſe one Inſtrument ſo tuned as to play along *Uniſon* with the Voice, and be in a *natural Key*, and in another ſo tuned as that, to go *uniſon* with the ſame Voice, it muſt take an artificial Key: But I ſhall have Occaſion to conſider this again in the next *Chapter*, where I

I shall also shew you what Letters or Notes must be taken in to make a true *diatonick Scale* of either Species proceeding from any one of the Twelve different Letters in this new *Scale*.

THE *diatonick* Series upon all Instruments, being kept distinct by the Seven distinct Letters, is always first learned; and because in every 8*ve* of the *diatonick Scale*, there are Two *Semitones* distant one from another by 2 Tones or 3, therefore if the first 8*ve* of the *diatonick* Series upon any Instrument is learned, by the Place of the Two *Semitones*, we shall easily know how we ought to name the first and lowest Note; for if the 3*d* and 7*th* Degrees are *Semitones*, then the first Note is *c*, if the 2*d* and 6*th* then it is *d*, and so of the rest, which are easily found by Inspection into a *Scale* carried to Two 8*ves*. And different Instruments begin at [*i. e.* their lowest Note is named by] different Letters; in some Cases because the *natural Series*, which is always most considerable, is more easily found if we begin with one particular Order of the Degrees; and in other Cases the Reason may be the making one Instrument *concord* to another. So *Flutes* begin in *f*, *Hautboys*, *Violins*, and some *Harpsichords* begin in *g*, tho' the last may be made to begin in any Letter. As to the *Violin*, let me here observe, that it is a Kind of mixt Instrument, having its Sounds partly fixed and partly unfixed: It has only Four fixt Sounds, which are the Sounds of the Four Strings untouched by the Finger, and are called *g*-*d*-*a*-*e*. and can with very small Trouble

Trouble be altered to a higher or lower Pitch, which is one Conveniency ; all the reſt of the Notes being made by ſhortning the String with one's Finger, are thereby unfixed Sounds, and a good Ear learns to take them in perfect Tune with reſpect to the preceeding Note ; ſo that from any Note up or down may be found any *Interval* propoſed ; and therefore we may begin a Song at any Note, with this Proviſion that it be moſt eaſy and convenient for the Hand ; yet a Habit of Practice in every *Key* may make this Condition unneceſſary. There is only this one Variation to be obſerved, that by making the Four open Strings true *5ths*, all continuous, *d-a* is here a true *5th*, which in the *diatonick* Series wants a *Comma* ; from this follow other Variations from the Order of the *diatonick Scale* ; as here, from *g* (the firſt Note of the *4th* String) to *a* is made a greater *Tone*, that it may be a true *8ve* below *a* the firſt Note of the *2d* String, which is occaſioned by making *d-a* a true *5th*, whereas in the *Scale g-a* is a leſſer *Tone* : And ſo from *a* to *b* will be made a leſſer *Tone*, tho' 'tis *t g.* in the *Scale*, that *g-b* may be made a true *3d g.* which are Advantages when we begin in *g.* The ſame happens in the *3d* String, whoſe firſt Note is *d*, from which to the next Note *e* will be made a *t g.* that it may be an *8ve* to the firſt Note of the firſt String, yet *d* : *e* in the *Scale* is a *t l.* *Again*, if having made *d-f* on the *3d* String a true *3d l.* we would riſe to a true *5th* above *d*, 'tis plain *f* : *g* muſt be a *t l.* to make *g.* a true *4th* to *d*, and then *g* : *a* will be be a *t g*, becauſe *d-a* is a *5th* in this Tuning; which is plainly inverting the Order of the *Scale*, for there *f* : *g* is *tg*. and *g* : *a* a *t l*. but ſtill this is an Advantage, that we can expreſs any Order of Degrees from any Note; ſo that ſometimes we can make that a *t g*. which at other times the *Melody* requires to be a *t l*. Yet let me obſerve in the *laſt* Place, that if all theſe intermedia e Notes betwixt the open Sounds of the Four Strings, be conſtantly made in the ſame Tune, they become thereby fixt Sounds; and this Inſtrument will then have as great Imperfections as any other; and indeed conſidering that the ſtopping of the String to take theſe Notes in Tune is a very mechanical Thing, at leaſt the doing of it right in a quick Succeſſion of Notes muſt proceed altogether from Habit, 'tis probable we take them always in the ſame Tune; nor do I believe that any Practiſer on this Inſtrument dare be very poſitive on the contrary; yet I don't ſay 'tis impoſſible to do otherwiſe, for I know a Habit of playing the ſame Piece in ſeveral *Keys* might make one ſenſible of the contrary, if obſerved with great Attention; and upon the larger Inſtruments of this Kind, that have Frets upon the Neck for directing to the right Note, it would be very ſenſible; and even upon the *Violin*, we find that ſome Songs go better from one Key than another; which proves that thoſe at leaſt to whom this happens, take theſe Notes always in the ſame Tune.

HAV-

HAVING done what I proposed for explaining the *Theory* of *Sounds* with respect to *Tune*, the Order seems to require, that I should next consider that of *Time*; but tho' this be very considerable in Practice, yet there is much less to be said about it in *Theory*; and therefore I chuse to explain next the *Art* of *writing Musick*, where I shall have Occasion to say what is needful with respect to the TIME.

CHAP. XI.

The Method *and* Art *of* Writing Musick, *particularly how the Differences of* Tune *are represented.*

§ 1. *A general Account of the* Method.

WHAT this Title imports has been explained in *Chap.* 1. § 2. And to come to the Thing it self, let us consider.

IT was not enough to have discovered so much of the Nature of Sound, as to make it serviceable to our Pleasure, by the various Combinations

binations of the Degrees of *Tune*, and Meaſures of *Time*; it was neceſſary alſo, for enlarging the Application, to find a Method how to repreſent theſe fleeting and tranſient Objects, by ſenſible and permanent Signs; whereby they are as it were arreſted; and what would otherwiſe be loſt even to the *Compoſer*, he preſerves for his own Uſe, and can communicate it to others at any Diſtance; I mean he can direct them how to raiſe the like Ideas to themſelves, ſuppoſing they know how to take Sounds in any Relation of *Tune* and *Time* directed; for the Buſineſs of this Art properly is, to repreſent the various Degrees and Meaſures of *Tune* and *Time* in ſuch a Manner, that the Connection and Succeſſion of the Notes may be eaſily and readily diſcovered, and the skilful Practiſer may at Sight find his Notes, or, as they ſpeak, read any Song.

As the Two principal Parts of *Muſick* are the *Tune* and *Time* of Sounds, ſo the Art of writing it is very naturally reduced to Two Parts correſponding to theſe. The firſt, or the Method of repreſenting the Degrees of *Tune*, I ſhall explain in this Chapter; which will lead me to ſay ſomething in general of the other, a more full and particular Account whereof you ſhall have in the next Chapter.

We have already ſeen how the Degrees of *Tune* or the *Scale* of *Muſick* may be expreſt by 7 Letters repeated as oft as we pleaſe in a different Character; but theſe, without ſome other Signs, do not expreſs the Meaſures of *Time*, unleſs we ſuppoſe all the

the Notes of a Song to be of equal Length. Now, ſuppoſing the Thing to be made not much more difficult by theſe additional Signs of *Time*, yet the Whole is more happily accompliſhed in the following Manner.

If we draw any Number of parallel Lines, as in *Plate* 1. *Fig.* 7. Then, from every Line to the next Space, and from every Space to the next Line up and down, repreſents a Degree of the *diatonick Scale*; and conſequently from every Line or Space to every other at greater Diſtance repreſents ſome other Degree of the Scale, according as the immediate Degrees from Line to Space, and from Space to Line are determined. Now to determine theſe we make Uſe of the Scale expreſt by 7 Letters, as already explained, *viz.* *c* : *d*; *e* . *f* : *g*; *a* : *b*. *c*— where the Tone greater is repreſented by a Colon (:) the Tone leſſer by a Semicolon (;) and the Semitone greater by a Point (.). If the Lines and Spaces are marked and named by theſe Letters, as you ſee in the Figure, then according to the Relations aſſigned to theſe Letters (*i. e.* to the Sounds expreſt by them) the Degrees and Intervals of Sound expreſt by the Diſtances of Lines and Spaces are determined.

As to the Extent of the *Scale* of *Muſick*, it is infinite if we conſider what is ſimply poſſible, but for Practice, it is limited; and in the preſent Practice 4 *Octaves*, or at moſt 4 *Octaves* with a *6th*, comprehending 34 *diatonick* Notes, is the greateſt Extent. There is ſcarcely any

one

one Voice to be found that reaches near ſo far, tho' ſeveral different Voices may; nor any one ſingle Piece of *Melody*, that comprehends ſo great an Interval betwixt its higheſt and loweſt Note: Yet we muſt conſider not only what *Melody* requires, but what the Extent of ſeveral Voices and Inſtruments is capable of, and what the *Harmony* of ſeverals of them requires; and in this reſpect the whole Scale is neceſſary, which you have repreſented in the Figure directed to; I ſhall therefore call it the *univerſal Syſtem*, becauſe it comprehends the whole Extent of modern Practice.

BUT the Queſtion ſtill remains, How any particular Order and Succeſſion of Sounds is repreſented? And this is done by ſetting certain Signs and Characters one after another, up and down on the Lines and Spaces, according to the Intervals and Relations of *Tune* to be expreſt; *that is*, any one Letter of the Scale, or the Line or Space to which it belongs, being choſen to ſet the firſt Note on, all the reſt are ſet up and down according to the Mind of the Compoſer, upon ſuch Lines and Spaces as are at the deſigned Diſtances, *i. e.* which expreſs the deſigned Interval according to the Number and Kind of the intermediate Degrees; and *mind* that the firſt Note is taken at any convenient Pitch of *Tune*; for the Scale, or the Lines and Spaces, ſerve only to determine the *Tune* of the reſt with relation to the firſt, leaving us to take that as we pleaſe: For *Example*, if the firſt Note is placed on the Line *c*, and the

the next designed a *Tone* or 2*d g.* above, it is set on the next Space above, which is *d*; or i it is designed a 3*d g.* it is set on the Line above which is *e*; or on the second Line above, if it was designed 5*th*, as you see represented in the 2*d* Column of the Scale in the preceeding Figure, where I have used this Character O for a Note. And here let me observe in general, that these Characters serve not only to direct how to take the Notes in their true *Tune*, by the Distance of the Lines and Spaces on which they are set; but by a fit Number and Variety of them, (to be explained in the next Chapter) they express the *Time* and Measure of Duration of the Notes; whereby 'tis plain that these Two Things are no way confounded; the relative Measures of *Tune* being properly determined by the Distances of Lines and Spaces, and the *Time* by the Figure of the Note or Character.

'T is easy to *observe* what an Advantage there is in this Method of Lines and Spaces, even for such *Musick* as has all its Notes of equal Length, and therefore needs no other Thing but the Letters of the Scale to express it; the Memory and Imagination are here greatly assisted, for the Notes standing upward and downward from each other on the Lines and Spaces, express the rising and falling of the Voice more readily than different Characters of Letters; and the Intervals are also more readily perceived.

OBSERVE in the next Place, That with reſpect to Inſtruments of Muſick, I ſuppoſe their Notes are all named by the Letters of the Scale, having the ſame Diſtances as already ſtated in the Relations of Sounds expreſt by theſe Letters; ſo that knowing how to raiſe a Series of Sounds from the loweſt Note of any Inſtrument by *diatonick* Degrees (which is always firſt learned) and naming them by the Letters of the Scale, 'tis eaſily conceived how we are directed to play on any Inſtrument, by Notes ſet upon Lines and Spaces that are named by the ſame Letters. It is the Buſineſs of the Maſters and Profeſſors of ſeveral Inſtruments to teach the Application more expreſly. And as to the *human Voice*, obſerve, the Notes thereof, being confined to no Order, are called *c* or *d*, &c. only with reſpect to the Direction it receives from this Method; and that Direction is alſo very plain; for having taken the firſt Note at any convenient Pitch, we are taught by the Places of the reſt upon the Lines and Spaces how to tune them in relation to the firſt, and to one another.

Again, as the *artificial* Notes which divide the *Tones* of the *natural* Series, are expreſt by the ſame Letters, with theſe Marks, ✱, ♭, already explained, ſo they are alſo plac'd on the ſame Lines and Spaces, on which the *natural* Note named by that Letter ſtands; thus *c*✱ and *c* belong to the ſame Line or Space, as alſo *d*' and *d*. And when the Note on any Line or Space ought to be the *artificial* one, it is marked

ked ✱ or ♭; and where there is no ſuch Mark it is always the *natural* Note. Thus, if from *a* (*natural*) we would ſet a 3*d g.* upward, it is *c*✱; or a 3*d l.* above *g*, it is *b flat* or ♭, as you ſee in the 2*d* Column of the preceeding Figure. Theſe artificial Notes are all determined on Inſtruments to certain Places or Poſitions, with reſpect to the Parts of the Inſtrument and the Hand; and for the Voice they are taken according to the Diſtance from the laſt Note, reckoned by the Number of *Tones* and *Semitones* that every greater *Interval* contains.

THE laſt general *Obſerve* I make here is, that as there are Twelve different Notes in the *ſemitonick Scale*, the Writing might be ſo ordered, that from every Line a Space to the next Space or Line ſhould expreſs a *Semitone*; but it is much better contrived, that theſe ſhould expreſs the *Degrees* of the *diatonick Scale* (i. e. ſome *Tones* ſome *Semitones*) for hereby we can much eaſier diſcover what is the true *Interval* betwixt any Two Notes, becauſe there are fewer Lines and Spaces interpoſed, and the Number of them ſuch as anſwers to the Denomination of the *Intervals*; ſo an *Octave* comprehends Four Lines and Four Spaces; a 5*th* comprehends Three Lines and Two Spaces, or Three Spaces and Two Lines; and ſo of others. I have already ſhewn, how it is better that there ſhould be but Seven different Letters, to name the Twelve Degrees of the *ſemitonick Scale*; but ſuppoſing there were Twelve Letters, it is plain we ſhould need no more Lines to comprehend an *Octave*, becauſe we might aſſign Two Letters to one Line or Space, as well as to make it, for *Example*, both *c*✳ and *c*, whereof the one belonging to the *diatonick Series*, ſhould mark it for ordinary, and upon Occaſions the other be brought in the ſame Way we now do the Signs ✳ and ♭.

---

§ 2. *A more particular Account of the Method; where, of the* Nature *and* Uſe *of* Clefs.

THO' the *Scale* extends to Thirty Four *diatcnick* Notes, which require Seventeen Lines with their Spaces, yet becauſe no one ſingle Piece of *Melody* comprehends near ſo many Notes, whatever ſeveral Pieces joyned in one *Harmony* comprehend among them; and becauſe every Piece or ſingle Song is directed or written diſtinctly by it ſelf; therefore we never draw more than Five Lines, which comprehend the greateſt Number of the Notes of any ſingle Piece; and for thoſe Caſes which require more, we draw ſhort Lines occaſionally, above or below the 5, to ſerve the Notes that go higher or lower. See an *Example* in *Plate* 1. *Fig.* 8.

Again, tho' every Line and Space may be marked at the Beginning with its Letter, as has been done in former Times; yet, ſince the Art has been improven, only one Line is marked, by which all the reſt are eaſily known, if we reckon up or down in the Order of the Letters; the

the Letter marked is called the *Clef* or *Key*, becauſe by it we know the Names of all the other Lines and Spaces, and conſequently the true Quantity of every *Degree* and *Interval*. But becauſe every Note in the *Octave* is called a *Key*, tho' in another Senſe, this Letter marked is called in a particular Manner the *ſigned Clef*, becauſe being written on any Line, it not only *ſigns* or marks that one, but explains all the reſt. And to prevent Ambiguity in what follows, by the Word *Clef*, I ſhall always mean that Letter, which, being marked on any Line, explains all the reſt; and by the Word *Key* the principal Note of any Song, in which the Melody cloſes, in the Senſe explained in the laſt *Chapter*. Of theſe *ſigned Clefs* there are Three, *viz.* *c*, *f*, *g*; and that we may know the Improvement in having but one *ſigned Clef* in one particular Piece, alſo how and for what Purpoſe Three different *Clefs* are uſed in different Pieces, conſider the following Definition.

A *Song* is either *ſimple* or *compound*. It is a *ſimple Song*, where only one Voice performs; or, tho' there be more, if they are all *Uniſon* or *Octave*, or any other *Concord* in every Note, 'tis ſtill but the ſame Piece of *Melody*, performed by different Voices in the ſame or different Pitches of *Tune*, for the *Intervals* of the Notes are the ſame in them all. A *compound Song* is where Two or more Voices go together, with a Variety of *Concords* and *Harmony*; ſo that the *Melody* each of them makes, is a diſtinct and different *ſimple Song*, and all together

ther make the *compound*. The *Melody* that each of them produces is therefore called a Part of the *Composition*; and all such *Compositions* are very properly called *symphonetick Musick*, or *Musick* in *Parts*; taking the Word *Musick* here for the *Composition* or *Song* it self.

Now, because in this *Composition* the *Parts* must be some of them higher and some lower, (which are generally so ordered that the same *Part* is always highest or lowest, tho' in modern *Compositions* they do frequently change,) and all written distinctly by themselves, as is very necessary for the Performance; therefore the Staff of Five Lines upon which each *Part* is written, is to be considered as a *Part* of the *universal System* or *Scale*, and is therefore called a *particular System*; and because there are but Five Lines ordinarily, we are to suppose as many above and below, as may be required for any single *Part*; which are actually drawn in the particular Places where they are necessary.

The highest *Part* is called the Treble, or Alt whose *Clef* is *g*, set on the 2*d* Line of the *particular System*, counting upward: The lowest is called the Bass, *i. e. Basis*, because it is the Foundation of the *Harmony*, and formerly in their *plain Compositions* the *Bass* was first made, tho' 'tis otherwise now; the *Bass-clef* is *f* on the 4*th* Line upward: All the other *Parts*, whose particular Names you'll learn from Practice, I shall call Mean Parts, whose *Clef* is *c*, sometimes on one, sometimes on another Line; and some that are really *mean*

Parts

Parts are ſet with the *g Clef.* See *Plate* 1. *Fig.* 8. where you'll obſerve that the *c* and *f Clefs* are marked with Signs no way reſembling theſe Letters; I think it were as well if we uſed the Letters themſelves, but Cuſtom has carried it otherwiſe; yet that it may not ſeem altogether a Whim, *Kepler* in *Chap.* *Book* 3*d* of his *Harmony*, has taken a critical Pains to prove, that theſe Signs are only Corruptions of the Letters they repreſent; the curious may conſult him.

We are next to conſider the Relations of theſe *Clefs* to one another, that we may know where each *Part* lies in the *Scale* or *general Syſtem*, and the natural Relation of the *Parts* among themſelves, which is the true Deſign and Office of the *Clefs*. Now they are taken 5*ths* to one another, *that is*, the *Clef f* is loweſt, *c* is a 5*th* above it, and *g* a 5*th* above *c*. See them repreſented in *Plate* 1. *Fig.* 7. the laſt Column of the *Scale*; and *obſerve*, that tho' in the *particular Syſtems*, the *Treble* or *g Clef* is ordinarily ſet on the 2*d* Line, the *Baſs* or *f Clef* on the 4*th* Line, and the *mean* or *c Clef* on the 3*d* Line (eſpecially when there are but Three *Parts*) yet they are to be found on other Lines; as particularly the *mean Clef*, which moſt frequently changes Place, becauſe there are many *mean Parts*, is ſometimes on the 1*ſt*, the 2*d*, the 3*d* or 4*th* Line; but on whatever Line in the ſeparate *particular Syſtem* any *Clef* is ſigned, it muſt be underſtood to belong to the ſame Place of the *general Syſtem*, and to be the

ſame

ſame individual Note or Sound on the Inſtrument which is directed by that *Clef*, as I have diſtinguiſh'd them in the *Scale* upon the Margin of the 3*d* Column; ſo that to know what Part of the *Scale* any particular *Syſtem* is, we muſt take its *Clef* where it ſtands ſigned in the *Scale* (*i. e.* the laſt mentioned *Fig.*) and take as many Lines above and below it, as there are in the particular *Syſtem*; or thus, we muſt apply the *particular Syſtem* to the *Scale*, ſo as the *Clef* Lines coincide, and then we ſhall ſee with what Lines of the *Scale* the other Lines of the particular *Syſtem* coincide: For *Example*, if we find the *Clef* on the 3*d* Line upward, in a *particular Syſtem*; to find the coincident Five Lines to which it refers in the *Scale*, we take with the *f Clef* Line, Two Lines above and Two below. Again, if we have the *c Clef* on the 4*th* Line, we are to take in the *Scale* with the *Clef* Line, One Line above and Three below, and ſo of others; ſo that according to the different Places of the *Clef* in a particular *Syſtem*, the Lines in the *Scale* correſpondent to that *Syſtem* may be all different, except the *Clef Line* which is invariable: And that you may with Eaſe find in the *Scale* the Five Lines coincident with every particular *Syſtem*, upon whatever Line of the Five the *Clef* may be ſet, I have drawn Nine Lines acroſs, which include each Five Lines of the *Scale*, in ſuch a Manner, that you have the *particular Syſtems* diſtinguiſhed for every relative Poſition of any of the Three ſigned *Clefs*.

As

As to the Reaſon of changing the relative Place of the *Clef*, *i. e.* its Place in the *particular* Syſtem, 'tis only to make this comprehend as many Notes of the Song as poſſible, and by that Means to have fewer Lines above or below it; ſo if there are many Notes above the *Clef* Note and few below it, this Purpoſe is anſwered by placing the *Clef* in the firſt or ſecond Line; but if the Song goes more below the *Clef*, then it is beſt placed higher in the Syſtem: *In ſhort*, according to the Relation of the other Notes to the *Clef* Note, the *particular Syſtem* is taken differently in the *Scale*, the *Clef* Line making one in all the Variety, which conſiſts only in this, *viz.* taking any Five Lines immediately next other, whereof the *Clef* Line muſt always be one.

By this conſtant and invariable Relation of the *Clefs*, we learn eaſily how to compare the particular Syſtems of ſeveral *Parts*, and know how they communicate in the *Scale*, *i. e.* which Lines are *uniſon*, and which are different, and how far, and conſequently what Notes of the ſeveral Parts are *uniſon*, and what not: For you are not to ſuppoſe that each *Part* has a certain Bounds within which another muſt never come; no, ſome Notes of the *Treble*, for *Example*, may be lower than ſome of the *mean Parts*, or even of the *Baſs*; and that not only when we compare ſuch Notes as are not heard together, but even ſuch as are. And if we would put together in one Syſtem, all the *Parts* of any Compoſition that are written ſeparately. The Rule

is

is plainly this, *viz.* Place the Notes of each Part at the ſame Diſtances above and below the proper *Clef*, as they ſtand in the ſeparate Syſtem. And becauſe all the Notes that are conſonant (or heard together) ought to ſtand, in this Deſign, perpendicularly over each other, therefore that the Notes belonging to each *Part* may be diſtinctly known, they may be made with ſuch Differences as ſhall not confuſe or alter their Significations with reſpect to Time, and only ſignify that they belong to ſuch a *Part* ; by this Means we ſhall ſee how all the *Parts* change and paſs thro' one another, *i. e.* which of them, in every Note, is higheſt or loweſt or *uniſon* ; for they do ſometimes change, tho' more generally the *Treble* is higheſt and the *Baſs* loweſt, the Change happening more ordinarily betwixt the *mean Parts* among themſelves, or theſe with the *Treble* or *Baſs*: The *Treble* and *Baſs Clefs* are diſtant an *Octave* and *Tone*, and their *Parts* do ſeldom interfere, the *Treble* moving more above the *Clef* Note, and the *Baſs* below.

WE ſee plainly then, that the Uſe of particular ſign'd *Clefs* is an Improvement with reſpect to the *Parts* of any *Compoſition* ; for unleſs ſome one Key in the particular Syſtems were diſtinguiſhed from the reſt, and referred invariably and conſtantly to one Place in the *Scale*, the Relations of the *Parts* could not be diſtinctly marked ; and that more than one is neceſſary, is plain from the Diſtance there muſt be among the Parts: Or if one Letter is choſen for all,

all, there muſt be ſome other Sign to ſhew what *Part* it belongs to, and the Relation of the Parts. Experience having approven the Number and Relations of the ſigned *Clefs* which are explained, I ſhall add no more as to that, but there are other Things to be here obſerved.

THE chooſing theſe Letters *f . c . g* for ſigned *Clefs*, is a Thing altogether arbitrary; for any other Letter within the Syſtem, will explain the reſt as well; yet 'tis fit there be a conſtant Rule, that the ſeveral *Parts* may be right diſtinguiſhed; and concerning this *obſerve* again, that for the Performance of any ſingle Piece the *Clef* ſerves only for explaining the *Invervals* among the Lines and Spaces, ſo that we need not mind what Part of any greater Syſtem it is, and we may take the firſt Note as high or low as we pleaſe: For as the proper Uſe of the *Scale* is not to limit the abſolute Degree of *Tone*, ſo the proper Uſe of the ſigned *Clef* is not to limit the Pitch, at which the firſt Note of any *Part* is to be taken, but to determine the *Tune* of the reſt with relation to the firſt, and, conſidering all the *Parts* together, to determine the Relations of their ſeveral Notes,by the Relations of their *Clefs* in the *Scale* : And ſo the Pitch of *Tune* being determined in a certain Note of one *Part*, the other Notes of that *Part* are determined, by the conſtant Relations of the Letters of the *Scale*; and alſo the Notes of the other *Parts*, by the Relations of their *Clefs*. To ſpeak particularly of the Way of tuning the Inſtruments that are employed in executing the

ſeveral

ſeveral *Parts*, is out of my Way ; I ſhall only ſay this, that they are to be ſo tuned as the *Clef* Notes, wherever they ly on the Inſtruments which ſerve each *Part*, be in the foremention-ed Relations to one another.

As the *Harpſichord* or *Organ* (or any other of the Kind) is the moſt extenſive Inſtrument, we may be helped by it to form a clearer *Idea* of theſe Things : For conſider, a *Harpſichord* contains in itſelf all the *Parts* of *Muſick*, I mean the whole *Scale* or *Syſtem* of the modern Practice ; the foremoſt Range of Keys contains the *diatonick* Series beginning, in the largeſt Kind, in *g*, and extending to *c* above the Fourth 8*ve*; which therefore we may well ſuppoſe repreſen-ted by the preceeding *Scale*. In Practice, upon that Inſtrument, the *Clef* Notes are taken in the Places repreſented in the Scheme ; and other In-ſtruments are ſo tuned, that, conſidering the *Parts* they perform, all their Notes of the ſame Name are *uniſon* to thoſe of the *Harpſichord* that belong to the ſame *Part*. I have ſaid, the *Harpſichord* contains all the *Parts* of Muſick ; and indeed any Two diſtinct *Parts* may be per-formed upon it at the ſame Time and no more; yet upon Two or more *Harpſichords* tuned *uni-ſons*, whereby they are in Effect but one, any Number of *Parts* may be executed : And in this Caſe we ſhould ſee the ſeveral *Parts* ta-ken in their proper Places of the Inſtrument, ac-cording to the Relations of their *Clefs* explain-ed : And as to the tuning the Inſtrument, I ſhall only add, that there is a certain Pitch to which

it

it is brought, that it may be neither too *high* nor too *low*, for the Accompaniment of other Inſtruments, and eſpecially for the human Voice, whether in *Uniſon* or taking a different *Part* ; and this is called the CONSORT PITCH. To have done, you muſt conſider, that for performing any one ſingle *Part*, we may take the *Clef* Note in any 8*ve*, *i. e.* at any Note of the ſame Name, providing we go not too high or too low for finding the reſt of the Notes of the Song: But in a *Conſort* of ſeveral *Parts*, all the *Clefs* muſt be taken, not only in the Relations, but alſo in the Places of the Syſtem already mentioned, that every Part may be comprehended in it : Yet ſtill you are to mind, That the *Tune* of the Whole, or the abſolute Pitch, is in it ſelf an arbitrary Thing, quite foreign to the Uſe of the *Scale* ; tho' there is a certain Pitch generally agreed upon, that differs not very much in the Practice of any one Nation or Set of Muſicians from another. And therefore,

WHEN I ſpeak of the Place of the *Clefs* in the *Scale* or *general Syſtem*, you muſt underſtand it with reſpect to a *Scale* of a certain determined Extent ; for this being undetermined, ſo muſt the Places of the *Clefs* be : And for any *Scale* of a certain Extent, the *Rule* is, that the *mean Clef c* be taken as near the Middle of the *Scale* as poſſible, and then the *Clef g* a 5*th* above, and *f* a 5*th* below, as it is in the preſent *general Syſtem* of Four 8*ves* and a 6*th*, repreſented in the preceeding Scheme, and actually determined upon *Harpſichords*.

IN

In the *laſt Place* conſider, that ſince the Lines and Spaces of the *Scale*, with the Degrees ſtated among them by the Letters, ſufficiently determine how far any Note is diſtant from another, therefore there is no Need of different Characters of Letters, as would be if the Scale were only expreſt by theſe Letters: And when we ſpeak of any Note of the *Scale*, naming it by *a* or *b*, &c. we may explain what Part of the *Scale* it is in, either by numbring the 8*ves* from the loweſt Note, and calling the Note ſpoken of (for *Example*) *c* in the loweſt 8*ve* or in the 2*d* 8*ve*, and ſo on: Or, we may determine its Place by a Reference to the Seat of any of the Three *ſigned Clefs*; and ſo we may ſay of any Note, as *f* or *g*, that it is ſuch a *Clef* Note, or the firſt or ſecond, *&c.* *f* or *g* above ſuch a *Clef*. Take this Application, ſuppoſe you ask me what is the higheſt Note of my Voice, if I ſay *d*, you are not the wiſer by this Anſwer, till I determine it by ſaying it is *d* in the fourth *Octave*, or the firſt *d* above the *Treble Clef*. But again, neither this Queſtion nor the Anſwer is ſufficiently determined, unleſs it have a Reference to ſome ſuppoſed Pitch of *Tune* in a certain fixt Inſtrument, as the ordinary *Conſort Pitch* of a *Harpſichord*, becauſe, as I have frequently ſaid, the *Scale* of *Muſick* is concerned only with the Relation of Notes and the Order of Degrees, which are ſtill the ſame in all Differences of *Tune*, in the whole Series.

§ 3. *Of the* Reaſon, Uſe, *and* Variety *of the* Signatures *of* Clefs.

I Have already ſaid, that the *natural* and *artificial* Note expreſſed by the ſame Letter, as *c* and *c*※, are both ſet on the ſame Line or Space. When there is no ※ or ♭ marked on any Line or Space, at the Beginning with the *Clef*, then all the Notes are natural; and if in any particular Place of the Song, the artificial Note is required, 'tis ſignified by the Sign ※ or ♭, ſet upon the Line a Space before that Note; but if a ※ or ♭ is ſet at the Beginning in any Line or Space with the *Clef*, then all the Notes on that Line or Space are the artificial ones, *that is*, are to be taken a *Semitone* higher or lower than they would be without ſuch a Sign; the ſame affects all their *8ves* above or below, tho' they are not marked ſo. And in the Courſe of the Song, if the natural Note is ſometimes required, it is ſignified by this Mark ♮. And the marking the *Syſtem* at the Beginning with Sharps or Flats, I call the *Signature* of the *Clef*.

In what's ſaid, you have the plain *Rule* for Application; but that we may better conceive the Reaſon and Uſe of theſe Signatures, it will be neceſſary to recollect, and alſo make a little clearer, what has been explained of the Nature of *Keys* or *Modes*, and of the Original and Uſe of the *ſharp* and *flat* Notes in the *Scale*. I have in in *Chap.* 9. explained what a *Key* and *Mode* in *Musick* is; I have diſtinguiſhed betwixt theſe Two, and ſhewn that there are and can be but Two different *Modes*, the *greater* and the *leſſer*, according to the Two *concinnous* Diviſions of the 8*ve*, *viz.* by the 3*d g.* or the 3*d l.* and their proper Accompanyments; and whatever Difference you may make in the abſolute Pitch of the whole Notes, or of the firſt Note which limites all the reſt, the ſame individual Song muſt ſtill be in the ſame *Mode*; and by the *Key* I underſtand only that Pitch or Degree of *Tune* at which the *fundamental* or cloſe Note of the *Melody*, and conſequently the whole 8*ve* is taken; and becauſe the *Fundamental* is the principal Note of the 8*ve* which regulates the reſt, it is peculiarly called the *Key*. Now as to the Variety of *Keys*, if we take the Thing in ſo large a Senſe as to ſignify the abſolute Pitch of *Tune* at which any fundamental Note may be taken, the Number is at leaſt indefinite; but in Practice it is limited, and particularly with reſpect to the Denominations of *Keys*, which are only Twelve, *viz.* the Twelve different Names or Letters of the *ſemitonick Scale*; ſo we ſay the *Key* of a Song is *c* or *d*, &c. which ſignifies that the *Cadence* or *Cloſe* of the *Melody* is upon the Note of that Name when we ſpeak of any Inſtrument; and with reſpect to the human Voice, that the cloſe Note is *Uniſon* to ſuch a Note on an Inſtrument; and generally, with reſpect both to Inſtruments and Voice, the Denomination of the *Key* is taken from the Place of the cloſe

close Note upon the written *Musick*, *i. e.* the Name of the Line or Space where it stands: Hence we see, that tho' the Difference of *Keys* refers to the Degree of *Tune*, at which the *Fundamental*, and consequently the whole 8*ve* is taken, in Distinction from the *Mode* or Constitution of an *Octave*, yet these Denominations determine the Differences only relatively, with respect to one certain Series of fixt Sounds, as a Scale of Notes upon a particular Instrument, in which all the Notes of different Names are different *Keys*, according to the general Definition, because of their different Degrees of *Tune*; but as the tuning of the whole may be in a different Pitch, and the Notes taken in the same Part of the Instrument, are, without respect to the tuning of the Whole, still called by the same Names *c* or *d*, &c. because they serve only to mark the Relation of *Tune* betwixt the Notes, therefore 'tis plain, that in Practice a Song will be said to be in the same *Key* as to the Denomination, tho' the absolute *Tune* be different, and to be in different *Keys* when the absolute *Tune* is the same; as if the Note *a* is made the *Key* in one Tuning, and in another the Note *d unison* to *a* of the former. Now, this is a Kind of Limitation of the general Definition, yet it serves the Design best for Practice, and indeed cannot be otherwise without infinite Confusion. I shall a little below make some more particular Remarks upon the Denominations of Sounds or Notes raised from Instruments or the human Voice: But from what has been explained, you'll easily

eaſily underſtand what Difference I put betwixt a *Mode* and a *Key*; of *Modes* there are only Two, and they reſpect what I would call the *Internal Conſtitution* of the 8*ve*, but *Keys* are indefinite in the more general and abſtract Senſe, and with regard to their Denominations in Practice they are reduced to Twelve, and have reſpect to a Circumſtance that's *external* and *accidental* to the *Mode*;and therefore a *Key* may be changed under the ſame *Mode*, as when the ſame Song,which is always in the ſame *Mode*, is taken up at different Notes or Degrees of *Tune*, and from the ſame *Fundamental* or *Key* a Series may proceed in a different *Mode*, as when different Songs begin in the ſame Note. But then becauſe common Uſe applies the Word *Key* in both Senſes, *i. e.* both to what I call a *Key* and a *Mode*, to prevent Ambiguity the Word *ſharp* or *flat* ought to be added when we would expreſs the *Mode*; ſo that a *ſharp Key* is the ſame as a greater *Mode*, and a *flat Key* a leſſer *Mode*; and when we would expreſs both *Mode* and *Key*, we joyn the Name of the *Key* Note, thus, we may ſay ſuch a Song is for *Example* in the *ſharp* or *flat Key c*, to ſignifie that the fundamental Note in which the Cloſe is made is the Note called *c* on the Inſtrument, or *uniſon* to it in the Voice; or generally, that it is ſet on the Line or Space of that Name in Writing; and that the 3*d g*. or 3*d l*. is uſed in the *Melody*, while the Song keeps within that *Key*; for I have alſo obſerved, that the ſame Song may be carried thro' different *Keys*, or make

make ſucceſſive *Cadences* in different Notes, which is commonly ordered by bringing in ſome Note that is none of the natural Notes of the former *Key*, of which more immediately: But when we hear of any *Key* denominated *c* or *d* without the Word *ſharp* or *flat*, then we can underſtand nothing but what I have called the *Key* in Diſtinction from the *Mode*, *i. e.* that the *Cadence* is made in ſuch a Note.

AGAIN, I have in *Chap.* 10. explained the Uſe of the Notes we call *ſharp* and *flat*, or *artificial* Notes, and the Diſtinction of *Keys* in that reſpect into *natural* and *artificial*; I have ſhewn that they are neceſſary for correcting the Defects of Inſtruments having fixt Sounds, that beginning at any Note we may have a true concinnous *diatonick* Series from that Note, which in a *Scale* of fixt Degrees in the 8*ve* we cannot have, all the Orders of Degrees proceeding from each of the Seven *natural* Notes being different, of which only Two are concinnous, *viz.* from *c* which makes a *ſharp Key*, and from *a* which makes a *flat Key*; and to apply this more particularly, you muſt underſtand the Uſe of theſe *ſharp* or *flat* Notes to be this, that a Song, which, being ſet in a *natural Key* or without *Sharps* and *Flats*, is either too high or too low, may be tranſpoſed or ſet in another more convenient *Key*; which neceſſarily brings in ſome of the artificial Notes, in order to make a *diatonick* Series from this new *Key*, like that from the other; and when the Song changes the *Key* before it come to the

final

final Close, tho' the principal *Key* be natural, yet some of these into which it changes may require artificial Notes, which are the essential and natural Notes of this new *Key*; for tho' this be called an artificial Key, 'its only so with respect to the Names of the Notes in the fixt *System*, which are still natural with respect to their proper *Fundamental*, viz. the *Key* into which the Piece is transposed, or into which it changes where the principal *Key* is natural.

AND even with respect to the human Voice, which is under no Limitation, I have shewn the Necessity of these Names, for the sake of a regular, distinct and easy Representation of Sounds, for directing the Voice in Performance. I shall next more particularly explain by some Examples, the Business of keeping in and going out of *Keys*. *Example*. Suppose a Song begins in *c*, or at least makes the first Close in it; if all the Notes preceeding that Close are in true musical Relation to *c* as a *Fundamental* in one Species, suppose as a *sharp Key*, *i. e.* with a 3*d g*. the Melody has been still in that *Key* (See *Example* 5. *Plate* 3.) But if proceeding, the Composer brings in the Note *f*✱ he leads the *Melody* out of the former *Key*, because *f*✱ is none of the natural Notes of the 8*ve c*, being a false 4*th* to *c*. Again, he may lead it out of the *Key* without any false Note, by bringing in one that belongs not to the Species in which the Melody was begun: Suppose after beginning in the *sharp Key c*, he introduces the Note *g*✱, which is a 6*th l.* to *c*, and therefore harmonious, yet it belongs

longs to it as a *flat Key*, and consequently is out of the *Key* as a *sharp* one: And because the same Song cannot with any good Effect be made to close twice in the same Note in a different Species, therefore after introducing the Note *g*※, the next Close must be in some other Note as *a*, and then the *Key* in both Senses will be changed, because *a* has naturally a 3*d l*; and therefore when any Note is said to be out of a *Key*, 'tis understood to be out of it either as making a false *Interval*, or as belonging to it in another Species than a supposed one, *i. e.* if it belong to it as a *sharp Key*, 'tis out of it as a *flat* one; so in *Example* 3. *Plate* 3. the first Close is in *a* as a *sharp Key*, all the preceeding Notes being natural to it as such; then proceeding in the same *Key*, you see *g* (*natural*) introduced, which belongs not to *a* as a *sharp Key*, and also *a*※, which is quite out of the former *Key*: By these Notes a Close is brought on in *b*, and the *Melody* is said to be out of the first *Key*, and is so in both Senses of the Word *Key*, for *b* here has a 3*d l*; then the *Melody* is carried on to a Close in *d*, which is a Third *Key*, and with respect to that Piece is indeed the *principal Key*, in which also the Piece begins; but I shall consider this again; it was enough to my Purpose here, that all the Notes from the Beginning to the first Close in *a* were natural to the *Octave* from *a* with a 3*d g*; and tho' the 3*d g.* above the Close is not used in the *Example*, yet the 6*th l.* below it is used, which is the same Thing in determining the Species.

I

I have explained already, that with the 3*d l.* the *6th l.* and *7th l*,or *6th g.* and *7th g.* are used in different Circumstances; and therefore you are to mind that the *6th g.*or *7th g.* being introduced upon a *flat Key*, does not make any Change of it; so that tho' the *6th l.* and *7th l.* is a certain Sign of a *flat Key*, yet the *6th g.* and *7th g.* belong to either Species; therefore the Species is only certainly determined by the 3*d* in both Cases; and so in the preceeding *Example*, where I suppose *g*※ is introduced upon the *sharp Key c*, the next Close cannot be in *c*, because *g*※ being a *6th l*, to *c*, requires a 3*d l.* which would altogether destroy that Unity of *Melody* which ought to be kept up in every Song; therefore when I say the same Song cannot close twice in one Note in different Species, the Determination of that Difference depends on the 3*d*, which being the *greater*, must always have the *6th g.* and *7th g.* but the 3*d l.* takes sometimes the *6th l.* and *7th l.* sometime the *6th g.* and *7th g.* See *Ex.* 6. *Plate* 3. where the whole keeps within the *flat Key a*, and closes twice in it; the first Close is brought on with the *6th l.*and *7th l.* the next Close in the *Octave* above is made with the *6th g.* and *8th g.* but a Close in *a*, using the 3*d g.* would quite ruine the Unity of the *Melody*; yet the same Song may be carried into different *Keys*, of which some are *sharp*, some *flat*, without any Prejudice; but of all these there must be one *principal Key*, in which the Song sets out, and makes most frequent *Cadences*, and at least the *final Cadence*.

THE

THE last Thing I shall *observe* upon this Subject of *Keys* is, that sometimes the *Key* is changed, without bringing the *Melody* to a *Cadence* in the *Key* to which it is transferred, *that is*, a Note is introduced, which belongs properly to another *Key* than that in which the *Melody* existed before, yet no *Cadenc* made in that *Key*; as if after a *Cadence* in the *sharp Key c*, the Note *g*✳ is brought in, which should naturally lead to a Close in *a*, yet the *Melody* may be turned off without any formal and perfect *Close* in *a*, and brought to its next Close in another *Key*.

I return now to explain the Reason and Use of the *Signatures* of *Clefs*. And *first*, Let us suppose any Piece of *Melody* confined strictly to one *Mode* or *Key*, and let that be the natural *sharp Key c*, from which as the Relation of the Letters are determined in the *Scale*, there is a true *musical* Series and Gradation of Notes, and therefore it requires no ✳ or ♭, consequently the Signature of the *Clef* must be plain: But let the Piece be transposed to the *Key d*, it must necessarily take *f*✳ instead of *f*, and *c*✳ for *c*, because *f*✳ is the true 3*d g.* and *c*✳ the true 7*th g.* to *d*. See an *Example* in *Plate* 3. *Fig.* 5. Now if the *Clef* be not signed with a ✳ on the Seat of *f* and *c*, we must supply it wherever these Notes occur thro' the Piece, but 'tis plainly better that they be marked once for all at the Beginning.

AGAIN, suppose a Piece of *Melody*, in which there is a Change of the *Key* or *Mode*; if the same

ſame *Signature* anſwer all theſe *Keys*, there is no more Queſtion about it; but if that cannot be, then the *Signature* ought to be adjuſted to the *principal Key*, rather than to any other, as in *Example* 3. *Plate* 3. in which the *principal Key* is *d* with a 3*dg*. and becauſe this demands *f*※ and *c*※ for its 3*d* and 7*th*, therefore the Signature expreſſeth them. The Piece actually begins in the *principal Key*, tho' the firſt Cloſe is made in the 5*th* above, *viz*. in *a*, by bringing in *g*※; which is very naturally managed, becauſe all the Notes from the Beginning to that Cloſe belong to both the *ſharp Keys d* and *a*, except that *g*※ which is the only Note in which they can differ; then you ſee the *Melody* proceeds for ſome time in Notes that are common to both theſe *Keys*, tho' indeed the Impreſſion of the laſt *Cadence* will be ſtrongeſt; and then by bringing *g* (natural) and *a*※, it leaves both the former *Keys* to cloſe in *b*; and here again there is as great a Coincidence with the *principal Key* as poſſible, for the *flat Key b* has every one of its eſſential Notes common with ſome one of theſe of the *ſharp Key d*, except *a*※ and *g*※ the *6thg*. and *7th g*. which that *flat Key* may occaſionally make uſe of; but as it is managed here, the *6th l*. is uſed, ſo that it differs from the *principal Key* only in one Note *a*※; then the *Melody* is after this Cloſe immediately transferred to the *principal Key*, making there the *final Cadence*. In what Notes every *Key* differs from or coincides with any other, you may learn from the *Scale* of *Semitones*; but

but you ſhall ſee this more eaſily in a following *Table*.

To proceed with our *Signatures*, you have, in what's ſaid, the true Uſe and Reaſon of the *Signatures* of *Clefs*; in reſpect of which they are diſtinguiſhed into *natural*, and *artificial* or *tranſpoſed Clefs*; the firſt is when no ※ or ♭ is ſet at the Beginning; and when there are, it is ſaid to be *tranſpoſed*. We ſhall next conſider the *Variety* of *Signatures* of *Clefs*, which in all are but 12. and the moſt reaſonable Way of making the artificial Notes, either in the general Signature, or where they occur upon the Change of the *Key*.

In the *ſemitonick Scale* there are 12 different Notes in an *Octave* (for the 13*th* is the ſame with the 1*ſt*) each of which may be made the *Fundamental* or *Key* of a Song, *i. e.* from each of them we can take a Series of Notes, that ſhall proceed *concinnouſly* by Seven *diatonick Degrees* of *Tones* and *Semitones* to an *Octave*, in the Species either of a *ſharp* or *flat Key*, or of a *greater* or *leſſer Mode* (the ſmall Errors of this *Scale* as it is fixt upon Inſtruments, being in all this Matter neglected.) Now, making each of theſe 12 Letters or Notes a *Fundamental* or *Key*-note, there muſt be in the Compaſs of an *Octave* from each, more or fewer, or different *Sharps* and *Flats* neceſſarily taken in to make a *concinnous* Series of the ſame Species, *i. e.* proceeding by the greater or leſſer 3*d* (for theſe ſpecify the *Mode*, and determine the other Differences, as has been explained); and ſince from every one of the 12 *Keys* we may proceed *concinnouſ-*

cinnously, either with a greater or leſſer 3*d*, and their Accompanyments, it appears at firſt Sight, that there muſt be 24 different *Signatures* of *Clefs*, but you'll eaſily underſtand that there are but 12. For the ſame *Signature* ſerves Two different *Keys*, whereof the one is a *ſharp* and the other a *flat Key*, as you ſee plainly in the Nature of the *diatonick Scale*, in which the *Octave* from *c* proceeds *concinnouſly* by a 3*dg*. and that from *a* (which is a 6*thg*. above, or a 3*dl*. below *c*) by a 3*dl*. with the 6*th l*. and 7*th l*. for its Accompanyments, which I ſuppoſe here eſſential to all *flat Keys*; conſequently, if we begin at any other Letter, and by the Uſe of ※ or ♭ make a *concinnous diatonick Series* of either Kind, we ſhall have in the ſame Series, continued from the 6*th* above or 3*d* below, an *Octave* of the other Species; therefore there can be but 12 different *Signatures* of *Clefs*, whereof 1 is *plain* or *natural*, and 11 *tranſpoſed* or *artificial*.

WHAT the proper Notes of theſe *tranſpoſed Clefs* are, you may find thus; let the *Scale* of *Semitones* be continned to Two *Octaves*, then begin at every Letter, and, reckoning Two *Semitones* to every *Tone*, take Two *Tones* and one *Semitone*, then Three *Tones* and one *Semitone*, which is the Order of a *ſharp Key* or of the natural *Octave* from *c*, the Letters which terminate theſe *Tones* and *Semitones*, are the eſſential or natural Notes of the *Key* or *Octave*, whoſe *Fundamental* is the Letter or Note you begin at: By this you'll find the Notes be onging to every *ſharp Key*; and theſe being conti-

nued,

nued, you'll have alſo the Notes belonging to every *flat Key*, by taking the *6th* above the *ſharp Key* for the *Fundamental* of the *flat*: But to ſave you the Trouble, I have collected them in one *Table*. See *Plate* 2. *Fig.* 1. The *Table* has Two Parts, and the upper Part contains 16 Columns: From the 3 to the 14 incluſive, you have expreſt in each an *Octave*, proceeding from ſome the 12 Notes of different Names within the *ſemitonick Scale*, the *Fundamental* whereof you take in the lower End of the Column, and reading it upward, you have all the Letters or Names belonging to that *Octave* in a diatonick Scale, in the Species of a *ſharp Key*: In the 1*ſt* Column on the left Hand you have the Degrees marked in *Tones* and *Semitones*, without any Diſtinction of greater and leſſer *Tone*: In the Fifth Column, you have the Denominations of the *Intervals* from the *Fundamental*. Then for the 12 *flat Keys* take, as I ſaid before, the *6ths* above the other, and they are the *Fundamentals* of the *flat Keys*, whoſe Notes are all found by continuing the Scale upward: But as to finding the Note where any *Interval* ends, 'tis as well done by counting downward; for ſince 'tis always an *Octave* from any Letter to the ſame again, and alſo ſince a *7th* upward falls in the ſame Letter with a *2d* downward, a *6th* upward in the ſame with a *3d* downward, and a *3d* upward in the ſame with a *6th* downward, alſo a *4th* or *5th* upward in the ſame with a *5th* or *4th* downward; therefore in the 16th Column, you ſee *Key flat* written

written againſt the Line in which the *6ths* of the 12 *ſharp Keys* ſtand; and the Denomination of the *Intervals* are written againſt theſe Notes where they terminate; and becauſe the Scale in that Table is carried but to one *Octave*, ſo that we have only a 3*d l.* above the *Fundamental* of the *flat Key*, therefore the reſt of the *Intervals* are marked at the Letters below, which will be eaſier underſtood if you'll ſuppoſe the Key to ſtand below, and theſe *Intervals* to be reckoned upwards. In the 2*d* Part of the *Table* you have a Syſtem of 5 Lines marked with the *Treble* or *g Clef*, in 13 Diviſions each anſwering to a Column of the upper Part; and theſe expreſs all the various *Signatures* of the *Clef*, *that is*, all the *accidental* or *ſharp* and *flat* Notes that belong to any of the 12 *Keys* of the *Scale*.

With Reſpect to the Names and Signatures in the Table, there remain ſome Things to be explained: I told you in the laſt *Chapter* that upon the main it was an indifferent Thing whether the artificial Notes in the Scale were named from the Note below with a ✱, or from that above with a ♭: Here you have each of them marked, in ſome Signatures ✱ and in others ♭; but in every particular Signature the Marks are all of one Kind ✱ or ♭, tho' one Signature is ✱, and another ♭; and theſe are not ſo ordered at random; the Reaſon I ſhall explain to you: In the firſt Place there is a greater Harmony with reſpect to the Eye; but this is a ſmall Matter, a better Reaſon follows; *conſider*,

der, every Letter has two Powers, *i. e.* is capable of repreſenting Two Notes, according as you take it *natural* or plain, as *c*, *d*, &c. or *tranſpoſed* as *c*※ or *d*♭; again, every Line and Space is the Seat of one particular Letter: Now if we take Two Powers of one Letter in the ſame *Octave* or *Key*, the Line or Space to which it belongs muſt have Two different Signs; and then when a Note is ſet upon that Line or Space, how ſhall it be known whether it is to be taken *natural* or *tranſpoſed?* This can only be done by ſetting the proper Signs at every ſuch Note; which is not only troubleſom, but renders the general Signature uſeleſs as to that Line or Space: This is the Reaſon why ſome Signatures are made ※ rather than ♭, and contrarily; for *Example*, take for the *Fundamental* *c*※, the reſt of the Notes to make a *ſharp Key* are *d*※ .*f* : *f*※ : *g*※ : *a*※ : *c*. where you ſee *f* and *c* are taken both *natural* and *tranſpoſed*, which we avoid by making all the artificial Note ♭, as in the Table, thus *d*♭ : *e*♭ .*f* : *g*♭ : *a*♭ : ♭: *c* . *d*♭. 'Tis true that this might be helped another Way, *viz.* by taking all the Notes ※ *i. e.* taking *e*※ for *f*, and *b*※ for *c*; but the Inconveniency of this is viſible, for hereby we force Two natural Notes out of their Places, whereby the Difficulty of performing by ſuch Direction is increaſed: In the other Caſes where I have marked all ♭ rather than ※, the ſame Reaſons obtain: And in ſome Caſes, ſome Ways of ſigning with ※ would have both theſe Inconveniencies. The ſame Reaſons make it

neceſſary

neceſſary to have ſome Signature ※ rather than ♭; but the *Octave* beginning in *g*♭ is ſingular in this Reſpect, that it is equal which Way it is ſigned, for in both there will be one natural Note diſplaced unavoidably; as I have it in the Table *b* natural is ſigned *c*♭, and if you make all the Signs ※, you muſt either take in Two Powers of one Letter, or take *e*※ for *f*. Now neither in this, nor any of the other Caſes will the mixing of the Signs remove the Inconveniencies; and ſuppoſe it could, another follows upon the Mixture, which leads me to ſhew why the ſame Clef is either all ※ or all ♭, the Reaſon follows.

THE Quantity of an *Interval* expreſt by Notes ſet upon Lines and Spaces marked ſome ※, ſome ♭, will not be ſo eaſily diſcovered, as when they are all marked one Way, becauſe the Number of intermediate Degrees from Line to Space, and from Space to Line, anſwers not to the Denomination of the *Interval*; for *Example*, if it is a 5*th*, I ſhall more readily diſcover it when there are 5 intermediate Degrees from Line to Space, than if there were but 4; *thus*, from *g*※ to *d*※ is a 5*th*, and will appear as ſuch by the Degrees, among the Lines and Spaces; but if we mark it *g*※, *e*♭, it will have the Appearance of a 4*th*; alſo from *f*※ to *a*※ is a 3*d*, and appears ſo, whereas from *f*※ to ♭ looks like a 4*th*; and for that Reaſon Mr. *Simpſon* in his *Compend of Muſick* calls it a leſſer 4*th*, which I think he had better called an apparent 4*th*; and ſo by making the Signs of the

Clef

Clef all of one Kind, this Inconveniency is ſaved with reſpect to all *Intervals* whoſe both Extremes have a tranſpoſed Letter; and as to ſuch *Intervals* which have one Extreme a *natural* Note, or expreſt by a plain Letter, and the other *tranſpoſed*, the Inconveniency is prevented by the Choice of the ※ in ſome *Keys*, and of the ♭ in others; for *Example*, from *d* to *f*※ is a 3*dg*. equal to that from *d* to *g*♭, but the firſt only appears like a 3*d*, and ſo of other *Intervals* from *d*, which therefore you ſee in the Table are all ſigned ※. *Again* from *f* to ♭ or *f* to *a*※ is a 4*th*, but the firſt is the beſt Way of marking it; there are no more tranſpoſed Notes in that *Octave*, nor any other *Octave*, whoſe *Fundamental* is a natural Note, that is marked with ♭.

It muſt be owned, after all, That whatever Way we chuſe the Signs of tranſpoſed Notes, the Sounds or Notes themſelves on an Inſtrument are individually the ſame; and marking them one Way rather than another, reſpects only the Conveniencies of repreſenting them to the Eye, which ought not to be neglected; eſpecially for the Direction of the human Voice, becauſe that having no fixt Sounds (as an Inſtrument has, whoſe Notes may be found by a local Memory of their Seat on the Inſtrument) we have not another Way of finding the true Note but computing the *Interval* by the intermediate *diatonick Degrees*, and the more readily this can be done, it is certainly the better.

Now

NOW you are to *obſerve*, that, as the *Signature* of the *Clef* is deſigned for, and can ſerve but one *Key*, which ought rather to be the *principal Key* or *Octave* of the Piece than any other, ſhewing what tranſpoſed Notes belong to it, ſo the Inconveniency laſt mentioned is remedied, by having the Signs all of one Kind, only for theſe *Intervals* one of whoſe Extremes is the *Key*-note, or Letter: But a Song may modulate or change from the *principal* into other *Keys*, which may require other Notes than the *Signature* of the *Clef* affords; ſo we find ※ and ♭ upon ſome particular Notes contrary to the *Clef*, which ſhews that the *Melody* is out of the *principal Key*, ſuch Notes being natural to ſome other *ſubprincipal Key* into which it is carried; and theſe Signs are, or ought always to be choſen in the moſt convenient Manner for expreſſing the *Interval*; for *Example*, the *principal Key* being *C* with a 3*d* *g*. which is a *natural Octave* (*i. e.* expreſſed all with plain Letters) ſuppoſe a Change into its 4*th f*; and here let a 4*th* upward be required, we muſt take it in ♭ or *a*※; the firſt is the beſt Way, but either of them contradicts the *Clef* which is *natural*; and we no ſooner find this than we judge the Key is changed. But again, a Change may be where this Sign of it cannot appear, *viz.* when we modulate into the 6*th* of a *ſharp principal Key*, or into the 3*d* of a *flat principal Keys*; becauſe theſe have the ſame Signature, as has been already ſhown, and have ſuch

ſuch a Connection that, unleſs by a Cadence, the Melody can never be ſaid to be out of the *principal Key*. And with reſpect to a *flat principal Key*, *obſerve*, That if the *6th g.* and *7th g.* are uſed, as in ſome Circumſtances they may, eſpecially towards a Cadence, then there will be neceſſarily required upon that *6th* and *7th*, another Sign than that with which its Seat is marked in the general Signature of the Clef, which marks all flat Keys with the leſſer *6ths* and *7ths*; and therefore in ſuch Caſe (*i. e.* where the principal *Key is flat*) this Difference from the *Clef* is not a Sign that the Melody leaves the *Key*, becauſe each of theſe belong to it in different Circumſtances; yet they cannot be both marked in the *Clef*, therefore that which is of more general Uſe is put there and the other marked occaſionally.

FROM what has been explained, you learn another very remarkable Thing, *viz.* to know what the *principal Key* of any Piece is, without ſeeing one Note of it; and this is done by knowing the Signature of the *Clef*: There are but Two Kinds of *Keys* (or *Modes* of *Melody*) diſtinguiſhed into *ſharp* and *flat*, as already explained; each of which may have any of the 12 different Notes or Letters of the *ſemitonick Scale* for its *Fundamental*; in the *1ſt* and *6th* Line of the upper Part of the preceeding Table you have all theſe *Fundamentals* or *Key*-notes, and under them reſpectively ſtand the Signatures proper to each, in which, as has been the often ſaid, the flat Keys have their *6th* and *7th* marked of the *leſſer* Kind; and therefore as by the *Key*, or *fundamental* Note, we know the Signature, ſo reciprocally by the Signature we can know the *Key*; but 'tis under this one Limitation that, becauſe one Signature ſerves Two Keys, a *ſharp* one, and a *flat*, which is the *6th* above or *3d* below the *ſharp* one, therefore we only learn by this, that it is one of them, but not which; for *Example*, if the *Clef* has no tranſpoſed Note but *f*✱, then the Key is *g* with a *3d g.* or *e* with a *3d l.* If the *Clef* has ♭ and *e*♭, the Key is ♭ with a *3d g.* or *g.* with a *3d l.* as ſo of others, as in the Table: I know indeed, for I have found it ſo in the Writing of the beſt Maſters, that they are not ſtrict and conſtant in obſerving this Rule concerning the Signature of the C ef, eſpecially when the principal Key is a *flat* one; in which Caſe you'll find frequently, that when the *6th l.* or *7th l.* to the Key, or both, are tranſpoſed Notes, they don't ſign them ſo in the *Clef*, but leave them to be marked as the Courſe of the Melody requires; which is convenient enough when the Piece is ſo conducted as to uſe the *leſſer 6th* and *7th* ſeldomer than the *greater*.

---

§ 4. *Of*

§ 4. *Of Transposition.*

THERE are Two Kinds of *Transposition*, the one is, the changing the Places or Seats of the Notes or Letters among the Lines and Spaces, but so as every Note be set at the same Letter; which is done by a Change with respect to the *Clef*: The other is the changing of the Key, or setting all the Notes of the Song at different Letters, and performing it consequently in different Notes upon an *Instrument*: Of these in Order.

1. *Of Transposition with respect to the Clef.*

THIS is done either by removing the same *Clef* to another Line; or by using another *Clef*; but still with the same Signature, because the Piece is still in the same Key: How to set the Notes in either Case is very easy: For the 1*st*, You take the first Note at the same Distance above or below the *Clef*-note in its new Position, as it was in the former Position, and then all the rest of the Notes in the same Relations or Distances one from another; so that the Notes are all set on Lines and Spaces of the same Name. For the 2*d*, or setting the *Musick* with

with a different *Clef*, you muſt mind that the Places of the Three *Clef*-notes are invariable in the *Scale*, and are to one another in theſe Relations, *viz.* the *Mean* a 5*th* above the Baſs; and the *Treble* a 5*th* above the *Mean*, and conſequently Two 5*ths* above the Baſs: Now when we would tranſpoſe to a new *Clef*, ſuppoſe from the *Treble* to the *Mean*, wherever we ſet that new *Clef*, we ſuppoſe it to be the ſame individual Note, in the ſame Place of the *Scale*, as if the Piece were that *Part* in a *Compoſition* to which this new *Clef* is generally appropriated, that ſo it may direct us to the ſame individual Notes we had before Tranſpoſition: Now from the fixt Relations of the Three *Clefs* in the Scale, it will be eaſy to find the Seat of the firſt tranſpoſed Note, and then all the reſt are to be ſet at the ſame mutual Diſtances they were at before; for *Example*, ſuppoſe the firſt Note of a Song is *d*, a 6*th* above the *Baſs-clef*, the Piece being ſet with that *Clef*, if it is tranſpoſed and ſet with the *Mean-clef*, then wherever that *Clef* is placed, the firſt Note muſt be the 2*d g.* above it, becauſe a 2*d g.* above the *Mean* is a 6*th g.* above the *Baſs-clef*, the Relation of theſe Two being a 5*th*; and ſo that firſt Note will ſtill be the ſame individual *d*: Again, let a Piece be ſet with the *Treble-clef*, and the firſt Note be *e*, a 3*d l.* below the *Clef*, if we tranſpoſe this to the *Mean-clef*, the firſt Note muſt be a 3*d g.* above it, which is the ſame individual Note *e* in that Scale, for a 3*d l.* and 3*d g.* make

make a *5th* the Diſtance of the *treble* and *mean Clefs*.

THE Uſe and Deſign of this *Tranſpoſition* is, That if a Song being ſet with a certain *Clef* in a certain Poſition, the Notes ſhall go far above or below the *Syſtem* of Five Lines, they may, by the Change of the Place of the ſame *Clef* in the particular *Syſtem*, or taking a new *Clef*, be brought more within the Compaſs of the Five Lines: That this may be effected by ſuch a Change is very plain; for *Example*, Let any Piece be ſet with the *Treble Clef* on the firſt Line, (counting upward) if the Notes lie much below the *Clef* Note, they are without the *Syſtem*, and 'tis plain they will be reduced more within it, by placing the *Clef* on any other Line above; and ſo in general the ſetting any *Clef* lower in a particular *Syſtem* reduces the Notes that run much above it; and ſetting it higher reduces the Notes that run far below. The ſame is effected by changing the *Clef* it ſelf in ſome Caſes, tho' not in all, *Thus*, if the *Treble Part*, or a Piece ſet with the *Treble Clef*, runs high above the *Syſtem*, it can only be reduced by changing the Place of the ſame *Clef*; but if it run without the *Syſtem* below, it can be reduced by changing to the *Mean* or *Baſs Clef*. If the *mean Part* run above its particular Syſtem, it will be reduced by changing to the *Treble Clef*; or if it run below, by changing to the *Baſs Clef*. *Laſtly*. If the *Baſs Part* run without its Syſtem below, it can only be reduced by changing the Place of the ſame *Clef*; but running

above

above, it may be changed into the *mean* or *treble Clef.* Now as to the Poſition of the new *Clef*, you muſt chooſe it ſo that the Deſign be beſt anſwered; and in every Change of the *Clef* the Notes will be on Lines and Spaces of the ſame Name, or denominated by the ſame Letter, they refer alſo to the ſame individual Place of the *Scale* or *general Syſtem*, differing only with reſpect to their Places in the particular *Syſtem* which depend on the Difference of the *Clefs* and their Poſitions, and therefore will always be the ſame individual Notes upon the ſame Inſtrument.

As to both theſe *Tranſpoſitions* I muſt *obſerve*, that they increaſe the Difficulty of Practice, becauſe the Relations of the Lines and Spaces change under all theſe *Tranſpoſitions*, and therefore one muſt be equally familiar with all the Three *Clefs*, and every Poſition of them, ſo that under any Change we may be able with the ſame Readineſs to find the Notes in their true Relations and Diſtances: And as this is not acquired without great Application, I think it is too cruel a Remedy for the Inconveniency to which it is applied: It is better, I ſhould think, to keep always the ſame *Clef* for the ſame *Part*, and the ſame Poſition of the *Clef*; but if one will be Maſter of ſeveral Inſtruments, and be able to perform any *Part*, then he muſt be equally well acquainted with all their proper *Clefs*, but ſtill the Poſition of the *Clef* in the particular *Syſtem* may be fixt and invariable.

2. Of

2. *Of* Tranſpoſition *from one* Key *to another.*

THE Deſign of this *Tranſpoſition* is, That a *Song*, which being begun in one Note is too high or low, or any other way inconvenient, as may be in ſome Caſes for certain Inſtruments, may be begun in another Note, and from that carried on in all its juſt *Degrees* and *Intervals.* The *Clef* and its Poſition are the ſame, and the Change now is of the Notes themſelves from one Letter and its Line or Space to another. In the former *Tranſpoſition* the Notes were expreſſed by the ſame Letters, but both removed to different Lines and Spaces; here the Letters are unmoved, and the Notes of the Song are transferred to or expreſſed by other Letters, and conſequently ſet alſo upon different Lines and Spaces, which it is plain will require a different *Signature* of the *Clef.* Now we are eaſily directed in this Kind of *Tranſpoſition*, by the preceeding *Table*, *Plate* 2. *Fig.* 1. For there we ſee the *Signature* and Progreſs of Notes in either *ſharp* or *flat Keys* beginning at every Letter: The lower Line of the upper Part of the *Table* contains the *fundamental Notes* of the Twelve *ſharp Keys*; and under them are their *Signatures*, ſhewing what *artificial* Notes are neceſſary to make a *concinnous diatonick* Series from theſe ſeveral *Fundamentals:* In the *6th* Line above are the ſame Twelve Letters, conſidered as *Fundamentals* of the Twelve *flat Keys*, which have the ſame Signatures with the

the *sharp Keys* standing in the under Line, and in the same Column: So that 'tis equal to make any of these Twelve Notes the *Key* Note, changing the *Signature* according to the *Table*: And *observe*, tho' the *Fundamentals* of the Twelve *flat Keys* stand in the Table as *6ths* to the Twelve *sharp Keys*, yet that is not to be understood as if the *flat Keys* must all be a *6th* above (or in their 8*ves* a 3*d* below) the *sharp Keys*; it happens so there only in the Order and Relation of the Degrees of the *Scale*: But as the Fundamentals of the Twelve *flat Keys* are the same Letters with those of the *sharp Keys*, they shew us that the same Key may either be the *sharp* or *flat*, with a different Signature.

But to make this Matter as plain as possible, I shall consider the Application of it in Two distinct Questions. 1*mo*. Let the *Fundamental* or *Key* Note to which you would *transpose* a Song be given, to find the proper Signature. *Rule*. In the first or *6th* Line of the upper Part, according as the Key is *sharp* or *flat*, find the given *Key* to which you would transpose, and under it you have the proper Signature. For *Example*, Suppose a Song in the *sharp Key c*, which is natural, if you would transpose it to *g*, the *Clef* must be signed with *f*※, or to *d* and it must have *f*※ and *c*※. *Again*, suppose a Song in a *flat Key* as *d* whose Signature has *b flat*, if you transpose it to *e* the *Signature* has *f*※, or to *g* and it has ♭ and *e*♭. 2*do*. Let any *Signature* be assigned to find the *Key* to which we must trans-

transſpoſe. *Rule.* In the upper Part of the Table in the ſame Column with the given *Signature* you'll find the *Key* ſought, either in the *1ſt* or *6th* Line according as the Key is *ſharp* or *flat*. But without conſidering the *Key*, or whether the *Signature* be regular or not, we may know how to *tranſpoſe* by conſidering the Signature as it is and the firſt Note, *thus*, find the *Signature* with which it is already ſet, and in the ſame Column in the upper Part find the Letter of the firſt Note; in that ſame Line (betwixt Right and Left) find the Letter where you deſire to begin, and under it is the proper *Signature* to be now uſed: Or having choſen a certain *Signature* you'll find the Note to begin at, in the ſame Column, and in the ſame Line with the Note it began in formerly. Having thus your *Signature*, and the Seat of the firſt Note, the reſt are eaſily ſet up and down at the ſame mutual Diſtances they were in formerly; and where any ※, ♭ or ♮ is occaſionally upon any Note, mark it ſo in the correſpondent Note in the Tranſpoſition; but mind that if a Note with a ※ or ♭ is tranſpoſed to a Letter which in the new *Signature* is contrarily ♭ or ※, then mark that Note ♮; and reciprocally if a Note marked ♮ is tranſpoſed to a Letter, which is natural in the new Signature, mark it ※ or ♭ according as the ♮ was the removing of a ♭ or ※ in the former *Signature*. In all other Caſes mark the tranſpoſed Note the ſame Way it was before. For *Examples* of this Kind of *Tranſpoſition*, ſee *Plate* 3. *Examples* 3 and 5.

§ 5. Of

§ 5. *Of* Sol-fa-*ing, with ſome other particular Remarks about the Names of Notes.*

IN the ſecond Column of the preceeding *Table*, you have theſe Syllables written againſt the ſeveral Letters of the *Scale*, *viz. fa, ſol, la, fa, ſol, la, mi, fa*, &c. Formerly theſe Six were in uſe, *viz. ut, re, mi, fa, ſol, la*; from the Application whereof the Notes of the *Scale* were called *G ſol re ut*, *A la mi re*, &c. and afterwards a *6th* was added, *viz. ſi*; but theſe Four *fa, ſol, la, mi* being only in Uſe among us at preſent, I ſhall explain their Uſe here, and ſpeak of the reſt, which are ſtill in Uſe with ſome Nations, in *Chap.*14. where you ſhall learn their Original. As to their Uſe, it is this in general; they relate chiefly to *Singing* or the human Voice, that by applying them to every Note of the *Scale* it might not only be pronounced more eaſily, but principally that by them the *Tones* and *Semitones* of the *natural Scale* may be better marked out and diſtinguiſhed.

THIS Deſign is obtain'd by the Four Syllables *fa, ſol, la, mi*, in this Manner; from *fa* to *ſol* is a *Tone*, alſo from *ſol* to *la*, and from *la* to *mi*, without diſtinguiſhing the greater and leſſer *Tone*;

Tone; but from *la* to *fa*, alſo from *mi* to *fa* is a *Semitone*: Now if theſe are applied in this Order, *fa*, *ſol*, *la*, *fa*, *ſol*, *la*, *mi*, *fa*, &c. they expreſs the natural Series from *c*, as in the Table; and if it is repeated to another 8*ve*, we ſee how by them to expreſs all the Seven different Orders of *Tones* and *Semitones* within the *diatonick Scale*. If the *Scale* is extended to Two 8*ves*, you'll perceive that by this Rule 'tis always true, tho' it were further extended *in infinitum*, that above *mi* ſtands *fa*, *ſol*, *la*, and below it the ſame reverſed *la*, *ſol*, *fa*; and that one *mi* is always diſtant from another by an *Octave*, (which no other Syllable is) becauſe after *mi* aſcending comes always *fa*, *ſol*, *la*, *fa*, *ſol*, *la*, which are taken reverſe deſcending. But now you'll ask a more particular Account of the Application of this; and that you may underſtand it, conſider, the firſt Thing in teaching to ſing is, to make one raiſe a *Scale* of Notes by *Tones* and *Semitones* to an *Octave*, and deſcend again by the ſame Notes, and then to riſe and fall by greater *Intervals* at a Leap, as a 3*d*, 4*th* and 5*th*, &c. And to do all this by beginning at Notes of different Pitch; then theſe Notes are repreſented by Lines and Spaces, as above explained, to which theſe Syllables are applied; 'tis ordinary therefore, to learn a Scholar to name every Line and Space by theſe Syllables: But ſtill you'll ask, to what Purpoſe? The Anſwer is, That while they are learning to *tune* the *Degrees* and *Intervals* of Sound expreſt by Notes ſet upon Lines and Spaces, or learn-

learning a Song to which no Words are applied, they may do it better by an articulate Sound; and chiefly that by knowing the *Degrees* and *Intervals* expreſt by theſe Syllables, they may more readily know the true Diſtance of their Notes. I ſhall firſt make an End of what is to be ſaid about the Application, and then ſhew what an uſeleſs Invention this is.

THE only Syllable that is but once applied in Seven Letters is *mi*, and by applying this to different Letters, the Seat of the Two *natural Semitones* in the 8*ve*,expreſſed by *la-fa* and *mi-fa*, will be placed betwixt different Letters (which is all we are to notice where the Difference of the greater and leſſer *Tone* is neglected, as in all this) But becauſe the Relation of the Notes expreſt by the ſeven plain Letters, *c*, *d*, *e*, *f*, *g*, *a*, *b*, which we call the *natural Scale*, are ſuppoſed to be fixt and unalterable, and the Degrees expreſt by theſe Syllables are alſo fixt, therefore the natural Seat of *mi* is ſaid to be *b*, becauſe then *mi-fa* and *la-fa* areapplied to the *natural Semitones* *b.c* and *e.f*, as you ſee in the Table: But if *mi* is applied to any other of the Seven *natural* Notes, then ſome of the *artificial* Notes will be neceſſary, to make a Series anſwering to the *Degrees* which we ſuppoſe are invariably expreſt by theſe Syllables; but *mi* may be applied not only to any of the Seven *natural* Notes, it may alſo be applied to any of the Five *artificial* Ones: And now to know in any Caſe (*i. e.* when *mi* is applied to any of the Twelve Letters of the *ſemitonick Scale*) to what Notes

Notes the other Syllables are applied, you need but look into the preceeding Table, where if you ſuppoſe *mi* applied to any Letter of that Line where it ſtands, the Notes to which *fa*, *ſol*, *la* are applied are found in the ſame Column with that Letter, and in the ſame Line with theſe Syllables. By this Means I hope you have an eaſy Rule for *ſol-fa-ing*, or naming the Notes by *ſol*, *fa*, &c. in any *Clef* and with any *Signature*.

BUT now let us conſider of what great Importance this is, either to the underſtanding or practiſing of *Muſick*. In the *firſt* Place, the Difficulty to the Learner is increaſed by the Addition of theſe Names, which for every different Signature of the *Clef* are differently applied; ſo that the ſame Line or Space is in one *Signature* called *fa*, in another *ſol*, and ſo on: And if a Song modulates into a new *Key*, then for every ſuch Change different Applications of theſe Names may be required to the ſame Note, which will beget much Confuſion and Difficulty: And if you would conceive the whole Difficulty, conſider, as there are 12 different Seats of *mi* in the *Octave*, therefore the naming of the Lines and Spaces of any particular *Syſtem* and *Clef* has the ſame Variety; and if one muſt learn to name Notes in every *Clef* and every Poſition of the *Clef*, then as there is one ordinary Poſition for the *Treble-clef*, one for the *Baſs*, and Four for the *mean*, if we apply to each of theſe the 12 different *Signatures*, and conſequent Ways of *ſol-fa-ing*, we have in in all 72 various Ways of applying the Names of *ſol*, *fa*, &c. to the Lines and Spaces of a particular *Syſtem*; not that the ſame Line can have 72 different Names, but in the Order of the Whole there is ſo great a Variety: And if we ſuppoſe yet more Poſitions of the *Clefs*, the Variety will ſtill be increaſed, to which you muſt add what Variety happens upon changing the *Key* in the Middle of any Song. Let us next ſee what the Learner has by this troubleſom Acquiſition: After conſidering it well, we find nothing at all; for as to naming the Notes, pray what want we more than the Seven Letters already applied, which are conſtant and certain Names to every Line and Space under all different *Signatures*, the *Clef* being the ſame and in the ſame Poſition; and how much more ſimple and eaſy this is any Body can judge. If it be complained that the Sounds of theſe Letters are harſh when uſed in raiſing a Series of Notes, then, becauſe this ſeems to make the Uſe of theſe Names only for the ſofter Pronounciation of a Note, let Seven Syllables as ſoft as poſſible be choſen and joyned invariably to the Letters or alphabetical Names of the *Scale*; ſo that as the ſame Line or Space is, in the ſame *Clef* and Poſition, always called by the ſame Letter, whether 'tis a *natural* or *artificial* Note, ſo let it be conſtantly named by the ſame Syllable; and thus we leave the true Diſtance or *Interval* to be found by the *Degrees* among the Lines and Spaces, as they are determined by the Letters applied to them; or rather, ſince the *In-*

tervals

tervals are fufficiently determined by the alphabetical Names applied to the Lines and Spaces, there is no Matter whether the fyllabical Names be conftant or not, or what Number there be of them, *that is*, we may apply to any Note at random any Syllable that will make the Pronounciation foft and eafy, if this be the chief End of them, as I think it can only be, becaufe the *Degrees* and *Intervals* are better and more regularly expreft by the *Clef* and *Signature*: Nay, 'tis plain, that there is no Certainty of any *Interval* expreft fimply by thefe Syllables, without confidering the Lines and Spaces with their Relations determined by the Letters; for *Example*, If you ask what Diftance there is betwixt *fol* and *la*, the Queftion has different Anfwers, for 'tis either a *Tone* or a 5*th*, or one of thefe compounded with 8*ve*, and fo of other *Examples*, as are eafily feen in the preceeding Scheme: But if you ask what is betwixt *fol* in fuch a Line or Space, and *la* in fuch a one above or below, then indeed the Queftion is determined; yet 'tis plain, that we don't find the Anfwer by thefe Names *fa*, *fol*, but by the Diftances of the Lines and Spaces, according to the Relations fettled among them by the Letters with which they are marked.

I know this Method has been in Credit, and I doubt will continue fo with fome People, who, if they don't care to have Things difficult to themfelves, may perhaps think it an Honour both to them and their Art, that it appear *myfterious*; and fome fhrewd Gueffers may poffibly alledge

alledge fomethiug elfe; but I fhall only fay that, for the Reafons advanced, I think this an impertinent Burden upon *Mufick*,

Further Reflections upon the Names of Notes.

As there is a Neceffity, that the Progreffion of the *Scale* of *Mufick*, and all its *Intervals*, with their feveral Relations, fhould be diftinctly marked, as is done by means of Letters reprefenting Sounds; fo it is neceffary for Practice, that the Notes and *Intervals* of Sound upon Inftruments fhould be named by the fame Letters, by which we have feen a clear and eafy Method of expreffing any Piece of *Melody*, for directing us how to produce the fame upon a mufical Inftrument: But then obferve, that as the *Scale* of *Mufick* puts no Limitations upon the abfolute *Degree* of *Tune*, only regulating the relative Meafures of one Note to another, fo the Notes of Inftruments are called *c*, *d*, &c. not with refpect to any certain Pitch of *Tune*, but to mark diftinctly the Relations of one Note to another; and, without refpect to the Pitch of the Whole, the fame Notes, *i. e.* the Sounds taken in the fame Part of the Inftrument, are always named by the fame Letters, becaufe the Whole makes a Series, which is conftantly in the fame Order and Relation of *Degrees*. For *Example*, Let the Four Strings of a Violin be tuned as high or low as you pleafe, being always *5ths* to one another, the Names of the Four open Notes are ftill called *g*,*d*,*a*,*e*, and fo of the

the other Notes; and therefore, if upon hearing any Note of an Inſtrument we ask the Name of it, as whether it is *c* or *d*, &c. the Meaning can only be, what Part of the Inſtrument is it taken in, and with what Application of the Hand? For with reſpect to the abſolute *Tune* it cannot be called by one Letter rather than another, for the Note which is called *c*, according to the foreſaid general Rule, may in one Pitch of *Tuning* be equal to the Note called *d*, in another Pitch.

BUT for the human Voice, conſider there is no fixt or limited Order of its *Degrees*, but an *Octave* may be raiſed in any Order; therefore the Notes of the Voice cannot be called *c* or *d*, &c. in any other Senſe than as being *uniſon* to the Note of that Name upon a fixt Inſtrument: Or if a whole *Octave* is raiſed in any Order of *Tones* and *Semitones*, contained within the *diatonick Scale*, ſuppoſe that from *c*, each of theſe Notes may be called *c*, *d*, &c. in ſo far as they expreſs the Relations of theſe Notes one to another. And *laſtly*, With reſpect to this Method of writing *Muſick*, when the Voice takes Direction from it, the Notes muſt at that Time be called by the Letters and Names that direct it in taking the *Degrees* and *Intervals* that compoſe the *Melody*; yet the Voice may begin ſtill in the ſame Pitch of *Tune*, whatever Name or Letter in the Writing the firſt Note is ſet at, becauſe theſe Letters ſerve only to mark the Relations of the Notes: But in Inſtruments, tho' the *Tune* of the Whole may be

higher

higher or lower, the ſame Notes in the Writing direct always to the ſame individual Notes with reſpect to the Name and the Place of the Inſtrument, which has nothing parallel to it in the human Voice. Again, tho' the Voice and Inſtruments are both directed by the ſame Method of Writing *Muſick*, yet there is one very remarkable Difference betwixt the Voice and ſuch Inſtruments as have fixt Sounds; for the Voice being limited to no Order of *Degrees*, has none of the Imperfections of an Inſtrument, and can therefore begin in *Uniſon* with any Note of an Inſtrument, or at any other convenient Pitch, and take any *Interval* upward or downward in juſt *Tune*: And tho' the unequal *Ratios* or *Degrees* of the *Scale*, when the Sounds are fixt, make many ſmall Errors on Inſtruments, yet the Voice is not ſubjected to theſe: But it will be objected, that the Voice is directed by the ſame *Scale*, whoſe Notes or Letters have been all along ſuppoſed under a certain determinate Relation to one another, which ſeems to lay the Voice under the ſame Limitations with Inſtruments having fixt Sounds, if it follow the preciſe Proportions of theſe Notes as they ſtand in the *Scale*: The Anſwer to this is, That the Voice will not, and I dare ſay cannot poſſibly follow theſe erroneous Proportions; becauſe the true harmonious Diſtances are much eaſier taken, to which a good Ear will naturally lead: Conſider again, that becauſe the Errors are ſmall in a ſingle Caſe, and the Difference of *Tones* or of *Semitones* ſcarce ſenſible, therefore they

are

are conſidered as all equal upon Inſtruments; and the ſame Number of *Tones* or *Semitones* is, every where thro' the *Scale*, reckoned the ſame or an equal *Interval*, and ſo it muſt paſs with ſome ſmall unavoidable Errors. Now that the Voice may be directed by the ſame *Scale* or *Syſtem* of Notes, the Singer will alſo conſider them as equal, and in like manner take the ſame Number for the ſame *Interval*; yet, by the Direction of a well tuned Ear, will take every *Interval* in its due Proportion, according to the Exigences of the *Melody*; ſo if the *Key* is *d*, and the Three firſt Notes of a Song were ſet in *d*, *e*, *f*, the Voice will take *d-e* a *t g.* and *e-f* a *ſ g.* in order to make *d-f* a true 3*d l.* which is defective a *Comma* in the *Scale*, becauſe *d-e* is a *t l.* In another Caſe the Voice would take theſe very Notes according to the *Scale*, as here, ſuppoſe the *Key c*, and the firſt Three Notes *c*, *d*, *f*, the Voice will take *c-d* a *t g.* becauſe that is a more perfect Degree than *t l.* and then will take *f* not a true 3*d l* to *d*, but a true 4*th* to the *Key c*, which the *Melody* requires rather than the other, whereby *d-f* is made a deficient 3*d l*; and if we ſuppoſe *e* is the third Note, and *f* the Fourth, the Voice will take *e* a *t l* above *d*, in order to make *c-e* a true 3*d g.* I don't pretend that theſe ſmall Differences are very ſenſible in a ſingle Caſe, yet 'tis more rational to think that a good Ear left to itſelf will take the Notes in the beſt Proportions, where there is nothing to determine it another Way, as the Accompanyment of an Inſtrument; and then it is demonſtrated by by this, that in the beſt tuned Inſtruments having fixt Sounds, the ſame Song will not go equally well from every Note; but let a Voice directed by a juſt Ear begin *uniſon* to any Note of an Inſtrument, there ſhall be no Difference: I own, that by a Habit of ſinging and uſing the Voice to one Pitch of *Tune*, it may become difficult to ſing out of it, but this is accidental to the Voice which is naturally capable of ſinging alike well in every Pitch within its Extent of Notes, being equally uſed to them all.

APPENDIX.

Concerning Mr. Salmon's *Propoſal for reducing all* Muſick *to one* Clef.

'TIS certainly the Uſe of Things that makes them valuable; and the more univerſal the Application of any Good is, it is the more to their Honour who communicate it: For this Reaſon, no doubt, it would very well become the Profeſſors of ſo generous an Art as *Muſick*, and I believe in every reſpect would be their Intereſt, to ſtudy how the Practice of it might be made as eaſy and univerſal as poſſible; and to encourage any Thing that might contribute towards this End.

It will be eaſily granted that the Difficulty of Practice is much increaſed by the Difference of *Clefs* in particular Syſtems, whereby the ſame Line or Space, *i. e.* the firſt or ſecond Line, *&c.* is is ſometimes called *c*, ſometimes *g* : With reſpect to *Inſtruments* 'tis plain ; for if every Line and Space keeps not conſtantly the ſame Name, the Note ſet upon it muſt be ſought in a different Place of the Inſtrument ; And with reſpect to the Voice, which takes all its Notes according to their Intervals betwixt the Lines and Spaces, if the Names of theſe are not conſtant neither are the Intervals conſtantly the ſame in every Place ; therefore for every Difference either in the Clef or Poſition of it, we have a new Study to know our Notes, which makes difficult Practice, eſpecially if the *Clef* ſhould be changed in the very middle of a Piece, as is frequently done in the modern Way of writing Muſick. Mr. *Salmon* reflecting on theſe Inconveniencies, and alſo how uſeful it would be that all ſhould be reduced to one conſtant *Clef*, whereby the ſame Writing of any Piece of Muſick would equally ſerve to direct the Voice and all Inſtruments, a Thing one ſhould think to be of very great Uſe, he propoſes in his *Eſſay to the Advancement of Muſick*, what he calls an univerſal Character, which I ſhall explain in a few Words. In the 1*ſt* Place, he would have the loweſt Line of every particular Syſtem conſtantly called *g*, and the other Lines and Spaces to be named according to the Order of the 7 Letters ; and becauſe theſe Poſitions of the Letters are ſuppoſed invariable, therefore he thinks there's no Need to mark any of them ; but then, 2*do*. That the Relations of ſeveral *Parts* of a Compoſition may be diſtinctly known ; he marks

marks the *Treble* with the Letter T at the Beginning of the Syſtem; the *Mean* with M. and the Baſs with B. And the *g*s that are on the loweſt Line of each of theſe Syſtems, he ſuppoſes to be *Octaves* to each other in Order. And then for referring theſe *Syſtems* to their correſponding Places in the general *Syſtem*, the *Treble g*, which determines all the reſt, muſt be ſuppoſed in the ſame Place as the *Treble* Clef of the common Method; but this Difference is remarkable, That tho' the *g* of the *Treble* and *Baſs* Syſtems are both on Lines in the general *Syſtem*, yet the *Mean g*, which is on a Line of the particular Syſtem, is on a Space in the general one, becauſe in the Progreſſion of the Scale, the ſame Letter, as *g*, is alternately upon a Line and a Space; therefore the *Mean* Syſtem is not a Continuation of any of the other Two, ſo as you could proceed in Order out of the one into the other by Degrees from Line to Space, becauſe the *g* of the *Mean* is here on a Line, which is neceſſarily upon a Space in the Scale; and therefore in referring the mean *Syſtem* to its proper relative Place in the *Scale*, all its Lines correſpond to Spaces, of the other and contrarily; but there is no Matter of that if the *Parts* be ſo written ſeparately as their Relations be diſtinctly known, and the Practice made more eaſy; and when we would reduce them all to one general *Syſtem*, it is enough we know that the Lines of the mean Part muſt be changed into Spaces, and its Spaces into Lines. *3tio.* If the Notes of any

Part

Part go above or below its *Syſtem*, we may ſet them as formerly on ſhort Lines drawn on Purpoſe: But if there are many Notes together above or below, Mr. *Salmon* propoſes to reduce them within the *Syſtem* by placing them on the Lines and Spaces of the ſame Name, and prefixing the Name of the *Octave* to which they belong. To underſtand this better, conſider, he has choſen three diſtinct *Octaves* following one another; and becauſe one *Octave* needs but 4 Lines therefore he would have no more in the particular Syſtem; and then each of the three particular Syſtems expreſſing a diſtinct *Octave* of the Scale, which he calls the proper *Octaves* of theſe ſeveral *Parts*, if the Song run into another *Octave* above or below, 'tis plain, the Notes that are out of the *Octave* peculiar to the *Syſtem*, as it ſtands by a general Rule marked *T* or *M* or *B*, may be ſet on the ſame Lines and Spaces; and if the *Octave* they belong to be diſtinctly marked, the Notes may be very eaſily found by taking them an *Octave* higher or lower than the Notes of the ſame Name in the proper *Octave* of the *Syſtem*. For *Example*, If the Treble *Part* runs into the *middle* or Baſs *Octave*, we prefix to theſe Notes the Letter *M* or *B*, and ſet them on the ſame Lines and Spaces, for all the Three Syſtems, have in this Hypotheſis the Notes of the ſame Name in the ſame correſpondent Places; if the *Mean* run into the *Treble* or *Baſs Octaves*, prefix the Signs *T* or *M*. And *laſtly*, Becauſe the *Parts* may comprehend more than 3 *O-*

ctaves

ctaves, therefore the Treble may run higher than an *Octave*, and the *Bass* lower; in such Cases, the higher *Octave* for the *Treble* may be marked *Tt.* and the lower for the *Bass* *Bb.* But if any Body thinks there be any considerable Difficulty in this Method, which yet I'm of Opinion would be far less than the changing of *Clefs* in the common Way, the Notes may be continued upward and downward upon new Lines and Spaces, occasionally drawn in the ordinary Manner, and tho' there may be many Notes far out of the *System* above or below, yet what's the Inconveniency of this? Is the reducing the Notes within 5 Lines, and saving a little Paper an adequate Reward for the Trouble and Time spent in learning to perform readily from different Clefs?

As to the *Treble* and *Bass*, the Alteration by this new Method is very small; for in the common Position of the *Bass-clef*, the lowest Line is already *g*; and for the Treble it is but removing the *g* from the 2*d* Line, its ordinary Position, to the first Line; the greatest Innovation is in the *Parts* that are set with the *c Clef*.

AND now will any Body deny that it is a great Advantage to have an universal Character in *Musick*, whereby the same Song or *Part* of any Composition may, with equal Ease and Readiness be performed by the Voice or any Instrument; and different *Parts* with alike Ease by the same Instrument? 'tis true that each *Part* is marked with its own *Octave*, but the Design of this is only to mark the Relation of the

the *Parts*, that ſeveral Voices or Inſtruments performing theſe in a Concert may be directed to take their firſt Notes in the true Relations which the Compoſer deſigned; but if we ſpeak of any one ſingle Part to be ſung or performed alone by any Inſtrument, the Performer in this caſe will not mind the Diſtinction of the *Part*, but take the Notes upon his Inſtrument, according to a general Rule, which teaches him that a Note in ſuch a Line or Space is to be taken in ſuch a certain Place of the Inſtrument. You may ſee the Propoſal and the Applications the Author makes of it at large in his Eſſay, where he has conſidered and anſwered the Objections he thought might be raiſed; and to give you a ſhort Account of them, conſider, that beſides the Ignorance and Superſtition that haunts little Minds, who make a Kind of Religion of never departing from received Cuſtoms, whatever Reaſon there may be for changing; or perhaps the Pride and Vanity of the greateſt Part of Profeſſors of this Art, joyned to a falſe Notion of their Intereſt in making it appear difficult, for the rational Part of any Set and Order of Men is always the leaſt; beſides theſe, I ſay, the greateſt Difficulty ſeems to be, the rendring what is already printed uſeleſs in part to them that ſhall be taught this new Method, unleſs they are to learn both, which is rather enlarging than leſſening their Task: But this new Method is ſo eaſy, and differs ſo little in the *Baſs* and *Treble Parts*, from what obtains already, that I think it would
add

add very little to their Task, who by the common Method, must learn to sing and play from all *Clefs* and Variety of Positions; and then *Time* would wear it out, when new *Musick* were printed, and the former reprinted in the Manner proposed. Mr. *Salmon* has been a Prophet in guessing what Fate it was like to have; for it has lain Fifty Years neglected: Nor do I revive it with any better Hope. I thought of nothing but considering it as a Piece of Theory, to explain what might be done, and inform you of what has been proposed. I cannot however hinder my self to complain of the Hardships of learning to read cleverly from all *Clefs* and Positions of them: If one would be so universally capable in *Musick* as to sing or play all *Parts*, let him undergo the Drudgery of being Master of the Three *Clefs*; but why may not the Positions be fixt and unalterable? And why may not the same *Part* be constantly set with the same *Clef*, without the Perplexity of changing, that those who confine themselves to one Instrument, or the Performance of one *Part*, may have no more to learn than what is necessary? This would save a great deal of Trouble that's but sorrily recompensed by bringing the Notes within or near the Compass of Five Lines, which is all can be alledged, and a very silly Purpose considering the Consequence.

CHAP.

CHAP. XII.

Of the Time *or* Duration *of Sounds in* Musick.

§ 1. *Of the* Time *in general, and its Subdivision into* absolute *and* relative; *and particularly of the* Names, Signs, *and* Proportions, *or relative* Measures *of Notes, as to* Time.

WE are now come to the second general Branch of the *Theory* of *Musick*, which is to consider the *Time* or *Duration* of Sounds in the same Degree of *Tune*.

TUNE and *TIME* are the Affections or Properties of Sound, upon whose Difference or Proportions *Musick* depends. In each of these singly there are very powerful Charms: Where the *Duration* of the Notes is equal, the Differences of *Tune* are capable to entertain us with an endless Variety of Pleasure, either in an artfull ful and well ordered Succeſſion of ſimple Sounds, which is *Melody*, or the beautiful *Harmony* of Parts in Conſonance: And of the Power of *Time* alone, *i. e.* of the Pleaſure ariſing from the various Meaſures of *long* and *ſhort*, or *ſwift* and *ſlow* in the Succeſſion of Sounds differing only in *Duration*, we have Experience in a *Drum*, which has no Difference of Notes as to *Tune*. But how is the Power of *Muſick* heightned, when the Differences of *Tune* and *Time* are artfully joined: 'Tis this Compoſition that can work ſo irreſiſtibly on the Paſſions, to make one heavy or cheerful; it can be ſuited to Occaſions of Mirth or Sadneſs; by it we can raiſe, and at leaſt indulge, the ſolemn compoſed Frame of our Spirits, or ſink them into a trifling Levity: But enough for Introduction.

IN explaining this Part there is much leſs to do than was in the former; the Cauſes and Meaſures of the Degrees of *Tune*, with the *Intervals* depending thereon: And all their various Connections and Relations, were not ſo eaſily diſcovered and explained, as we can do what relates to this, which is a far more ſimple Subject.

THE *Reaſon* or *Cauſe* of a long or ſhort Sound is obvious in every Caſe; and I may ſay, in general, it is owing to the continued Impulſe of the efficient Cauſe, for a longer or ſhorter Time upon the ſonorous Body; for I ſpeak here of the artful Duration of Sound. See *Page* 17. where I have explained the Diſtinction betwixt natural and artificial Duration, to which I ſhall here

here add the Confideration of thofe Inftruments that are ftruck with a Kind of inftantaneous Motion, as *Harpfichords* and *Bells*, where the Sounds cannot be made longer or fhorter by Art; for the Stroke cannot be repeated fo oft as to make the Sound appear as one continued Note; and therefore this is fupplied by the Paufe and Diftance of *Time* betwixt the ftriking one Note and another, *i. e.* by the Quicknefs or Slownefs of their Succeffion; fo that *long* and *fhort*, *quick* and *flow* are the fame Things in *Mufick*; therefore under this Title of the *Duration* of Sounds, muft be comprehended that of the Quicknefs or Slownefs of their Succeffion, as well as the proper Notion of *Length* and *Shortnefs*: And fo the Time of a Note is not computed only by the uninterrupted Length of the Sound, but alfo by the Diftance betwixt the Beginning of one Sound and that of the next. And mind that when the Notes are in the ftrict Senfe long and fhort Sounds, yet fpeaking of their Succeffion we fay alfo, that it is quick or flow, according as the Notes are fhort or long; which Notion we have by confidering the Time from the Beginning of one Note to that of another.

NEXT, as to the Meafure of the *Duration* of a Note, if we chufe any fenfibly equal Motion, as the Pulfes of a well adjufted Clock or Watch, the *Duration* of any Note may be meafured by this, and we may juftly fay, that it is equal to 2, 3 or 4, *&c.* Pulfes; and if any other Note is compared to the fame Motion, we we ſhall have the exact Proportion of the *Times* of the Two, expreſt by the different Number of Pulſes. Now, I need give no Reaſon to prove, that the *Time* of a Note is juſtly meaſured by the ſucceſſive Parts of an equable Motion; for tis ſelf-evident, that it cannot be better done; and indeed we know no other Way of meaſuring *Time*, but by the Succeſſion of Ideas in our own Minds.

WE come now to examine the particular Meaſures and Proportions of *Time* that belong to *Muſick*; for as in the Matter of *Tune*, every Proportion is not fit for obtaining the Ends of *Muſick*, ſo neither is every Proportion of *Time*; and to come cloſe to our Purpoſe, obſerve,

TIME in *Muſick* is to be conſidered either with reſpect to the *abſolute Duration* of the Notes, *i. e.* the Duration conſidered in every Note by it ſelf, and meaſured by ſome external Motion foreign to the *Muſick*; in reſpect of which the Succeſſion of the whole is ſaid to be quick or ſlow: Or, it is to be conſidered with reſpect to the *relative* Quantity or Proportion of the Notes, compared one with another.

NOW, to explain theſe Things, we muſt firſt know what are the *Signs* by which the *Time* of Notes is repreſented. The Marks and Characters in the modern Practice are theſe Six, whoſe Figures and Names you ſee in *Plate* 2. *Fig.* 3. And *obſerve*, when Two or more *Quavers* or *Semiquavers* come together, they are made with one or Two Strokes acroſs their

Tails

Tails, and then they are called *tied Notes.* Theſe Signs expreſs no *abſolute Time*, and are in different Caſes of different Lengths, but their Meaſures and how they are determined, we ſhall learn again, after we have conſidered,

The relative Quantity or Proportions of Time.

THIS Proportion I have ſignified by Numbers written over the Notes or *Signs* of *Time*; whereby you may ſee a *Semibreve* is equal to Two *Minims*, a *Minim* equal to Two *Crotchets*, a *Crotchet* equal to Two *Quavers*, a *Quaver* equal to Two *Semiquavers*, a *Semiquaver* equal to Two *Demi-ſemiquavers*. The Proportions of Length of each of theſe to each other are therefore manifeſt: I have ſet over each of them Numbers which expreſs all their mutual Proportions; ſo a *Minim* is to a *Quaver* as 16 to 4, or 4 to 1, *i. e.* a *Minim* is equal to Four *Quavers*, and ſo of the reſt. Now theſe Proportions are double, (*i. e.* as 2 : 1) or compounded of ſeveral Doubles, ſo 4 : 1 contains 2 : 1 twice ; but there is alſo the Proportion of 3 : 1 uſed in *Muſick* : Yet that this Part may be as ſimple and eaſy as poſſible, theſe Proportions already ſtated among the Notes, are fixt and invariable ; and to expreſs a Proportion of 3 to 1 we add a Point (.) on the right Side of any Note, which is equal to a Half of it, whereby a pointed *Semibreve* is equal to Three *Minims*, and ſo of the reſt, as yon ſee in the *Figure.* From theſe ariſe other Proportions, as of 2 to 3, which is betwixt any Note (as a *Crotchet*)

Crotchet) plain, and the ſame pointed; for the plain *Crotchet* is Two *Quavers*, and the pointed is Three. Alſo we have the Proportion of 3 to 4, betwixt any Note pointed, and the Note of the next greater Value plain, as betwixt a pointed *Crotchet* and a plain *Minim*. And of theſe ariſe other Proportions, but we need not trouble our ſelves with them, ſince they are not directly uſeful; and that we may know what are ſo, ſuffer me to repeat a little of what I have ſaid elſewhere, *viz.* that

THINGS that are deſigned to affect our Senſes muſt bear a due Proportion with them; and ſo where the Parts of any Object are numerous, and their Relations perplext, and not eaſily perceived, they can raiſe no agreeable Ideas; nor can we eaſily judge of the Difference of Parts where it is great; therefore, that the Proportion of the *Time* of Notes may afford us Pleaſure, they muſt be ſuch as are not difficultly perceived: For this Reaſon the only *Ratios* fit for *Muſick*, beſides that of Equality, are the double and triple, or the *Ratios* of 2 to 1 and 3 to 1; of greater Differences we could not judge, without a painful Attention; and as for any other *Ratios* than the multiple Kind (*i. e.* which are as 1 to ſome other Number) they are ſtill more perplext. 'Tis true, that in the Proportions of *Tune* the *Ratios* of 2 : 3, of 3 : 4, *&c.* produce *Concord*; and tho' we conclude theſe to be the Proportions, from very good Reaſons, yet the Ear judges of them after a more ſubtil Manner; or rather indeed we are conſcious of no ſuch Thing

Thing as the Proportions of the different Numbers of Vibrations that constitute the *Intervals* of Sound, tho' the Agreeableness or Disagreeableness of our Sensations seem to depend upon it, by some secret Conformity of the Organs of Sense with the Impulse made upon them in these Proportions; but in the Business of *Time*, the good Effect depends entirely upon a distinct Perception of the Proportions.

Now, the Length of Notes is a Thing merely accidental to the Sound, and depends altogether upon our Will in producing them: And to make the Proportions distinct and perceivable, so that we may be pleased with them, there is no other Way but to divide the Two Notes compared into equal Parts; and as this is easier done in multiple Proportions, because the shorter Note needs not be divided, being the Divisor or Measure of the imaginary Parts of the other so 'tis still easier in the first and more simple Kind as 2 to 1, and 3 to 1; and the Necessity of such simple Proportions in the *Time* is the more, that we have also the *Intervals* of *Tune* to mind along with it. But observe, that when I say the *Ratio* of Equality, and those of 2 to 3 and 3 to 1, are the only *Ratios* of *Time* fit for *Musick*, I do not mean that there must not be, in the same Song, Two Notes in any other Proportion; but you must take it this Way, *viz.* that of Two Notes immediately next other, these ought to be the *Ratios*, because only the Notes in immediate Succession are or can be directly minded, in proporportioning the Time, whereof one being taken at any Length, the other is meaſured with relation to it, and ſo on: And the Proportions of other Notes at Diſtances I call accidental Proportions. Again *obſerve*, that even betwixt Two Notes next to other, there may be other Proportions of greater Inequality, but then it is betwixt Notes which the Ear does not directly compare, which are ſeparate by ſome Pauſe, as the one being the End of one Period of the Song, and the other the Beginning of another; or even when they are ſeparate by a leſs Pauſe, as a *Bar* (which you'll have explained preſently.) Sometimes alſo a Note is kept out very long, by connecting ſeveral Notes of the ſame Value,and directing them to be taken all as one, but this is always ſo ordered that it can be eaſily ſubdivided in the Imagination, and eſpecially by the Movement of ſome other *Part* going along, which is the ordinary Caſe where theſe long Notes happen, and then the *Melody* is in the moving *Part*, the long Note being deſigned only for *Harmony* to it; ſo that this Caſe is no proper Exception to the Rule, which relates to the *Melody* of ſucceſſive Sounds, but here the *Melody* is transferred from the one *Part* to another. And *laſtly*, conſider that it is chiefly in brisk Movements, where neither of the Two Notes is long, that no other Proportions betwixt them than the ſimple ones mentioned are admitted.

§ 2. *Of*

§ 2. *Of the* absolute Time; *and the various* Modes, *or* Constitution *of Parts of a Piece of* Melody, *on which the different Airs in* Musick *depend, and particularly of the Distinction of* common *and* triple Time, *and the Description of the* Chronometer *for measuring it.*

FROM the Principles mentioned in the last Article, we conclude that there are certain Limits beyond which we must not go, either in Swiftness or Slowness of *Time*, i.e. Length or Shortness of Notes; and therefore let us come to Particulars, and explain the various Quantities, and the Way of measuring them.

IN order to this we must here consider another Application of the preceeding Principles, which is, that a Piece of *Melody* being a Composition of many Notes successively ranged, and heard one after another, is divisible into several Parts; and ought to be contrived so as the several Members may be easily distinguished, that the Mind, perceiving this Connection of Parts constituting one Whole, may be delighted with it; for 'tis plain where we perceive there are Parts, the Mind will endeavour to distinguish them, and when that cannot be easily done, we must be so far disappointed of our Pleasure. Now a Division into equal Parts is, of all others, the most simple and easily perceived; and in the present Case, where so many other Things require our Attention, as the various Com-

Combinations of *Tune* and *Time*, no other Division can be admitted: Therefore,

EVERY *Song* is actually divided into a certain Number of equal Parts, which we call *Bars* (from a Line that separates them, drawn straight across the Staff, as you see in *Plate* 2.) or *Measures*, because the Measure of the *Time* is laid upon them, or at least by means of their Subdivisions we are assisted in measuring it; and therefore you have this Word *Measure* used sometime for a *Bar*, and sometime for the *absolute* Quantity of *Time*; and to prevent Ambiguity, I shall afterwards write it in *Italick* when I mean a *Bar*.

BY saying the *Bars* are all equal I mean that, in the same Piece of *Melody*, they contain each the same Number of the same Kind of Notes, as *Minims* or *Crotchets*, &c. or that the Sum of the Notes in each (for they are variously subdivided) reckoned according to their *Ratios* one to another already fixt, is equal; and every Note of the same Name, as *Crotchet*, &c. must be made of the same *Time* through the whole Piece, consequently the *Times* in which the several *Bars* are performed are all equal; see the *Examples* of *Plate* 3. But what that *Time* is, we don't yet know; and indeed I must say it is a various and undetermined Thing. Different Purposes, and the Variety which we require in our Pleasures, make it necessary that the Measures of a *Bar*, or the Movement with respect to quick and slow, be in some Pieces greater, and in others lesser;

leſſer; and this might be done by having the Quantity of the Notes of *Time* fixt to a certain Meaſure, ſo that wherever any Note occurred it ſhould always be of the ſame *Time*; and then when a quick Movement were deſigned, the Notes of ſhorter *Time* would ſerve, and the longer for a ſlow *Time*; and for determining theſe Notes we might uſe a Pendulum of a certain Length, whoſe Vibration being the fixt Meaſure of any one Note, that would determine the reſt; and it would be beſt if a *Crotchet* were the determined Note, by the Subdiviſion or Multiplication whereof, we could eaſily meaſure the other Notes; and by Practice we might eaſily become familiar with that Meaſure; but as this is not the Method agreed upon, tho' it ſeems to be a very rational and eaſy one, I ſhall not inſiſt upon it here.

In the preſent Practice, tho' the ſame Notes of *Time* are of the ſame Meaſure in any one Piece, yet in different Pieces they differ very much, and the Differences are in general marked by the Words *ſlow*, *briſk*, *ſwift*, &c. written at the Beginning; but ſtill theſe are uncertain Meaſures, ſince there are different Degrees of *ſlow* and *ſwift*; and indeed the true Determination of them muſt be learnt by Experience from the Practice of Muſicians; yet there are ſome Kind of general Rules commonly delivered to us in this Matter, which I ſhall ſhew you, and at the ſame Time the Method uſed for aſſiſting us to give each Note its true Proportion, according to the Meaſure or determined

Quantit

Quantity of *Time*, and for keeping this equal thro' the Whole. But in order to this, there is another very confiderable Thing to be learnt, concerning the *Mode* or *Conftitution* of the *Meafure* ; and firft *obferve*, That I call this Difference in the abfolute Time the different *Movements* of a Piece, a Thing very diftinct from the different *Meafure* or *Conftitution* of the *Bar*, for feveral Pieces may have the fame *Meafure*, and a different *Movement*. Now by this *Conftitution* is meant the Difference with refpect to the Quantity of the *Meafure*, and the particular Subdivifion and Combination of its Parts; and by the total Quantity, I underftand that the Sum of all the Notes in the *Meafure* reckoned according to their fixt Relation, is equal to fome one or more determined Notes, as to one *Semibreve* or to Three *Minims* or *Crotchets*, &c. which yet without fome other Determination is but relative: And in the Subdivifion of the *Meafure* the Thing chiefly confidered is, That it is divifible into a certain Number of equal Parts, fo that, counting from the Beginning of the *Meafure*, each Part fhall end with a Note, and not in the Middle of one (tho' this is alfo admitted for Variety;) for *Example*, if the Meafure contain 3 *Minims*, and ought to be divided into Three equal Parts, then the Subdivifion and Combination of its leffer Parts ought to be fuch, that each Part, counting from the Beginning, fhall be compofed of a precife Number of whole Notes, without breaking in upon any Note; fo if the firft Note were

were a *Crotchet*, and the ſecond a *Minim*, we could not take the firſt 3*d* Part another Way than by dividing that *Minim*.

WE conſidered already how neceſſary it is that the *Ratios* of the *Time* of ſucceſſive Notes be ſimple, which for ordinary are only as 2 to 1, or 3 to 1, and in any other Caſes are only the Compounds of theſe *Ratios*, as 4 to 1; ſo in the *Conſtitution* of the *Meaſure*, we are limited to the ſame *Ratios*, i. e. the Meaſures are only ſubdivided into 2 or 3 equal Parts; and if there are more, they muſt be Multiples of theſe Numbers as 4 to 6, is compoſſed of 2 and 3; again *obſerve*, the *Meaſures* of ſeveral Songs may agree in the total Quantity, yet differ in the Subdiviſion and Combination of the leſſer Notes that fill up the *Meaſure*; alſo thoſe that agree in a ſimilar or like Combination or Subdiviſion of the *Meaſure*, may yet differ in the total Quantity. But to come to Particulars.

Of common *and* triple Time.

THESE *Modes* are divided into Two general Kinds, which I ſhall call the *common* and *triple Mode*, called ordinarily *common* and *triple Time*.

1. *COMMON TIME* is of Two Species; the 1*ſt* where every *Meaſure* is equal to a *Semibreve*, or its Value in any Combination of Notes of a leſſer relative Quantity; the 2*d*, where every *Meaſure* is equal to a *Minim*, or its Value in leſſer Notes. The *Movements* of this Kind of *Meaſure* are very various; but there are Three common Diſtinctions, the firſt is *ſlow*, ſignified

at

at the Beginning by this Mark C, the 2*d* is *brisk*, ſignified by this ₵, the 3*d* is very *quick* ſignified by this Ȼ; but what that *ſlow*, *brisk*, and *quick* is, is very uncertain, and, as I have ſaid already, muſt be learned by Practice: The neareſt Meaſure I know, is to make a *Quaver* the Length of the Pulſe of a good Watch, and ſo the *Crotchet* will be equal to 2 Pulſes, a *Minim* equal to 4, and the whole *Meaſure* or *Semibreve* equal to 8 Pulſes; and this is very near the Meaſure of the brisk *common Time*, the ſlow *Time* being near as long again, as the quick is about half as long. Some propoſe to meaſure it thus, *viz.* to imagine the *Bar* as actually divided into 4 *Crotchets* in the firſt Species, and to make the whole as long as one may diſtinctly pronounce theſe Four Words, *One*, *two*, *three*, *four*, all of equal Length; ſo that the firſt *Crotchet* may be applied to One, the 2*d* to Two, *&c.* and for other Notes proportionally; and this they make the brisk Movement of *common Time*; and where the *Bar* has but Two *Crotchets*, then 'tis meaſured by *one*, *two*: But this is ſtill far from being a certain Meaſure. I ſhall propoſe ſome other Method preſently, mean while

LET us ſuppoſe the Meaſure or Quantity fixt, that we may explain the ordinary Method practiſed as a Help for perſerving it equal thro' the whole Piece.

THE total *Meaſure* of *common Time* is equal to a *Semibreve* or *Minim*, as already ſaid; but theſe are variouſly ſubdivided into Notes of leſſer

leſſer Value. Now to keep the *Time* equal, we make uſe of a Motion of the Hand, or Foot (if the other is employed,) thus; knowing the true *Time* of a *Crotchet*, we ſhall ſuppoſe the *Meaſure* actually ſubdivided into 4 *Crotchets* for the firſt Species, and the half *Meaſure* will be 2 *Crotchets*, therefore the Hand or Foot being up, if we put it down with the very Beginning of the firſt Note or *Crotchet*, and then raiſe it with the Third, and then down with the Beginning of the next *Meaſure*, this is called *Beating* the *Time*; and by Practice we acquire a Habit of making this Motion very equal, and conſequently of dividing the *Meaſure* in Two equal Parts: Now whatever other Subdiviſion the *Meaſure* conſiſts of, we muſt calculate, by the Relation of the Notes, where the firſt Half ends, and then applying this equable Motion of the Hand or Foot, we make the firſt as long as the Motion down (or as the Time betwixt its being down and raiſed again, for the Motion is frequently made in an Inſtant; and the Hand continues down for ſome Time,) and the other Half as long as the Motion up (or as the Hand remains up,) and having the half *Meaſure* thus determined, Practice very ſoon learns us to take all the Notes that compoſe it in their true Proportion one to another, and ſo as to begin and end them preciſely with the *beating*. In the *Meaſure* of Two *Crotchets*, we beat down the firſt and the ſecond up.

OBSERVE, That ſome call each Half of the *Meaſure*, in *common Time*, A TIME; and

and ſo they call this the *Mode* or *Meaſure* of Two *Times*, or the *Dupla-meaſure.* Again you'll find ſome mark the *Meaſure* of Two *Crotchets* with a 2 or $\frac{2}{4}$, ſignifying that 'tis equal to Two Notes, whereof 4 make a *Semibreve*; and ſome alſo marked $\frac{4}{8}$ which is the very ſame Thing, *i. e.* 4 Quavers.

2. *TRIPLE TIME* conſiſts of many different Species, whereof there are in general 4, each of which have their Varieties under it; and the common Name of *Triple* is taken from this, that the Whole or Half *Meaſure* is diviſible into 3 equal Parts, and ſo beat.

THE 1*ſt* *Species* is called the *ſimple Triple*, whoſe *Meaſure* is equal either to 3 *Semibreves*, to 3 *Minims*, or to 3 *Crotchets*, or to 3 *Quavers*, or laſtly to 3 *Semiquavers*; which are marked thus, *viz.* $\frac{3}{1}$ or $\frac{3}{2}$ or $\frac{3}{4}$ $\frac{3}{8}$ $\frac{3}{16}$, but the laſt is not much uſed, nor the firſt, except in Church-muſick. The *Meaſure* in all theſe, is divided into 3 equal Parts or *Times*, called from that properly *Triple-time*, or the *Meaſure* of 3 *Times*, whereof 2 are beat down, and the 3*d* up.

THE 2*d* *Species* is the *mixt Triple:* its *Meaſure* is equal to 6 *Crotchets* or 6 *Quavers* or 6 *Semiquavers*, and accordingly marked $\frac{6}{4}$ or $\frac{6}{8}$ or $\frac{6}{16}$, but the laſt is ſeldom uſed. Some Authors add other Two, *viz.* 6 *Semibreves* and 6 *Minims*, marked $\frac{6}{1}$ or $\frac{6}{2}$ but theſe are not in uſe. The *Meaſure* here is ordinarily divided into Two equal Parts or *Times*, whereof one is beat down, and one up; but it may alſo be divided into 6 *Times*, whereof the firſt Two are beat

beat down, and the 3*d* up, then the next Two down and the laſt up, *that is*, beat each Half of the Meaſure like the *ſimple Triple* (upon which Account it may alſo be called a *compound Triple*,) and becauſe it may be thus divided either into Two or 6 *Times* (*i. e.* Two *Triples*) 'tis called *mixt*, and by ſome called the Meaſure of 6 *Times*.

THE 3*d Species* is the *compound Triple*, conſiſting of 9 *Crotchets*, or *Quavers* or *Semiquavers* marked thus $\frac{9}{4}$, $\frac{9}{8}$, $\frac{9}{16}$; the firſt and the laſt are little uſed, and ſome add $\frac{9}{1}$ $\frac{9}{2}$ which are never uſed. This *Meaſure* is divided either into 3 equal Parts or *Times*, whereof Two are beat down and one up; or each Third Part of it may be divided into 3 *Times*, and beat like the *ſimple Triple*, and for this 'tis called the Meaſure of 9 *Times*.

THE 4*th Species* is a *Compound* of the 2*d Species*, containing 12 *Crotchets* or *Quavers* or *Semiquavers* marked $\frac{12}{4}$ $\frac{12}{8}$ $\frac{12}{16}$, to which ſome add $\frac{12}{1}$ and $\frac{12}{2}$ that are not uſed; nor are the 1*ſt* and 3*d* much in Uſe, eſpecially the 3*d*. The *Meaſure* here may be divided into Two *Times*, and beat one down and one up; or each Half may be divided and beat at the 2*d* Species, either by Two or Three, in which Caſe it will make in all 12 *Times*, hence called the Meaſure of 12 *Times*. See Examples of the moſt ordinary Species in *Plate* 3*d*.

NOW as to the Movement of theſe ſeveral Kinds of *Meaſures* both *duple* and *triple*, 'tis various and as I have ſaid, it muſt be learned by by Practice; yet ere I leave this Part, I shall make these general *Observations, First.* That the *Movement* in every Piece is ordinarily marked by such Words as *slow, swift*, &c. But because the *Italian* Compositions are the Standard and Model of the better Kind of modern *Musick*, I shall explain the Words by which they mark their Movements, and which are generally used by all others in Imitation of them: They have 6 common Distinctions of *Time*, expressed by these Words, *grave, adagio, largo, vivace, allegro, presto*, and sometimes *prestissimo*. The first expresses the slowest Movement, and the rest gradually quicker; but indeed they leave it altogether to Practice to determine the precise Quantity. 2*do*. The Kind of *Measure* influences the *Time* exprest by these Words, in respect of which we find this generally true, that the Movements of the same Name, as *adagio* or *allegro*, &c. are swifter in *triple* than in *common Time*. 3*tio*. We find *common Time* of all these different Movements; but in the *triple*, there are some Species that are more ordinarily of one Kind of Movement than another: Thus the triple $\frac{3}{2}$ is ordinarily *adagio*, sometimes *vivace*; the $\frac{3}{4}$ is of any Kind from *adagio* to *allegro*; the $\frac{3}{8}$ is *allegro*, or *vivace*; the $\frac{6}{4}$ $\frac{6}{8}$ $\frac{9}{8}$ are more frequently *allegro*; the $\frac{12}{8}$ is sometimes *adagio* but oftner *allegro*. Yet after al, the *allegro* of one Species of *triple* is a quicker Movement than that of another, so very uncertain these Things are.

There is another very considerable Thing to be minded here, *viz.* that the Air or Humour

mour of a *Song* depends very much upon theſe different *Modes* of *Time*, or *Conſtitutions* of the *Meaſure*, which joined with the Variety of Movements that each *Mode* is capable of, makes this Part of *Muſick* wonderfully entertaining; but we muſt be acquainted with *practical Muſick* to underſtand this perfectly; yet the following general Things concerning the Species of *Triple*, may be of ſome Uſe to remark.

1mo. As to the Differences in each Species, ſuch as $\frac{3}{2}$; $\frac{3}{4}$. $\frac{3}{8}$ in the *ſimple triple*, there is more Caprice than Reaſon; for the ſame Piece of *Melody* may be ſet in any of theſe Ways without loſing any Thing of its true Air, ſince the *Relation* of the Notes are invariable, and there is no certain Quantity of the *abſolute Time*, which is left to the arbitrary Direction of theſe Words, *adagio*, *allegro*, &c.

2do. Of the ſeveral Species of *triple*, there are ſome that are of the ſame *relative Meaſure*, as $\frac{3}{2}$. $\frac{6}{4}$. $\frac{12}{8}$; and $\frac{3}{4}$. $\frac{6}{8}$; theſe are ſo far of the ſame *Mode* as the Meaſure of each contains the ſame total Quantity; for Three *Minims* and Six *Crotchets* and Twelve *Quavers* are equal, and ſo are Three *Crotchets* equal to Six *Quavers*; but the different *Conſtitutions* of the *Meaſure*, with reſpect to the Subdiviſions and Connections of the Notes, make a moſt remarkable Difference in the Air: For *Example*, The Time of $\frac{3}{2}$ conſiſts generally of *Minims*, and theſe ſometimes mixt with *Semibreves* or with *Crotchets*, and ſome *Bars* will be all *Crotchets*; but is contrived ſo that the Air requires the

Meaſure

Meaſure to be divided and beat by Three *Times*, and will not do another Way without manifeſtly changing and ſpoiling the Humour of the Song: Suppoſe we would beat it by Two *Times*, the firſt Half will always (except when the *Meaſure* is actually divided into Six *Crotchets*, which is very ſeldom) end in the Middle, or within the *Time* of ſome Note; and tho' this is admitted ſometimes for Variety (whereof afterwards) yet it is rare compared with the general Rule, which is, to contrive the Diviſion of the *Meaſure* ſo that every Down and Up of the *Beating* ſhall end with a particular Note; for upon this depends very much the Diſtinctneſs and, as it were, the Senſe of the *Melody*; and therefore the Beginning of every *Time*, or *Beating* in the *Meaſure*, is reckoned the *accented* Part thereof. For the Time $\frac{6}{4}$ it conſiſts of *Crotchets* ſometimes mixt with *Quavers*, and even with *Minims*, but ſo ordered that 'tis either *dupla* or *tripla*, as above explained, which makes a great Difference in the Air. The *Time* $\frac{12}{8}$ is alſo mixt of *dupla* and *tripla*, and conſiſts generally of *Quavers*, and ſometimes of *Crotchets*, but theſe are tied always by Three; and we have the *Bar* frequently compoſed of Twelve *Quavers* tied Three and Three; which, if we ſhould ty Two and Two, would quite alter the Air: The Reaſon is, That in this *Mode* there are in each *Bar* Four remarkably accented Parts, which are diſtant from each other by Three *Quavers*; and the true Reaſon of tying the *Quavers* in that manner, ſeems to me me to be, the marking out these distinct Parts of the *Measure*; but when the *Quavers* are tied in even Numbers by Two or Four, or by Six, it supposes the Accent upon the 1*st*, 3*d*, and 5*th Quaver*; which gives another Air to the *Melody*, and always a wrong one, when the skilful Composer designed it otherwise. The same Reasons take place in the Difference of these Times $\frac{3}{4}$. $\frac{6}{8}$; the first consists more ordinarily of *Crotchets*, and *Quavers* tied in even Numbers, because 'tis divided into Three Parts or *Times*; but the other is mixt of *dupla* and *tripla*, and therefore 'tis tied in Threes, unless it be subdivided into *Semiquavers*, and then these are tied in even Numbers, because Two *Semiquavers* make a *Quaver*.

AGAIN, there is another Question to be considered here, *viz.* What is the real Difference betwixt $\frac{3}{4}$ and $\frac{6}{4}$, and betwixt $\frac{3}{8}$, $\frac{6}{8}$ and $\frac{12}{8}$? The Lengths of the several Strains, or more general Periods of the Song, depend upon these, which make a considerable Difference; but their principal Difference lies in the proper Movements of each, and a certain Choice of the successive Notes that agree only with that Movement; so $\frac{6}{4}$ is always *allegro*, and would have no agreeable Air if it were performed *adagio* or *largo*: Another Thing is, that the Beginning of each *Bar* is a more distinct and accented Part than the Beginning of any *Time* in the Middle of a *Bar*, and therefore if we should take a Piece set $\frac{6}{4}$, and subdivide its *Bars* to make it $\frac{3}{4}$, there would be Hazard of separat-

ing

ing Things that ought to ſtand in a cloſer Connection; and if we put Two *Bars* in one of a Piece ſet $\frac{3}{4}$, to make it $\frac{6}{4}$, then we ſhould joyn Things that ought to be diſtinct: But I doubt I have already ſaid more than can be well underſtood without ſome Acquaintance with the Practice; yet there is one Thing I cannot omit here, *viz.* that in *common Time* we have in ſome Caſes *Quavers* tied by Threes, and the Number 3 written over them, to ſignify that theſe Three are only the Time of other Two *Quavers* of that Meaſure.

OBSERVE, in explaining what a *Bar* or *Meaſure* is, I have ſaid that all the *Meaſures* of the ſame Piece of *Melody* or *Song*, are of equal *relative* Value; and the Differences in this reſpect are brought under the Diſtinction of different *Modes* and *Species*; but that is taking the Unity of the Piece in the ſtricteſt Senſe. We have alſo a Variety of ſuch Pieces united in one principal *Key*, and ſuch an Agreement of Air as is conſiſtent with the different *Modes* of *Time*; and ſuch a Compoſition of different Airs is called, in a large Senſe, one Piece of *Melody*, under the general Name of *Sonata* if 'tis deſigned only for Inſtruments, or *Cantata* if for the Voice; and theſe ſeveral leſſer Pieces have alſo different Names, ſuch as *Allemanda*, *Gavotta*, &c. (which are always *common Time*) *Minuet*, *Sarabanda*, *Giga*, *Corrante*, *Siciliana*, &c. which are *triple Time*.

Of

Of the CHRONOMETER.

I have ſpoken a little already of the meaſuring the *abſolute Time*, or determining the *Movement* of a Piece by means of a *Pendulum*, a Vibration of which being applied to any one Note, as a *Crotchet*, the reſt might be eaſily determined by that. Monſieur *Loulie* in his *Elemens, ou Principes de Muſique*, propoſes for this Purpoſe a very ſimple and eaſy Machine of a *Pendulum*, which he calls a CHRONOMETER; it conſiſts of one large Ruler or Piece of Board, Six Foot or Seventy Two Inches long, to be ſet on End; it is divided into its Inches, and the Numbers ſet ſo as to count upward; and at every Diviſion there is a ſmall round Hole, thro' whoſe Center the Line of Diviſion runs. At Top of this Ruler, about an Inch above the Diviſion 72, and perpendicular to the Ruler is inſerted a ſmall Piece of Wood, in the upper Side of which there is a Groove, hollowed along from the End that ſtands out to that which is fixt in the Ruler, and near each End of it a Hole is made: Thro' theſe Holes a *Pendulum* Chord is drawn, which runs in the Groove; at that End of the Chord that comes thro' the Hole furtheſt from the Ruler the Ball is hung, and at the other End there is a ſmall wooden Pin which can be put in any of the Holes of the Ruler; when the Pin is in the upmoſt Hole at 72, then the *Pendulum* from the Top to the Center of the

the Ball, muſt be exactly Seventy Two Inches; and therefore whatever Hole of the Ruler it is put in, the *Pendulum* will be juſt ſo many Inches as that Figure at the Hole denotes. The Uſe of this Machine is; the Compoſer lengthens or ſhortens his *Pendulum* till one Vibration be equal to the deſigned Length of his *Bar*, and then the *Pin* ſtands at a certain Diviſion, which marks the Length of the *Pendulum*; and this Number being ſet with the *Clef*, at the Beginning of the Song, is a Direction to others how to uſe the *Chronometer* in meaſuring the Time according to the Compoſer's Deſign; for, with the Number is ſet the Note (*Crotchet* or *Minim*) whoſe Value he would have the Vibration to be; which in brisk *common Time* is beſt a *Minim* or half *Bar*, or even a whole *Bar* when that is but a *Minim*, and in ſlow *Time* a *Crotchet*: In *triple Time* it will do well to be the 3*d* Part, or Half or 4*th* Part of a *Bar*; and in the *ſimple Triples* that are *allegro*, let it be a whole *Bar*. And if in every *Time* that is *allegro*, the Vibration is applied to a whole or half *Bar*, Practice will teach us to ſubdivide it juſtly and equally. And mind, to make this Machine of univerſal Uſe, ſome canonical Meaſure of the Diviſions muſt be agreed upon, that the Figure may give a certain Direction for the Length of the *Pendulum*.

§ 3. Con-

§ 3. *Concerning* Refts *or* Paufes *of* Time ; *and fome other neceffary Marks in writing* Mufick.

AS Silence has very powerful Effects in *Oratory*, when it is rightly managed, and brought in agreeable to Circumftances, fo in *Mufick*, which is but another Way of expreffing and exciting Paffions, Silence is fometimes ufed to good Purpofe : And tho it may be neceffary in a fingle Piece of *Melody* for expreffing fome Paffion, and even for the Pleafure depending on Variety, where no Paffion is directly minded, yet it is ufed more generally in *fymphonetick* Compofitions ; for the fake of that Beauty and Pleafure we find in hearing one Part move on while another refts, and this interchangeably; which being artfully contrived, has very good Effects. But my Bufinefs in this Place is only to let you know the Signs or Marks by which this Silence is expreffed.

THESE *Refts* are either for a whole *Bar*, or more than one *Bar*, or but the Part of a *Bar* : When it is for a Part of a *Bar*, then it is expreffed by certain Signs correfponding to the Quantity of certain Notes of *Time*, as *Minim*, *Crotchet*, &c. and are accordingly called *Minim-refts*, *Crotchet-refts*, &c. See their Figure in *Plate* 2. *Fig*. 3. where the Note and correfponding Reft are put together ; and

and when any of theſe occur either on Line or Space, for 'tis no Matter where they are ſet, that Part is always ſilent for the *Time* of a *Minim* or *Crotchet*, &c. according to the Nature of the *Reſt*. A *Reſt* will be ſometimes for a *Crotchet* and *Quaver*, or for other Quantities of *Time*, for which there is no particular Note; in this Caſe the Signs of Silence are not multiplied or made more difficult than thoſe of Sound, but ſuch a Silence is marked by placing together as many *Reſts* of different *Time* as make up the whole deſigned *Reſt*; which makes the Practice more eaſy, for by this we can more readily divide the Meaſure, and give the juſt Allowance of *Time* to the *Reſts*: But let Practice ſatisfie you of theſe Things.

WHEN the *Reſt* is for a whole *Bar*, then the *Semibreve Reſt* is always uſed, both in *common* and *triple Time*. If the Reſt is for Two *Meaſures*, then it is marked by a Line drawn croſs a whole Space, and croſs a Space and an Half for Three *Meaſures*, and croſs Two Spaces for Four *Meaſures*, and ſo on as you ſee marked in the Place above directed. But to prevent all Ambiguity, and that we may at Sight know the Length of the *Reſt*, the Number of *Bars* is ordinarily written over the Place where theſe Signs ſtand.

I know ſome Writers ſpeak differently about theſe *Reſts*, and make ſome of them of different Values in different Species of *triple Time*: For *Example*, they ſay, that the Figure of what is the *Minim-reſt* in *common Time*, expreſſes the

Reſt

Reſt of Three *Crotchets* ; and that in the *Triples* $\frac{6}{8}$ $\frac{6}{16}$ $\frac{12}{8}$ $\frac{12}{16}$ it marks always an half *Meaſure*, however different theſe are among themſelves : Again, that the *Reſt* of a *Crotchet* in *common Time* is a *Reſt* of Three *Quavers* in the *Triple* $\frac{9}{8}$, and that the *Quaver-reſt* of *common Time* is equal to Three *Semiquavers* in the *triple* $\frac{9}{16}$. But this Variety in the Uſe of the ſame Signs is now generally laid aſide, if ever it was much in Faſhion ; at leaſt there is a good Reaſon why it ought to be out, for we can obtain our End eaſier by one conſtant Value of theſe Marks of Silence, as they are above explained.

THERE are ſome other Marks uſed in writing of *Muſick*, which I ſhall explain, all of which you'll find in *Plate* 2. A *ſingle Bar* is a Line acroſs the Staff, that ſeparates one *Meaſure* from another. A *double Bar* is Two parallel Lines acroſs the Staff, which ſeparates the greater Periods or Strains of any particular or *ſimple Piece*. A *Repeat* is a Mark which ſignifies the Repetition of a Part of the Piece; which is either of a whole Strain, and then the double *Bar*, at the End of that Strain, which is repeated, is marked with Points on each Side of it ; and ſome make this the Rule, that if there are Points on both Sides, they direct to a Repetition both of the preceeding and following Strain, *i. e.* that each of them are to be play'd or ſung twice on End ; but if only one of theſe Strains ought to be repeated, then there muſt be Points only on that Side, *i. e.* on the left, if

it

it is the preceeding, or the Right if the following Strain: When only a Part of a Strain is to be repeated, there is a Mark ſet over the Place where that Repetition begins, which continues to the End of the Strain.

A *Direct* is a Mark ſet at the End of a Staff, eſpecially at the Foot of a Page, upon that Line or Space where the firſt Note of the next Staff is ſet.

YOU'LL find a Mark, like the Arch of a Circle drawn from one Note to another, comprehending Two or more Notes in the ſame or different Degrees; if the Notes are in different Degrees, it ſignifies that they are all to be ſung to one Syllable, for Wind-inſtruments that they are to be made in one continued Breath, and for ſtringed Inſtruments that are ſtruck with a Bow, as Violin, that they are made with one Stroke. If the Notes are in the ſame Degree, it ſignifies that 'tis all one Note, to be made as long as the whole Notes ſo connected; and this happens moſt frequently betwixt the laſt Note of one *Bar* and the firſt of the next, which is particularly called *Syncopation*, a Word alſo applied in other Caſes: Generally, when any *Time* of a *Meaſure* ends in the Middle of a Note, *that is*, in *common Time*, if the Half or any of the *4th* Parts of the *Bar*, counting from Beginning, ends in the Middle of a Note, in the *ſimple Treble* if any *3d* Part of the *Meaſure* ends within a Note, in the *compound Treble* if any *9th* Part, and in the Two *mixt Triples*, if any *6th* or *12th* Part ends in the Middle of

any

any Note, 'tis called *Syncopation*, which properly ſignifies a ſtriking or breaking of the *Time*, becauſe the Diſtinctneſs of the ſeveral *Times* or Parts of the *Meaſure* is as it were hurt or interrupted hereby, which yet is of good Uſe in *Muſick* as Experience will teach.

YOU'LL find over ſome ſingle Notes a Mark like an Arch, with a Point in the Middle of it which has been uſed to ſignifie that that Note is to be made longer than ordinary, and hence called a *Hold*; but more commonly now it ſignifies that the *Song* ends there, which is only uſed when the *Song* ends with a Repetition of the firſt Strain or a Part of it; and this Repetition is alſo directed by the Words, *Da capo*, *i. e.* from the Beginning.

OVER the Notes of the *Baſs-part* you'll find Numbers written, as 3 . 5, *&c.* theſe direct to the *Concords* or *Diſcords*, that the Compoſer would have taken with the Note over which they are ſet, which are as it were the Subſtance of the *Baſs*, theſe others being as Ornaments, for the greater Variety and Pleaſure of the *Harmony*.

CHAP.

CHAP. XIII.

Containing the general Principles and Rules of HARMONICK COMPOSITION.

§ I. *DEFINITIONS.*

1. *Of* Melody *and* Harmony *and their* Ingredients.

THO' theſe, and alſo the next *Definition* concerning the *Key*, have been already largely explained; yet 'tis neceſſary they be here repeated with a particular View to the Subject of this Chapter.

MELODY is the agreeable Effect of different *muſical* Sounds, ſucceſſively ranged and diſpoſed; ſo that *Melody* is the Effect only of one ſingle Part; and tho' it is a Term chiefly applicable to the *Treble*, as the *Treble* is moſtly to be diſtinguiſhed by its *Air*, yet in ſo far as the *Baſs* may be made airy, and to ſing well, it may be alſo properly ſaid to be *melodious*.

HAR-

HARMONY is the agreeable Reſult of the Union of Two or more *muſical* Sounds heard at one and the ſame Time; ſo that *Harmony* is the Effect of Two Parts at leaſt: As therefore a continued Succeſſion of *muſical* Sounds produces *Melody*, ſo does a continued Combination of theſe produce *Harmony*.

Of the Twelve *Intervals* of *muſical* Sounds, known by the Names of *Second leſſer*, *Second greater*, *Third leſſer*, *Third greater*, *Fourth*, *falſe Fifth*, (which is called *Tritone* or *Semidiapente* in *Chap.* 8. § 4.) *Fifth*, *Sixth leſſer*, *Sixth greater*, *Seventh leſſer*, *Seventh greater* and *Octave*, all *Melody* and *Harmony* is compoſed; for the *Octaves* of each of theſe are but Replications of the ſame Sounds; and whatever therefore is or ſhall be ſaid of any or of all of theſe Sounds, is to be underſtood and meant as ſaid alſo of their *Octaves*.

These *Intervals*, as they are expreſſed by Notes, ſtand, as in *Example* 1. *C* being the *fundamental* Note from which the reſt receive their Denominations: Or they may ſtand as in the Second *Example*, where *g* is the *fundamental* Note; for whatever be the *Fundamental*, the Diſtances of Sound are to it, and reciprocally to each other the ſame.

Of theſe *Intervals* Two, *viz.* the *Octave* and *Fifth*, are called *perfect Concords*; Four, *viz.* the Two 3*ds* and Two 6*ths*, are called *imperfect Concords*; Five *viz.* the falſe *Fifth*, the Two *Seconds* and Two *Sevenths*, are *Diſcords*. The *Fourth* is in its own Nature a *perfect Concord*

cord; but becauſe of its Situation, lying betwixt the 3*d* and the 5*th*, it can never be made uſe of as a *Concord*, but when joined with the 6*th* with which it ſtands reciprocally in the Relation of a 3*d*; it is therefore commonly claſſed among the *Diſcords*, not on account of the Nature of the *Interval*, but becauſe of its little Uſe in the *Harmony* of *Concords*.

2. *Of the principal* Tone *or* Key.

The *Key* in every Piece and in every Part of each Piece of *muſical* Compoſition is that *Tone* or Sound which is predominant and to which all the reſt do refer (See above *Chap.* 9.)

Every Piece of *Muſick*, as a *Concerto*, *Sonata* or *Cantata* is framed with due regard to one particular Sound called the *Key*, and in which the Piece is made to begin and end; but in the Courſe of the *Harmony* of any ſuch Piece, the Variety which in *Muſick* is ſo neceſſary to pleaſe and entertain, requires the introducing of ſeveral other *Keys*.

It is enough here to conſider, that every the leaſt Portion of any Piece of *Muſick* has its *Key*; which rightly to comprehend we are to take Notice, that a well tuned Voice, tho' unaccuſtomed to *Muſick*, aſcending by Degrees from any Sound aſſigned, will naturally proceed from ſuch Sound to the 2*d g.* from thence to the

the 3*d l.* or to the 3*d g.* indifferently from either of theſe to the 4*th*, from thence to the 5*th*, from thence to the 6*th l.* or 6*th g.* accordingly as it has before either touched at the 3*d l.* or 3*d g.* from either of theſe to the 7*th g.* and from thence into the *Octave*: From which it is inferred, that of the 12 *Intervals* within the Compaſs of the *Octave* of any Sound aſſigned, ſeven are only *natural* and *melodious* to that Sound, *viz.* the 2*d g.* 3*d g.* 4*th*, 5*th*, 6*th g.* 7*th g.* and 8*ve*, if the proceeding be by the 3*d g.* but if it is by the 3*d l.* the Seven natural Sounds are the 2*d g.* 3*d l.* 4*th*, 5*th*, 6*th l.* 7*th g.* and 8*ve*, as they are expreſs'd in the *Examples*, 3*d* and 4*th*.

As therefore the 3*d* and 6*th* may be either greater or leſſer, from thence it is that the *Key* is denominated *ſharp* or *flat*; the *ſharp Key* being diſtinguiſhed by the 3*d g.* and the *Flat* by the 3*d l.*

In ſuch a Progreſſion of Sounds, the *fundamental* one to which the others do refer, is the *principal Tone* or *Key*; and as here *C* is the *Key*, ſo may any other Note be the *Key*, by being made the *fundamental* Note to ſuch like Progreſſion of Notes, as is already exemplified.

Whatever be the *Key*, none but the Seven *natural* Notes can enter into the Compoſition of its *Harmony*: The Five other Notes that are within the Compaſs of the *Octave* of the *Key*, *viz.* the 2*d l.* 3*d l.* falſe 5*th*, 6*th l.*

7*th l.*

7th l. in a *ſharp Key*; and the *2d l. 3d g. falſe 5th, 6th g.* and *7th l.* in a *flat* one, are always extraneous to the *Key*.

WHEN theſe Seven Notes ſhall happen to be mentioned in the *Baſs* as Notes, I ſhall for Diſtinction's ſake expreſs them by the Names of *2d Fundamental* or *2d f. 3d f. 4th f. 5th f. 6th f. 7th f.* the *Octave* being a Replication of the *Key*, will need no other Name than the *Key f.* But when any of the *Octaves* of theſe Seven Notes ſhall happen to be mentioned as Ingredients of the *Treble*, I ſhall deſcribe them by the ſimple Names of *2d, 3d, 4th, 5th,* &c. Thus, when the *3d f.* or its *Octave*, which is the ſame Thing, ſhall happen to be conſidered as a *Treble* Note, it is to be marked ſimply thus (*3d*) as being a *Third* to the *Key Fund.* Thus the *5th f.* or its *Octave*, when conſidered as a Note in the *Treble*, is to be ſimply marked thus (*5th*) as being a *5th* to the *Key f:* Or thus (*3d*) as being a *3d* to the *3d f:* Or thus (*6th*) as being a *6th* to the *7th f.* and ſo of the reſt.

EACH of the Seven *natural* Notes therefore in each *Key*, conſidered as *fundamental*, or as Notes of the *Baſs*, have their reſpective *3ds 5ths, 6ths,* &c. which reſpective *3ds, 5ths, 6ths,* &c. muſt be ſome one, or *Octaves* to ſome one or other of the 7 *fundamental* Notes that are *natural* to the Key; becauſe, as was ſaid before, nothing can enter into the *Harmony* of any *Key*, but its Seven *natural* Notes and their *Octaves*.

2. *Of*

3. *Of Composition.*

UNDER this Title of *Composition* are justly comprehended the *practical Rules.* 1*mo.* Of *Melody*, or the Art of making a single *Part*, i. e. contriving and disposing the single Sounds, so that their Succession and Progress may be agreeable; and 2*do.* Of *Harmony*, or the *Art* of disposing and conserting several single *Parts* so together, that they may make one agreeable Whole. And here *observe*, the Word *Harmony* is taken somewhat larger than above in *Chap.* 7. for *Discords* are used with *Concords* in the *Composition* of *Parts*, which is here exprest in general by the Word *Harmony*; which therefore is distinguished into the *Harmony* of *Concords* in which no *Discords* are used, and that of *Discords* which are always mixt with *Concords*. *Observe* also that this Art of *Harmony* has been long known by the Name of *Counterpoint*; which arose from this, That in the Times when *Parts* were first introduced, their *Musick* being so simple that they used no Notes of different Time, that Difference depending upon the Quantity of Syllables of the Words of a Song, they marked their *Concords* by Points set against one another. And as there were no different Notes of Time, so the *Parts* were in every Note made *Concord*: And this afterwards was called *simple* or *plain Counterpoint*, to distinguish it from another Kind, wherein Notes of different Value were used, and *Discords* brought in in betwixt the *Parts*, which was called *figurate Counterpoint*.

OBSERVE again, *Melody* is chiefly the Buſineſs of the Imagination; ſo that the Rules of *Melody* ſerve only to preſcribe certain Limits to it, beyond which the Imagination, in ſearching out the Variety and Beauty of Air, ought not to carry us: But *Harmony* is the Work of Judgment; ſo that its Rules are more certain, extenſive, and in Practice more difficult. In the Variety and Elegancy of the *Melody*, the Invention labours a great deal more than the Judgment; but in *Harmony* the Invention has nothing to do, for by an exact Obſervation of the Rules of *Harmony* it may be produced without that Aſſiſtance from the Imagination.

IT may not be impertinent here to obſerve, that it is the great Buſineſs of a Compoſer not to be ſo much attach'd to the Beauty of *Air*, as to neglect the ſolid Charms of *Harmony*; nor ſo ſervilly ſubjected to the more minute Niceties of *Harmony*, as to detract from the *Melody*; but, by a juſt Medium, to make his Piece conſpicuous, by preſerving the united Beauty both of *Air* and *Harmony*.

---

§ 2. *Rules of* Melody.

I. ANY Note being choſen for the *Key*, and its Quality of *ſharp* or *flat* determined, no Notes muſt be uſed in any *Part* but the *natural*

tural and *essential* Notes of the *Key*, as these are already shewn: And for changing or *modulating* from one *Key* to another, which may also be done, you'll find Rules below in §. 5.

II. Concerning the Succession of *Intervals* in the several *Parts*, you have these general Rules.

1. THE *Treble* ought to proceed by as little *Intervals*, as is possibly consistent with that Variety of *Air*, which is its distinguishing Character.

2. THE *Bass* may proceed either gradually or by larger *Intervals*, at the Will of the Composer.

3. THE ascending by the Distance of a *false 5th* is forbid, as being harsh and disagreeable; but descending by such a Distance is often practised especially in the *Bass*.

4. TO proceed by the Distance of a spurious *2d*, *that is*, from any Note that is ✻, to the Note immediately above or below it that is ♭; or from any Note ♭ to the Note immediately above or below it ✻, is very offensive. As we are in greatest Danger of transgressing this Rule in a *flat Key*, because of the *6th l.* and *7th g.* which are Two of the *natural* Notes of the *Harmony*, we are therefore to take Care, that descending from the *Key* we may proceed by the *7th l.* to the *6th l.* and ascending to it we may proceed by the *6th g.* to the *7th g.* For altho' the *6th g.* and *7th l.* are not of the Seven Notes of a

a *flat Key*, yet they may be thus made Uſe of as Tranſitions, without any Offence.

5. THE proceeding by the Diſtance of a *7th l.* in any of the Parts, is very harſh.

THUS far may Rules be given to correct the Irregularities of Invention in point of *Air*; but to acquire or improve it, nothing leſs is neceſſary than to be acquainted with the *Melody* of the more celebrated Compoſers, ſo as to have the more ordinary, and, as it were, common Places of their *Melody*, familiar to the Ear; and what is further neceſſary will, in due Time, naturally follow a Genius turned that Way.

---

§ 3. *Of the Harmony of* Concords, *or ſimple* Counterpoint.

THE *Harmony* of *Concords* is compoſed of the *imperfect*, as well as of the *perfect Concords*; and therefore may be ſaid to be *perfect* and *imperfect*, according as the *Concords* are of which it is compoſed; thus the *Harmony* that ariſes from a Conjunction of any Note with its *5th* and *Octave* is *perfect*, but with its 3*d* and *6th* is *imperfect*.

IT has been already ſhewn what may enter into the *Harmony* of any *Key*, and what may not. I proceed to ſhew how the Seven natural Notes, and their *Octaves* in any *Key*, may ſtand together in a *Harmony* of *Concord*; and how

how the ſeveral *Concords* may ſucceed other; and then make ſome particular Application, which will finiſh what is deſi g d on this Branch.

I. *How the* Concords *may ſtand together.*

1. To apply, *firſt*, the preceeding Diſtinction of *perfect* and *imperfect* Harmony, take this *general Rule*, *viz.* to the *Key f.* to the *4th f.* and to the *5th f.* a *perfect Harmony* muſt be joyned. To the *2d f.* to the *3d f.* and to the *7th f.* an *imperfect Harmony* is in all Caſes indiſpenſably required. To the *6th f.* a perfect or *imperfect Harmony* is arbitrary.

OBSERVE, In the Compoſition of Two *Parts*, tho' a 3*d* appears only in the *Treble* upon the *Key f.* the *4th f.* and the *5th f.* yet the perfect *Harmony* of the *5th* is always ſuppoſed, and muſt be ſupplied in the Accompanyments of the *thorough Baſs* to theſe fundamental Notes.

2. BUT more particularly in the *Compoſition* of Two Parts.

The RULES *are*,

1. THE *Key f.* may have either its *Octave*, its 3*d* or its *5th*.

2. THE *4th f.* and *5th f.* may have either their reſpective 3*ds* or *5ths*; and the firſt may have its *6th*; as, to favour a contrary Motion, the laſt may have its *Octave*.

3. THE

3. THE *6th f.* may have either its *3d*, its *5th* or its *6th*.

4. THE *2d f.* *3d f.* and *7th f.* may have either their reſpective *3ds* or *6ths*; and the laſt may, on many Occaſions, have its *falſe 5th*.

THESE Rules are ſtill the ſame whether the the *Key* is *ſharp* or *flat*, as they are exemplified in *Example* 5, 6, 7, 8, 9, 10, 11.

AFTER having conſidered what are the ſeveral *Concords*, that may be *harmoniouſly* applied to the ſeven *fundamental* Notes; it is next to be learned, how theſe ſeveral *Concords* may ſucceed each other, for therein lies the greateſt Difficulty of *muſical Compoſition*.

II. *The general* Rules *of* Harmony, *reſpecting the Succeſſion of* Concords.

1. THAT as much as can be in *Parts* may proceed by a contrary Movement, *that is*, when the *Baſs* aſcends, the *Treble* may at the ſame Time *deſcend*, & *vice verſa*; but as it is impoſſible this can always be done, the Rule only preſcribes the doing ſo as frequently as can be, *Exam.* 12.

2. The *Parts* moving the ſame Way either upwards or downwards, Two *Octaves* or Two *5ths* muſt never follow one another immediately, *Exam.* 13.

3. TWO *6ths l.* muſt never ſucceed each other immediately; the Danger of tranſgreſſing which lies chiefly in a *ſharp Key*, where the *6th* to the *6th f.* and to the *7th f.* are both *leſſer*. *Exam.* 14.

4. WHENEVER

4. WHENEVER the *Octave* or *5th* is to be made use of, the *Parts* must proceed by a contrary Movement to each other; except the *Treble* move into such *Octave* or *5th* gradually; which Rule must be carefully observed, because the Occasions of transgressing it do most frequently occur, *Ex.* 15.

5. If in a *sharp Key*, the *Bass* descends gradually from the *5th f.* to the *4th f*; the last must never in that Case have its proper *Harmony* applied to it, but the Notes that were *Harmony* to the preceeding *5th f.* must be continued upon the *4th f. Exam.* 16.

6. *THIRDS* and *6ths* may follow one another immediately, as often as one has a Mind. *Exam.* 17.

HERE then are the *Rules* of *Harmony* plainly exhibited, which tho' few in Number, yet the Beginner will find the Observance of them a little difficult, because Occasions of transgressing do most frequently offer themselves.

IN the former *Article* it is shewn what *Concords* may be applied to each *Fundamental* or *Bass*-note; and here is taught how the *Parts* may proceed joyntly, the *Section 2d* shewing how they may proceed singly, and what in either Case is to be avoided. It remains therefore now to make the Application.

III. *A particular Application of the preceeding* Rules, *to two* Parts.

WHEREAS it is natural to Beginners, first to imagine the *Treble*, and then to make a *Bass* to to it, the *Treble* being the ſhining Part,in which the Beauty of *Melody* is chiefly to appear; in Compliance therewith, I ſhall, by inverting as it were the Rules in the foregoing Section, ſet forth,in the following Rules, which of the Seven *fundamental* Notes, in the *ſharp* and *flat Keys*, can properly be made uſe of to each of theSeven *natural* Notes that may enter into the *Treble*; of which an exact Remembrance will very much facilitate the attaining a Readineſs in the Practice of *ſingle Counterpoint*.

RULES *for making a* Baſs *to a* Treble, *in the* ſharp *as well as* flat Key.

1. The *Key* may have for its *Baſs*, either the *Key f.* the *4th f.* to which it is a *5th*, the *3d f.* to which it is a *6th*, or the *6th f.* to which it is a *3d*.

2. The *2d* may have for its *Baſs*, either the *7th f.* to which it is a *3d*, or the *5th f.* to which is is a *5th*, and ſometimes the *4th f.* to which it is a *6th*.

3. The *3d* can rarely have any other *Baſs* but the *Key f.* tho' ſometimes it may have the *6th f.* to which it is a *5th*.

4. The *4th* may have for its *Baſs* either the *2d f.* to which it is a *3d*, or the *6th f.* to which it is a *6th*, and ſometimes, to favour a contrary Movement of the *Parts*, it may have the *7th f.* to which it is a falſe *5th*, which ought to reſolve in the *3d*, the *Baſs* aſcending

to

to the *Key*, and the *Treble* defcending to the 3*d*.

5. THE 5*th* may have for its *Bafs*, either the 3*d f.* to which it is a 3*d*, the *Key* to which it is a 5*th*, the 7*th f.* to which it is a 6*th*; or, fometimes, to favour a contrary Movement of the *Parts*, it may have the 5*th f.* to which it is an *Octave*.

6. THE 6*th* may only have for its *Bafs* the 4*th f.* to which it is a 3*d*.

7. THE 7*th* may have for its *Bafs*, either the 5*th f.* to which it is a 3*d*, or the 2*d f.* to which it is a 6*th*.

I have carefully avoided the mentioning the 3*ds* and 6*ths*, particularly as they are *greater* or *leffer*, which would inevitably puzzle a Beginner: According to the Plan I have followed, there is no need to be fo particular, becaufe when a 3*d* and 6*th* are mentioned here in general, one is always to underftand fuch a 3*d* and fuch a 6*th* as makes one of the Seven *natural* Notes of the *Key*; thus when I fay that in a *fharp Key* the 5*th* is a 3*d*, to the 3*d f.* I muft neceffarily mean that it is a 3*d l.* to it, becaufe the 3*d g.* to the 3*d f.* is one of the Five extraneous Notes; juft fo when I fay that in a *flat Key* the 5*th* is a 3*d* to the 3*d f.* I muft needs mean that it is a 3*d g.* to it, becaufe the 3*d l.* to it is one of the Five extraneous Notes: Thus when I fay that the 3*d f.* in either *Key* may have a 3*d* or a 6*th* for its *Treble* Note, it muft be underftood as if I faid that fuch 3*d* and 6*th* in

a

a *ſharp Key* muſt be both leſſer, and in a *flat Key*, they muſt be both greater, becauſe in the firſt or *ſharp Key* the 3*d g.* and 6*th g.* of the 3*d f.* are extraneous, and ſo are the 3*d l.* and the 6*th l.* of the 3*d f.* in a *flat Key*: But conſidering how much it would embaraſs and multiply the Rules, to have characterized the 3*ds* and 6*ths* ſo particularly, I have therefore contrived the Plan I proceed upon, ſo as to avoid both theſe Inconveniencies, and by being general make the ſame Rules rightly underſtood, ſerve both for a *ſharp* and a *flat Key*.

BUT now that the Contents of the foregoing Rules may be the more eaſily committed to the Memory, I ſhall therefore convert them into this Scheme, where the *Aſteriſm* is intended to denote what is but uſed ſometimes.

Scheme *drawn from the preceeding Rules.*

The Octaves *of the*		*may ſtand in the* Treble *either as a*		*to the*	
	Key		3*d*, 5*th*, 6*th*, or 8*ve*.		6*f*. 4*f*. 3*f*. *Kf*.
	2*d*		3*d*, 5*th*, 6*th**		7*f*. 5*f*. 4*f*.
	3*d*		3*d*, 5*th**		*Kf*. 6*f*.
	4*th*		3*d*, 5*th l*.* 6*th*.		2*f*. 7*f*. 6*f*.
	5*th*		3*d*, 5*th*, 6*th*, 8*ve*.		3*f*. *Kf*. 7*f*. 5*f*.
	6*th*		3*d*,		4*f*.
	7*th*		3*d*, 6*th*.		5*f*. 2*f*.

See this exemplified, *Example* 18.

Theſe Rules being well underſtood, and exactly committed to the Memory, the *Treble* in *Ex.* 19. is ſuppoſed to be aſſign'd, and the *Baſs* compoſed to it according to theſe and the former Rules.

THE

THE first Thing I am to observe in the *Treble* is, that its *Key* is *c natural, i. e.* with the 3*d g.* because it begins and ends in *c* without touching any Note but the Seven that belong to the *Harmony* of that *Key*.

THE second Note in the *Treble* is the *second* in the *Harmony* of the *Key*; which, according to the Rules, might have stood as a 3*d* to the *Bass*, as well as a 5*th*; to which therefore the *Bass* might have been *b*, as well as *g.* but I rather chused the latter, because having begun pretty high with the *Bass*, I foresaw I should want to get down to *c* below, for a *Bass* to the 3*d* Note in the *Treble*; and therefore I chused *g* here rather than *b*, being a more natural and melodious Transition to *c* below.

THE third Note in the *Treble*, and 3*d* in the *Harmony* of the *Key*, has *c* the *Key f.* for its *Bass*, because it is almost the only *Bass* it can have: And I chused to take the *Key* below for the Reason I just now mentioned.

THE fourth Note in the *Treble* and 4*th* in the *Harmony* of the *Key*, has the 2*d f.* for its *Bass*, which here is *d*; it is capable of having for its *Bass* the 6*th f.* but considering what behoved to follow, it would not have been so natural.

THE fifth Note in the *Treble* and 5*th* in the *Harmony* of the *Key*, has for its *Bass* the 3*d f.* which is here *e.* it might have had *c* the *Key* for its *Bass*, and the going to *f* afterwards would have sung as well; but I chused to ascend gradually

gradually with the *Baſs*, to preſerve an Imitation that happens to be between the Parts, by the *Baſs* aſcending gradually to the 5*th f.* from the Beginning of the ſecond *Bar*, as the *Treble* does from the Beginning of the firſt *Bar*.

THE ſixth Note in the *Treble*, and *Key* in the *Harmony*, ſtands as a 5*th* ; and has for its *Baſs* the 4*th f.* rather than any other it might have had, for the Reaſon juſt now mentioned.

THE ſeventh Note in the *Treble*, and 7*th* in the *Harmony* of the *Key*, has the 5*th f.* rather than the 2*d f.* for its *Baſs*, not only on account of the Imitation I took Notice of, but to favour the contrary Movement of the *Parts* ; and beſides, conſidering what behoved to follow in the *Baſs*, the 2*d f.* would not have done ſo well here ; and the Tranſition from it to the *Baſs* Note that muſt neceſſarily follow, would not have been ſo natural. As to the following Notes of the *Baſs* I need ſay nothing ; for the Choice of them will appear to be from one of theſe Two Conſiderations, either that they are the only proper *Baſs* Notes that the *Treble* could admit of, or that one is choſen rather than another to favour the contrary Movement of the *Parts*.

I chuſed rather to be particular in ſetting forth one *Example* than to perplex the Beginner with a Multitude of them; I have therefore only added a ſecond, which I refer to the Student's own Examination ; both which are ſo contrived, as to be capable of being tranſpoſed into

into a *flat Key*, with the Alteration of the 3*d* and 6*th*.

WHEN these *Examples* are thoroughly examined, the next Step I would advise the Beginner to make, would be to transpose these *Trebles* into other *Keys*; and then endeavour to make a *Bass* to them in these other *Keys*: For to him, the same *Treble* in different *Keys* will be in some Measure like so many different *Trebles*, and will be equally conducive to his Improvement. And when he has finished the *Bass* in these other *Keys*, let him cast his Eyes on the *Example*, and transpose the *Bass* here into the same *Keys*, that he may observe wherein they differ, and in what they agree; by which Comparison he will be able to discover his Faults, and become a Master to himself. And by the Time that he can with Facility write a *Bass* to these Two *Trebles*, in all the usual *Keys*, which upon Examination he shall find to coincide with the *Examples*, I may venture to assure him that he has conquered the greatest Difficulty.

NOTWITHSTANDING the infinite Variety of *Air* there may be in *Musick*, I take it for granted, that there are a great many common Places in point of *Air*, equally familiar to all Composers, which necessarily produce correspondent common Places in *Harmony*; thus it most frequently happens that the *Treble* descends from the 3*d* to the *Key*, as at the *Example* 20, as often will the *Treble* descend from the

the *7th* to the *5th*. *Examples* 21, 22, and in this Caſe the *Baſs* is always the 5 *f*. as in that the *Baſs* is always the *Key f*. Thus frequently in the *Treble*, after a Series of Notes the *Air* will terminate and come to a Kind of *Reſt* or *Cloſe* upon the *2d* or *7th*; in both which the *Baſs* muſt always be the *5th f*. as in *Examples* 23, 24. Some other common Places will appear ſufficiently in the *Examples*, and others,for the Beginner's Inſtruction, he will beſt gather himſelf from the Works of Authors, particularly of *Corelli*.

As a thorough Acquaintance with ſuch common Places, will be a great Aſſiſtance to the Beginner, I would firſt recommend to him the Practice of thoſe here ſet forth, in all the *uſual Keys ſharp* as well as *flat*, till they are become very familiar to him: But in tranſpoſing them to *flat Keys*, the Variation of the *3d* and *6th* is to be carefully adverted to.

After *ſimple Counterpoint*, wherein nothing but *Concords* have Place, the next Step is to that *Counterpoint* wherein there is a Mixture of *Diſcord*; of which there are Two Kinds, that wherein the *Diſcords* are introduced occaſionally to ſerve only as Tranſitions from *Concord* to *Concord*, or that wherein the *Diſcord* bears a chief Part in the *Harmony*.

§ 4. Of

§ 4. *Of the Uſe of* Diſcords, *or* Figurate Counterpoint.

1. *Of the* tranſient Diſcords *that are ſubſervient to the* Air, *but make no Part of the* Harmony.

EVERY *Bar* or *Meaſure* has its accented and unaccented Parts: The Beginning and Middle, or the Beginning of the firſt Half of the *Bar*, and Beginning of the latter Half thereof in *common Time*;and the Beginning,or the firſt of the Three Notes in *triple Time*, are always the accented Parts of the *Meaſure*. So that in *common Time* the firſt and third *Crotchet* of the *Bar*, or if the Time be very ſlow, the *1ſt*, *3d*, *5th* and *7th Quavers* are on the accented Parts of the *Meaſure*, the reſt are upon the unaccented Parts of it. In the various Kinds of *Triple* whether $\frac{3}{2}$ $\frac{3}{4}$ $\frac{3}{8}$ or $\frac{6}{8}$ $\frac{12}{8}$ the Notes go always Three and Three, and that which is in the Middle of every Three is always unaccented, the firſt and laſt accented; but the Accent on the firſt is ſo much ſtronger, that, in ſeveral Caſes, the laſt is accounted as if it had no Accent ; ſo that a *Diſcord* duly prepared never ought to come upon it.

THE *Harmony* muſt always be full upon the accented Parts of the *Meaſure*, but upon the unaccented Parts that is not ſo requiſite: Wherefore *Diſcords* may tranſiently paſs there without

out any Offence to the Ear : This the *French* call *Suppoſition*, becauſe the tranſient *Diſcord* ſuppoſes a *Concord* immediately to follow it, which is of infinite Service in *Muſick*, as contributing mightily to that infinite Variety of *Air* of which *Muſick* is capable.

OF SUPPOSITION there are ſeveral Kinds. The firſt Kind is when the Parts proceed gradually from *Concord* to *Diſcord*, and from *Diſcord* to *Concord* as in the *Examples* 25 and 26. where the intervening *Diſcord* ſerves only as a Tranſition to the following *Concord*.

BY imagining all the *Crotchets* in the *Treble* to be *Minims*, and all the *Semibreves* in the *Baſs* of the *Example* 25. to be pointed, it will ſerve as an *Example* of this Kind of *Suppoſition* in *triple Time*.

THERE is another Kind, when the Parts do not proceed gradually from the *Diſcord* to the *Concord*, but deſcend to it by the Diſtance of a 3*d*. as in the *Examples* 27 and 28. where the *Diſcord* is eſteem'd as a Part of the preceeding *Concord*.

THERE is a third Kind reſembling the ſecond, when the riſing to the *Diſcord* is gradual, but the deſcending from it to the following *Concord* is by the Diſtance of a 4*th*, as in *Example* 29. in which the *Diſcord* is alſo conſidered as a Part, or Breaking of the preceeding *Concord*.

THERE

THERE is a fourth Kind very different from the Three former, when the *Discord* falls upon the accented Parts of the *Measure*, and when the rising to it is by the Distance of a *4th*; but then it is absolutely necessary to follow it immediately by a gradual Descent into a *Concord* that has just been heard before the *Harmony*; by which the *Discord* that preceeds gives no Offence to the Ear, serving only as a Transition into the *Concord*, as in *Example* 30.

THUS far was necessary to be taught by way of *Institution* upon the Subject of SUPPOSITION; what further Liberties may be taken that Way in making Divisions upon holding Notes, as in *Example* 31. may be easily gathered from what has been said; observing this as a Principle never to be departed from, that the less one deviates from the Rules, for the sake of *Air*, the better.

2. *Of the* HARMONY *of* DISCORDS.

THE *Harmony* of *Discords* is, that wherein the *Discords* are made use of as a solid and substantial Part of the *Harmony*; for by a proper Interposition of a *Discord* the succeeding *Concords* receive an additional Lustre. Thus the *Discords* are in *Musick* what the strong Shades are in Painting; for as the Lights there, so the *Concords* here, appear infinitely more beautiful by the Opposition.

THE DISCORDS are 1*mo*. the 5*th* when joyn'd with the 6*th*, to which it stands in relation as

a

a *Diſcord*, and is therefore treated as a *Diſcord* in that Place; not as it is a *5th* to the *Baſs* in which View it is a perfect *Concord*, but as being joyn'd with the Note immediately above it, there ariſes from thence a Senſation of *Diſcord*.

2do. THE *4th*, tho' in its own Nature it is a *Concord* to the *Baſs*, yet being joyn'd with the *5th*, which is immediately above it, is alſo uſed as a *Diſcord* in that Caſe.

3tio. THE *Ninth* which is in effect the *2d*, and is only called the *Ninth* to diſtinguiſh it from the *2d*, which under that Denominati-on is uſed in a different Manner, is in its own Nature a *Diſcord*.

4to. THE *7th* is in its own Nature a *Diſcord*.

5to. THE *2d* and *4th* is made uſe of when the *Baſs* ſyncopates, in a very different Manner from that of uſing thoſe above mentioned, as will appear in the *Examples*.

AS I treat only of Compoſition in Two Parts, there is no Occaſion to name the *Concords* with which, in Compoſition of Three or more *Parts*, the *Diſcords* are accompanied; theſe, I take for granted, are known to the Performer of the *thorough Baſs*; and tho' in Compoſition of Two *Parts* they cannot appear, yet they are always ſuppoſed and ſupplied by the Accom-panyments of the *Baſs*.

Of

Of Preparation *and* Refolution *of* Difcords.

THE *Difcords* here treated of are introduced into the *Harmony* with due Preparation; and they muft be fucceeded by *Concords*, commonly called the *Refolution* of the *Difcord.*

THE *Difcord* is *prepared*, by fubfifting firft in the *Harmony* in the Quality of a *Concord*, *that is*, the fame Note which becomes the *Difcord* is firft a *Concord* to the *Bafs* Note immediately preceeding that to which it is a *Difcord*; the *Difcord* is *refolved*, by being immediately fucceeded by a *Concord* defcending from it by the Diftance only of 2*d g.* or 2*d l.*

AS the *Difcord* makes a fubftantial Part of the *Harmony*, fo it muft always poffefs an accented Part of the *Meafure*: So that in *common Time* it muft fall upon the 1*ft* and 3*d Crotchet*; or, if the Time be extremely flow, upon the 1*ft*, 3*d*, 5th or 7*th Quaver* of the *Bar*; and in *triple Time* it muft fall on the firft of every Three *Crotchets*, or of every Three *Minims*, or of every Three *Quavers*, according as the *triple Time* is, there being various Kinds of it.

IN order then to know how the *Difcords* may be properly introduced into the *Harmony*, I fhall examine what *Concords* may ferve for their *Preparation* and *Refolution*; *that is*, Whether the *Concords* going before and following fuch and fuch a *Difcord* may be a 5*th*, 6*th*, 3*d* or *Octave*.

THE

THE *5th* may be *prepared*, by being either an *8ve*, *6th* or *3d*; it may be *resolved* either into the *6th* or *3d*, but most commonly into the *3d*. *Example* 32.

THE *4th* may be *prepared* in all the *Concords*; and may be *resolved* into the *6th*, *3d* or *8ve*, but most commonly into the *3d*. *Example* 33.

THE *9th* may be *prepared* in all the *Concords* except the *8ve*, and may be *resolved* into the *6th*, *3d* or *8ve*, but most commonly into the *8ve*. *Example* 34.

THE *7th* may be *prepared* in all the *Concords*; and may be *resolved* into the *3d*, *6th* or *5th*, but most commonly into the *6th* or *3d*. *Example* 35.

THE *2d* and *4th* are made use of after a quite different Manner from the other *Discords*, being *prepared* and *resolved* in the *Bass*. *Thus*, when the *Bass* descends by the Distance of a *2d*, and the first Half of the Note falls upon an unaccented Part of the *Measure*, then either the *4th* or the *2d* may be applied to the last or accented Half of the Note; if the *2d*, it is continued upon the following Note in the *Bass*, and becomes the *3d* to it; if the *4th* is applied, the *Treble* rises a Note, and becomes a *6th* to the *Bass*. *Example* 36.

FROM all which I must observe, that the *5th* and *7th* are *Discords* of great Use, because, even in Two Parts, they may be made use of successively for a pretty long Series of Notes without Interruption, especially the *7th*, as producing

ducing a most beautiful *Harmony*. The *4th* is not useful in Two Parts in this successive Way, but is otherwise very useful. The *9th* in the same Manner is only useful as the *4th* is.

HAVING once distinctly understood how the *Discords* are introduced and made a Part of the *Harmony*, by the *Examples* that I have exhibited in plain Notes, it may not be amiss to take a View, in the *Examples* here set forth, how these plain Notes may be broke into Notes of less Value; and being so divided, how they may be disposed to produce a Variety of *Air*: Which *Examples* may suffice to give the Beginner an *Idea* how the *Discords* may be divided into Notes of small Value, for the sake of *Air*. Of the Manner of doing it there is an infinite Variety, and therefore to have shewn all the possible Ways how it may be done, would have required an infinite Number of *Examples*: I shall therefore only give one Caution, that in all such Breakings the first Part of the discarding Note must distinctly appear, and after the remaining Part of it has been broke into a Division of Notes of less Value, according to the Fancy of the Composer, such Division ought to lead naturally into the *resolving Concord* that it may be also distinctly heard. See *Example* 37.

HAVING now considered the Matter of *Harmony* as particularly as is necessary to do by way of *Institution*, to qualify the Student for reading and receiving Instruction from the Works

Works of the more celebrated Composers, which is the utmost that any *Treatise* in my Opinion ought to aim at, I proceed to describe the Nature of *Modulation*, and to give the Rules for guiding the Beginner in the Practice of it.

---

§ 5. *Of* MODULATION; *and*

1mo. *What it is.*

ALTHO' every Piece of *Musick* has one particular *Key* wherein it not only begins and ends, but which prevails more through the whole Piece; yet the Variety that is so necessary to the Beauty of *Musick* requires the frequent changing of the *Harmony* into several other *Keys*; on Condition always that it return again into the *Key* appropriated to the Piece, and terminate often there by middle as well as final *Cadences*, especially if the Piece be of any Length, else the middle *Cadences* in the *Key* are not so necessary.

THESE other *Keys*, whether *sharp* or *flat* into which the *Harmony* may be changed, must be such whose *Harmonies* are not remote to the *Harmony* of the *principnl Key* of the Piece; because otherwise the Transitions from the *principal Key* to those other intermediate ones, would be unnatural and inconsistent with that

Analo-

Analogy which ought to be preſerved between all the Members of the ſame Piece. Under the Term of *Modulation* may be comprehended the regular Progreſſion of the ſeveral Parts thro' the Sounds that are in the *Harmony* of any particular *Key* as well as the proceeding naturally and regularly with the *Harmony* from one *Key* to another: The Rules of *Modulation* therefore in that Senſe are the Rules of *Melody* and *Harmony*, of which I have already treated; ſo that the Rules of *Modulation* only in this laſt Senſe is my preſent Buſineſs.

SINCE every Piece muſt have one *principal Key*, and ſince the Variety that is ſo neceſſary in *Muſick* to pleaſe and entertain, forbids the being confin'd to one *Key*, and that therefore it is not only allowable but requiſite to *modulate* into and make *Cadences* upon ſeveral other *Keys*, having a Relation and Connection with the *principal Key*, I am firſt to conſider what it is that conſtitutes a Connection between the *Harmony* of one *Key* and that of another, that from thence it may appear into what *Keys* the *Harmony* may be led with Propriety: And in order to comprehend the better wherein this Connection between the *Harmony* of different *Keys* may conſiſt, I ſhall firſt ſhew what it is that occaſions an Inconſiſtency between the *Harmony* of one *Key* and that of another.

2. *Of the* Relation *and* Connection *of* Keys.

IT has been already ſet forth, that each *Key* has Seven Notes belonging to it and no more. In

In a *ſharp Key* theſe are fix'd and unalterable; but in a *flat Key* there is one that varies, *viz.* the *7th.* Hitherto I have accounted the *7th g.* one of the Seven natural Notes in a *flat Key*, and I behoved to do ſo in the Matter of *Harmony*, becauſe the *7th g* is the *3d g.* to the *5th*, without the Help of which there would be no *Cadence* on the *Key*; and beſides, it is alone by the Help of it that one can aſcend into the *Key*. But here when I conſider not the particular Exigencies of the *Harmony* in a *flat Key*, but the general Analogy there is between the *Harmony* of one *Key* and that of another, I muſt reckon that the *7th* which is eſſential in a *flat Key* is the *7th l.* becauſe both the *3d* and *6th* in a *flat Key* are leſſer, therefore as to our preſent Enquiry the *7th g.* in a *flat Key* muſt be henceforth accounted extraneous.

THE diſtinguiſhing Note in each *Key*, next to the *Key*-note it ſelf, is the *3d*; any *Key* therefore that has for its *3d* any one of the Five extraneous Notes of another *Key*, under what Denomination ſoever of ※ or ♭ is diſcrepant with that other *Key* to which ſuch *3d* is extraneous. Thus the extraneous Notes of the *ſharp Key c* being *c*※, *d*※, *f*※, *g*※, *a*※, or as the ſame Notes may happen to be differently denominated *d*♭, *e*♭, *g*♭, *a*♭, ♭: The *ſharp Key a* therefore having *c*※ for its *3d*, the *ſharp Key b* having *d*※ for its *3d*, the *ſharp Key e* having *g*※ for its *3d*, the *ſharp Key f*※ having *a*※ for its *3d*, or the *flat Key* ♭ having *d*♭ for its *3d*, the *flat Key c* having *e*♭ for its *3d*, the *flat Key e*♭ having *g*♭ for

for its 3*d*, the *flat Key f* having *a*♭ for its 3*d*, and the *flat Key g* having ♭ for its 3*d*, are all, I ſay, diſcrepant with the *ſharp Key c*, becauſe the 3*ds* which are the diſtinguiſhing Notes of theſe other *Keys* are all extraneous Notes to *c*, with a 3*dg*. and ſince any *Key* which has for its 3*d* any one of the Five extraneous Notes of another *Key*, is diſcrepant with that other *Key*, *a fortiori* therefore any one of the Five extraneous Notes of a *Key* being a *Key* it ſelf, is utrerly diſcrepant with a *Key*, to which ſuch *Key*-note it ſelf is extraneous; thus therefore *c*※, *d*※, *f*※, *g*※, *a*※, or, *d*♭, *e*♭, *g*♭, *a*♭, ♭ being conſidered as *Keys*, whether with 3*dg*. or 3*dl*. are utterly diſcrepant to *c* with a 3*dg*. becauſe they are all extraneous to it.

A *Key* then being aſſign'd as a *principal Key*, as none of its five extraneous Notes can either be *Keys* themſelves, or 3*ds* to *Keys* that can have any Connexion with it, ſo it will from thence follow, that the Seven *natural* Notes of the *Key* aſſigned, being conſtituted *Keys* with ſuch 3*ds* as are one or other of the Seven *natural* Notes of the ſaid *Key* aſſign'd, may be accounted conſonant to it; provided they do not eſſentially introduce the *principal Key* or its 3*d* under a new Denomination, *that is*, the *Key* aſſign'd being for *Example* the *ſharp Key c*, no *Key* can be conſonant to it, that introduces neceſſarily and eſſentially *c*※, which is the Key under a new Denomination, or *e*※, which is its 3*d* under a new Denomination, and different from what they were in the *Key* aſſign'd; therefore

fore to the *sharp Key c*, which I shall take for the *principal Key* assign'd, the *flat Keys d*, *e* and *a*, also the *sharp Keys f* and *g* are consonant; but the *flat Key b*, altho' both it self and its 3*d* are Two of the Seven *natural* Notes of the *Key* assigned, is not consonant to it, because it would essentially introduce *c*※ for its 2*d*, which being the *Key* assign'd under a new Denomination, would produce a very great Inconsistency with it. And here, lest from thence the Beginner may form this Objection against the *flat Key d*, being reckoned consonant to the *sharp Key c*, as I have done, because that *Key d* does introduce *c*※ for its 7*th g*. I must inform him, as I have before observed, that the 7*th g.* to a *flat Key* is only occasionally made Use of; and that the 7*th l.* is the 7*th* that is essential in a *flat Key*.

THE *flat Key c* being the *principal flat Key* assigned, the *flat Keys f* and *g*, also the *sharp Keys e♭*, *a♭* and *♭* are consonant to it, but the *flat Key d*, tho' both it self and its 3*d* are of the *natural* Notes of the *Key* assigned, yet as this *flat Key d* being constituted a *Key*, behoved to have *e* for its Second, which is the 3*d* of the *Key* assigned, under a different Denomination, therefore it cannot be admitted as a consonant *Key* to it.

TO the *Harmony* therefore of a *flat principal Key*, as well as of a *sharp one*, there are Five *Keys* that are consonant, that, with all the Elegancy and Property imaginable, may be introduced in the Course of the Modulation of any

any one Piece of *Musick*. To all *sharp principal Keys* the Five consonant *Keys* are the 2*d*, 3*d*, 4*th*, 5*th* and 6*th* to the *principal Key*, with their respective 3*ds*, viz. with the 2*d*, the 3*dl*. 3*d*, 3*dl*. 4*th*, 3*dg*. 5*th*, 3*dg*. 6*th*, 3*dl*. To all *flat principal Keys* the Five consonant *Keys* are the 3*d*, 4*th*, 5*th*, 6*th* and 7*th* to the *principal Key*, with their respective 3*ds*, viz. with the 3*d*, the 3*dg*. 4*th*, 3*dl*. 5*th*, 3*dl*. 6*th*, 3*dg*. 7*th*, 3*dg*. each of which consonant *Keys*, tho' reckoned dependent upon their *principal Key* with regard to the Structure of the whole Piece, yet with respect to the particular Places where they prevail, they are each of them *principal* so long as the *Modulation* continues in them, and the Rules of *Melody* and *Harmony* are the same way to be observed in them as in the *principal Key*; for all *Keys* of the same Kind are the same, and this Subordination here discoursed of is only *accidental*; for no *Key* in its own Nature is more to be accounted *principal* than another.

THE several *Keys* then that may enter into the Composition of the same Piece being known, it is material next to learn in what Order they may be introduc'd; and herein one must have Recourse to the current Practice of the Masters of *Composition*; from which, tho' indeed no certain Rules can be gathered, because the Order of introducing the consonant *Keys* is very much at the Discretion of the Composer, and in the Work of the same Author is often various, yet generally the Order is thus.

IN

IN a *sharp principal Key*, the first *Cadence* is upon the *principal Key* it self often; then follow in Order *Cadences* on the *5th*, *3d*, *6th*, *2d*, *4th*, concluding at last with a *Cadence* on the *principal Key*. In a *flat principal Key* the intermediate *Cadences* are on the *3d*, *5th*, *7th*, *4th* and *6th*. Now, whatever Liberty may be taken in varying from this Order, yet the beginning and ending with the *principal Key* is a Principle never to be departed from; and as far as I have observed, it ought to be a Rule also, that in a *sharp principal Key*, the *5th*, and in a *flat* one the *3d*, ought to have the next Place to the *principal Key*.

3tio. How the *Modulation* is to be performed.

IT now remains to shew, how to *modulate* from one *Key* to another, so that the Transitions may be easy and natural; but how to teach this Kind of *Modulation* by Rules is the Difficulty; for altho' it is chiefly performed by the Help of the *7th g*. of the *Key* into which we are resolved to change the *Harmony*, whether it be *sharp* or *flat*; yet the Manner of doing it is so various and extensive, as no Rules can circumscribe: Wherefore in this Matter, as well as in other Branches of my Subject, I must think it enough to explain the Nature of the Thing so, and to give the Beginner such general Notions of it, as he may be able to gather by his own Observation, in the Course of his Studies of this Kind, what no Rules can teach.

THE

THE *7th g.* in either *sharp* or *flat Key* is the *3d g.* to the *5th f.* of the *Key*, by which the *Cadence* in the *Key* is chiefly perform'd; and by being only a *Semitone* under the *Key*, is therefore the most proper Note to lead into it, which it does in the most natural Manner that can be imagin'd; insomuch that the *7th g.* is never heard in any of the *Parts*, but the Ear expects the *Key* should succeed it; for whether it be used as a *3d* or as a *6th*, it doth always affect us with such an imperfect Sensation, that we naturally expect something more perfect to follow, which cannot be more easily and smoothly accomplished, than by the small *Interval* of a *Semitone*, to pass into the perfect *Harmony* of the *Key*; from hence it is that the Transition into any *Key* is best effected, by introducing its *7th g.* which so naturally leads to it; and how this *7th g.* may be introduced, will best appear in the *Examples*.

IN *Ex.* 38. the *Key* is first the *sharp Key* c, but *f*※, which is the 7*th g.* to *g*, introduces and leads the *Harmony* into the first consonant *Key* of *c* with a 3*d g.* In this *Example f*※ stands in the *Treble* a *6th*; but it may also stand a 3*d g.* as in *Ex.* 39. or it may be introduced into the *Bass* with its proper *Harmony* of a 3*d* or *6th*, as in *Examples* 40 and 42. or it may, as a *6th g.* or 3*d g.* in the *Treble*, be the resolving *Concord* of a preceeding *Discord*, as in *Examples* 41 and 44. or it may stand in the *Treble* as a 4*th g.* accompanied also in that Case with a 2*d*, or supposed to be so as in *Ex.* 46.

46. or otherwife ufed as in *Examples* 45 and 47. The *Modulation* changes from the *fharp Key c* into the *flat Key a*, one of its confonant *Keys*, whofe *7thg.* is introduced in the Quality of a *6thg.* and *3dg.* ferving as the *Refolutions* of preceeding *Difcords.* In *Examples* 48 and 51. the *6th* is applied to the *Key*, which is always a good Preparation to lead the *Harmony* out of it; for a *Key* can be no longer a *Key* when a *6th* is applied. The remaining *Examples* fhew how the *Harmony* may pafs through feveral *Keys* in the Compafs of a few Notes.

FROM thefe *Examples* I fhall deduce fome few Obfervations, that may ferve as fo many Rules to guide the Beginner in this firft Attempt.

1ft. THE *7thg.* of the *Key* into which we intend to lead the *Harmony*, is introduced into the *Treble* either as a *3dg.* or *6thg.* or as a *4thg.* with its fuppofed Accompanyments of *4th* and *6th*; and as *3dg.* or *6thg.* it is commonly the *Refolution* of a preceeding *Difcord.*

2d. WHEN this *7thg.* comes into the *Treble* in what Quality foever, as *3dg. 6thg.* &c. it is either fucceeded immediately by that Note which is the *Key* whereto it immediately leads, or immediately preceeded by it, and moft commonly the laft; in which Cafe the *Treble* muft of confequence defcend to it by the Diftance of a *Semitone.* Thus, when we are to change the *Harmony* from the *fharp Key c* to the *flat Key a*, that is, from a *fharp principal Key* into its

6th,

6th, we use it in the *Treble* as the *6th* to the *principal Key c*, or as the *5th* to *d*, or as the *3d* to *f*; and being once upon the Note which we design to be the *Key*, the falling half a Note to its *7th g.* for fixing the *Harmony* fairly in the *Key*, is most easily perform'd; thus were we to go from a *principal Key* into the *3d*, we should use a *6th* on the *5 f.*; or were we to go into the *2d*, we should use a *6th* on the *4 f.* and the rather, because in the *Key* whereto we design to go, a *6th* is the proper *Harmony*, for that *5th f.* of the *principal Key* becomes the *3d f.* of the *3d*, when it is constitute a *Key*; and so does the *4th f.* of the *principal Key* become the *3d f.* of the *2d*, when constitute a *Key*.

3tio. WHEN the *7th g.* of the *Key*, into which we design to change the *Harmony*, is introduced in the *Bass*, it is always immediately succeeded by the *Key*; and then the Transition to the *7th g.* is most part gradual, by the *Interval* of a *Tone* or *Semitone*, or by the *Interval* of a *3d l.* But most commonly it is introduced into the *Bass*, by proceeding to it from the *natural* Note of the same Name, *that is*, from a Note that is *natural* in the *Key*, as from *f* to *f*✱ in the *sharp Key c*, or from ♭ to *b* in the *flat Key d*.

4to. WHEN the *7th g.* of the *Key* to which we design to lead the *Harmony*, is one of the Seven *natural* Notes of the *Key* wherein the *Harmony* already is, the introducing it into the *Bass* is most *natural*, as being of course; this happens when we would *modulate* from a *sharp Key* into its *4th*, or from a *flat Key* into its

3d.

3*d*. In which Cafes the 7*th g.* is introduced into the *Bafs*, and in the *Treble* the *falfe* 5*th* is applied to it, which refolves into the 3*d g.*

5*to*. WHEN this 7*th g.* comes into the *Bafs*, it muft of neceffity have either a 3*d l.* 6*th l.* or *falfe* 5*th* in the *Treble*; if a 3*d l.* it refolves into the 8*ve*, if a 6*th l.* it commonly paffes into the *falfe* 5*th*, and from thence refolves into the 3*d* of the *Key*.

6*to*. BY applying the 6*th* to any Note of the *Key*, to which the 5*th* is a more *natural Harmony*, as for *Example*, to the *Key* it felf, to the 4*th f.* or 5*th f.* a Preparation is thereby made for going into another *Key*, viz. into that Note which is fo made Ufe of, as a 6*th* to any of thefe *fundamental* Notes, as in the *Examples*.

HAVING thus explained the Nature of *Modulation* from one *Key* to another, it may feem natural to treat now of *Cadences*; but of thefe I cannot fuppofe a Performer of the *Thorough-bafs* ignorant, they being fo frequent in *Mufick*; all I fhall therefore fay of them is, that they muft always be finifhed with an accented Part of the *Meafure*. As to what concerns *Fugues* and *Imitations* I am to fay nothing, becaufe thefe are to be learnt more by a Courfe of Obfervation than by Rule. What I propofed was, to fet forth the *Principles* of *Compofition* in Two Parts, by way of *Inftitution* only, not daring to proceed any further than the fmall Knowledge I have of *Mufick* would lead me with Safety.

CHAP.

CHAP. XIV.

Of the ANCIENT MUSICK.

§ 1. *Of the* Name, *with the various* Definitions *and* Divisions *of the* Science.

THE Word MUSICK comes to us from the Latin Word *Musica*, if not immediately from a Greek Word of the same Sound, from whence the *Romans* probably took theirs; for they got much of their Learning from the *Greeks*. Our Criticks teach us, that it comes from the Word *Musa*, and this from a Greek Word which signifies to search or find out, because the *Muses* were feigned to be Inventresses of the *Sciences*, and particularly of *Poetry* and these *Modulations* of Sound that constitute *Musick*. But others go higher, and tell us, the Word *Musa* comes from a Hebrew Word, which signifies *Art* or *Discipline*; hence *Musa* and *Musica* anciently signified *Learn-*

Learning in general, or any Kind of *Science*; in which Senſe you'll find it frequently in the Works of the ancient Philoſophers. But *Kircher* will have it from an *Egyptian* Word; becauſe the Reſtoration of it after the Flood was probably there, by reaſon of the many Reeds to be found in their Fens, and upon the Banks of the *Nile*. *Heſychius* tells us, that the *Athenians* gave the Name of *Muſick* to every *Art*. From this it was that the *Poets* and *Mythologiſts* feigned the nine *Muſes* Daughters of *Jupiter*, who invented the Sciences, and preſide over them, to aſſiſt and inſpire theſe who apply to ſtudy them, each having her particular Province. In this geneal Senſe we have it defin'd to be, the orderly Arangement and right Diſpoſition of Things; in ſhort, the Agreement and *Harmony* of the Whole with its Parts, and of the Parts among themſelves. *Hermes Triſmegiſtus* ſays, *That* Muſick *is nothing but the Knowledge of the Order of all Things*; which was alſo the Doctrine of the *Pythagorean* School, and of the *Platonicks*, who teach that every Thing in the Univerſe is *Muſick*. Agreeable to this wide Senſe, ſome have diſtinguiſhed Muſick into *Divine* and *Mundane*; the firſt reſpects the Order and Harmony that obtains among the Celeſtial Minds; the other reſpects the Relations and Order of every other Thing elſe in the Univerſe. But *Plato* by the *divine Muſick* underſtands, that which exiſts in the *divine* Mind, *viz.* theſe archetypal Ideas of Order and Symmetry, according to which GOD formed all Things; and as this Order exiſts

exists in the Creatures, it is called *Mundane Musick*: Which is again subdivided, the remarkable Denominations of which are, *First*, *Elementary* or the Harmony of the first Elements of Things; and these according to the Philosophers, are Fire, Air, Water, and Earth, which tho' seemingly contrary to one another, are, by the Wisdom of the Creator, united and compounded in all the beautiful and regular Forms of Things that fall under our Senses. 2*d. Celestial*, comprehending the Order and Proportions in the Magnitudes, Distances, and Motions of the heavenly Bodies, and the Harmony of the Sounds proceeding from these Motions: For the *Pythagoreans* affirmed that they produce the most perfect *Consort*; the Argument, as *Macrobius* in his Commentary on *Cicero*'s *Somnium Scipionis* has it, is to this Purpose, *viz.* Sound is the Effect of Motion, and since the heavenly Bodies must be under certain regular and stated Laws of Motion, they must produce something musical and concordant; for from random and fortuitous Motions, governed by no certain Measure, can only proceed a grating and unpleasant Noise: And the Reason, says he, why we are not sensible of that Sound, is the Vastness of it, which exceeds our Sense of Hearing; in the same Manner as the Inhabitants near the Cataracts of the *Nile*, are insensible of their prodigious Noise. But some of the Historians, if I remember right, tell us that by the Excessiveness of the Sounds, these People are rendred quite deaf, which makes that

Denon-

Demonſtration ſomewhat doubtful, ſince we hear every other Sound that reaches to us. Others alledge that the Sounds of the Spheres, being the firſt we hear when we come into the World, and being habituated to them for a long Time, when we could ſcarcely think or make Reflection on any Thing, we become incapable of perceiving them afterwards. But *Pythagoras* ſaid he perceived and underſtood the Celeſtial Harmony by a peculiar Favour of that Spirit to whom he owed his Life, as *Jamblichus* reports of him, who ſays, That tho' he never ſung or played on any Inſtrument himſelf, yet by an inconceivable Sort of Divinity, he taught others to imitate the Celeſtial Muſick of the Spheres, by Inſtruments and Voice: For according to him, all the Harmony of Sounds here below, is but an Imitation, and that imperfect too, of the other. This Species is by ſome called particularly the *Mundane Muſick*. 3*d*. *Human*, which conſiſts chiefly in the Harmony of the Faculties of the human Soul, and its various Paſſions; and is alſo conſidered in the Proportion and Temperament, mutual Dependence and Connection, of all the Parts of this wonderful Machine of our Bodies. 4*th*. Is what in a more limited and peculiar Senſe of the Word was called *Muſick*; which has for its Object *Motion*, conſidered as under certain regular Meaſures and Proportions, by which it affects the Senſes in an agreeable Manner. All Motion belongs to Bodies, and Sound is the Effect of Motion, and cannot be without it; but all Motion does

not

not produce Sound, therefore this was again ſubdivided. Where the Motion is without Sound, or as it is only the Object of Seeing, it was called *Muſica Orcheſtria* or *Saltatoria*, which contains the Rules for the regular Motions of *Dancing*; alſo *Hypocritica*, which reſpects the Motions and Geſtures of the *Pantomimes*. When Motion is perceived only by the Ear, *i. e.* when Sound is the Object of *Muſick*, there are Three Species; HARMONICA, which conſiders the Differences and Proportion of Sounds, with reſpect to *acute* and *grave*; RYTHMICA, which reſpects the Proportion of Sounds as to Time, or the Swiftneſs and Slowneſs of their Succeſſions; and METRICA, which belongs properly to the *Poets*, and reſpects the verſifying Art: But in common Acceptation 'tis now more limited, and we call nothing *Muſick* but what is heard; and even then we make a Variety of *Tones* neceſſary to the Being of *Muſick*.

ARISTIDES QUINTILIANUS, who writes a profeſt Treatiſe upon *Muſick*, calls it the Knowledge of ſinging, and of the Things that are joyned with ſinging (*'επιϛήμη μέλȣς καὶ τῶν περὶ μελος συμβαινόντων*, which *Meibomius* tranſlates, *Scientia cantus, eorumq; quæ circa cantum contingunt*) and theſe he calls the Motions of the Voice and Body, as if the *Cantus* it ſelf conſiſted only in the different Tones of the Voice. *Bacchius* who writes a ſhort Introduction to Muſick in Queſtion and Anſwer, gives the ſame Definition. Afterwards, *Ariſtides* conſiders

siders *Musick* in the largest Sense of the Word, and divides it into *Contemplative* and *Active*. The first, he says, is either *natural* or *artificial*; the *natural* is *arithmetical*, because it considers the Proportion of Numbers, or *physical* which disputes of every Thing in Nature; the *Artificial* is divided into *Harmonica*, *Rythmica* (comprehending the dumb Motions) and *Metrica*: The *active*, which is the Application of the *artificial*, is either *enunciative* (as in Oratory,) *Organical* (or Instrumental Performance,) *Odical* (for Voice and singing of Poems,) *Hypocritical* (in the Motions of the *Pantomimes*.) To what Purpose some add *Hydraulical* I do not understand, for this is but a Species of the *Organical*, in which Water is some way used for producing or modifying the Sound. The musical Faculties, as they call them, are, *Melopœia* which gives Rules for the *Tones* of the Voice or Instrument, *Rythmopœia* for Motions, and *Poesis* for making of Verse. Again, explaining the Difference of *Rythmus* and *Metrum*, he tells us, That *Rythmus* is applied Thee Ways; either to immoveable Bodies, which are called *Eurythmoi*, when their Parts are right proportioned to one another, as a well made Statue; or to every Thing that moves, so we say a Man walks handsomly (*composite*,) and under this *Dancing* will come, and the Business of the *Pantomimes*; or particularly to the Motion of Sound or the Voice, in which the *Rythmus* consists of long and short Syllables or Notes, (which he calls *Times*) joyned together (in

Suc-

Succeſſion) in ſome kind of Order, ſo that their Cadence upon the Ear may be agreeable; which conſtitutes in *Oratory* what is called a numerous Stile, and when the *Tones* of the Voice are well choſen 'tis an *harmonious* Stile. RYTHMUS is perceived either by the Eye or the Ear, and is ſomething general, which may be without *Metrum*; but this is perceived only by the Ear, and is but a Species of the other, and cannot exiſt without it: The firſt is perceived without Sound in Dancing; and when it exiſts with Sounds it may either be without any Difference of *acute* and *grave*, as in a *Drum*, or with a Varitey of theſe, as in a Song, and then the *Harmonica* and *Rythmica* are joyned; and if any *Poem* is ſet to *Muſick*, and ſung with a Variety of *Tones*, we have all the Three Parts of *Muſick* at once. *Porphyrius* in his Commentaries on *Ptolemey's Harmonicks*, inſtitutes the Diviſion of *Muſick* another Way; he takes it in the limited Senſe, as having *Motion* both dumb and ſonorous for its Object; and, without diſtinguiſhing the *ſpeculative* and *practical*, he makes its Parts theſe Six, *viz.* *Harmonica*, *Rythmica*, *Metrica*, *Organica*, *Poetica*, *Hypocritica*; he applies the *Rythmica* to Dancing, *Metrica* to the Enunciative, and *Poetica* to Verſes.

ALL the other ancient Authors agree in the ſame threefold Diviſion of *Muſick* into *Harmonica*, *Rythmica* and *Metrica*: Some add the *Organica*, others omit it, as indeed it is but an accidental Thing to *Muſick*, in what Species of Sounds

Sounds it is exprest. Upon this Division of *Musick*, the more ancient Writers are very careful in the Inscription or Titles of their Books, and call them only *Harmonica*, when they confine themselves to that Part, as *Aristoxenus*, *Euclid*, *Nicomachus*, *Gaudentius*, *Ptolomey*, *Bryennius*; but *Aristides* and *Bacchius* call theirs *Musica*, because they profess to treat of all the Parts. The *Latines* are not always so accurate, for they inscribe all theirs *Musica*, as *Boethius*, tho' he only explains the *Harmonica*; and St. *Augustin*, tho' his Six Books *de Musica* speak only of the *Rythmus* and *Metrum*; *Martianus Capella* has a better Right to the Title, for he makes a Kind of Compend and Translation of *Aristides Quintil.* tho' a very obscure one of as obscure an Original. *Aurelius Cassiodorus* needs scarcely be named, for tho' he writes a Book *de Musica*, 'tis but barely some general Definitions and Divisions of the Science.

THE *Harmonica* is the Part the Ancients have left us any tolerable Account of, which are at least but very general and *Theorical*; such as it is I purpose to explain it to you as distinctly as I can; but having thus far settled the Definition and Division of *Musick* as delivered by the Ancients, I chuse next to consider histo rically.

§ 2. *The*

§ 2. *The Invention and Antiquity of* Musick, *with the Excellency of the Art in the various Ends and Uses of it.*

OF all human Arts *Musick* has justest Pretences to the Honour of *Antiquity*: We scarce need any Authority for this Assertion; the Reason of the Thing demonstrates it, for the Conditions and Circumstances of human Life required some powerful Charm, to bear up the Mind under the Anxiety and Cares that Mankind soon after his Creation became subject to; and the Goodness of our blessed *Creator* soon discovered it self in the wonderful Relief that *Musick* affords against the unavoidable Hardships which are annexed to our State of being in this Life; so that *Musick* must have been as early in the World as the most necessary and indispensable Arts. For

IF we consider how natural to the Mind of Man this kind of Pleasure is, as constant and universal Experience sufficiently proves, we cannot think he was long a Stranger to it. Other Arts were revealed as bare Necessity gave Occasion, and some were afterwards owing to Luxury; but neither Necessity nor Luxury are the Parents of this heavenly Art; to be pleased with it seems to be a Part of our Constitution; but 'tis made so, not as absolutely necessary to our Being, 'tis a Gift of GOD to us for our more happy and comfortable Being; and therefore we can make no doubt that this Art was among the very first that were known to Men. It is reason-

reaſonable to believe, that as all other Arts, ſo this was rude and ſimple in its Beginning, and by the Induſtry of Man, prompted by his natural Love of Pleaſure, improven by Degrees. If we conſider, again, how obvious a Thing Sound is, and how manifold Occaſions it gives for Invention, we are not only further confirmed in the Antiquity of this Art, but we can make very ſhrewd Gueſſes about the firſt Diſcoveries of it. *Vocal Muſick* was certainly the firſt Kind; Man had not only the various *Tones* of his own Voice to make his Obſervations upon, before any other Arts or Inſtruments were found, but being daily entertained by the various natural Strains of the winged Choirs, how could he not obſerve them, and from hence take Occaſion to improve his own Voice, and the Modulations of Sound, of which it is capable? 'Tis certain that whatever theſe Singers were capable of, they poſſeſt it actually from the Beginniug of the World; we are ſurpriſed indeed with their ſagacious Imitations of human Art in Singing, but we know no Improvements the Species is capable of; and if we ſuppoſe that in theſe Parts where Mankind firſt appeared, and eſpecially in theſe firſt Days, when Things were probably in their greateſt Beauty and Perfection, the Singing of Birds was a more remarkable Thing, we ſhall have leſs Reaſon to doubt that they led the Way to Mankind in this charming Art: But this is no new Opinion; of many ancient Authors, who agree in this very juſt Conjecture, I ſhall only let you hear *Lucretius Lib.* 5.

At

At liquidas avium voces imitarier ore
Ante fuit multo, quam lævia carmina cantu
Concelebrare homines possent, aureisque juvare.

THE first Invention of Wind-instruments he ascribes to the Observation of the Whistling of the Winds among the hollow Reeds.

Et Zephyri cava per calamorum sibila primum
Agresteis docuere cavas inflare cicutas,
Inde minutatim dulceis didicere querelas,
Tibia quas fundit digitis pulsata canentum.

or they might also take that Hint from some Thing that might happen accidentally to them in their handling of Corn-stalks or the hollow Stems of other Plants. And other Kinds of Instruments were probably formed by such like Accidents: There were so many Uses for Chords or Strings, that Men could not but very soon observe their various Sounds, which might give Rise to stringed Instruments: And for the pulsatile Instruments, as Drums and Cymbals, they might arise from the Observation of the hollow Noise of concave Bodies. To make this Account of the Invention of Instruments more probable, *Kircher* bids us consider, That the first Mortals living a pastoral Life, and being constantly in the Fields, near Rivers and among Woods, could not be perpetually idle; 'tis probable therefore, says he, That the Invention of Pipes and Whistles was owing to their Diversions and

and Exercises on these Occasions; and because Men could not be long without having Use for Chords of various Kinds, and variously bent, these, either by being exposed to the Wind, or necessarily touched by the Hand, might give the first Hint of stringed Instruments; and because, even in the first simple Way of Living, they could not be long without some *fabrile* Arts, this would give Occasion to observe various Sounds of hard and hollow Bodies, which might raise the first Thought of the *pulsatile* Instruments; hence he concludes that *Musick* was among the first Arts.

IF we consider *next*, the Opinion of those that are Ancients to us, who yet were too far from the Beginning of Things to know them any other way than by Tradition and probable Conjecture; we find an universal Agreement in this Truth, That *Musick* is as ancient as the World it self, for this very Reason, that it is natural to Mankind. It will be needless to bring many Authorities, one or Two shall serve: *Plutarch* in his *Treatise of Musick*, which is nothing but a Conversation among Friends, about the Invention, Antiquity and Power of *Musick*, makes one ascribe the Invention to *Amphion* the Son of *Jupiter* and *Antiopa*, who was taught by his Father; but in the Name of another he makes *Apollo* the Author, and to prove it, alledges all the ancient Statues of this God, in whose Hand a musical Instrument was always put. He adduces many Examples to prove the natural Influence *Musick* has upon the

the Mind of Man, and ſince he makes no leſs than a *God* the Inventor of it, and the *Gods* exiſted before Men, 'tis certain he means to prove, both by Tradition and the Nature of the Thing, that it is the moſt ancient as well as the moſt noble Science. *Quintilian* (*Lib.* 1. *Cap.* 11.) alledges the Authority of *Timagenes* to prove that *Muſick* is of all the moſt ancient Science; and he thinks the Tradition of its Antiquity is ſufficiently proven by the ancient *Poets*, who repreſent *Muſicians* at the Table of *Kings*, ſinging the Praiſes of the Gods and Heroes. *Homer* ſhews us how far *Muſick* was advanced in his Days, and the Tradition of its yet greater Antiquity, while he ſays it was a Part of his Hero's Education. The Opinion of the divine Original and Antiquity of Muſick, is alſo proven by the Fable of the Muſes, ſo univerſal among the Poets; and by the Diſputes among the Greek Writers concerning the firſt Authors, ſome for *Orpheus*, ſome for *Amphion*, ſome for *Apollo*, &c. As the beſt of the Philoſophers own'd the Providence of the Gods, and their particular Love and Benevolence to Mankind, ſo they alſo believed that *Muſick* was from the Beginning a peculiar Gift and Favour of Heaven; and no Wonder, when they looked upon it as neceſſary to aſſiſt the Mind to a raiſed and exalted Way of praiſing the Gods and good Men.

I ſhall add but one Teſtimony more, which is that of the *ſacred Writings*; where *Jubal* the Sixth from *Adam*, is called *the Father*

ther of ſuch as handle the Harp and Organ; whether this ſignifies that he was the Inventor, or one who brought theſe Inſtruments to a good Perfection, or only one who was eminently skilled in the Performance, we have ſufficient Reaſon to believe that *Muſick* was an Art long before his Time; ſince it is rational to think that *vocal Muſick* was known long before *Inſtrumental*, and that there was a gradual Improvement in the Art of modulating the Voice; unleſs *Adam* and his Sons were inſpired with this Knowledge, which Suppoſition would prove the Point at once. And if we could believe that this Art was loſt by the Flood, yet the ſame Nature remaining in Man, it would ſoon have been recovered; and we find a notable Inſtance of it in the Song of Praiſe which the *Iſraelites* raiſed with their Voices and Timbrels to GOD, for their Deliverance at the *Red Sea*; from which we may reaſonably conjecture it was an Art well known, and of eſtabliſhed Honour long before that Time.

IT may be expected I ſhould, in this Place, give a more particular Hiſtory of the *Inventors* of *Muſick* and *muſical Inſtruments*, and other famous *Muſicians* ſince the Flood. As to the Invention, I think there is enough ſaid already to ſhow that *Muſick* is natural to Mankind; and therefore inſtead of *Inventors*, the Enquiry ought properly to be about the *Improvers* of it; and I own it would come in very naturally here: But the Truth is, we have ſcarce any Thing left

left us we can depend upon in this Matter; or at leaſt we have but very general Hints, and many of them contrary to each other, from Authors that ſpeak of theſe Things in a tranſient Manner: And as we have no Writings of the Age in which *Muſick* was firſt reſtored after the Flood, ſo the Accounts we have are ſuch uncertain Traditions, that no Two Authors agree in every Thing. *Greece* was the Country in *Europe* where Learning firſt flouriſhed; and tho' we believe they drew from other Fountains, as *Egypt* and the more Eaſtern Parts, yet they are the Fountains to us, and to all the Weſtern World: Other Antiquities we neither know ſo well, nor ſo much of, at leaſt of ſuch as have any Pretence to a greater Antiquity; except the *Jewiſh*; and tho' we are ſure they had *Muſick*, yet we have no Account of the Inventors among them, for 'tis probable they learned it in *Egypt*; and therefore this Enquiry about the *Inventors* of *Muſick* ſince the Flood, muſt be limited to *Greece*. PLUTARCH, JULIUS POLLUX, ATHENEUS, and a few more, are the Authorities we have principally to truſt to, who take what they ſay from other more ancient Authors of their Tradition. I hope to be forgiven if I am very ſhort in the Account of Things of ſuch Uncertainty.

AMPHION, the *Theban*, is by ſome reckoned the moſt ancient *Muſician* in *Greece*, and the Inventor of it, as alſo of the *Lyra*. Some ſay *Mercury* taught him, and gave him a *Lyre* of Seven Strings. He is ſaid to be the firſt who

taught

taught to play and ſing together. The Time he lived in is not agreed upon.

CHIRON the *Pelithronian*, reckoned a *Demigod*, the Son of *Saturn* and *Phyllira*, is the next great Maſter; the Inventor of Medicine; a famous *Philoſopher* and *Muſician*, who had for his Scholars *Æſculapius*, *Jaſon*, *Hercules*, *Theſeus*, *Achilles*, and other Heroes.

DEMODOCUS is another celebrated *Muſician*, of whom already.

HERMES, or MERCURY TRISMEGISTUS, another *Demigod*, is alſo reckoned amongſt the Inventors or Improvers of *Muſick* and of the *Lyra*.

LINUS was a famous *Poet* and *Muſician*. Some ſay he taught *Hercules*, *Thamyris* and *Orpheus*, and even *Amphion*. To him ſome aſcribe the Invention of the *Lyra*.

OLYMPUS the *Myſian* is another Benefactor to *Muſick*; he was the Diſciple of *Marſyas* the Son of *Hyagnis* the *Phrygian*; this *Hyagnis* is reckoned the Inventor of the *Tibiæ*, which others aſcribe to the Muſe *Euterpe*, as *Horace* inſinuates, -- *Si neque tibias* Euterpe *cohibet*.

ORPHEUS the *Thracian* is alſo reckoned the Author, or at leaſt the Introducer of various Arts into *Greece*, among which is *Muſick*; he pactiſed the *Lyra* he got from *Mercury*. Some ſay he was Maſter to *Thamyris* and *Linus*.

PHEMIUS of *Ithaca*. *Ovid* uſes his Name for any excellent Muſician; *Homer* alſo names him honourably.

TER-

TERPANDER the *Lesbian*, liv'd in the Time of *Lycurgus*, and ſet his Laws to *Muſick*. He was the firſt who among the *Spartans* applied *Melody* to *Poems*, or taught them to be ſung in regular Meaſures. This is the famous *Muſician* who quelled a Sedition at *Sparta* by his *Muſick*. He and his Followers are ſaid to have firſt inſtituted the *muſical Modes*, uſed in ſinging Hymns to the *Gods*; and ſome attribute the Invention of the *Lyre* to him.

THALES the *Cretan* was another great Maſter, honourably entertain'd by the *Lacedemonians*, for inſtructing their Youth. Of the Wonders he wrought by his Muſick, we ſhall hear again.

THAMYRIS the *Thracian* was ſo famous, that he is feigned to have contended with the *Muſes*, upon Condition he ſhould poſſeſs all their Power if he overcame, but if they were Victors he conſented to loſe what they pleaſed; and being defeat, they put out his Eyes, ſpoiled his Voice, and ſtruck him with Madneſs. He was the firſt who uſed *inſtrumental Muſick* without Singing.

THESE are the remarkable Names of *Muſicians* before *Homer*'s Time, who himſelf was a *Muſician*; as was the famous Poet *Pindar*. You may find the Characters of theſe mentioned at more large, in the firſt Book of *Fabritius*'s *Bibliotheca Græca*.

WE find others of a later Date, who were famous in *Muſick*, as *Laſus Hermionenſis*, *Melanippides*, *Philoxenus*, *Timotheus*, *Phrynnis*, *Epi-*

Epigonius, *Lyſander*, *Simmicus*, *Diodorus* the *Theban*; who were Authors of a great Variety and luxurious Improvements in *Muſick*. *Laſus*, who lived in the Time of *Darius Hyſtaſpes*, is reckoned the firſt who ever wrote a Treatiſe upon *Muſick*. *Epigonius* was the Author of an Inſtrument called *Epigonium*, of 40 Strings; he introduced Playing on the *Lyre* with the Hand without a *Plectrum* ; and was the firſt who joyned the *Cithara* and *Tibia* in one Concert, altering the Simplicity of the more ancient *Muſick*; as *Lyſander* did by adding a great many Strings to the *Cithara*. *Simmicus* alſo invented an Inſtrument called *Simmicium* of 35 Strings. *Diodorus* improved the *Tibia*, which at firſt had but Four Holes, by contriving more Holes and Notes.

TIMOTHEUS, for adding a String to his *Lyre* was fined by the *Lacedemonians*, and the String ordered to be taken away. Of him and *Phrynnis*, the Comic Poet *Pherecrates* makes bitter Complaints in the Name of *Muſick*, for corrupting and abuſing her, as *Plutarch* reports: For, among others, they chiefly had completed the Ruin of the ancient ſimple *Muſick*, which, ſays *Plutarch*, was nobly uſeful in the Education and forming of Youth, and the Service of the *Temples*, and uſed principally to theſe Purpoſes, in the ancient Times of greateſt Wiſdom and Virtue ; but was ruined after theatrical Shews came to be ſo much in Faſhion, ſo that ſcarcely the Memory of theſe ancient Modes remained in his Time. You ſhall have ſome

Account

Account afterwards of the ancient Writers of *Musick.*

As we have but uncertain Accounts of the Inventors of *musical Instruments* among the Ancients, so we have as imperfect an Account of what these Instruments were, scarce knowing them any more than by Name. The general Division of Instruments is into *stringed* Instruments, *Wind* Instruments and the *pulsatile* Kind; of this last we hear of the *Tympanum* or *Cymbalum*, of the Nature of our Drum; the *Greeks* gave it the last Name from its Figure, resembling a Boat.

There were also the *Crepitaculum*, *Tintinabulum*, *Crotalum*, *Sistrum*; but, by any Accounts we have, they look rather like Childrens Rattles and Play Things than *musical Instruments*.

Of *Wind*-instruments we hear of the *Tibia*, so called from the Shank-bone of some Animals, as Cranes, of which they were first made. And *Fistula* made also of Reeds. But these were afterwards made of Wood and also of Mettal. How they were blown, whether as *Flutes* or *Hautboys* or otherwise, and which the one Way, and which the other, is not sufficiently manifest. 'Tis plain, some had Holes, which at first were but few, and afterwards increased to a greater Number; some had none. Some were single Pipes, and some a Combination of severals, particularly Pan's *Syringa*, which consisted of Seven Reeds joyned together side-

ſideways; they had no Holes, each giving but one Note, in all Seven diſtinct Notes; but at what mutual Diſtances is not very certain, tho' perhaps they were the Notes of the natural or *diatonick Scale*; but by this Means they would want an 8*ve*, and therefore probably otherwiſe conſtituted. Sometimes they played on a ſingle Pipe, ſometimes on Two together, one in each Hand. And leſt we ſhould think there could little *Muſick* be expreſt by one Hand, *Iſ. Voſſius* alledges, they had a Contrivance by which they made one Hole expreſs ſeveral Notes, and cites a Paſſage of *Arcadius* the Grammarian to prove it: That Author ſays, indeed, that there were Contrivances to ſhut and open the Holes, when they had a Mind, by Pieces of Horn he calls *Bombyces* and *Opholmioi* (which *Julius Pollux* alſo mentions as Parts of ſome Kind of *Tibiæ*) turning them upwards or downwards, inwards or outwards: But the Uſe of this is not clearly taught us, and whether it was that the ſame Pipe might have more Notes than Holes, which might be managed by one Hand: Perhaps it was no more than a like Contrivance in our common Bagpipes, for tuning the Drones to the *Key* of the Song. We are alſo told that *Hyagnis* contrived the joyning of Two Pipes, ſo that one Canal conveyed Wind to both, which therefore were always ſounded together.

We hear alſo of *Organs*, blown at firſt by a Kind of Air-pump, where alſo Water was ſome way uſed, and hence called *Organum Hydraulicum*; but afterwards they uſed Bellows. *Vitruvius*

vius has an obſcure Deſcription of it, which *Iſ. Voſſius* and *Kircher* both endeavour to clear.

THERE were *Tubæ*, and *Cornua*, and *Litui*, of the Trumpet Kind, of which there were different Species invented by different People. They talk of ſome Kind of *Tubæ*, that without any Art in the *Modulation*, had ſuch a prodigious Sound, that was enough to terrify one.

OF *ſtringed Inſtruments* the firſt is the *Lyra* or *Cithara* (which ſome diſtinguiſh :) *Mercury* is ſaid to be Inventor of it, in this Manner; after an Inundation of the *Nile* he found a dead Shell-fiſh, which the *Greeks* call *Chelone*, and the *Latins Teſtudo*; of this Shell he made his *Lyre*, mounting it with Seven Strings, as *Lucian* ſays; and added a Kind of *jugum* to it, to lengthen the Strings, but not ſuch as our Violins have, whereby one String contains ſeveral Notes; by the common Form this *jugum* ſeems no more than Two diſtinct Pieces of Wood, ſet parallel, and at ſome Diſtance, but joyn'd at the farther End, where there is a Head to receive Pins for ſtretching the Strings. *Boethius* reports the Opinion of ſome that ſay, the *Lyra Mercurii* had but Four Strings, in Imitation of the mundane *Muſick* of the Four Elements: But *Diodorus Siculus* ſays, it had only Three Strings, in Imitation of the Three Seaſons of the Year, which were all the ancient *Greeks* counted, *viz.* Spring, Summer and Winter. *Nicomachus*, *Horace*, *Lucian* and others ſay, it had Seven Strings, in Imitation of the Seven Planets. Some reconcile *Diodorus*

dorus

odorus, with the laſt, thus, they ſay the more ancient *Lyre* had but Three or Four Strings, and *Mercury* added other Three, which made up Seven. *Mercury* gave this Seven-ſtringed *Lyre* to *Orpheus*, who being torn to Pieces by the *Bacchanals*, the *Lyre* was hung up in *Apollo*'s Temple by the *Lesbians*: But others ſay, *Pythagoras* found it in ſome Temple of *Egypt*, and added an eighth String. *Nicomachus* ſays, *Orpheus* being killed by the *Thracian* Women, for contemning their Religion in the *Bacchanalian* Rites, his *Lyre* was caſt into the Sea, and thrown up at *Antiſſa* a City of *Leſbos*; the Fiſhers finding it gave it to *Terpander*, who carrying it to *Egypt*, gave it to the Prieſts, and call'd himſelf the Inventor. Thoſe who call it Four-ſtring'd, make the Proportions thus, betwixt the *1ſt* and *2d*, the *Interval* of a *4th*, 3 : 4, betwixt the *2d* and *3d*, a *Tone* 8 : 9, and betwixt the 3*d* and 4*th* String another 4*th*: The Seven Strings were *diatonically* diſpoſed by *Tones* and *Semitones*, and *Pythagoras*'s eighth String made up the *Octave*.

The Occaſion of aſcribing the Invention of this Inſtrument to ſo many Authors, is probably, that they have each in different Places invented Inſtruments much reſembling other. However ſimple it was at firſt, it grew to a great Number of Strings; but 'tis to no Purpoſe to repete the Names of theſe who are ſuppoſed to have added new Strings to it.

From this Inſtrument, which all agree to be firſt of the ſtringed Kind in *Greece*, aroſe a Multitude

titude of others, differing in their Shape and Number of Strings, of which we have but indistinct Accounts. We hear of the *Psalterium, Trigon, Sambuca, Pectis, Magadis, Barbiton, Testudo* (the Two last used by *Horace* promiscuously with the *Lyra* and *Cithara*) *Epigonium, Simmicium, Pandura*, which were all struck with the Hand or a *Plectrum*; but it does not appear that they used any Thing like the Bows of Hair we have now for Violins, which is a most noble Contrivance for making long and short Sounds, and giving them a thousand Modifications 'its impossible to produce by a *Plectrum.*

Kircher also observes, that in all the ancient Monuments, where Instruments are put in the Hands of *Apollo* and the Muses, as there are many of them at *Rome* says he, there is none to be found with such a *jugum* as our Violins have, whereby each String has several Notes, but every String has only one Note: And this he makes an Argument of the Simplicity and Imperfection of their Instruments. Besides several Forms of the *Lyra* Kind, and some *Fistulæ*, he is positive they had no Instruments worth naming. He considers how careful they were to transmit, by Writing and other Monuments, their most trifling Inventions, that they might not lose the Glory of them; and concludes, if they had any Thing more perfect, we should certainly have heard of it, and had it preserved, when they were at Pains to give us the Fi-

gure

gure of their trifling Reed-pipes, which the Shepherds commonly uſed. But indeed I find ſome Paſſages, that cannot be well underſtood, without ſuppoſing they had Inſtruments in which one String had more than one Note: Where *Pherecrates* (already mention'd) makes *Muſick* complain of her Abuſes from *Timotheus*'s Innovations; ſhe ſays, he had deſtroyed her who had Twelve *Harmonies* in Five Strings; whether theſe *Harmonies* ſignify ſingle Notes or Conſonances, 'tis plain each String muſt have afforded more than one Note. And *Plutarch* aſcribes to *Terpander* a *Lyre* of Three Chords, yet he ſays it had Seven Sounds, *i. e.* Notes.

I have now done as much as my Purpoſe required. If you are curious to hear more of this, and ſee the Figures of Inſtruments both ancient and modern, go to *Merſennus* and *Kircher*.

---

§ 3. *Of the* Excellency *and various* Uſes *of* Muſick.

THo' the Reaſons alledged for the Antiquity of *Muſick*, ſhew us the Dignity of it, yet I believe it will be agreeable, to enter into a more particular Hiſtory of the Honour *Muſick* was in among the Ancients, and of its various Ends and Uſes, and the pretended Virtues and Powers of it.

The

THE Reputation this Art was in with the *Jewish* Nation, is I suppose well known by the *sacred History*. Can any Thing shew the Excellency of an Art more, than that it was reckoned useful and necessary in the Worship of GOD; and as such, diligently practised and cultivated by a People, separated from the rest of Mankind, to be Witnesses for the Almighty, and preserve the true Knowledge of GOD upon the Earth? I have already mentioned the Instance of the *Israelites* Song, upon their Delivery at the Red Sea, which seems to prove that *Musick* both *vocal* and *instrumental*, was an approven and stated Manner of worshipping GOD: And we cannot doubt that it was according to his Will, for *Moses* the Man of GOD, and *Miriam* the Prophetess, were the Chiefs of this sacred Choir: And that from this Time to that of the Royal Prophet *David*, the Art was honoured and encouraged by them both publickly and privately, we can make no Doubt; for when *Saul* was troubled with an evil Spirit from the LORD, he is advised to call for a cunning Player on the *Harp*, which supposes it was a well known Art in that Time; and behold, *David*, yet an obscure and private Person, being famous for his Skill in *Musick*, was called; and upon his playing, Saul *was refreshed and was well, and the evil Spirit departed from him.* Nor when *David* was advanced to the Kingdom thought he this Exercise below him, especially the religious Use of it. When the *Ark* was brought from *Kirjath-jearim*, David *and* *all*

all Ifrael *played before GOD with all their Might, and with Singing, and with Harps, and with Pfalteries, and with Timbrels, and with Cymbals, and with Trumpets*, 1 Chron. 13. 8. And the Ark being fet up in the City of *David*, what a folemn Service was inftituted for the publick Worfhip and Praife of God; Singers and Players on all Manner of Inftruments, *to minifter before the Ark of the LORD continually, to record, and to thank, and praife the Lord GOD of* Israel. Thefe feem to have beeen divided into Three *Choirs*, and over them appointed Three *Choragi* or Mafters, *Afaph*, *Heman* and *Jeduthun*, both to inftruct them, and to prefide in the Service: But *David* himfelf was the chief *Mufician* and *Poet* of *Ifrael*. And when *Solomon* had finifhed the *Temple*, behold, at the Dedication of it, *the* Levites *which were the Singers, all of them of* Afaph, *of* Heman, *of* Jeduthun, *having Cymbals, and Pfalteries, and Harps, ftood at the Eaft-end of the Altar, praifing and thanking the LORD.* And this Service, as *David* had appointed before the *Ark*, continued in the *Temple*; for we are told, that the King and all the People having dedicated the Houfe to God,—*The Priefts waited on their Offices: the Levites alfo with Inftruments of* Mufick *of the LORD, which* David *the King had made to praife the LORD.*

The Prophet *Elifha* knew the Virtue of *Mufick*, when he called for a Minftrel to compofe his Mind (as is reafonably fuppofed) before *the Hand of the LORD came upon him.*

To

To this I ſhall add the Opinion and Teſtimony of St. *Chryſoſtom*, in his Commentary on the 40*th Pſalm.* He ſays to this Purpoſe, 'That GOD knowing Men to be ſlothful and 'backward in ſpiritual Things, and impatient 'of the Labour and Pains which they require, 'willing to make the Task more agreeable, 'and prevent our Wearineſs, he joyn'd *Melody* 'or *Muſick* with his Worſhip; that as we are 'all naturally delighted with *harmonious* Num-'bers, we might with Readineſs and Cheerful-'neſs of Mind expreſs his Praiſe in ſacred 'Hymns. For, ſays he, nothing can raiſe the 'Mind, and, as it were, give Wings to it, free 'it from Earthlineſs, and the Confinement 'tis 'under by Union with the Body, inſpire it with 'the Love of Wiſdom, and make every thing 'pertaining to this Life agreeable, as well mo-'dulated Verſe and divine Songs *harmoniouſly* 'compoſed. Our Natures are ſo delighted with '*Muſick*, and we have ſo great and neceſſary 'Inclination and Tendency to this Kind of Plea-'ſure, that even Infants upon the Breaſt are 'ſoothed and lulled to Reſt by this means. A-gain he ſays, 'Becauſe this Pleaſure is ſo fami-'liar and connate with our Minds, that we 'might have both Profit and Pleaſure, GOD 'appointed Pſalms, that the Devil might not 'ruine us with prophane and wicked Songs. And tho' there be now ſome Difference of Opinion about its Uſe in ſacred Things, yet all Chriſtians keep up the Practice of ſinging Hymns and Pſalms, which is enough to confirm the ge-neral

neral Principle of *Musick*'s Suitableness to the Worship of GOD.

IN St. *John*'s Vision, the Elders are represented with *Harps* in their Hands; and tho' this be only representing Things in Heaven, in a Way easiest for our Conception, yet we must suppose it to be a Comparison to the best Manner of worshipping GOD among Men, with respect at least to the Means of composing and raising our Minds, or keeping out other Ideas, and thereby fitting us for entertaining religious Thoughts.

LET us next consider the Esteem and Use of it among the ancient *Greeks* and *Romans*. The Glory of this Art among them, especially the *Greeks*, appears first, according to the Observation of *Quintilian*, by the Names given to the *Poets* and *Musicians*, which at the Begining were generally the same Person, and their Characters thought to be so connected, that the Names were reciprocal; they were called *Sages* or *Wisemen*, and the *inspired*. *Salmuth* on *Pancirollus* cites *Aristophanes* to prove, that by *citharæ callens*, or one that was skilled in playing on the *Cithara*, the Ancients meant a Wiseman, who was adorned with all the Graces; as they reckoned one who had no Ear or Genius to *Musick*, stupid, or whose Frame was disordered, and the Elements of his Composition at War among themselves. And so high an Opinion they had of it, that they thought no Industry of Man could attain to such an excellent Art; and hence they believed this Faculty

to

to be an Inſpiration from the Gods; which alſo appears particularly by their making *Apollo* the Author of it, and then making their moſt ancient *Muſicians*, as *Orpheus*, *Linus*, and *Amphion*, of divine Offspring. *Homer*, who was himſelf both *Poet* and *Muſician*, could have ſuppoſed nothing more to the Honour of his Profeſſion, than making the Gods themſelves delighted with it; after the fierce Conteſt that happened among them about the *Grecian* and *Trojan* Affairs, he feigns them recreating themſelves with *Apollo*'s Muſick; and after this, 'tis no Wonder he thought it not below his *Hero* to have been inſtructed in, and a diligent Practiſer of this Godlike Art. And do not the *Poets* univerſally teſtify this Opinion of the Excellency of *Muſick*, when they make it a Part of the Entertainment at the Tables of Kings; where to the Sound of the *Lyre* they ſung the Praiſes of the Gods and Heroes, and other uſeful Things: As *Homer* in the *Odyſſea* introduces *Demodocus* at the Table of *Alcinous*, King of *Phæacea*, ſinging the *Trojan* War and the Praiſes of the Heroes: And *Virgil* brings in *Jopas* at the Table of *Dido*, ſinging to the Sound of his golden *Harp*, what he had learned in natural Philoſophy, and particularly in Aſtronomy from *Atlas*; upon which *Quintilian* makes this Reflection, that hereby the *Poet* intends to ſhew the Connection there is betwixt *Muſick* and heavenly Things; and *Horace* teaches us the ſame Doctrine, when addreſſing his *Lyre*, he cries out, *O decus Phœbi, & dapibus ſupremi, grata teſtudo, Jovis.*

AT the Beginning, *Muſick* was perhaps ſought only for the ſake of innocent Pleaſure and Recreation; in which View *Ariſtotle* calls it the Medicine of that Heavineſs that proceeds from Labour; and *Horace* calls his Lyre *laborum dulce lenimen:* And as this is the firſt and moſt ſimple, ſo it is certainly no deſpicable Uſe of it; our Circumſtances require ſuch a Help to make us undergo the neceſſary Toils of Life more cheerfully. *Wine and Muſick cheer the Heart*, ſaid the wiſe Man; and that the ſame Power ſtill remains, does plainly appear by univerſal Experience. Men naturally ſeek Pleaſure, and the wiſer Sort ſtudying how to turn this Deſire into the greateſt Advantage, and mix the *utile dulci*, happily contrived, by bribing the Ear, to make Way into the Heart. The ſevereſt of the Philoſophers approved of *Muſick*, becauſe they found it a neceſſary Means of Acceſs to the Minds of Men, and of engaging their Paſſions on the Side of Virtue and the Laws; and ſo *Muſick* was made an Handmaid to Virtue and Religion.

JAMBLICHUS in the Life of *Pythagoras* tells us, That Muſick was a Part of the Diſcipline by which he formed the Minds of his Scholars. To this Purpoſe he made, and taught them to make and ſing, Verſes calculated againſt the Paſſions and Diſeaſes of their Minds; which were alſo ſung by a Chorus, ſtanding round one that plaid upon the Lyre, the Modulations whereof

whereof were perfectly adapted to the Design and Subject of the Verses. He used also to make them sing some choice Verses out of *Homer* and *Hesiod.* Musick was the first Exercise of his Scholars in the Morning; as necessary to fit them for the Duties of the Day, by bringing their Minds to a right Temper; particularly he designed it as a Kind of Medicine against the Pains of the Head, which might be contracted in Sleep: And at Night, before they went to rest, he taught them to compose their Minds after the Perturbations of the Day, by the same Exercise.

WHATEVER Virtue the *Pythagoreans* ascribed to *Musick*, they believed the Reason of it to be, That the Soul it self consisted of Harmony; and therefore they pretended by it to revive the primitive Harmony of the Faculties of the Soul. By this primitive Harmony they meant that which, according to their Doctrine, was in the Soul in its pre-existent State in Heaven. *Macrobius*, who is plainly *Pythagorean* in this Point, affirms, That every Soul is delighted with *musical* Sounds; not the polite only but the most barbarous Nations practise *Musick*, whereby they are excited to the Love of Vertue, or dissolved in Softness and Pleasure: The Reason is, says he, That the Soul brings into the Body with it the Memory of the *Musick* which it was entertained with in Heaven: And there are certain Nations, says he, that attend the Dead to their Burial with Singing; because they believe the Soul returns to Heaven the Fountain

or

or Original of *Musick*, *Lib.* 2. in *Somnium Scipionis*. And because this Sect believed the *Gods* themselves to have celestial Bodies of a most perfect harmonious Composition, therefore they thought the *Gods* were delighted with it; and that by our Use of it in sacred Things, we not only compose our Minds, and fit them better for the Contemplation of the *Gods*, but imitate their Happiness, and thereby are acceptable to them, and open for our selves a Return into *Heaven*.

ATHENAEUS reports of one *Clinias* a *Pythagorean*, who, being a very cholerick and wrathful Man, as soon as he found his Passion begin to rise, took up his Lyre and sung, and by this means allayed it. But this Discipline was older than *Pythagoras*; for *Homer* tells us, That *Achilles* was educated in the same manner by *Chiron*, and feigns him, after the hot Dispute he had with *Agamemnon*, calming his Mind with his Song and Lyre: And tho' *Homer* should be the Author of this Story, it shews however that such an Use was made of *Musick* in his Days; for 'tis reasonable to think he had learned this from Experience.

THE virtuous and wise *Socrates* was no less a Friend to this admirable Art; for even in the Decline of his Age he applied himself to the Lyre, and carefully recommended it to others. Nor did the divine *Plato* differ from his great Master in this Point; he allows it in his *Common-wealth*; and in many Places of his Works speaks with the greatest Respect of it, as a most useful Thing in Society;
he

he ſays it has as great Influence over the Mind, as the Air has over the Body; and therefore he thought it was worthy of the Law to take Care of it: He underſtood the Principles of the Art ſo well that, as *Quintilian* juſtly obſerves, there are many Paſſages in his Writings not to be underſtood without a good Knowledge of it. *Ariſtotle* in his *Politicks* agrees with *Plato* in his Sentiments of *Muſick*.

Aristides the Philoſopher and Muſician, in the Introduction to his Treatiſe on this Subject, ſays, 'tis not ſo confined either as to the Subject Matter or Time as other Arts and Sciences, but adds Ornament to all the Parts and Actions of human Life: Painting, ſays he, attains that Good which regards the Eye, Medicine and Gymnaſtick are good for the Body, Dialectick and that Kind helps to acquire Prudence, if the Mind be firſt purged and prepared by *Muſick*: Again, it beautifies the Mind with the Ornaments of Harmony, and forms the Body with decent Motions: 'Tis fit for young ones, becauſe of the Advantages got by Singing; for Perſons of more Age, by teaching them the Ornaments of modulate Diction, and of all Kinds of Eloquence; to others more advanced it teaches the Nature of Number, with the Variety of Proportions, and the Harmony that thereby exiſts in all Bodies, but chiefly the Reaſons and Nature of the Soul. He ſays, as wiſe Husband-men firſt caſt out Weeds and noxious Plants, then ſow the good Seed, ſo Muſick is uſed to compoſe the Mind, and fit it for receiving

receiving Inſtruction: For Pleaſure, ſays he, is not the proper End of Muſick, which affords Recreation to the Mind only by accident, the propoſed End being the inſtilling of Virtue. Again, he ſays, if every City, and almoſt every Nation loves Decency and Humanity, Muſick cannot poſſibly be uſeleſs.

It was uſed at the Feaſts of Princes and Heroes, ſays *Athenæus*, not out of Levity and vain Mirth; but rather as a Kind of Medicine, that by making their Minds cheerful, it might help their Digeſtion: There, ſays he, they ſung the Praiſes of the Gods and Heroes and other uſeful and inſtructive Compoſures, that their Minds might not be neglected while they took Care of their Bodies; and that from a Reverence of the Gods, and by the Example of good Men, they might be kept within the Bounds of Sobriety and Moderation.

But we are not confined to the Authority and Opinion of Philoſophers or any particular Perſons; we have the Teſtimony of whole Nations where it had publick Encouragement, and was made neceſſary by the Law; as in the moſt Part of the *Grecian* Common-wealths.

Athenaeus aſſures us, That anciently all their Laws divine and civil, Exhortations to Vertue, the Knowledge of divine and human Things, the Lives and Actions of illuſtrious Men, and even Hiſtories and mentions *Herodotus*, were written in Verſe and publickly ſung by a *Chorus*, to the Sound of Inſtruments; they found this by Experience an effectual means to im-

impreſs Morality, and a right Senſe of Duty: Men were attentive to Things that were propoſed to them in ſuch a ſweet and agreeable Manner, and attracted by the Charms of harmonious Numbers, and well modulated Sounds, they took Pleaſure in repeating theſe Examples and Inſtructions, and found them eaſier retained in their Memories. *Ariſtotle* alſo in his *Problems* tells us, That before the Uſe of Letters, their Laws were ſung *muſically*, for the better retaining them in Memory. In the Story of ORPHEUS and AMPHION, both of them *Poets* and *Muſicians*, who made a wonderful Impreſſion upon a rude and uncultivated Age, by their virtuous and wiſe Inſtructions, inforced by the Charms of *Poetry* and *Muſick*: The ſucceeding Poets, who turned all Things into Myſtery and Fable, feign the one to have drawn after him, and tamed the moſt ſavage Beaſts, and the other to have animated the very Trees and Stones, by the Power of *Muſick*. *Horace* had received the ſame Traditions of all the Things I have now narrated, and with theſe mentions other Uſes of *Muſick*: The Paſſage is in his Book *de arte Poetica*, and is worth repeating.

Silveſtres homines, ſacer interpreſq; deorum,
Cædibus & victu fædo, deterruit Orpheus:
Dictus ob hoc lenire tigres, rabidoſq; leones:
Dictus & Amphion, Thebanæ conditor arcis,
Saxa movere ſono teſtudinis, & prece blanda
Ducere quo vellet. Fuit hæc ſapientia quondam,
Pub-

Publica privatis secernere, sacra profanis:
Concubitu prohibere vago: dare sacra maritis:
Oppida moliri: leges incidere ligno:
Sic honor, & nomen divinis vatibus, atque
Carminibus venit. Post hos insignis Homerus,
Tyrtæusq; *mares animos in martia bella*
Versibus exacuit. Dictæ per carmina sortes:
Et vitæ monstrata via est: & gratia regum
Pieriis tentata modis: ludusq; repertus,
Et longorum operum finis: ne forte pudori,
Sit tibi musa lyræ solers, & cantor Apollo.

From these Experiences I say, the Art was publickly honour'd by the Governments of *Greece*. It was by the Law made a necessary Part of the Education of Youth. *Plato* assures us it was thus at *Athens*; in his first *Alcibiades*, he mentions to that great Man, in *Socrates*'s Name, how he was taught *to read and write, to play on the Harp, and wrestle.* And in his *Crito*, he says, did not the *Laws* most reasonably appoint that your Father should educate you in *Musick* and *Gymnastick?* And we find these Three *Grammar*, *Musick* and *Gymnastick* generally named together, as the known and necessary Parts of the Education of Youth, especially of the better Sort: *Plutarch* and *Athenæus* give abundant Testimony to this; and *Terence* having laid the Scene of his Plays in *Greece*, or rather only translated, and at most but imitated *Menander*, gives us another Proof, in the *Act* 3. *Scene* 2. of his *Eunuch. Fac periculum in literis, fac in palæstra, in musicis. Quæ liberum scire æquum est adolescentem solertem dabo.*

The

THE Uſe of *Muſick* in the Temples and ſolemn Service of their *Gods* is paſt all queſtion. *Plato* in his *Dialogues* concerning the Laws, gives this Account of the ſacred Muſick. 1*mo*. That every Song conſiſt of pious Words. 2*do*. That we pray to God to whom we ſacrifice. 3*tio*. That the Poets, who know that Prayers are Petitions or Requeſts to the Gods, take good Heed they don't ask Ill inſtead of Good, and do nothing but what's juſt, honeſt, good and agreeable to the Laws of the Society; and that they ſhew not their Compoſitions to any private Perſon, before thoſe have ſeen and approven them who are appointed Judges of theſe Things, and Keepers of the Laws: Then, Hymns to the Praiſes of the Gods are to be ſung, which are very well connected with Prayer; and after the Gods, Prayers and Praiſes are to be offered to the *Dæmons* and *Heroes*.

AS they had poetical Compoſitions upon various Subjects for their publick Solemnities, ſo they had certain determinate *Modes* both in the *Harmonia* and *Rythmus*, which it was unlawful to alter; and which were hence called *Nomi* or *Laws*, and *Muſica Canonica*. They were jealous of any Innovations in this Matter, fearing that a Liberty being allowed, it might be abuſed to Luxury; for they believed there was a natural Connection betwixt the publick Manners and *Muſick*: *Plato* denied that the *muſical Modes* or Laws could be changed without a Change of the publick Laws; he meant, the

In-

Influence of *Musick* was so great, that the Changes in it would necessarily produce a proportional Change of Manners and the publick Constitution.

THE Use of it in *War* will easily be allowed to have been by publick Authority; and the Thing we ought to remark is, that it was not used as a mere Signal, but for inspiring Courage, raising their Minds to the Ambition of great Actions, and freeing them from base and cowardly Fear; and this was not done without great Art, as *Virgil* shews when he speaks of *Misenus*,

— Quo non præstantior alter,
Ære ciere viros, martemque accendere cantu.

FROM *Athens* let us come to *Lacedemon*, and here we find it in equal Honour. Their Opinion of its natural Influence was the same with that of their Neighbours: And to shew what Care was taken by the Law, to prevent the Abuse of it to Luxury, the Historians tell us that *Timotheus* was fined for having more than Seven Strings on his *Lyre*, and what were added ordered to be taken away. The *Spartans* were a warlike People, yet very sensible of the Advantage of fighting with a cool and deliberate Courage; therefore as *Gellius* out of *Thucydides* reports, they used not in their Armies, Instruments of a more vehement Sound, that might inflame their Temper and make them more furious, as the *Tuba*, *Cornu* and *Lituus*, but

but the more gentle and moderate Sounds and Modulations of the *Tibia*, that their Minds being more composed, they might engage with a rational Courage. And *Gellius* tells us, the *Cretans* used the *Cithara* to the same Purpose in their Armies. We have already heard how this People entertain'd at great Expence the famous *Thales* to instruct their Youth in *Musick*; and after their Musick had been thrice corrupted, thrice they restored it.

If we go to *Thebes*, *Epaminondas* will be a Witness of the Esteem it was in, as *Corn. Nepos* informs us.

Athenæus reports, upon the Authority of *Theopompus*, that the *Getan* Ambassadors, being sent upon an Embassy of Peace, made their Entry with *Lyres* in their Hands, singing and playing to compose their Minds, and make themselves Masters of their Temper. We need not then doubt of its publick Encouragement among this People.

But the most famous Instance in all *Greece*, is that of the *Arcadians*, a People, says *Polybius*, in Reputation for Virtue among the *Greeks*; especially for their Devotion to the Gods. *Musick*, says he, is esteem'd every where, but to the *Arcadians* it is necessary, and allowed a Part in the Establishment of their State, and an indispensable Part of the Education of their Children. And tho' they might be ignorant of other Arts and Sciences without Reproach, yet none might presume to want Knowledge in Musick,

ſick, the Law of the Land making it neceſſary; and Inſufficiency in it was reckoned infamous among that People. It was not thus eſtabliſhed, ſays he, ſo much for Luxury and Delight, as from a wiſe Conſideration of their toilſom and induſtrious Life, owing to the cold and melancholy Air of their Climate; which made them attempt every Thing for ſoftning and ſweetning thoſe Auſterities they were condemned to. And the Neglect of this Diſcipline he gives as the Reaſon of the Barbarity of the *Cynæthians* a People of *Arcadia*.

We ſhall next conſider the State of Muſick among the ancient *Romans*. Till Luxury and Pride ruin'd the Manners of this brave Nation, they were famous for a ſevere and exact Virtue. And tho' they were convinced of the native Charms and Force of *Muſick*, yet we don't find they cheriſhed it to the ſame Degree as the *Greeks*; from which one would be tempted to think they were only afraid of its Power, and the ill Uſe it was capable of; a Caution that very well became thoſe who valued themſelves ſo much, and juſtly, upon their Piety and good Manners.

Corn. Nepos, in his Preface, takes Notice of the Differences betwixt the *Greek* and *Roman Cuſtoms*, particularly with reſpect to *Muſick*; and in the Life of *Epaminondas*, he has theſe Words, *Scimus enim muſicum noſtris moribus abeſſe a principis perſona; ſaltare etiam in vitiis poni, quæ omnia apud* Græcos *& gratia & laude digna ducuntur.*

Cice-

CICERO in the Beginning of the firſt Book of his *Tuſculan* Queſtions, tells us, that the old *Romans* did not ſtudy the more ſoft and polite Arts ſo much as the *Greeks*;being more addicted to the Study of Morality and Government: Hence Muſick had a Fate ſomewhat different at *Rome*.

BUT the ſame *Cicero* ſhews us plainly his own Opinion of it. *Lib.* 2. *de Legibus*; *Aſſentior enim* Platoni, *nihil tam facile in animos teneros atque molles influere quam varios canendi ſonos. Quorum dici vix poteſt quanta ſit vis in utramque partem, namque & incitat languentes, & languefacit incitatos, & tum remittit animos, tum contrahit.* Certainly he had been a Witneſs to this Power of Sound, before he could ſpeak ſo; and I ſhall not believe he had met with the Experiment only at *Athens*. A Man ſo famous for his Eloquence, muſt have known the Force of harmonious Numbers, and well proportioned *Tones* of the Voice.

QUINTILIAN ſpeaks honourably of *Muſick*. He ſays, *Lib.* I. *Chap.* II. Nature ſeems to have given us this Gift for mitigating the Pains of Life, as the common Practice of all labouring Men teſtifies. He makes it neceſſary to his Orator, becauſe, ſays he, *Lib.* 8. *Chap.* 4. it is impoſſible that a Thing ſhould reach the Heart which begins with choking the Ear; and becauſe we are naturally pleaſed with Harmony, otherwiſe Inſtruments of Muſick that cannot expreſs Words would not make ſuch ſurpriſing and

and various Effects upon us. And in another Place, where he is proving *Art* to be only Nature perfected, he says, *Musick* would not otherwise be an *Art*, for there is no Nation which has not its *Songs* and *Dances*.

SOME of the first Rank at *Rome* practised it. *Athenæus* says of one *Masurius* a Lawyer, whom he calls one of the best and wisest of Men, and inferior to none in the Law, that he applied himself to Musick diligently. And *Plutarch* places *Musick*, *viz.* singing and playing on the *Lyre*, among the Qualifications of *Metella* the Daughter of *Scipio Metellus*.

MACROBIUS in the 10 *Chap. Lib.* 2. of his *Saturnalia* shews us, that neither Singing nor Dancing were reckoned dishonourable Exercises even for the Quality among the ancient *Romans*; particularly in the Times betwixt the Two *Punick* Wars, when their Virtue and Manners were at the best; providing they were not studied with too much Curiosity, and too much Time spent about them; and observes that it is this, and not simply the Use of these that *Salust* complains of in *Sempronia*, when he says she knew *psallere & saltare elegantius quam necesse erat probæ*. What an Opinion *Macrobius* himself had of *Musick* we have in part shewn already; to which let us add here this remarkable Passage in the Place formerly cited. *Ita denique omnis habitus animæ cantibus gubernatur, ut & ad bellum progressui & etiam receptui canatur, cantu & excitante & rursus sedante virtutem; dat somnos adimitque, nec-*

necnon curas & immittit & retrahit, iram suggerit, clementiam suadet, corporum quoque morbis medetur. Hinc est quod ægris remedia præstantes præcinere dicuntur. The Abuse of it, which 'tis probable lay chiefly in their idle, ridiculous and lascivious Dancing, or perhaps their spending too much Time even in the most innocent Part of it, and not applying it to the true Ends, made the wiser Sort cry out, and brought the Character of a *Musician* into some Discredit. But we find that the true and proper *Musick* was still in Honour and Practice among them: Had *Rome* ever such Poets, or were they ever so honoured as in *Augustus*'s Reign? *Horace*, tho' he complains of the Abuse of the Theatre and the *Musick* of it, yet in many Places he shews us, that it was then the Practice to sing Verses or *Odes* to the Sound of the *Lyre*, or of *Pipes*, or of both together; *Lib.* 4. *Ode* 9. *Verba loquor socianda chordis. Lib.* 2. *Ep.* 2. *Hic ego verba lyræ motura sonum connectere digner?* In the first *Ode*, *Lib.* 1. he gives us his own Character as a Poet and *Musician*, *Si neque tibias* Euterpe *cohibet, &c.* He shews us that it was in his Time used both publickly in the Praise of the *Gods* and Men, and privately for Recreation, and at the Tables of the Great, as we find clearly in these Passages. *Lib.* 4. *Ode* 11. *Condisce modos amanda voce quos reddas, minuentur atræ carmine curæ.* Lib. 3. Ode 28. *Nos cantabimus invicem* Neptunum, *tu curva recines lyra* Latonam, *&c.* Lib. 4. Ode 15. *Nosque & profestis lucibus & sacris - Rite*

Deos

Deos prius adprecati, virtute functos more patrum duces, Lydis *remisto carmine tibiis* Trojamque, *&c. canemus.* Epode 9. *Quando repostum cæcubum ad festas dapes tecum. – Beate* Mecænas *bibam? Sonante mistis tibiis carmen lyra.* Lib. 3. Ode 11. *Tuque testudo – Nunc & divitum mensis & amica templis.*

FOR all the Abuses of it, there were still some, even of the best Characters, that knew how to make an innocent Use of it: *Sueton* in *Titus*'s Life, whom he calls *Amor ac deliciæ generis humani*, among his other Accomplishments adds, *Sed ne* Musicæ *quidem rudis, ut qui cantaret & psalleret jucunde scienterque.*

THERE is enough said to shew the real Value and Use of *Musick* among the Ancients. I believe it will be needless to insist much upon our own Experience; I shall only say, these Powers of *Musick* remain to this Day, and are as universal as ever. We use it still in *War* and in *sacred Things*, with Advantages that they only know who have the Experience. But in common Life almost every Body is a Witness of its sweet Influences.

WHAT a powerful Impression musical Sounds make even upon the *Brute* Animals, especially the feathered Kind, we are not without some Instances. But how surprising are the Accounts we meet with among the old Writers? I have reserved no Place for them here. You may see a Variety of Stories in *Ælian*'s History of Animals;

mals, *Strabo*, *Pliny*, *Marcianus Capella*, and others.

BEFORE I leave this, I muſt take Notice of ſome of the extraordinary Effects a cribed to *Muſick*. *Pythagoras* is ſaid to have had an abſolute Command of the human Paſſions, to turn them as he pleaſed by *Muſick*: They tell us, that meeting a young Man who in great Fury was running to burn his Rival's Houſe, *Pythagoras* allayed his Temper, and diverted the Deſign, by the ſole Power of *Muſick*. The Story is famous how *Timotheus*, by a certain Strain or Modulation, fired *Alexander's* Temper to that Degree, that forgetting himſelf, in a warlike Rage he killed one of the Company; and by a Change of the *Muſick* was ſoftned again, even to a bitter Repentance of what he had done. But *Plutarch* ſpeaks of one *Antigenides* a *Tibicen* or Piper, who by ſome warlike Strain had tranſported that *Hero*, ſo far that he fell upon ſome of the Company. *Terpander* quelled a Sedition at *Sparta* by means of *Muſick*. *Thales* being called from *Crete*, by Advice of the Oracle, to *Sparta*, cured a raging Peſtilence by the ſame Means. The Cure of Diſeaſes by *Muſick* is talked of with enough of Confidence. *Aulus Gellius Lib.* 4. *Chap.* 13. tells us it was a common Tradition, that thoſe who were troubled with the *Sciatica* (he calls them *Iſchiaci*) when their Pain was moſt exquiſite, were eaſed by certain gentle Modulations of *Muſick* performed upon the *Tibiæ*; and ſays, he had read in *Theophraſtus* that, by certain artful Modu-

Modulations of the ſame Kind of Inſtrument, the Bites of Serpents or Vipers had been cured. *Clytemneſtra* had her vicious Inclinations to Unchaſtity corrected by the Applications of *Muſicians*. And a virtuous Woman is ſaid to have diverted the wicked Deſign of two Rakes that aſſaulted her, by ordering a Piece of *Muſick* to be performed in the *Spondean* Mode. The Truth and Reality of theſe Effects ſhall be conſidered afterwards.

---

§ 4. *Explaining the* HARMONICK Principles *of the* Ancients; *and their* Scale *of* Muſick.

Indroduction. *Of the ancient Writers on* Muſick.

THESE Principles are certainly to be found no where, but among thoſe who have written profeſſedly upon the Subject; I ſhall therefore introduce what I'm to deliver, with a ſhort Account of the ancient Writers upon *Muſick*.

I have already obſerved, that the firſt Writer upon *Muſick* was *Laſus Hermionenſis*; but his Work is loſt, as are the Works of very many more, both *Greek* and *Latin*, of which you'll find a large Catalogue in the 3*d* Book of *Fabritius*'s *Bibliotheca græca*; where you'll alſo find an Account of ſome others, that are pretended to be ſtill in Manuſcript in ſome Libraries.

ries. Here I ſhall only ſay a few Words concerning theſe Authors that are ſtill extant and already made publick.

ARISTOXENUS the Diſciple of *Ariſtotle*, is the eldeſt Writer extant on this Subject; he calls his Book *Elements* of *Harmonicks*; and tho' in his *Diviſion* he ſpeaks of the reſt of the Parts, yet he explains there only the *Harmonica*. He wrote a Treatiſe upon the other Parts, which is loſt.

EUCLID, the Author of the *Elements* of *Geometry*, is next to *Ariſtoxenus*, he writes an *Introduction* to *Harmonicks*.

ARISTIDES QUINTILIANUS wrote after *Cicero*'s Time; he calls his Book, *Of Muſick*, becauſe he treats of both the *Harmonica* and *Rythmica*.

ALYPIUS ſtands next, who writes only an Account of the Greek *Semeiotica*, or of the Signs by which the various Degrees of *Tune* were noted in any Song.

GAUDENTIUS the Philoſopher makes a Kind of ſhort Compend of *Ariſtoxenus*, which he calls an *Introduction* to *Harmonicks*.

NICOMACHUS the *Pythagorean* writes a Compend. of *Harmonicks*, which he ſays was done at the Requeſt of ſome great Woman, and promiſes a more complete Treatiſe of *Muſick*. 'tis ſuppoſed that *Boethius* had ſeen and made Uſe of it, from ſeveral Paſſages he cites, which are not in this Compend; but 'tis loſt ſince.

BACCHIUS a Follower of *Ariſtoxenus*, writes a very ſhort *Introduction* to the *Art* of *Muſick* in Dialogue.

OF

OF these Seven *Greek* Authors, we have a fair Copy, with Tranſlation and Notes, by *Meibomius*.

CLAUDIUS PTOLOMAEUS the famous Mathematician, about the Time of the Emperor *Antoninus Pius*, writes in *Greek* Three Books of *Harmonicks*. He ſtrikes a Medium betwixt the *Pythagoreans* and *Ariſtoxenians*, in explaining the *harmonick* Principles. Of this Author, with his prolix Commentator *Porphyrius*, we have a fair Copy with Tranſlations and Notes, by the learned Doctor *Wallis*. Vol. III. of his mathematical Works. And from the ſame Hand we have alſo, with Tranſlation and Notes.

MANUEL BRYENNIUS, long after any of the former, who writes of *Harmonicks*. In his firſt Book he follows *Euclid*, and in his 2*d* and 3*d Ptolomy*.

I have ſpoken of *Plutarch*'s Book de *Muſica*, in the § 1.

OF the *Latins* we have

BOETHIUS, in the Time of *Theodorick* the *Goth*, he writes *de muſica*, but explains only the *harmonick* Principles; 'tis with his other Works.

MARTIANUS CAPELLA in the 9*th* Book of his Treatiſe *de nuptiis Philologiæ & Veneris*, writes *de muſica*, in which he is but a ſorry Copier from *Ariſtides*. We have this Work with *Meibomius*'s Collection of the *Greek* Writers.

St.

St. AUGUSTIN writes *de musica*, but he treats only of the *Rythmi* and *pedes metrici*; 'tis among his Works.

AURELIUS CASSIODORUS, in the Time of *Theodorick*, among his other Works, and particularly *de artibus ac disciplinis liberalium literarum*, treats *de musica*; 'tis a very short Sketch, amounting to no more than some general Definitions and Divisions.

THERE are one or Two more Authors, which I have not seen: But these mentioned contain the whole Doctrine that's left us by the Ancients; and perhaps we might spare severals of these without great Loss, Two or Three of them containing the Whole; so true it is what *Gerhard Vossius* remarks of them, *nempe alii alios illaudato more exscripserunt.*

THESE then are the Authorities and Originals, from which I have taken the following Account of the ancient *System* of *Musick*. It will be needless therefore, after I have told you this, to make a troublesom and tedious Citation for every Thing I mention.

Of the ancient HARMONICA.

HOW the ancient Writers *defined* and *divided* MUSICK has been explained in § 1. of this *Ch.* and needs not be repeted. My Business here is with the Part they called *Harmonica*, which treats of Sounds and their Differences, with respect to *acute* and *grave*. *Ptolomy* calls it *a Power or Faculty perceptive of the Difference*

of

of Sounds, with respect to Acuteneſs *and* Gravity; and *Bryennius* calls it a ſpeculative and practical Science, of the Nature of the *harmonick* Agreement in Sounds.

THEY reduce the Doctrine of *Harmonicks* into Seven Parts, *viz.* 1*ſt.* Of *Sounds.* 2*d.* Of *Intervals.* 3*d.* Of *Syſtems.* 4*th.* Of the *Genera* or different Kinds, with reſpect to the Conſtitution and Diviſion of the *Scale.* 5*th.* Of the *Tones* or *Modes.* 6*th.* Of *Mutations* or *Changes.* 7*th.* Of the *Melopœia* or Art of making *Melody* or Songs. Of theſe in Order.

I. OF SOUND. This *Ptolomy* conſiders in a large Senſe, comprehending the whole Object of Hearing, and calls it by a general Name ψοφος, *i. e. Strepitus*, or any Kind of Sound. As it is capable of a Difference in *Acuteneſs* and *Gravity*, *Ariſtoxenus* calls it Φονὴ, *i. e. Vox*, or Voice. As to the Nature and Cauſe of Sound, they agree that it is the Effect of the Percuſſion of the Air, whoſe Motion is propagated to the Ear, and there raiſes a Perception. The principal Difference they conſider in Sounds is of *Acuteneſs* and *Gravity*, which is produced by a quicker or ſlower Motion in the Vibrations of the Air. A Sound conſidered in a certain determinate Degree of *Acuteneſs* or *Gravity*, they call Φθόγγος, *i. e. Sonus*; and they define it thus, *Ariſtox.* Φωνῆς πτῶσις ἐπὶ μίαν τάσιν, ὁ Φθόγγος, *i. e. Sonus eſt vocis caſus in unam tenſionem. Ariſtides* conſiders it with regard to its Uſe, and calls it τάσιν μελωδικὴν, *tenſionem melodicam. Nicomachus* defines it,

Φωνῆς

φωνῆς ἐμμελῆς ἀπλατῆ τάσιν, *vocis ad cantum aptæ tensionem, latitudinis expertem.* Thus they distinguished Sounds, according as their Degree of *Acuteness* or *Gravity* was fit or not for Song; such as were fit were also called *concinnous* Sounds, and others *inconcinnous*. These Words *wanting Latitude*, were added to contradict a Notion of *Lasus* and the *Epigonians*, that a Voice could not possibly remain for any determinate Time in one Degree, but made continually some little Variations up and down, tho' not very sensible.

THEN they consider a Voice as changing from *acute* to *grave*, or from this to that; and hereby form the Notion of a Motion of the Voice, which they say is Twofold; the one *concinnous*, by which we change the Voice in common Speaking, the other *discrete*, as in Singing. See above *Ch.* 2. And some added a Third and middle Kind, whereby, say they, we read a Poem.

IN Sounds (Φθόγγοι) they consider Three Things, *Tension*, which is the Rest or Standing of the Voice in any Degree, *Intension* and *Remission* are the Motions of the Voice upward and downward, whereby it acquires *Acuteness* or *Gravity*: And when it moves, all the Distance or Difference betwixt the first and last Degree or *Tension*, they called the *Place* thro' which it moved. Then there is *Distension* or Difference of *acute* and *grave*, in which the Quantity that is the mathematical Object consists; this they said is naturally infinite, but with respect either to our Senses, or what Sounds we can

can poſſibly raiſe by any Means, it is limited; and this brings us to the Second Head.

II. OF INTERVALS. An *Interval* is the Difference of Two Sounds, in reſpect of *acute* and *grave*; or, that imaginary Space which is terminated by Two Sounds differing in *Acuteneſs* or *Gravity*. *Intervals* were conſidered as differing, 1*mo*. in Magnitude. 2*do*. As the Extremes were *Concord* or *Diſcord*. 3*tio*. As compoſite or incompoſite, *that is*, ſimple or compound. 4*to*. As belonging to the different *genera* (of which again.) 5*to*. As rational or irrational, *i. e.* ſuch as we can diſcern and meaſure, and which neither exceed our Capacities in Greatneſs or Littleneſs.

AS to the meaſuring of *Intervals*, and, as *Ptolomy* calls it, the *Criterions* in *Harmonicks*, there was a notable Difference among the *Philoſophers*, which divided them into Two Sects, the *Pythagoreans* and *Ariſtoxenians*; betwixt whom *Ptolomy* ſtriking a Midſt, made a Third Sect.

PYTHAGORAS and his Followers meaſured all the Differences of *Acuteneſs* and *Gravity*, by the *Ratios* of Numbers. They ſuppoſed theſe Differences to depend upon the different Velocities of the Motions that cauſe Sound; and thought therefore, that they could only be accurately meaſured by the *Ratios* of theſe Velocities. Which *Ratios* were firſt inveſtigate by *Pythagoras*, as *Nicomachus* and others inform us, in this Manner, *viz*. Paſſing by a Smith's Shop, he perceived a Concord or Agreement betwixt the

the Sounds of Hammers ſtriking the Anvil: He went in, and made ſeveral Experiments, to find upon what the Difference really depended; and at laſt making Experiments upon Strings, which he ſtretched by various Weights, he found, ſay they, that if Four Chords, in every Thing elſe equal and alike, are ſtretched by Four Weights, as 6 . 8 . 9 . 12. they yield the *Concord* of *Octave* betwixt the firſt and laſt, a *4th* betwixt the firſt and Second, as alſo betwixt the Third and laſt, a *5th* betwixt the firſt and Third, and alſo betwixt the Second and laſt; and that betwixt the Second and Third was exactly the Difference of *4th* and *5th*; being all proven by the Judgment of a well tuned Ear: Hence he determined theſe to be the true *Ratios* that accurately expreſs theſe *Intervals*.

BUT we have found an Error in this Account, which *Vincenzo Galileo*, in his Dialogues of the ancient and modern *Muſick*, is, for what I know, the firſt who obſerves; and from him *Meibomius* repetes it in his Notes upon *Nicomachus*. We know, that if Four Strings are in Length, as theſe Numbers 6 . 8 . 9 . 12. (*cæteris paribus*) their Sounds make the *Intervals* mentioned. But whatever *Ratio* of Length makes any *Interval*, to make the ſame by Two Chords, in every other Thing equal, but ſtretcht by different Weights, theſe Weights muſt be as the Squares of the unequal Lengths, *i. e.* for an *Octave* 1 : 4, for a *5th* 4 : 9, and for a *4th* 9 : 16. (See above *Ch.* 2.) Hence by the *Ratios* of the Lengths of Chords, which are reciprocally as the

the Numbers of Vibrations, all the Differences of *acute* and *grave* are meaſured. The *Pythagoreans* juſtly reckoned that the minute Differences could by no means be truſted to the Ear, and therefore judged and meaſured all by *Ratios*.

ARISTOXENUS on the contrary, thought Reaſon had nothing to do in the Caſe; that Senſe was the only Judge; and that the other was too ſubtil, to be of any good Uſe: He therefore took the *8ve*, *5th* and *4th*, which are the firſt and moſt ſimple *Concords* by the Ear. By the Difference of the *4th* and *5th* he found the *Tonus*: And this being once ſettled as an *Interval* the Ear could judge of, he pretended to meaſure every *Interval* by various Additions and Subductions made of theſe mentioned, one with another. Particularly, he calls *Diateſſaron* equal to Two *Tones* and a Half; and taking Two *Tones*, or *Ditonum*, out of *Diateſſaron*, the Remainder is the *Hemitonium*; then the Sum of *Tonus* and *Hemitonium* is the *Triemitonium*. To get an Idea of the Method of bringing out theſe *Intervals*, ſuppoſe Six Sounds *a* : *b* : *c* : *d* : *e* : *f*. If *a* is the loweſt, we can by the Ear take *d* a *4th* and *e* a *5th* upward; then from *e* downward we can take *b* a *4th*, ſo that *a* : *b* and *d* : *e* are each the *Tonus* or Difference of *4th* and *5th*; alſo from *b* we can take upward *f* a *5th*, and downward from *f* a *4th* at *c*; hence we have other Two *Tones* *b* : *c* and *e* : *f*, alſo a *Hemitonium* *c* . *d*, a *Ditonum* *a* - *c* or *d* - *f*, a *Triemitonium* *b* - *d* or *c* - *e*. But

But the Inaccuracy of this Method of determining *Intervals* is very great.

PTOLOMEY argues ſtrongly againſt the laſt Sect, that while they own theſe different Ideas of *acute* and *grave*, which ariſe from the Relations of the Sounds among themſelves; and that the Differences in the Lengths of Chords which yield theſe Sounds, are the ſame; yet they neither know nor enquire into the Relation: But as if the *Interval* were the real Thing, and the Sound the imaginary, they only compare the Differences of the *Intervals*, making by this Means a Shew of doing ſomething in *Muſick* by Number and Proportion; which yet, ſays he, they act contrary to; for they don't determine what every Species is in it ſelf; as we define a *Tone* to be the Difference of Two Sounds which are to one another as 8 : 9; but they ſend us to another Thing as indeterminate, when they call it the Difference of a 4*th* and 5*th*. Whereas if we would raiſe a *Tone* exactly, we need neither 4*th* nor 5*th*. And if we aſk how great that Difference is, they cannot tell us; if perhaps they don't ſay, 'tis equal to Two ſuch Intervals, whereof *Diateſſaron* contains 5, or *Diapaſon* 12, and ſo of the reſt; but what that is they determine not. Again, by conſidering the mere Interval, they do nothing at all; for the mere Diſtance is neither Concord nor concinnous, nor any Thing real; whereas by comparing Two Sounds together we determine the *Ratio* or Relation, and the Quality of their Difference, *i. e.* whether it conſtitutes Concord or or Difcord, by the Form of that *Ratio*. Next, he fhews the Fallacy of *Ariftoxenus*'s Demonftration, whereby he pretended to prove that a *4th* was equal to Two *Tones* and a Half. I need not trouble you with it here; for we have learnt already that a *Tone* 8 : 9 is not divifible into Two equal Parts. But then he alfo finds fault with the *Pythagoreans* for fome falfe Speculations about the Proportions; and having too little Regard to the Judgment of the Ear, while they refufe fome *Concords* that the Ear approves, only becaufe the *Ratio* does not agree with their arbitrary Rule; as we fhall hear immediately.

THEREFORE he would have Senfe and Reafon always taken together in all our Judgments, about Sounds, that they may mutually help and confirm one another. And of all the Methods to prove and find the *Ratios* of Sounds, he recommends as the moft accurate, this, *viz.* to ftretch over a plain Table an evenly well made String, fixt and raifed equally at both Ends, over Two immoveable Bridges of Wood, fet perpendicularly to the Table, and parallel to each other; betwixt them a Line is to be drawn on the Table, and divided into as many equal Parts as you need, for trying all Manner of *Ratios*; then a moveable Bridge runs betwixt the other Two, which juft touches the String, and being fet at the feveral Divifions of the Line, it divides the Chord into any *Ratio* of Parts; whofe Sounds are to be compared together, or with

with the Sound of the Whole. This he calls *Canon Harmonicus*. And those who determined the *Intervals* this Way, were particularly called *Canonici*, and the others by the general Name of *Musici*.

OF CONCORDS. They defined this, An Agreement of Two Sounds that makes them, either successively or jointly heard, pleasant to the Ear. They owned only these Three simple ones, *viz.* the *Fourth* 3 : 4, and *Fifth* 2 : 3 called *Dia-tessaron* and *Dia-pente*, and the *Octave* 1 : 2, which they called *Dia-pason*; the Reason of these Names we shall hear again. Of *compound Concords*, the *Pythagoreans* owned only the Sum of the *5th* and 8*ve* 1 : 3, and the double 8*ve* 1 : 4 or *Dis-dia-pason*, but others owned also the Sum of *4th* and 8*ve*, 3 : 8. The Reason why the *Pythagoreans* rejected the compound *4th*, 3 : 8 was, That they admitted nothing for *Concord* but the *Intervals* whose *Ratios* were *multiple* or *superparticular*, i. e. where the greater Term contained the other a precise Number of Times, as 3 : 1, or where the greater exceeded the lesser only by 1, as 3 : 2 or 4 : 3. because these are the most simple and perfect Forms of Proportion: But *Ptolomy* argues against them from the Perfection of the *Dia-pason*, whereby 'tis impossible that any Sound should be *Concord* to its one Extreme, and Discord to the other. The Extremes *Dia-pason* and *Disdia-pason*, *Ptolomy* calls *Omophoni* or *Unisons*, because they agree as one Sound. The *4th* and *5th* and their Com-

Compounds he calls *Synphoni* or *consonant*; the other *Intervals* belonging to *Musick* he calls *Emmeli* or *concinnous*. Others call those of equal Degree *Omophoni*, the 8*ves* *Antiphoni*, the 4*ths* and 5*ths* *Paraphoni*; others call the 5*ths* only *Paraphoni*, and the 4*ths* *Synphoni*, but all agree to call the Discords *Diaphoni*.

THE abstract Reasonings of the *Pythagoreans* about the *Ratios* of the *Concords*, you have in *Ptolomy*; but more particularly in *Euclid*'s *Sectio Canonis*. The *fundamental Principle* is, That every *Concord* arises either from a *Multiple* or *superparticular Ratio*. The other necessary Premisses are. 1*mo*. That a *multiple Ratio* twice compounded, (*i. e.* multiplied by 2,) makes the Total a *multiple Ratio*. *Euclid* proves it his own Way; but to our Purpose it is shorter done thus $a : ra$, and $ra : rra$, are both *Multiples*, and in the same *Ratio*; then $a : rra$ is the Compound of these Two, and is also *multiple*. 2*do*. The Converse is true, that if any *Ratio* twice compounded makes the total *Multiple*, that *Ratio* is it self multiple. 3*tio*. A *superparticular Ratio*, admits neither of one or more geometrical mean Proportionals: Which I thus demonstrate, *viz.* the Difference of the Terms being 1, 'tis plain there can be no middle Term in whole Numbers; but the first of any Number (^{n}) of *geometrical* Means betwixt a and $a+1$, (which represents any *superparticular Ratio*) is the $\overline{n+1}$ Root of this Quantity $\overline{a}^{n}\times\overline{a+1}$ which being a whole Number, if it have no Root in whole Numbers, cannot have one in

a

a mixt Number, *that is*, can have no Root at all; and consequently there can be no Mean betwixt a and $a+1$. Nor can the Matter be mended by multiplying the Terms of the *Ratio*, as if for $a : a+1$ we take $ra : ra + r$; because if we have not here a *Mean* in whole Numbers, we cannot have it at all; and if we have it in whole Numbers, then all the Series as well as the Extremes, will reduce to radical Terms contrary to the last *Demonstr.* 4*to*. From the 2*d* and 3*d* follows, that a *Ratio* not multiple being twice compounded, the Total is a *Ratio*, neither *multiple* nor *superparticular*. Again, from the 2*d* follows, that if any *Ratio* twice composed make not a *multiple Ratio*, it self is not *multiple*. 5*to*, The *multiple Ratio* 2 : 1 (which is the least and most simple of the Kind) is composed of the Two greatest *superparticular Ratios* 3 : 2 and 4 : 3, and cannot be composed of any other Two that are *superparticular*. From these Premisses the Concords are deduced thus: *Diatessaron* and *Diapente* are *Concords*; and they must be *superparticular Ratios*, for neither of them twice composed makes a *Concord*; the Sum therefore not being *multiple*, the simple *Ratio* is not *multiple*; yet this *Ratio* being *Concord*, must be *superparticular*. *Diapason* and *Disdiapason* are both *Concords*, and they are also *multiple*: The *Disdiapason* cannot be *superparticular*, because it has a *Mean* (which is the *Diapason*,) therefore 'tis *multiple*; and *diapason* is *multiple*, because being twice composed, it makes a *Multiple*, *viz.* the *Disdiapason* *pafon*; then he proves that *Diapafon* is duple 2 : 1. Thus, it cannot be any greater *Multiple* as 1 : 3; for it is compofed of Two *fuperparticulars, viz. Diateffaron* and *Diapente*: But 2 : 1 is compofed of the Two greateft *fuperparticulars* 3 : 2 and 4 : 3. Now if the Two greateft *fuperparticulars* make the leaft Multiple 2 : 1, no other Two are equal to it, and far lefs to a greater; and the 8*ve* being multiple, and compofed of Two *fuperparticulars*, muft therefore be 2 : 1. From this 'tis alfo concluded that *Diateffaron* is 4 : 3, *Diapente* 3 : 2, and *Difdiapafon* 1 : 4; and the reft are deduced from thefe.

DISCORDS are either (*Emmeli*) *concinnous*, i. e. fit for *Mufick*, which is by fome alfo applied to *Concords*, or (*Ecmeli*) *inconcinnous*. Of the *Concinnous* they numbred thefe, *viz. Diefis*, *Hemitonium*, *Tonus*, *Triemitonium*, *Ditonum*. There are different Species of each; and of their Quantities we fhall hear again.

THE *fimple Intervals* are called *Diaftems*, which are different according to the *Genera*, of which below; the *Compound* are called *Syftems*, of which next.

III. OF SYSTEMS. A *Syftem* is an *Interval* compofed, or conceived as compofed, of feveral leffer. As there is no leaft *Interval* in the Nature of the Thing, fo we can conceive any given *Interval* as compofed of, or equal to the Sum of others; but here a *Syftem* is an *Interval* which is actually divided in Practice; and where

where along with the Extremes we conceive always ſome intermediate Terms. As *Syſtems* are only a Species of *Intervals*, ſo they have all the ſame Diſtinctions, except that of *Compoſite* and *Incompoſite*. They were alſo diſtinguiſhed ſeveral other Ways not worth Pains to repeat. But there are Two we cannot paſs over, which are theſe, *viz.* into *concinnous* and *inconcinnous*; the firſt compoſed of ſuch Parts, and in ſuch Order as is fit for *Melody*; the other is of an oppoſite Nature. Then into *perfect* and *imperfect*: Any *Syſtem* leſs than *Diſdiapaſon* was reckoned *imperfect*; and that only called *Perfect*, becauſe within its Extremes are contained Examples of the ſimple and original *Concords*, and in all the Variety of Order, in which their *concinnous* Part ought to be taken; which Differences conſtitute what they call'd the *Species* or *Figuræ conſonantiarum*; which were alſo different according to the *Genera*: It was alſo called the *Syſtema maximum*, or *immutatum*, becauſe they thought it was the greateſt Extent, or Difference of *Tune*, that we can go in making good *Melody*; tho' ſome added a 5*th* to the *Diſdiapaſon* for the greateſt Syſtem; and ſome ſuppoſe Three 8*ves*; but they all owned the *Diapaſon* to be the moſt *perfect*, with reſpect to the Agreement of its Extremes; and that however many 8*ves* we put in the *Syſtema maximum*, they muſt all be conſtituted or ſubdivided the ſame Way as the firſt: And therefore when we know how 8*ve* was divided, we know the Nature of their *Diagramma*, which we now call

call the *Scale of Musick*; the Variety of which constitutes what they called the *Genera melodiæ*, which were also subdivided into *Species*; and these must next be explained.

IV. OF the GENERA. By this Title is meant the various Ways of subdividing the consonant *Intervals* (which are the chief Principles of *Melody*) into their *concinnous* Parts. As the *Octave* is the most perfect Interval, and all other *Concords* depend upon it; so according to the modern *Theory* we consider the Division of this *Interval*, as containing the true Division of the whole Scale: (See above *Chap.* 8.) But the Ancients went to work with this somewhat differently: The *Diatessaron* or *4th* was the least *Interval* they admitted as *Concord*; and therefore they sought first how that might be most concinnously divided; from which they constituted the *Diapente* or *5th*, and *Diapason* or *8ve*: Thus, the Sum of *4th* and *5th* is an *Octave*, and their Difference is a *Tonus*; if therefore to the same Fundamental, suppose *a*, we take a *4th b*, *5th c*, and *8ve d*, then also *b*-*d* is a *5th*, and *c*-*d* a *4th*, and *b*: *c* is the *Tonus*; which they called particularly the *Tonus diazeucticus*, because it separates or stands in the Middle betwixt Two *4ths*, one on either Hand, *a*-*b*, and *c*-*d*. This *Tonus* they reckoned indispensable in rising to a *5th*: And therefore, the Division of the *4th* being made, the Addition of this *Tone* made the *5th*; and adding another *4th*, the same Way divided as the first, completed the *8ve*. Now the *Diatessaron* being

as

as it were the Root or Foundation of their Scale, what they call'd the *Genera* arose from its various Divisions: Hence they defined the GENUS (*modulandi*) *the manner of dividing the* TETRACHORD, *and disposing its four Sounds* (as to their Succession:) And this Definition shews us in general, That the *4th* was divided into *3 Intervals* by two middle Terms, so as to contain 4 Sounds betwixt the Extremes: Hence we have the Reason of the Name *Diatessaron*, (i. e. *per quatuor*;) and because from the *4th* to the *5th* was always the *Tone*, the *5th* contained 5 Notes, and hence called *Diapente* (i. e, *per quinque*:) And with respect to the *Lyra* and its Strings, these Intervals were called *Tetrachordum* and *Pentechordum*. But the *8ve* was called *Diapason*, (as it were *per omnes*) because it contains in a manner all the different Notes of Musick; for after one *Octave* all the rest of the Notes of the Scale were reckoned but as it were Repetitions of it: Yet with respect to the Lyre, it was also called *Octochordum*. The *Disdiapason* and all other Names of this Kind being now plain enough, need not be insisted on: And we shall proceed.

BY universal Consent the *Genera* were Three, *viz.* the *Enharmonick*, *Chromatick* and *Diatonick*. The Reasons of these Names we shall have presently; but the two last were variously subdivided into different *Species*; and even the first, tho' 'tis commonly reckoned to be without any Species, yet different Authors proposed different

ferent Divisions, under that Name, tho' without distinguishing Names of Species, as were added to the other Two.

ARISTOXENUS who measured all by the Ear, expressed his Constitutions of the *Genera* in this Manner: He supposes the *Tonus* (*diazeucticus*) or Difference of the 4*th* and 5*th*, to be divided into 12 equal Parts; which, to prevent Fractions, *Ptolomy*, when he explains them, doubles, and makes 24; so that the whole 4*th* must contain 60 of them. A certain Number of these *imaginary* Intervals he assigned to each of the Three Parts into which the 4*th* is to be divided; and all together made up these Six following Divisions, which I take with the common Latin Names.

		4*th*: *a* -- *b* -- *c* -- *d*.
Enharmonium		6 + 6 + 48 = 60
Chroma.	*Molle*	8 + 8 + 44 = 60
	Hemiolion	9 + 9 + 42 = 60
	Tonicum	12 + 12 + 36 = 60
Diatonum	*Molle*	12 + 18 + 30 = 60
	Intensum	12 + 24 + 24 = 60

IN the *Enharmonium*, suppose *a*, (marked at the Top of the Table) the first and lowest Note of the *Tetrachord*, from that to the 2*d* *b*, is 6 of the Parts mentioned; to the 3*d* *c*, is other 6, and from the 3*d* to the acutest Note *d*, is an Interval equal to 48 of these Parts: In this Manner you can explain all the rest. Six of them he called a *Diesis Enharmonica*; 8 a *Diesis*

Diesis trientalis, 9 a *Diesis quadrantalis*, 12 a *Hemitonium*, 24 a *Tonus*, 36 a *Triemitonium*, and 48 a *Ditonum*; but to measure all these accurately by the Ear was an extravagant Pretence. Let us consider the Divisions that were made by *Ratios*.

Besides some particular *Ratios* of *Archytas*, *Eratosthenes* and *Didymus*, (who were all Musicians) which I pass by, *Ptolomy* gives us an Account of the following 8 Divisions of the *Tetrachord*; where the Fractions express the *Ratio* betwixt each Sound (marked by the Letters standing above) and the next, in order from *a* the lowest, *i. e.* suppose any of the lower Notes *a*, *b* or *c* to be 1. the Fraction betwixt that and the next expresses the Proportion of that next to it.

		Diatessaron. *a* -- *b* -- *c* -- *d.*
Enharmonium		$\frac{45}{46} \times \frac{23}{24} \times \frac{4}{5} = \frac{3}{4}$
Chroma	*Molle* or *Antiquum*	$\frac{27}{28} \times \frac{14}{15} \times \frac{5}{6} = \frac{3}{4}$
	Intensum	$\frac{21}{22} \times \frac{11}{12} \times \frac{6}{7} = \frac{3}{4}$
Diatonum	*Molle*	$\frac{20}{21} \times \frac{9}{10} \times \frac{7}{8} = \frac{3}{4}$
	Tonicum	$\frac{27}{28} \times \frac{7}{8} \times \frac{8}{9} = \frac{3}{4}$
	Ditonicum or *Pythagor.*	$\frac{243}{256} \times \frac{8}{9} \times \frac{8}{9} = \frac{3}{4}$

Diatonum { *Intensum* or *Syntonum* } $\frac{15}{16} \times \frac{8}{9} \times \frac{9}{10} = \frac{3}{4}$
Æquabile. $\frac{11}{12} \times \frac{10}{11} \times \frac{9}{10} = \frac{3}{4}$

THESE different *Species* were alſo called the *Colores* (*Chroai*) *generum* : *Molle* expreſſes a Progreſſion by ſmall Intervals, as *Intenſum* by greater ; the other Names are plain enough. The Two firſt Intervals of the *Enharmonium*, are called each a *Dieſis* ; the Third is a *Ditonum*, and particularly the 3*d g.* already explained. The Two firſt of the *Chromatick* are called *Hemitones*, and the Third is *Triemitonium* ; and in the *Antiquum* it is the 3*d l.* above explained. The firſt in the *diatonick* is called *Hemitonium*, and the other Two are *Tones*; particularly the $\frac{243}{256}$ is called *Limma* (*Pythagoricum*;) $\frac{7}{8}$ is the greateſt of the *Tones*, and $\frac{10}{11}$ the leaſt ; but the $\frac{8}{9}$ and $\frac{9}{10}$ are the *Tonus major* and *minor* above explained.

AS to the Names of the *Genera* themſelves, the *Enharm.* was ſo called as by a general Name ; or ſome ſay for its Excellence (tho' where that lies we don't well know.) The *Diatonum*, becauſe the *Tones* prevail in it. The *Chromatick* was ſo called, ſay ſome, from χρόα *color*, becauſe as Colour is ſomething betwixt Black and White, ſo the *Chrom.* is a *medium* betwixt the other Two.

BUT

But now to what Purpose all these Divisions were contrived, we cannot well learn by any Thing that they have told us. The *Enharm.* was by all acknowledged to be so difficult, that few could practise it, if indeed any ever could do it accurately; and they own much the same of the *Chromatick*. Such Inequalities in the Degrees of the *Scale*, might be used for attacking the Fancy, and humouring some disorderly Motions: But what true Melody could be made of them, we cannot conceive. All acknowledged, that the *Diatonick* was the true Melody which Nature had formed all Mens Ears to receive and be satisfied with; and therefore it was the general Practice; tho' in their Speculations of the Proportions they had the Differences you see in the *Table*. And tho' *Diatonick* was the prevailing Kind, yet still a Question remained among them, Whether it should be *Aristoxenus*'s *Diatonum intensum*, or the *Pythagorick*, which *Eratosthenes* contended for: (But here observe, the *Pythagoreans* departed from their Principles, by admitting the *Limma*, which is neither multiple nor superparticular;) or what *Ptolomy* calls the *Syntonum* or *intensum*, which *Didymus* maintain'd. The *Aristox.* could give no Proof of theirs, because it was impossible for the Ear to determine the Difference accurately: The other Two might be tried and proven by the *Canon harmonicus*; but if they tuned by the Ear, they might dispute on without any Certainty of the Kind they followed. As to the Species we now make

make Uſe of, the ſame may be ſaid; but I ſhall conſider it afterwards.

NOW, theſe Parts of the *Diateſſaron* are what they called the *Diaſtems* of the ſeveral *Genera*, upon which their Differences depend: Which are called in the *Enharm.* the *Dieſis* and *Ditonum*; in the *Chromatick*, the *Hemitonium* and *Triemitonium*; in the *Diaton.* the *Hemitonium* (or *Limma*) and the *Tonus*; but under theſe general Names, which diſtinguiſh the *Genera*, there are ſeveral different *Intervals* or *Ratios*, which conſtitute the *colores generum*, or Species of *Enharm. Chrom.* and *Diatonick*, as we have ſeen: And we are alſo to *obſerve*, that what is a *Diaſtem* in one *genus* is a *Syſtem* in another: But the *Tonus diazeuƈticus* 8 : 9 is eſſential in all the *Kinds*, not as a neceſſary Part of every Tetrachord, but neceſſary in every Syſtem of 8*ve*, to ſeparate the 4*th* and 5*th*, or disjoin the ſeveral *Tetrachords* one from another.

Of the DIAGRAMMA *or* Scale.

WE have already ſeen the eſſential Principles, of which the ancient *Scale* or *Diagramma*, which they called their *Syſtema perfeƈtum*, was compoſed, in all its different Kinds. Let us now conſider the Conſtruction of it; in order to which I ſhall take the *Tetrachords diatonically*. I have already ſaid, that the Extent of it is a *Diſdiapaſon*, or Two 8*ves* in the *Ratio*

tio 1:4.: But in that Space they make Eighteen Chords, tho' they are not all different Sounds. And, to explain it, they represent to us Eighteen Chords or Strings of an Instrument, as the *Lyre*, supposed to be tuned according to the Proportions explained in any one *Genus*. To each of these Chords (or Sounds) they gave a particular Name, taken from its Situation in the *Diagramma*, or also in the *Lyre*; which Names are commonly used by the *Latins* without any Change. They are these, *Proslambanomenos*, *Hypate-hypaton*, *parhypate-hypaton*, *Lichanos-hypaton*, *Hypate-meson*, *parhypate-meson*, *Lichanos-meson*, *Mese*, *Trite-synemmenon*, *Paranete-synemmenon*, *Nete-synemmenon*, *Paramese*, *Trite-diezeugmenon*, *Paranete-diezeugmenon*, *Nete-diezeugmenon*, *Trite-hyperbolæon*, *Paranete-hyperbolæon*, *Nete-hyperbolæon*.

THAT you may understand the Order and Constitution of their *Scale* and the Sense of these Names, take this short History of it. While the *Lyre* was *Tetra.* (or had but Four Strings) these were called in order from the *gravest* Sound *Hypate*, *Parhypate*, *Paranete*, *Nete*; which Names are taken from their Place in the *Diagram*, in which anciently they set the *gravest* uppermost, or their Situation in the *Lyre*, hence called *Hypate*, *i. e. suprema*, (*Chorda*, *scil.*) the next is *parhypate*, *i. e. subsuprema* or *juxta upremam*; then *Paranete*, *i. e. penultima* or *juxta ultimam*, and then *Nete*, *i.e. ultima*, as here.

THIS

Hypate
ſ:
Parhypate
t:
Paranete
t:
Nete

This reſpects the ancient *Lyra*, whoſe Chords were dedicate to, or made ſymbolical of the Four Elements: Which according to ſome contained an 8*ve*, but ſome ſay only a *Diateſſaron* 3 : 4, and the Degrees I have marked by ſ for *Semitone*, and *t* for a *Tone*, without Diſtinction.

Hypate
ſ·
Parhypate
t:
Lichanos
t:
Meſe
ſ:
Trite
t:
Paranete
t:
Note

Next to this ſucceeded the *Septichord Lyre* of *Mercury*, which ſtands thus. *Meſe* is *media*. *Lichanos*, ſo called from the *digitus index* with which the Chord was ſtruck,as ſome ſay, or from its being the *Index* of the *Genus*, according to its Diſtance from *Hypate*;it was alſo called *Hypermeſe*, *i. e. ſupra mediam*. *Trite* ſo called as the Third from *Nete* ; and it is alſo called *Parameſe*, *i. e. juxta mediam*. This contains Two Tetrachords conjunct in *Meſe*, which is common to both, and are particularly called the Tetrachords *Hypaton*, and *Neton* ; ſo that theſe which were formerly Names of ſingle Chords, are now Names of whole Tetrachords; but as yet there was no great Neceſſity for the Diſtinction, as we ſhall ſee afterwards.

Hy-

Hypate	
ſ:	
Parhypate	
t:	
Lichanos	
t:	
Meſe	
t:	
Parameſe	
ſ:	
Trite	
t:	
Paranete	
t:	
Nete	

BUT *Pythagoras* finding the Imperfection of this *Syſtem*, added an 8*th* Chord to complete an 8*ve*: And this he did by ſeparating the Two Tetrachords by the *Tonus diazeucticus*; ſo the Whole ſtood thus. Where we have Two Tetrachords, one from *Hypate* to *Meſe*, and the other from *Parameſe* to *Nete*; the *Tonus diazeucticus* coming betwixt them, *i. e.* betwixt *Meſe* and *Parameſe*. So here *Parameſe* and *Trite* are different Chords, which were the ſame before.

BUT there was another *octichord Lyre* attributed to *Terpander*; where inſtead of disjoining the Two Tetrachords of the *ſeptichord Lyre*, he added another Chord a *Tone* lower than *Hypate*, called *Hyper-hypate*, *i. e. ſuper ſupremam*, becauſe it ſtood above in the *Diagram*; or *Proſlambanomenos*, *i. e. aſſumptus*, becauſe it belonged to none of the Two Tetrachords: The reſt of the Names were unchanged.

OBSERVE, the *ſeptichord Lyre* was made ſymbolical of the Seven Planets. *Hypate* repreſented *Saturn*, with reſpect to his periodical Revolution, which is ſlower than that of any of the reſt, as the graveſt Sounds are always produced by ſloweſt Vibrations, and ſo of the reſt

reſt gradually. But others make *Nete* repreſent *Saturn* with reſpect to his diurnal Motion round the Earth (in the old Aſtronomy) which is the ſwifteſt, as the acuteſt Sounds are alſo produced by quickeſt Vibrations, and ſo of the reſt. When the 8*th* Chord was added, it repreſented the *Cœlum ſtelliferum.*

AFTERWARDS a third Tetrachord was added to the *ſeptichord Lyre*; which was either conjunct with it, making Ten Chords, or disjunct, making Eleven. The Conjunct was particularly diſtinguiſhed by the Name *Synemmenon, i. e. Tetrachordum conjunctarum*; and the other by the Name of *Diezeugmenon, i. e. disjunctarum.* And now the middle Tetrachord was called *Meſon* (*mediarum*;) and to the Words *Hypate*, *Parhypate*, *Lichanos*, *Trite*, *Paranete*, *Nete*, are now added the Name of the Tetrachord, which is neceſſary for Diſtinction; and the Whole ſtands thus,

Tetra. Hyp.	*Hypate, hypaton.*			
	Parhypate, hyp.			
	Lichanos, hyp.			
	Hypate, meſon,			
Meſ.	*Parh, Meſ.*			
	Lich. Meſ.			
	Meſe - - -		*Meſe.*	*Tonus diezeuct.*
Syn.	*Trite Synem.*	*Diezeug.*	*Parameſe*	
	Paranete, Syn.		*Trite Diezeug.*	
	Nete, Syn.		*Paranete Diezeug.*	
			Nete Diezeug.	

At length another Tetrachord was added, called *Hyperbolæon* (*i. e. excellentium* or *excedentium*) the acuteſt of all; which being conjunct with the *Diezeugmenon*, the *Nete Diezeugmenon* was its graveſt Chord, the other Three being called *Trite*, *Paranete*, and *Nete Hyperbolæon*; and now the Four Tetrachords *Hypaton*, *Meſon*, *Diezeugmenon*, *Hyperbolæon*, made in all Fourteen Chords, to which, to complete the *Diſdiapaſon*, a *Proſlambanomenos* was added; all which with the *Trite Paranete*, and *Nete Synemmenon* make up the Eighteen Chords mentioned; which yet are but Sixteen different Sounds, for the *Paranete Syn.* coincides in the *Trite Diez.* as the *Nete Syn.* with the *Paranete Diez.* So that theſe Two differ only in the *Trite Syn.* and *Parameſe* betwixt which there is a *Semitone*. And now ſee the whole *Diagram* together in the following Page; where to favour the Imagination more, inſtead of marking the *Tone* and *Semitone* by *ſ* and *t*. the Chords that have a *Tone* betwixt them are ſet further aſunder than thoſe that have a *Semitone*. At the ſame Time I have annexed the Letters by which the *modern Scale* is above explained, that you may ſee to what Part of that this ancient *Scale* correſponds. And becauſe we place the graveſt Notes in the lower Part of our *Diagram* (as the ancient *Latins* came at laſt to do, tho' they ſtill applied *Hypate* to the *graveſt*, and *Nete* to the *acuteſt*, to prevent Confuſion) I ſhall do it ſo here.

DIA-

DIAGRAMMA VETERUM.

Synemmenon.		
	aa *Nete, Hyperbol.*	*Tetrachor. Hyperbolæon.*
	g *Paranete, Hyperbol.*	
	f *Trite, Hyberbol.*	
	e *Nete, Diezeug.*	
Nete, Synem.	d *Paranete Diezeug.*	*Diezeugmenon.*
Paranete, Syn.	c *Trite, Diezeug.*	
	b *Paramese.*	
Trite, Synem.	♭	
Mese.	a *Mese.*	*Meson.*
	G *Lichanos, Meson,*	
	F *Parhypate, Meson,*	
	E *Hypate, Meson.*	
	D *Lichanos, hypaton.*	*Hypaton.*
	C *Parhypate, hypaton.*	
	B *Hypate, hypaton.*	
	A *Proslambanomenos.*	

YOU ſee, that by twice applying *Hypate*, *Parhypate* and *Lichanos*; alſo *Trite*, *Paranete* and *Nete* Three Times; the Difficulty of too many Names is avoided: And by the Diſtinction of *Tetrachords* with theſe particular Names for the reſpective Chords, 'tis eaſily imagined in what Place of the *Diagram* any Chord ſtands. But if we conſider every *Tetrachord* by it ſelf, then we may apply theſe common Names to its Chords, *viz.* *Hypate*, *Parhypate* (or *Trite*) *Licha-*

Lichanos (or *Paranete*) and *Nete*: And then when Two *Tetrachords* are conjunct, the *Hypate* of the one is the *Nete* of the other, as *Hypate meson* is equivalent to *Nete hypaton*; and in the *Diagram*, *Mese* is the *Nete meson* and the *Hypate synem.* and *Paramese* is the *Hypate diezeug.* And lastly, *Nete diezeug.* is equal to *Hypate hyperbolæon.* We shall know the Use of the *Tetrachord synemmenon*, when we come to explain the Business of their *Mutations.* The Rest of the *Diagram* from *Proslamban.* is a concinnous Series, answering to the *flat Series* of the *diatonick Genus*, explained in the *Ch.* 8. and the Order from *Parhypate hypaton* contains the *sharp Series* above explained. Observe, tho' there are certain *Systems*, particularly distinguished as *Tetrachords*, yet we have *Tetrachords* (*i. e. Intervals* of Four Sounds) in other Parts of the *Scale*, that are true *4ths* 3 : 4. Again, if to any true *4th* a *Tonus diazeug.* is added, we have the *Diapente*, as from *Proslamb.* to *Hypate meson.*

I have explained the *Diagram* in the *diatonick genus*; but the same Names are applied to all the Three *Genera*; and according to the Differences of these, so are the Relations of the several Chords to one another. But since the Constitution of the *Scale* by *Tetrachords* is the same in all, and that the *Genera* differ only in the *Ratios* which the Two middle Chords of the *Tetrachord* bear to the Extremes; therefore these Extremes were called *standing* or *immoveable Sounds* (ἑςῶτες *soni stantes*) and all the middle ones

ones were called *moveable* (κινητοὶ *soni mobiles*) for to raise a Series from a given *Fundamental* or *Proslambanomenos*, the first and last Chord of each *Tetrachord* is invariably the same, or common to every *Genus*; but the middle Chords vary according to the *Genus*. So the *Parhypate* or *Trite*, *Lichanos* or *Paranete* of each *Tetrachord* is variable, and all the rest of the Chords of the *Diagram* are invariable.

THE next Thing to be considered is, what they called the *Figures* or *Species* of the *consonant Systems*, viz. of the *4th*, *5th* and *8ve* (for they extended this Speculation no further than the *simple Concords*.) The *colores generum* differed according to the Difference of the constituent Parts of the *Diatessaron*; but the *figuræ* or *species consonantiarum* differ only according to the Order and Position of the *concinnous* Parts of the *System*: So that in the same *Diagram* (or Series) and under every Difference of *Genus* and *Color*, there are Differences of the *Figuræ*. Now, tho' of a certain Number of different constituent Parts, there will be a certain Number of different Positions or Combinations of the Whole; yet in every *Genus* there is a certain *Diastem* agreed upon to be the *Characteristick*; and according to the Position of this in the *System*, so are the different *Figuræ* reckoned; the Combinations proceeding from the Differences of the other *Diastems* being neglected in this Matter. *Ptolomy* makes the *Characteristick* of the *Diatessaron*, the *Ratio* of the Two *acutest* Chords in every *Genus*; and

of

of the *Diapason*, the *Tonus diezeucticus* But *Euclid* reckons them otherwise, and applies the same Mark to 4*th*, and 5*th* and 8*ve*; thus in the *Enharmonick* the *Ditonum* is the Characteristick; in the *Chromatick* it is the *Triemitonium*; and in the *Diatonick* the *Semitone*. If we take Two conjunct *Tetrachords*, as from *Hypate-hypaton* to *Mese*, we shall find in that all the Figures of the *Diatessaron*, which are only Three; for there are but Three Places of the *Diatessaron* in which the Characteristick can exist; there are Four Figures of the *Diapente* which are to be found in Two disjunct *Tetrachords*, betwixt *Hypate-meson* and *Nete-diezeugmenon*. The 8*ve* is composed of the 4*th* and 5*th*, and the Three Species of 4*th* joined to each of the Four Species of 5*th*, make in all 12 Species of 8*ves*; but we consider here only those Connections of 4*th* and 5*th*, that are actually in the *System*, which are only Seven, to be found from *Proslambanomenos* to *Nete-hyperbolæon*, *i. e.* in the Compass of a *Disdiapason*. *Proslambanomenos* being the lowest Chord of the first 8*ve*, and *Lichanos-meson* of the last 8*ve*; for *Mese* begins another Revolution of the *Diapason*, proceeding the same Way as from *Proslambanomenos*: And because this *System* of *Disdiapason* contains all the Species of the *Concords* it was called *perfect*. And observe, that in every 8*ve* *Euclid's* *Characteristick* occurs twice, and they are always asunder by Two and Three *Dieses*, or *Hemitones*, or *Tones* (according to the *Genus*) alternatively. What was the Order they thought

thought moſt *concinnous* and *harmonious*, we ſhall ſee preſently.

V. Of Tones or Modes. They took the Word *Tone* in four different Senſes. 1. For a ſingle Sound, as when they ſaid the *Lyra* has Seven *Tones*, i. e. Notes. 2. For a certain *Interval*, as the Difference of the 4*th* and 5*th*. 3. For the *Tenſion* of the Voice, as when we ſay, One ſings with an *acute* or a *grave* Voice. 4. For a certain *Syſtem*, as when they ſaid, The *Dorick* or *Lydian Mode*, or *Tone*; which is the Senſe to be particularly conſidered in this Place.

This is the Part of the ancient *Harmonica* which we wiſh they had explained more clearly to us; for it muſt be owned there is an unaccountable Difference among the Writers, in their Definitions, Diviſions and Names of the *Modes*. As to the Definition, I find an Agreement in this, that a *Mode*, or *Tone* in this Senſe, is a certain *Syſtem* or *Conſtitution* of Sounds; and they agree too, that an *Octave* with all its intermediate Sounds is ſuch a Conſtitution: But the ſpecifick Differences of them ſome place in the Manner of Diviſion or Order of its *concinnous* Parts; and others place merely in the *Tenſion* of the Whole, *i. e.* as the whole Notes are *acuter* or *graver*, or ſtand higher and lower in the *Scale* of *Muſick*, as *Bryennius* ſays very expreſly. *Boethius* has a very ambiguous Definition, he firſt tells us, that the *Modes* depend on the Seven different Species of the *Diapaſon*, which are alſo called *Tropi*; and theſe, ſays he, are *Con-*

ſtitu-

ſtitutiones in totis vocum ordinibus, vel gravitate vel acumine differentes. Again he ſays, *Conſtitutio eſt plenum veluti modulationis corpus, ex conſonantiarum conjunctione conſiſtens, quale eſt* Diapaſon, &c. *Has igitur conſtitutiones, ſi quis totas faciat acutiores, vel in gravius totas remittat ſecundum ſupradictas* Diapaſon *conſonantiæ ſpecies, efficiet modos ſeptem.* This is indeed a very ambiguous Determination, for if they depend on the Species of 8*ves*, to what Purpoſe is the laſt Clauſe; and if they differ only by the Tenor or Place of the whole 8*ve*, i. e. as 'tis taken at a higher or lower Pitch, what Need the Species of 8*ves* be at all brought in: His Meaning perhaps is only to ſignify, that the different Orders or Species of 8*ves* ly in different Places, *i. e.* higher and lower in the *Scale*. *Ptolomy* makes them the ſame with the Species of *Diapaſon*; but at the ſame Time he ſpeaks of their being at certain Diſtances from one another. Some contended for Thirteen, ſome for Fifteen *Modes*, which they placed at a *Semitone's* Diſtance from each other; but 'tis plain, theſe underſtood the Differences to be only in their Place or Diſtances one from another; and that there is one certain *harmonious* Species of *Octave* applied to all, *viz.* that Order which proceeds from *Proſlamb.* of the *Syſtema immutatum*, or the *A* of the modern *Syſtem*. *Ptolomy* argues, that if this be all, they may be infinite, tho' they muſt be limited for Uſe and Practice; but indeed the Generality define them by the *Species diapaſon*, and there-

fore

fore make only Seven Modes; but to what they tend, and the true Uſe, is ſcarcely well explained, and we are left to gueſs and reaſon about it; I ſhall conſider them upon both the Suppoſitions, and firſt as they are the Species of *Octaves*, and here I ſhall follow *Ptolomy*.

The *Tones* have no different Denominations from the *Genera*; and what's ſaid of them in one *Genus* is applicable to all; and I ſhall here take the *diatonick*. The *Syſtem* of *Diſdiapaſon* already explained in the *Diagram* (coinciding with the Series from *A* of the modern *Scale*) is the *Syſtema immutatum*; which I ſhall, in what follows here, call the *Syſtem* without Diſtinction. The Seven Species of *Octaves*, as they proceed in Order from *A* . *B* . *C* . *D* . *E* . *F* . *G*, are the Seven *Tones*, which differ in their Modulations, *i. e.* in the Diſtances of the ſucceſſive Sounds, according to the fixt *Ratios* in the *Syſtem*. Theſe Seven *Ptolomy* calls, The 1*ſt*, *Dorick*, the ſame with the *Syſtem*, or beginning in *A* or *Proſlamb*. 2*d*, *Hypo-lydian*, beginning in and following the Order from *B* or *Hyp-hyp*. 3*d*, *Hypophrygian*, beginning at *C* or *Parh-hy*. 4*th*, *Hypodorian* at *D*. 5*th*, *Mixolydian* in *E*. 6*th*, *Lydian* in *F*. 7*th*, *Phrygian* in *G*. The laſt Three he takes in the *Octaves* above, for a Reaſon will preſently appear. Now, every *Mode* being conſidered by it ſelf as a diſtinct *Syſtem*, may have the Names *Proſlamb*. *hyp-hyp*. &c. applied to it; for theſe ſignify only in general the Poſitions of the Chords in any particular *Syſtem*; if they are ſo applied, he calls them the *Poſitions*; for

Ex-

Example, the firſt Chord, or graveſt Note of any *Mode* is called its *Proſlamb. poſitione*, and ſo of the reſt in Order. But again theſe are conſidered as coinciding, or being uniſon, with certain Chords of the *Syſtem*; and theſe Chords are called the *poteſtates*, with reſpect to that *Mode*; for *Example*, the *Hypodorian* begins in *D*, or *Lichanos hypaton* of the *Syſtem*, which therefore is the *poteſtas* of its *Proſlamb.* as *Hyp-meſon* is the *poteſtas* of its *hyp-hyp.* and ſo of others, *that is*, theſe Two Chords coincide and differ only in Name; and we alſo ſay, that ſuch a numerical Chord as *Proſl. poſitione* of any Mode is ſuch a Chord, as *hyp-hyp. poteſtate*, which is equivalent to ſaying, that *hyp-hyp.* of the *Syſtem* is the *Poteſtas* of the *Proſlamb. poſitione* of that Mode.

You'll eaſily find what Chord of the *Syſtem* or *Dorick Mode* is the 2*d*, 3*d*, &c. Chord of any other Mode, by counting up from the Chord of the *Syſtem* in which that Mode begins. Or contrarily, to know what numerical Chord of any Mode correſponds to any Chord of the *Syſtem*, count from this Chord to that in which the Mode begins, and you have the Number of the Chord; to which you may apply the Names *Proſlamb.* &c. or *a*, *b*, &c. And the Chords of any Mode being thus named to you, you'll ſolve the preceeding *Problems* eaſieſt, by finding what numerical Chord of the *Mode*, that is the Name of; for *Example*, to find what Chord of the *Mode Hypodorian* coincides with the *Parhypate-meſon* of the *Syſtem* (or *Dorick Mode*)

The

The *Hypo-dor. Mode* begins, or has its *Proslamb. positione*, in *D* or *Lichanos-hyp.* of the *System*, betwixt which and *Parhy-mes.* are Three Chords (inclusive) therefore the Thing sought is the Third Chord, or *Parhyp-hyp. positione* of the *hyperdorian Mode.* Again, to find what Chord of the *System* is the *potestas* of the *Lych-hyp* or *4th* Chord of the *Hypo-phr. Mode.* This begins in *C* or *Parhyp-hyp.* of the *System*, and the *4th* above is *Parhy-meson* or F the Thing sought. But more universally, to find what Chord of any Mode corresponds to any Chord of any other Mode; you may easily solve this by the *Table Plate* 2. *Fig.* 1. explained above in *Chap.* 11. § 3. Thus, find in the Column of plain Letters, the Letters at which the Modes proposed begin, against which in the same Lines you must find the Letter *a*, which is the *Proslamb. positione*, or first Chord of these Modes; and then these respective Columns compared, shew what Chord of the one corresponds to any of the other. *Observe* also, that were it proposed to begin in any Chord of any *Mode* (*i. e.* at any Chord of the *System*, or Letter of the *plain Scale*) and make a Series proceeding from that, in the Order of any other *Mode*; we easily know by this *Table* what Chords of the *System* must be altered to effect this; for *Example*, to begin in *e*, (which is *Hyp-meson* of the *System* or *dorick Mode*, *Proslamb.* of the *Phrygian Mode*, &c.) if we would proceed from this in the Order of the *Hypo-lydian*, which begins at *b* of the *System*, we must find *e* in the Column of plain Letters, and

and in the ſame Line find *b*; the Signature of the Letters of that Column where *b* ſtands, ſhews what Chords are to be changed: And by this *Table* you ſolve all theſe *Problems*, with a great deal more Eaſe, than by the long and perplext Schemes which ſome of the Ancients give us: But let us return.

PTOLOMY in *Chap.* 10. *Lib.* 2. propoſes to have his *Modes* at theſe Diſtances, *viz. tone, tone, limma, tone, tone, limma*. The *Hypodorian* being ſet loweſt, then *Hypo-phr. Hypolyd. Dorick, Phrygian* and *Mixolydian*, yet according to the Syſtem they won't ſtand at theſe Diſtances, nor in that Order. But in the next *Chap.* it appears that he means only to take them ſo as their *Meſe-poteſtate* (or theſe Chords of each which is the firſt of a Series ſimilar to the *Syſtema immutatum*,) ſhall ſtand in that Order; and to this Purpoſe he makes the *Dorick* the *Syſtema immut.* and the *Proſl.* of the reſt in order as already mentioned; only he takes *Mixolyd. Lyd.* and *Phryg.* in the 8*ve* above, *i. e.* at *Nete diez. Trite hyperbol. Paramhyperbol.* whereby their *Meſes poteſtate* ſtand in the Order mentioned; otherwiſe they had ſtood in an Order juſt reverſe of their *proſlamb. poſitione*. And now, if we would know at what Diſtances the *Meſes poteſtate* of theſe *Modes* are let us find what numerical Chord of each *Mode* is its *Meſe poteſtate*, and let it be expreſt by the Letters applied *poſitione*, as already explained: Then we muſt ſuppoſe that from *a* of the *Syſtem* (or *Dorick Mode*) a Series proceeds in each of the

the Seven different Orders; and by the Table laſt mentioned, we ſhall know, in the Manner alſo explained, what Chords are to be altered for each; therefore taking theſe Chords that are the *Meſes poteſtate* of each Mode, we ſhall ſee their mutual Diſtances. As *Ptolomy* has placed the *Proſlambanomenos*, or *a*, *poſitione* of each Mode, their *Meſes poteſtate* are in the Chords *e* : *f*※. *g* : *a* : *b* : *c*※. *d*. in order from *Hypo-dor*. as above mentioned, *that is*, when all the Orders are transferred to the *Proſlamb*. of the *Dorick Mode*, the neceſſary Variety of Signatures cauſes the *f* and *c* to be marked ※ for the *Hypo-phr*. and *Lydian* Modes, and theſe *f*※ and *c*※ are the *Meſes poteſtate* of theſe Modes; all the reſt are plain; therefore the *mutual* Diſtances of theſe *Meſes poteſtate* are expreſſed in the Scheme by (:) which ſignifies a *Tone*, (.) a *Semitone* or *limma*, which are different from what he had formerly propoſed.

DOCTOR *Wallis* in explaining theſe by the modern *Syſtem*, chuſes the Signature for the *Lydian* Mode, ſo that *a* (its *Proſlamb*.) has a *flat* Sign, and the *Meſe-poteſtate* of it is *c plain*: But ſince this explained is the only Senſe according to which the Diſtances of theſe *Meſes-poteſtate* can be found, and ſince 'tis more rational, that when any *Mode* is to be transferred to the *Proſl-poſitione* of another, that *Proſl*. ſhould not be altered; for otherwiſe it is transferred to another Note; therefore I was obliged to differ from the Doctor in that Particular: But neither does his Method ſet the *Meſes poteſtate* at the Diſtances

Distances which *Ptolomy* mentions, and which by Examination I find cannot possibly be done without changing the *Prosl.* of the *Systema immutatum*.

Anciently there were but Three *Modes*, the *Dorick*, *Lydian* and *Phrygian*, so called from the Countries that used them, and particularly called *Tones* because they were at a *Tone's* Distance from each other; and afterwards the rest were added and named from their Relations to the former, particularly the *Hypodorian*, as being below the *Dorian*, and so of the rest; for which Reason 'tis by some placed first, and they make its *Proslambanomenos* the lowest Sound that can be distinctly heard. But we should be easy about their Names or Order, if we understood the true Nature and Use of them.

If the *Modes* are indeed nothing else but the Seven Species of *Octaves*, the Use of them we can only conceive to be this, *viz.* That the *Prosl.* of any Mode being made the principal Note of any Song, there may be different Species of Melody answering to these different Constitutions; but then we are not to conceive that the *Prosl.* or Fundamental of any Mode is fixt to one particular Chord of the *System*, for *Ex.* the *Phrygian* to *g*; so that we must always begin there, when we would have a Piece of Melody of that Species: When we say in general that such a *Mode* begins in *g.* 'tis no more than to signifie the Species of 8*ve*, according as they appear

appear in a certain fixt *Syſtem* ; but we may begin in any Chord of the *Syſtem*, and make it the *Proſl.* of any *Mode*, by adding new Chords, or altering the Tuning of the old (in the Manner already mentioned:) If the Deſign is no more, but that a Song may be begun higher or lower, that may be done by beginning at the ſame Chord, which is the *Proſl.* of any Mode in the *Syſtem*, and altering the *Tune* of the Whole, keeping ſtill the fixt Order (which as I have already ſaid, is that in our modern natural Scale, from *a*) but it will be eaſier to begin in a Chord which is already higher or lower, and transfer the *Mode* in which the Song is, to that Chord. If every Song kept in one *Mode*, there was Need for no more than one *diatonick* Series, and by occaſional changing the Tune of certain Chords, theſe Tranſpoſitions of every Mode to every Chord may be eaſily performed ; and I have ſpoken already of the Way to find what Chords are to be altered in their tuning to effect this,by the various Signatures of ✻ and ♭: But if we ſuppoſe that in the Courſe of any Song a new Species is brought in, this can only be effected by having more Chords than in the fixt *Syſtem*, ſo as from any Chord of that,any Order or Species of 8*ve* may be found.

If this be the true Nature and Uſe of the *Tones*, I ſhall only obſerve here, that according to the Notions we have at preſent of the Principles and Rules of *Melody*, as they have been explained in ſome of the preceeding *Chapters*, moſt of theſe Modes are imperfect, and incapable

pable of good Melody; becauſe they want ſome of thoſe we reckon the eſſential and natural Notes of a true *Mode* (or *Key*) of which we reckon only Two Species, *viz.* that from *c* and *a*, or the *Parhypate-hypaton* and *Proſlambanomenos* of the ancient fixt Syſtem.

Again, if the eſſential Difference of the *Modes* conſiſts only in the *Gravity* or *Acuteneſs* of the whole 8*ve*; then we muſt ſuppoſe there is one Species or concinnous Diviſion of the 8*ve*, which being applied to all the Chords of the *Syſtem*, makes them true *Fundamentals* for a certain Series of ſucceſſive Notes. Theſe Applications may be made in the Manner already mentioned; by changing the *Tune* of certain Chords in ſome Caſes; but more univerſally, by adding new Chords to the *Syſtem*, as the artificial or *ſharp* and *flat* Notes of the modern Scale above explained. But in this Caſe, again, where we ſuppoſe they admitted only one *concinnous* Species, we muſt ſuppoſe it to be correſponding to the 8*ve a*, of what we call the *natural* Scale; becauſe they all ſtate the Order of the *Syſtema immutatum* in the *Diagram*, ſo as it anſwers to that 8*ve*.

But what a ſimple *Melody* muſt have been produced by admitting only one concinnous Series, and that too wanting ſome uſeful and neceſſary Chords? We have above explained, that the *flat* Series, ſuch as that beginning in *a*, has Two of its Chords that are variable, *viz.* the *6th* and *7th*, whereof ſometimes the greater, ſometimes the leſſer is uſed; and therefore a

Syſtem

System that wants this Variety must be so far imperfect: And what has been explained in *Chap.* 13. shews how impossible it is to make any good Modulation or Change from one *Key* to another, unless both the Species of *sharp* and *flat Key* be admitted in the *System*; which Experience and all the Reasonings in the preceeding *Chapters* demonstrate to be necessary.

Ptolomy has a Passage relating to the *Modes*, with which I shall end this Head, *Lib.* 2. *Chap.* 7. of the *Mutations with respect to what they call* Tones. He says, these Mutations with respect to *Tones* was not introduced for the sake of *acuter* or *graver* Sounds, which might be produced by raising or lowering the whole Instrument or Voice, without any Change in the Song; but upon this Account, that the same Voice beginning the same Song now in a higher Note then in a lower, may make a Kind of Change of the *Mode*. This, to make any Sense, must signify that the same Song might be contrived so, as several Notes higher or lower might be used as *Fundamentals* to a certain Number of successive Notes; and all together make one Song; like what I explained of our modern Songs making Cadences in different Notes, so as the Song may be said to begin there again. If this is not the Sense, then what he says is plainly a Contradiction. But this may be the true Use of the *Tones*, in either of the Hypotheses concerning their essential Differences. He says in the Beginning of that *Chap.* "The *Mutations* which are made

" by

" by whole *Systems*, which we properly call " *Tones*, because these Differences consist in " *Tension*, are infinite with respect to Possibility, " as Sounds are, but actually and with respect " to Sense they are finite." All this seems plainly to put the Difference of the *Tones* only in the *Acuteness* or *Gravity* of the Whole, else how do their Differences consist in *Tension*, which signifies a certain Tenor or Degree of *Tune*; and how can they be called *infinite*, if they depend on the different Constitutions of the 8*ve*. Yet elsewhere he argues, that they are no other than the Species of 8*ves*, and as such makes their Number Seven; and accordingly, in all his Schemes, sets down their different Modulations: But in *Chap.* 6. he seems more plainly to take in both these Differences, for he says, there are Two principal Differences with respect to the Change of the *Tone*, one whereby the whole Song is sung higher or lower, the other wherein there is a Change of the *Melody* to another Species than it was begun in; but this he thinks is rather a Change of the Song or *Melos* than of the *Tone*, as if again he would have us think this depended only on the *Acuteness* and *Gravity* of the Whole; so obscurely has the best of all the ancient Writers delivered himself on this Article that deserved to have been most clearly handled. But that I may have done with it, I shall only say, it must be taken in one of the Senses mentioned, if not in both, for another I think cannot be found. Let me me alſo add, that the Moderns who have endeavoured to explain the ancient Muſick take theſe *Modes* for the Species of *8ves*. If you'll except *Meibomius*, who, in his Notes upon *Ariſtides*, affirms that the Differences of the *Modes* upon which all the different Effects depended, were only in the Tenſion or Acuteneſs and Gravity of the whole *Syſtem*. But there are *Modes* I call the *Antiquo-modern Modes*, which ſhall be conſidered afterwards.

OBSERVE. The *Tetrachord Synemmenon*, which makes what they called the *Syſtema conjunctum*, was added for joyning the upper and lower *Diapaſon* of the *Syſtema immutatum*; that when the Song having modulated thro' Two conjunct Tetrachords, and being come to *Meſe*, might for Variety paſs either into the disjunct Tetrachord *Diezeugmenon* or the conjunct *Synemmenon*. 'Tis made in our *Syſtem* by *b flat*, *i. e.* putting only a *Semitone* betwixt *a* and *b*; ſo that from *b* to *d* (in *8ve*,) makes Three conjunct Tetrachords; and the Uſe of that new Chord ♭ with us is properly for perfecting ſome *8ve* from whoſe Fundamental in the fixt *Scale* there is not a right concinnous Series.

VI. OF MUTATIONS. This ſignifies the Changes or Alterations that happen in the Order of the Sounds that compoſe the *Melody*. *Ariſtox.* ſays, 'tis as it were a certain *Paſſion* in the Order of the *Melody*. It properly belongs to the *Melopœia* to explain this, but is always put by it ſelf as a diſtinct Part of the *Harmonica*.

nica. Theſe Changes are Four. 1. In the *Genus*; when the Song begins in one as the *Chromatick*, and paſſes into another as the *Diatonick.* 2. In the *Syſtem*, as when the Song paſſes out of one Tetrachord, as *Meſon*, into another, as *Diezeugmenon*; or more generally, when it paſſes from a high Place of the *Scale* to a low, or contrarily, *that is*, the Whole is ſung ſometimes high, ſometimes low; or rather, a Part of it is high, and a Part of it low. 3. In the *Mode* or *Tone*, as when the Song begins in one, as the *Dorick*, and paſſes into another, as the *Lydian*: What this Change of the *Mode* ſignifies according to the modern Theory has been explained already. 4. In the *Melopœia*, that is, when the Song changes the very *Air*, ſo as from gay and ſprightly to become ſoft and languiſhing, or from a *Manner* that expreſſes one Paſſion or Subject to the Expreſſion of ſome other; and therefore ſome of them call this a Change in the *Manner* (*ſecundum morem*): But to expreſs Paſſion, or to have what they called *Pathetick Muſick*, the various *Rythmus* is abſolutely neceſſary to be join'd; and therefore among the *Mutations* ſome place this of the *Rythmus*, as from *Jambick* to *Choraick*; but this belongs properly to the *Rythmica.* Now theſe are at beſt but mere Definitions, the Rules when and how to uſe theſe Changes, ought to be found in the *Melopœia.*

VII. Of the Melopoeia, or Art of making *Melody* or Songs. After the End and Principles of any Art are ſuppoſed to be diſtinctly enough

enough shewn, the Thing to be expected is, that the *Rules* of Application be clearly set forth. But in this, I must say it, the Ancients have left us little else than a Parcel of Words and Names; such a Thing they call such a Name; but the Use of that Thing they leave you to find. The Substance of their Doctrine according to *Euclid* is this. After he has said that the *Melopœia* is the Use of the Parts (or Principles) already explained. He tells us, it consists of Four Parts, first αγογη, which the *Latins* called *ductus*, *that is*, when the Sounds or Notes proceed by continuous Degrees of the *Scale*, as *a. b. c.* 2*d.* πλοκὴ, *nexus*, which is, when the Sounds either ascending or descending are taken alternately, or not immediately next in the *Scale*, as *a, c, b, d.* or *a, d, b, e, c, f,* or these reversely *d, b, c, a.* 3*d.* πεττεία, *Petteia*, (for the *Latins* made this *Greek* Name their own) when the same Note was frequently repeated together, as *a, a, a.* 4*th*, τονὴ, *Extensio*, when any one Note was held out or sounded remarkably longer than the rest. This is all *Euclid* teaches us about it. But *Aristides Quintilianus*, who writes more fully than any of them, explains the *Melopœia* otherwise. He calls it the *Faculty* or *Art* of making *Songs*, which has Three Parts, *viz.* λῆψις, μιξίς, χρῆσις, which the *Latins* call *sumtio*, *mistio*, *usus*.

NOT to trouble our selves with long *Greek* Passages, I shall give you the Definitions of these in *Meibomius*'s Words, 1. SUMTIO *est per quam musico datur a quali vocis loco Systema sit faci-*

faciendum, utrum ab Hypatoide *an reliquorum aliquo.* 2. MISTIO, *per quam aut ſonos inter ſe aut vocis locos coagmentamus, aut modulationis genera, aut modorum Syſtema.* 3. USUS, *certa quædam modulationis confectio, cujus ſpecies tres,* viz. *Ductus, Petteia, Nexus.* As to the Definitions of the Three principal Parts, the Author of the *Dictionaire de Muſique* puts this Senſe upon them, *viz. Sumtio* teaches the Compoſer in what Syſtem he ought to place his Song, whether high or low, and conſequently in what *Mode* or *Tone*, and at what Note to begin and end. *Miſtio,* ſays he, is properly what we call the Art of *Modulating* well, *i. e.* after having begun in a convenient Place, to proſecute or conduct the Song, ſo as the Voice be always in a convenient *Tenſion*; and that the eſſential Chords of the *Mode* be right placed and uſed, and that the Song be carried out of it, and return again agreeably. *Uſus* teaches the Compoſer how the Sounds ought to follow one another, and in what Situations each may and ought to be in, to make an agreeable *Melody*, or a good *Modulation*. For the Species of the *Uſus*: *Ariſtides* defines the *ductus* and *nexus* the ſame Way as *Euclid* does; and adds, that the *ductus* may be performed Three Ways, or is threefold, *viz. ductus rectus,* when the Notes aſcend, as *a, b, c*; *revertens,* when they deſcend *c, b, a*; or *circumcurrens,* when having aſcended by the *ſyſtema disjunctum,* they immediately deſcend by the *ſyſtema conjunctum,* or move downwards betwixt the ſame Extremes, in in a different Order of the intermediate Degrees, as having aſcended thus, *a : b : c : d*, the Deſcent is *d : c : ♭ : a*, or *c : d : e : f*, and *f : e♭. d : c*. But the *Petteia* he defines, *Qua cognoſcimus quinam ſonorum omittendi, & qui ſunt adſumendi, tum quoties illorum ſinguli : porro a quonam incipiendum, & in quem definiendum: atque hæc quoque morem exhibet*. In ſhort, according to this Definition the *Petteia* is the whole Art.

THERE were alſo what they called, The *modi melopœiæ*, of which *Ariſtides* names theſe, *Dithyrambick*, *Nomick*, and *Tragick*; called *Modes* for their expreſſing the ſeveral Motions and Affections of the Mind. The beſt Notion we can form of this is, to ſuppoſe them ſomething like what we call the different Stiles in *Muſick*, as the *Eccleſiaſtick*, the *Choraick*, the *Recitative*, &c. But I think the *Rythmus* muſt have a conſiderable or the greateſt Share in theſe Differences.

BUT now if you'll ask where are the particular practical Rules, that teach when and how all theſe Things are to be done and uſed, I muſt own, I have found nothing of this Kind particular enough to give me a diſtinct *Idea* of their Practice in *Melody*. It is true, that *Ariſtoxenus* employs his whole 3*d* Book very near, in ſomething that ſeems deſigned for Rules, in the right Conduct of Sounds for making *Melody*. But Truth is, all the tedious and perplext Work he makes of it, amounts to no more than ſhewing,

ing, what general Limitations we are under, with reſpect to the placing of *Intervals* in Succeſſion, according to the ſeveral *Genera*, and the Conſtitution of the *Syſtema immutatum*, or what we call the naturally *concinnous* Series. You'll underſtand it by One or Two *Examples*: Firſt, in the *Diatonick* Kind, he ſays, That Two *Semitones* never follow other immediately, and that a *Hemitone* is not to be placed immediately above and below one *Tone*, but may be placed above and below Two or Three *Tones*; and that Two or Three *Tones* may be placed together but no more. Then as to the Two other *Genera*, to underſtand what he ſays, *obſerve*, that the lower Part of the *Tetrachord* containing Two *Dieſes* in the One, and Two *Hemitones* in the other *Genus* (whoſe Sums are always leſs than the remaining *Ditone* or *Triemitone* that makes up the *Diateſſaron*) is called πυκνὸν *ſpiſſum*, becauſe the *Intervals* being ſmall, the Sounds are as it were ſet thick and near other; oppoſite to which is απυκνὸν *non ſpiſſum* or *rarum*: Notice too, that the Chords that belonged to the *ſpiſſum* were called πυκνὸι, and particularly the loweſt or *graveſt* of the Three in every *Tetrachord* were called βαρὺπυκνοι, (from βάρυς *gravis*,) the middle μεσόπυκνοι (from μεσος *medius*) the acuteſt ὀξύπυκνοι (from ὀξύς *acutus*). Thoſe that belonged not to the πυκνὸν were called απυκνὸι, *extra ſpiſſum*. Now then, with reſpect to the *Enharmonick* and *Chromatick* we are told, that Two *Spiſſa*, or

Two

Two *Ditones*, *Triemitones*, or *Tones* cannot be put together; but that a *Ditone* may ſtand betwixt Two *ſpiſſa*; that a *Tone* (it muſt be the *diazeucticus* betwixt Two *Tetrachords*) may be placed immediately above the *Ditone* or *Triem.* but not below, and below the *Spiſſum* but not above. There is a World more of this kind, that one ſees at Sight almoſt in the *Diagram*, without long tedious Explications; and at beſt they are but very general Rules. There is a Heap of other Words and Names mentioned by ſeveral Authors, but not worth mentioning.

BUT at laſt I muſt obſerve and own, That any Rules that can poſſibly be given about this Practice, are far too general, either to teach one to compoſe different Species of *Melody*, or to give a diſtinct Idea of the Practice of others; and that 'tis abſolutely neceſſary for theſe Purpoſes that we have a Plenty of *Examples* in actual Compoſitions, which we have not of the Ancients. There is a natural Genius, without which no Rules are ſufficient: And indeed what Rules can be given, when a very few general Principles are capable of ſuch an infinite Application; therefore Practice and Experience muſt be the Rule; and for this Reaſon we find both among the Ancients and Moderns, ſo very few, and theſe very general Rules for the Compoſition of Melody. Beſides the Knowledge of the *Syſtem*, and what we call Modulation or keeping in and changing the *Mode* or *Key*; there are other general Principles that Nature teacheth

teacheth us, and which muſt be attended to, if we would produce good Effects, either for the Entertainment of the Fancy with the Variety we find ſo indiſpenſable in our Pleaſures, or for imitating Nature, and moving the Affections: Theſe are, *firſt*, the different Species of Sounds abſtract from the Acuteneſs, as Drums, Trumpets, Violins, Flutes, Voice, *&c.* which as they give different Senſations, ſo they are fit for expreſſing different Things, and raiſing or humouring different Paſſions; to which we may add the Differences of ſtrong and weak, or loud and low Sounds. 2*do*. Tho' a Piece of Melody is ſtrictly the ſame, whether it is performed by an acute or grave Voice; yet 'tis certain, That acute Sounds and grave, have different Effects; ſo that the one is more applicable to ſome Subjects than the other; and we know that, in general, *acute* Sounds (which are owing to quicker Vibrations) have ſomething more brisk and ſprightly than the graver, which are better applied to the more calm Affections, or to ſad and melancholy Subjects; but there is a great Variety betwixt the Extremes; and different Cuſtoms and Manners may alſo make a Difference: We find by Experience a lively Motion in our Blood and Nerves, under ſome Affections of Mind, as Joy and Gladneſs; and in the more boiſterous Paſſions, as Anger, that Motion is ſtill greater; but others are accompanied with more calm and ſlow Motions; and ſince Bodies communicate their Motion, and the Effect is proportional to the Cauſe, we ſee a natural

natural Reaſon of theſe different Effects of acute and grave Sounds. 3*tio*. The Effects of Melody have a great Dependence on the alternate Paſſage or Movement of the Sounds up and down, *i. e.* from acute to grave, and contrarily; or its continuing for leſs or more Time in one Place; but the Variety here is infinite; yet Experience teaches ſome general Leſſons; for *Example*, if a Man in the Middle of a Diſcourſe turns angry, 'tis natural to raiſe his Voice; this therefore ought to be expreſt by raiſing the Melody from grave to acute; and contrarily a ſinking of the Mind to Melancholy muſt be imitated by the falling of the Sounds; a more evenly State by a like Conduct of the Melody. Again, the taking of the Sounds by immediate Degrees, or alternatively, or repeating the ſame Note, and the moving by greater or leſſer Intervals, have all their proper and different Effects: Theſe, and their various Combinations, muſt all be under the Compoſer's Conſideration; but who can poſſibly give Rules for the infinite Variety in the State and Temper of human Minds, and the proper Application of Sounds for expreſſing or exciting theſe? And when Compoſitions are deſigned only for Pleaſure in general, what an infinite Number of Ways may this be produced?

AGAIN it muſt be minded, That the *Rythmus* is a very principal Thing in *Muſick*, eſpecially of the *pathetick* Kind; for 'tis this Variety of Movements in the quick or ſlow Succeſſions, or Length and Shortneſs of Notes, that's the

the conſpicuous Part of the *Air*, without which the other can produce but very weak Effects; and therefore moſt of the Ancients uſed to call the *Rythmus* the *Male*, and the *Harmonica* the *Female*. And as to this I muſt take Notice here, That the Ancients ſeem to have uſed none but the long and ſhort Syllables of the Words and Verſes which were ſung, and always made a Part of their *Muſick*; therefore the *Rythmica* was nothing with them but the Explication of the *metrical Feet*, and the various Kinds of Verſes which were made of them: And for the *Rythmopœia*, or the Art of applying theſe, I am confident no Body will affirm they have left us any more than very general Hints, that can ſcarce be called *Rules*: The reading of *Ariſtides* and St. *Auguſtin* will, I believe, convince you of this; and all the reſt put together have not ſaid as much about it. I ſuppoſe the ancient Writers, who in their Diviſions of *Muſick*, make the *Rythmica* one Part, and in their Explications of this ſpeak of no other than that which belongs to the Words and Verſes of their Songs, I ſay theſe will be a ſufficient Proof that they had no other. But you'll ſee it further confirmed immediately, when we conſider the *ancient* Notes or Writing of *Muſick*. As to the *modern Rythmus*, I need ſay little about it; that it is a Thing very different from the ancient, is manifeſt to any Body who conſiders what I have ſaid of theirs, and has but the ſmalleſt Acquaintance with our Muſick. That the *Meaſures* and *Modes* of TIME explained

in

in *Ch.* 12. and all the poſſible Subdiviſions and Conſtitutions of them, are capable to afford an endleſs Variety of *Rythmus*, and expreſs any Thing that the Motion of Sound is capable of, is equally certain to the experienced; and therefore I ſhall ſay no more of it here: Only *obſerve*, That as I ſaid about the *Harmonica*, ſo of this 'tis certainly true, That the Rules are very general: We know that quick and ſlow Movements ſuit different Objects; when we are gay and cheerful we love airy Motions; and to different Subjects and Paſſions different Movements muſt be applied, for which Nature is our beſt Guide: Therefore the *practical Writers* leave us to our own Obſervations and Experience, to learn how to apply theſe Meaſures of Time, which they can only deſcribe in general, as I have done, and refer us to Examples for perfecting our Idea of them, and what they are capable of.

Of the ancient Notes, *and* Writing *of* Muſick.

WE learn from *Alipius* (*vid. Meibom. Edition.*) how the *Greeks* marked their Sounds. They made uſe of the Letters of their Alphabet: And becauſe they needed more Signs than there were Letters, they ſupplied that out of the ſame Alphabet; by making the ſame Letter expreſs different Notes, as it was placed upright or reverſed, or otherwiſe put out of the common Poſition; and alſo making them imperfect, by cutting off ſomething, or by doubling ſome Strokes. For *Example*, the Letter *Pi* expreſſes

expreſſes different Notes in all theſe Poſitions and Forms, *viz.* Π . Ш . ⊏ . ⊐ Γ . ˥, *&c.* But that we may know the whole Task a Scholar had to learn, conſider, that for every *Mode* there were 18 Signs (becauſe they conſidered the *Tetrachordum ſynemmenon*, as if all its Chords had been really different from the *Diezeugmenon*) and for every one of the Three *Genera* they were alſo different; again the Signs that expreſſed the ſame Note were different for the Voice and for the Inſtruments. *Alipius* gives us the Signs for 15 different Modes, which with the Differences of the 3 *Genera*, and the Diſtinction betwixt Voice and Inſtrument, makes in all 1620; not that theſe are all different Characters, for the ſame Character is uſed ſeveral Times, but then it has differerent Significations; for *Example*, in the *diatonick Genus* Φ is *Lichanos hypaton* of the *Lydian* Mode, and *Hypate meſon* of the *Phrygian*, both for the Voice; ſo that they are in effect as different Characters to a Learner. What a happy Contrivance this was for making the Practice of *Muſick* eaſy, every Body will judge who conſiders, that 15 Letters with ſome ſmall Variation for the *Chordæ mobiles*, in order to diſtinguiſh the *Genera*, was ſufficient for all. In *Boethius*'s Time the *Romans* were wiſe enough to eaſe themſelves of this unneceſſary Difficulty; and therefore they made uſe only of the firſt 15 Letters of their Alphabet: But afterwards Pope *Gregory* the Great, conſidering that the 8*ve* was the ſame in effect with the firſt, and that the Order of Degrees was the ſame

ſame in the upper and lower 8*ve* of the *Diagram*, he introduced the Uſe of 7 Letters, which were repeated in a different Character. But hitherto there was no ſuch Thing as any Mark of *Time*; theſe Characters expreſſing only the Degrees of *Tune*, which therefore were always placed in a Line, and the Words of the Song under them, ſo that over every Syllable ſtood a Note to mark the Accent of the Voice: And for the *Time*, that was according to the long and ſhort Syllable of the Verſe; tho' in ſome very extraordinary Caſes we hear of ſome particular Marks for altering the natural or ordinary Quantity.

I ſhall end this Part with obſerving that among all the ancient Writers on *Muſick*, there is not one Word to be found relating to *Compoſition* in *Parts*, or joining ſeveral different *Melodies* in one *Harmony*, as what we call *Treble*, *Tenor*, *Baſs*, &c. But this ſhall be more particularly examined in the next *Section*.

---

§ 5. *A ſhort HISTORY of the Improvements in MUSICK.*

FOR what Reaſons the *Greek* Muſicians made ſuch a difficult Matter of their Notes and Signs we cannot gueſs, unleſs they did it deſignedly to make their Art myſterious, which is an odious Suppoſition; but one can ſcarcely think it was otherwiſe, who conſiders how obvious

vious it was to find a more eaſy Method. This was therefore the firſt Thing the *Latins* corrected in the *Greek Muſick*, as we have already heard was done by *Boethius*, and further improved by *Gregory* the Great.

THE next Step in this Improvement is commonly aſcribed to *Guido Aretinus* a *Benedictin* Monk, of *Aretium* in *Tuſcany*, who, about the Year 1024, (tho' there are ſome Differences about the Year) contrived the Uſe of a Staff of 5 Lines, upon which, with its Spaces he marked his Notes, by ſetting Points (.) up and down upon them, to denote the Riſe and Fall of the Voice, (but as yet there were no different Marks of *Time*;) he marked each Line and Space at the Beginning of the Staff, with *Gregory*'s 7 Letters, and when he ſpake of the Notes, he named them by theſe inſtead of the long *Greek* Names of *Proſlambanomenos*, &c. The Correſpondence of theſe Letters to the Names of the Chords in the *Greek Syſtem* being ſettled, ſuch as I have already repreſented in their *Diagram*, the Degrees and Intervals betwixt any Line or Space, and any other were hereby underſtood. But this Artifice of Points and Lines was uſed before his Time, by whom invented is not known; and this we learn from *Kircher*, who ſays he found in the *Jeſuites* Library at *Meſſina* a Greek manuſcript Book of Hymns, more than 700 Years old; in which ſome Hymns were written on a Staff of 8 Lines, marked at the Beginning with 8 Greek Letters; the Notes or Points were ſet upon the Lines, but no Uſe made

made of the Spaces: *Vincenzo Galileo* confirms us alſo in this. But whether *Guido* knew this, is a Queſtion; and tho' he did, yet it was well contrived to uſe the Spaces and Lines both, by which the Notes ly nearer other, fewer Lines are needful for any Interval, and the Diſtances of Notes are eaſier reckoned.

BUT there is yet more of *Guido*'s Contrivance, which deſerves to be conſidered; *Firſt.* He contrived the 6 muſical Syllables, *ut*, *re*, *mi*, *fa*, *ſol*, *la*, which he took out of this Latin Hymn.

UT queant laxis RE ſonare fibris
MIra geſtorum FAmuli tuorum,
SOLve polluti LAbii reatum,
O pater alme.

In repeating this it came into his Mind, by a Kind of divine Inſtinct ſays *Kircher*, to apply theſe Syllables to his Notes of *Muſick*: A wonderful Contrivance certainly for a *divine Inſtinct!* But let us ſee where the Excellency of it lies: *Kircher* ſays, by them alone he unfolded all the Nature of *Muſick*, diſtinguiſhed the *Tones* (or *Modes*) and the Seats of the Semitones: Elſewhere he ſays, That by the Application of theſe Syllables he cultivated *Muſick*, and made it fitter for Singing. In order to know how he applied them, there is another Piece of the Hiſtory we muſt take along, *viz.* That finding the *Greek Diagram* of too ſmall Extent, he added 5 more Chords or Notes in this Manner; having

having applied the Letter A to the *Proslambanomenos*, and the rest in Order to *Nete Hyperbolæon*, he added a Chord, a *Tonus* below *Proslam.* and called it *Hypo-proslambanomenos*, and after the Latins *g.* but commonly marked with the Greek *Gamma* Γ; to shew by this, say some, that the Greeks were the Inventors of *Musick*; but others say he meant to record himself (that Letter being the first in his Name) as the Improver of *Musick*; hence the *Scale* came to be called the *Gamm*. Above *Nete Hyperbolæon* he added other 4 Chords, which made a new disjunct *Tetrachord*, he called *Hyper-hyperbolæon*; so that his whole *Scale* contained 20 *diatonick Notes*, (for this was the only *Genus* now used) besides the *b* flat, which corresponded to the *Trite Synemmenon* of the Ancients, and made what was afterwards called the Series of *b molle*, as we shall hear.

Now the Application of these Syllables to the *Scale* was made thus: Betwixt *mi* and *fa* is a *Semitone*; *ut* : *re*, *re* : *mi*, *fa* : *sol*, and *sol* : *la* are Tones (without distinguishing greater and lesser;) then because there are but 6 Syllables, and 7 different Notes or Letters in the 8*ve*; therefore, to make *mi* and *fa* fall upon the true Places of the natural Semitones, *ut* was applied to different Letters, and the rest of the 6 in order to the others above; the Letters to which *ut* was applied are *g* . *c* . *f*. according to which he distinguished three Series, *viz.* that which begun with *ut* in *g*, and he called it the Series of *b durum*, because *b* was a whole Tone above

a,

a; that which begun with *ut* in *c* was the Series of *b* natural, the ſame as the former; and when *ut* was in *f*, it was called *b molle*, wherein *b* was only a *Semitone* above *a*. See the whole Scale in the following Scheme, where *obſerve*, the Series of *b* natural ſtands betwixt the other two, and communicates with both; ſo that to name the Chords of the Scale by theſe Syllables, if we would have the Semitones in their natural Places, *viz.* *b* . *c*, and *e* . *f*, then we apply *ut* to *g*, and after *la*, we go into the Series of *b* natural at *fa*, and after *la* of this, we return to the former at *mi*, and ſo on; or we may begin at *ut* in *c*, and paſs into the firſt Series at *mi*, and then back to the other at *fa*: By which Means the one Tranſition is a Semitone, *viz.* *la* . *fa*, and the other a Tone *la* : *mi*. To follow the Order of *b molle*

GUIDO's SCALE.

	B dur.	*nat.*	*molle*
ee	*la*	*mi*	
dd	*ſol*	*re*	*la*
cc	*fa*	*ut*	*ſol*
bb	*mi*		
♭♭			*fa*
aa	*re*	*la*	*mi*
g	*ut*	*ſol*	*re*
f		*fa*	*ut*
e	*la*	*mi*	
d	*ſol*	*re*	*la*
c	*fa*	*ut*	*ſol*
b	*mi*		
♭			*fa*
a	*re*	*la*	*mi*
G	*ut*	*ſol*	*re*
F		*fa*	*ut*
E	*la*	*mi*	
D	*ſol*	*re*	
C	*fa*	*ut*	
B	*mi*		
A	*re*		
Γ*amm*	*ut*		

b molle, we may begin with *ut* in *c* or *f*, and make Tranſitions the ſame Way as formerly: Hence came the barbarous Names of *Gammut*, *Are*, *Bmi*, &c. with which the Memories of Learners uſed to be oppreſſed. But now what a perplext Work is here, with ſo many different Syllables applied to every Chord, and all for no other Purpoſe but marking the Places of the Semitones, which the ſimple Letters, *a* . *b* . *c*, &c. do as well and with infinite more Eaſe. Afterwards ſome contrived better, by making Seven Syllables, adding *Si* in the Blanks you ſee in the Series betwixt *la* and *ut*, ſo that *mi-fa* and *ſi-ut* are the two natural Semitones: Theſe 7 completing the 8*ve*, they took away the middle Series as of no Uſe, and ſo *ut* being in *g* or *f*, made the Series of *B durum* (or natural, which is all one) and *B molle*. But the *Engliſh* throw out both *ut* and *ſi*, and make the other 5 ſerve for all in the Manner explained in *Chap.* 11. where I have alſo ſhewn, the Unneceſſarineſs of the Difficulty that the beſt of theſe Methods occaſions, and therefore ſhall not repete it here. This wonderful Contrivance of *Guido*'s 6 Syllables, is what a very ingenious Man thought fit to call *Crux tenellorum ingeniorum*; but he might have ſaid it of any of the Methods; for which Reaſon, I believe, they are laid aſide with very many, and, I am ſure, ought to be ſo with every Body.

But to go one with *Guido*; the Letters he applied to his Lines and Spaces, were called *Keys*, and at firſt he marked every Line and

and Space at the Beginning of a Staff with its Letter; afterwards marked only the Lines, as ſome old Examples ſhew; and at laſt marked only one, which was therefore called the *ſigned Clef*; of which he diſtinguiſhed Three different ones, *g*, *c*, *f*; (the three Letters he had placed his *ut* in) and the Reaſon of this leads us to another Article of the Hiſtory, *viz.* That *Guido* was the Inventor of *Symphonetick Compoſition*, (for if the Ancients had it, it was loſt; but this ſhall be conſidered again) the firſt who joyned in one *Harmony* ſeveral diſtinct *Melodies*, and brought it even the length of 4 *Parts*, *viz. Baſs*, *Tenor*, *Counter*, *Treble*; and therefore to determine the Places of the ſeveral *Parts* in the general *Syſtem*, and their Relations to one another, it was neceſſary to have 3 different ſigned Clefs (*vid. Chap.* 11.)

HE is alſo ſaid to be the Contriver of thoſe Inſtruments they call *Polyplectra*, as *Spinets* and *Harpſichords*: However they may now differ in Shape, he contrived what is called the *Abacus* and the *Palmulæ*, that is, the *Machinery* by which the String is ſtruck with a Plectrum made of Quills. Thus far go the Improvements of *Guido Aretinus*, and what is called the *Guidonian Syſtem*; to explain which he wrote a Book he calls his *Micrologum*.

THE next conſiderable Improvement was about 300 Years after *Guido*, relating to the *Rythmus*, and the Marks by which the Duration of every Note was known; for hitherto they had but imitated the Simplicity of the Ancients, and

and barely followed the Quantity of the Syllables, or perhaps not ſo accurate in that, made all their Notes of equal Duration, as ſome of the old *Eccleſiaſtick Muſick* is an Inſtance of. To produce all the Effects *Muſick* is capable of, the Neceſſity of Notes of different Quantity was very obvious; for the *Rythmus* is the Soul of *Muſick*; and becauſe the natural Quantity of the Syllables was not thought ſufficient for all the Variety of Movements, which we know to be ſo agreeable in *Muſick*, therefore about the Year 1330 or 1333, ſays *Kircher*, the famous *Joannes de Muris*, Doctor at *Paris*, invented the different Figures of Notes, which expreſs the *Time*, or Length of every Note, at leaſt their true relative Proportions to one another; you ſee their Names and Figures in *Plate*, 2 *Fig.* 3. as we commonly call them. But anciently they were called, *Maxima*, *Longa*, *Brevis*, *Semibrevis*, *Minima*, *Semiminima*, *Chroma*, (or *Fuſa*) *Semichroma*. What we call the *Demiſemiquaver* is of modern Addition. But whether all theſe were invented at once is not certain, nor is it probable they were; at firſt 'tis like they uſed only the *Longa* and *Brevis*, and the reſt were added by Degrees. Now alſo was invented the Diviſion of every Song in ſeparate and diſtinct *Bars* or *Meaſures*. Then for the Proportion of theſe *Notes* one to another it was not always the ſame; ſo a *Long* was in ſome Caſes equal to Two *Breves*, ſometimes to Three, and ſo of others; and this Difference was marked generally at the Beginning; and ſometimes by the Poſition

Position or Way of joyning them together in the Middle of the Song; but this Variety happened only to the first Four. *Again*, respecting the mutual Proportions of the Notes, they had what they called *Modes*, *Prolations* and *Times*: The Two last were distinguished into *Perfect* and *Imperfect*; and the first into *greater* and *lesser*, and each of these into *perfect* and *imperfect*: But afterwards they reduced all into 4 *Modes* including the *Prolations* and *Times*. I could not think it worth Pains to make a tedious Description of all these, with their Marks or Signs, which you may see in the already mentioned *Dictionaire de Musique*: I shall only observe here, That as we now make little Use of any Note above the *Semibreve*, because indeed the remaining 6 are sufficient for all Purposes, so we have cast off that Difficulty of various and changeable Proportions betwixt the same Notes: The Proportions of 3 to 1 and 2 to 1 was all they wanted, and how much more easy and simple is it to have one Proportion fixt, *viz.* 2 : 1 (*i. e.* a *Large* equal to Two *Longs*, and so on in Order) and if the Proportion of 3 : 1 betwixt Two successive Notes is required, this is, without any Manner of Confusion or Difficulty, expressed by annexing a Point (.) on the Right Hand of the greatest of the Two Notes, as has been above explained; so that 'tis almost a Wonder how the Elements of *Musick* were so long involved in these Perplexities, when a far easier Way of coming to the same End was not very hard to find.

WE

We shall observe here too, That till these *Notes* of various *Time* were invented, instrumental Performances without Song must have been very imperfect if they had any; and what a wonderful Variety of Entertainments we have by this Kind of Composition, I need not tell you.

There remain Two other very considerable Steps, before we come to the present State of the Scale of Musick. *Guido* first contrived the joyning different *Parts* in one *Concert*, as has been said, yet he carried his *System* no further than 20 *diatonick* Notes: Now for the more simple and plain Compositions of the Ecclesiastick Stile, which is probable was the most considerable Application he made of Musick, this Extent would afford no little Variety: But Experience has since found it necessary to enlarge the *System* even to 34 diatonick Notes, which are represented in the foremost Range of Keys on the Breast of a *Harpsichord*; for so many are required to produce all that admirable Variety of Harmony, which the Parts in modern Compositions consist of, according to the many different Stiles practised: But a more considerable Defect of his System is, That except the Tone betwixt *a* and *b*, which is divided into Two Semitones by ♭ (flat) there was not another Tone in all the Scale divided; and without this the System is very imperfect, with respect to fixt Sounds, because without these there can be no right Modulation or Change from

Key

Key to *Key*, taking Mode or *Key* in the Senſe which I have explained in *Chap.* 9. Therefore the *modern Syſtem* has in every 8*ve* 5 artificial Chords or Notes which we mark by the Letters of the *natural* Chords, with the Diſtinction of ※ or ♭, the Neceſſity and true Uſe of which has been largely explained in *Chap.* 8. and therefore not to be inſiſted on here ; I ſhall only *obſerve*, That by theſe additional Chords, we have the *diatonick* and *chromatick Genera* of the Ancients mixed ; ſo that Compoſitions may be made in either Kind, tho' we reckon the *diatonick* the true natural Species ; and if at any Time, Two *Semitones* are placed immediately in Succeſſion ; for *Example*, if we ſing *c* . *c*※. *d*, which is done for Variety, tho' ſeldom, ſo far this is a Mixture of the *Chromatick*; but then to make it pure *Chromatick*, no ſmaller Interval can be ſung after Two *Semitones* aſcending than a *Triemitone*, nor deſcending leſs than a *Tone*; becauſe in the pure *chromatick* Scale the *Spiſſum* has always above it a *Triemitone*, and below it either a *Triemitone* or a *Tone*.

THE laſt Thing I ſhall conſider here is, how the *Modes* were defined in theſe Days of Improvement ; and I find they were generally characterized by the Species of 8*ve* after *Ptolomy*'s Manner, and therefore reckoned in all 7. But afterwards they conſidered the *harmonical* and *arithmetical* Diviſions of the 8*ve*, whereby it reſolves into a 4*th* above a 5*th*, or a 5*th* above a 4*th* a *4th*. And from this they conſtituted 12 *Modes*, making of each *8ve* two different Modes according to this different Diviſion; but becauſe there are Two of them that cannot be divided both Ways, therefore there are but 12 Modes. To be more particular, conſider, in the natural Syſtem there are 7 different *Octaves* proceeding from theſe 7 Letters, *a*, *b*, *c*, *d*, *e*, *f*, *g*; each of which has Two middle Chords, which divide it *harmonically* and *arithmetically*, except *f*, which has not a true *4th*, (becauſe *b* is Three Tones above it, and a *4th* is but Two *Tones* and a *Semitone*) and *b*, which conſequently wants the true *5th* (becauſe *f* is only Two *Tones* and Two *Semitones* above it, and a true *5th* contains 3 *Tones* and a *Semitone*) therefore we have only 5 *Octaves* that are divided both Ways, *viz.* *a*, *c*, *d*, *e*, *g*, which make 10 Modes according to theſe different Diviſions, and the other Two *f* and *b* make up the 12. Theſe that are divided harmonically, *i. e.* with the *5ths* loweſt were called *authentick*, and the other *plagal* Modes. See the following Scheme.

To theſe Modes they gave the Names of the ancient *Greek Tones*, as *Dorian*, *Phrygian*: But ſeveral Authors differ in the Application of theſe Names, as they do about the Order, as, which they ſhall call the firſt and ſecond, &c. which being arbitrary Things, as far as I can underſtand, it were as idle to pretend to recon-

MODES.

Plagal.			*Authentick.*	
8*ve.*			8*ve.*	
4*th.*		5*th.*		4*th.*
g	--- *c*	--- *g*	--- *c*	
a	--- *d*	--- *a*	--- *d*	
b	--- *e*	--- *b*	--- *e*	
c	--- *f*	--- *c*	--- *f*	
d	--- *g*	--- *d*	--- *g*	
e	--- *a*	--- *e*	--- *a*	

cile them, as it was in them to differ about it. The material Point is, if we can find it, to know what they meant by these Distinctions, and what was the real Use of them in *Musick*; but even here where they ought to have agreed, we find they differed. The best Account I am able to give you of it is this: They considered that an 8*ve* which wants a 4*th* or 5*th*, is imperfect; these being the *Concords* next to 8*ve*, the Song ought to touch these Chords most frequently and remarkably; and because their *Concord* is different, which makes the Melody different, they established by this Two Modes in every natural *Octave*, that had a true 4*th* and 5*th*: Then if the Song was carried as far as the *Octave* above, it was called a *perfect Mode*; if less, as to the 4*th* or 5*th*, it was *imperfect*; if it moved both above and below, it was called a *mixt Mode*: Thus some Authors speak about these *Modes*. Others considering how indispensable a Chord the 5*th* is in every *Mode*, they took for the *final* or *Key*-note in the arithmetically divided *Octaves*, not the lowest Chord of that *Octave*, but that very 4*th*; for *Example*, the *Octave* g is arithmetically divided thus, *g* - *c* - *g*, *c* is a 4*th* above the lower *g*, and a 5*th* below the upper

per *g*, this *c* therefore they made the *final* Chord of the Mode, which therefore properly ſpeaking is *c* and not *g*; the only Difference then in this Method, betwixt the *authentick* and *plagal Modes* is, that the *Authentick* goes above its Final to the *Octave*, the other aſcends a *5th*, and deſcends a *4th*, which will indeed be attended with different Effects, but the Mode is eſſentially the ſame, having the ſame Final to which all the Notes refer. We muſt next conſider wherein the Modes of one Species, as *Authentick* or *Plagal*, differ among themſelves: This is either by their ſtanding higher or lower in the Scale, *i. e.* the different Tenſion of the whole *Octave*; or rather the different Subdiviſion of the *Octave* into its concinnous Degrees; there is not another. Let us conſider then whether theſe Differences are ſufficient to produce ſo very different Effects, as have been aſcribed to them, for *Example*, one is ſaid to be proper for Mirth, another for Sadneſs, a Third proper to Religion, another for tender and amorous Subjects, and ſo on: Whether we are to aſcribe ſuch Effects merely to the Conſtitution of the *Octave*, without Regard to other Differences and Ingredients in the Compoſition of Melody, I doubt any Body now a Days will be abſurd enough to affirm; theſe have their proper Differences, 'tis true, but which have ſo little Influence, that by the various Combinations of other Cauſes, one of theſe Modes may be uſed to different Purpoſes. The greateſt and moſt influencing Difference is that of

theſe

these *Octaves*, which have the 3*d l.* or 3*d g.* making what is above called the *sharp* and *flat Key* But we are to notice, that of all the 8*ves*, except *c* and *a*, none of them have all their essential Chords in just Proportion, unless we neglect the Difference of Tone greater and lesser, and also allow the *Semitone* to stand next the Fundamental in some flat Keys (which may be useful, and is sometimes used;) and when that is done, the *Octaves* that have a flat 3*d* will want the *6th g.* and *7th g.* which are very necessary on some Occasions ; and therefore the artificial Notes ※ and ♭ are of absolute Use to perfect the *System*. *Again*, if the Modes depend upon the Species of 8*ves*, how can they be more than 7? And as to this Distinction of *authentick* and *plagal*, I have shewn that it is imaginary, with respect to any essential Difference constituted hereby in the Kind of the Melody; for tho' the carrying the Song above or below the *Final*, may have a different Effect, yet this is to be numbred among the other Causes, and not ascribed to the Constitution of the *Octaves*. But 'tis particularly to be remarked, that these Authors who give us *Examples* in actual Composition of their 12 Modes, frequently take in the artificial Notes ※ and ♭ to perfect the *Melody* of their *Key*; and by this Means depart from the Constitution of the 8*ve*, as it stands in the fixt natural System. So we can find little certain and consistent in their Way of speaking about these Things; and their Modes are all reducible to Two, *viz.* the *sharp* and *flat* ; other

ther Differences refpecting only the Place of the Scale where the Fundamental is taken: I conclude therefore that the true Theory of *Modes* is that explained in *Chap. 9.* where they are diftinguifhed into Two Species, *fharp* and *flat*, whofe Effects I own are different; but other Caufes (*vid. Pag.* 547, &c.) muft concur to any remarkable Effect; and therefore 'tis unreafonable to talk as if all were owing to any one Thing. Before I have done there is another Thing you are to be informed of, *viz.* That what they called the Series of *b molle*, was no more than this, That becaufe the 8*ve* *f* had a 4*th* above at *b*, *exceffive* by a *Semitone*, and confequently the 8*ve* *b* had a 5*th* above as much deficient, therefore this artificial Note *b flat* or ♭, ferved them to tranfpofe their *Modes* to the Diftance of a 4*th* or 5*th*, above or below; for taking ♭ a Semitone above *a*, the reft keeping their *Ratios* already fixt, the Series proceeding from *c* with *b* natural (*i. e.* a Tone above *a*) is in the fame Order of Degrees, as that from *f* with *b flat* (i. e, ♭ a Semitone above *a*;) but *f* is a 4*th* above *c*, or a 5*th* below; therefore to tranfpofe from the Series of *b* natural to *b molle* we afcend a 4*th* or defcend a 5*th*; and contrarily from *b molle* to the other: This is the whole Myftery; but they never fpeak of the other Tranfpofitions that may be made by other artificial Notes.

You may alfo *obferve*, that what they called the *Ecclefiaftick Tones*, are no other than certain

tain Notes in the *Organ* which are made the *Final* or *Fundamental* of the Hymns; and as Modes they differ, ſome by their Place in the Scale, others by the *ſharp* and *flat* 3*d*; but even here every Author ſpeaks not the ſame Way: 'Tis enough we know they can differ no other Way, or at leaſt all their Differences can be reduced to theſe. At firſt they were Four in Number, whoſe *Finals* were *d*, *e*, *f*, *g* conſtituted *authentically*: This Choice, we are told, was firſt made by St. *Ambroſe* Biſhop of *Milan*; and for being thus choſen and approven, they pretend the Name *Authentick* was added: Afterwards *Gregory* the *Great* added Four *Plagals* *a*, *b*, *c*, *d*, whoſe Finals are the very ſame with the firſt Four, and in effect are only a Continuation of theſe to the 4*th* below; and for this Connection with them were called *plagal*, tho' the Derivation of the Word is not ſo plain.

BUT 'tis Time to have done; for I think I have ſhewn you the principal Steps of the Improvement of the *Syſtem* of *Muſick*, to the preſent State of it, as that is more largely explained in the preceeding *Chapters*. I have only one Word to add, that in *Guido*'s Time and long after, they ſuppoſed the Diviſion of the *Tetrachord* to be *Ptolomy*'s *Diatonum diatonicum*, *i. e.* Two *Tones* 8 : 9, and *a limma* $\frac{243}{256}$; till *Zarlinus* explained and demonſtrated, that it ought to be the *intenſum*, containing the Tone greater 8 : 9, leſſer 9 : 10, and *Semitone* 15 : 16; which *Kepler* ſtrongly argues for; as he alſo ſhews

ſhews how inconſiſtently they ſpake about the *Modes*, where he reduces all to the Two Species of *ſharp* and *flat*. 'Tis true, *Galileo* approves the other, as common Practice ſhewed that the Difference was inſenſible; yet it muſt be meant only with reſpect to common Practice. I have already explained, how this Difference in fixt Inſtruments is the very Reaſon of their Imperfection after the greateſt Pains to correct them; and how the natural Voice will, without any Direction, and even without perceiving it, chooſe ſometimes a greater, ſometimes a leſſer *Tone*: Therefore I think Nature guides us to the Choice of this Species: If the commenſurate *Ratios* of Vibrations are the Cauſe of *Concord* then certainly 4 : 5 is better than 64 : 81. The firſt ariſes from the Application of a ſimple general Rule upon which the more perfect *Concords* depend; the other comes in as it were arbitrarily. How the Proportions happen upon Inſtruments depends upon the Method of tuning them; of which enough has been already ſaid.

---

§ 6. *The* ancient *and* modern Muſick *compared.*

THE laſt Age was famous for the War that was raiſed, and eagerly maintain'd by two different Parties, concerning the ancient and modern *Genius* and *Learning*. Among the diſputed Points *Muſick* was one. I know of nothing

thing new to be advanced on either Side; so that I might refer you to those who have examined the Question already: But that nothing in my Power may be wanting to make this Work more acceptable, I shall put the Substance of that Controversy into the best Form I can, and shall endeavour to be at the same Time short and distinct.

THE Question in general is, Whether the *Ancients* or the *Moderns* best understood and practised *Musick?* Some affirm that the *ancient* Art of *Musick* is quite lost, among other valuable Things of Antiquity, *vid. Pancirollus, de Musica.* Others pretend, That the true Science of *Harmony* is arrived to much greater Perfection than what was known or practised among the Ancients. The Fault with many of the Contenders on this Point is, that they fight at long Weapons; I mean they keep the Argument in *generals*, by which they make little more of it than some innocent Harangues and Flourishes of Rhetorick, or at most make bold Assertions upon the Authority of some misapplied Expressions and incredible Stories of ancient Writers, for I'm now speaking chiefly of the Patrons of the ancient Musick.

IF Sir *William Temple* was indeed serious, and had any Thing else in his View, but to shew how he could declaim, he is a notable Instance of this. *Says he*, "What are become "of the Charms of Musick, by which "Men and Beasts were so frequently inchanted, "and

" and their very Natures changed, by which
" the Passions of Men were raised to the greatest
" Height and Violence, and then as suddenly
" appeased, so as they might be *justly* said, to
" be turned into Lions or Lambs, into Wolves
" or into Harts, by the Power and Charms of
" this admirable Art?" And he might have added too, by which the Trees and Stones were animated; in Spite of the Sense which *Horace* puts upon the Stories of *Orpheus* and *Amphion*. But this Question shall be considered presently. Again he says, " 'Tis agreed by the Learned, that
" the Science of Musick, so admired of the
" Ancients, is wholly lost in the World, and
" and that what we have now, is made up out
" of certain Notes that fell into the Fancy or
" Observation of a poor Friar, in chanting his
" Mattins. So that those Two divine Excel-
" lencies of *Musick* and *Poetry*, are grown in a
" Manner, but the one *Fiddling* and the other
" *Rhyming*, and are indeed very worthy the Ig-
" norance of the *Friar*, and the Barbarousness
" of the *Goths* that introduced them among us."
Some learned Men indeed have said so; but as learned have said otherwise: And for the Description Sir *William* gives of the modern *Musick*, it is the poorest Thing ever was said, and demonstrates the Author's utter Ignorance of Musick: Did he know what Use *Guido* made of these Notes? He means the Syllables, *ut, re, mi, &c.* for these are the Notes he invented. If the modern *Musick* falls short of the ancient, it

it muſt be in the Uſe and Application; for the Materials and Principles of *Harmony* are the ſame Thing, or rather they are improven; for *Guido*'s Scale to which he applied theſe Syllables, is the ancient *Greek* Scale only carried to a greater Extent; and which is much improven ſince.

As I have ſtated the Queſtion, we are firſt to compare the *Principles* and then the *Practice*. As to the *Principles* I have already explained them pretty largely, at leaſt as far as they have come to our Knowledge, by the Writings on this Subject that have eſcaped the Wrack of Time. Nor is there any great Reaſon to ſuſpect that the beſt are loſt, or that what we have are but Sketches of their Writings: For we have not a few Authors of them, and theſe written at different Times; and ſome of them at good Length; and by their Introductions they propoſe to handle the Subject in all its Parts and Extent, and have actually treated of them all.

MEIBOMIUS, no Enemy to the ancient Cauſe, ſpeaking of *Ariſtides*, calls him, *Incomparabilis antiquæ muſicæ Auctor, & vere exemplar unicum*, who, he ſays, has taught and explained all that was ever known or taught before him, in all the Parts' We have *Ariſtoxenus*; and for what was written before him, he affirms to have been very deficient: Nor do the later Writers ever complain of the Loſs of any valuable Author that was before them.

NOW I ſuppoſe it will be manifeſt to the unprejudiced, who conſider what has been explained

plained both of the ancient and modern Principles and Theory of *Harmonicks*, that they have not known more of it than we do, plainly becauſe we know all theirs; and that we have improven upon their Foundation, will be as plain from the Accounts I have given of both, and the Compariſon I have drawn all along in explaining the *ancient Theory*; therefore I need inſiſt no more upon this Part. The great Diſpute is about the Practice.

To underſtand the ancient *Practice* of *Muſick*, we are firſt to conſider what the Name ſignified with them. I have already explained its various Significations; and ſhewn, that in the moſt particular Senſe, *Muſick* included theſe Three Things, *Harmony*, *Rythmus* and *Verſe*: If there needs any Thing to be added, take theſe few Authorities. In *Plato*'s firſt *Alcibiades*, *Socrates* asks what he calls that Art which teaches to *ſing*, *play* on the *Harp*, and *dance*? and makes him Anſwer, *Muſick*: But ſinging among them was never without Verſe. This is again confirmed by *Plutarch*, who ſays, "That in "judging of the Parts of *Muſick*, Reaſon and "Senſe muſt be employed; for theſe three "muſt always meet in our Hearing, *viz. Sound*, "whereby we perceive *Harmony*; *Time*, "whereby we perceive *Rythmus*; and *Letters* "or *Syllables*, by which we underſtand what "is ſaid." Therefore we reaſonably conclude, that their Muſick conſiſted of Verſes ſung by one or more Voices, alternately, or in Choirs; ſometimes

times with the Sound of Inſtruments, and ſometimes by Voices only; and whether they had any *Muſick* without Singing, ſhall be again conſidered.

LET us now conſider what *Idea* their Writers give us of the *practical Muſick*: I don't ſpeak of the Effects, which ſhall be examined again, but of the *practical Art*. This we may expect, if 'tis to be found at all, from the Authors who write *ex profeſſo* upon Muſick, and pretend to explain it in all its Parts. I have already ſhewn, that they make the *muſical Faculties* (as they call them) theſe, *viz. Melopœia*, *Rythmopœia*, and *Poeſis*. For the *Firſt*, to make the Compariſon right, I ſhall conſider it under theſe Two Heads, *Melody* and *Symphony*, and begin with the laſt. I have obſerved, in explaining the Principles of the ancient *Melopœia*, that it contains nothing but what relates to the Conduct of a ſingle Voice, or making what we call *Melody*: There is not the leaſt Word of the *Concert* or *Harmony* of Parts; from which there is very great Reaſon to conclude, that this was no Part of the ancient Practice, and is altogether a modern Invention, and a noble one too; the firſt Rudiments of which I have already ſaid we ow to that ſame poor Friar (as Sir *William Temple* calls him) *Guido Aretinus*. But that there be no Difference about mere Words, obſerve, that the Queſtion is not, Whether the Ancients ever joyned more Voices or Inſtruments together in one *Symphony*; but, whether ſeveral Voices were joyned, ſo as each

had

had a diſtinct and proper *Melody*, which made among them a Succeſſion of various *Concords*; and were not in every Note *Uniſons*, or at the ſame Diſtance from each other, as 8ves? which laſt will agree to the general Signification of the Word *Symphonia*; yet 'tis plain, that in ſuch Caſes there is but one Song, and all the Voices perform the ſame individual *Melody*; but when the *Parts* differ, not by the Tenſion of the Whole, but by the different Relations of the ſucceſſive Notes, This is the modern Art that requires ſo peculiar a Genius, and good Judgment, in which therefore 'tis ſo difficult to ſucceed well. The ancient *Harmonick* Writers, in their Rules and Explications of the *Melopœia*, ſpeak nothing of this Art: They tell us, that the *Melopœia* is the Art of making Songs; or more generally, that it is the Uſe of all the Parts and Principles that are the Subjects of *harmonical Contemplation*. Now is it at all probable, that ſo conſiderable an Uſe of theſe Principles was known among the Ancients, and yet never once mentioned by thoſe who profeſſed to write of *Muſick* in all its Parts? Shall we think theſe concealed it, becauſe they envied Poſterity ſo valuable an Art? Or, was it the Difficulty of explaining it that made them ſilent? They might at leaſt have ſaid there was ſuch an Art; the Definition of it is eaſy enough: Is it like the reſt of their Conduct to neglect any Thing that might redound in any Degree to their own Praiſe and Glory? Since we find no Notice of this Art

Art under the *Melopœia*, I think we cannot expect it in any other Part. If any Body ſhould think to find it in the Part that treats of *Syſtems*, becauſe that expreſſes a Compoſition of ſeveral Things, they'll be diſappointed: For theſe Authors have conſidered Syſtems only as greater *Intervals* betwixt whoſe Extremes other Notes are placed, dividing them into leſſer *Intervals*, in ſuch Manner as a ſingle Voice may paſs agreeably from the one Extreme to the other. But in diſtinguiſhing *Syſtems* they tell us, ſome are σύμφωνα ſome διάφωνα, *i. e.* ſome *conſonant* ſome *diſſonant*: Which Names expreſſed the Quality of theſe *Syſtems*, *viz.* that of the firſt, the Extremes are fit to be heard together, and the other not; and if they were not uſed in Conſonance, may ſome ſay, theſe Names are wrong applied: But tho' they ſignified that Quality, it will not prove they were uſed in Conſonance, at leaſt in the modern Way: Beſides, when they ſpeak plainly and expreſly of their Uſe in Succeſſion or *Melody*, they uſe the ſame Names, to ſignify their Agreement: And if they were uſed in Conſonance in the Manner deſcribed, why have we not at leaſt ſome general Rules to guide us in the Practice? Or rather, does not their Silence in this demonſtrate there was no ſuch Practice? But tho' there is nothing to be found in thoſe who have written more fully and expreſly on Muſick, yet the Advocates for the ancient Muſick find Demonſtration enough, they think, in ſome Paſſages of Authors that have given tranſient Deſcriptions of Muſick:

But

But if theſe Paſſages are capable of any other good Senſe than they put upon them, I think the Silence of the profeſſed Writers on *Muſick* will undoubtedly caſt the Balance on that Side. To do all Juſtice to the Argument, I ſhall produce the principal and fulleſt of theſe Kind of Paſſages in their Authors Words. *Ariſtotle* in his Treatiſe concerning the World, περι κοσμȣ, *Lib.* 5. anſwers that Queſtion, If the World is made of contrary Principles, how comes it that it is not long ago diſſolved? He ſhews that the Beauty and Perfection of it conſiſts in the admirable Mixture and Temperament of different Things, and among his Illuſtrations brings in *Muſick* thus, Μȣσικὴ δε ὀξεῖς ἅμα και βαρεῖς, μακρύς τε και βραχεῖς Φθόγγȣς μίξασα, ἐν διαφόραις Φωναῖς, μίαν ἀπετέλεσεν ἁρμονίαν, which the Tranſlators juſtly render thus, *Muſica acutis & gravibus ſonis, longiſque & brevibus una permixtis in diverſis vocibus, unum ex illis concentum reddit*, *i. e. Muſick*, by a Mixture of acute and grave, alſo of long and ſhort Sounds of different Voices, yields one abſolute or perfect *Concert. Again*, in *Lib.* 6. explaining the Harmony of the celeſtial Motions, where each Orb, ſays he, has its own proper Motion, yet all tend to one harmonious End, as they alſo proceed from one Principle, making a *Choir* in the Heavens by their Concord, and he carries on the Compariſon with Muſick thus: Καθάπερ δε ἐν χορῷ κορυφαίȣ καταρξαντες, συνεπηχεῖ πᾶς ὁ χορὸς ἀνδρων ἔθ ὅτε καὶ γυναικων εν διαφὸραις Φωναῖς ὀξυτέραις καὶ βαρυτέραις μιαν ἁρμονίαν ἐμμελῆ κεραννύντων.

νύντων. *Quemadmodum fit in* Choro, *ut auſpicianti præſuli aut præcentori, accinat omnis chorus, e viris interdum fœminiſque compoſitus, qui diverſis ipſis vocibus, gravibus ſcilicet & acutis concentum attemperant. i. e.* As in a *Choir*, after the *Præcentor* the whole *Choir* ſings, compoſed ſometimes of Men and Women, who by the different Acuteneſs and Gravity of their Voices, make one *concinnous* Harmony.

LET *Seneca* appear next, *Epiſtle* 84. *Non vides quam multorum vocibus Chorus conſtet? Unus tamen ex omnibus ſonus redditur, aliqua illic acuta eſt, aliqua gravis, aliqua media. Accedunt viris fœminæ, interponuntur tibiæ, ſingulorum latent voces, omnium apparent. i. e.* Don't you ſee of how many Voices the *Chorus* conſiſts? yet they make but one Sound: In it ſome are acute, ſome grave, and ſome middle: Women are joyned with Men, and Whiſtles alſo put in among them: Each ſingle Voice is concealed, yet the Whole is manifeſt.

CASSIODORUS ſays, *Symphonia eſt temperamentum ſonitus gravis ad acutum, vel acuti ad gravem, modulamen efficiens, ſive in voce ſive in percuſſione, ſive in flatu. i. e. Symphony* is an Adjuſtment of a grave Sound to an acute, or an acute to a grave, making *Melody*.

NOW the moſt that can be made of theſe Paſſages is, That the Ancients uſed *Choirs* of ſeveral Voices differing in Acuteneſs and Gravity; which was never denied: But the Whole of theſe Definitions will be fully anſwered, ſuppoſing

posing they sung all the same *Part* or *Song* only in different Tensions, as 8*ve* in every Note. And from what was premised I think there is Reason to believe this to be the only true Meaning.

But there are other considerable Things to be said that will put this Question beyond all reasonable Doubt. The Word *Harmonia* signifies more generally the Agreement of several Things that make up one Whole; but so do several Sounds in Succession make up one *Song*, which is in a very proper Sense a Composition. And in this Sense we have in *Plato* and others several Comparisons to the *Harmony* of Sounds in *Musick*. But 'tis also used in the strict Sense for *Consonance*, and so is equivalent to the Word *Symphonia*. Now we shall make *Aristotle* clear his own Meaning in the Passages adduced: He uses *Symphonia* to express Two Kinds of *Consonance*; the one, which he calls by the general Name *Symphonia*, is the Consonance of Two Voices that are in every Note *unison*, and the other, which he calls *Antiphonia*, of Two Voices that are in every Note 8*ve*: In his *Problems*, § 19. *Prob.* 16. He asks why *Symphonia* is not as agreeable as *Antiphonia*; and answers, because in *Symphonia* the one Voice being altogether like or as *One* with the other, they eclipse one another. The *Symphoni* here plainly must signify *Unisons*, and he explains it elsewhere by calling them *Omophoni*: And that the 8*ve* is the *Antiphoni* is plain, for it was a common Name to 8*ve*; and *Aristotle* himself

explains

explains the *Antiphoni* by the Voice of a Boy and a Man that are as *Nete* and *Hypate*, which were 8*ve* in *Pythagoras*'s Lyre. *Again*, I own he is not ſpeaking here of *Uniſon* and 8*ve* ſimply conſidered, but as uſed in *Song* : And tho' in modern *Symphonies* it is alſo true, that *Uniſon* cannot be ſo frequently uſed with as good Effect as 8*ve*, yet his Meaning is plainly this, *viz.* that when Two Voices ſing together one Song, 'tis more agreeable that they be 8*ve* than *uniſon* with one another, in every Note: This I prove from the 17*th Probl.* in which he asks why *Diapente* and *Diateſſaron* are never ſung as the *Antiphoni* ? He anſwers, becauſe the *Antiphoni*, or Sounds of 8*ve*, are in a Manner both the ſame and different Voices ; and by this Likeneſs, where at the ſame Time each keeps its own diſtinct Character, we are better pleaſed: Therefore he affirms, that the 8*ve* only can be ſung in *Symphony* (διὰ πασῶν συμφωνία μόνη ἄδεται.) Now that by this he means ſuch a *Symphony* as I have explained, is certain, becauſe in modern *Counterpoint* the 4*th*, and eſpecially the 5*th* are indiſpenſable ; and indeed the 5*th* with its Two 3*ds*, are the Life of the Whole. *Again*, in *Probl.* 18. he asks why why the *Diapaſon* only is *magadiſed* ? And anſwers, becauſe its Terms are the only *Antiphoni* : Now that this ſignifies a Manner of Singing, where the Sounds are in every Note 8*ve* to one another, is plain from this Word *magadiſed*, taken from the Name of an Inſtrument μαγάδιος, in which Two Strings were always ſtruck toge-

together for one Note. *Athenæus* makes the *Magadis* the ſame with the *Barbiton* and *Pectis*; and *Horace* makes the Muſe *Polyhymnia* the Inventor of the *Barbiton.* — *Nec Polyhymnia* Lesboum *refugit tendere* Barbiton.— And from the Nature of this Inſtument, that it had Two Strings to every Note, ſome think it probable the Name *Polyhymnia* was deduced. *Athenæus* reports from *Anacreon*, that the *Magadis* had Twenty Chords; which is a Number ſufficient to make us allow they were doubled; ſo that it had in all Ten Notes: Now anciently they had but Three *Tones* or *Modes*, and each extended only to an 8*ve.* and being a *Tone* aſunder, required preciſely Ten Chords; therefore *Athenæus* corrects *Poſſidonius* for ſaying the Twenty Chords were all diſtinct Notes, and neceſſary for the Three *Modes*. But he further confirms this Point by a Citation from the Comick Poet *Alexandrides*, who takes a Compariſon from the *Magadis*, and ſays, *I am, like the* Magadis, *about to make you underſtand a Thing that is at the ſame Time both ſublime and low*; which proves that Two Strings were ſtruck together, and that they were not *uniſon*. He reports alſo the Opinion of the Poet *Jon*, that the *Magadis* conſiſted of Two Flutes, which were both ſounded together. From all this 'tis plain, That by *magadiſed*, *Ariſtotle* means ſuch a Conſonance of Sounds as to be in every Note at the ſame Diſtance, and conſequently to be without *Symphony* and Parts according to the modern Practice. *Athenæus* reports alſo of

of *Pindar*, that he called the Muſick ſung by a Boy and a Man *Magadis* ; becauſe they ſung together the ſame Song in Two *Modes*. Mr. *Perault* concludes from this, that the Strings of the *Magadis* were ſometimes 3*ds*, becauſe *Ariſtotle* ſays, the 4*th* and 5*th* are never *magadiſed* : But why may not *Pindar* mean that they were at an 8*ve*'s Diſtance ; for certainly *Ariſtotle* uſed that Compariſon of a Boy and a Man to expreſs an 8*ve* : Mr. *Perault* thinks it muſt be a 3*d* becauſe of the Word *Mode*, whereof anciently there were but Three; and confirms it by a Paſſage out of *Horace*, Epod. 9. *Sonante miſtum tibiis carmen lyra*; *hac* Dorium *illis* Barbarum: By the *Barbarum*, ſays he, is to be underſtood the *Lydian*, which was a *Ditone* above the *Dorian* : But the Difficulty is, that the Ancients reckoned the *Ditone* at beſt a *concinnous Diſcord*; and therefore 'tis not probable they would uſe it in ſo remarkable a Manner: But we have enough of this. The Author laſt named obſerves, that the Ancients probably had a Kind of ſimple Harmony, in which Two or Three Notes were tuned to the principal Chords of the *Key*, and accompanied the Song. This he thinks probable from the Name of an Inſtrument *Pandora* that *Athenæus* mentions; which is likely the ſame with the *Mandora*, an Inſtrument not very long ago uſed, ſays he, in which there were Four Strings, whereof one ſerved for the Song, and was ſtruck by a *Plectrum* or Quill tied to the Fore-finger: The other Three were tuned
ſo

ſo as Two of them were an 8*ve*, and the other a Middle dividing the 8*ve* into a 4*th* and 5*th:* They were ſtruck by the Thumb, and this regulated by the *Rythmus* or Meaſure of the Song, *i. e.* Four Strokes for every Meaſure of common Time, and Three for Triple. He thinks *Horace* points out the Manner of this Inſtrument in *Ode 6.* Lesbium *ſervate pedem, meique pollicis ictum,* which he thus tranſlates. *Take Notice, you who would joyn your Voice to the Sound of my Lyre, that the Meaſure of my Song is* Sapphick, *which the ſtriking of my Thumb marks out to you.* This Inſtrument is parallel to our common Bagpipe.

THE Paſſages of *Ariſtotle* being thus cleared, I think *Seneca* and *Caſſiodorus* may be eaſily given up. *Seneca* ſpeaks of *vox media*, as well as *acuta* and *gravis* ; but this can ſignify nothing, but that there might be Two 8*ves*, one betwixt the Men and Women and the ſhrill *Tibiæ* might be 8*ve* above the Women : But then the latter Part of what he ſays deſtroys their Cauſe ; for *ſingulorum voces latent* can very well be ſaid of ſuch as ſing the ſame Melody *Uniſon* or *Octave*, but would by no Means be true of ſeveral Voices performing a modern *Symphony*, where every Part is conſpicuous, with a perfect Harmony in the Whole. For *Caſſiodorus*, I think what he ſays has no Relation to *Conſonance*, and therefore I have tranſlated it, *An Adjuſtment of a grave Sound to an acute, or an acute to a grave making Melody* : If it be alledged that *temperamentum* may ſignifie a Mixture, I ſhall yield

yield it; but then he ought to have ſaid, *Temperamentum ſonitus gravis & acuti*; for what means *ſonitus gravis ad acutum*, and again *acuti ad gravem?* But in the other Caſe this is well enough, for he means, That Melody may conſiſt either in a Progreſs from acute to grave, or contrarily: And then the Word *Modulamen* was never applied any other way than to ſucceſſive Sounds. There is another Paſſage which *Iſ. Voſſius* cites from *Ælian* the *Platonick*, Συμφωνία δὲ ἐςι δυοῖν ἢ πλειόνων φθόγγων ὀξύτητι καὶ βαρύτητι διαφερόντων κατα τὸ ἀυτὸ πτῶσις καὶ κρᾶσις, i. e. Symphony conſiſts of Two or more Sounds differing in Acuteneſs and Gravity, with the ſame Cadence and Temperament: But this rather adds another Proof that what Symphonies they had were only of ſeveral Voices ſinging the ſame *Melody* only in a different Tone.

After ſuch evident Demonſtrations, I think there needs no more to be ſaid to prove that *Symphonies* of different *Parts* are a modern Improvement. From their rejecting the 3*ds* and 6*ths* out of the Number of *Concords*, the ſmall Extent of their Syſtem being only Two *Octaves*, and having no Tone divided but that betwixt *Meſe* and *Parameſe*, we might argue that they had no different *Parts*: For tho ſome ſimple Compoſitions of Parts might be contrived with theſe Principles, yet 'tis hard to think they would lay the Foundations of that Practice, and carry it no further; and much harder to believe they would never ſpeak one Word of ſuch an Art and Practice, where they profeſs to explain all the

the Parts of Musick. But for the *Symphonies* which we allow them to have had, you'll ask why these Writers don't speak of them, and why it seems so incredible that they should have had the other Kind without being ever mentioned, when they don't mention these we allow? The Reason is plain, because the Musician's Business was only to compose the *Melody*, and therefore they wanted only Rules about that; but there was no Rule required to teach how several Voices might joyn in the same Song, for there is no Art in it: Experience taught them that this might be done in *Unison* or *Octave*; and pray what had the Writers more to say about it? But the modern *Symphony* is a quite different Thing, and needs much to be explained both by Rules and Examples. But tis Time to make an End of this Point: I shall only add, That if plain *Reason* needs any Authority to support it, I can adduce many Moderns of Character, who make no Doubt to say, That after all their Pains to know the true State of the ancient *Musick*, they could not find the least Ground to believe there was any such Thing in these Days as *Musick* in *Parts*. I have named *Perrault*, and shall only add to him *Kircher* and Doctor *Wallis*, Authors of great Capacity and infinite Industry.

OUR next Comparison shall be of the *Melody* of the Ancients and Moderns; and here comes in what's necessary to be said on the other Parts of *Musick*, viz. the *Rythmus* and *Verse*. In order to this Comparison, I shall distinguish *Melody*

Melody into *vocal* and *inſtrumental*. By the firſt I mean *Muſick* ſet to Words, eſpecially Verſes; and by the other *Muſick* compoſed only for Inſtruments without Singing. For the *vocal* you ſee by the Definition that *Poetry* makes a neceſſary Part of it: This was not only of ancient Practice, but the chief, if not their only Practice, as appears from their Definitions of *Muſick* already explain'd. 'Tis not to be expected that I ſhould make any Compariſon of the ancient and modern Poetry; 'tis enough for my Purpoſe to obſerve, That there are admirable Performances in both; and if we come ſhort of them, I believe 'tis not for want either of Genius or Application: But perhaps we ſhall be obliged to own that the *Greek* and *Latin* Languages were better contrived for pleaſing the Ear. We are next to conſider, that the *Rythmus* of their *vocal Muſick* was only that of the Poetry, depending altogether on the Verſe, and had no other Forms or Variety than what the metrical Art afforded: This has been already ſhewn, particularly in explaining their muſical Notes; to which add, That under the Head of *Mutations*, thoſe who conſider the *Rythmus* make the Changes of it no other than from one Kind of *metrum* or *Verſe* to another, as from *Jambick* to *Choraick*: And we may notice too, That in the more general Senſe, the *Rythmus* includes alſo their Dancings, and all the theatrical Action. I conclude therefore that their vocal *Muſick* conſiſted of Verſes, ſet to *muſical Tones*, and ſung by one or more Voices

Voices in Choirs or alternately; ſometimes with and alſo without the Accompanyment of Inſtruments: To which we may add, from the laſt Article, That their Symphonies conſiſted only of ſeveral Voices performing the ſame Song in different Tones as *Uniſon* and *Octave*. For *inſtrumental Muſick* (as I have defined it) 'tis not ſo very plain that they uſed any: And if they did, 'tis more than probable the *Rythmus* was only an Imitation of the poetical Numbers, and conſiſted of no other Meaſures than what were taken from the Variety and Kinds of their Verſes; of which they pretended a ſufficient Variety for expreſſing any Subject according to its Nature and Property: And ſince the chief Deſign of their *Muſick* ſeems to have been to move the Heart and Paſſions, they needed no other *Rythmus*. I cannot indeed deny that there are many Paſſages which fairly inſinuate their Practice upon Inſtruments without Singing; ſo *Athenæus* ſays, *The* Synaulia *was a Conteſt of Pipes performing alternately without ſinging.* And *Quintilian* hath this Expreſſion, *If the Numbers and Airs of* Muſick *have ſuch a Vertue, how much more ought eloquent Words to have?* That is to ſay, the other has Virtue or Power to move us, without Reſpect to the Words. But if they had any *Rythmus* for inſtrumental Performances, which was different from that of their *poetical Meaſures*, how comes it to paſs that thoſe Authors who have been ſo full in explaining the Signs by which their Notes of *Muſick* were repreſented, ſpeak not

not a Word of the Signs of Time for Instruments? Whatever be in this, it must be owned that Singing with Words was the most ancient Practice of *Musick*, and the Practice of their more solemn and perfect Entertainments, as appears from all the Instances above adduced, to prove the ancient Use and Esteem of *Musick*: And that it was the universal and common Practice, even with the Vulgar, appears by the pastoral Dialogues of the Poets, where the Contest is ordinarily about their Skill in *Musick*, and chiefly in Singing.

LET us next consider what the present Practice (among *Europeans* at least) consists of. We have, *first*, *vocal Musick*; and this differs from the ancient in these Respects, *viz.* That the Constitution of the *Rythmus* is different from that of the Verse, so far, that in setting Musick to Words, the Thing principally minded is, to accommodate the long and short Notes to the Syllables in such Manner as the Words may be well separated, and the accented Syllable of every Word so conspicuous, that what is sung may be distinctly understood: The Movement and Measure is also suited to the different Subjects, for which the Variety of Notes, and the Constitutions or Modes of Time explained in *Chap.* 12. afford sufficient means. Then we differ from the Ancients in our instrumental Accompanyments, which compose Symphonies with the Voice, some in *Unison*, others making a distinct *Melody*; which produces a ravishing Entertainment they were not blest with, or at least

with

without which we ſhould think ours imperfect. Then there is a delightful Mixture of pure inſtrumental Symphonies, performed alternately with the Song. *Laſtly*, We have Compoſitions fitted altogether for Inſtruments: The Deſign whereof is not ſo much to move the Paſſions, as to entertain the Mind and pleaſe the Fancy with a Variety of Harmony and *Rythmus*; the principal Effect of which is to raiſe Delight and Admiration. This is the plain State of the ancient and modern *Muſick*, in reſpect of Practice: But to determine which of them is moſt perfect, will not perhaps be ſo eaſily done to ſatisfie every Body. Tho' we believe theirs to have been excellent in its Kind, and to have had noble Effects; this will not pleaſe ſome, unleſs we acknowledge ours to be barbarous, and altogether ineffectual. The Effects are indeed the true Arguments; but how ſhall we compare theſe, when there remain no Examples of ancient Compoſition to judge by? ſo that the Defenders of the ancient *Muſick* admire a Thing they don't know; and in all Probability judge not of the modern by their perſonal Acquaintance with it, but by their Fondneſs for their own Notions. Thoſe who ſtudy our *Muſick*, and have well tuned Ears, can bear Witneſs to its noble Effects: Yet perhaps it will be replied, *That this proceeds from a bad Taſte, and ſomething natural, in applauding the beſt Thing we know of any Kind.* But let any Body produce a better, and we ſhall heartily applaud it. They bid us bring back the ancient *Muſicians*,

and

and then they'll effectually shew us the Difference; and we bid them learn to understand the *modern Musick*, and believe their own Senses: In short we think we have better Reason to determine in our own Favours, from the Effects we actually feel, than any Body can have from a Thing they have no Experience of, and can pretend to know no other Way than by Report: But we shall consider the Pretences of each Party a little nearer. I have already observed, that the principal End the Ancients proposed in their *Musick*, was to move the Passions; and to this purpose Poetry was a necessary Ingredient. We have no Dispute about the Power of poetical Compositions to affect the Heart, and move the Passions, by such a strong and lively Representation of their proper Objects, as that noble Art is capable of: The Poetry of the Ancients we own is admirable; and their Verses being sung with harmonious Cadences and Modulations, by a clear and sweet Voice, supported by the agreeable Sound of some Instrument, in such Manner that the Hearer understood every Word that was said, which was all delivered with a proper Action, *that is*, Pronunciation and Gestures suitable to, or expressive of the Subject, as we also suppose the Kind of Verse, and the Modulation applied to it was; taking their vocal *Musick* in this View, we make no Doubt that it had admirable Effects in exciting Love, Pity, Anger, Grief, or any Thing else the Poet had a Mind to: But then they must be allowed to affirm, who pretend to have the Experience of

it,

it, That the modern *Musick* taking it in the same Sense, has all these Effects. *Whatever* Truth may be in it, I shall pass what Doctor *Wallis* alledges, *viz. That these ancient Effects were most remarkably produced upon Rusticks, and at a Time when* Musick *was new, or a very rare Thing*: But I cannot however miss to observe with him, That the Passions are easily wrought upon. The deliberate Reading of a Romance well written will produce Tears, Joy, or Indignation, if one gives his Imaginations a Loose; but much more powerfully when attended with the Things mentioned: So that it can't be thought so very mysterious and wonderful an Art to excite Passion, as that it should be quite lost. Our Poets are capable to express any moving Story in a very pathetick Manner: Our *Musicians* too know how to apply a suitable Modulation and *Rythmus*: And we have those who can put the Whole in Execution; so that a Heart capable of being moved will be forced to own the wonderful Power of *modern Musick*. The *Italian* and *English* Theatres afford sufficient Proof of this; so that I believe, were we to collect Examples of the Effects that the *acting of modern Tragedies* and *Operas* have produced, there would be no Reason to say we had lost the Art of exciting Passion. But 'tis needless to insist on a Thing which so many know by their own Experience. If some are obstinate to affirm, *That we are still behind the Ancients in this Art, because they have never felt such Effects of it*; I shall ask them if

they

they think every Temper and Mind among the Ancients was equally disposed to relish, and be moved by the same Things? If Tempers differed then, why may they not now, and yet the Art be at least as powerful as ever? Again have we not as good Reason to believe those who affirm they feel this Influence, as you who say you have never experienced it? And if you put the Matter altogether upon the Authority of others, pray, is not the Testimony of the Living for the one, as good as that of the Dead for the other?

But still there are Wonders pretended to have been performed by the ancient *Musick*, which we can produce nothing like; such as those amazing Transports of Mind, and hurrying of Men from one Passion to another, all on a sudden, like the moving of a Machine, of which we have so many Examples in History, *See Page* 495. For these I shall answer, That what we reckon incredible in them may justly be laid upon the Historians, who frequently aggravate Things beyond what's strictly true, or even their Credulity in receiving them upon weak Grounds; and most of these Stories are delivered to us by Writers who were not themselves Witnesses of them, and had them only by Tradition and common Report. If nothing like this had ever been justly objected to the ancient Historians, I should think my self obliged to find another Answer: But since 'tis so, we may be allowed to doubt of these Facts, or suspect at least that they are in a great Degree *hyperbolical*. Consider but the

Circumſtances of ſome of them as they are told, and if they are literally true, and can be accounted for no other Way but by the Power of Sound, I muſt own they had an Art which is loſt: For *Example*, the quelling of a Sedition; let us repreſent to our ſelves a furious Rabble, envenomed with Diſcontent, and enraged with Oppreſſion; or let the Grounds of their Rebellion be as imaginary as you pleaſe, ſtill we muſt conſider them as all in a Flame; ſuppoſe next they are attacked by a skilful Muſician, who addreſſes them with his Pipe or Lyre; how likely is it that he ſhall perſwade them by a Song to return to their Obedience, and lay down their Arms? Or rather how probable is it that he may be torn to Pieces, as a ſolemn Mocker of their juſt Reſentment? But that I may allow ſome Foundation for ſuch a Story, I ſhall ſuppoſe a Man of great Authority for Virtue, Wiſdom and the Love of Mankind, comes to offer his humble and affectionate Advice to ſuch a Company; I ſuppoſe too, he delivers it in Verſe, and perhaps ſings it to the Sound of his Lyre, (which ſeems to have been a common Way of delivering publick Exhortations in more ancient Times, the *Muſick* being uſed as a Means to gain their Attention.) I don't think it impoſſible that this Man may perſwade them to Peace, by repreſenting the Danger they run, aggravating the Miſchief they are like to bring upon themſelves and the Society, or alſo correcting the falſe Views they may have had of Things. But then will any Body ſay, all this

is

is the proper Effect of *Musick*, unless Reasoning be also a Part of it? And must this be an *Example* of the Perfection of the ancient Art, and its Preference to ours? In the same Manner may other Instances alledged be accounted for, such as *Pythagoras*'s diverting a young Man from the Execution of a wicked Design, the Reconcilement of Two inveterate Enemies, the curing of *Clytemnestra*'s vicious Inclinations, *&c.* *Horace*'s Explication of the Stories of *Orpheus* and *Amphion*, makes it probable we ought to explain all the rest the same Way. For the Story of *Timotheus* and *Alexander*, as commonly represented, it is indeed a very wonderful one, but I doubt we must here allow something to the Boldness or Credulity of the Historian: That *Timotheus*, by singing to his Lyre, with moving Gesture and Pronunciation, a well composed Poem of the Atchievements of some renowned Hero, as *Achilles*, might awaken *Alexander*'s natural Passion for warlike Glory, and make him express his Satisfaction with the Entertainment in a remarkable Manner, is nowise incredible: We are to consider too the Fondness he had for the *Iliad*, which would dispose him to be moved with any particular Story out of that: But how he should forget himself so far, as to commit Violence on his best Friend, is not so easily accounted for, unless we suppose him at that Time as much under the Power of *Bacchus* as of the *Muses*: And that a softer Theme sung with equal Art, should please a Hero who was
not

not insensible of *Venus*'s Influences is no Mystery, especially when his Mistress was in Company: But there is nothing here above the Power of modern *Poetry* and *Musick*, where it meets with a Subject the same Way disposed, to be wrought upon. To make an End of this, I must observe, that the Historians, by saying too much, have given us Ground to believe very little. What do you think of curing a raging Pestilence by *Musick?* For curing the Bites of Serpents, we cannot so much doubt it, since that of the *Tarantula* has been cured in *Italy*. But then they have no Advantage in this Instance: And we must mind too that this Cure is not performed by exquisite Art and Skill in *Musick*; it does not require a *Correlli* or *Valentini*, but is performed by Strains discovered by random Trials without any Rule: And this will serve for an Answer to all that's alledged of the Cure of Diseases by the ancient *Musick*.

'TIS Time to bring this Comparison to an End; and after what's explained I shall make no Difficulty to own, that I think the State of *Musick* is much more perfect now than it was among the ancient *Greeks* and *Romans*. The Art of *Musick*, and the true Science of *Harmony* in Sounds is greatly improven. I have allowed their *Musick* (including Poetry and the theatrical Action) to have been very moving; but at the same Time I must say, their *Melody* has been a very simple Thing, as their *System* or *Scale* plainly shews, whose Difference from the modern I have already explained.

And

And the confining all their *Rythmus* to the poetical Numbers, is to me another Proof of it, and ſhews that there has been little Air in their *Muſick*; which by this appears to have been only of the recitative Kind, *that is*, only a more *muſical* Speaking, or *modulated* Elocution; the Character of which is to come near Nature, and be only an Improvement of the natural Accents of Words by more pathetick or emphatical *Tones*; the Subject whereof may be either Verſe or Proſe. And as to their Inſtruments of *Muſick*, for any Thing that appears certain and plain to us, they have been very ſimple. Indeed the publick Laws in *Greece* gave Check to the Improvement of the Art of *Harmony*, becauſe they forbade all Innovations in the primitive ſimple Muſick; of which there are abundance of Teſtimonies, ſome whereof have been mentioned in this *Chapter*, and I ſhall add what *Plato* ſays in his Treatiſe of the Laws, *viz.* That they entertain'd not in the City the Makers of ſuch Inſtruments as have many Strings, as the *Trigonus* and *Pectis*; but the *Lyra* and *Cithara* they uſed, and allowed alſo ſome ſimple *Fiſtulæ* in the Country. But 'tis certain, that primitive Simplicity was altered; ſo that from a very few Strings, they uſed a greater Number: But there is much Uncertainty about the Uſe of them, as whether it was for mixing their *Modes*, and the *Genera*, or for ſtriking Two Chords together as in the *Magadis*. Since I have mentioned *Inſtruments*, I muſt obſerve Two Things, *Firſt*, That they pretend to have had *Tibiæ* of diffe-

different Kinds, whose specifick Sounds were excellently chosen for expressing different Subjects. *Then*, there is a Description of the *Organum hydraulicum* in *Tertullian*, which some adduce to prove how perfect their *Instruments* were. — *Specta portentosam* Archimedis *munificentiam ; organum hydraulicum dico, tot membra, tot partes, tot compagines, tot itinera vocum, tot compendia sonorum, tot commercia modorum, tot acies tibiarum, & una moles erunt omnia* ; where he had learnt this pompous Description of it I know not ; for one can get but a very obscure *Idea* of it from *Vitruvius*, even after *Kircher* and *Vossius*'s Explications. But I hope it will not be pretended to have been more perfect than our modern Organs: And what have they to compare of the stringed Kind, with our Harpsichords; and all the Instruments that are struck with a Bow ?

After all, if our *Melody* or Songs are only equal to the Ancients, I hope the Art of *Musick* is not lost as some pretend. But then, what an Improvement in the Knowledge of pure *Harmony* has been made, since the Introduction of the modern *Symphonies?* Here it is, that the Mind is ravished with the Agreement of Things seemingly contrary to one another. We have here a Kind of Imitation of the Works of Nature, where different Things are wonderfully joyned in one harmonious Unity : And as some Things appear at first View the farthest removed from Symmetry and Order, which from the Course of Things we learn to be absolutely necessary for the Perfection on and Beauty of the Whole ; so *Discords* being artfully mixed with *Concords*, make a more perfect Composition, which surprises us with Delight. If the Mind is naturally pleased with perceiving of Order and Proportion, with comparing several Things together, and discerning in the midst of a seeming Confusion, the most perfect and exact Disposition and united Agreement; then the modern *Concerts* must undoubtedly be allowed to be Entertainments worthy of our Natures: And with the Harmony of the Whole we must consider the surprising Variety of Air, which the modern *Constitutions* and *Modes* of *Time* or *Rythmus* afford; by which, in our instrumental Performances, the Sense and Imagination are so mightily charmed. Now, this is an Application of Musick to a quite different Purpose from that of moving Passion : But is it reasonable upon that Account, to call it idle and insignificant, as some do, who I therefore suspect are ignorant of it ? It was certainly a noble Use of *Musick* to make it subservient to Morality and Virtue ; and if we apply it less that Way, I believe 'tis because we have less Need of such Allurements to our Duty: But whatever be the Reason of this, 'tis enough to the present Argument, that our *Musick* is at least not inferior to the ancient in the pathetick Kind: And if it be not a low and unworthy Thing for us to be pleased with Proportion and Harmony, in which there is properly an intellectual Beauty, then it must be confessed, that the modern *Musick* is more perfect than the ancient. But why must

muſt the moving of particular Paſſions be the only Uſe of *Muſick ?* If we look upon a noble Building, or a curious Painting, we are allowed to admire the Deſign, and view all its Proportions and Relation of Parts with Pleaſure to our Underſtandings, without any reſpect to the Paſſions. We muſt obſerve again, that there is ſcarce any Piece of *Melody* that has not ſome general Influence upon the Heart ; and by being more ſprightly or heavy in its Movements, will have different Effects ; tho' it is not deſigned to excite any particular Paſſion,and can only be ſaid in general to give Pleaſure, and recreate the Mind. But why ſhould we diſpute about a Thing which only Strangers to *Muſick* can ſpeak ill of? And for the *Harmony* of different Parts, the Defenders of the ancient *Muſick* own it to be a valuable Art, by their contending for its beingancient : Let me therefore again affirm, that the *Moderns* have wonderfully improven the Art of *Muſick.* It muſt be acknowledged indeed, that to judge well, and have a true Reliſh of our more elaborate and complex *Muſick*, or to be ſenſible of its Beauty, and taken with it,requires a peculiar Genius, and much Experience, without which it will ſeem only a confuſed Noiſe ; but I hope this is no Fault in the Thing. If one altogether ignorant of Painting looks upon the moſt curious Piece, wherein he finds nothing extraordinary moving to him, becauſe the Excellency of it may ly in the Deſign and admirable Proportion and Situation of the Parts which he takes no Notice of : Muſt we therefore

fore ſay, it has nothing valuable in it, and capable to give Pleaſure to a better Judge? What, in *Muſick* or *Painting*, would ſeem intricate and confuſed, and ſo give no Satisfaction to the unskilled, will raviſh with Admiration and Delight, one who is able to unravel all the Parts, obſerve their Relations and the united *Concord* of the Whole. But now, if this be ſuch a real and valuable Improvement in *Muſick*, you'll ask, How it can be thought the Ancients could be ignorant of it, and ſatisfy themſelves with ſuch a ſimple *Muſick*, when we conſider their great Perfection in the Siſter Arts of Poetry and Painting, and all other Sciences. I ſhall anſwer this by asking again, How it comes that the Ancients left us any thing to invent or improve? And how comes it that different Ages and Nations have Genius and Fondneſs for different Things. The Ancients ſtudied only how to move the Heart, to which a great many Things neceſſarily concurred, as *Words*, *Tune* and *Action*; and by theſe we can ſtill produce the ſame Effects; but we have alſo a new Art, whoſe End is rather to entertain the Underſtanding, than to move particular Paſſions. What Connection there is betwixt their improving other Sciences and this, is not ſo plain as to make any certain Concluſion from it. And as to their *Painting*, there have been very good Reaſons alledged to prove, That they followed the ſame Taſte there as in the *Muſick*, *i. e.* the ſimple obvious Beauties, of which every Body might judge and be ſenſible. Their End was to pleaſe and move the People, which is bet-

better done by the Senſes and the Heart than by the Underſtanding; and when they found ſufficient Means to accompliſh this, why ſhould we wonder that they proceeded no further, eſpecially when to have gone much beyond, would likely have loſed their Deſign. But, ſay you, this looks as if they had been ſenſible there were Improvements of another Kind to be made: Suppoſe it was ſo, yet they might ſtop when their principal End was obtained. And *Plutarch* ſays as much, for he tells us it was not Ignorance that made the ancient Muſick ſo ſimple, but it was ſo out of Politick: Yet he complains, that in his own Time, the very Memory of the ancient Modes that had been ſo uſeful in the Education of Youth, and moving the Paſſions was loſt thro' the Innovations and luxurious Variety introduced by later Muſicians; and now, when a full Liberty ſeems to have been taken, may we not wonder that ſo little Improvement was made, or at leaſt ſo little of it explained and recorded to us by theſe who wrote of Muſick, after ſuch Innovations were ſo far advanced.

I ſhall end this Diſpute, which is perhaps too tedious already, with a ſhort Conſideration of what the boldeſt Accuſer of the modern *Muſick*, *Iſaac Voſſius*, ſays againſt it, in his Book *de poematum cantu & viribus Rythmi*. He obſerves, what a wonderful Power Motion has upon the Mind, by Communication with the Body; how we are pleaſed with *rythmical* or *regular Motion*; then he obſerves, that the ancient *Greeks* and *Latins* perceiving this, took an infinite

Pains

Pains to cultivate their Language, and make it as harmonious, eſpecially in what related to the *Rythmus*, or Number, and Combination of long and ſhort Syllables, as poſſible; to this End particularly were the *pedes metrici* invented, which are the Foundations of their Verſification; and this he owns was the only *Rythmus* of their *Muſick*, and ſo powerful, that the whole Effect of *Muſick* was aſcribed to it, as appears, ſays he, by this Saying of theirs, *τὸ πᾶν παρά μȣσικοῖς ὁ ρυθμὸς*: And to prove the Power attributed to the *Rythmus*, he cites ſeveral other Paſſages. That it gives Life to *Muſick*, eſpecially the *pathetick*, will not be denied; and we ſee the Power of it even in plain Proſe and Oratory: But to make it the *Whole*, is perhaps attributing more than is due: I rather reckon the Words and Senſe of what's ſung, the principal Ingredient; and the other a noble Servant to them, for raiſing and keeping up the Attention, becauſe of the natural Pleaſure annexed to theſe Senſations. 'Tis very true, that there is a Connection betwixt certain Paſſions, which we call Motions of the Mind, and certain Motions in our Bodies; and when by any external Motion theſe can be imitated and excited, no doubt we ſhall be much moved; and the Mind, by that Influence, becomes either gay, ſoft, briſk or drowſy: But how any particular Paſſion can be excited without ſuch a lively Repreſentation of its proper Object, as only Words afford, is not very intelligible; at leaſt this appears to me the moſt juſt and effectual Way. But let us the hear what Notion others had of this Matter, *Quintilian* ſays, *If the Numbers of Muſick have ſuch Influence, how much more ought eloquent Words to have ?* And in all the ancient *Muſick* the greateſt Care was taken, that not a Syllable of the Words ſhould be loſt, for ſpoiling the Senſe, which *Voſſius* himſelf obſerves and owns. *Pancirollus*, who thinks the Art loſt, aſcribes the chief Virtue of it to the Words. -- *Siquidem una cum melodia integra percipiebantur verba :* And the very Reaſon he gives, that the modern *Muſick* is leſs perfect, is, that we hear Sounds without Words, by which ſays he, the ear is a little pleaſed, without any Entertainment to the Underſtanding: But all this has been conſidered already. *Voſſius* alledges the *mimick* Art, to prove, that the Power of Motion was equal to the moſt eloquent Words ; but we ſhall be as much ſtraitned to believe this, as the reſt of their Wonders. Let them believe it who will, that a *Pantomime* had Art to make himſelf eaſily underſtood without Words, by People of all Languages: And that *Roſcius* the Comedian, could expreſs any Sentence by his Geſtures, as ſignificantly and variouſly, as *Cicero* with all his Oratory. Whatever this Art was, 'tis loſt, and perhaps it was ſomething very ſurpriſing ; but 'tis hard to believe theſe Stories literally. However to the Thing in Hand, we are concerned only to conſider the *muſical* or *poetical Rythmus.*

Voſſius ſays, that *Rythmus* which does not contain and expreſs the very Forms and Figures of of Things, can have no Effect; and that the ancient poetical Numbers alone are juſtly contrived for this End. And therefore the modern Languages and Verſe are altogether unfit for *Muſick*; and we ſhall never have, ſays he, any right *vocal Muſick*, till our Poets learn to make Verſes that are capable to be ſung, *that is*, as he explains it, till we new model our Languages, reſtore the ancient metrical Feet, and baniſh our barbarous Rhimes. Our Verſes, ſays he, run all as it were on one Foot, without Diſtinction of Members and Parts, in which the Beauty of Proportion is to be found; therefore he reckons, that we have no *Rythmus* at all in our Poetry; and affirms, that we mind nothing but to have ſuch a certain Number of Syllables in a Verſe, of whatever Nature, and in whatever Order. Now, what a raſh and unjuſt Criticiſm is this! if it was ſo in his Mother Tongue, the *Dutch*, I know not; but I'm certain it is otherwiſe in *Engliſh*. 'Tis true, we don't follow the metricalCompoſition of the Ancients; yet we have ſuch a Mixture of ſtrong and ſoft, long and ſhort Syllables, as makes our Verſes flow, rapid, ſmooth, or rumbling, agreeable to the Subject. Take any good *Engliſh* Verſe, and by a very ſmall Change in the Tranſpoſition of a Word or Syllable, any Body who has an Ear will find, that we make a very great Matter of the *Nature* and *Order* of the Syllables. But why muſt the ancient be the only proper *Metre* for *Poetry* and *Muſick?* He ſays, their *Odes* were ſung, as to the *Rythmus*, in the ſame Manner

as

as we ſcan them, every *pes* being a diſtinct Bar or Meaſure, ſeparate by a diſtinct Pauſe; but in the bare Reading, that Diſtinction was not accurately obſerved, the Verſe being read in a more continuous Manner. Again he notices, that after the Change of the ancient Pronunciation, and the Corruption of their Language, the *Muſick* decayed till it became a poor and inſignificant Art. Their *Odes* had a regular Return of the ſame Kind of Verſe; and the ſame Quantity of Syllables in the ſame Place of every ſimiar Verſe: But there's nothing, ſays he, but Confuſion of Quantities in the modern *Odes*; ſo that to follow the natural Quantity of our Syllables, every Stanza will be a different Song, otherwiſe than in the ancient Verſes: (He ſhould have minded, that every Kind of *Ode* was not of this Nature; and how heroick Verſes were ſung, if this was neceſſary, I cannot ſee, becauſe in them the *Dactylus* and *Spondeus* are ſometimes in one Place of the Verſe, and ſometimes in another.) But inſtead of this, he ſays, the *Moderns* have no Regard to the natural Quantity of the Syllables, and have introduced an unnatural and barbarous Variety of long and ſhort Notes, which they apply without any Regard to the Subject and Senſe of the Verſe, or the natural Pronunciation: So that nothing can be underſtood that's ſung, unleſs one knows it before; and therefore, no wonder, ſays he, that our *vocal Muſick* has no Effects. Now here is indeed a heavy Charge, but Experience gives me Authority to affirm it to be abſolutely falſe. We have

have *vocal Musick* as pathetick as ever the ancient was. If any Singer don't pronounce intelligibly, that is not the Fault of the *Musick*, which is always so contrived, as the Sense of the Words may be distinctly perceived. But this is impossible, says he, if we don't follow the natural Pronunciation and Quantity; which is I think, precariously said; for was the Singing of the ancient *Odes* by separate and distinct Measures of metrical Feet, in which there must frequently be a Stop in the very Middle of a Word, Was this I say the natural Pronunciation, and the Way to make what was sung best understood? Himself tells us, they read their Poems otherwise. And if Practice would make that distinct enough to them, will it not be as sufficient in the other Case. Again, to argue from what's strictly natural, will perhaps be no Advantage to their Cause; for don't we know, that the Ancients admitted the most unnatural Positions of Words, for the sake of a numerous Stile, even in plain Prose; and took still greater Liberties in Poetry, to depart from the natural Order in which Ideas ly in our Mind; far otherwise than it is in the modern Languages, which will therefore be moe easily and readily understood in Singing, if pronounced distinctly, than the ancient Verse could be, wherein the Construction of the Words was more difficult to find, because of the Transpositions. Again the Difference of long and short Syllables in common Speaking, is not accurately observed; not even in the ancient Languages; for *Example*, in common Speaking, who

who can diſtinguiſh the long and ſhort Syllables in theſ e Words, *ſatis*, *nivis*, *miſit*. The Senſe of a Word generally depends upon the right Pronunciation of one Syllable, or Two at moſt in very long Words; and if theſe are made conſpicuous, and the Words well ſeparated by a right Application of the long and ſhort Notes, as we certainly know to be done, then we follow the natural Pronunciation more this Way than the other. If 'tis replied, that ſince we pretend to a poetical *Rythmus*, ſuitable to different Subjects, why don't we follow it in our *Muſick?* I ſhall anſwer, that tho' that *Rythmus* is more diſtinguiſhed in the Recitation of Poems, yet our *muſical Rythmus* is accommodated alſo to it; but with ſuch Liberty as is neceſſary to make good *Melody*; and even to produce ſtronger Effects than a ſimple Reciting can do; and I would aſk, for what other Reaſon the Ancients ſung their Poems in a Manner different from the bare reading of them? Still he tells us, that we want the true *Rythmus*, which can only make pathetick *Muſick*; and if there is any Thing moving in our Songs, he ſays, 'tis only owing to the Words; ſo that Proſe may be ſung as well as Verſe: That the Words ought naturally to have the greateſt Influence, has been already conſidered; and I have ſeen no Reaſon why the ancient poetical *Rythmus* ſhould have the only Claim to be pathetick; as if they had exhauſted all the Combinations of long and ſhort Sounds, that can be moving or agreeable: But indeed the Queſtion is about

about Matter of Fact, therefore I ſhall appeal to Experience, and leave it; after I have minded you, that by this Defence of the *modern Muſick*, I don't ſay it is all alike good, or that there can be no juſt Objection laid againſt any of our Compoſitions, eſpecially in the ſetting of *Muſick* to Words; I only ſay, we have admirable Compoſitions, and that the Art of *Muſick*, taken in all that it is capable of, is more perfect than it was among the old *Greeks* and *Romans*, at leaſt for what can poſſibly be made appear.

FINIS.

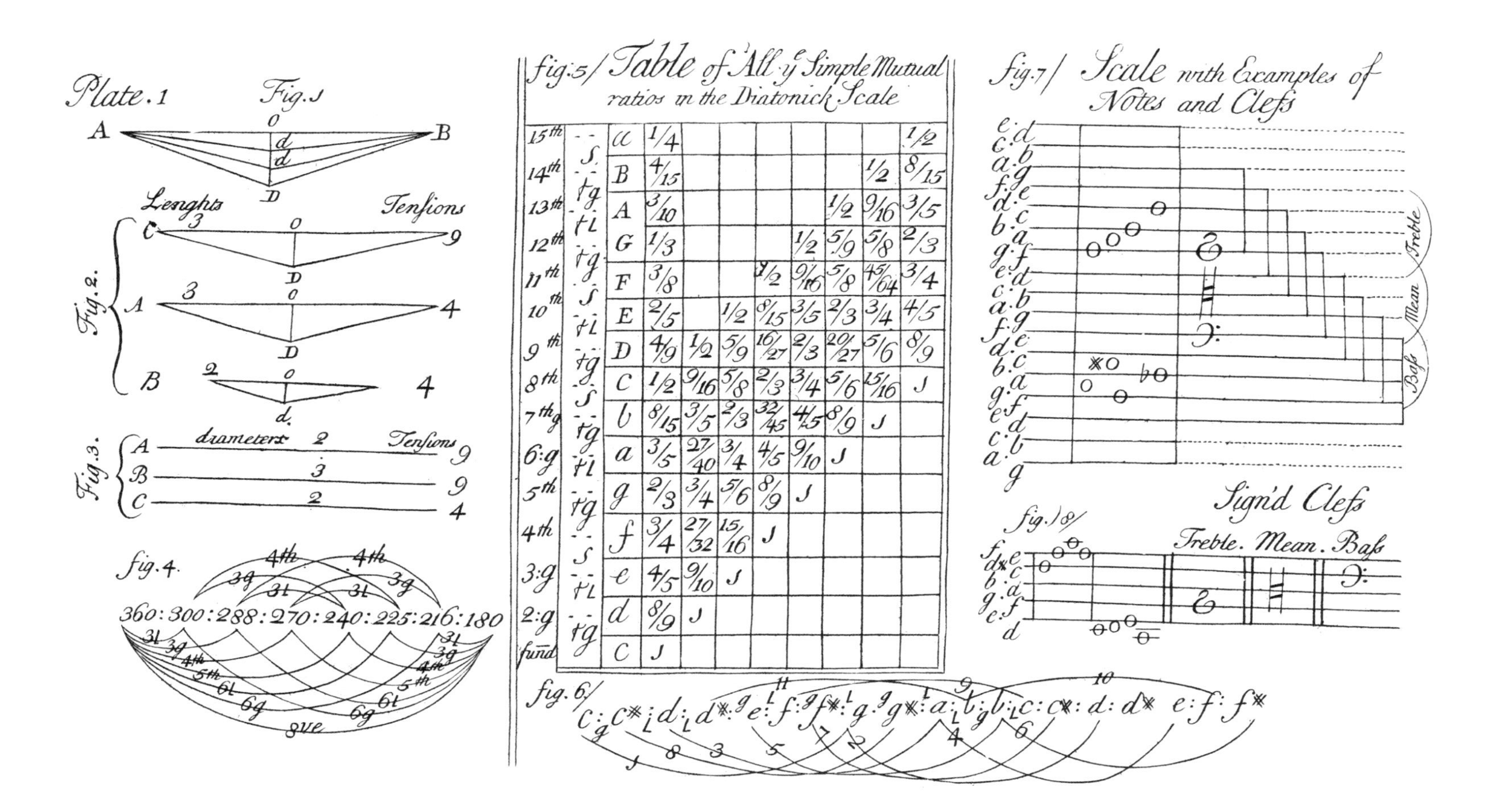

fig. 5/ Table of All ye Simple Mutual ratios in the Diatonick Scale

15th	- -	a	1/4							1/2
14th	S	B	4/15						1/2	8/15
13th	tg	A	3/10					1/2	9/16	3/5
12th	tl	G	1/3				1/2	5/9	5/8	2/3
11th	tg	F	3/8			1/2	9/16	5/8	45/64	3/4
10th	S	E	2/5		1/2	8/15	3/5	2/3	3/4	4/5
9th	tl	D	4/9	1/2	5/9	16/27	2/3	20/27	5/6	8/9
8th	tg	C	1/2	9/16	5/8	2/3	3/4	5/6	15/16	1
7th	S	b	8/15	3/5	2/3	32/45	4/5	8/9	1	
6:g	tg	a	3/5	27/40	3/4	4/5	9/10	1		
5th	tl	g	2/3	3/4	5/6	8/9	1			
4th	tg	f	3/4	27/32	15/16	1				
3:g	S	e	4/5	9/10	1					
2:g	tl	d	8/9	1						
fund	tg	C	1							

Plate 2 Fig. 1.

Universal Table of the Signatures of Clefs; Shewing how to transpose from any key to any other; and how to Sol-fa any Song.

														Sharp key	Flat key
	fa	c	d♭	d	e♭	e	f	g♭	g	a♭	a	♭	b	8ve	3d L
Sem:	mi	♭	c	c*	d	d*	e	f	f*	g	g*	a	a*	7th g	2d g
tone	la	a	♭	b	c	c*	d	e♭	e	f	f*	g	g*	6th g	Fund
tone	Sol	g	a♭	a	♭	b	c	d♭	d	e♭	e	f	f*	5th	7th L
tone	fa	f	g♭	g	a♭	a	♭	c♭	c	d♭	d	e♭	e	4th	6th L
Sem.	la	e	f	f*	g	g*	a	♭	b	c	c*	d	d*	3d g	5th
tone	Sol	d	e♭	e	f	f*	g	a♭	a	♭	b	c	c*	2d g	4th
tone	fa	c	d♭	d	♭e	e	f	g♭	g	a♭	a	♭	b	Fund	3d L

fig. 2 / Table of False Intervals in the Hemitonick Scale

Ratios	3d L : 6th g (8ve)	Ratios
64:75 =	c* – e – c*	= 75:128. e
id =	d* – f* – d*	= idem.
id =	g* – b – g*	= id
27:32 =	d – f – d	= 16:27. e
id =	f* – a – f*	= id.
id. =	g – b – g	= id.
	3d g 6th L	
25:32 =	e – g* – e	= 16:25. d
id =	a – c* – a	= id.
id =	b – d – b	= id.
405:512 =	f* – b – f*	= 256:405. d
64:81 =	b – d – b	= 81:128. d
	4th : 5th	
512:675 =	c* – f* – c*	= 675:1024. e
20:27 =	a – d – a	= 27:40. d
id =	b – d* – b	= id
	Tritone Tritone	
32:45 =	c – f* – c	= 45:64
id =	c* – g – c*	= id
id =	f – b – f	= id
id =	g* d – g*	= id
id =	a* – e – a*	= id
25 36 =	a – d* – a	= 18:25

fig 3/ Names, Figures and proportions of Notes.

8 · 4 · 2 · 1 · 1/2 · 1/4 · 1/8 · 1/16 · 1/32

Large. Long. breve Semibrive. Minim. Crotchet. quaver. Semiquaber: demisemiqr

or or

Rests

or

Single bar

double bar

Repeat

repeat

close

tye

tye

direct

Ex.a 1

Adagio

Ex.a 2

Allegro

Ex. 3d

Allegro

Ex. 3d. transposd

Allegro

Ex. 4th.

Allegro

Ex. 5th.

Adagio

Ex. 5th. transposd.

Adagio

Ex. 6th.

Largo

Ex.a 7th.

Vivace

Ex. 8th.

Allegro

Ex. 9th.

Allegro

Ex. 10

Allegro

Ex. 11.

Allegro

Plate 4th.
Ex. 1.
Ex. 2.
Ex. 3.
Ex. 4.
Ex. 5th
8 5 3 maj. 3 Min 3
Key f
Ex. 6.
6 3
2d f
Ex. 7
6 3 6
3d f
Ex. 8
5 3 3
4th. f
Ex 9
5 3
5th f
Ex. 10
5 6 3 5 6 3
6th f
Ex. 11
3 6 5♭
7th f
Ex. 12
Ex. 13.
Ex. 14.
Ex. 15.
Ex. 16
bad bad bad bad good bad good good
Ex. 17
Ex. 18.
Ex. 19. first Lesson.

(Ex. 19) 1st Leſſon, tranſported to a flat-key.
Plate 5.
Ex. 19. 2d. Leſſon.
2d. Leſſon, tranſported to a flat-key.
Ex. 20
21

Ex. 22
23
24
Ex. 25
26
27
28
29
30
31

Plate 6.th

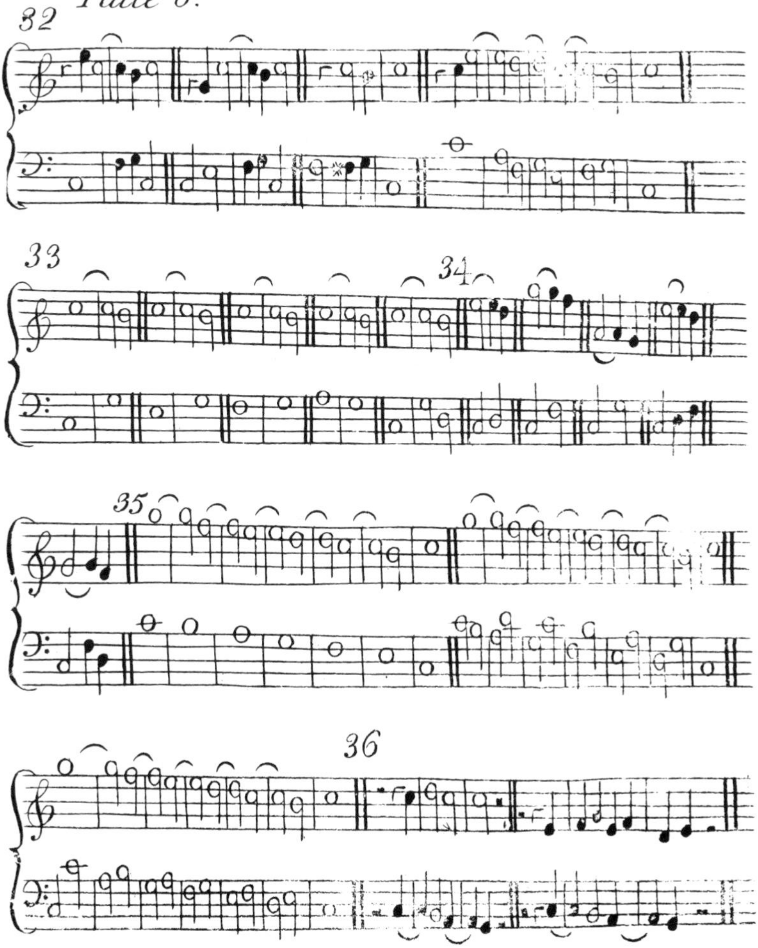

32

33

34

35

36

37
38
39
40
41
42
43
44
45
46
47
48

49
50
51
52
53
54
55
56
57
58